MISS QUINCES

KAT FAJARDO

Color by Mariana Azzi

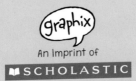

An Imprint of

SCHOLASTIC

All rights reserved. Published by Graphix, an imprint of
Scholastic Inc., *Publishers since 1920.* SCHOLASTIC, GRAPHIX,
and associated logos are trademarks and/or registered
trademarks of Scholastic Inc.

Library of Congress Control Number: 2021937053

ISBN 978-1-338-53558-7 (hardcover)
ISBN 978-1-338-53559-4 (paperback)

10 9 8 7 6 5 4 3 2 1   22 23 24 25 26

Printed in China   62
First edition, April 2022

Edited by Cassandra Pelham Fulton
Lettering by E. K. Weaver
Book design by Shivana Sookdeo
Creative Director: Phil Falco
Publisher: David Saylor

For Mami, Papi, and
Clau, and for my fans,
Pablo and Gloria

CHAPTER ONE

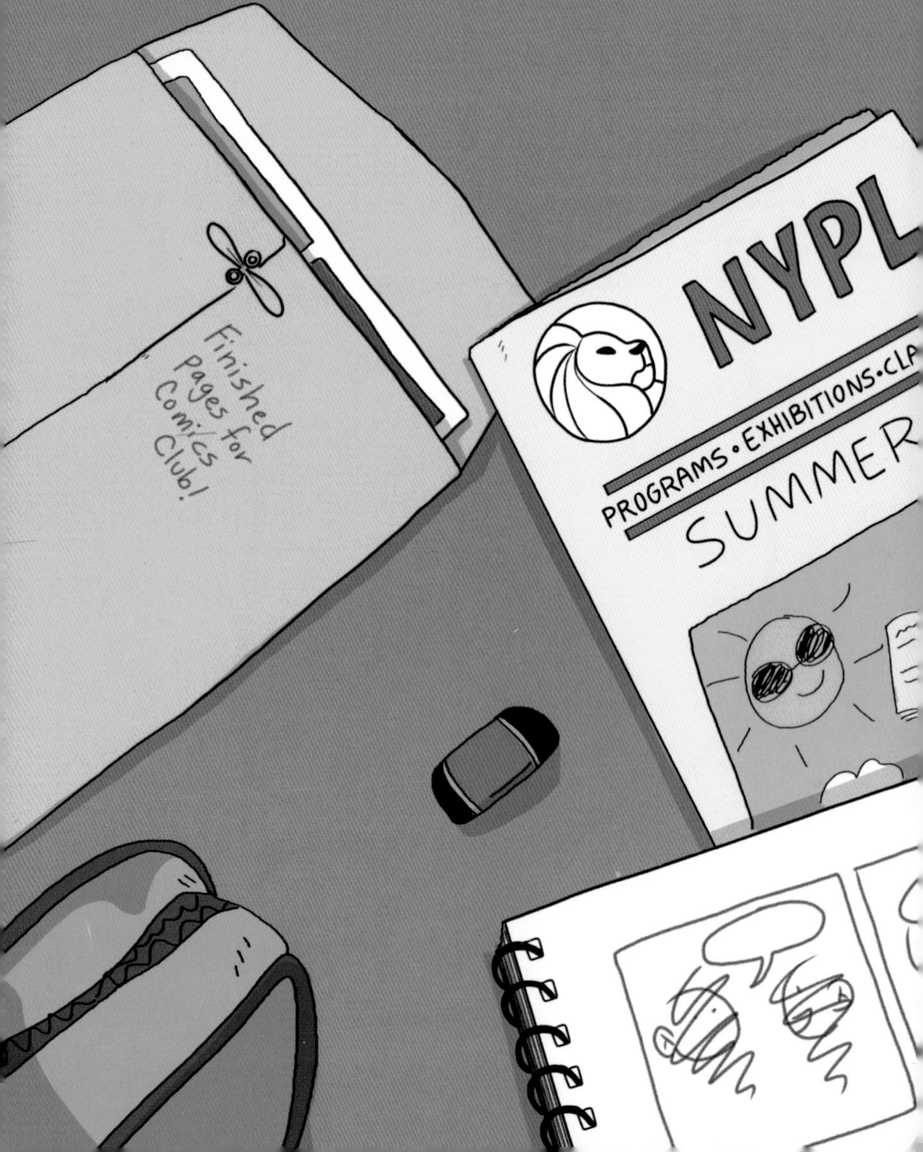
Finished pages for Comics Club!
NYPL
PROGRAMS • EXHIBITIONS •
SUMMER

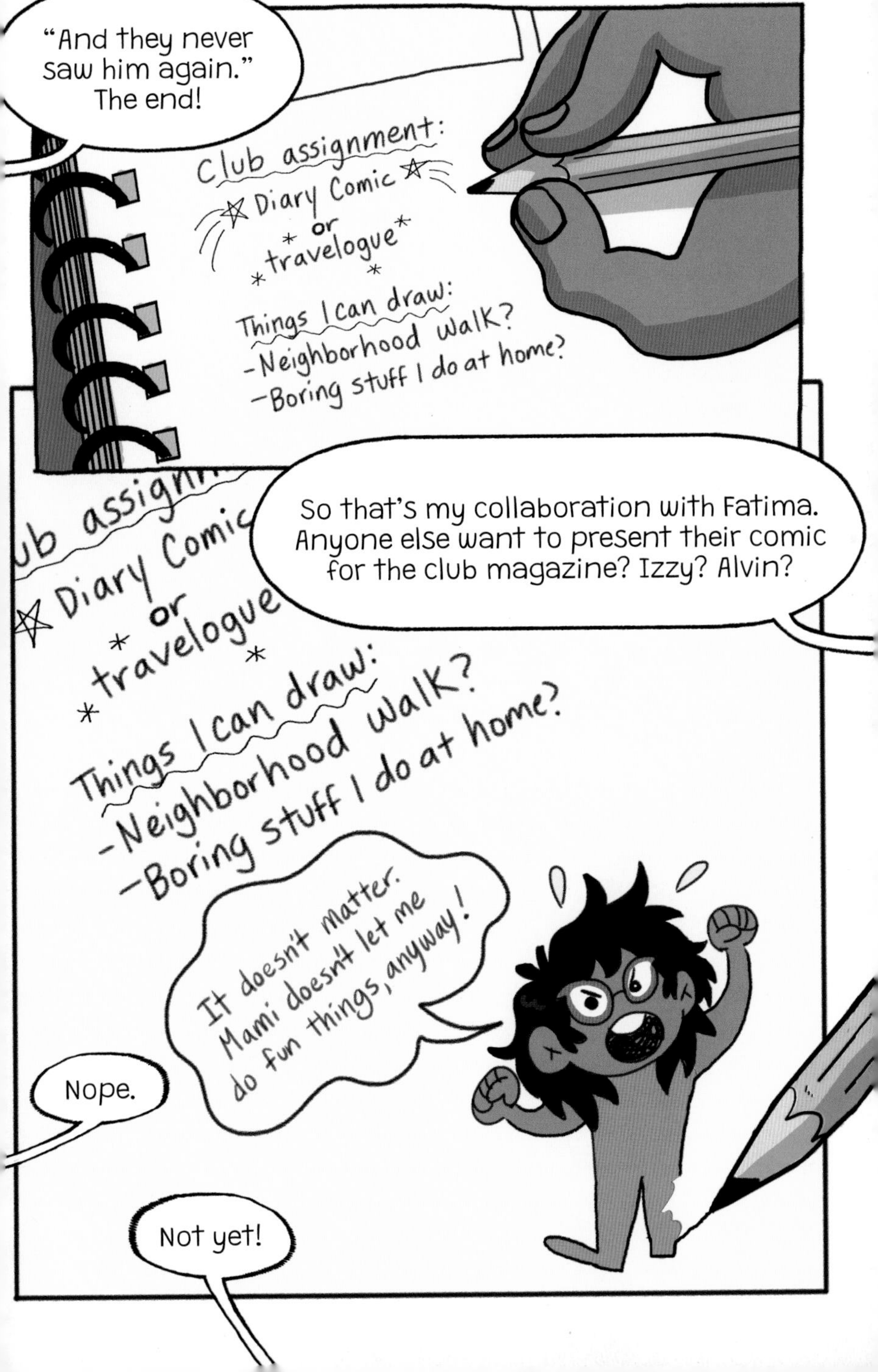
"And they never saw him again." The end!
Club assignment:
Diary Comic
or
travelogue
Things I can draw:
-Neighborhood walk?
-Boring stuff I do at home?
So that's my collaboration with Fatima. Anyone else want to present their comic for the club magazine? Izzy? Alvin?
It doesn't matter. Mami doesn't let me do fun things, anyway!
Nope.
Not yet!

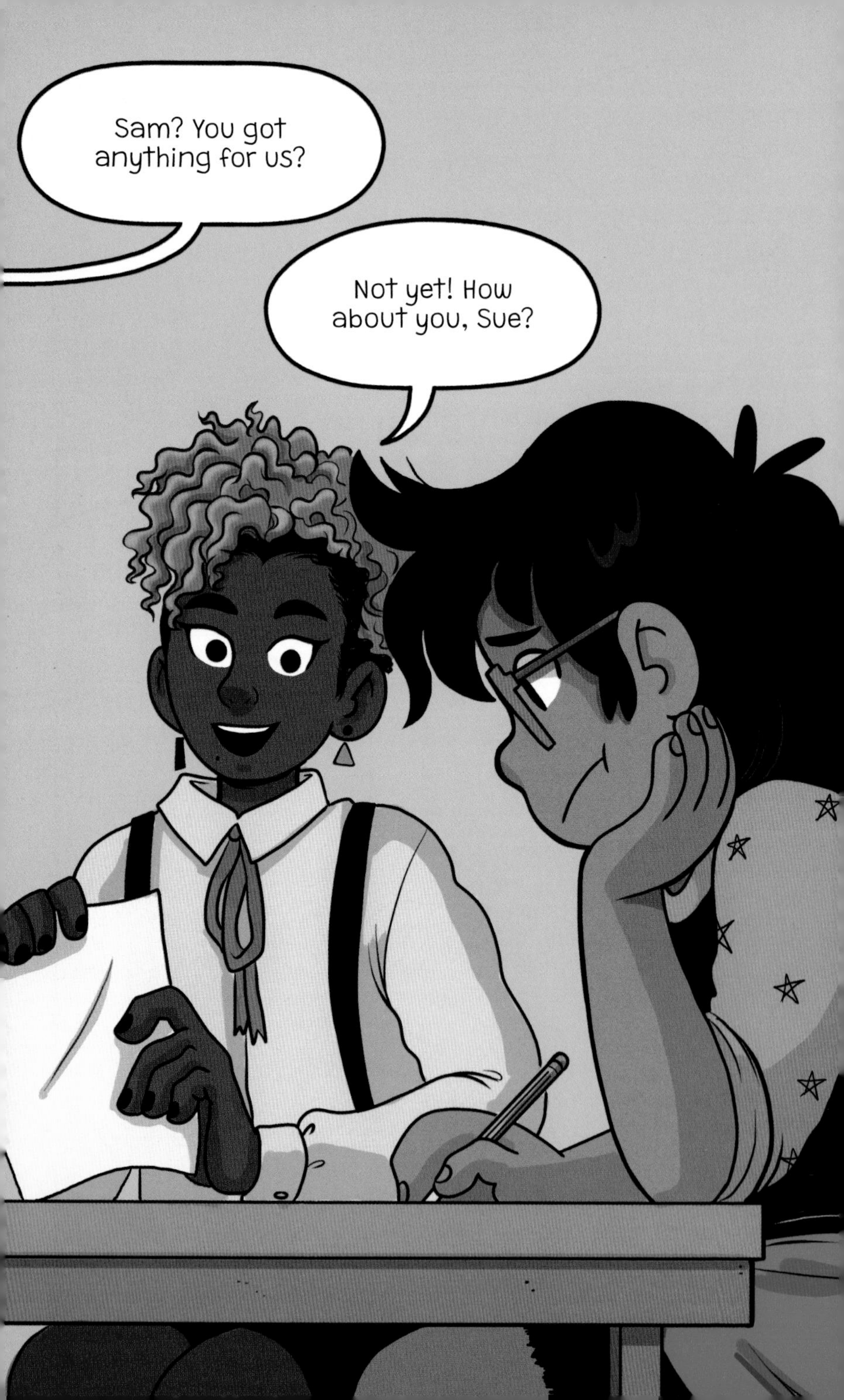
Sam? You got anything for us?
Not yet! How about you, Sue?

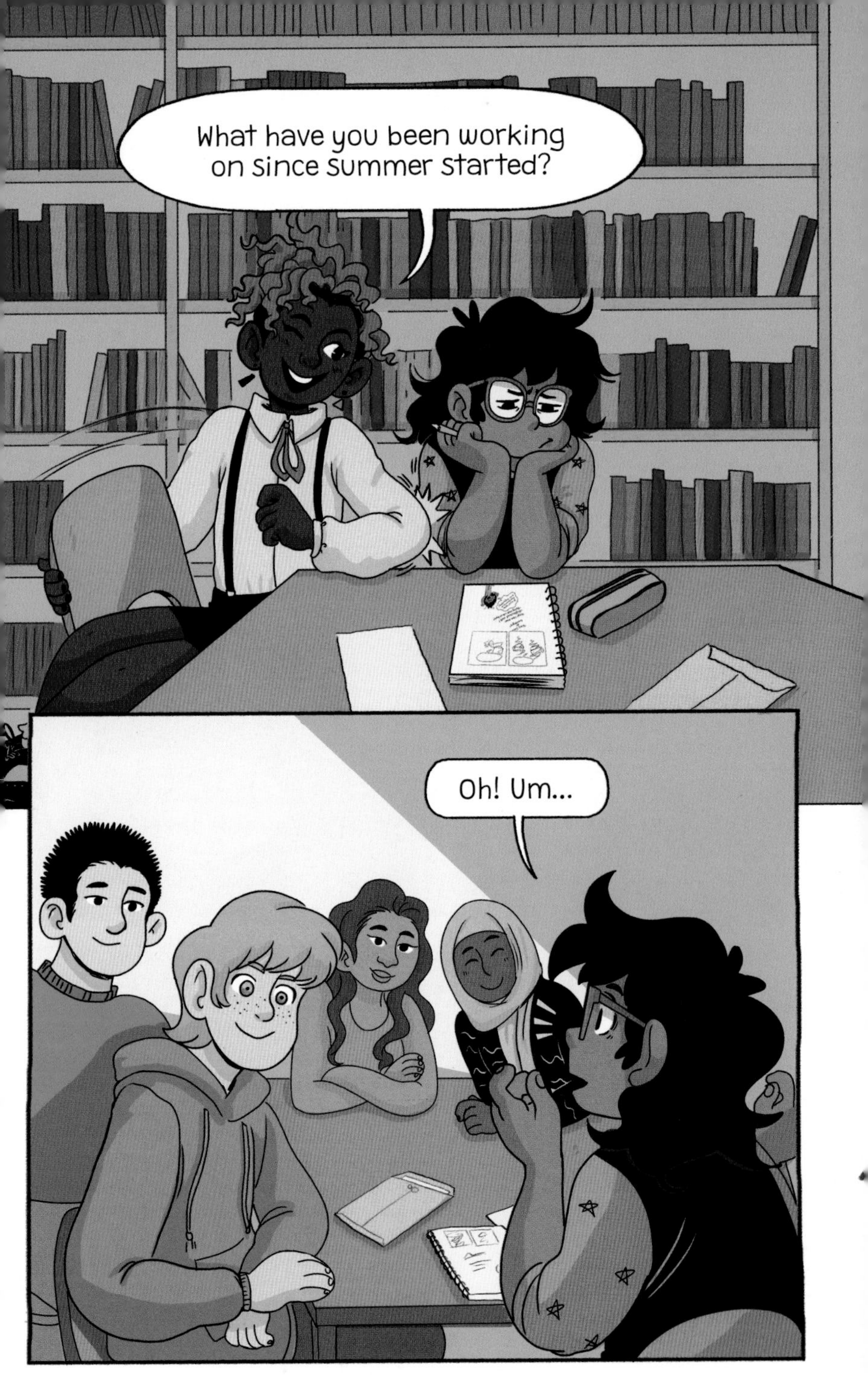
What have you been working on since summer started?
Oh! Um...

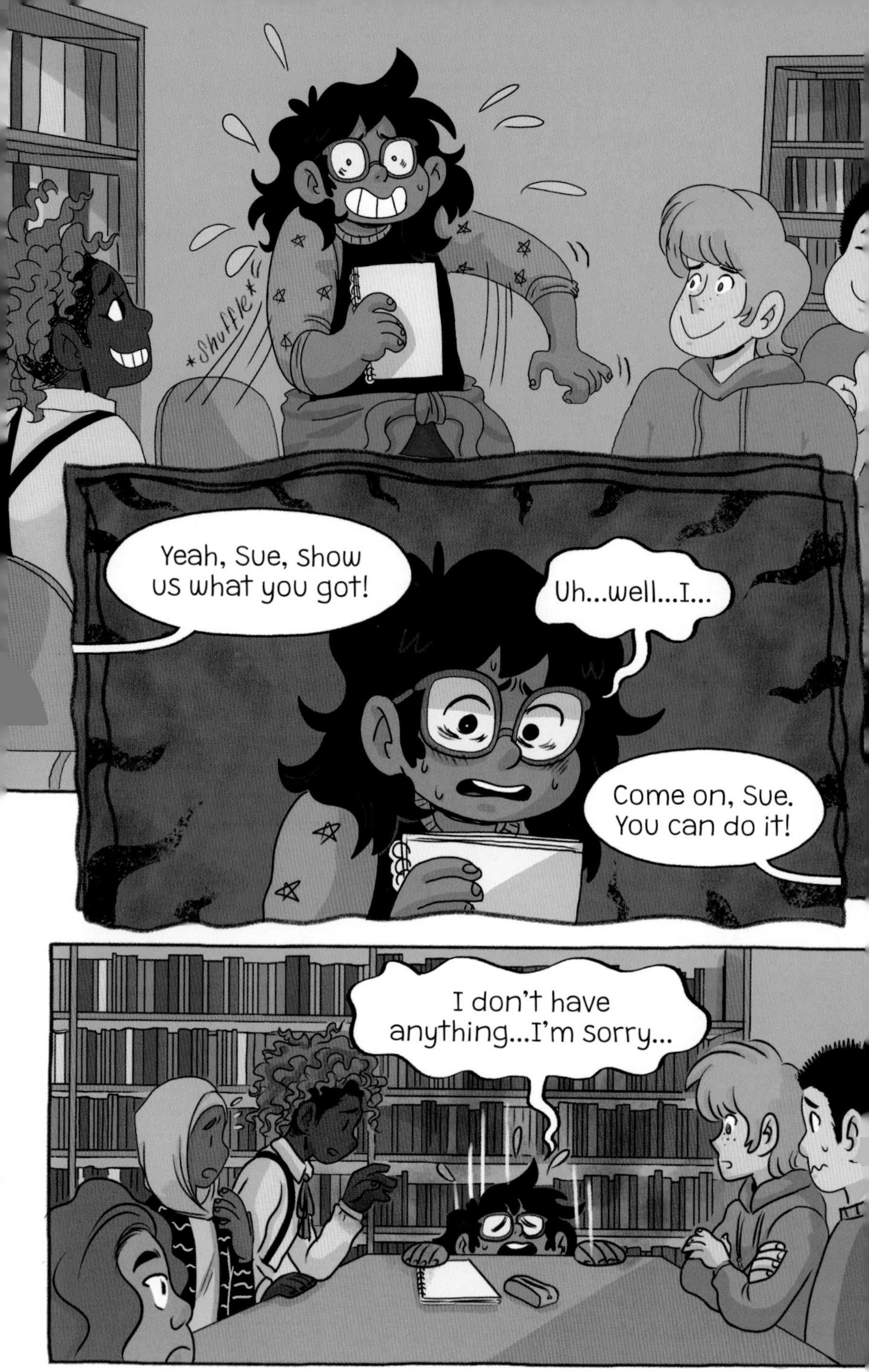
Shuffle
Yeah, Sue, show us what you got!
Uh...well...I...
Come on, Sue. You can do it!
I don't have anything...I'm sorry...

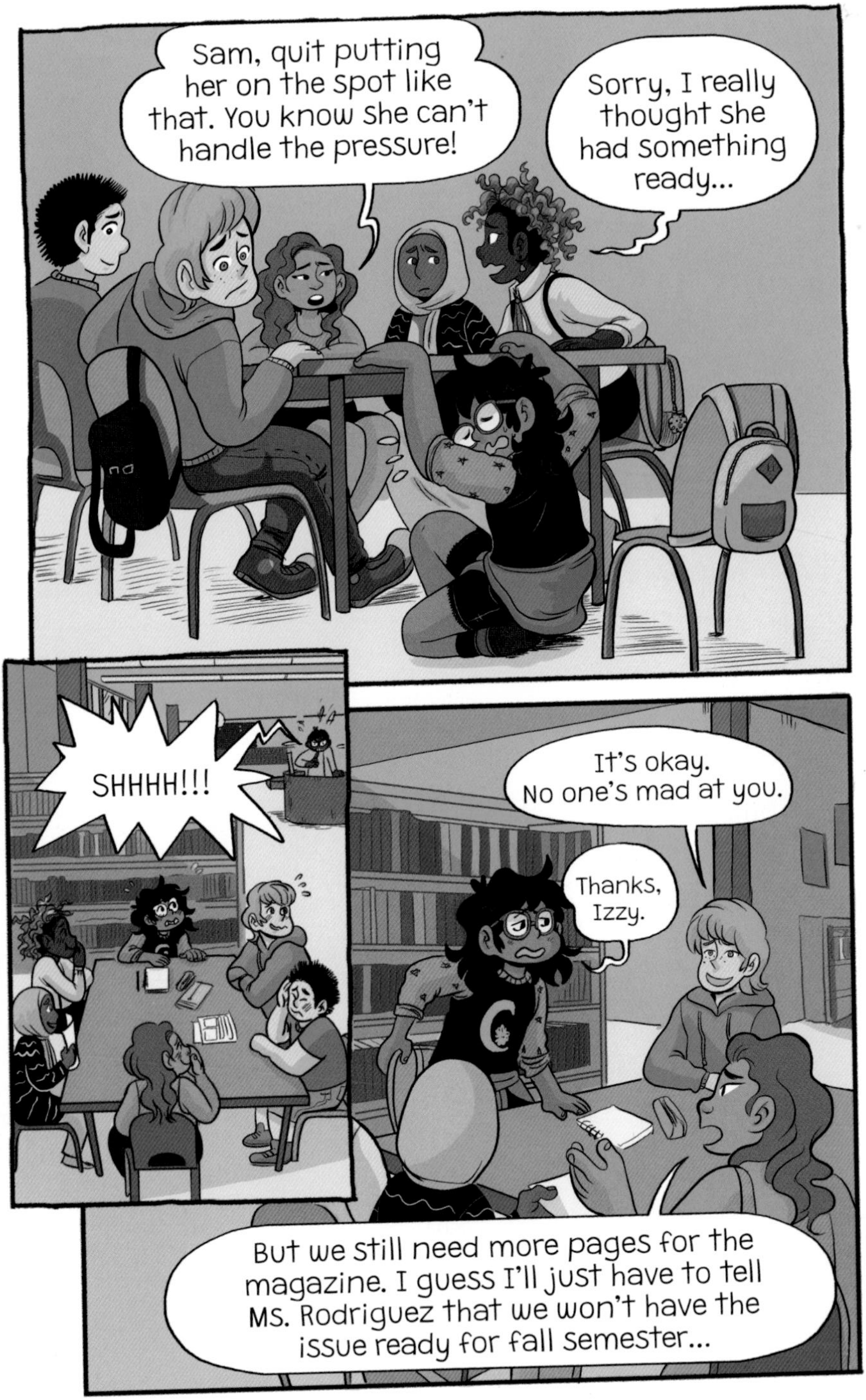
Sam, quit putting her on the spot like that. You know she can't handle the pressure!
Sorry, I really thought she had something ready...
SHHHH!!!
It's okay. No one's mad at you.
Thanks, Izzy.
But we still need more pages for the magazine. I guess I'll just have to tell Ms. Rodriguez that we won't have the issue ready for fall semester...

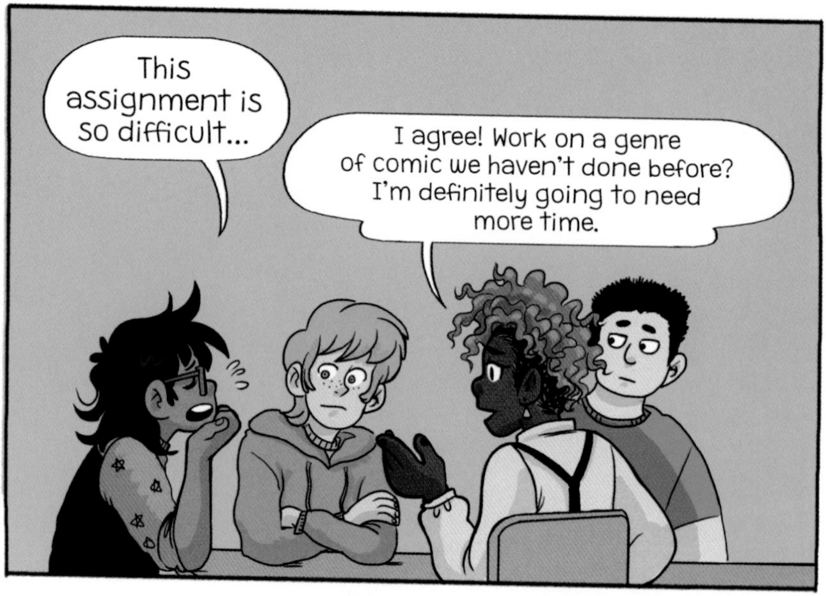
This assignment is so difficult...
I agree! Work on a genre of comic we haven't done before? I'm definitely going to need more time.

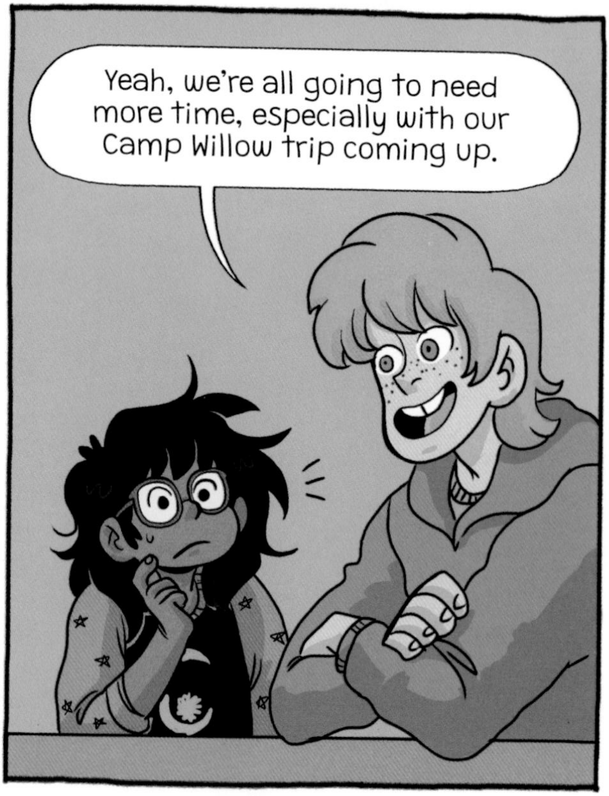
Yeah, we're all going to need more time, especially with our Camp Willow trip coming up.

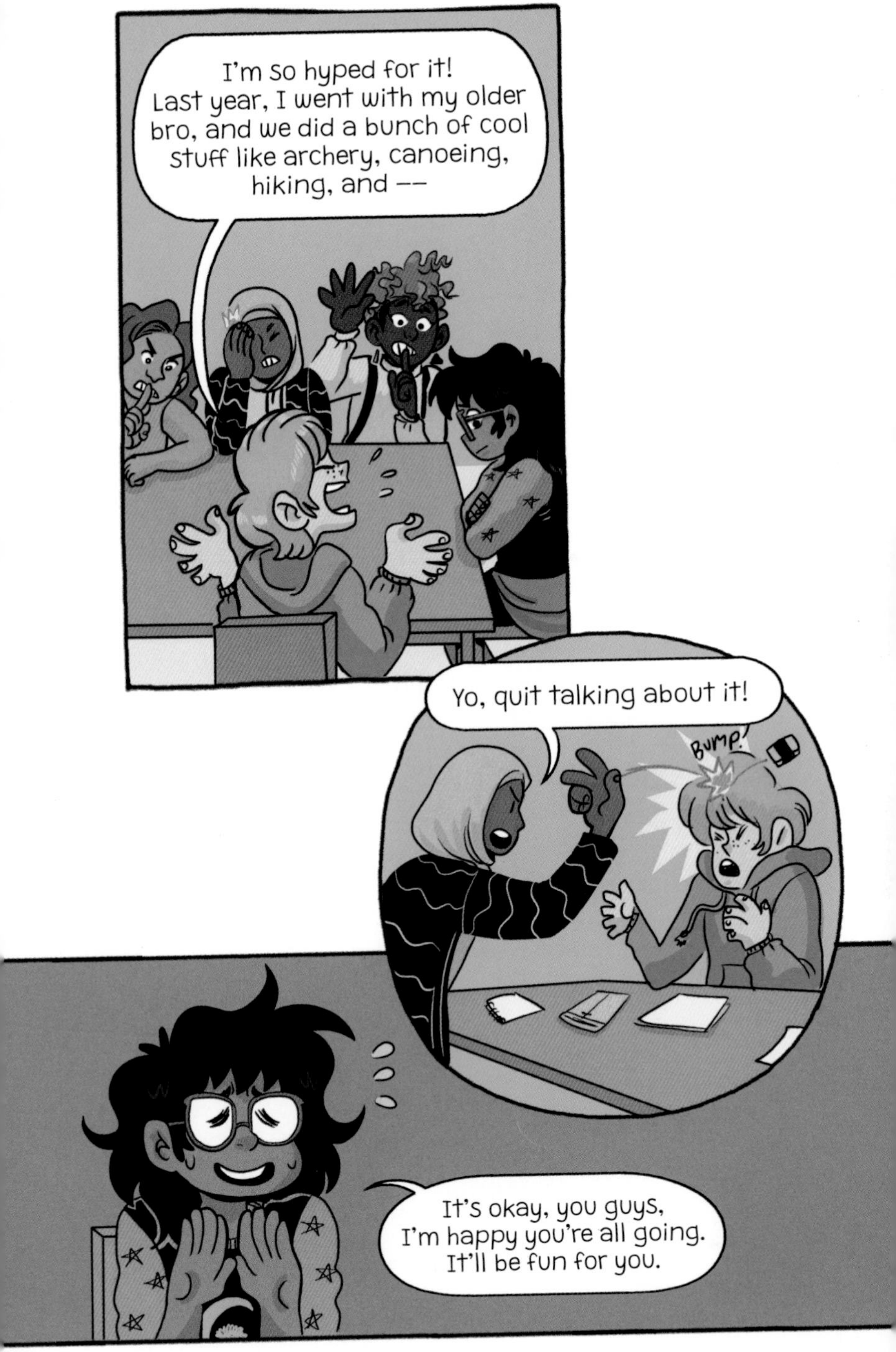
I'm so hyped for it! Last year, I went with my older bro, and we did a bunch of cool stuff like archery, canoeing, hiking, and --
Yo, quit talking about it!
BUMP!
It's okay, you guys, I'm happy you're all going. It'll be fun for you.

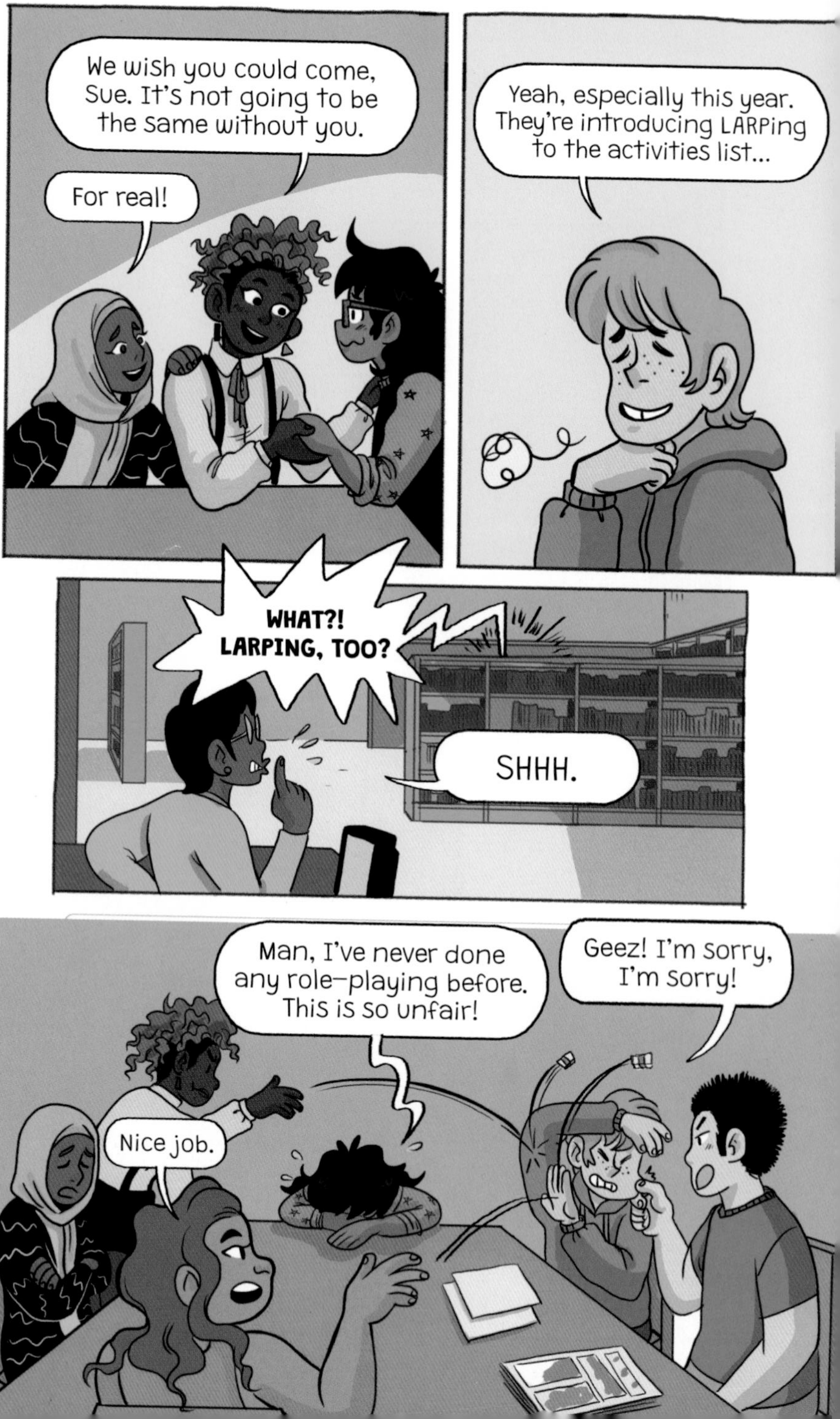
We wish you could come, Sue. It's not going to be the same without you.
For real!
Yeah, especially this year. They're introducing LARPing to the activities list...
WHAT?! LARPING, TOO?
SHHH.
Man, I've never done any role-playing before. This is so unfair!
Geez! I'm sorry, I'm sorry!
Nice job.

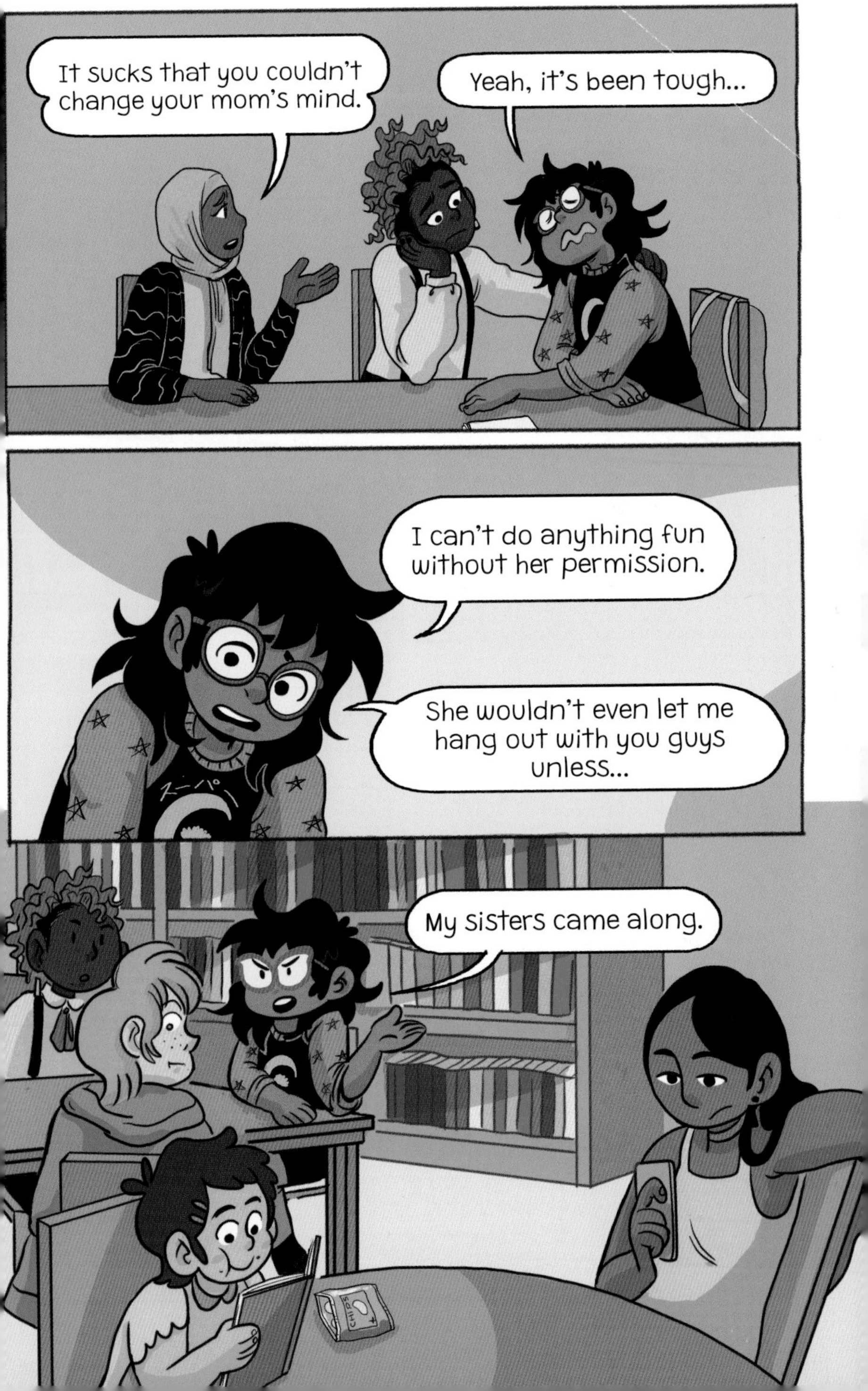
It sucks that you couldn't change your mom's mind.
Yeah, it's been tough...
I can't do anything fun without her permission.
She wouldn't even let me hang out with you guys unless...
My sisters came along.
CHIPS

I didn't know you had sisters...

Ester! You can't eat in the library. Carmen, stop her!

CRUNCH

Let her eat it or she's going to be cranky on the way home and I don't want to deal with that.

CRUNCH

CHIPS!

Yeah, I've got two sisters and they're both way too annoying.

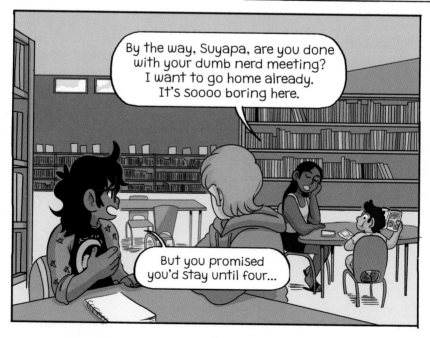

By the way, Suyapa, are you done with your dumb nerd meeting? I want to go home already. It's soooo boring here.

But you promised you'd stay until four...

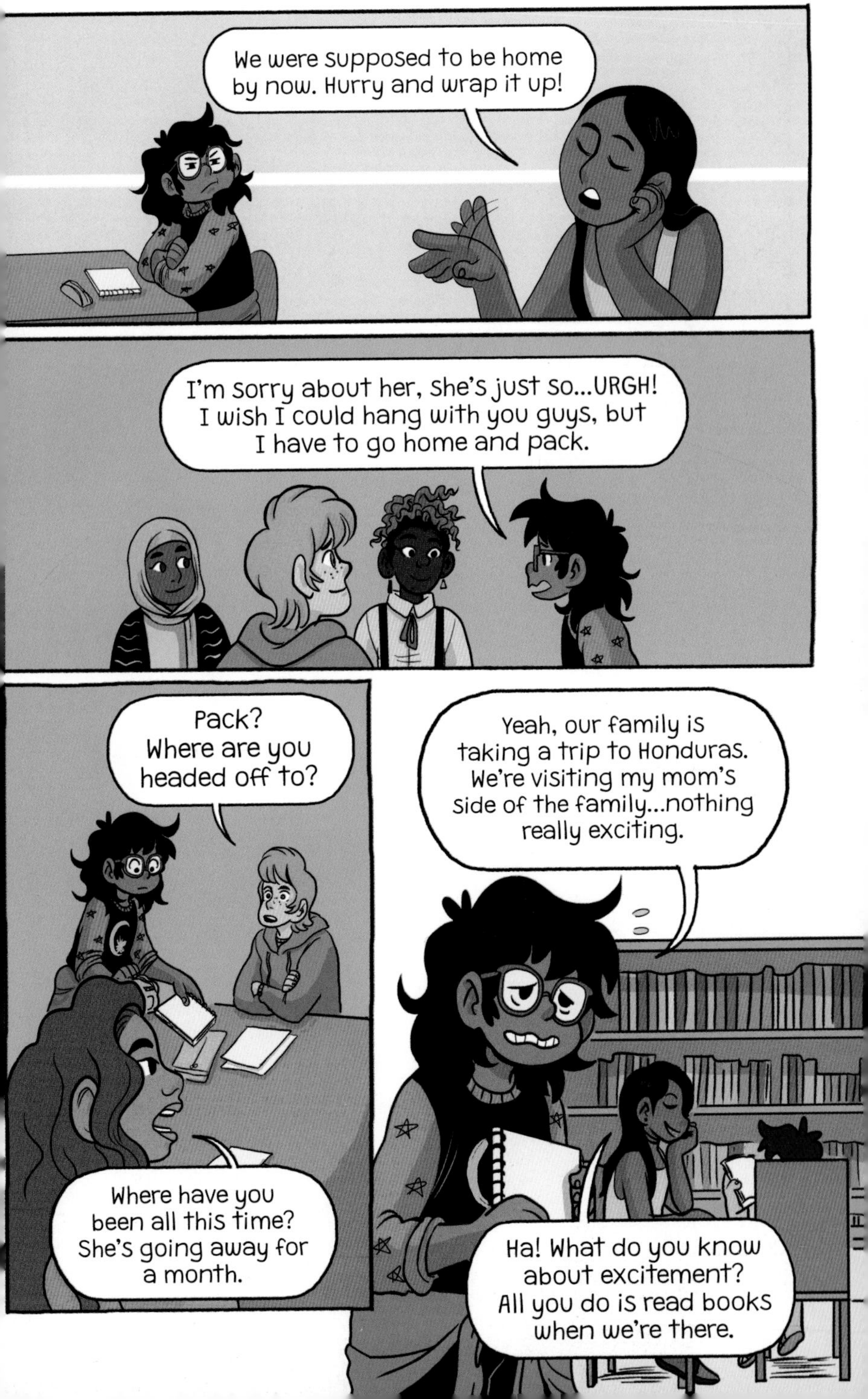
We were supposed to be home by now. Hurry and wrap it up!
I'm sorry about her, she's just so...URGH! I wish I could hang with you guys, but I have to go home and pack.
Pack? Where are you headed off to?
Where have you been all this time? She's going away for a month.
Yeah, our family is taking a trip to Honduras. We're visiting my mom's side of the family...nothing really exciting.
Ha! What do you know about excitement? All you do is read books when we're there.

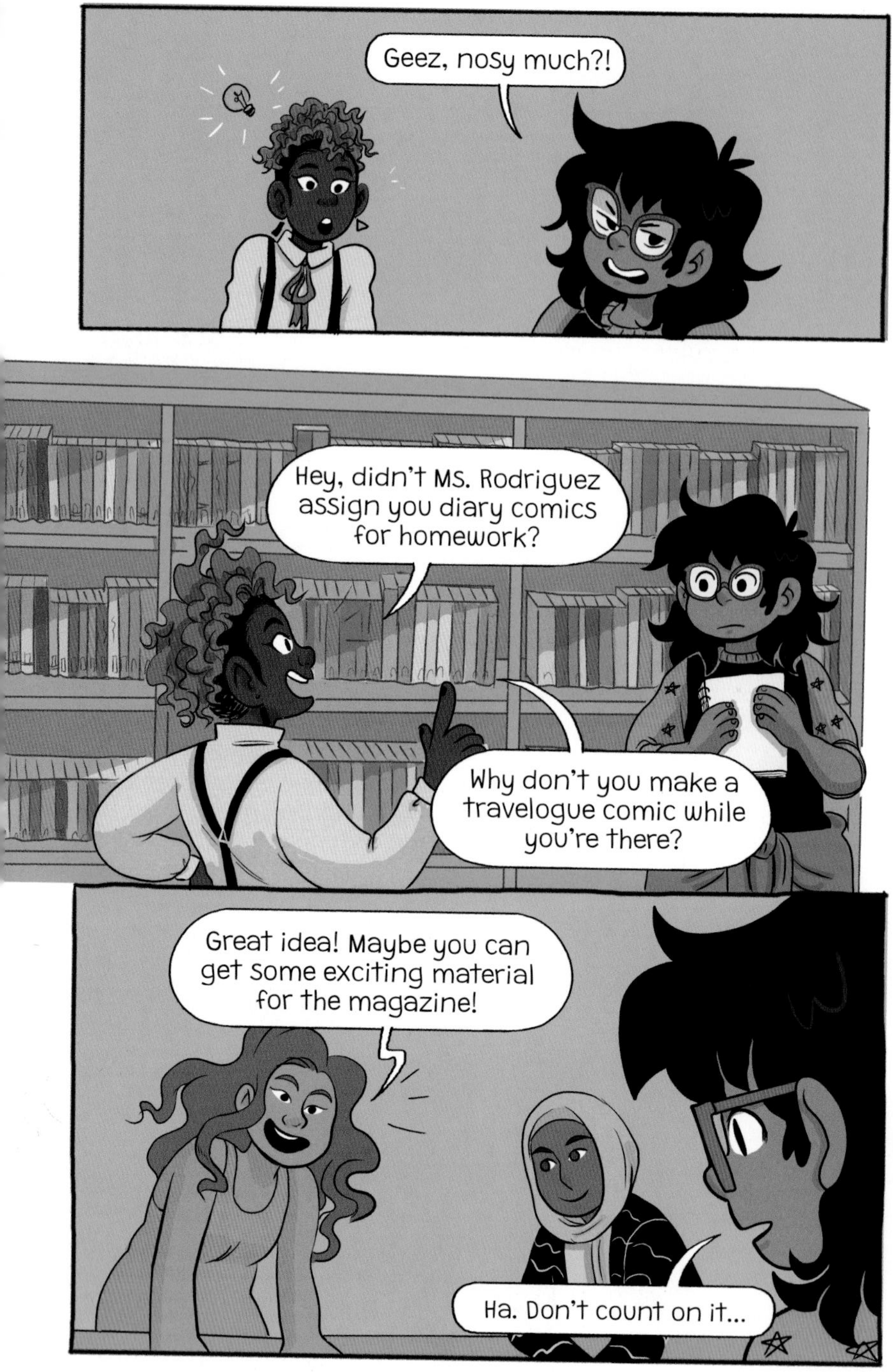
Geez, nosy much?!
Hey, didn't MS. Rodriguez assign you diary comics for homework?
Why don't you make a travelogue comic while you're there?
Great idea! Maybe you can get some exciting material for the magazine!
Ha. Don't count on it...

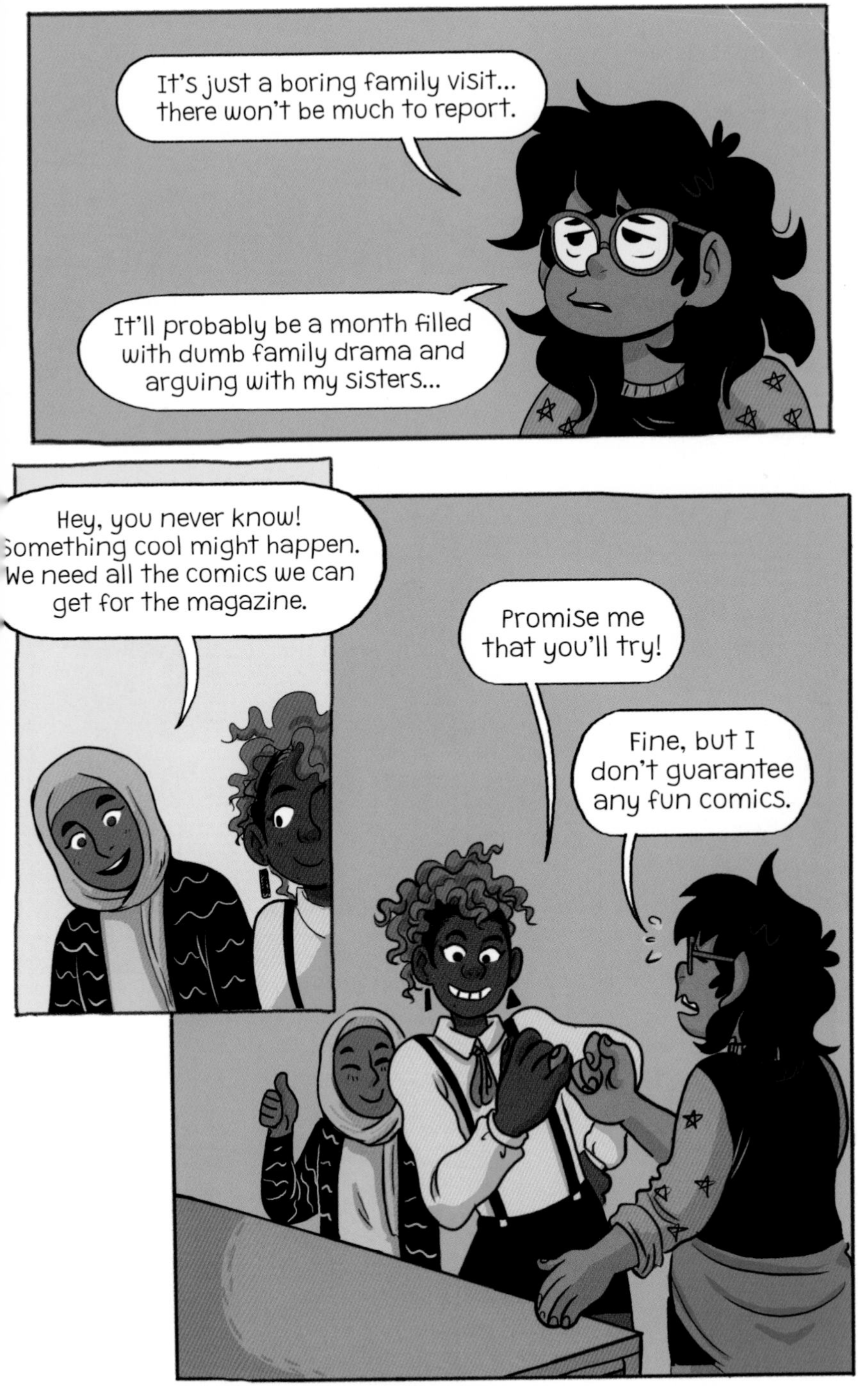
It's just a boring family visit... there won't be much to report.
It'll probably be a month filled with dumb family drama and arguing with my sisters...
Hey, you never know! Something cool might happen. We need all the comics we can get for the magazine.
Promise me that you'll try!
Fine, but I don't guarantee any fun comics.

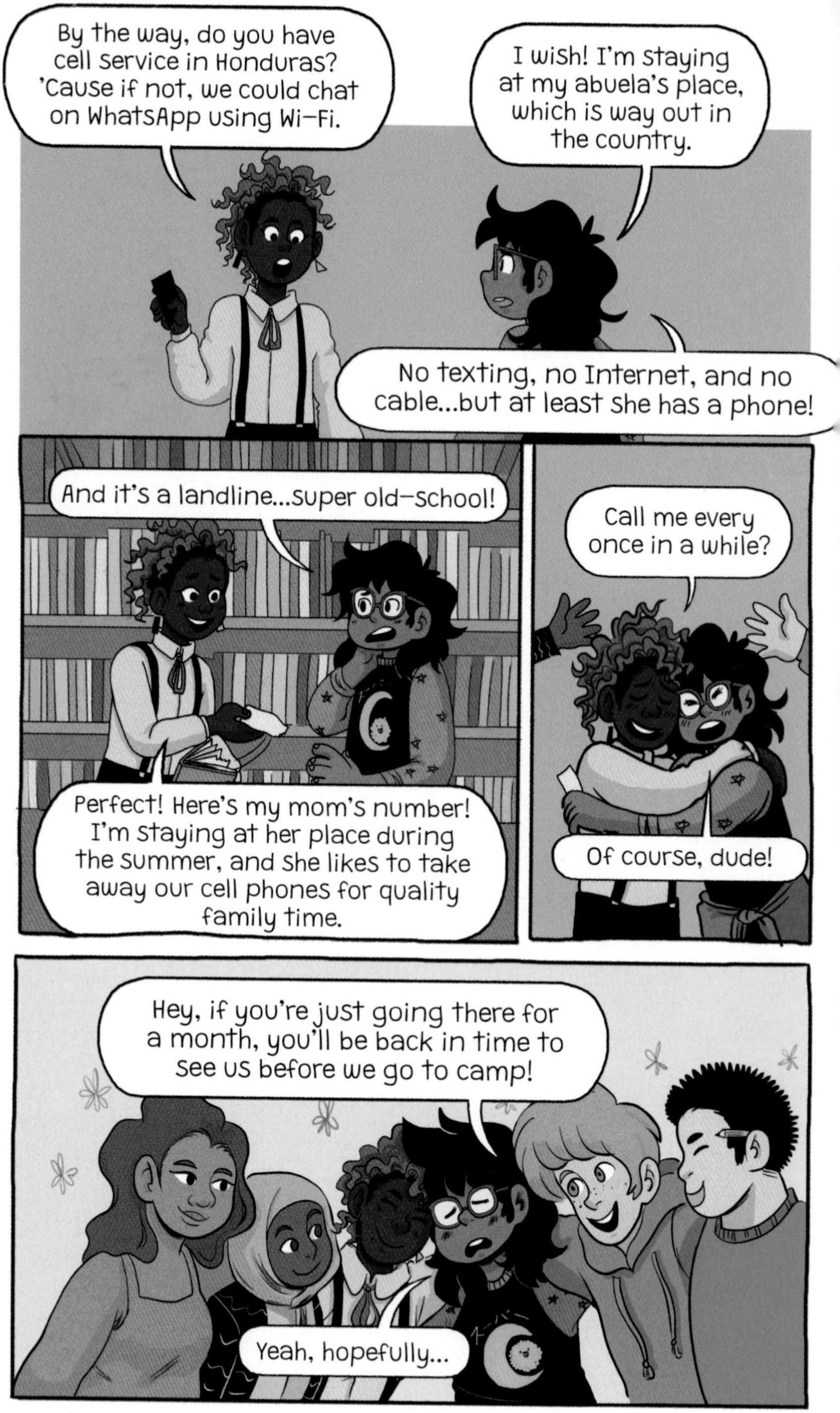
By the way, do you have cell service in Honduras? 'Cause if not, we could chat on WhatsApp using Wi-Fi.
I wish! I'm staying at my abuela's place, which is way out in the country.
No texting, no Internet, and no cable...but at least she has a phone!
And it's a landline...super old-school!
Perfect! Here's my mom's number! I'm staying at her place during the summer, and she likes to take away our cell phones for quality family time.
Call me every once in a while?
Of course, dude!
Hey, if you're just going there for a month, you'll be back in time to see us before we go to camp!
Yeah, hopefully...

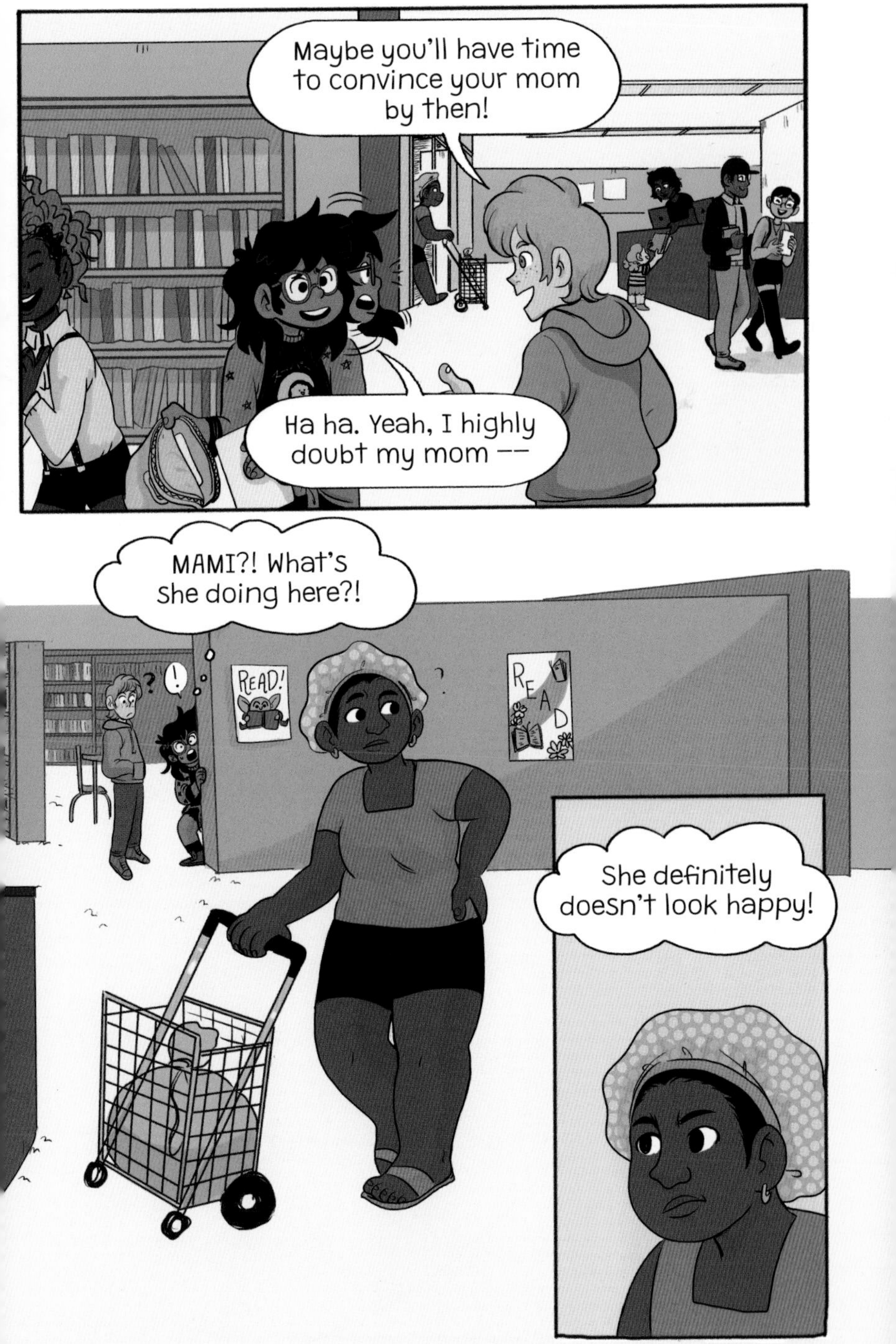
Maybe you'll have time to convince your mom by then!
Ha ha. Yeah, I highly doubt my mom --
MAMI?! What's she doing here?!
READ!
READ
She definitely doesn't look happy!

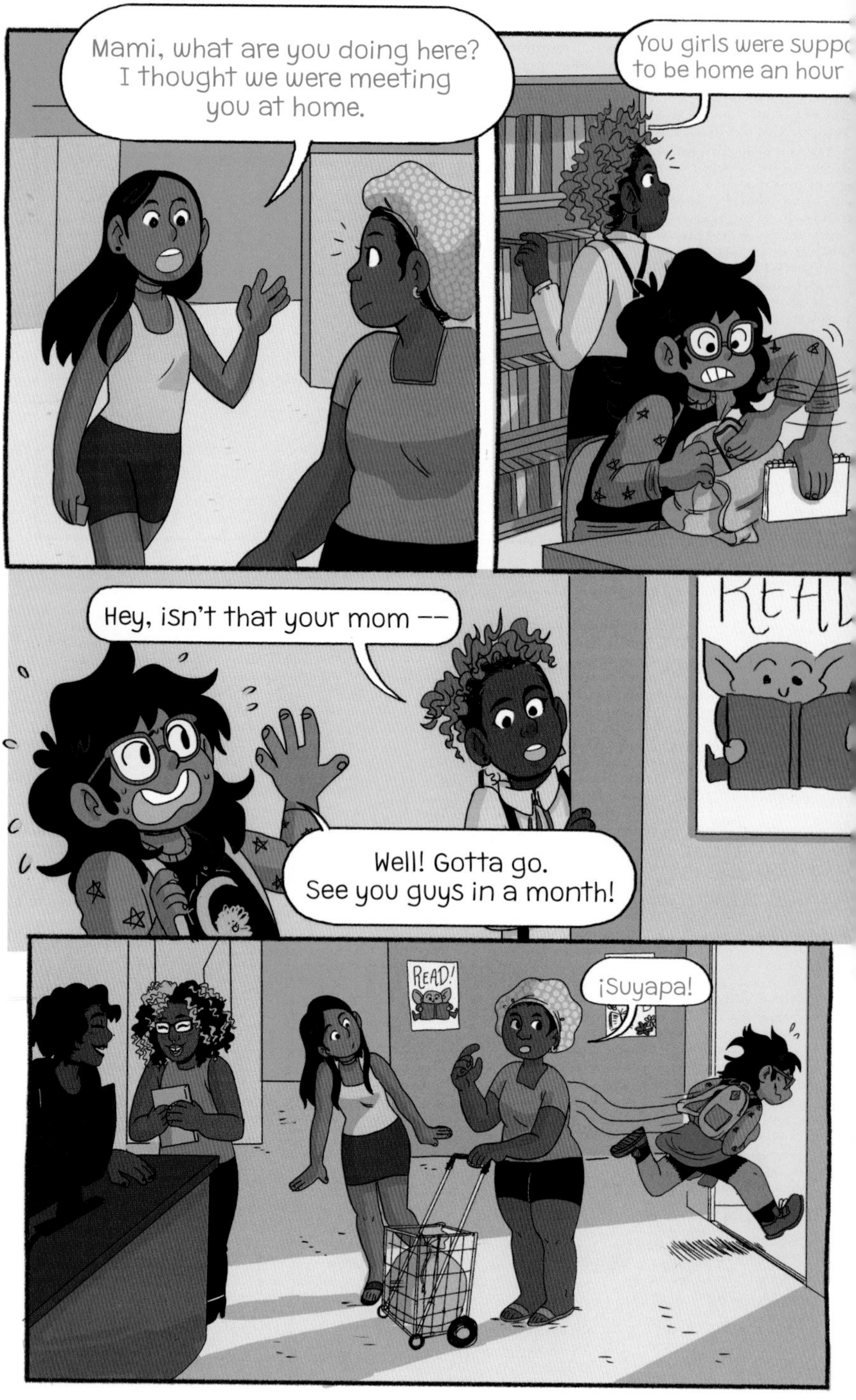
Mami, what are you doing here? I thought we were meeting you at home.
You girls were suppc to be home an hour
Hey, isn't that your mom --
Well! Gotta go. See you guys in a month!
READ!
¡Suyapa!

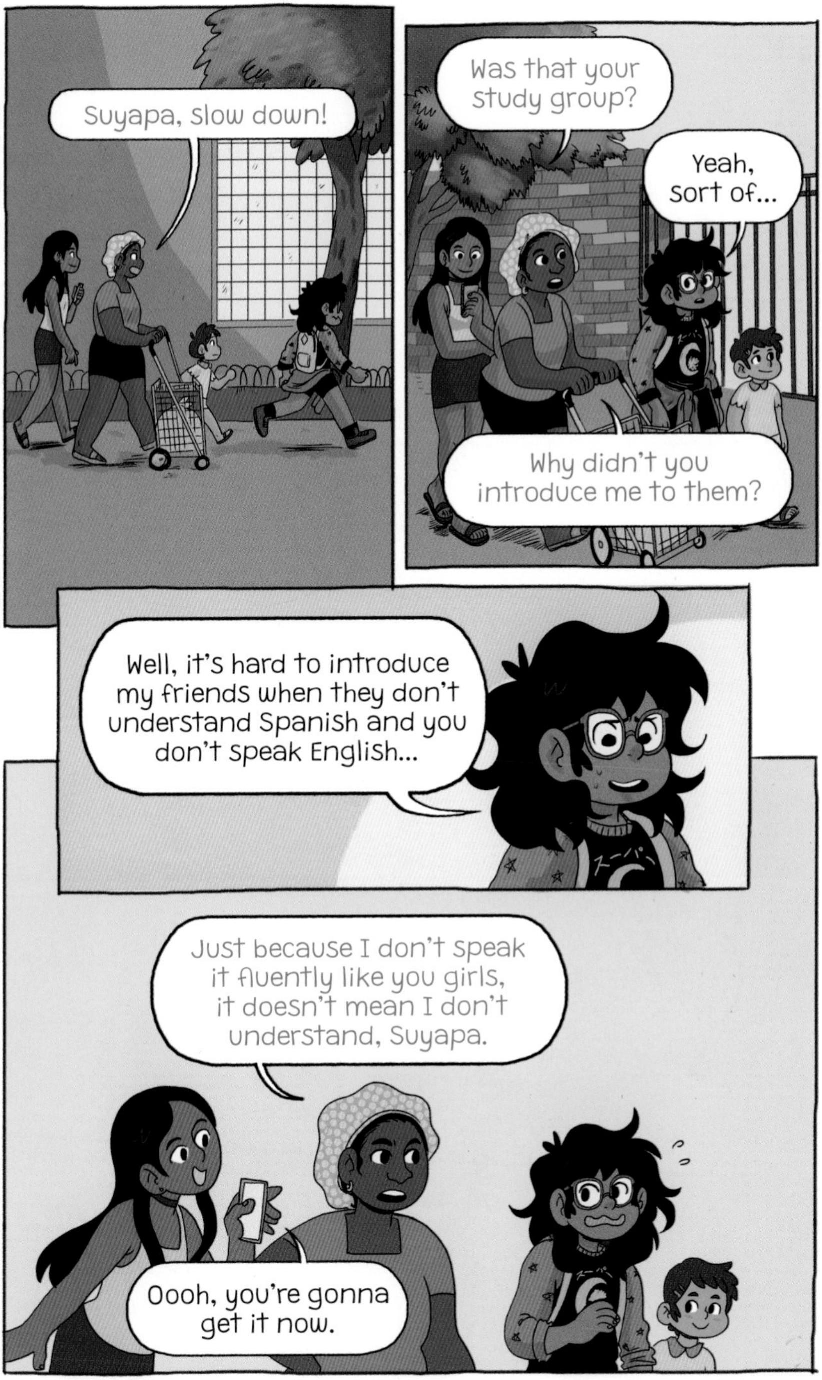
Suyapa, slow down!
Was that your study group?
Yeah, sort of...
Why didn't you introduce me to them?
Well, it's hard to introduce my friends when they don't understand Spanish and you don't speak English...
Just because I don't speak it fluently like you girls, it doesn't mean I don't understand, Suyapa.
Oooh, you're gonna get it now.

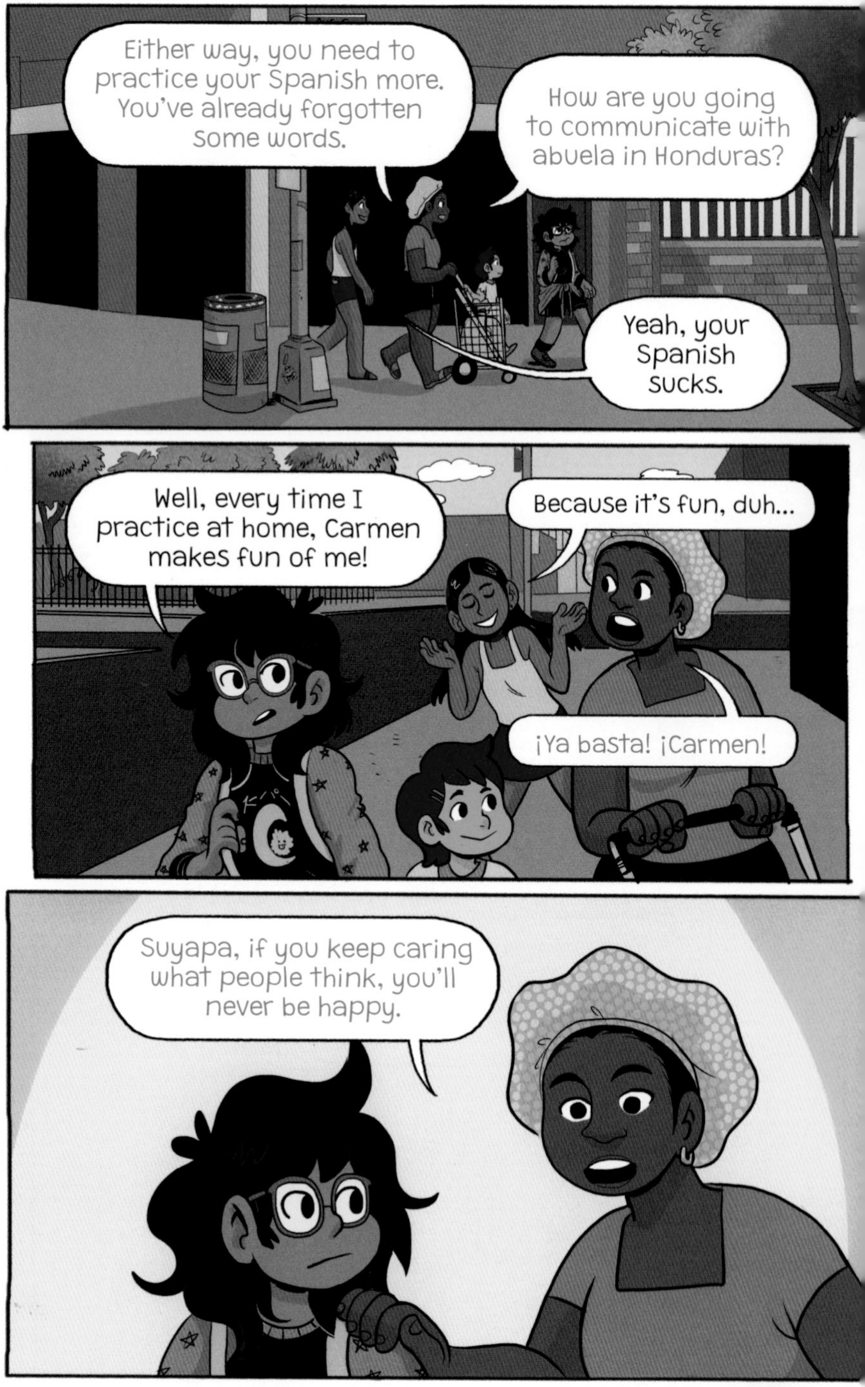
Either way, you need to practice your Spanish more. You've already forgotten some words.
How are you going to communicate with abuela in Honduras?
Yeah, your Spanish sucks.
Well, every time I practice at home, Carmen makes fun of me!
Because it's fun, duh...
¡Ya basta! ¡Carmen!
Suyapa, if you keep caring what people think, you'll never be happy.

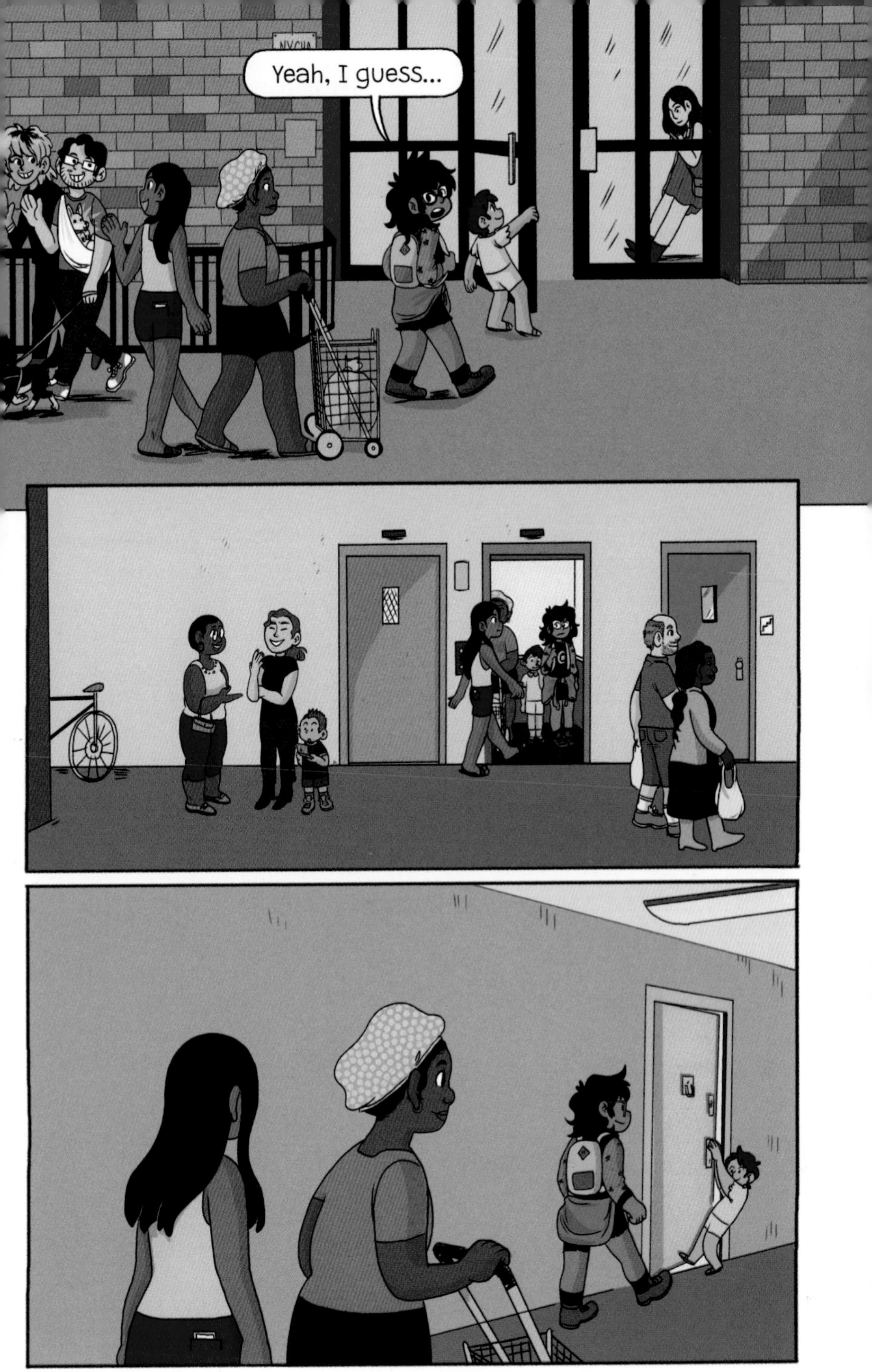
Yeah, I guess...

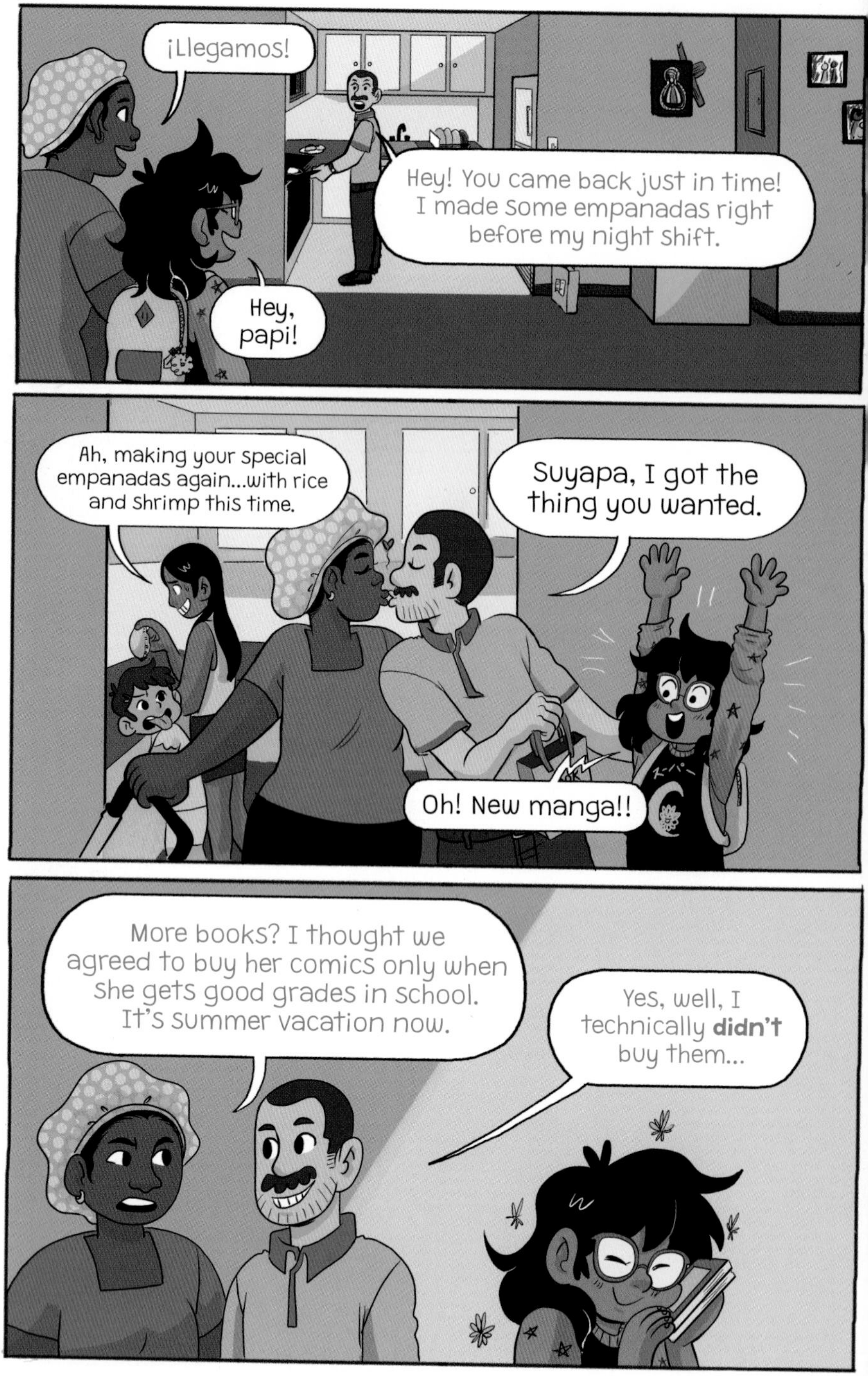

¡Llegamos!
Hey! You came back just in time! I made some empanadas right before my night shift.
Hey, papi!
Ah, making your special empanadas again...with rice and shrimp this time.
Suyapa, I got the thing you wanted.
Oh! New manga!!
More books? I thought we agreed to buy her comics only when she gets good grades in school. It's summer vacation now.
Yes, well, I technically **didn't** buy them...

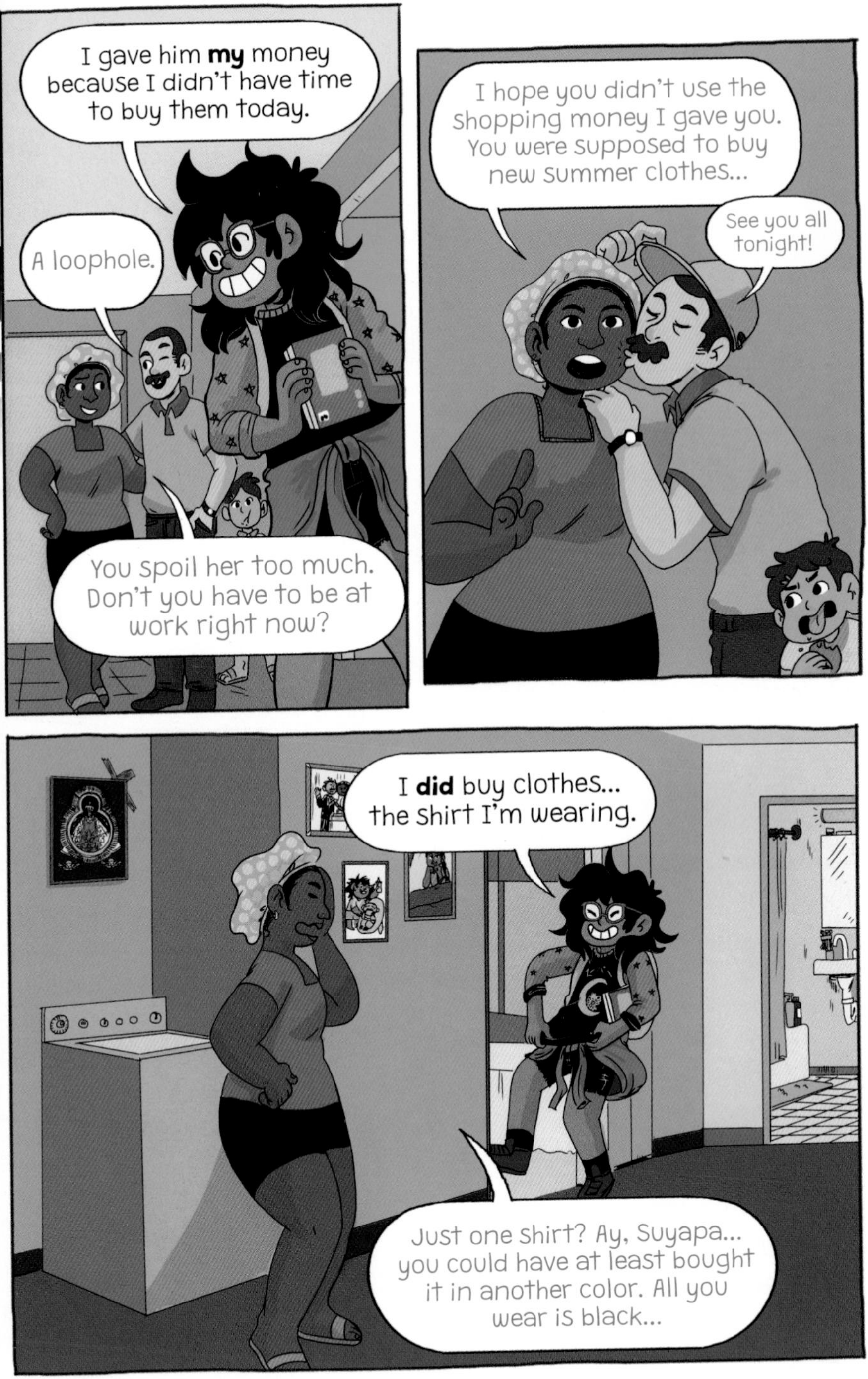
I gave him **my** money because I didn't have time to buy them today.
A loophole.
You spoil her too much. Don't you have to be at work right now?
I hope you didn't use the shopping money I gave you. You were supposed to buy new summer clothes...
See you all tonight!
I **did** buy clothes... the shirt I'm wearing.
Just one shirt? Ay, Suyapa... you could have at least bought it in another color. All you wear is black...

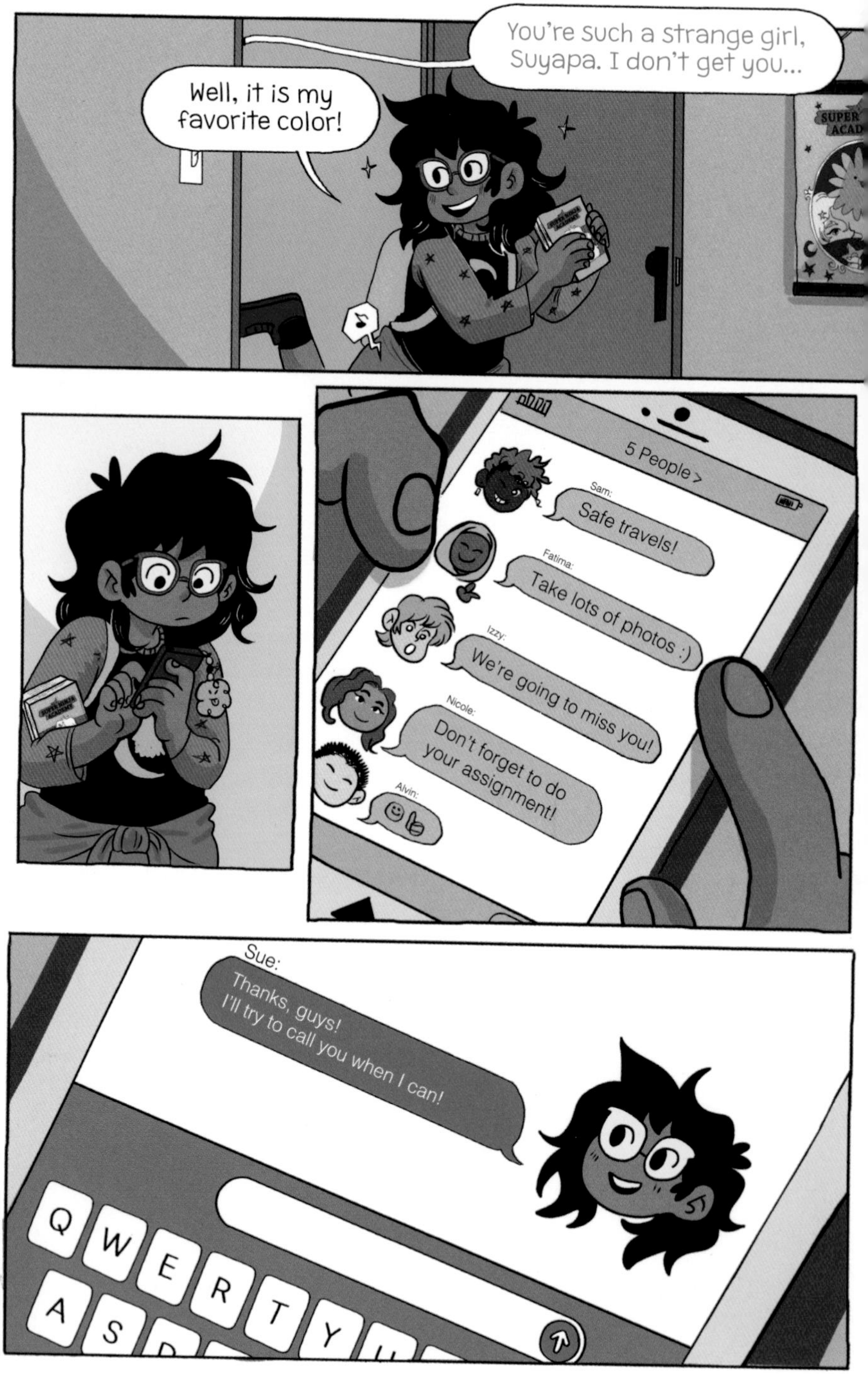
You're such a strange girl, Suyapa. I don't get you...
Well, it is my favorite color!
SUPER ACAD
5 People >
Sam:
Safe travels!
Fatima:
Take lots of photos :)
Izzy:
We're going to miss you!
Nicole:
Don't forget to do your assignment!
Alvin:
Sue:
Thanks, guys! I'll try to call you when I can!
QWERTY
AS

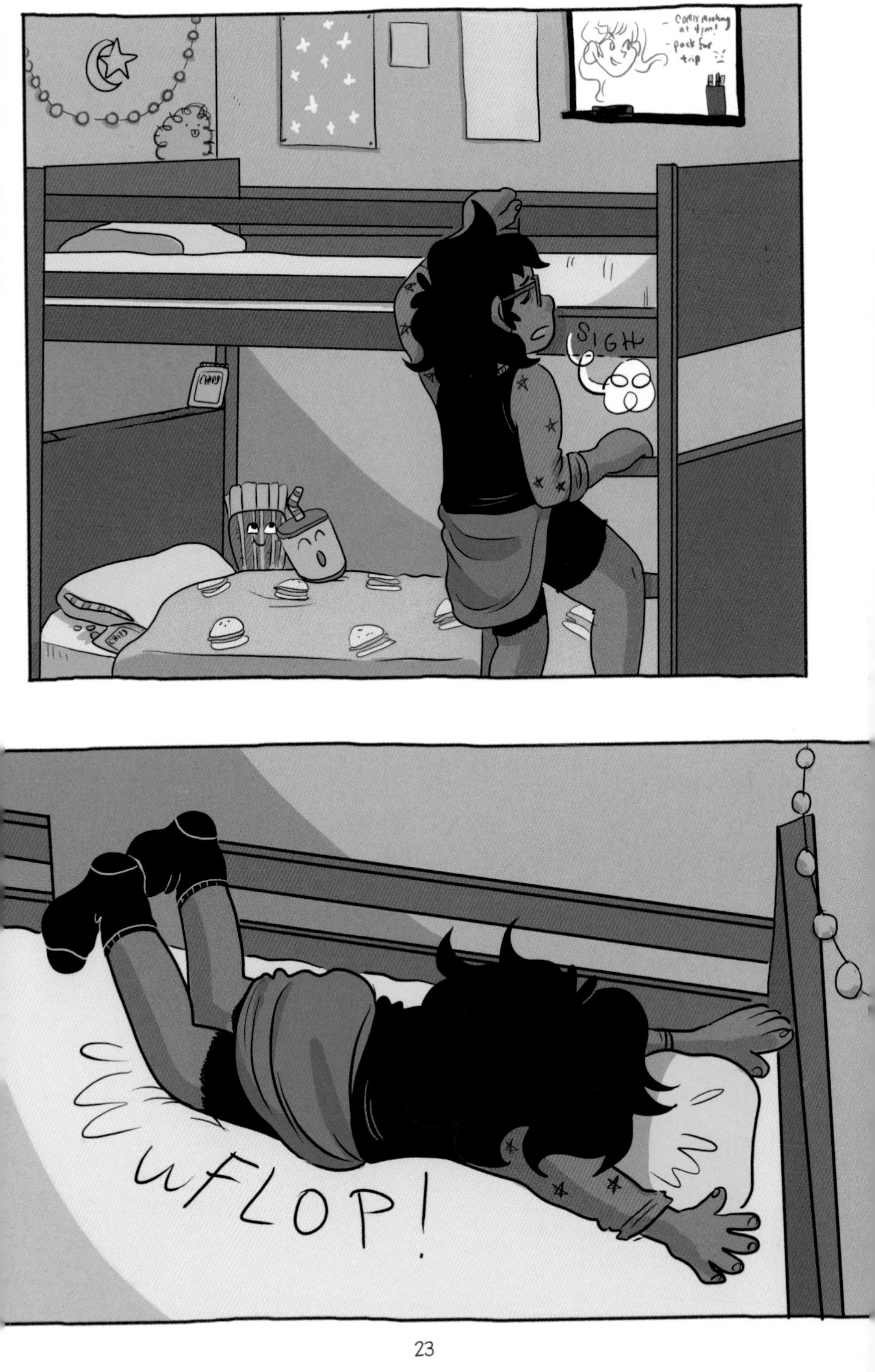
- COMIX meeting at 4pm!
- pack for trip
CHIPS
SIGH
FLOP!

CHAPTER TWO

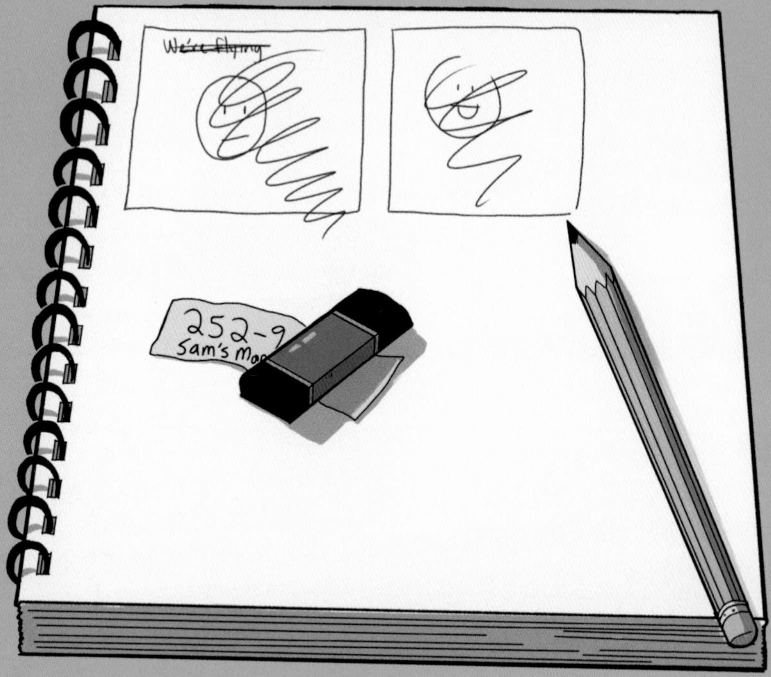

We're flying
252-9
Sam's Ma

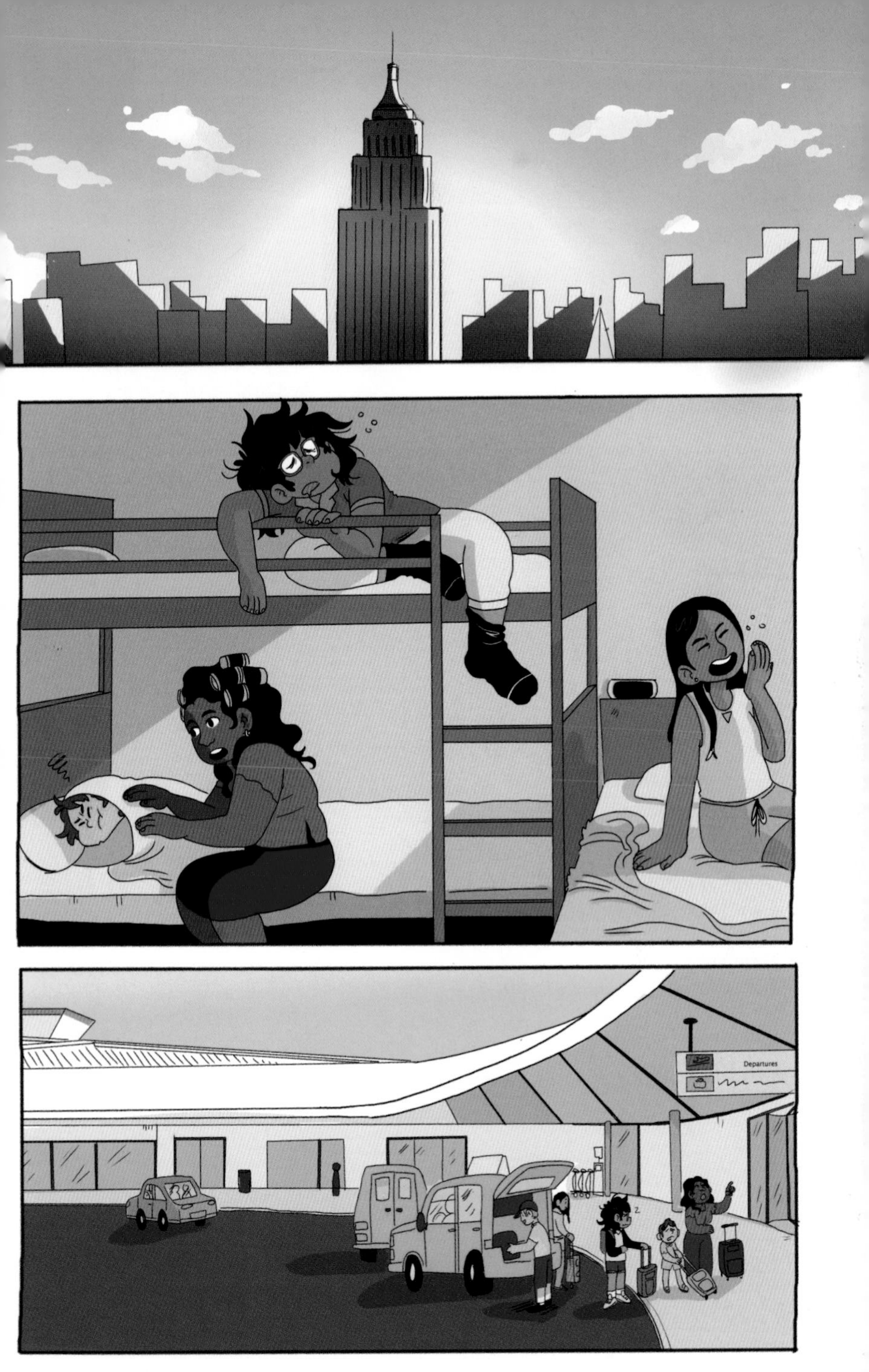
Departures

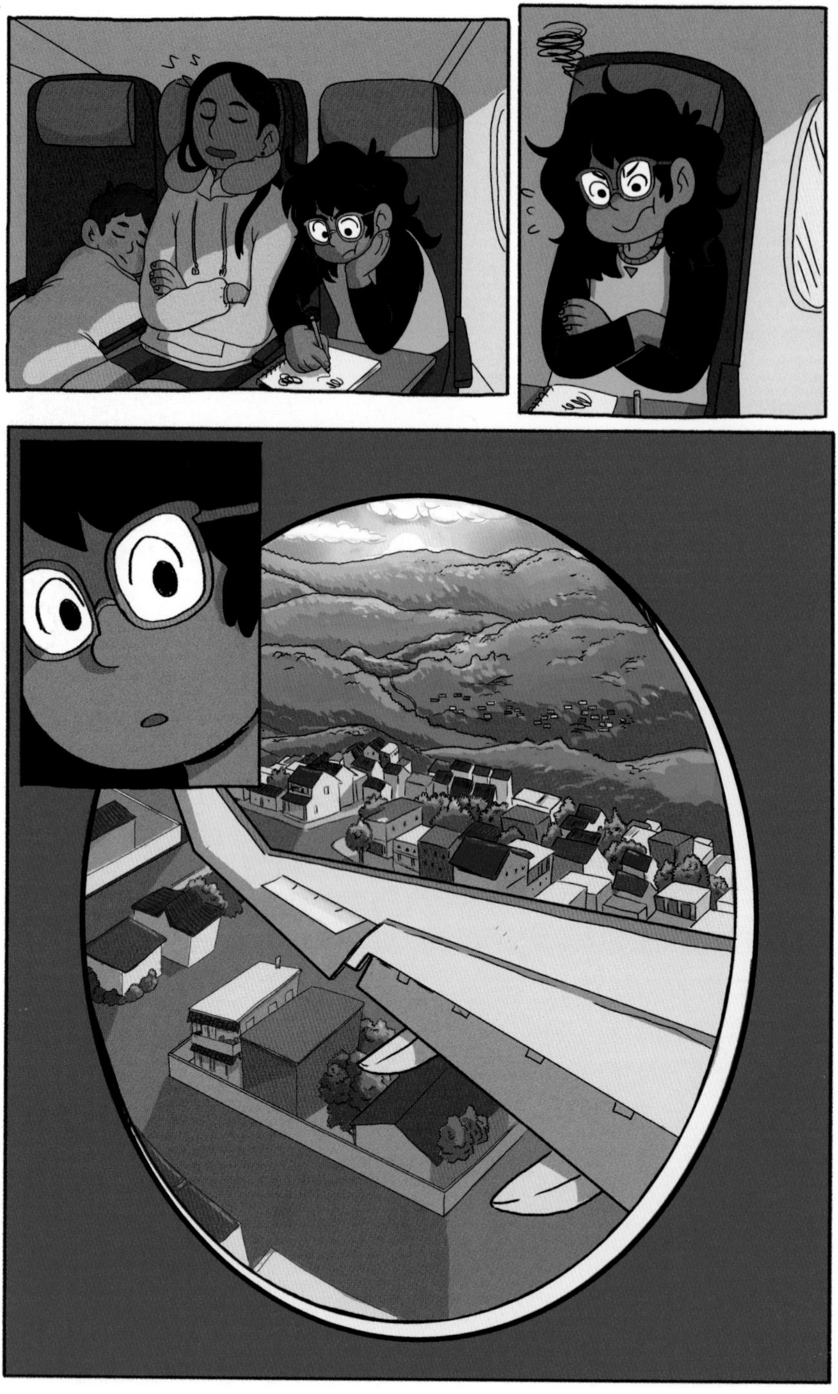

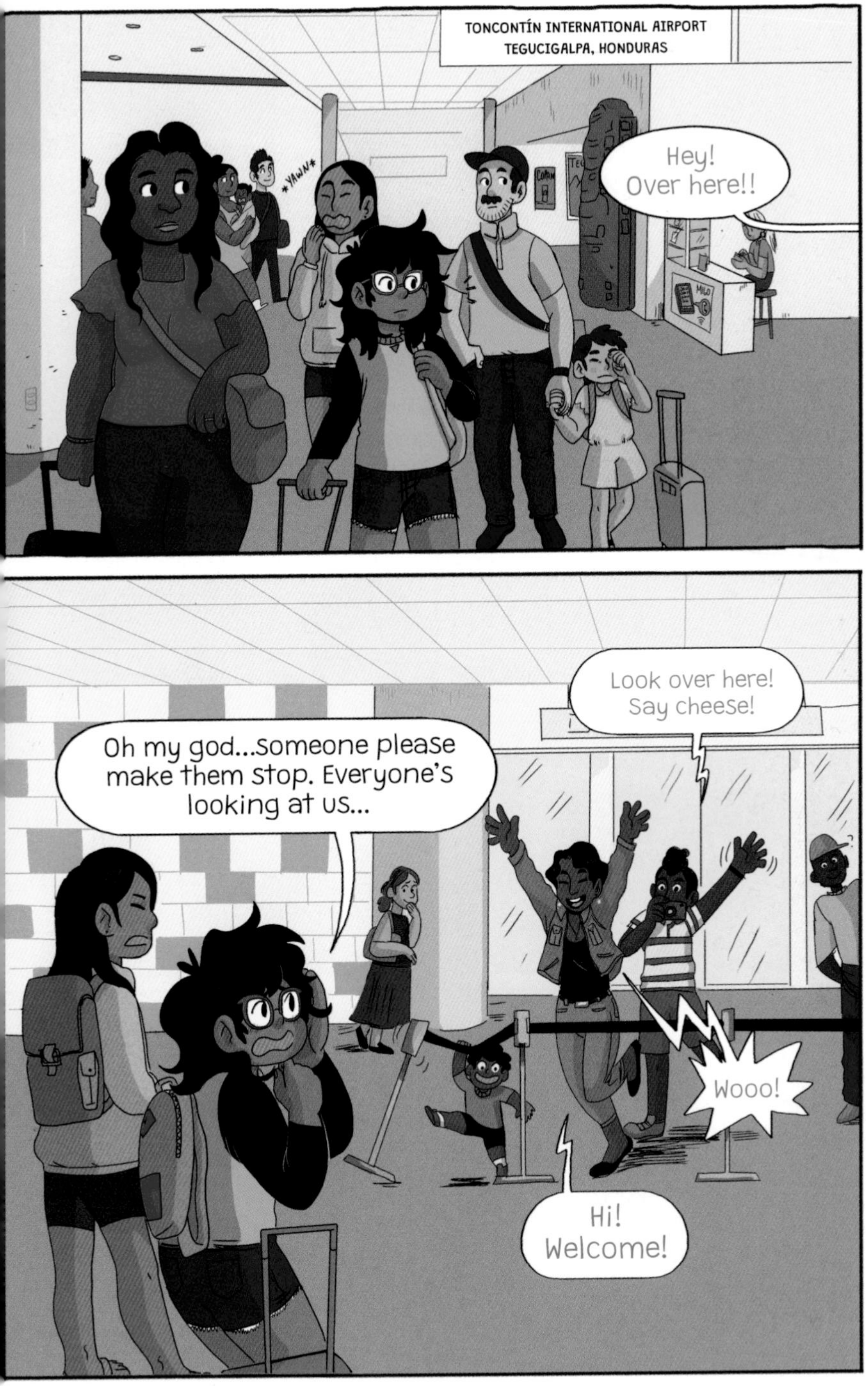
TONCONTÍN INTERNATIONAL AIRPORT
TEGUCIGALPA, HONDURAS
YAWN
Hey! Over here!!
Look over here! Say cheese!
Oh my god...someone please make them stop. Everyone's looking at us...
Wooo!
Hi! Welcome!

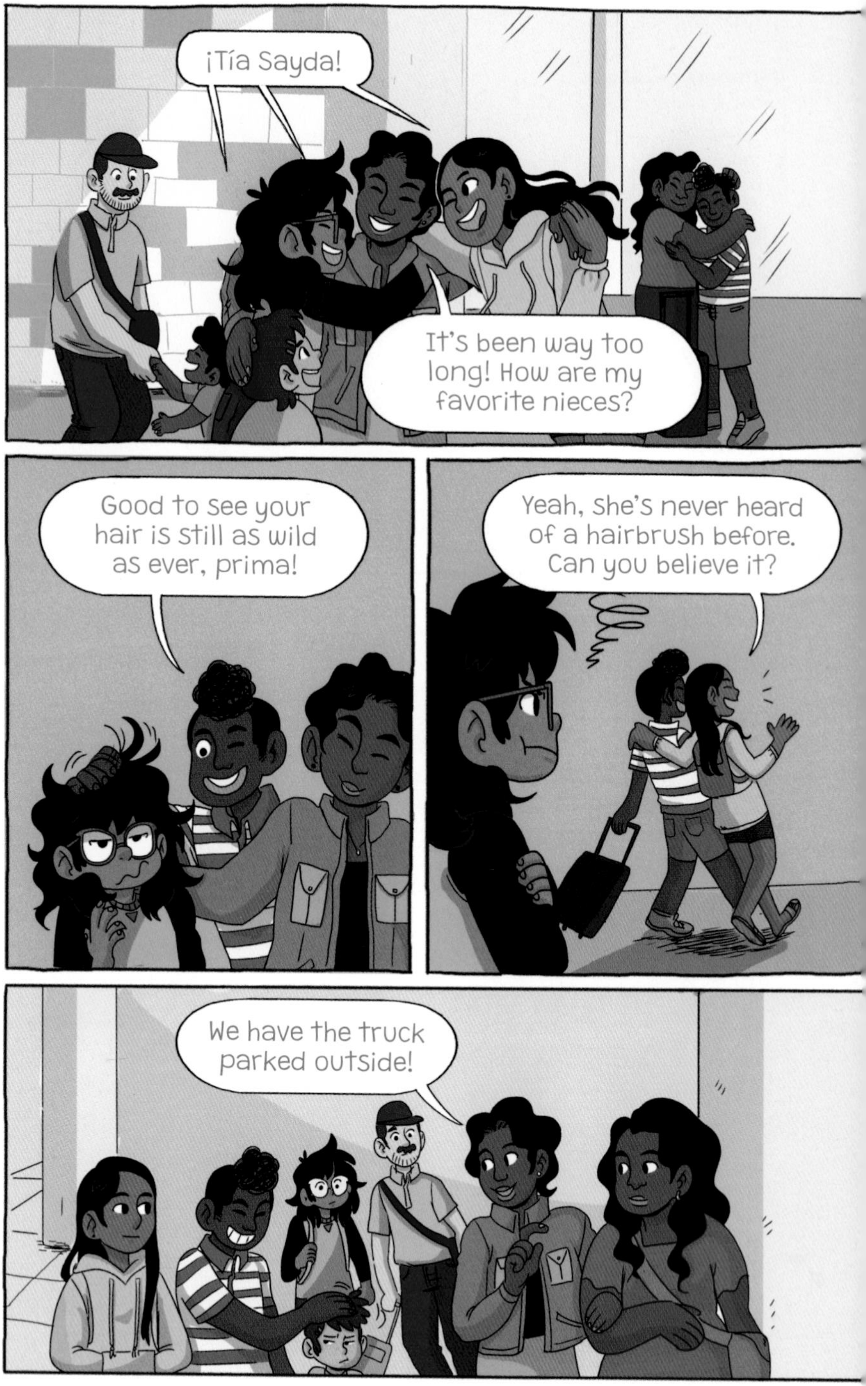
¡Tía Sayda!
It's been way too long! How are my favorite nieces?
Good to see your hair is still as wild as ever, prima!
Yeah, she's never heard of a hairbrush before. Can you believe it?
We have the truck parked outside!

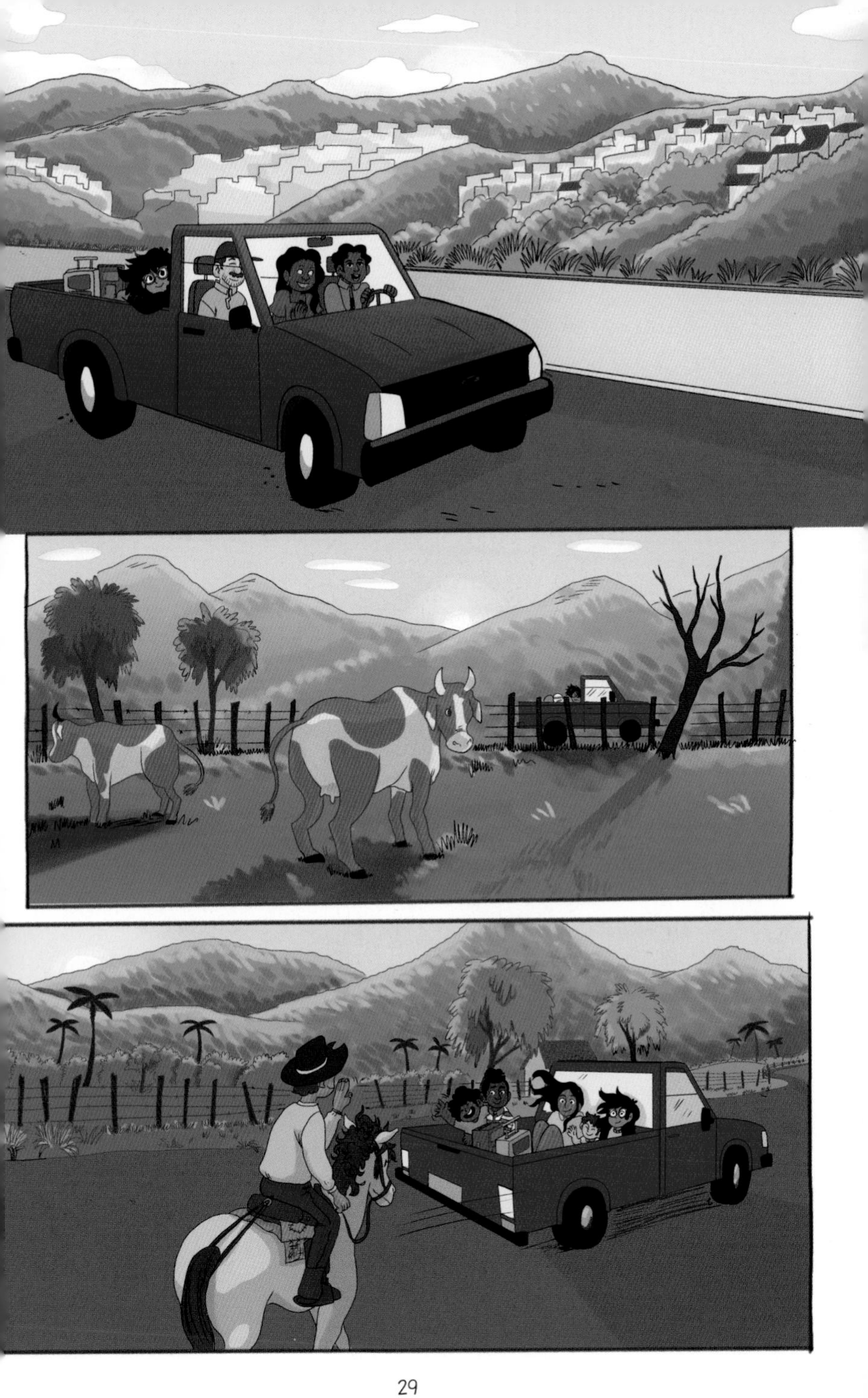

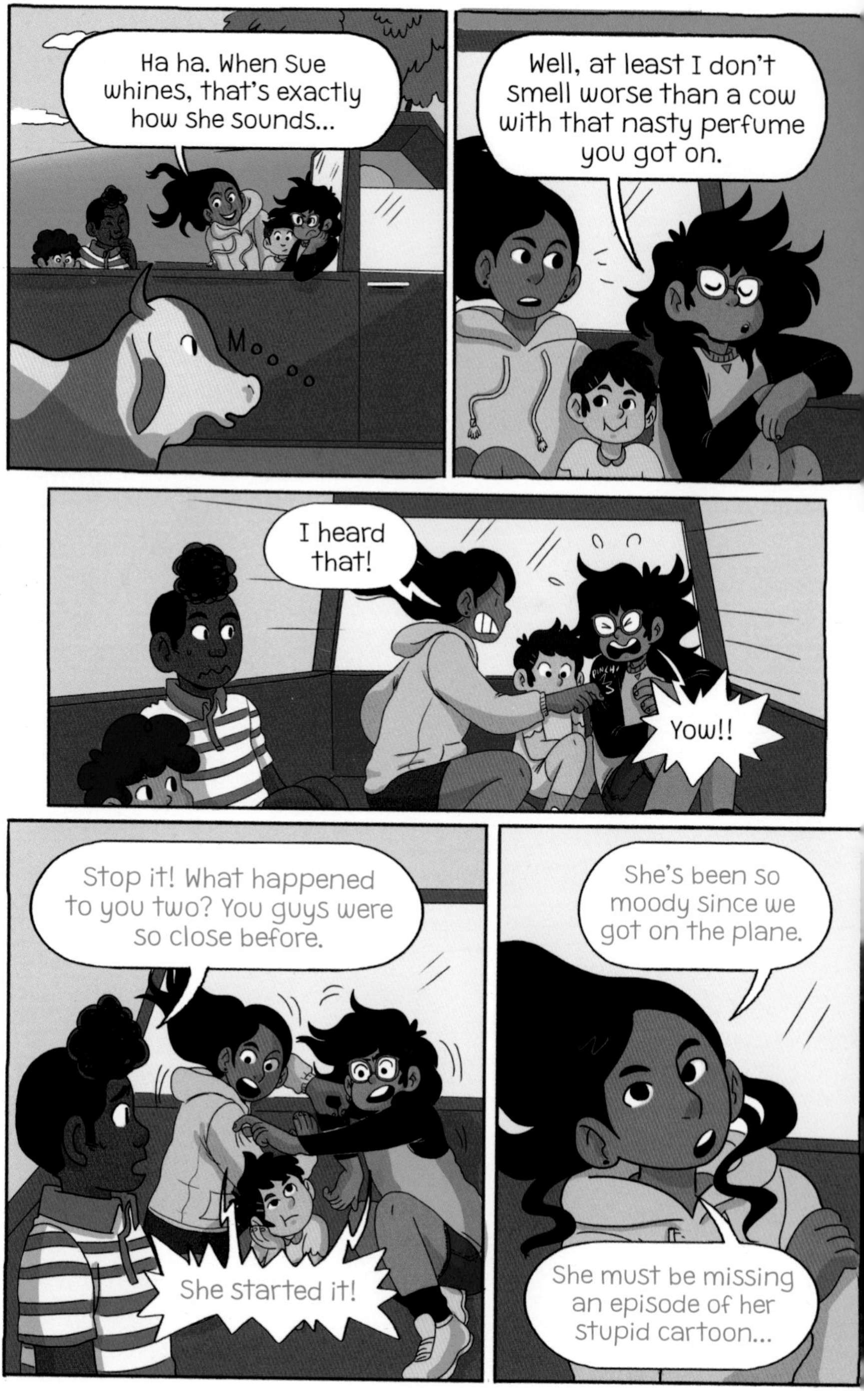
Ha ha. When Sue whines, that's exactly how she sounds...
Mooooo
Well, at least I don't smell worse than a cow with that nasty perfume you got on.
I heard that!
PINCH
Yow!!
Stop it! What happened to you two? You guys were so close before.
She started it!
She's been so moody since we got on the plane.
She must be missing an episode of her stupid cartoon...

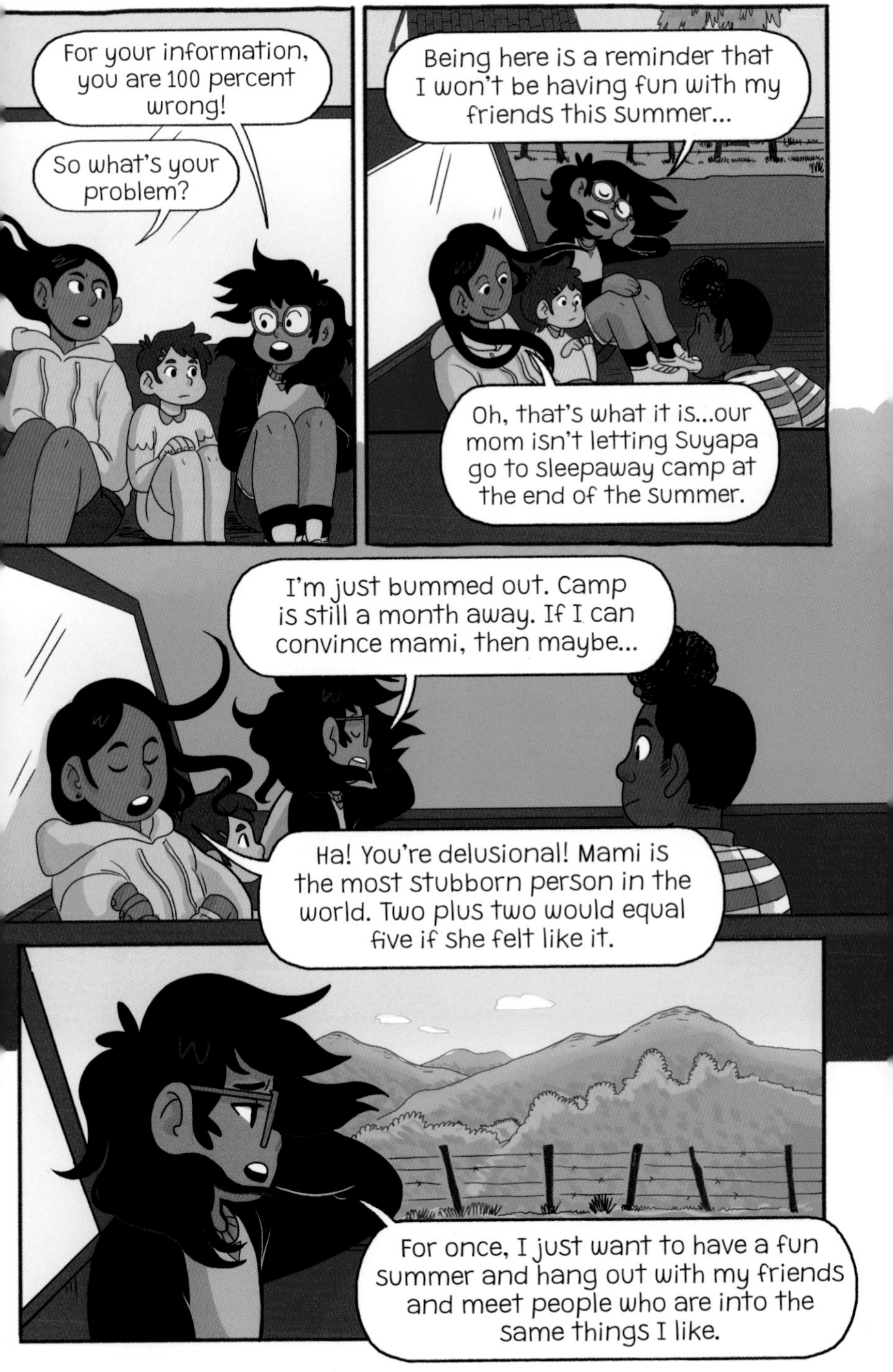
For your information, you are 100 percent wrong!
So what's your problem?
Being here is a reminder that I won't be having fun with my friends this summer...
Oh, that's what it is...our mom isn't letting Suyapa go to sleepaway camp at the end of the summer.
I'm just bummed out. Camp is still a month away. If I can convince mami, then maybe...
Ha! You're delusional! Mami is the most stubborn person in the world. Two plus two would equal five if she felt like it.
For once, I just want to have a fun summer and hang out with my friends and meet people who are into the same things I like.

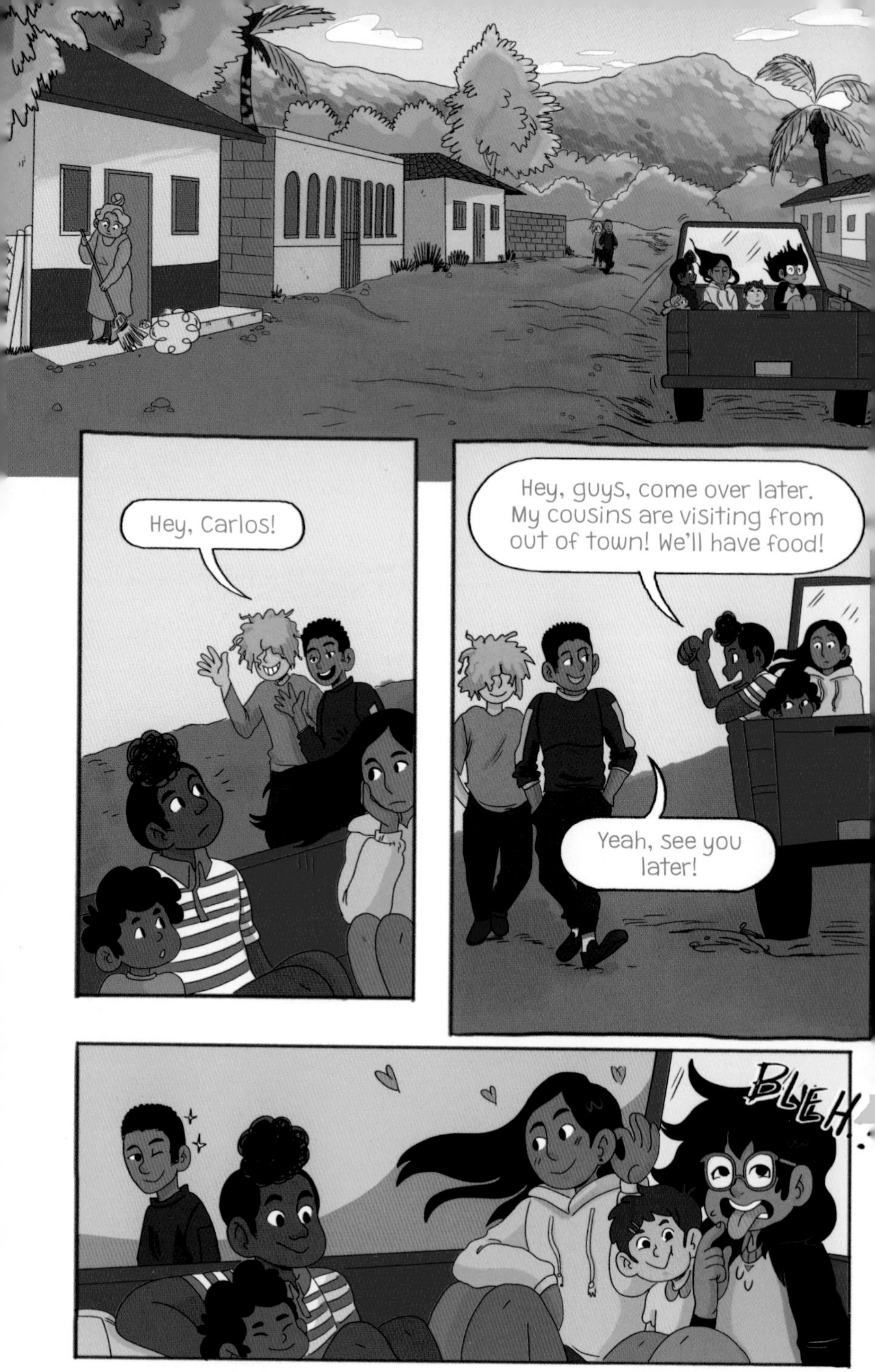
Hey, Carlos!
Hey, guys, come over later. My cousins are visiting from out of town! We'll have food!
Yeah, see you later!
BLEH

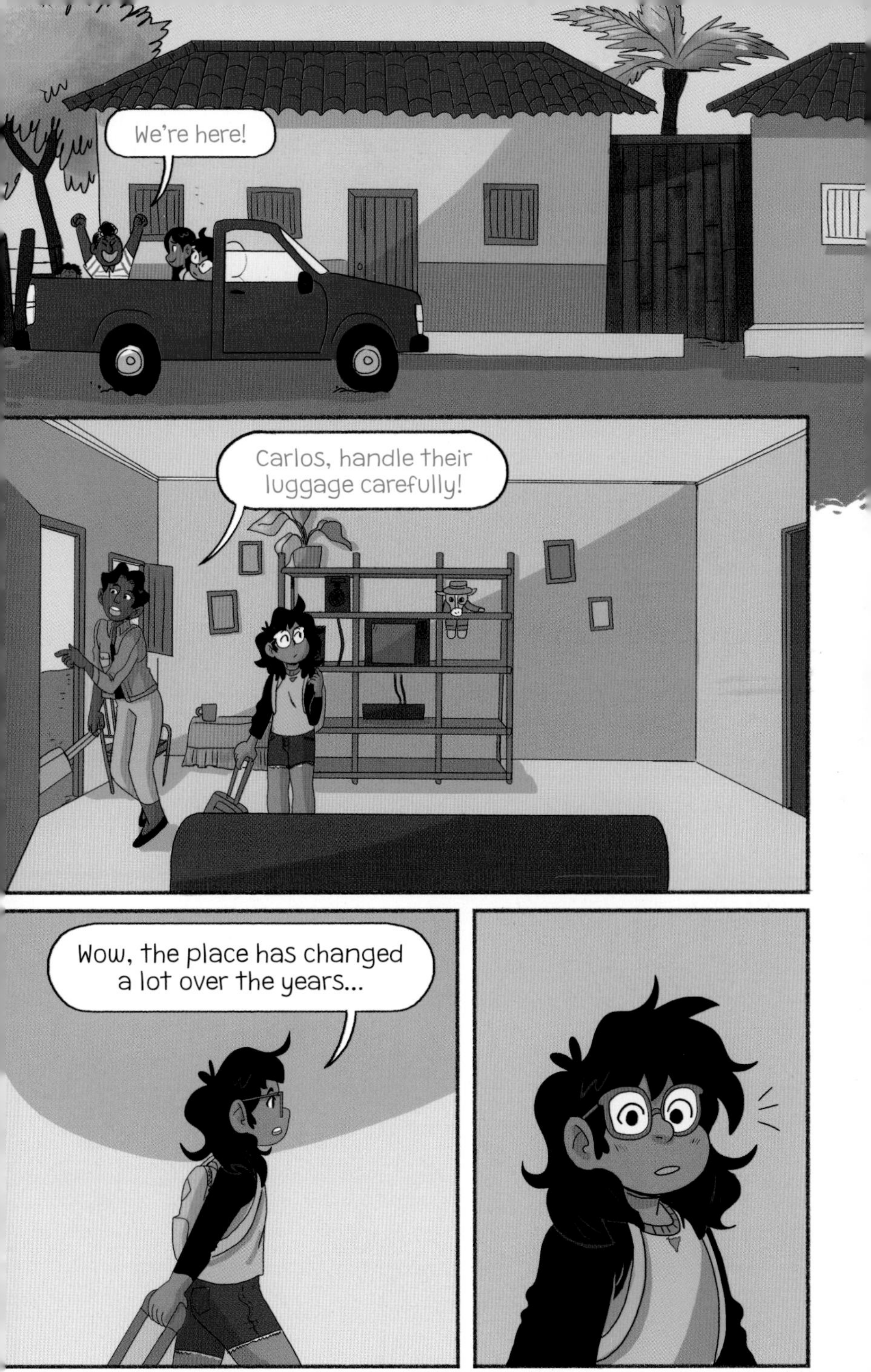
We're here!
Carlos, handle their luggage carefully!
Wow, the place has changed a lot over the years...

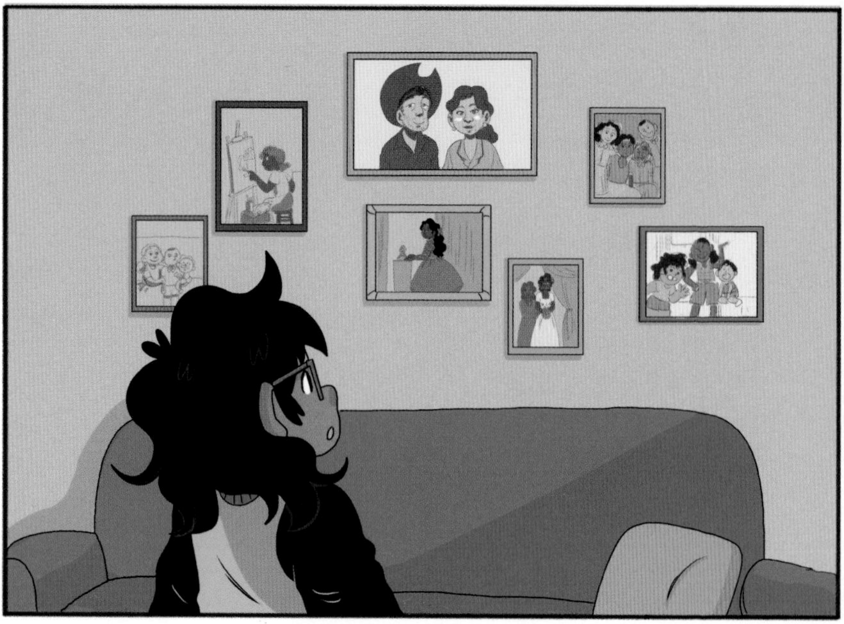
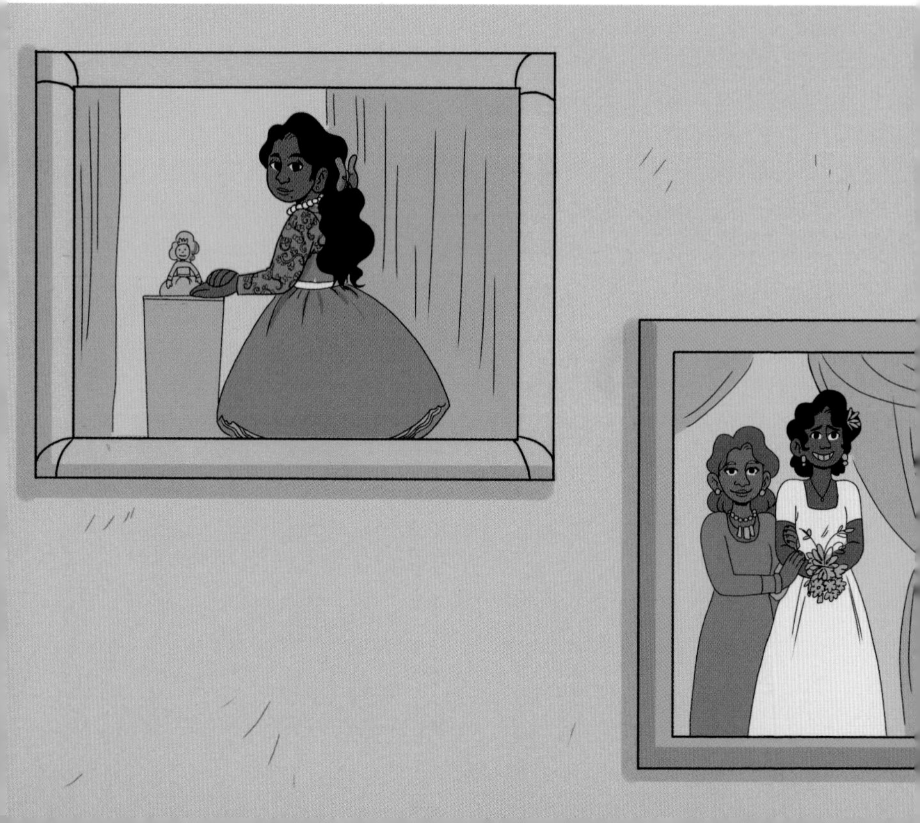

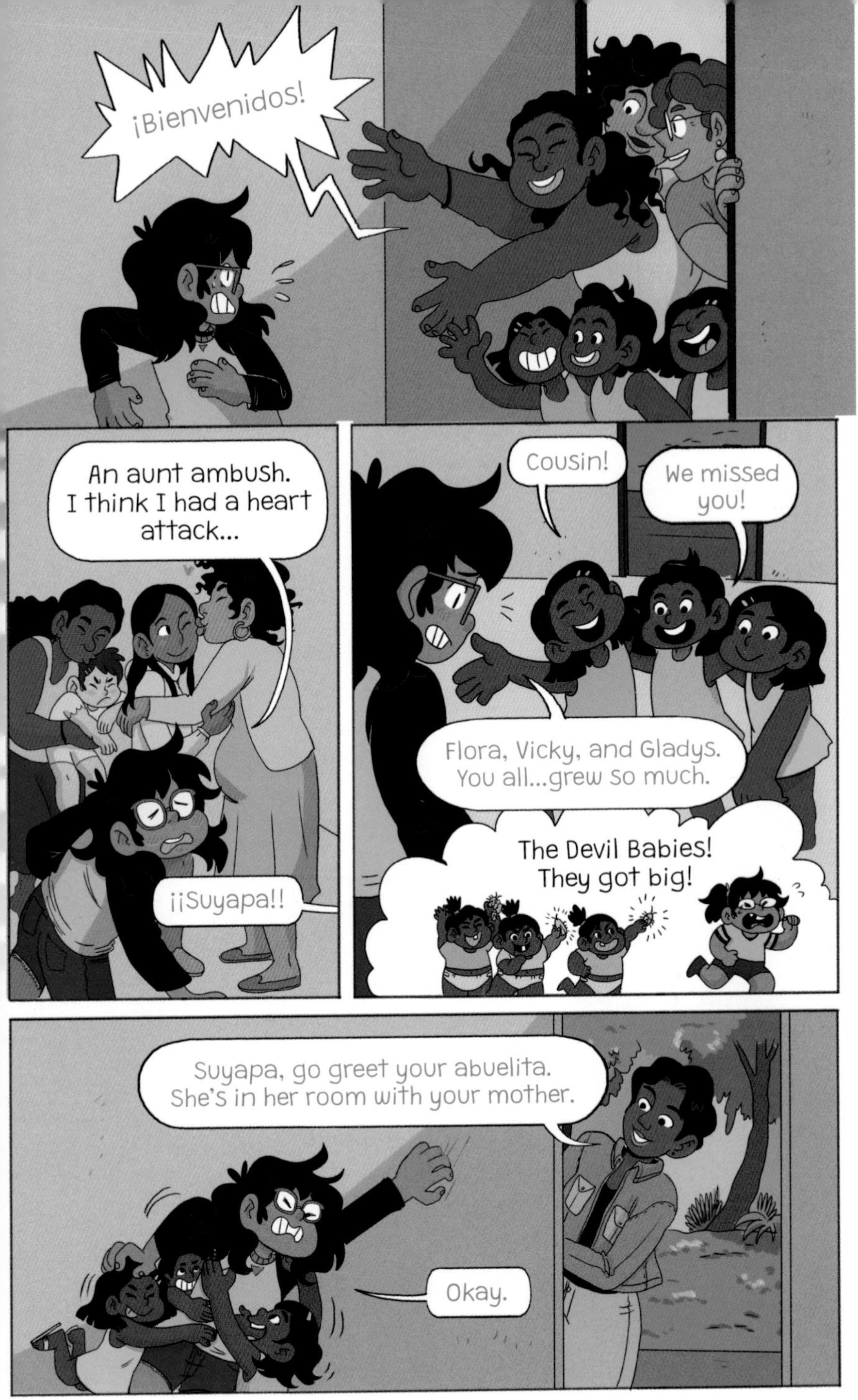
¡Bienvenidos!
An aunt ambush. I think I had a heart attack...
¡¡Suyapa!!
Cousin!
We missed you!
Flora, Vicky, and Gladys. You all...grew so much.
The Devil Babies! They got big!
Suyapa, go greet your abuelita. She's in her room with your mother.
Okay.

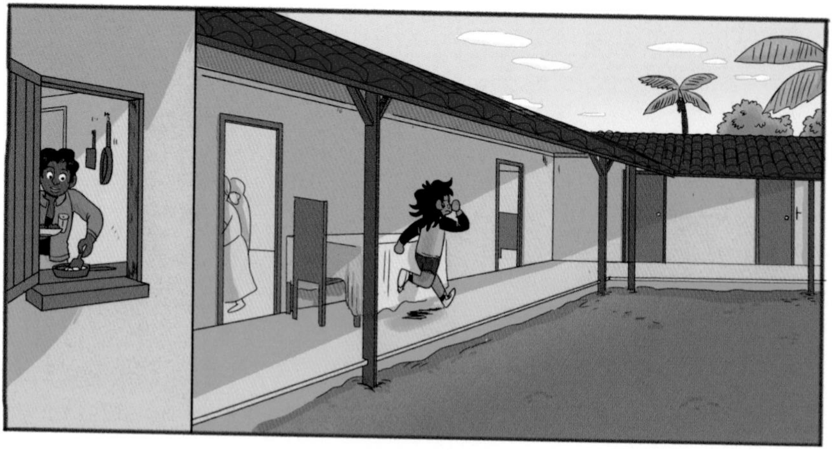

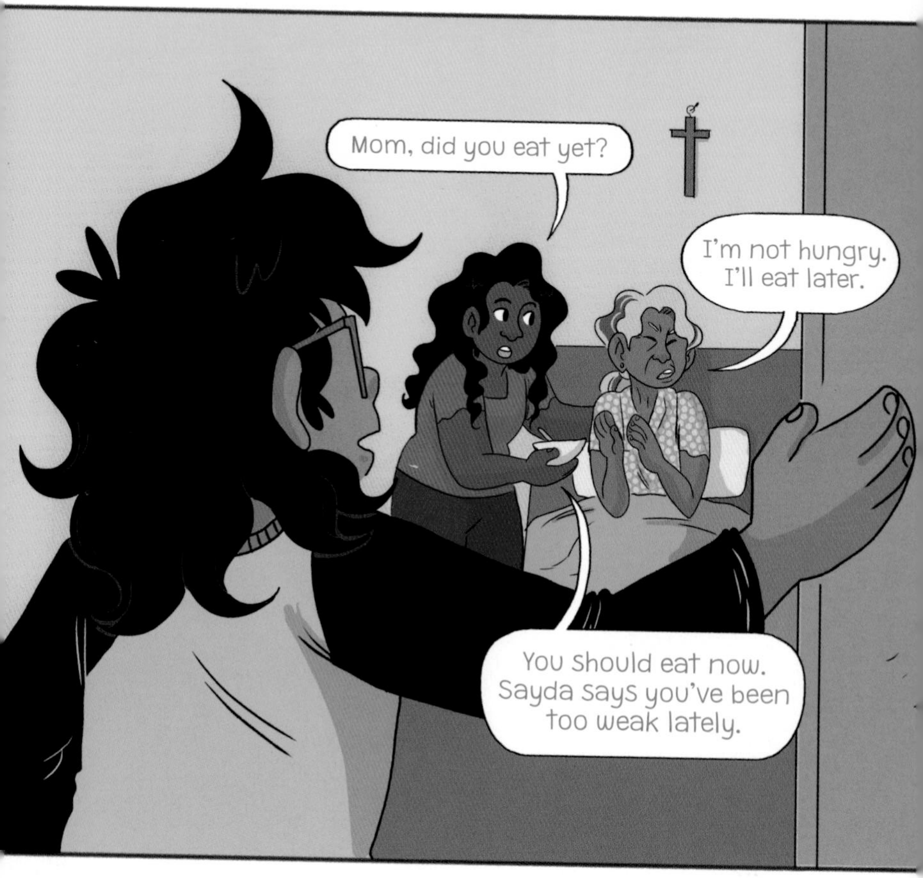

Mom, did you eat yet?
I'm not hungry. I'll eat later.
You should eat now. Sayda says you've been too weak lately.

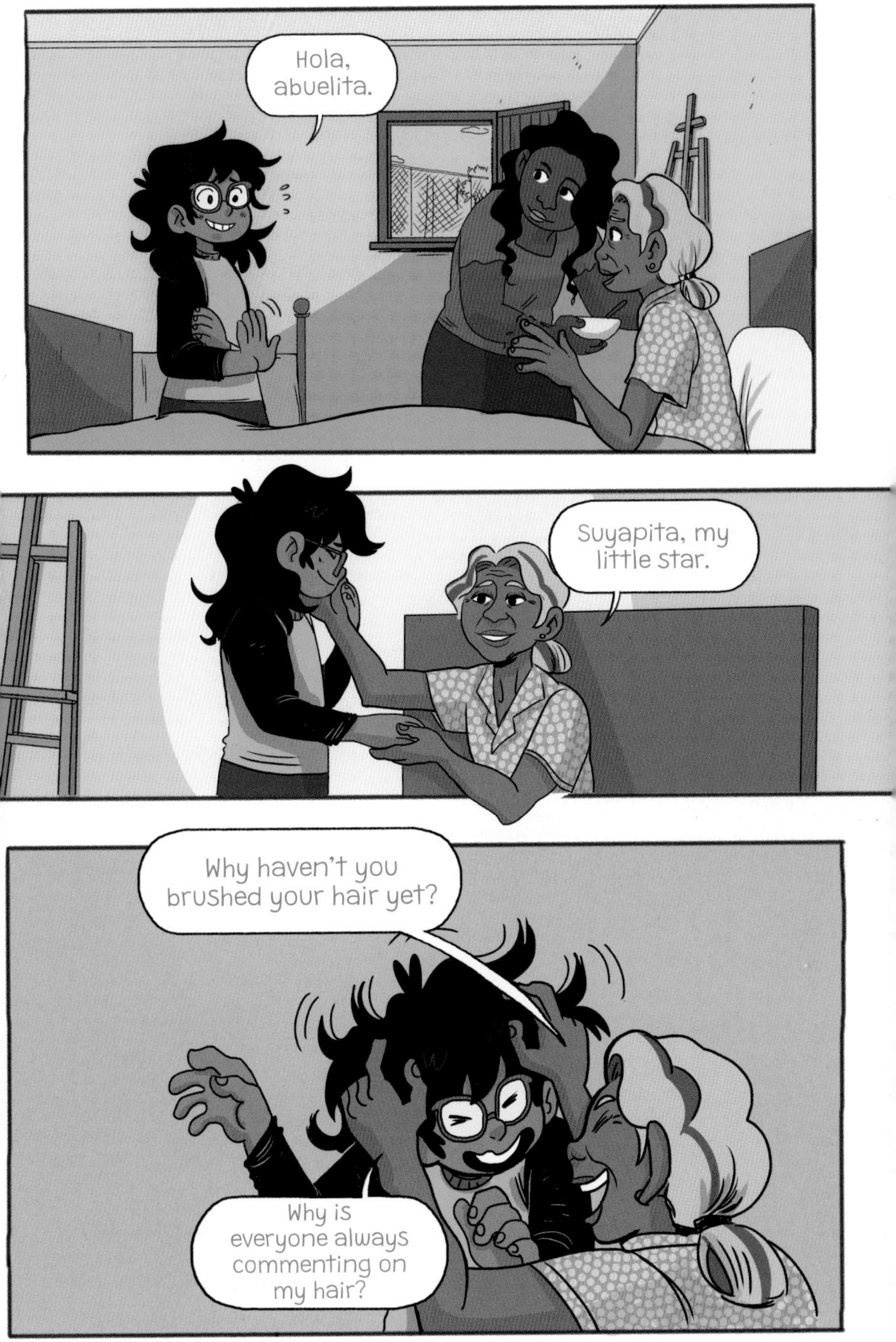
Hola, abuelita.
Suyapita, my little star.
Why haven't you brushed your hair yet?
Why is everyone always commenting on my hair?

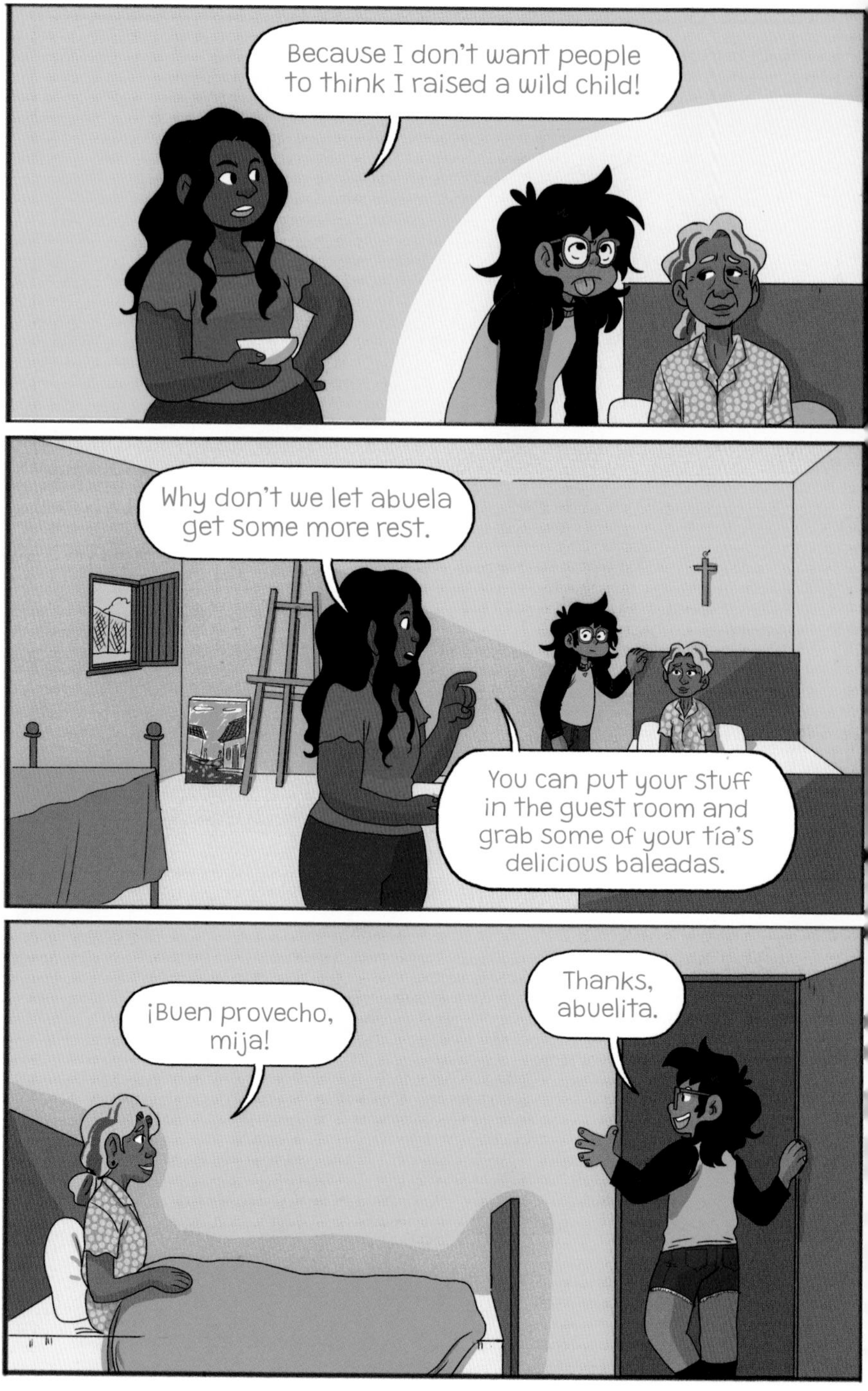
Because I don't want people to think I raised a wild child!
Why don't we let abuela get some more rest.
You can put your stuff in the guest room and grab some of your tía's delicious baleadas.
¡Buen provecho, mija!
Thanks, abuelita.

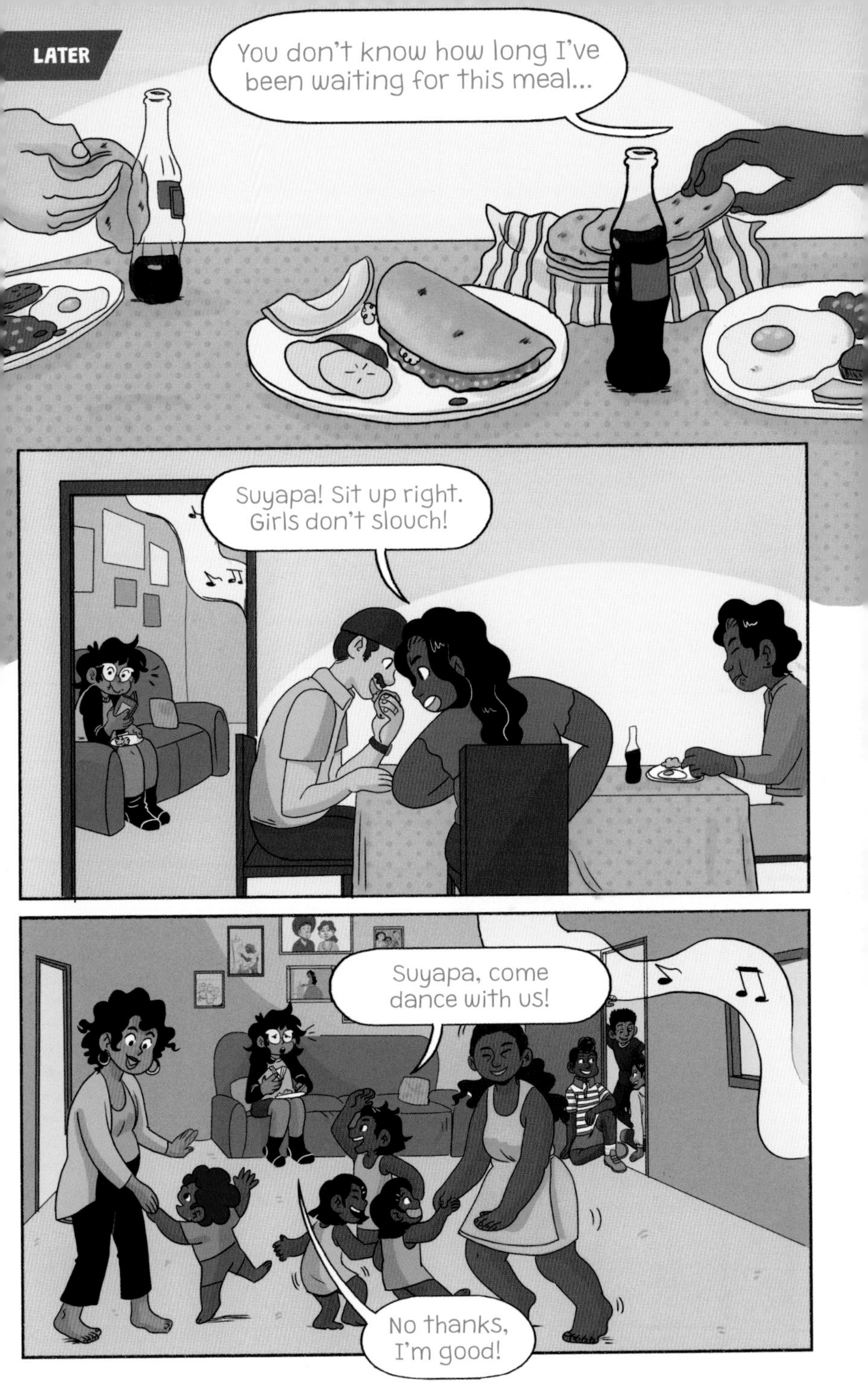
LATER
You don't know how long I've been waiting for this meal...
Suyapa! Sit up right. Girls don't slouch!
Suyapa, come dance with us!
No thanks, I'm good!

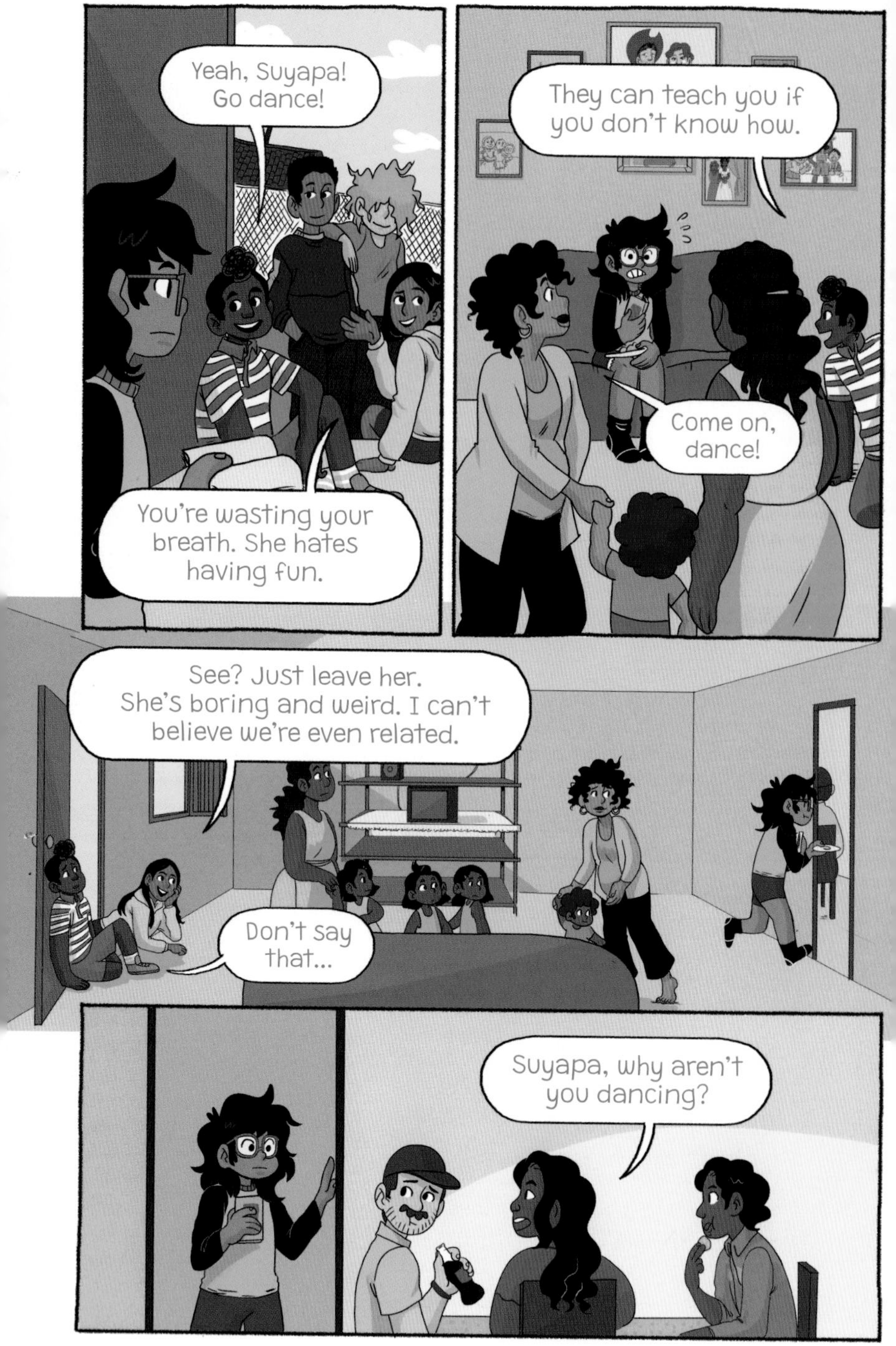
Yeah, Suyapa!
Go dance!
You're wasting your breath. She hates having fun.
They can teach you if you don't know how.
Come on, dance!
See? Just leave her. She's boring and weird. I can't believe we're even related.
Don't say that...
Suyapa, why aren't you dancing?

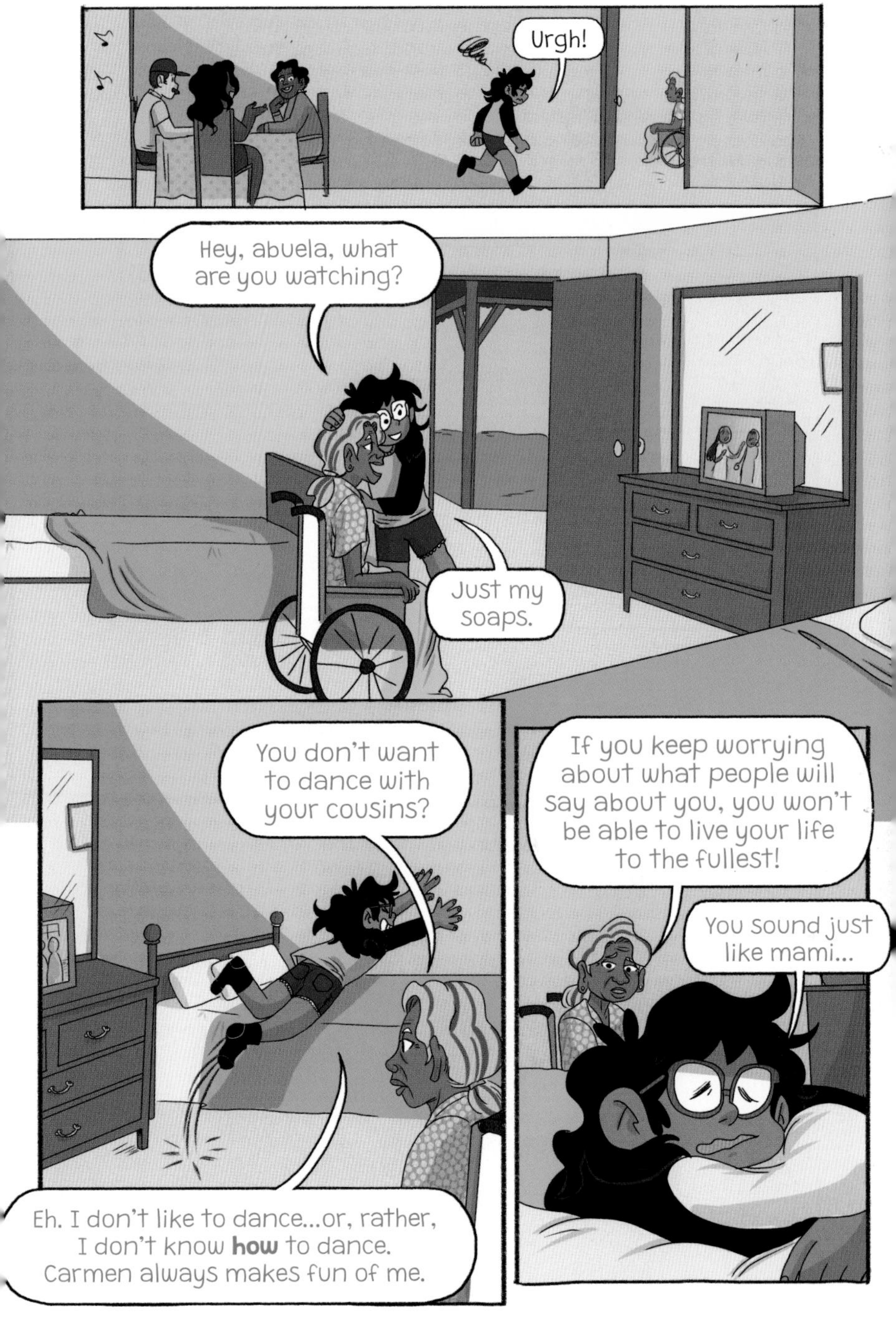
Urgh!
Hey, abuela, what are you watching?
Just my soaps.
You don't want to dance with your cousins?
Eh. I don't like to dance...or, rather, I don't know **how** to dance. Carmen always makes fun of me.
If you keep worrying about what people will say about you, you won't be able to live your life to the fullest!
You sound just like mami...

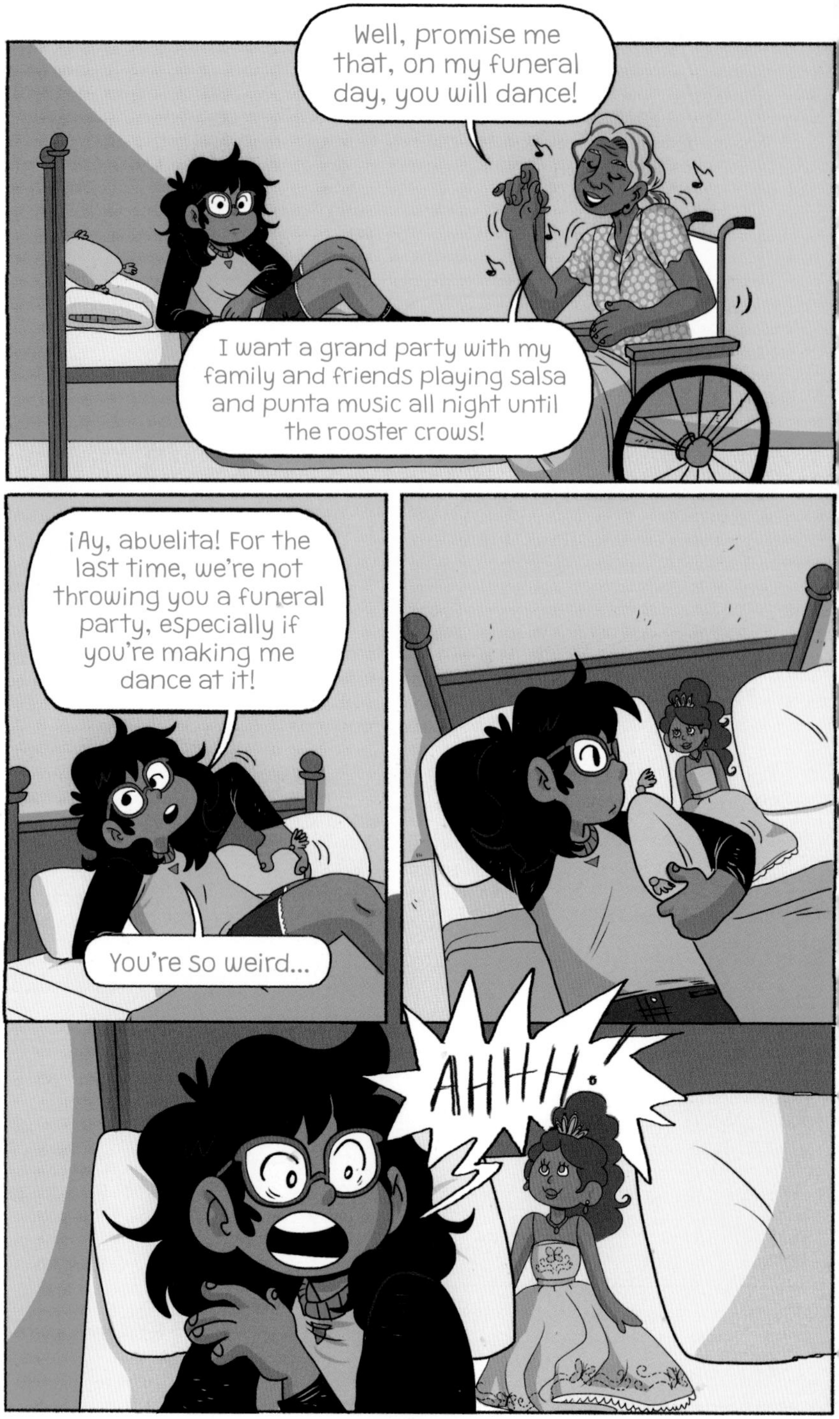
Well, promise me that, on my funeral day, you will dance!
I want a grand party with my family and friends playing salsa and punta music all night until the rooster crows!
¡Ay, abuelita! For the last time, we're not throwing you a funeral party, especially if you're making me dance at it!
You're so weird...
AHHH!

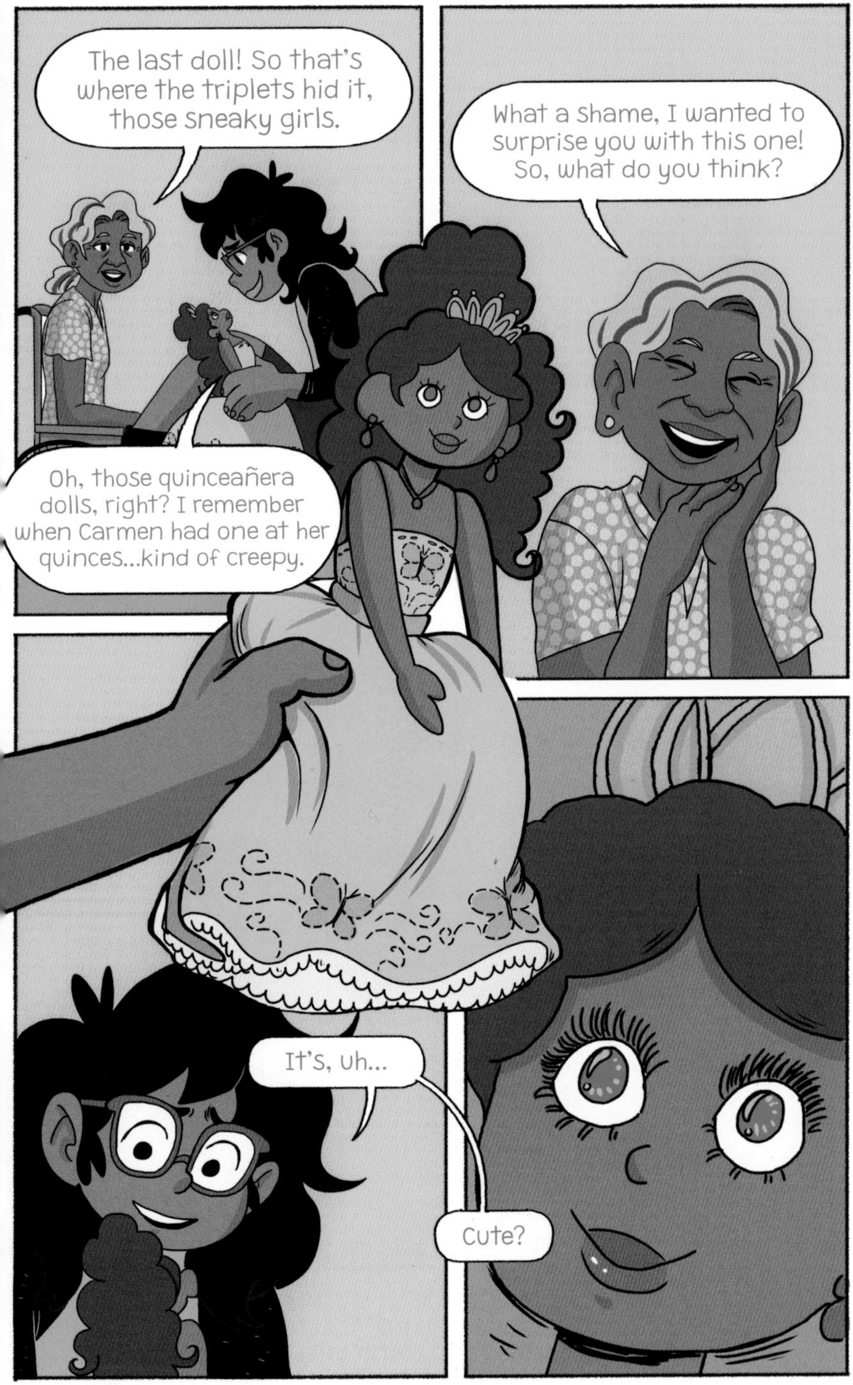
The last doll! So that's where the triplets hid it, those sneaky girls.
Oh, those quinceañera dolls, right? I remember when Carmen had one at her quinces...kind of creepy.
What a shame, I wanted to surprise you with this one! So, what do you think?
It's, uh...
Cute?

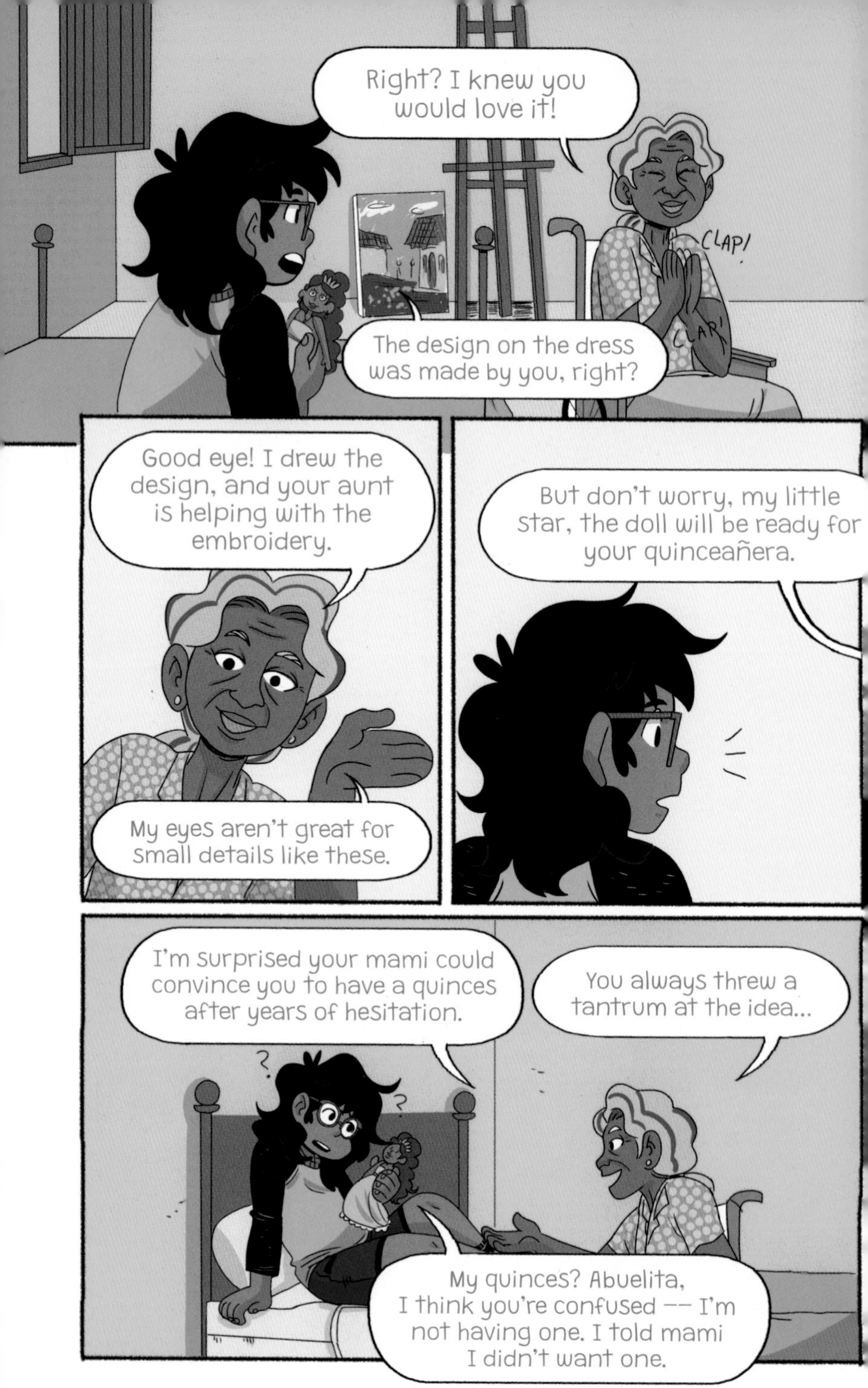
Right? I knew you would love it!
CLAP!
CLAP!
The design on the dress was made by you, right?
Good eye! I drew the design, and your aunt is helping with the embroidery.
My eyes aren't great for small details like these.
But don't worry, my little star, the doll will be ready for your quinceañera.
I'm surprised your mami could convince you to have a quinces after years of hesitation.
You always threw a tantrum at the idea...
?
?
My quinces? Abuelita, I think you're confused -- I'm not having one. I told mami I didn't want one.

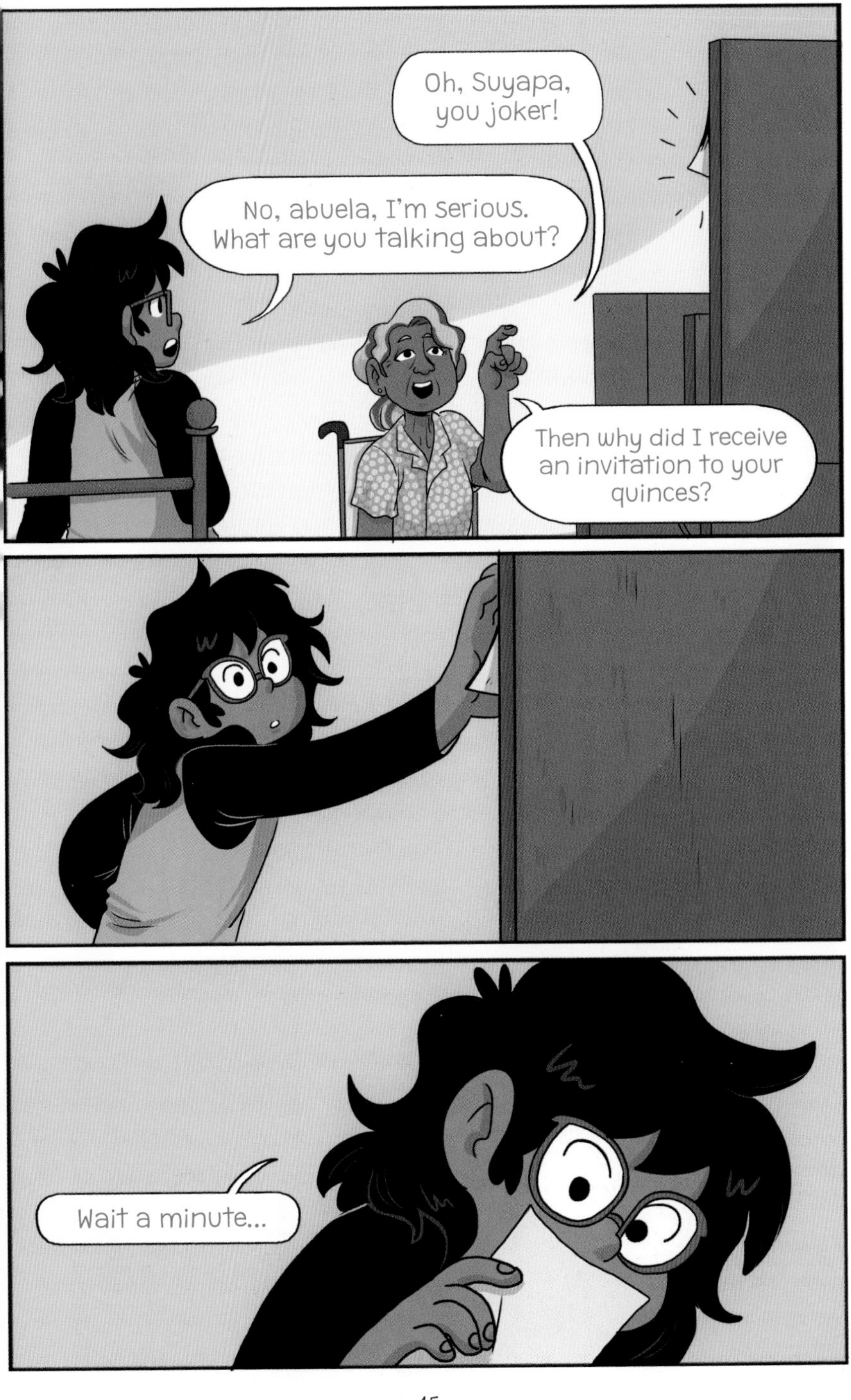
No, abuela, I'm serious. What are you talking about?
Oh, Suyapa, you joker!
Then why did I receive an invitation to your quinces?
Wait a minute...

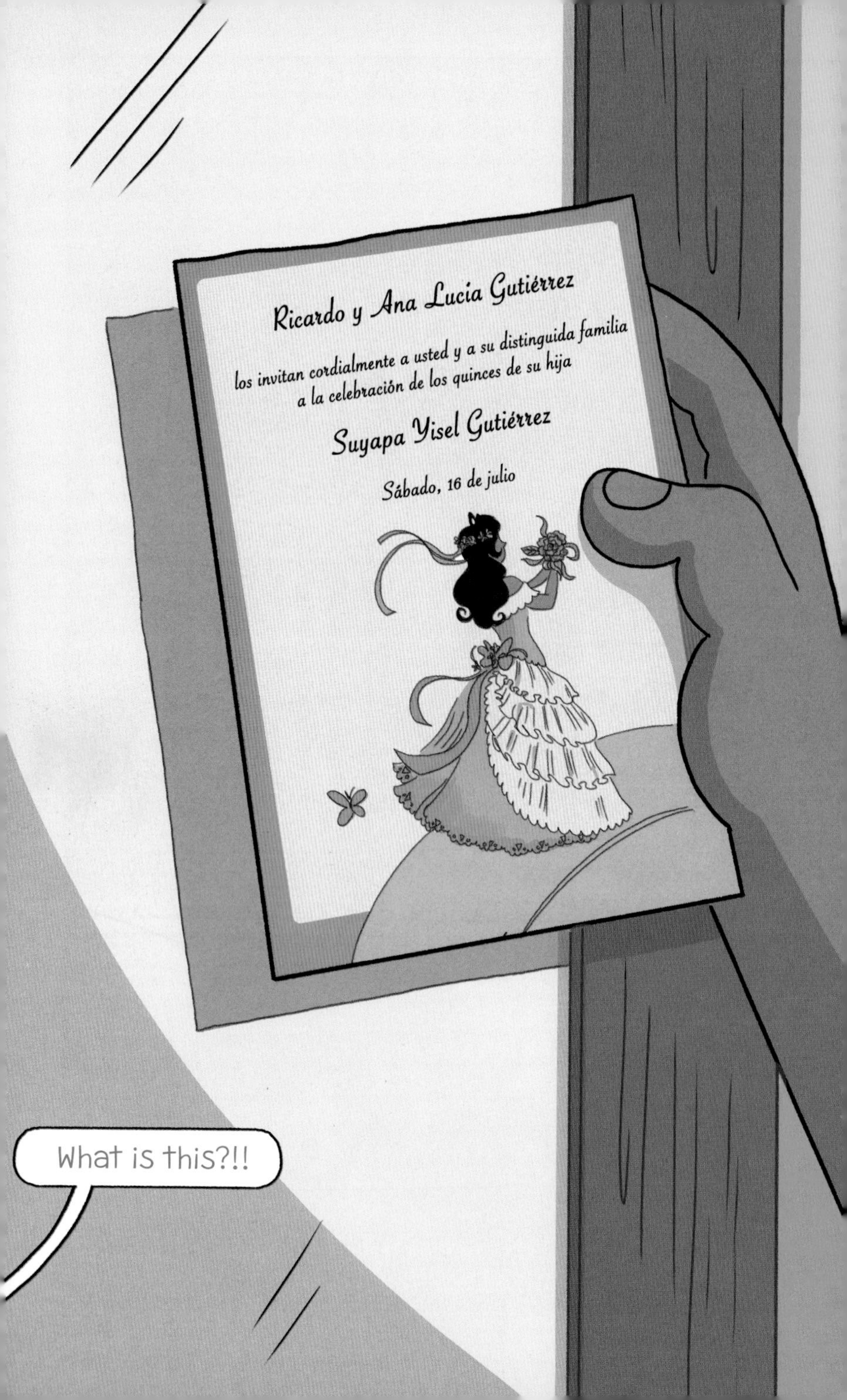
Ricardo y Ana Lucia Gutiérrez
los invitan cordialmente a usted y a su distinguida familia
a la celebración de los quinces de su hija
Suyapa Yisel Gutiérrez
Sábado, 16 de julio
What is this?!!

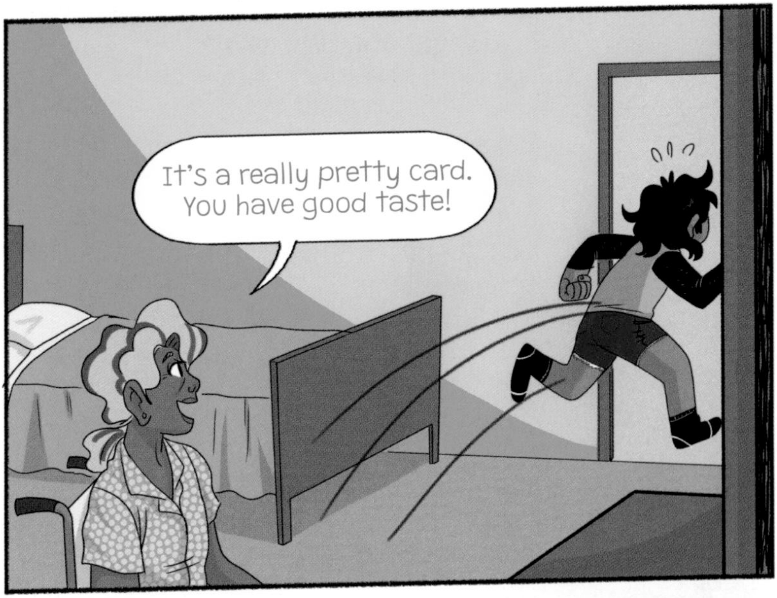
It's a really pretty card. You have good taste!

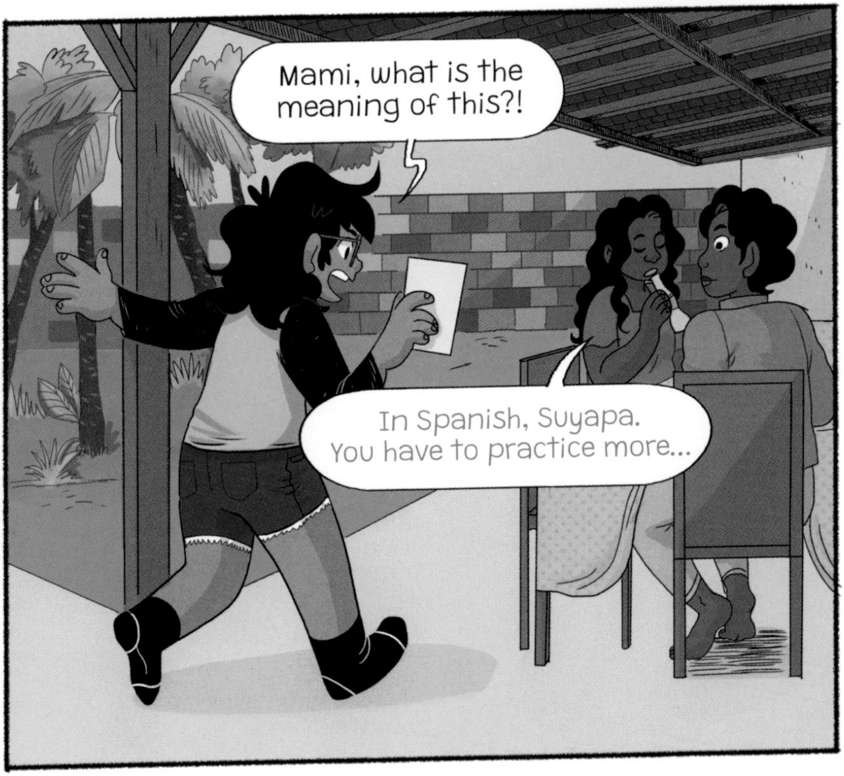
Mami, what is the meaning of this?!
In Spanish, Suyapa. You have to practice more...

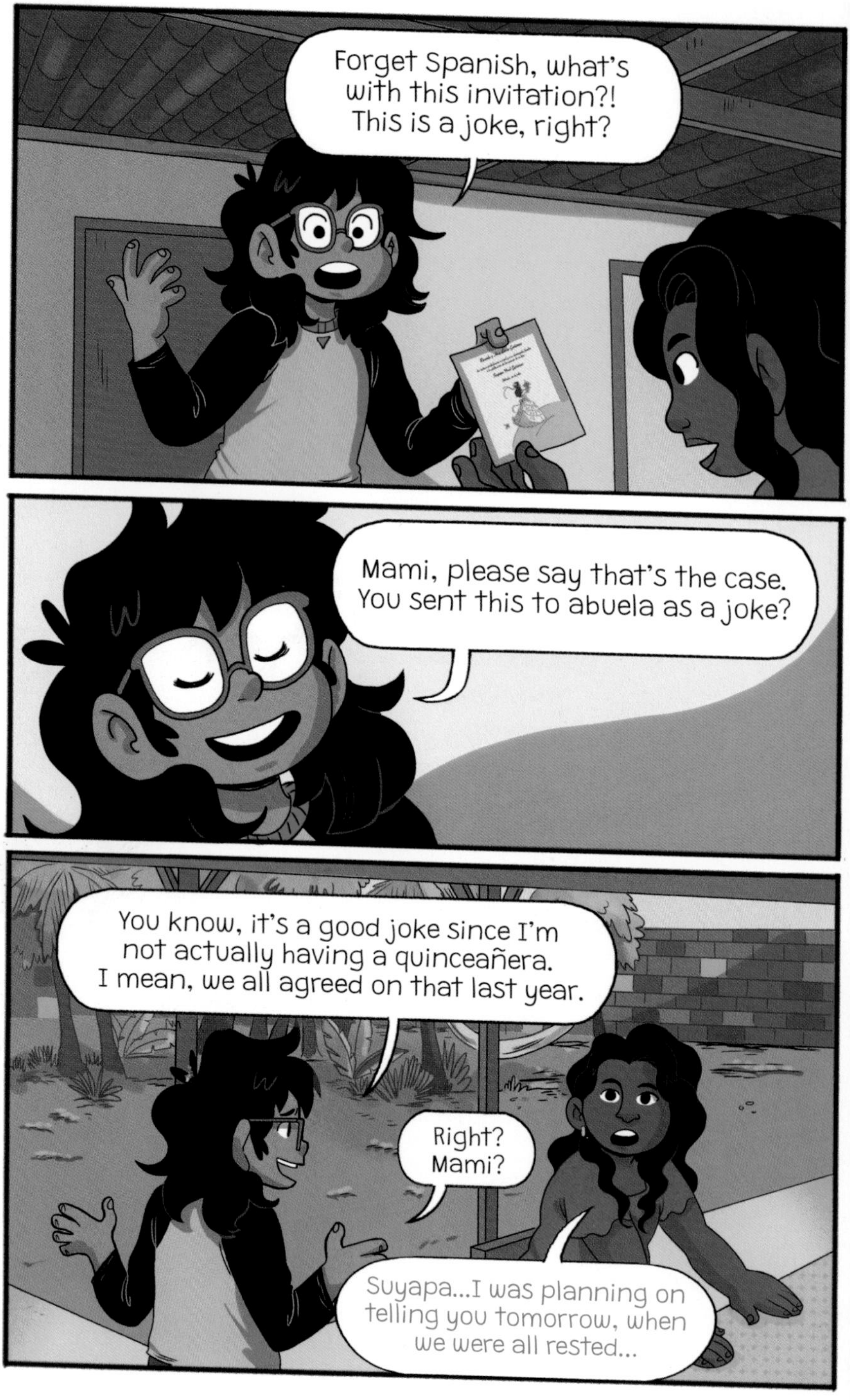
Forget Spanish, what's with this invitation?! This is a joke, right?
Mami, please say that's the case. You sent this to abuela as a joke?
You know, it's a good joke since I'm not actually having a quinceañera. I mean, we all agreed on that last year.
Right? Mami?
Suyapa...I was planning on telling you tomorrow, when we were all rested...

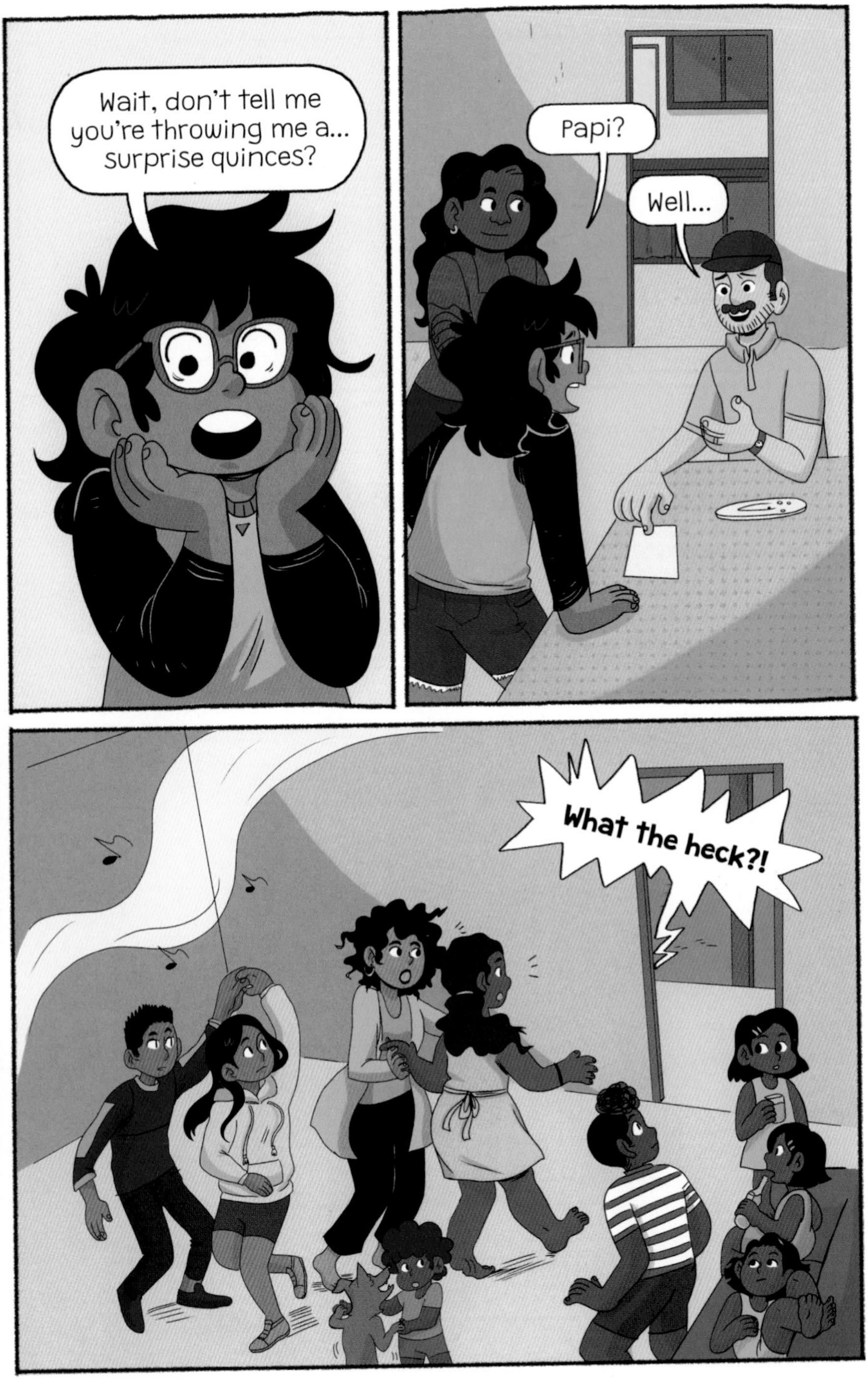
Wait, don't tell me you're throwing me a... surprise quinces?
Papi?
Well...
What the heck?!

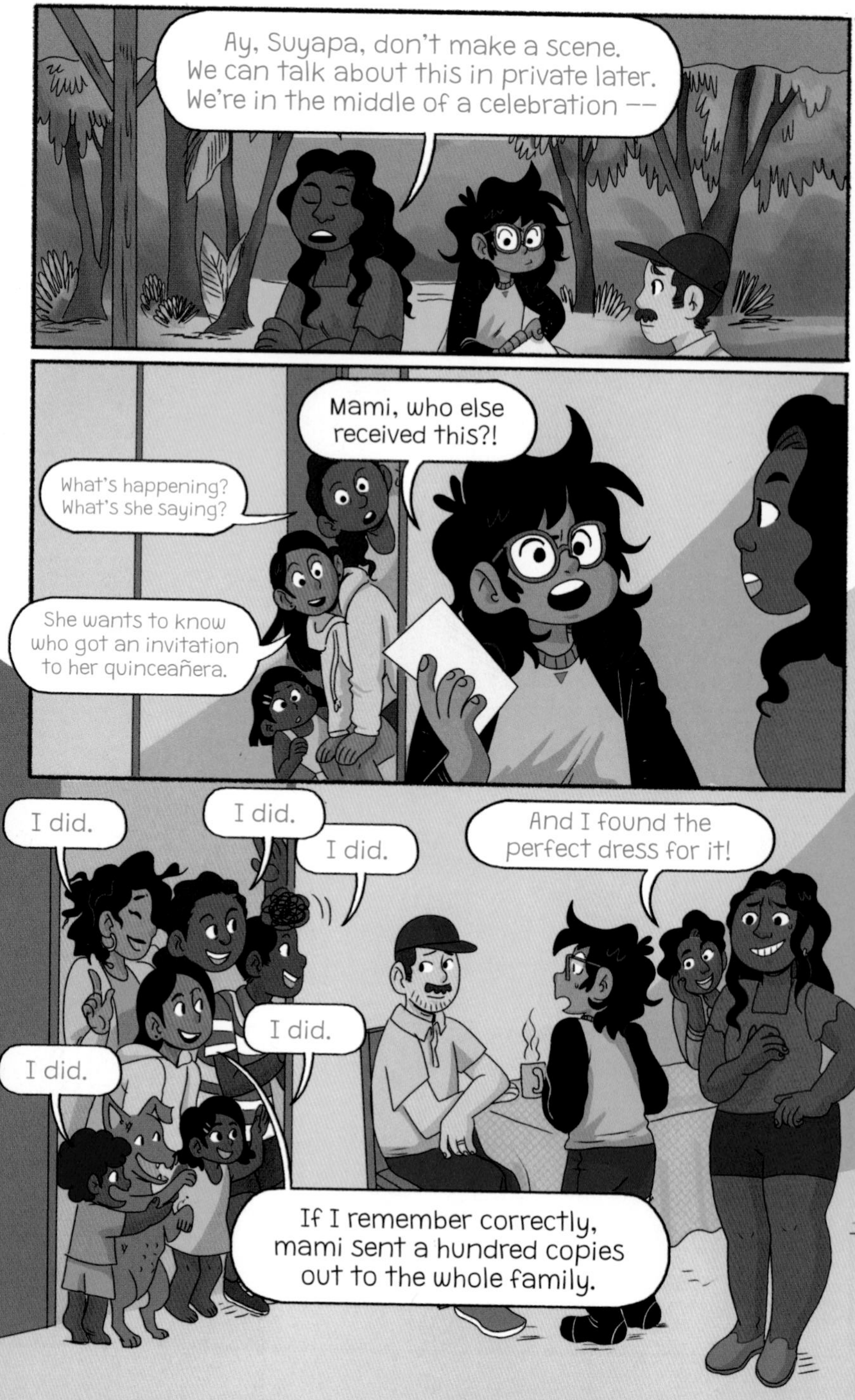
Ay, Suyapa, don't make a scene. We can talk about this in private later. We're in the middle of a celebration --
Mami, who else received this?!
What's happening? What's she saying?
She wants to know who got an invitation to her quinceañera.
I did.
I did.
I did.
And I found the perfect dress for it!
I did.
I did.
If I remember correctly, mami sent a hundred copies out to the whole family.

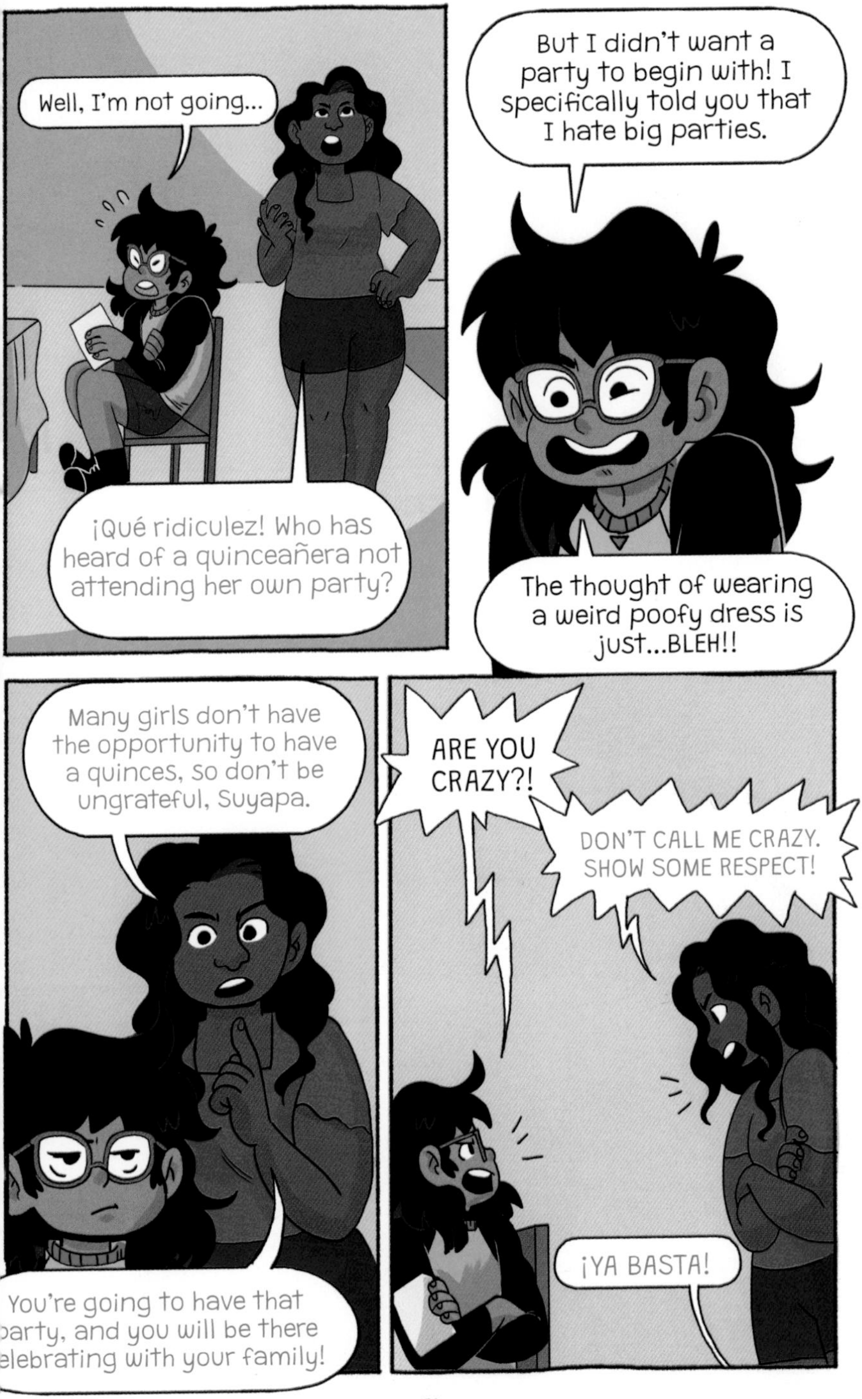
Well, I'm not going...
¡Qué ridiculez! Who has heard of a quinceañera not attending her own party?
But I didn't want a party to begin with! I specifically told you that I hate big parties.
The thought of wearing a weird poofy dress is just...BLEH!!
Many girls don't have the opportunity to have a quinces, so don't be ungrateful, Suyapa.
You're going to have that party, and you will be there celebrating with your family!
ARE YOU CRAZY?!
DON'T CALL ME CRAZY. SHOW SOME RESPECT!
¡YA BASTA!

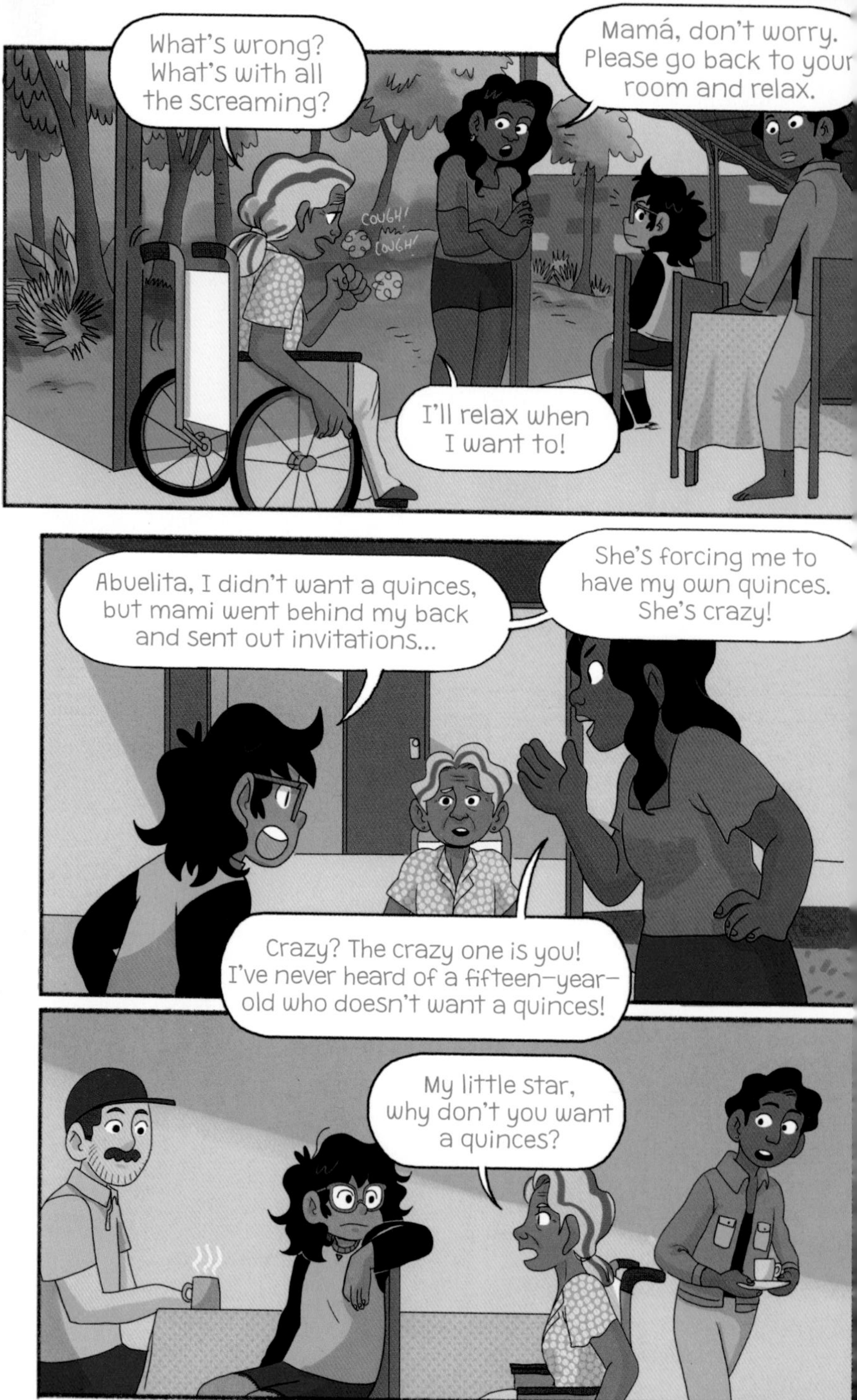

What's wrong? What's with all the screaming?
COUGH! COUGH!
Mamá, don't worry. Please go back to your room and relax.
I'll relax when I want to!
Abuelita, I didn't want a quinces, but mami went behind my back and sent out invitations...
She's forcing me to have my own quinces. She's crazy!
Crazy? The crazy one is you! I've never heard of a fifteen-year-old who doesn't want a quinces!
My little star, why don't you want a quinces?

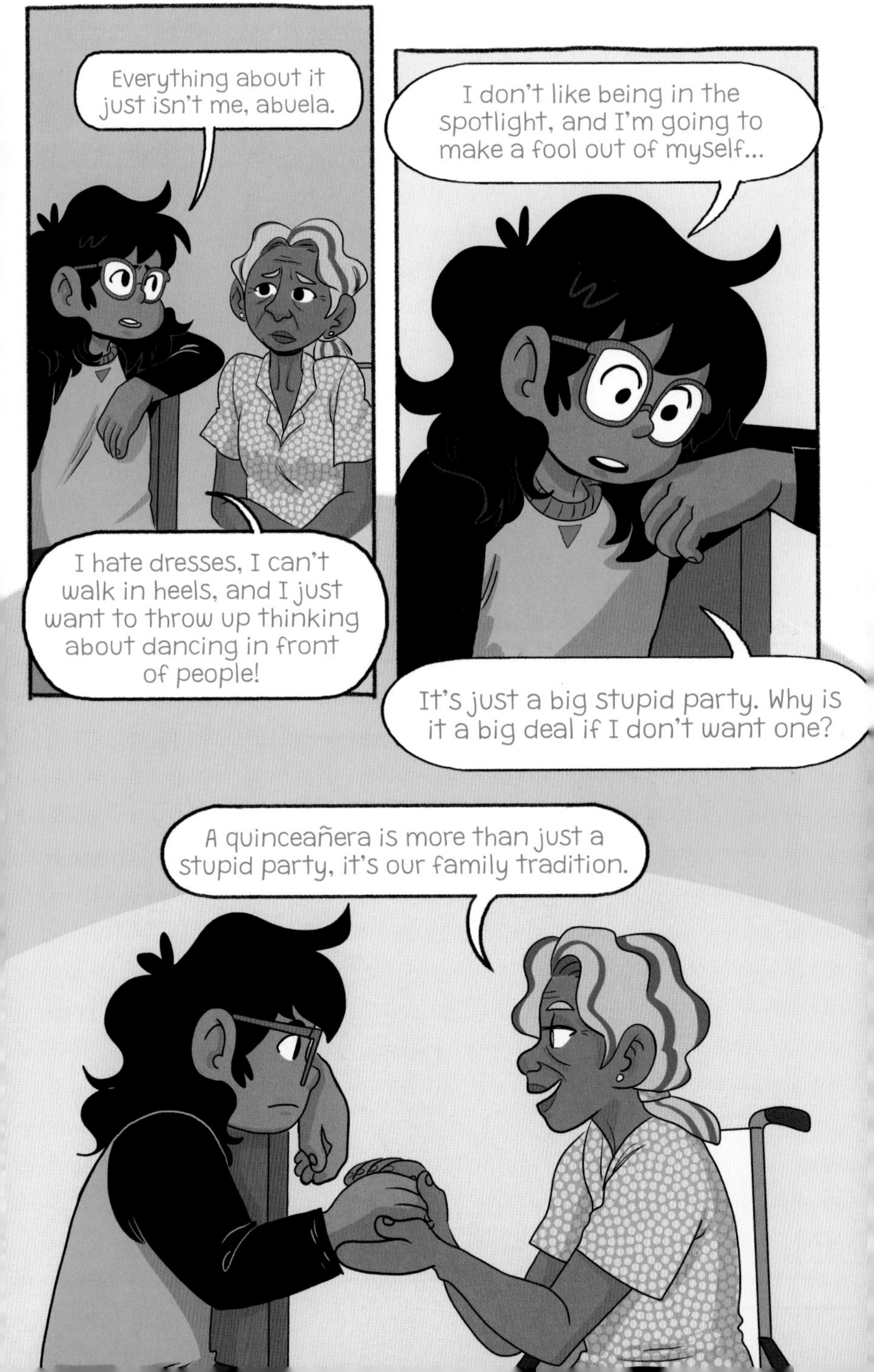
Everything about it just isn't me, abuela.
I hate dresses, I can't walk in heels, and I just want to throw up thinking about dancing in front of people!
I don't like being in the spotlight, and I'm going to make a fool out of myself...
It's just a big stupid party. Why is it a big deal if I don't want one?
A quinceañera is more than just a stupid party, it's our family tradition.

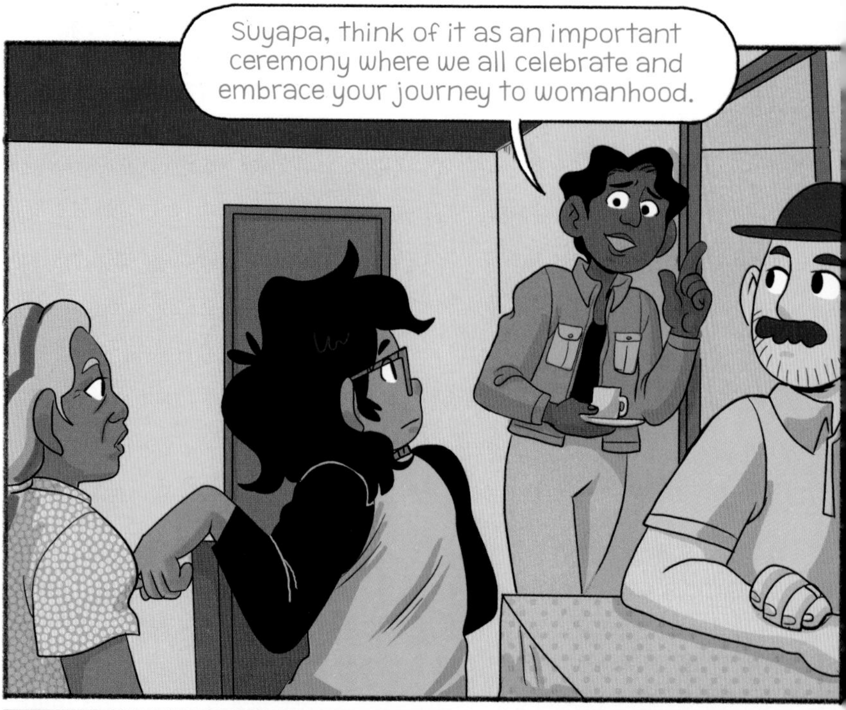
Suyapa, think of it as an important ceremony where we all celebrate and embrace your journey to womanhood.

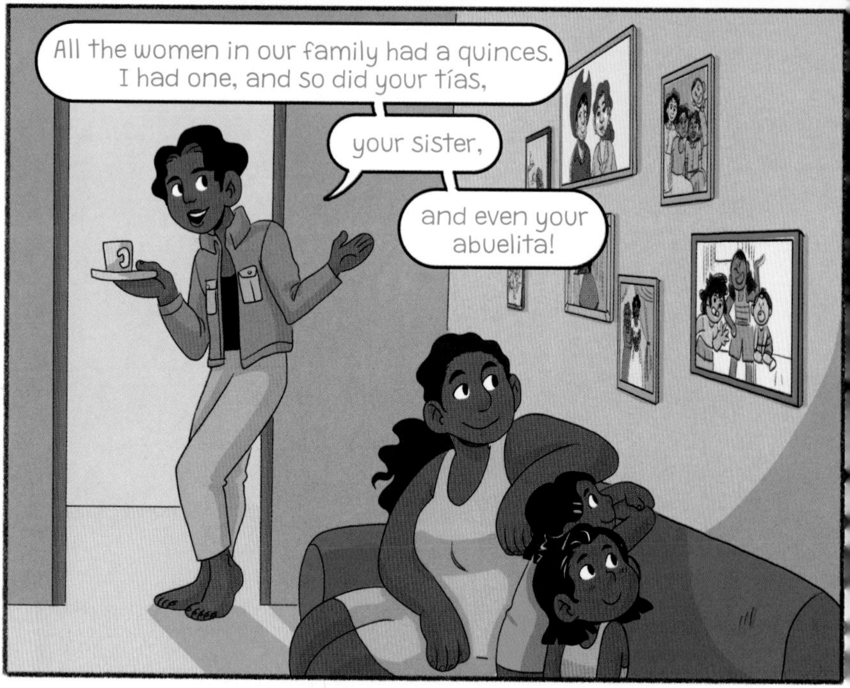
All the women in our family had a quinces. I had one, and so did your tías,
your sister,
and even your abuelita!

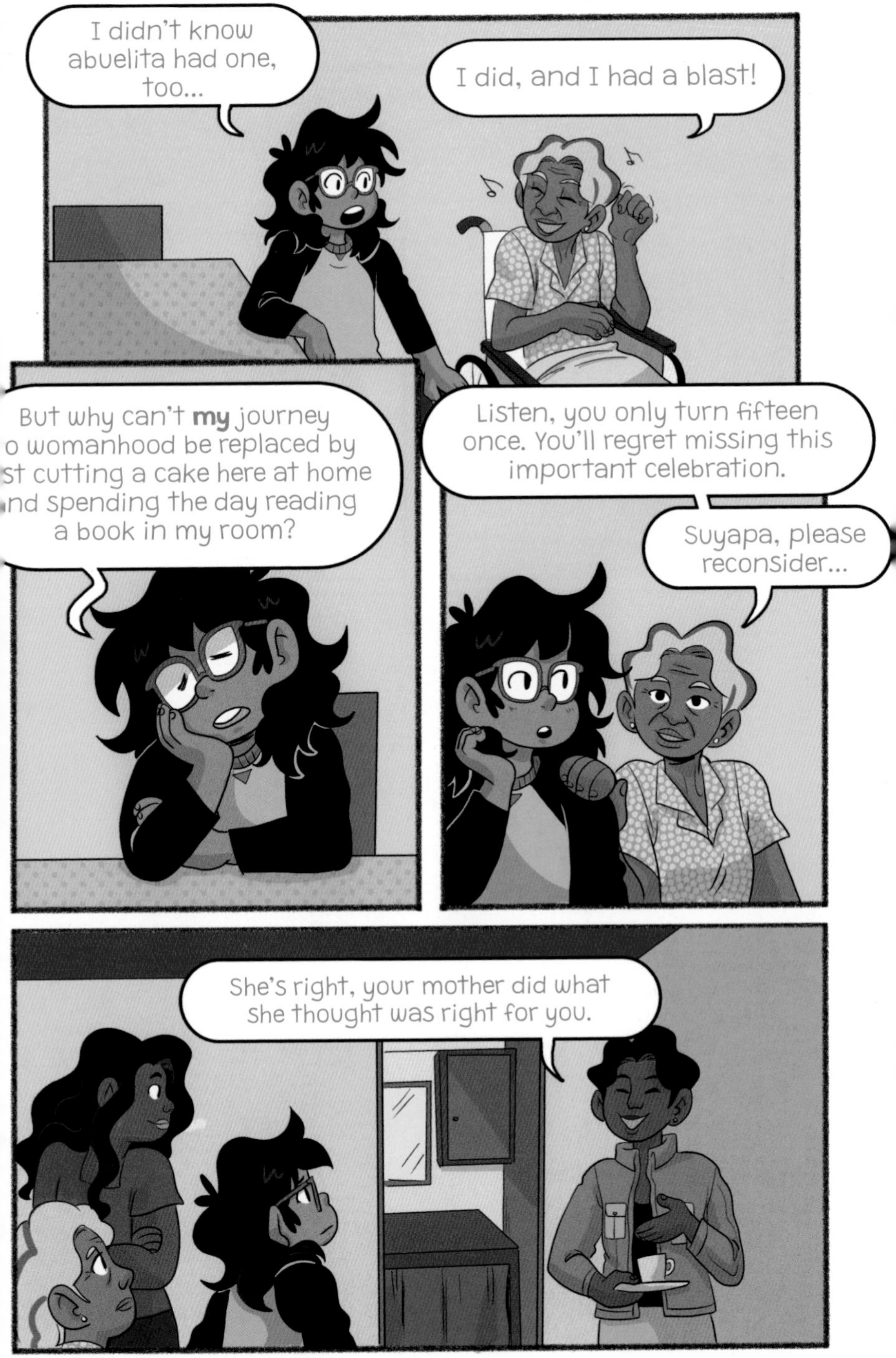
I didn't know abuelita had one, too...
I did, and I had a blast!
But why can't **my** journey
o womanhood be replaced by
st cutting a cake here at home
nd spending the day reading
a book in my room?
Listen, you only turn fifteen once. You'll regret missing this important celebration.
Suyapa, please reconsider...
She's right, your mother did what she thought was right for you.

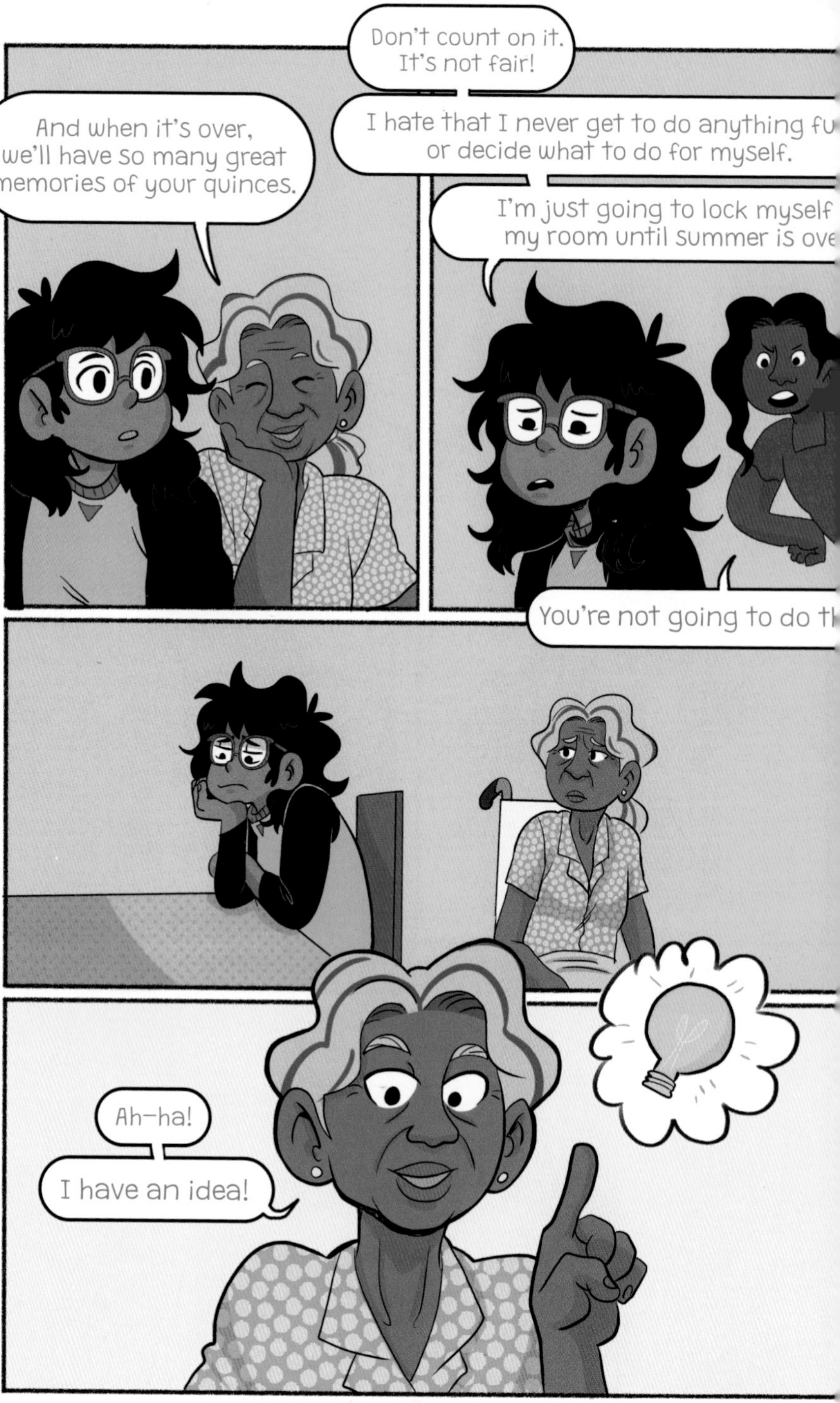
And when it's over, we'll have so many great memories of your quinces.
Don't count on it. It's not fair!
I hate that I never get to do anything
or decide what to do for myself.
I'm just going to lock myself
my room until summer is
You're not going to do
Ah-ha!
I have an idea!

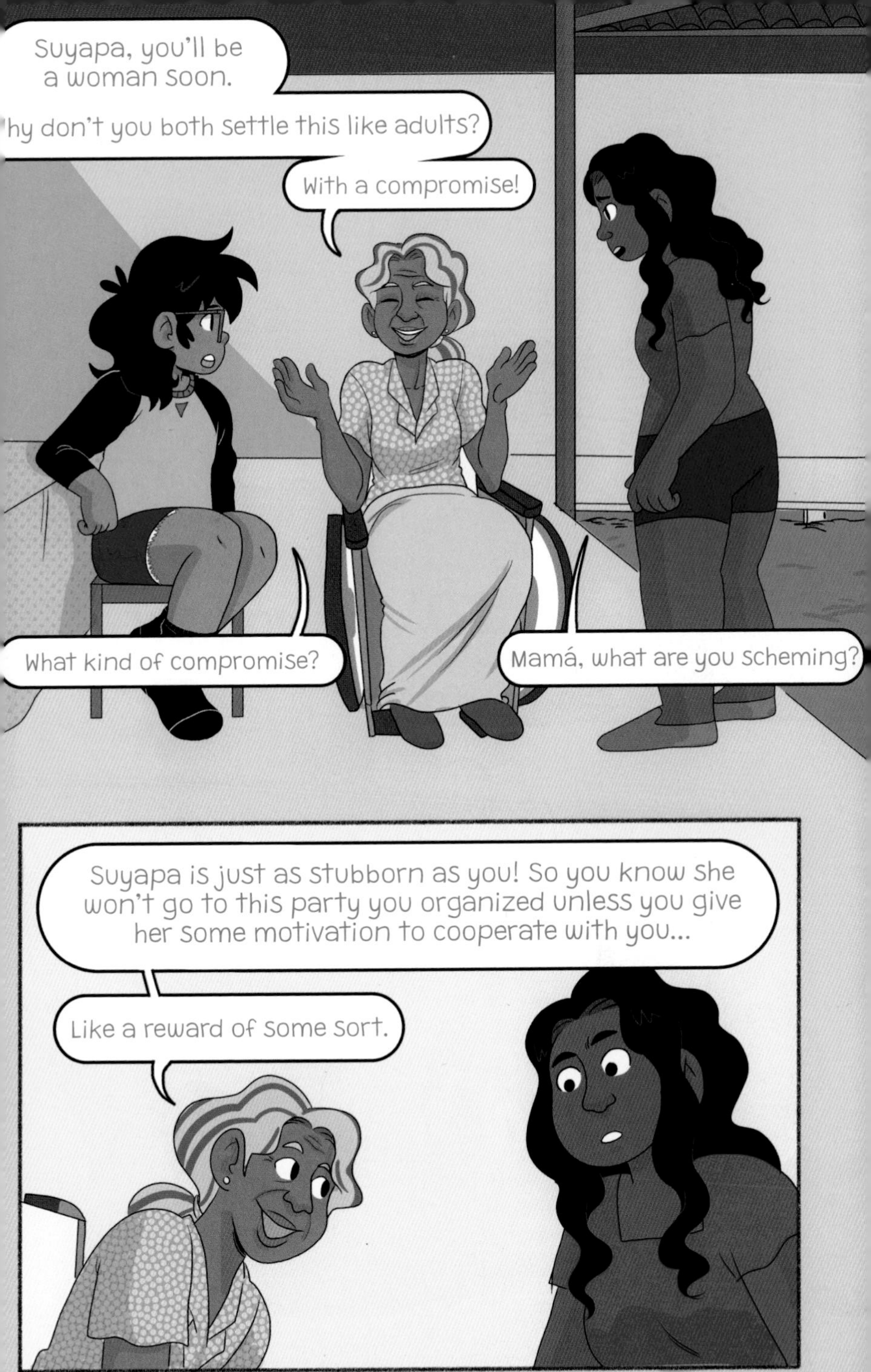
Suyapa, you'll be a woman soon.
hy don't you both settle this like adults?
With a compromise!
What kind of compromise?
Mamá, what are you scheming?
Suyapa is just as stubborn as you! So you know she won't go to this party you organized unless you give her some motivation to cooperate with you...
Like a reward of some sort.

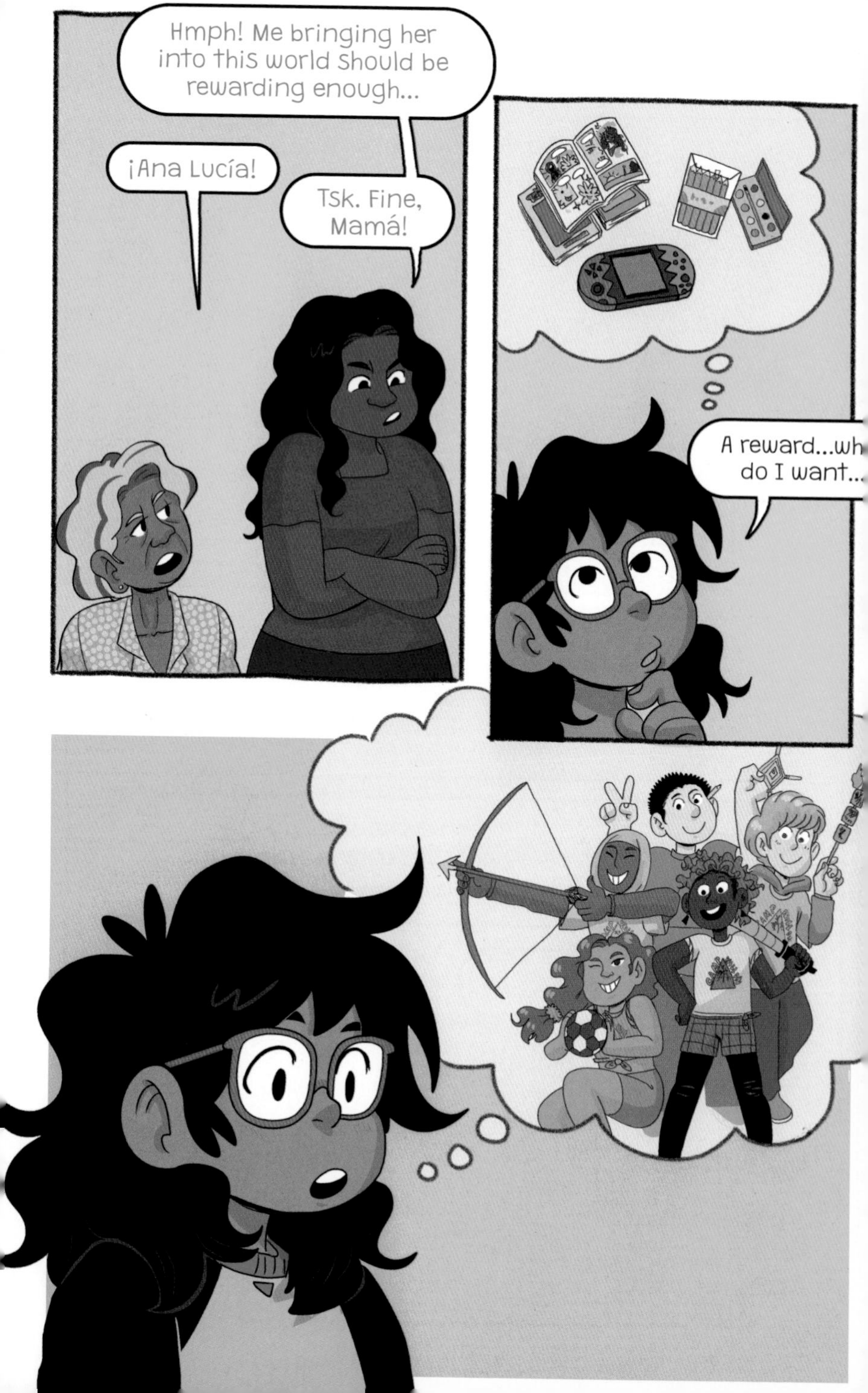
Hmph! Me bringing her into this world should be rewarding enough...
¡Ana Lucía!
Tsk. Fine, Mamá!
A reward...wh do I want...

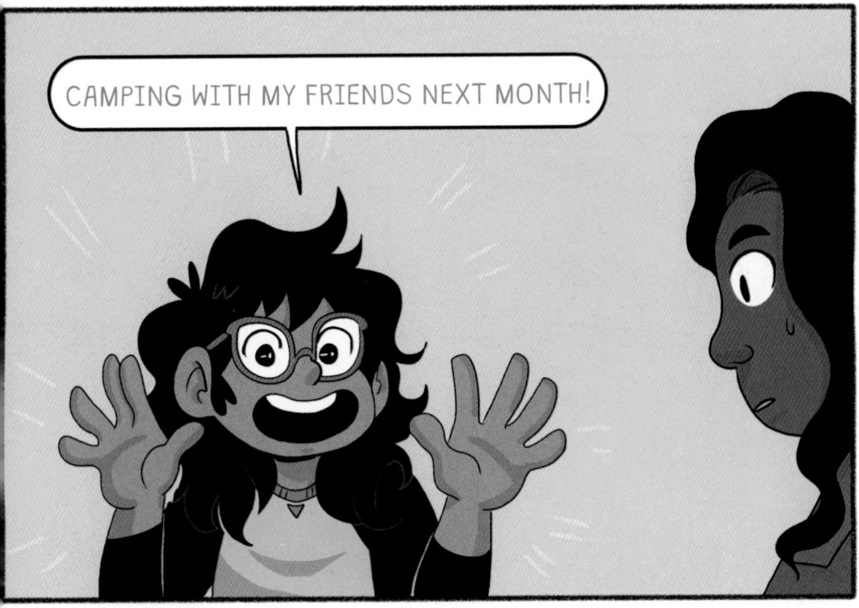
CAMPING WITH MY FRIENDS NEXT MONTH!

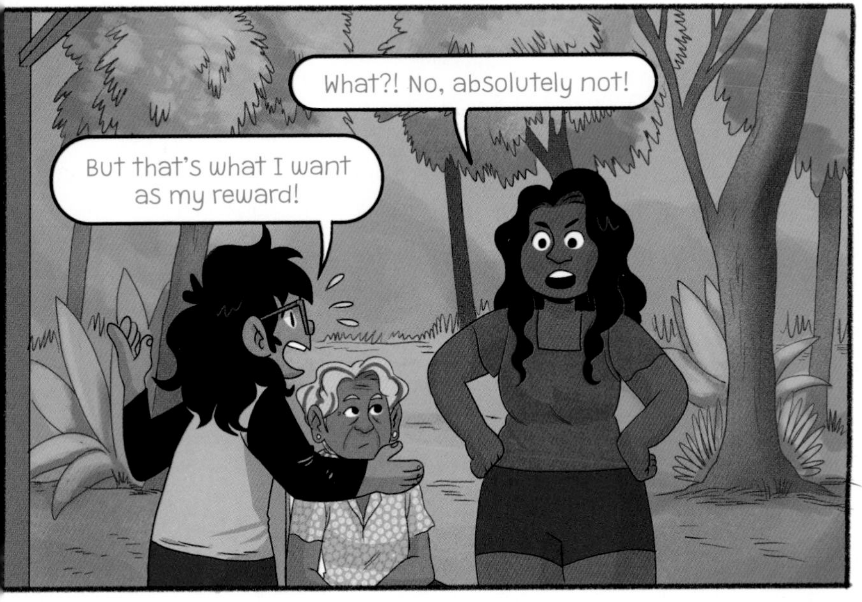
What?! No, absolutely not!
But that's what I want as my reward!

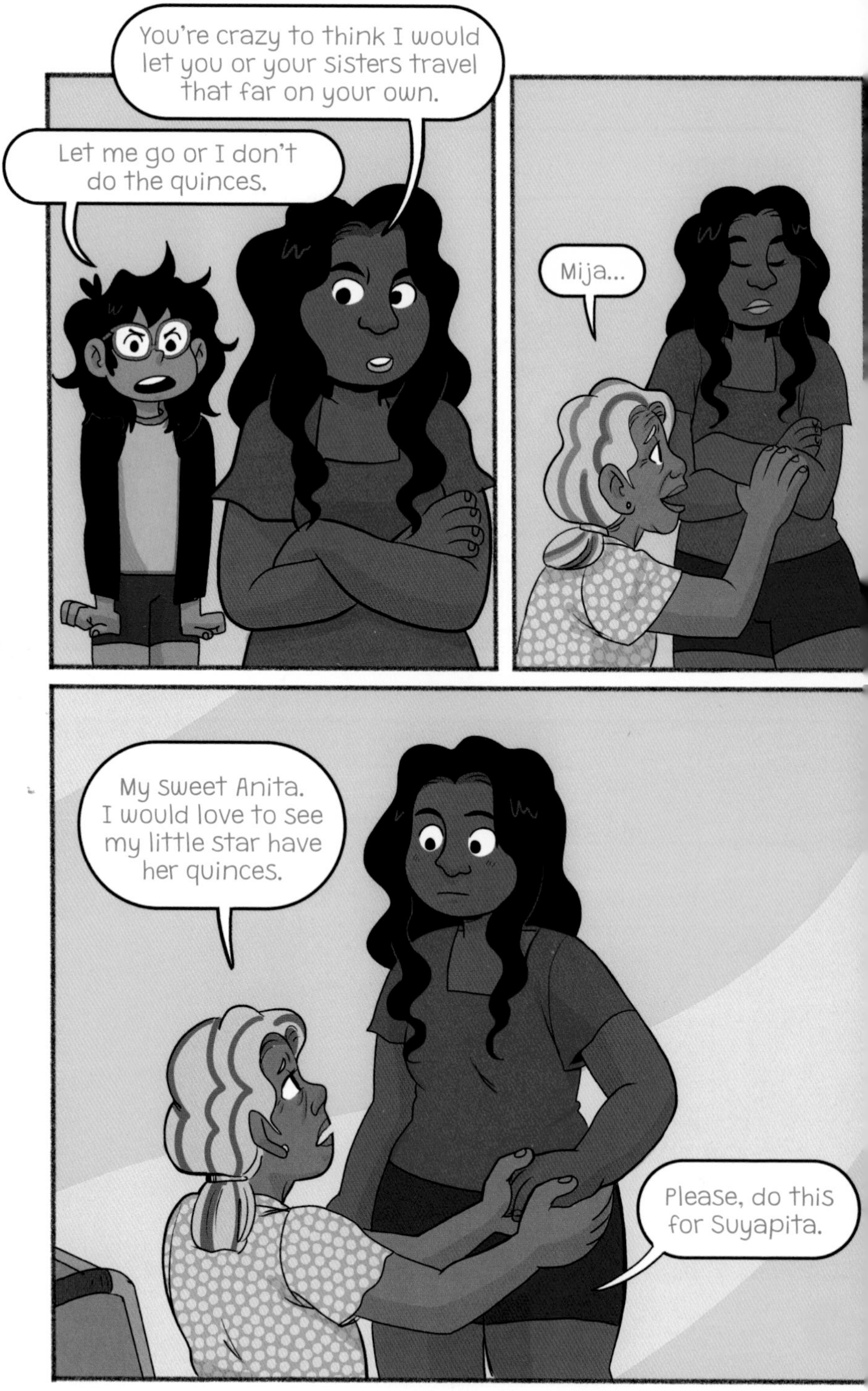
You're crazy to think I would let you or your sisters travel that far on your own.
Let me go or I don't do the quinces.
Mija...
My sweet Anita. I would love to see my little star have her quinces.
Please, do this for Suyapita.

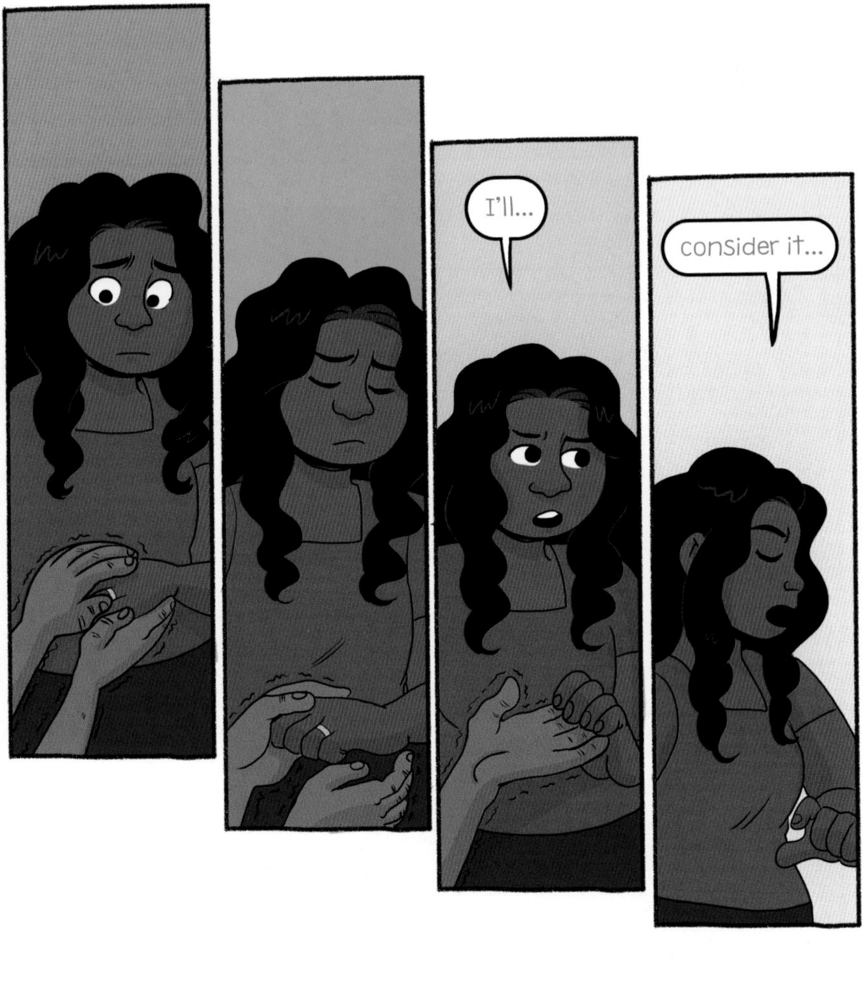
I'll...
consider it...

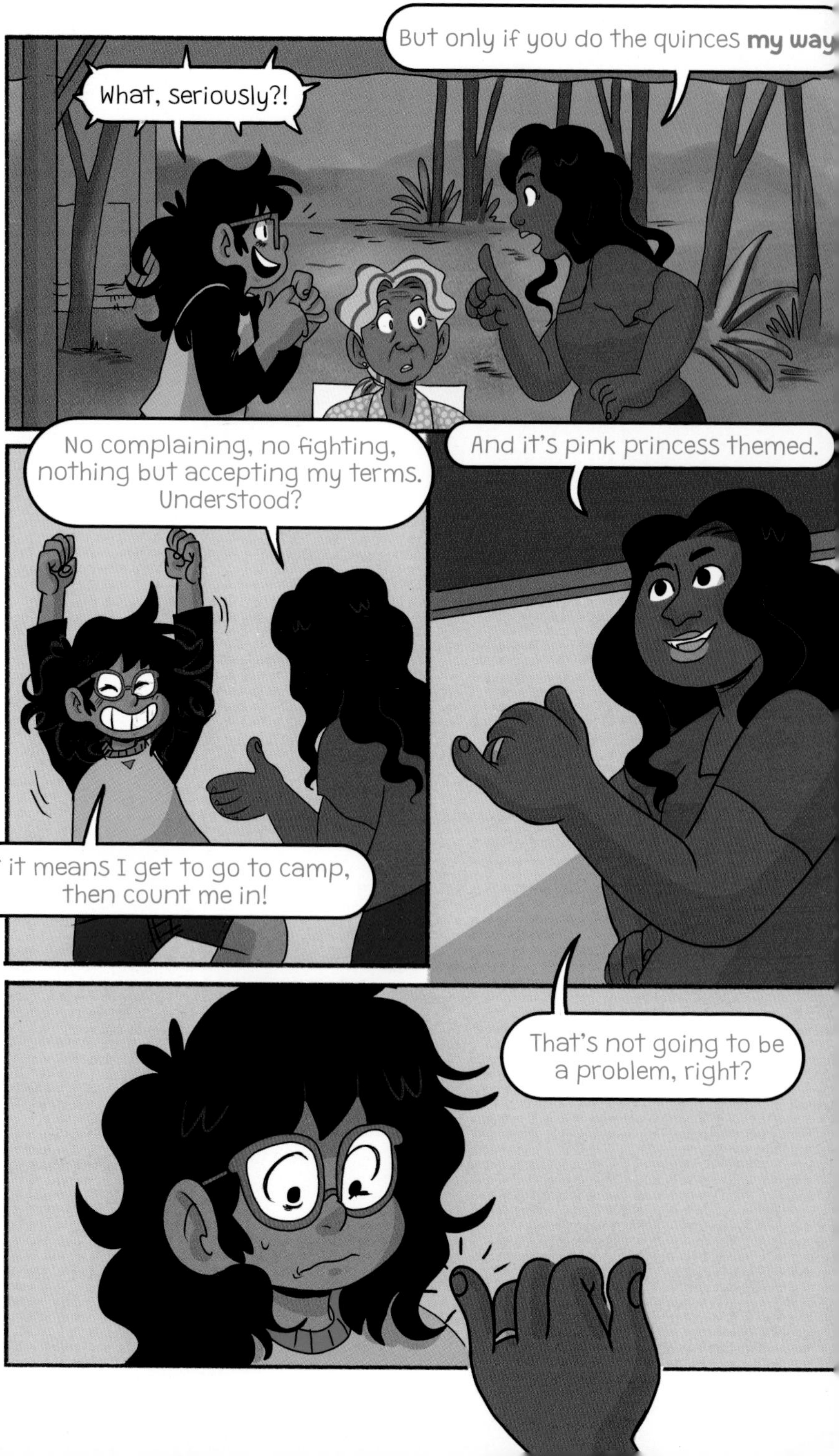
What, seriously?!
But only if you do the quinces **my way**
No complaining, no fighting, nothing but accepting my terms. Understood?
If it means I get to go to camp, then count me in!
And it's pink princess themed.
That's not going to be a problem, right?

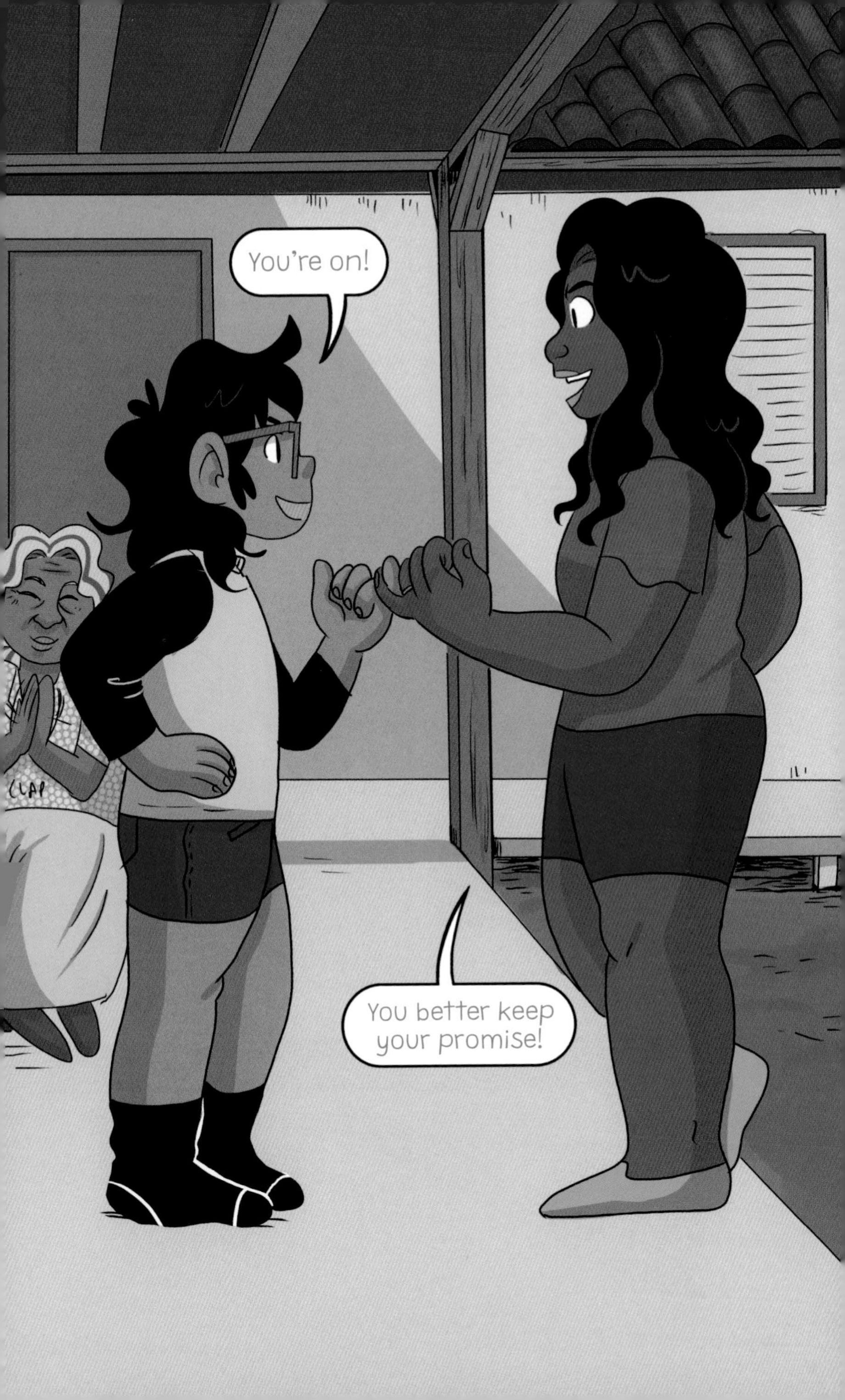

You're on!
CLAP
You better keep your promise!

CHAPTER THREE

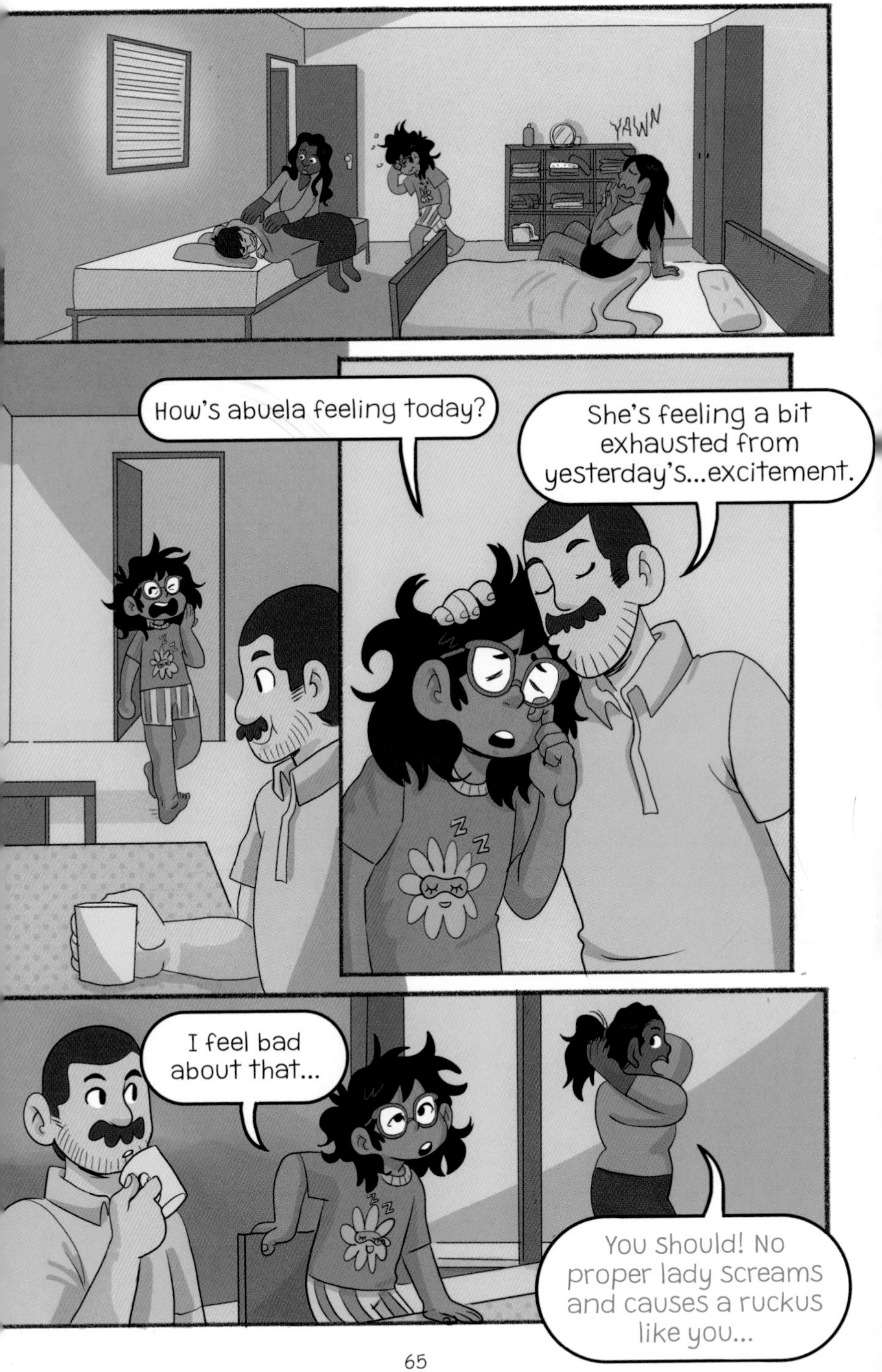
YAWN
How's abuela feeling today?
She's feeling a bit exhausted from yesterday's...excitement.
I feel bad about that...
You should! No proper lady screams and causes a ruckus like you...

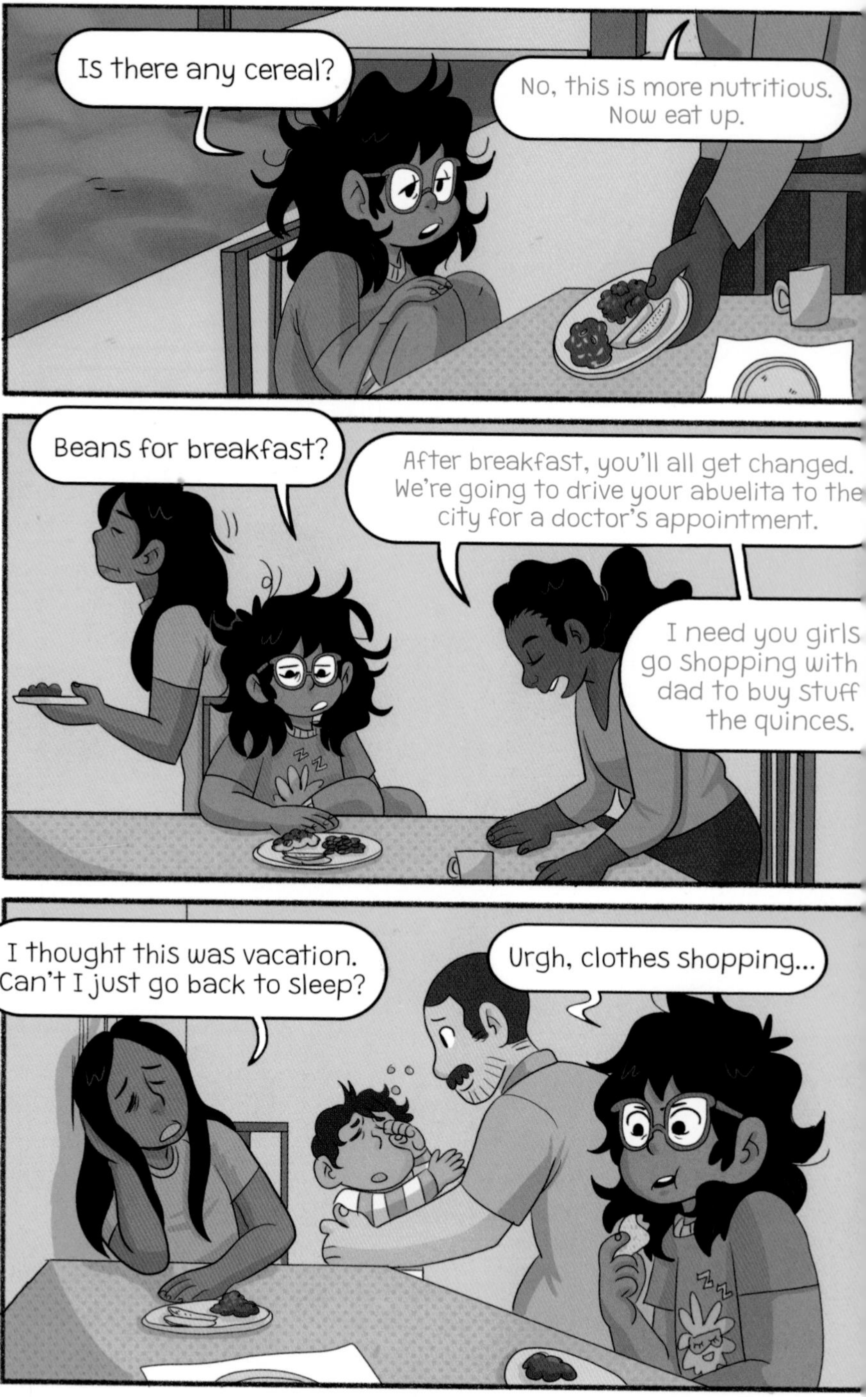
Is there any cereal?
No, this is more nutritious. Now eat up.
Beans for breakfast?
After breakfast, you'll all get changed. We're going to drive your abuelita to the city for a doctor's appointment.
I need you girls go shopping with dad to buy stuff the quinces.
I thought this was vacation. Can't I just go back to sleep?
Urgh, clothes shopping...

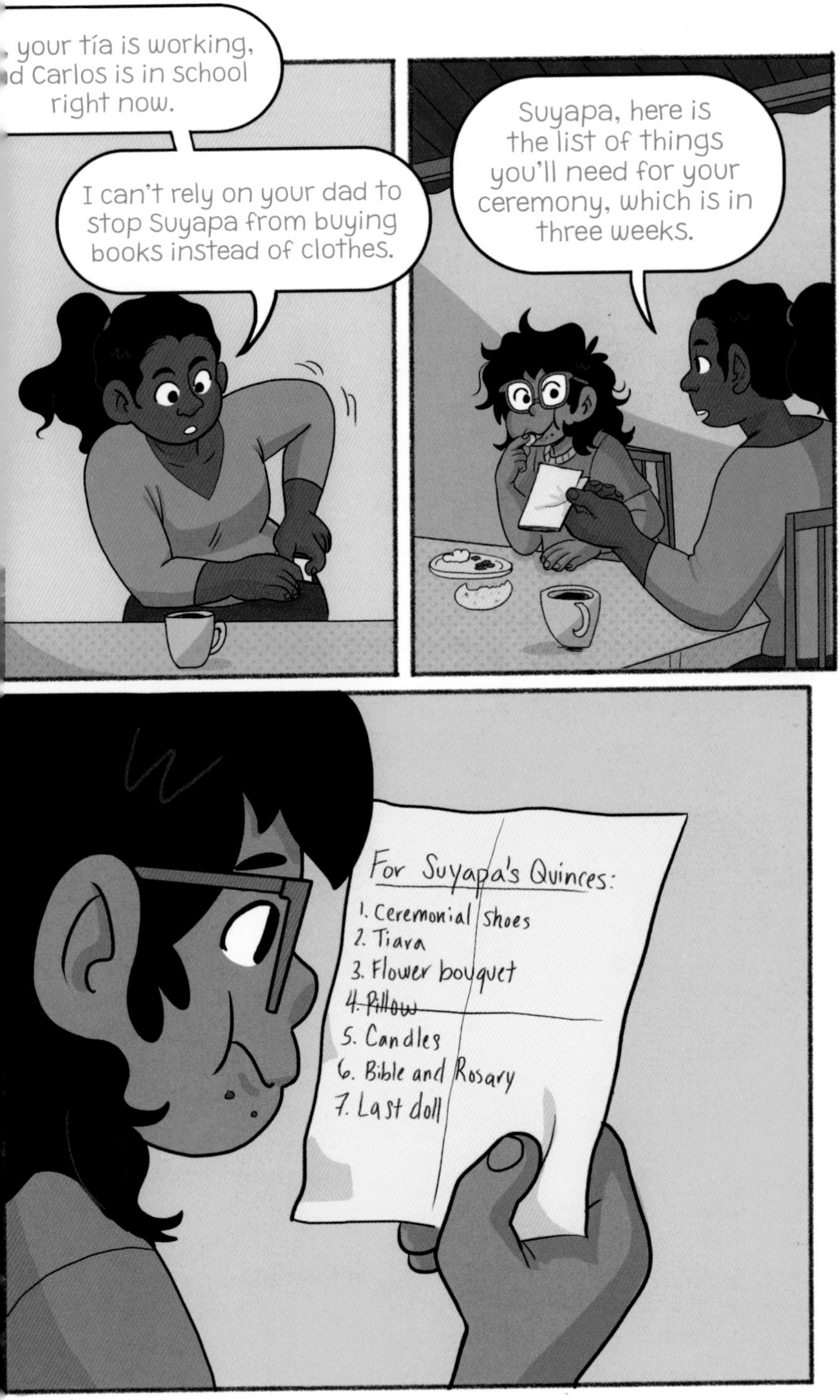

your tía is working,
d Carlos is in school
right now.
I can't rely on your dad to
stop Suyapa from buying
books instead of clothes.
Suyapa, here is
the list of things
you'll need for your
ceremony, which is in
three weeks.
For Suyapa's Quinces:
1. Ceremonial shoes
2. Tiara
3. Flower bouquet
4. Pillow
5. Candles
6. Bible and Rosary
7. Last doll

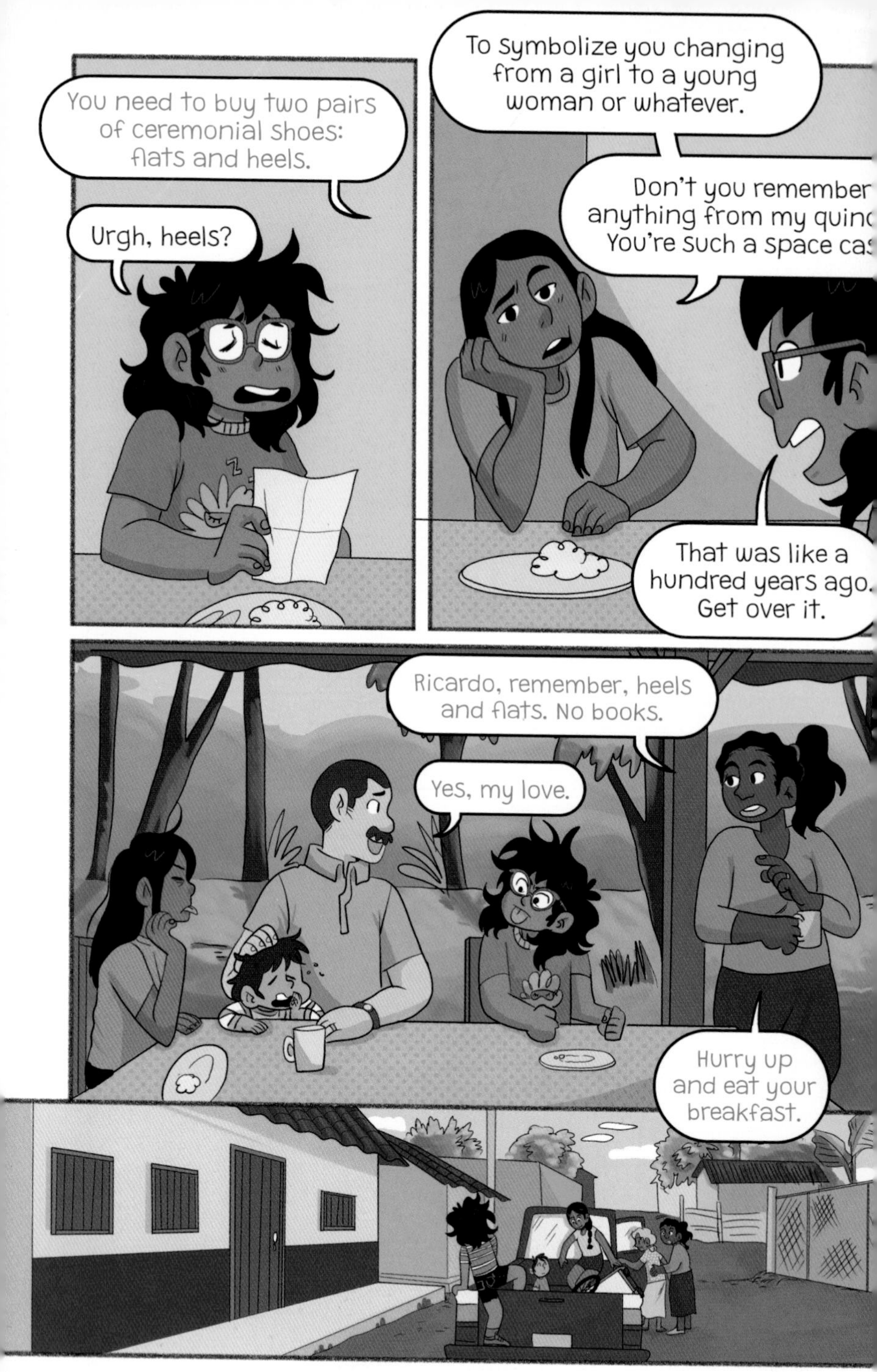
You need to buy two pairs of ceremonial shoes: flats and heels.
Urgh, heels?
To symbolize you changing from a girl to a young woman or whatever.
Don't you remember anything from my quinc You're such a space cas
That was like a hundred years ago. Get over it.
Ricardo, remember, heels and flats. No books.
Yes, my love.
Hurry up and eat your breakfast.

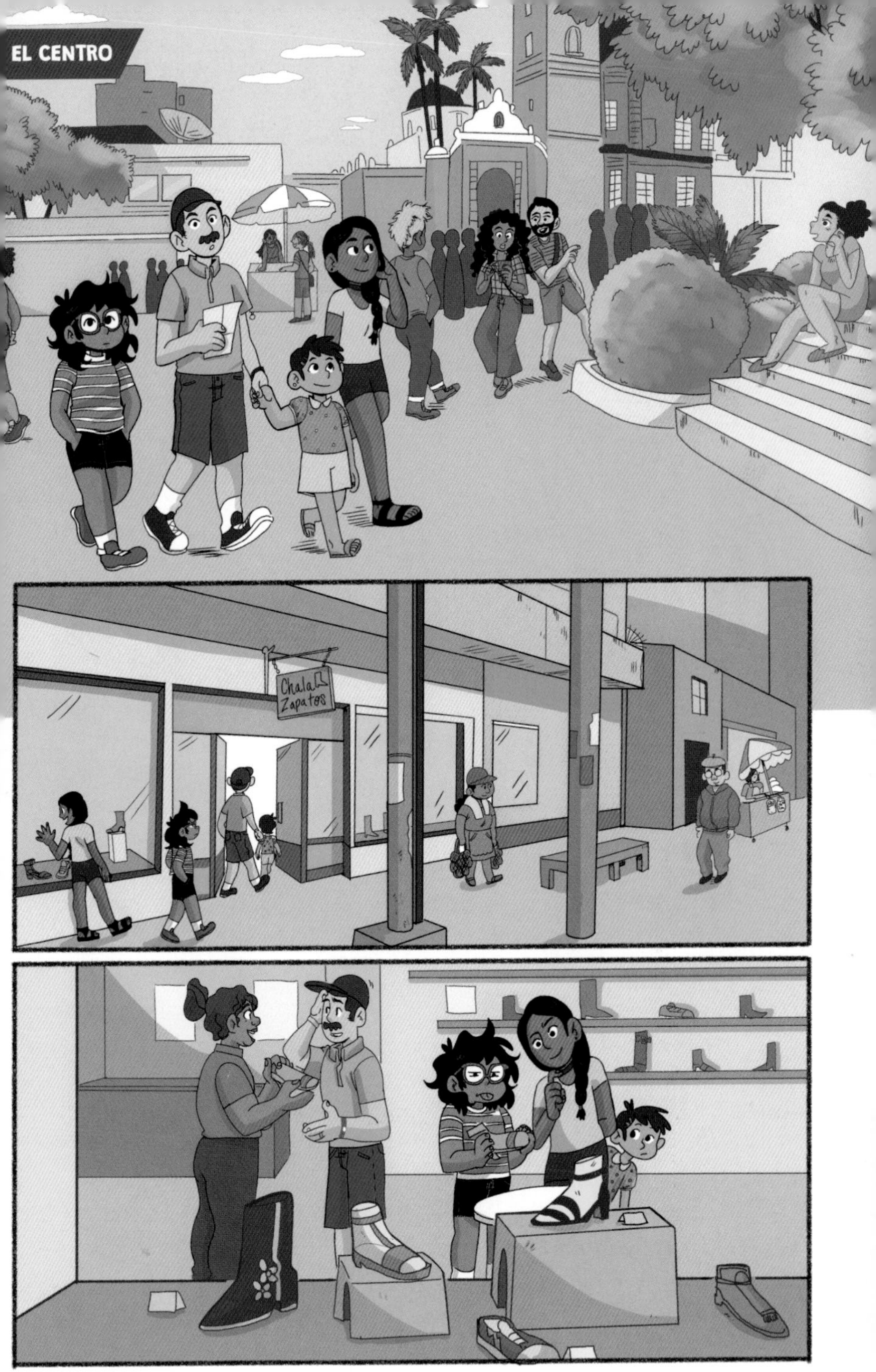
EL CENTRO
Chala Zapatos

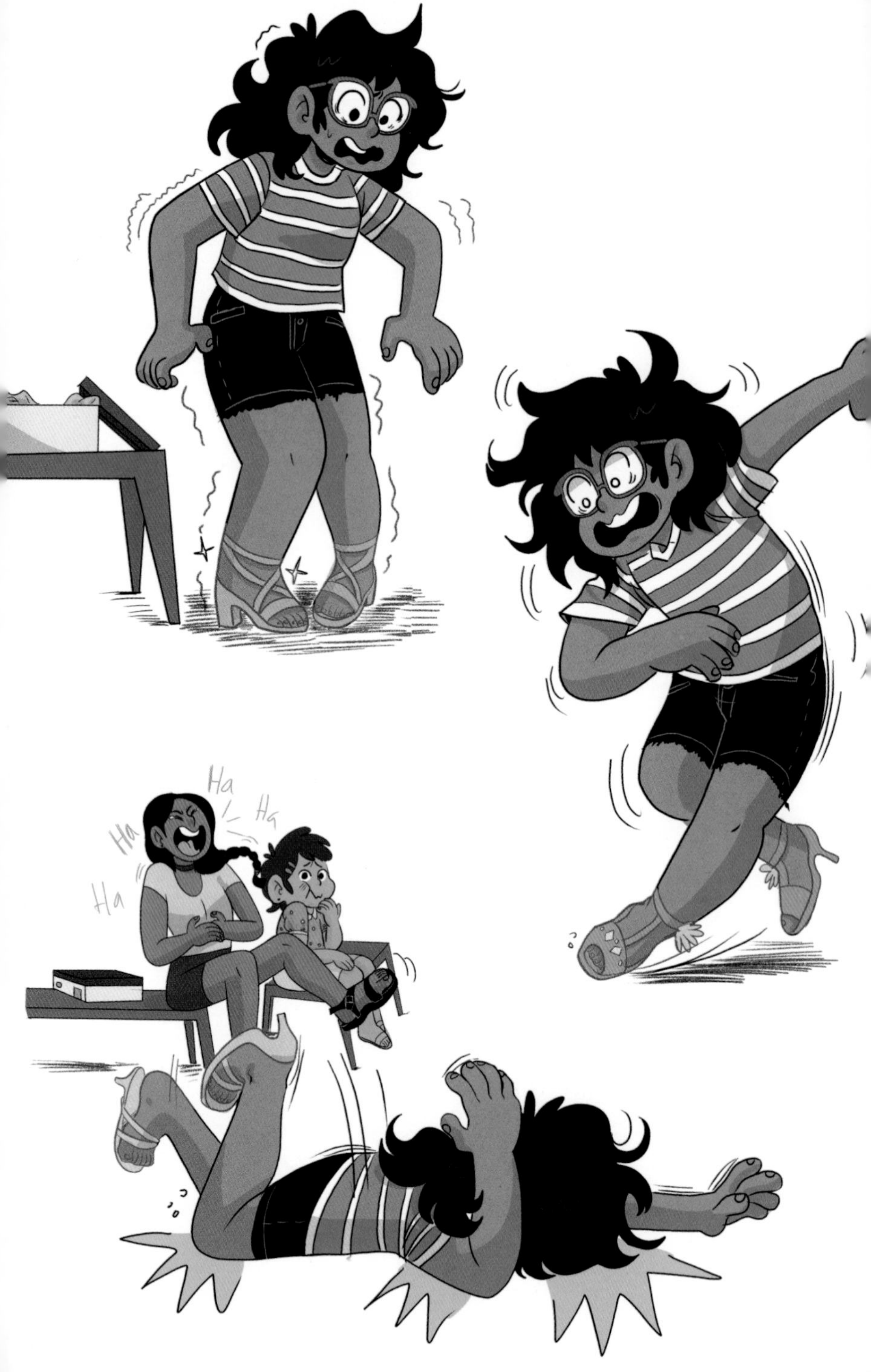
Ha
Ha
Ha
Ha

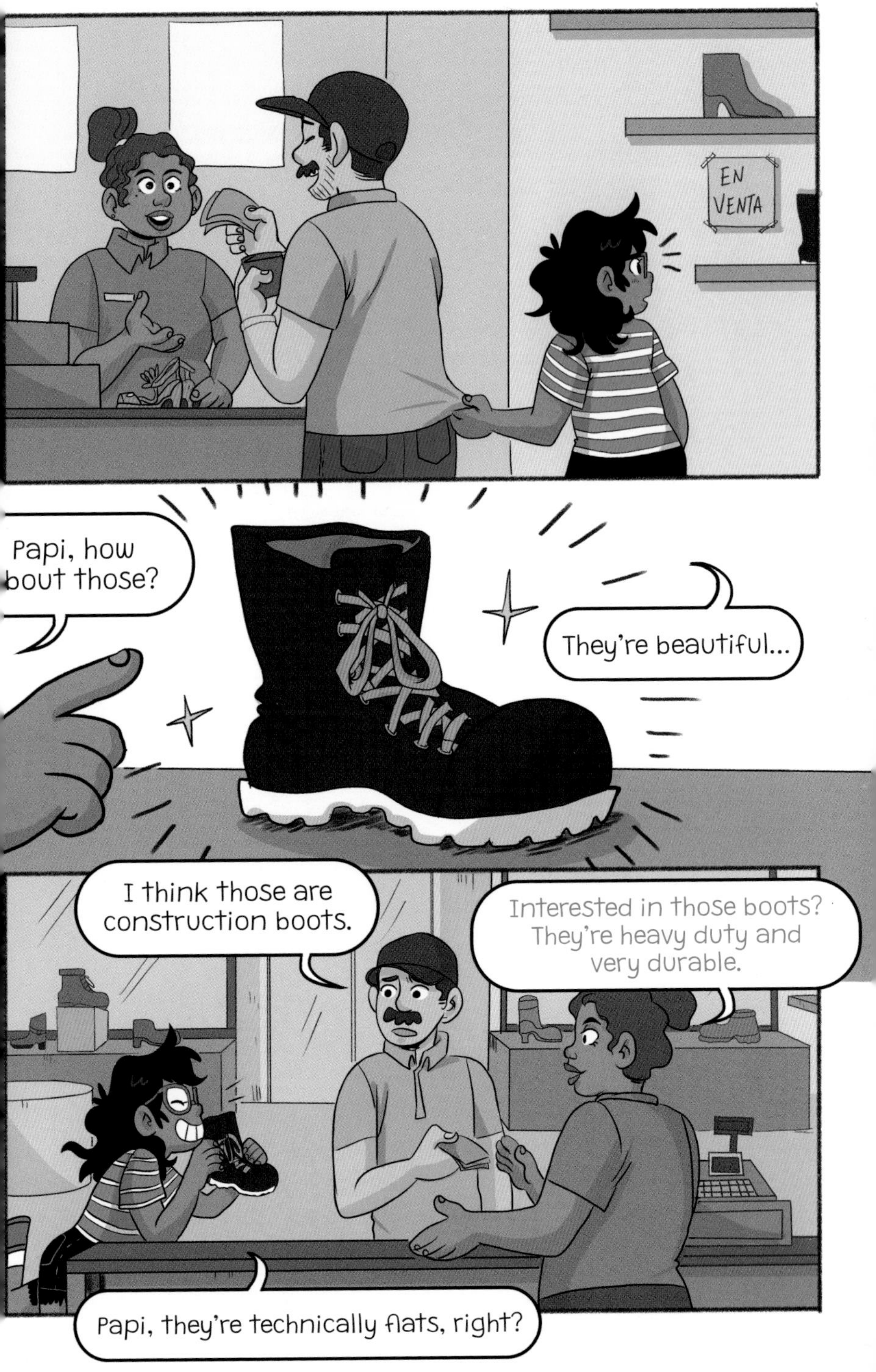
EN VENTA
Papi, how bout those?
They're beautiful...
I think those are construction boots.
Interested in those boots? They're heavy duty and very durable.
Papi, they're technically flats, right?

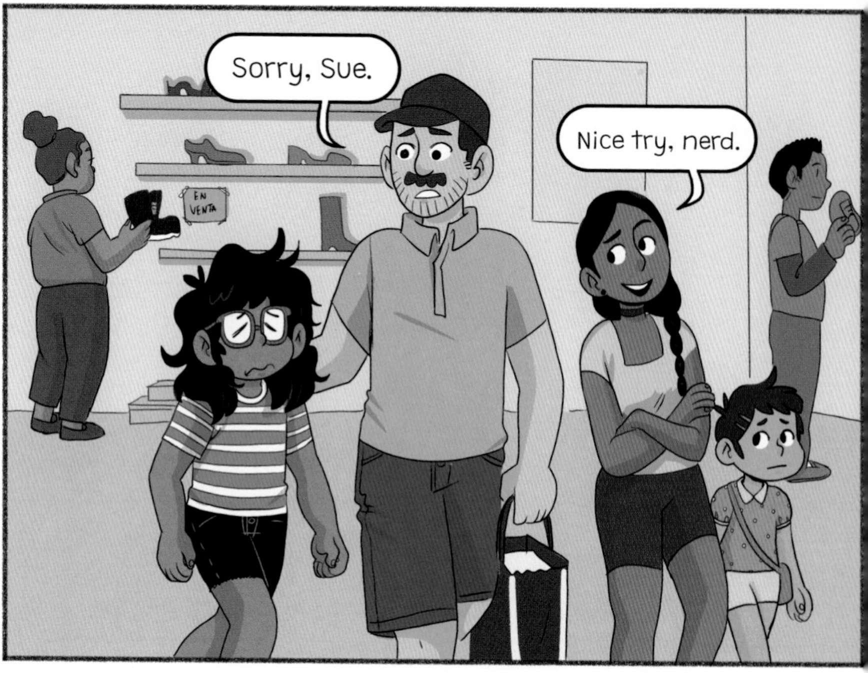
Sorry, Sue.
Nice try, nerd.
EN VENTA

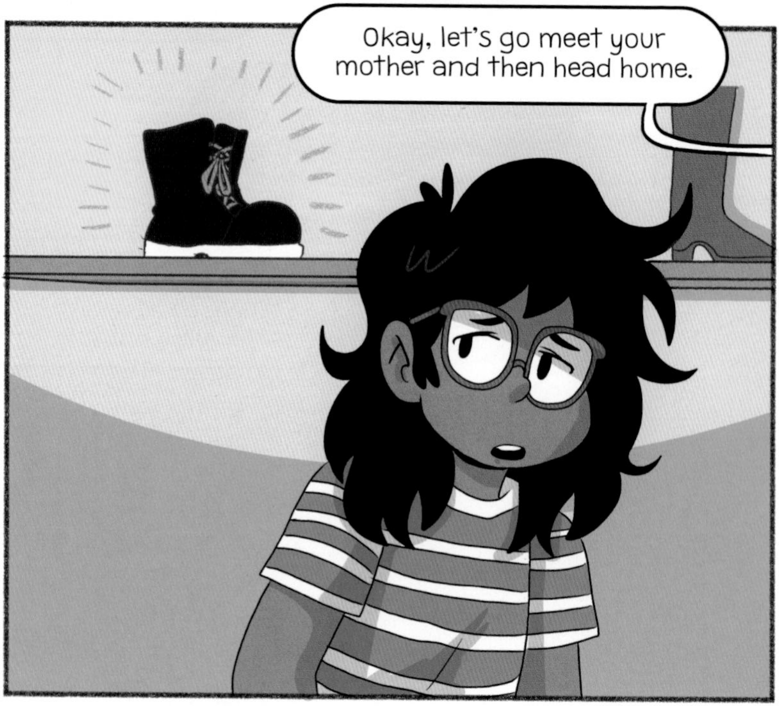
Okay, let's go meet your mother and then head home.

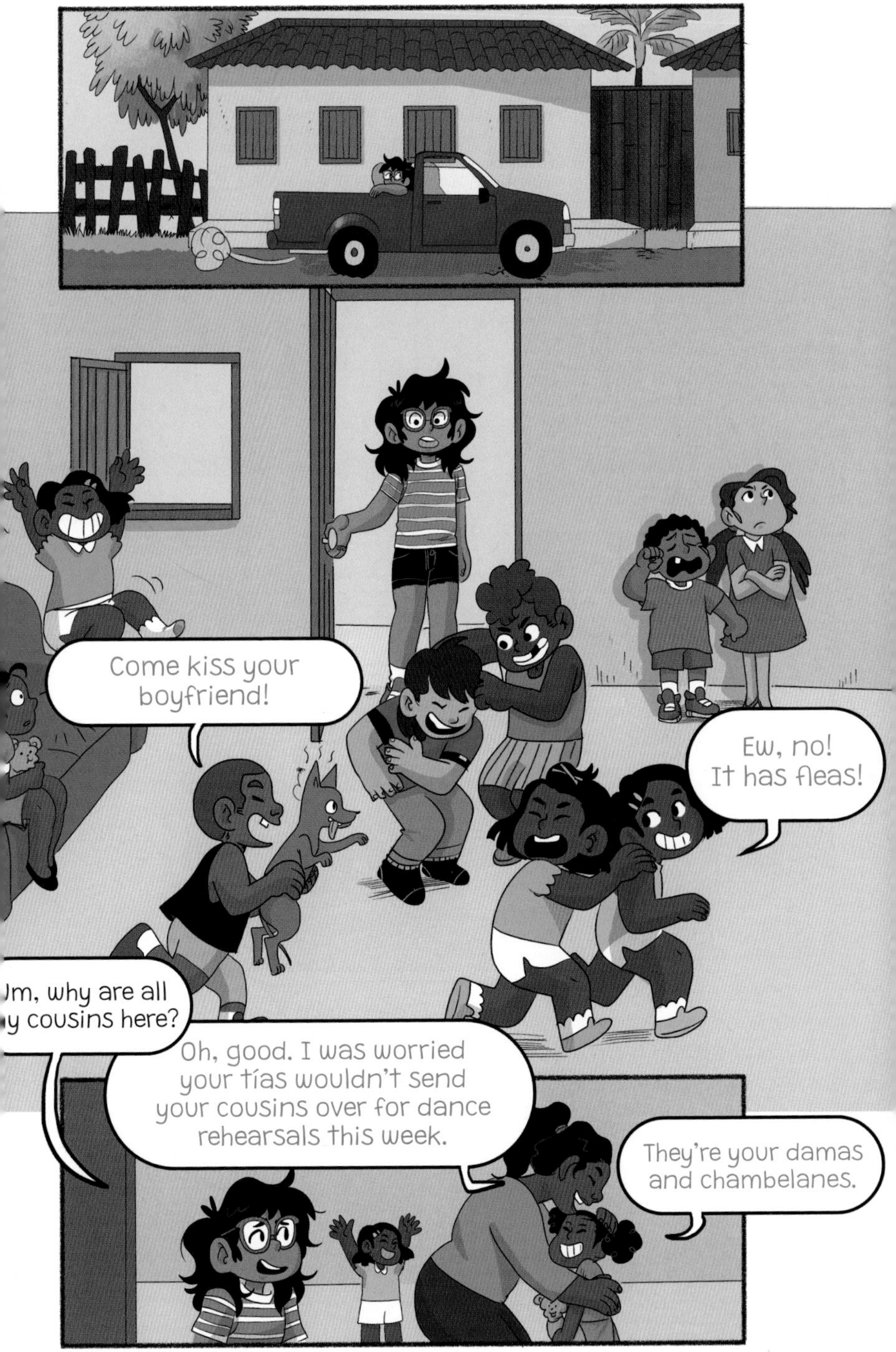
Come kiss your boyfriend!
Ew, no! It has fleas!
Jm, why are all y cousins here?
Oh, good. I was worried your tías wouldn't send your cousins over for dance rehearsals this week.
They're your damas and chambelanes.

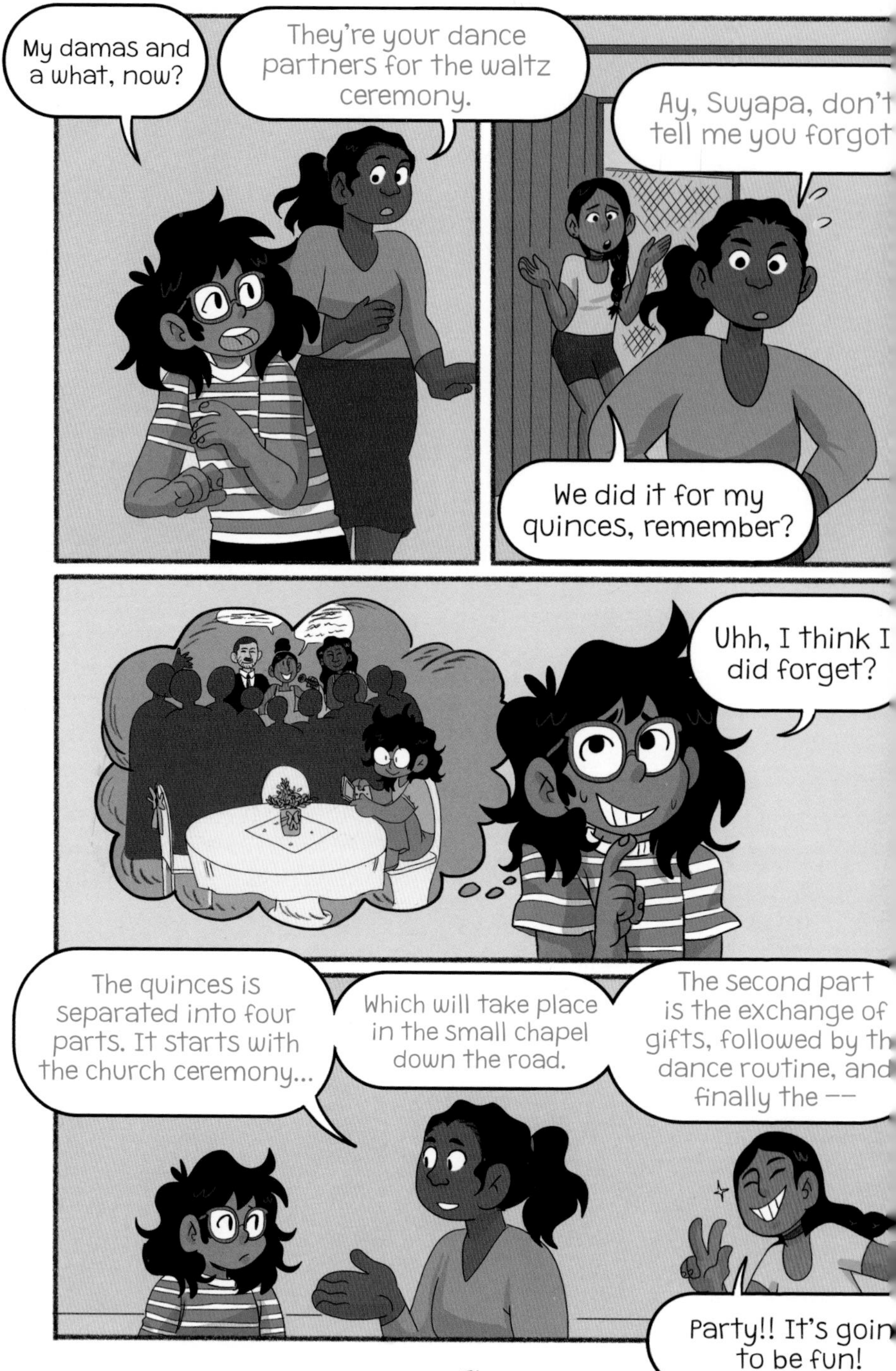
My damas and a what, now?
They're your dance partners for the waltz ceremony.
Ay, Suyapa, don't tell me you forgot
We did it for my quinces, remember?
Uhh, I think I did forget?
The quinces is separated into four parts. It starts with the church ceremony...
Which will take place in the small chapel down the road.
The second part is the exchange of gifts, followed by th dance routine, and finally the --
Party!! It's goin to be fun!

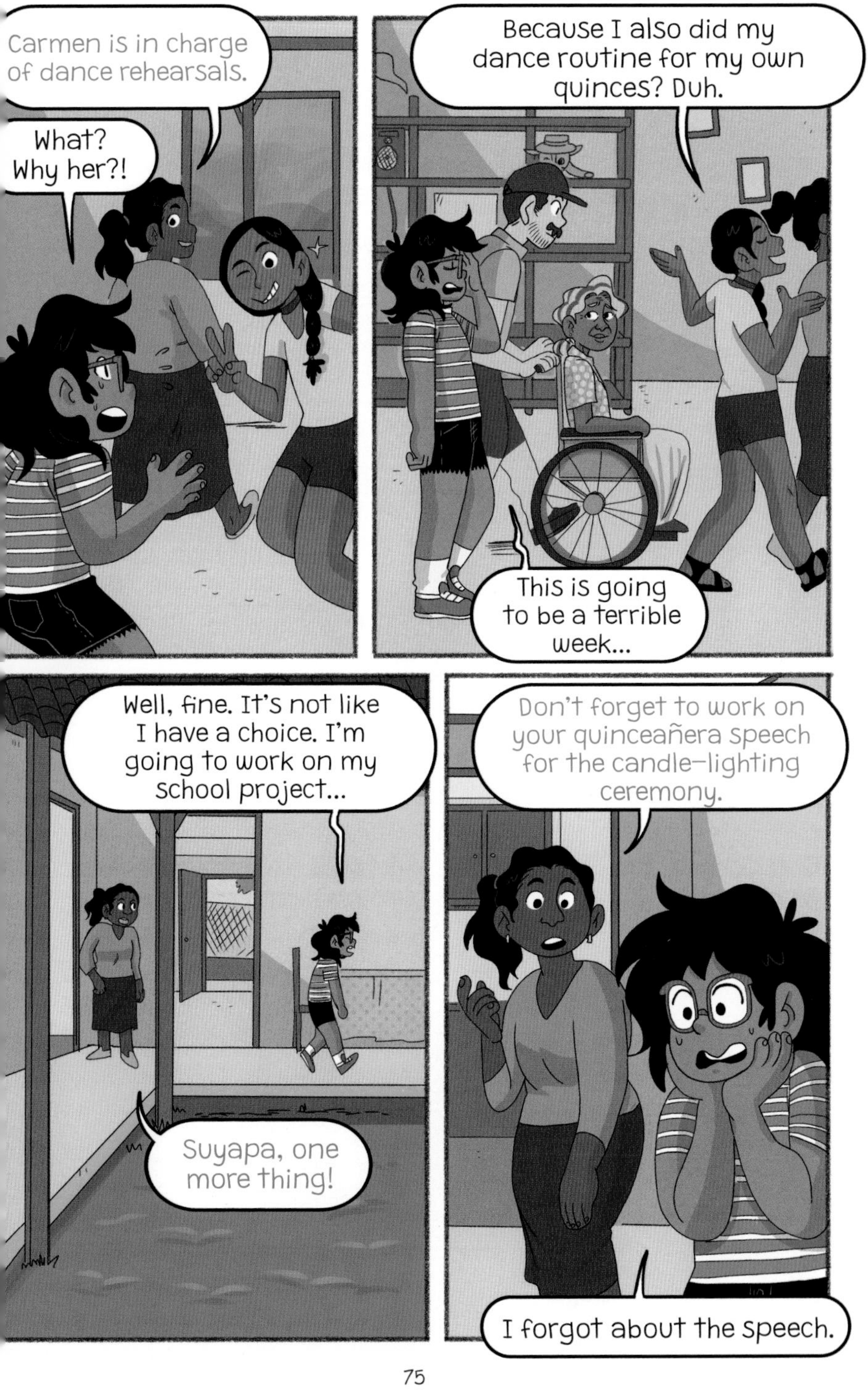
Carmen is in charge of dance rehearsals.
What? Why her?!
Because I also did my dance routine for my own quinces? Duh.
This is going to be a terrible week...
Well, fine. It's not like I have a choice. I'm going to work on my school project...
Suyapa, one more thing!
Don't forget to work on your quinceañera speech for the candle-lighting ceremony.
I forgot about the speech.

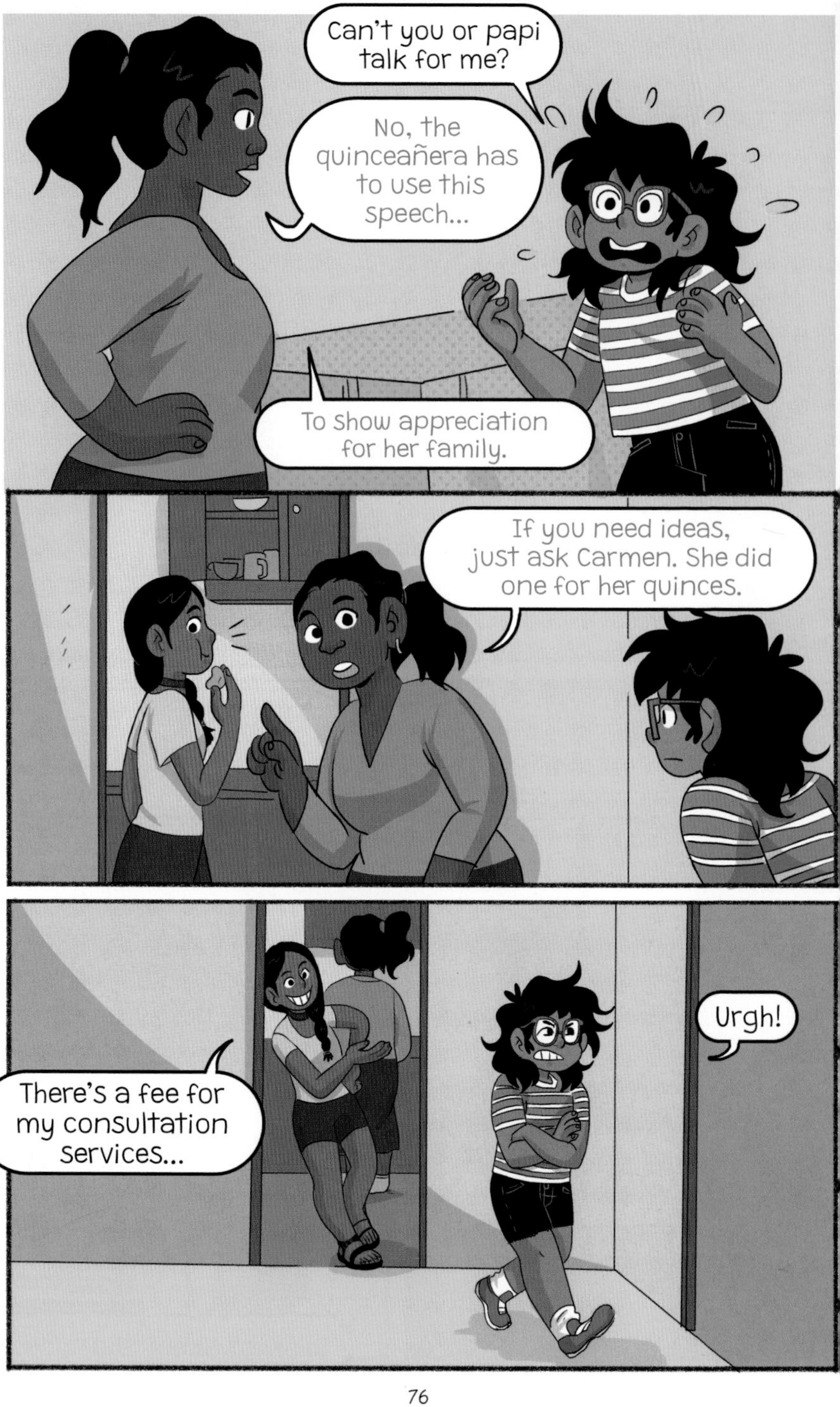
Can't you or papi talk for me?
No, the quinceañera has to use this speech...
To show appreciation for her family.
If you need ideas, just ask Carmen. She did one for her quinces.
There's a fee for my consultation services...
Urgh!

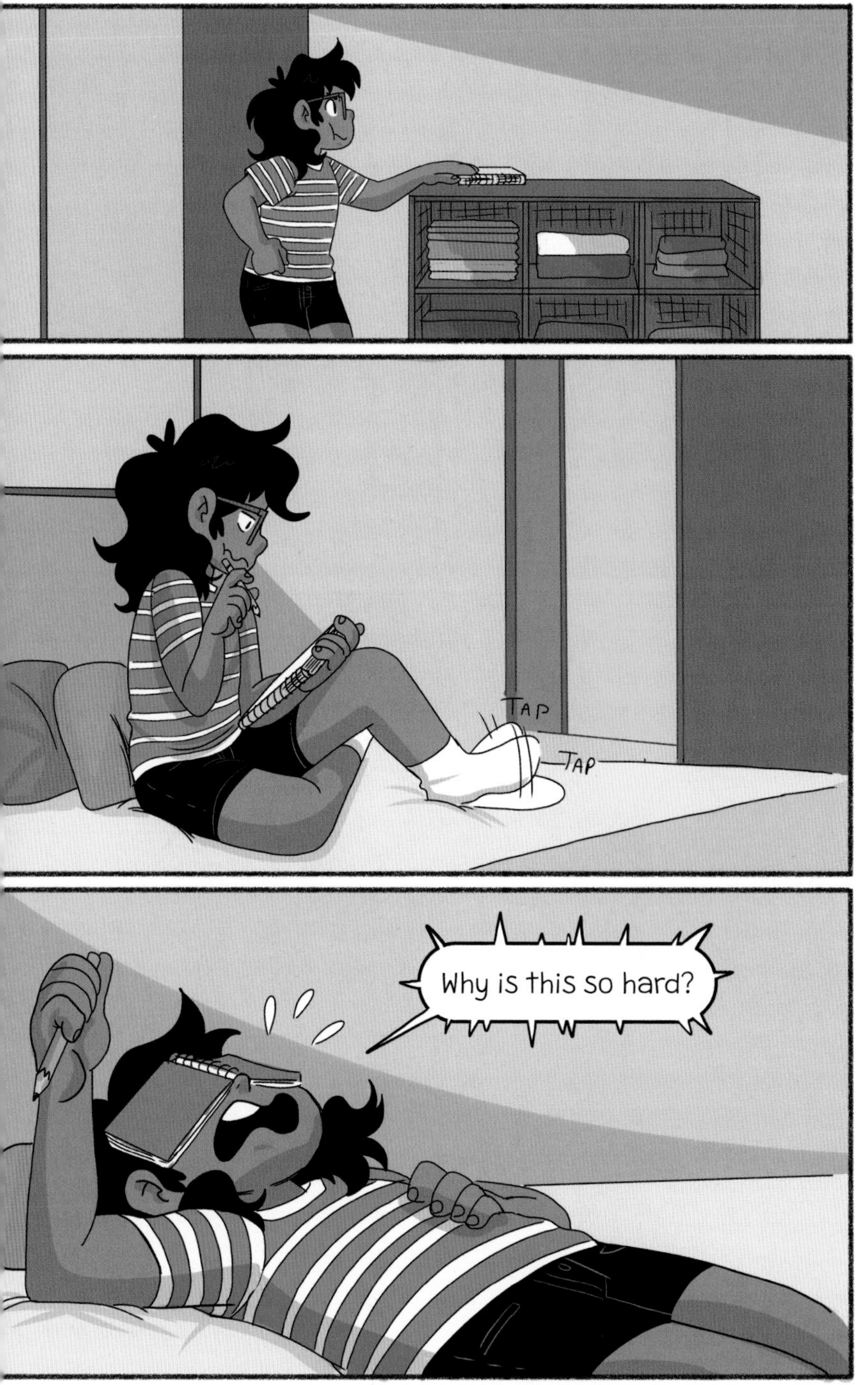
TAP
TAP
Why is this so hard?

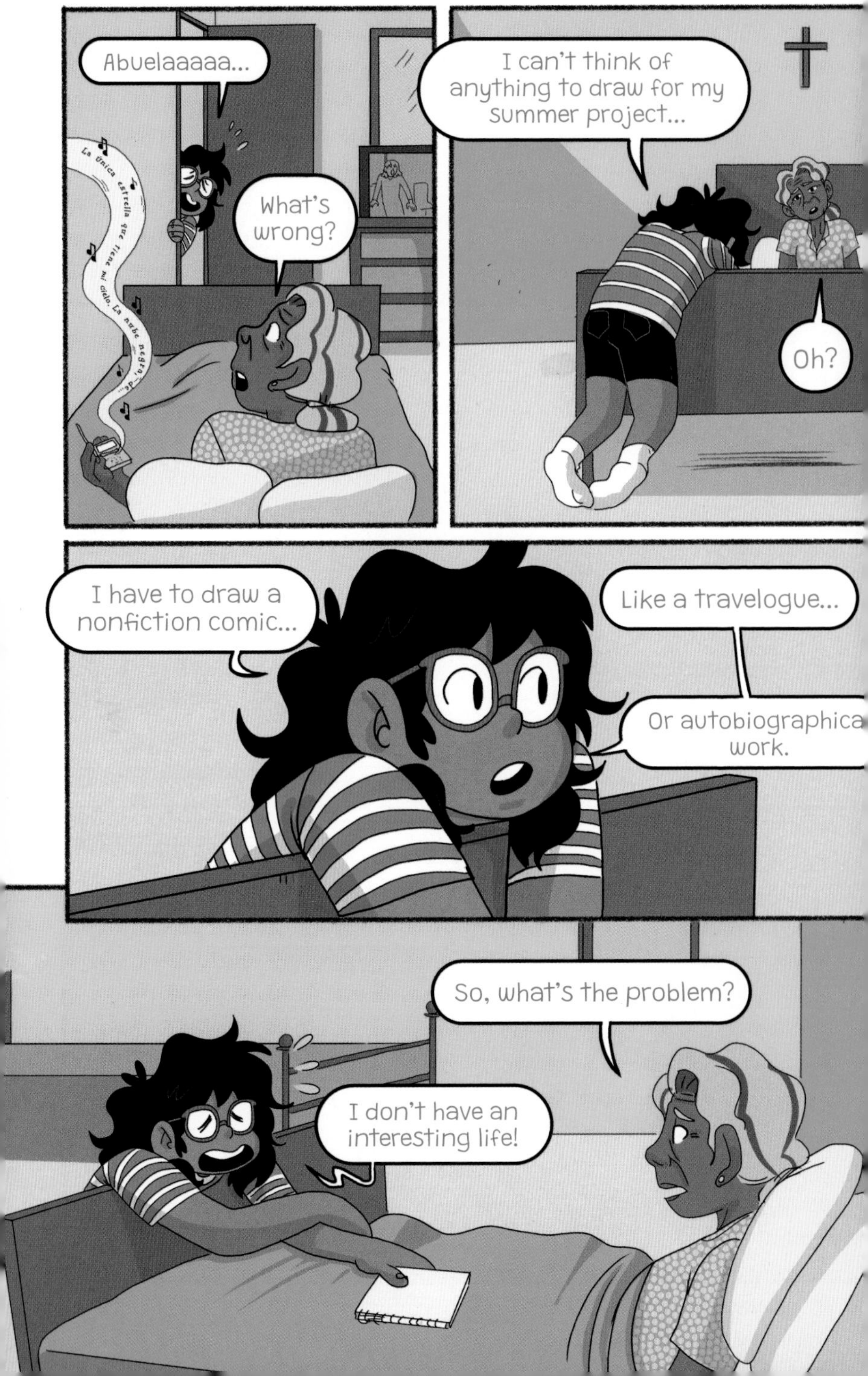
Abuelaaaaa...
La única estrella que tiene mi cielo. La nube negra, de...
What's wrong?
I can't think of anything to draw for my summer project...
Oh?
I have to draw a nonfiction comic...
Like a travelogue...
Or autobiographica work.
So, what's the problem?
I don't have an interesting life!

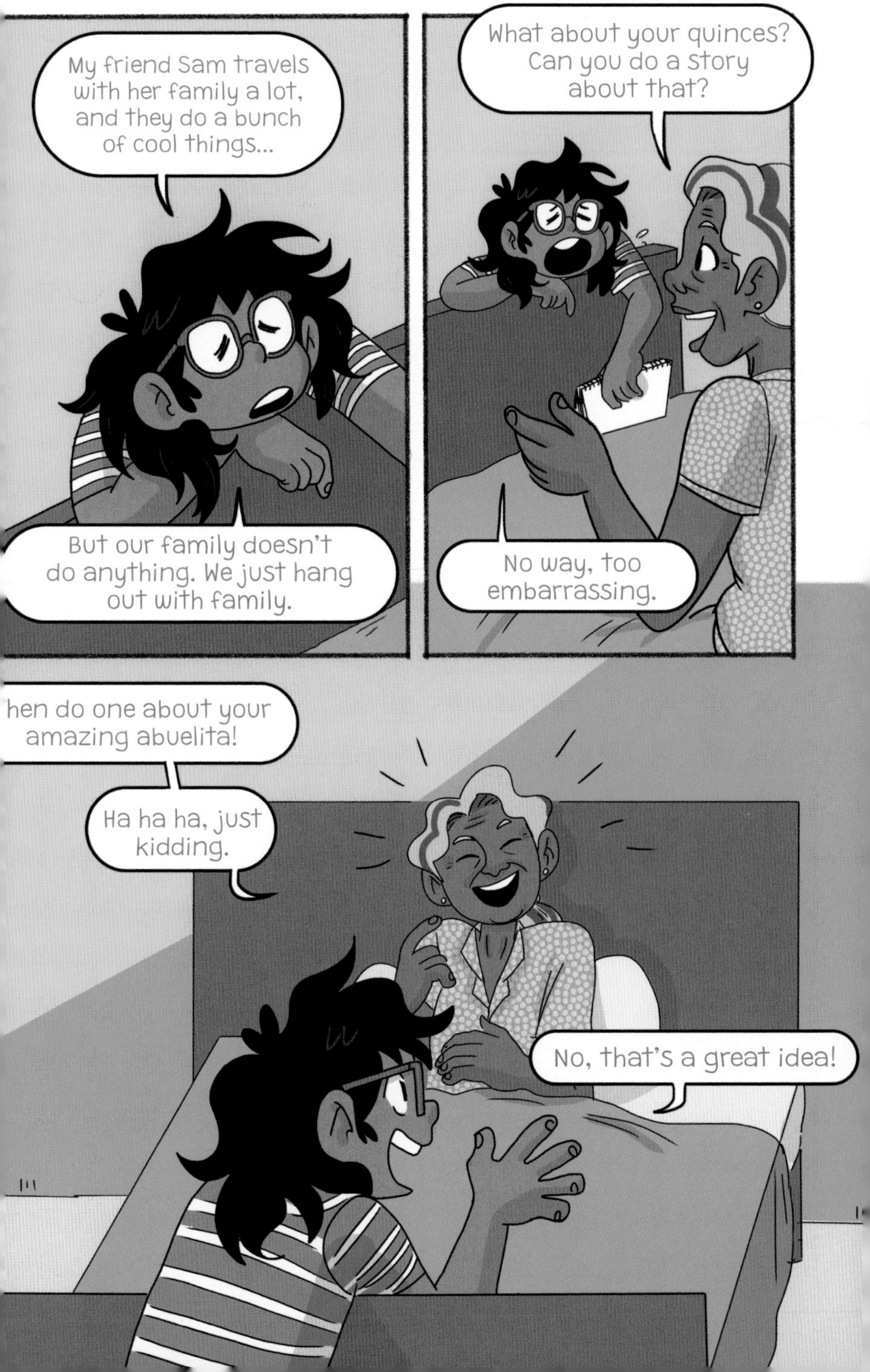

My friend Sam travels with her family a lot, and they do a bunch of cool things...
But our family doesn't do anything. We just hang out with family.
What about your quinces? Can you do a story about that?
No way, too embarrassing.
hen do one about your amazing abuelita!
Ha ha ha, just kidding.
No, that's a great idea!

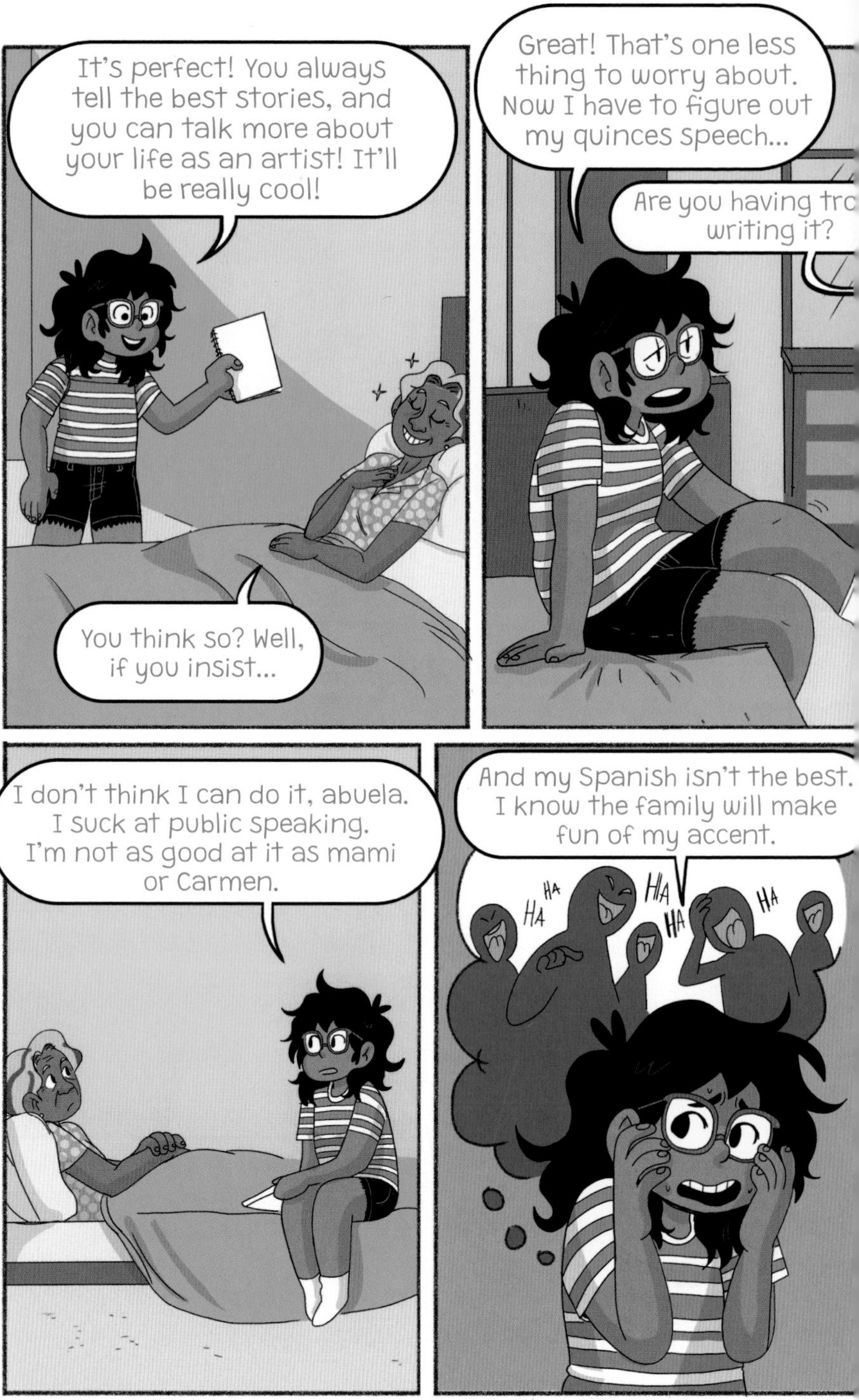
It's perfect! You always tell the best stories, and you can talk more about your life as an artist! It'll be really cool!
You think so? Well, if you insist...
Great! That's one less thing to worry about. Now I have to figure out my quinces speech...
Are you having tro
writing it?
I don't think I can do it, abuela. I suck at public speaking. I'm not as good at it as mami or Carmen.
And my Spanish isn't the best. I know the family will make fun of my accent.
HA HA HA HA HA HA

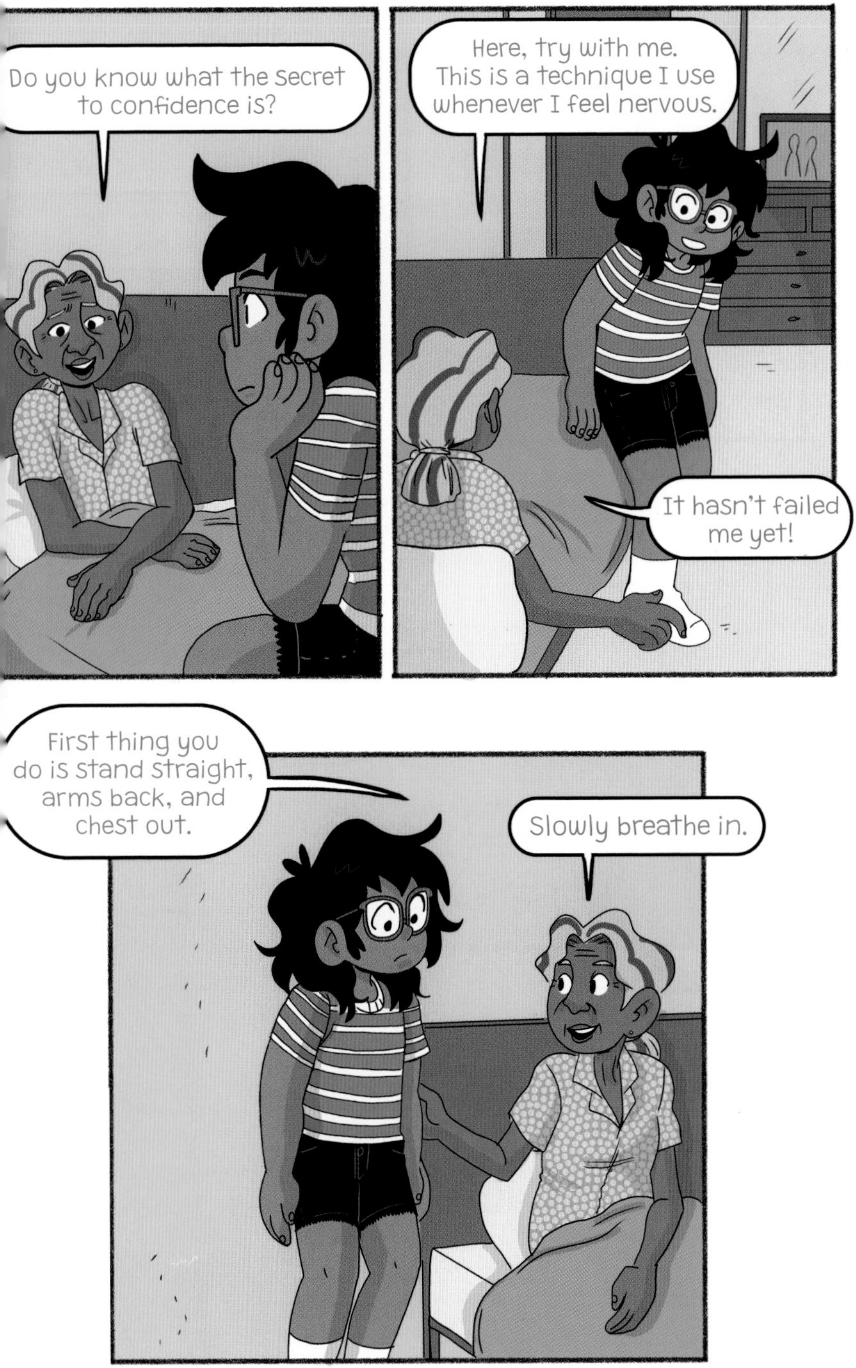
Do you know what the secret to confidence is?
Here, try with me. This is a technique I use whenever I feel nervous.
It hasn't failed me yet!
First thing you do is stand straight, arms back, and chest out.
Slowly breathe in.

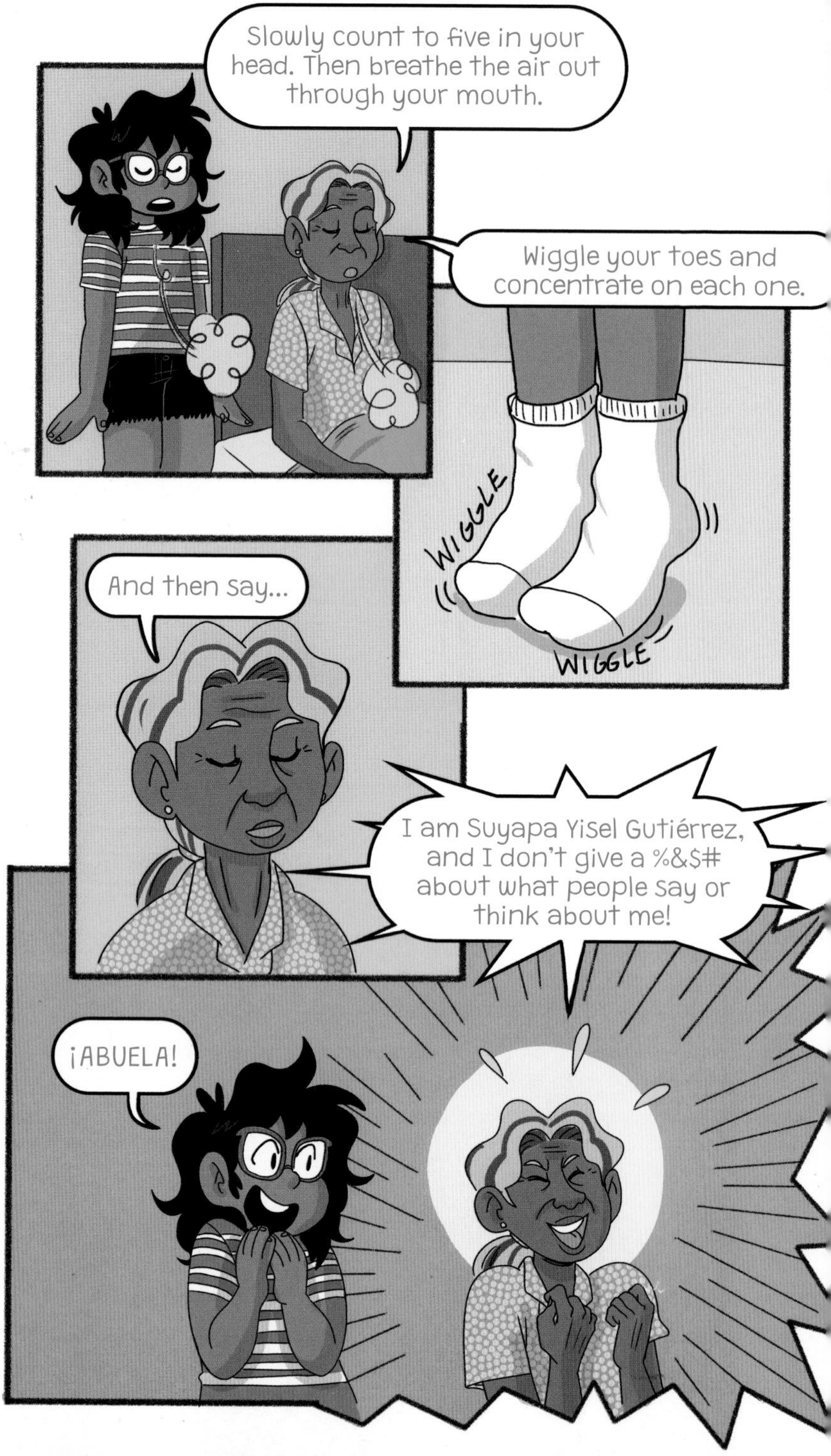
Slowly count to five in your head. Then breathe the air out through your mouth.
Wiggle your toes and concentrate on each one.
WIGGLE
WIGGLE
And then say...
I am Suyapa Yisel Gutiérrez, and I don't give a %&$# about what people say or think about me!
¡ABUELA!

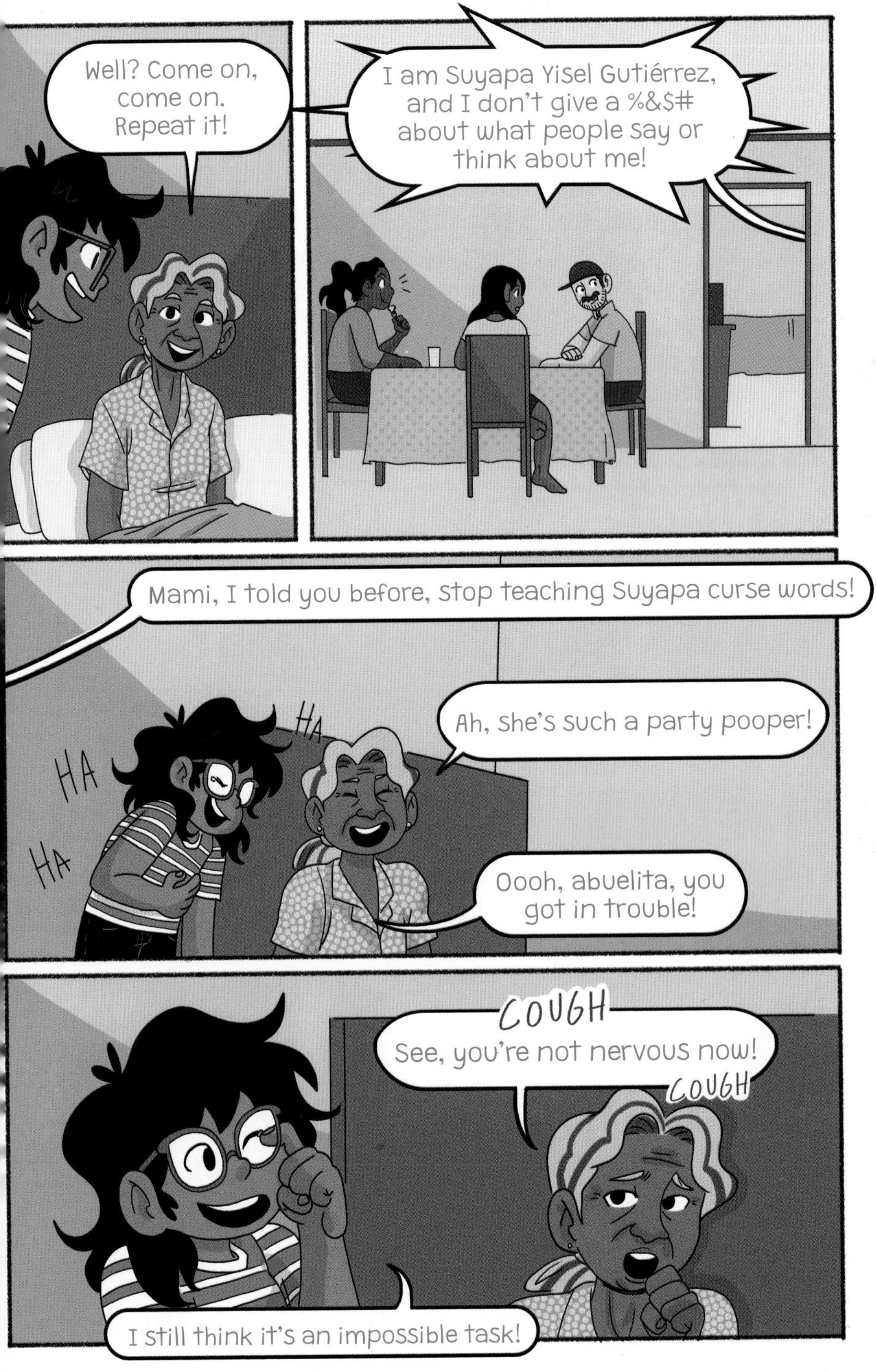
Well? Come on, come on. Repeat it!
I am Suyapa Yisel Gutiérrez, and I don't give a %&$# about what people say or think about me!
Mami, I told you before, stop teaching Suyapa curse words!
HA
HA
HA
Ah, she's such a party pooper!
Oooh, abuelita, you got in trouble!
COUGH
See, you're not nervous now!
COUGH
I still think it's an impossible task!

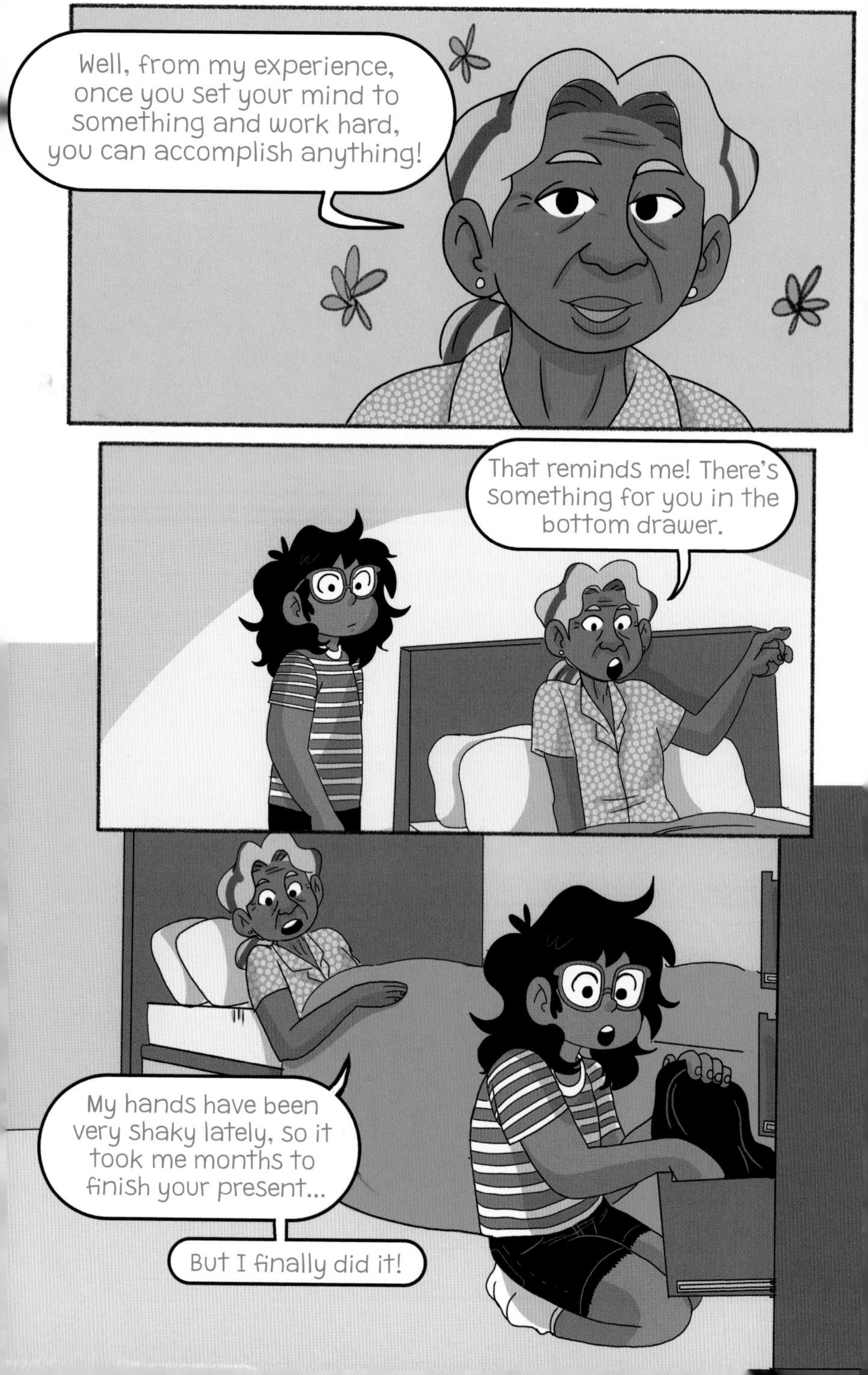
Well, from my experience, once you set your mind to something and work hard, you can accomplish anything!
That reminds me! There's something for you in the bottom drawer.
My hands have been very shaky lately, so it took me months to finish your present...
But I finally did it!

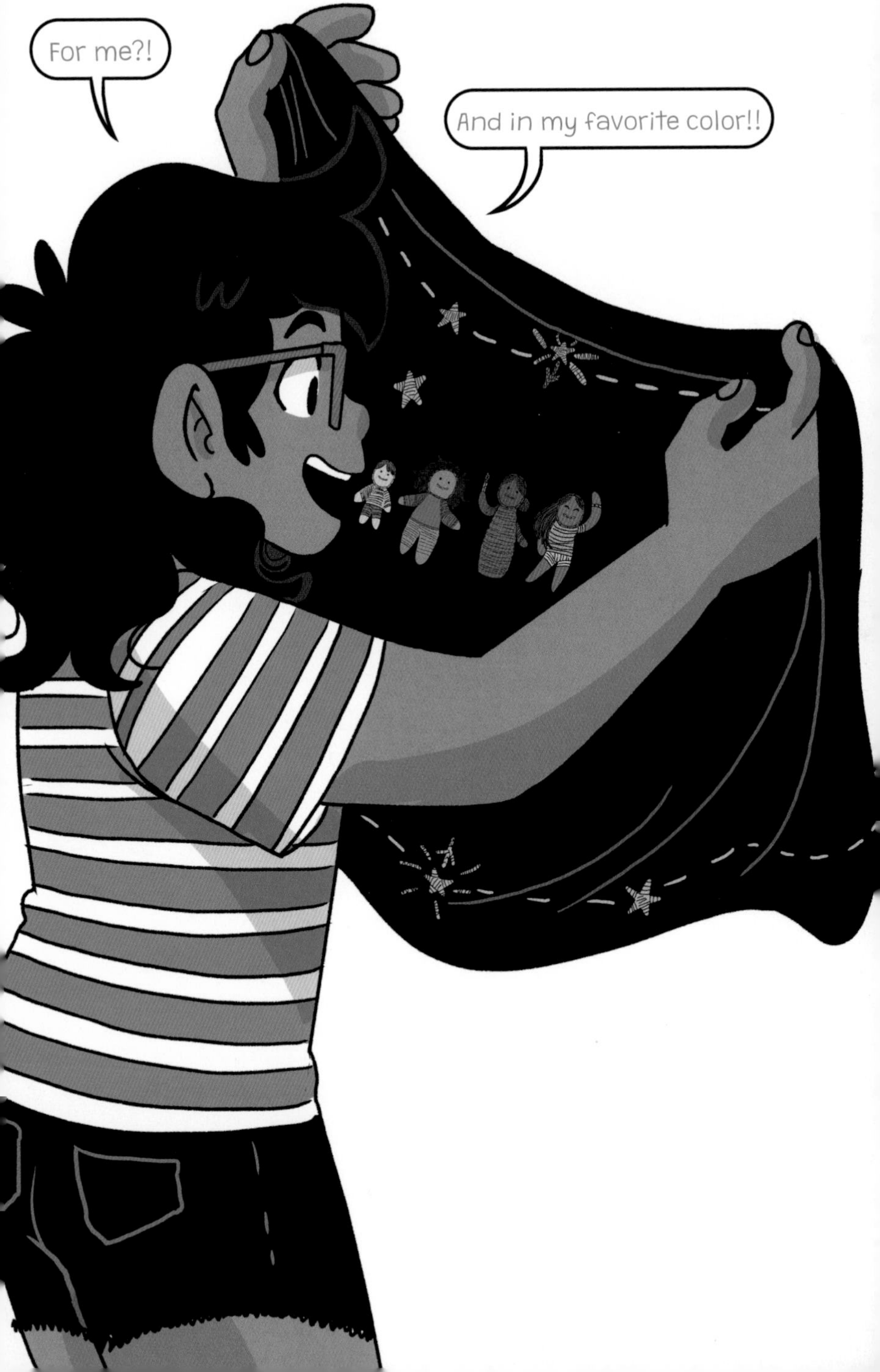
For me?!
And in my favorite color!!

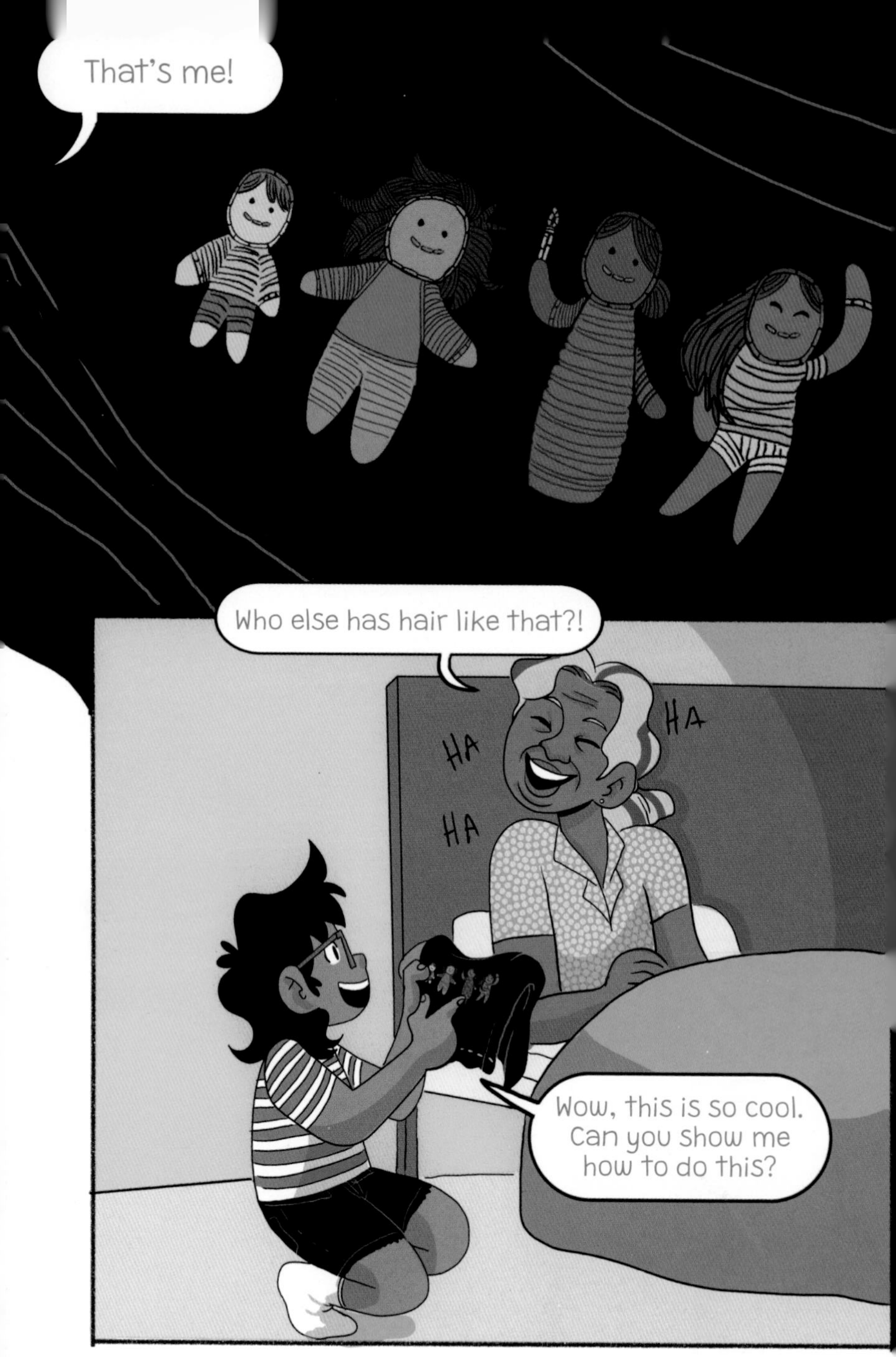
That's me!
Who else has hair like that?!
HA
HA
HA
Wow, this is so cool. Can you show me how to do this?

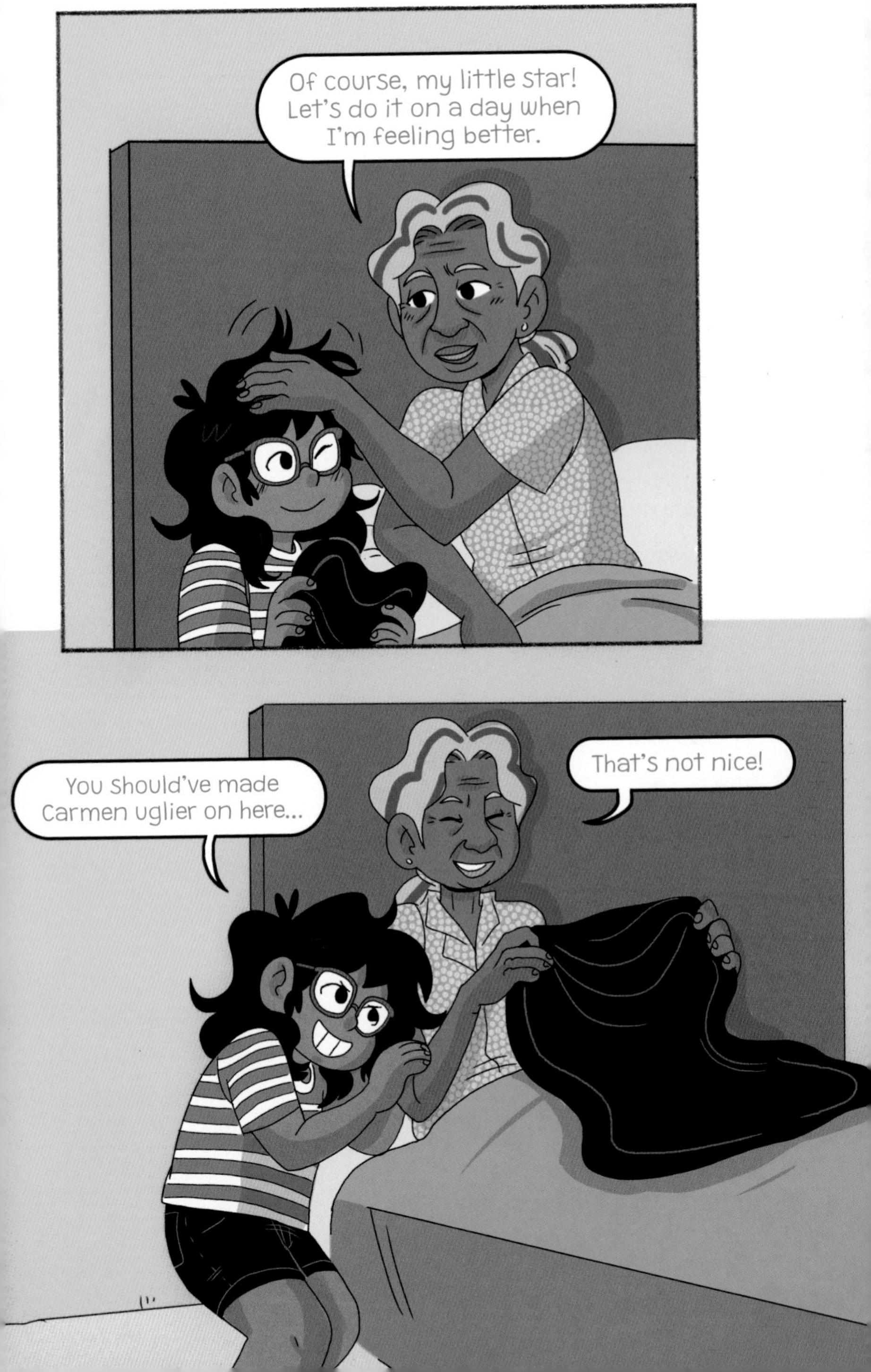
Of course, my little star! Let's do it on a day when I'm feeling better.
You should've made Carmen uglier on here...
That's not nice!

CHAPTER FOUR

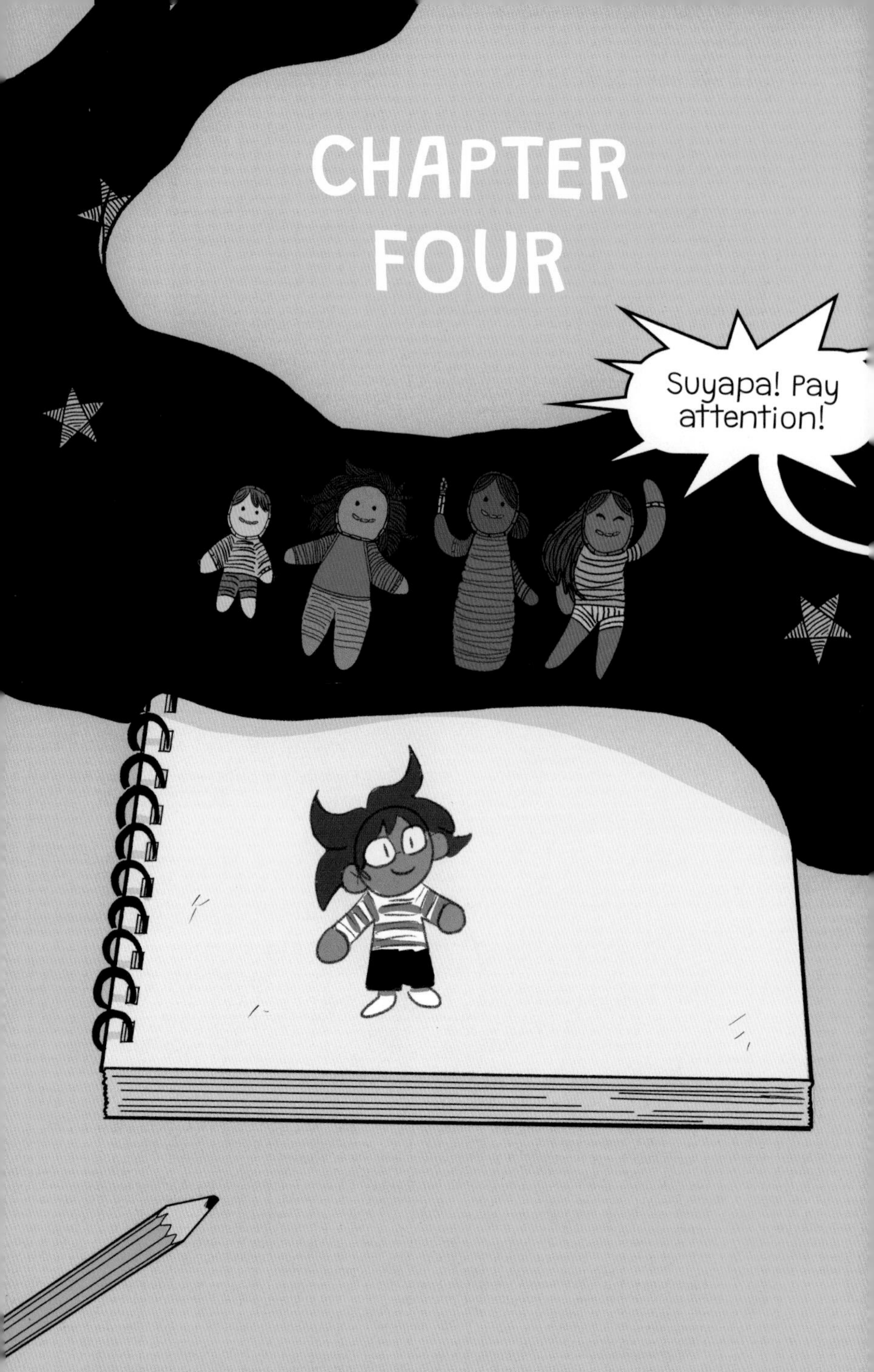
Suyapa! Pay attention!

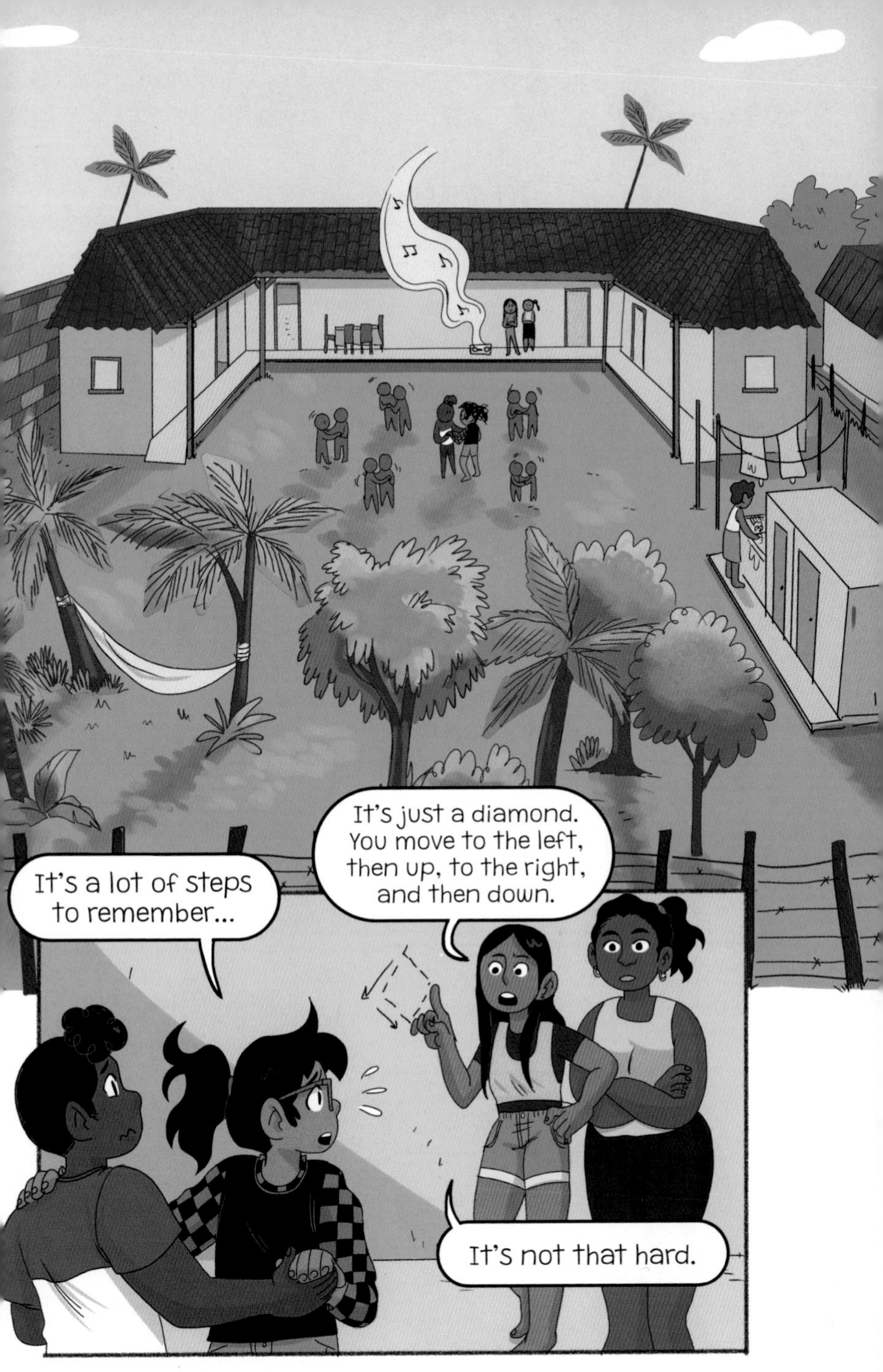
It's a lot of steps to remember...
It's just a diamond. You move to the left, then up, to the right, and then down.
It's not that hard.

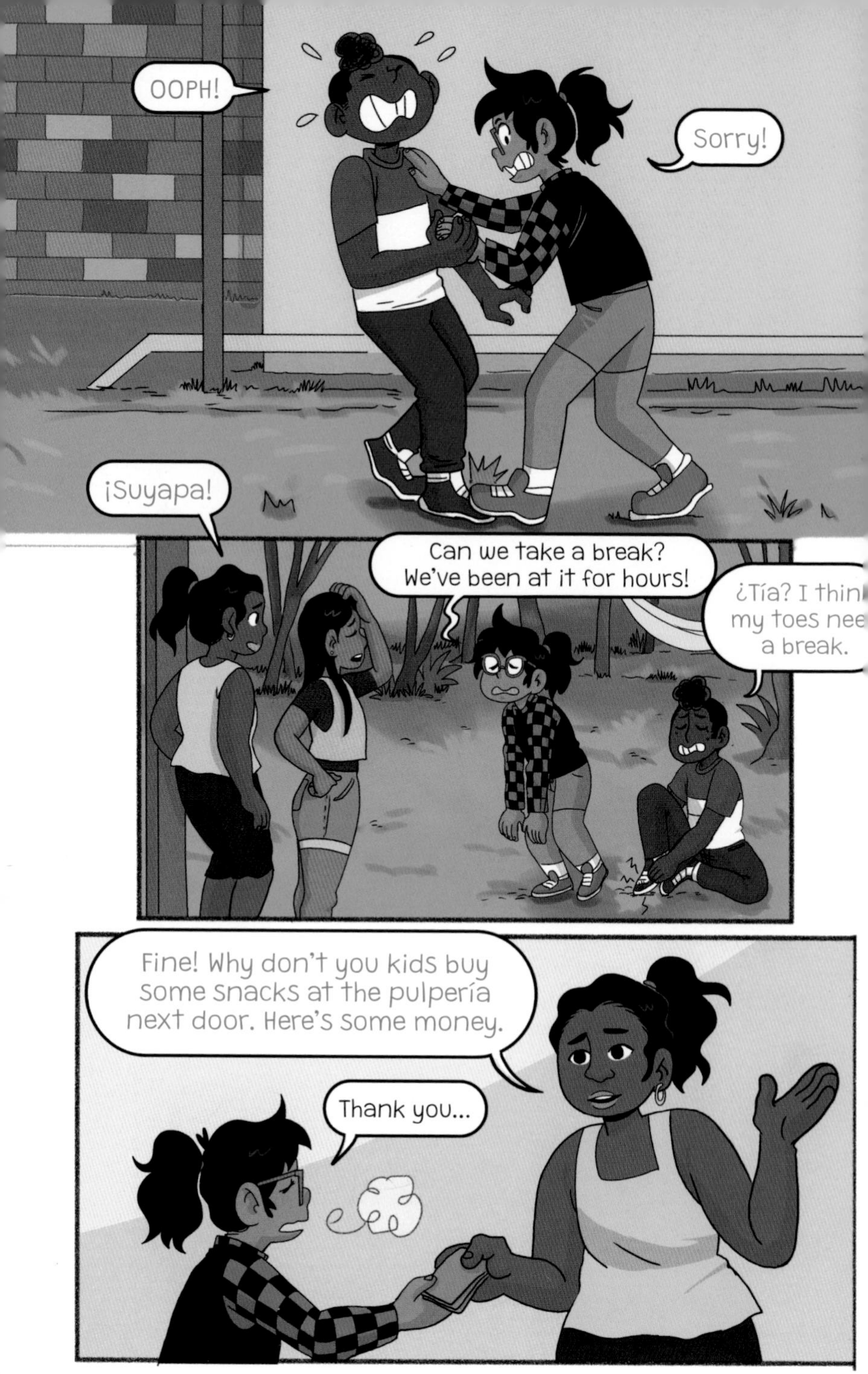
OOPH!
Sorry!
¡Suyapa!
Can we take a break? We've been at it for hours!
¿Tía? I thin my toes nee a break.
Fine! Why don't you kids buy some snacks at the pulpería next door. Here's some money.
Thank you...

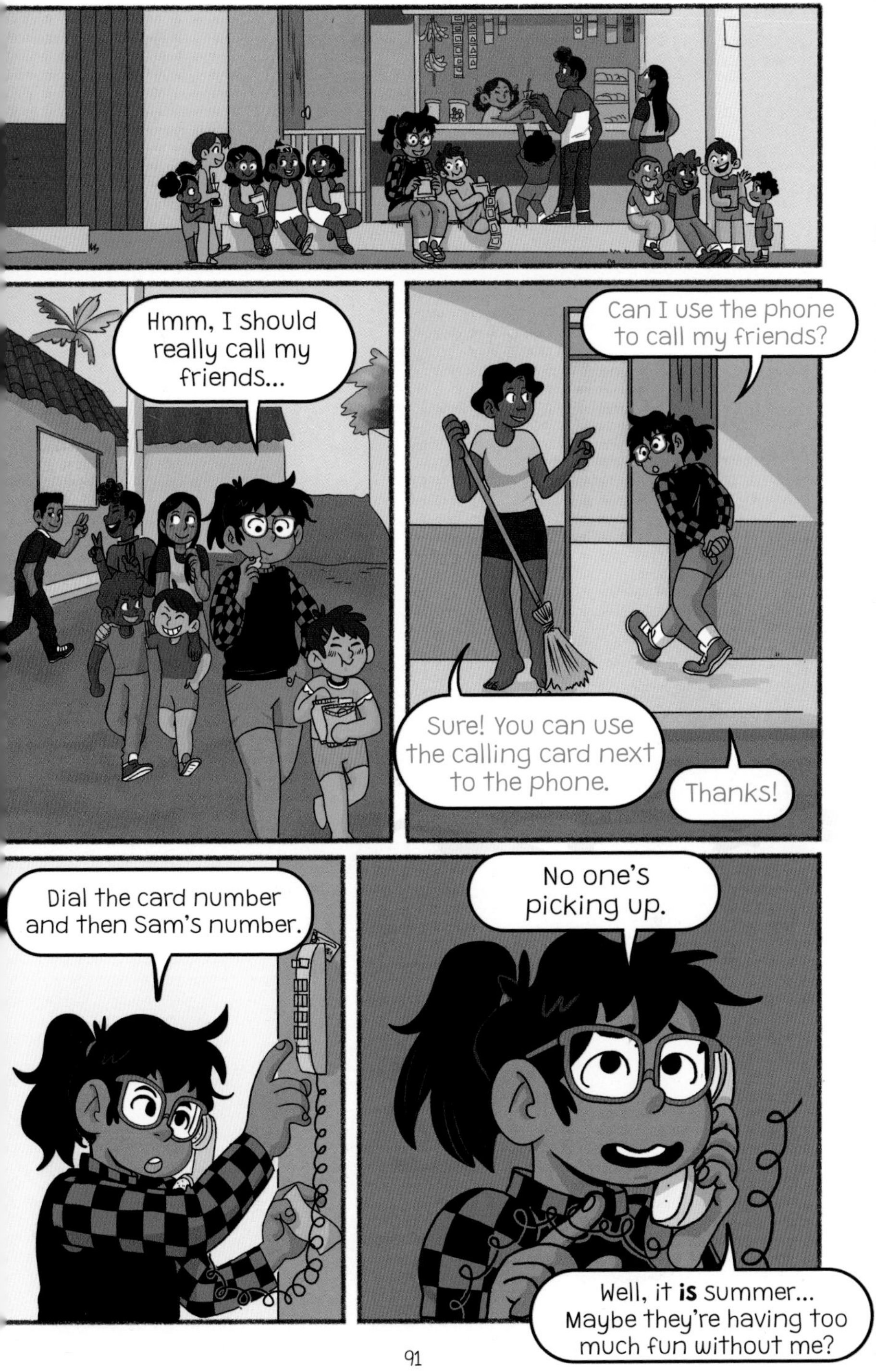
Hmm, I should really call my friends...
Can I use the phone to call my friends?
Sure! You can use the calling card next to the phone.
Thanks!
Dial the card number and then Sam's number.
No one's picking up.
Well, it **is** summer... Maybe they're having too much fun without me?

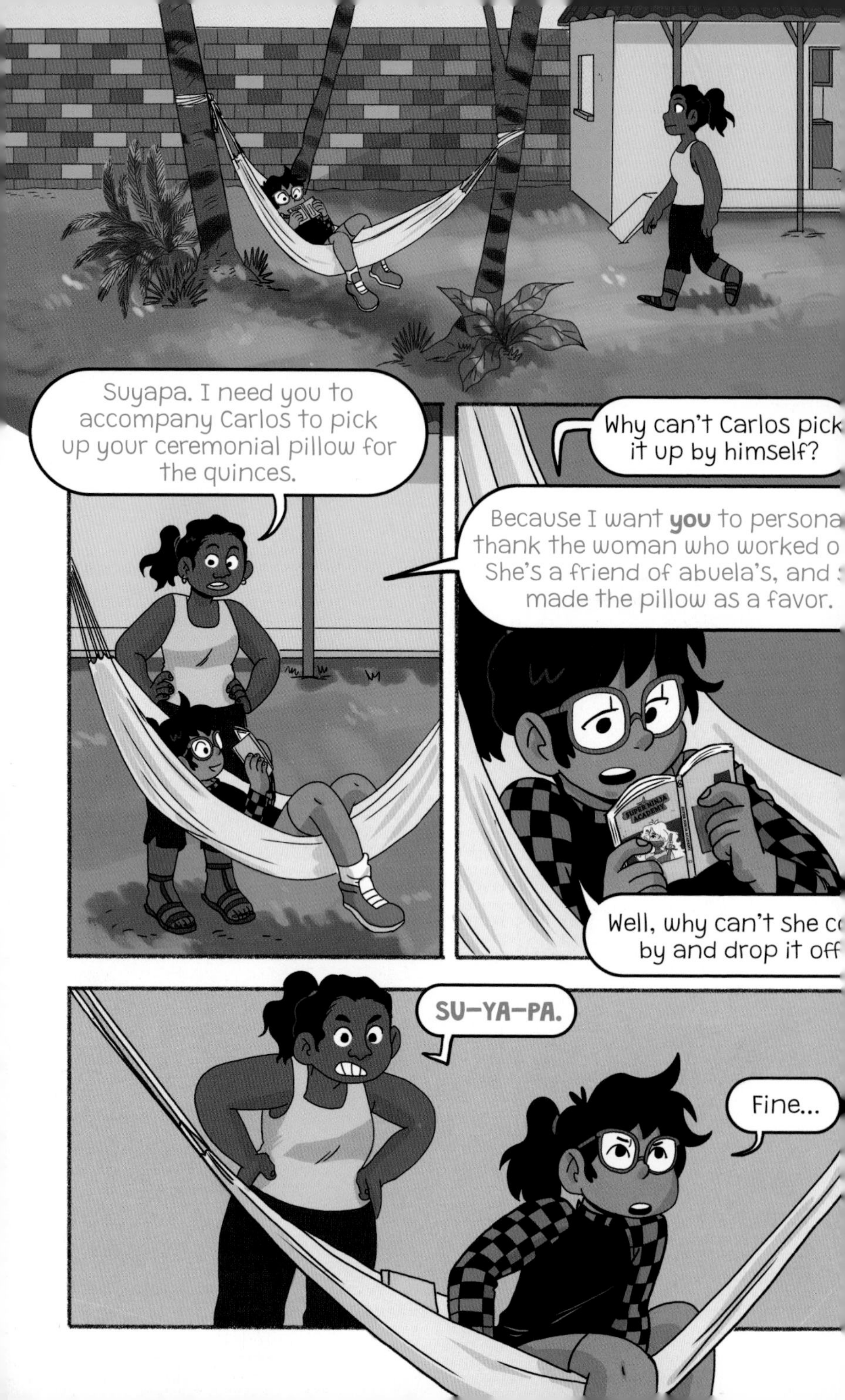
Suyapa. I need you to accompany Carlos to pick up your ceremonial pillow for the quinces.
Why can't Carlos pick it up by himself?
Because I want **you** to persona thank the woman who worked o She's a friend of abuela's, and made the pillow as a favor.
Well, why can't she c by and drop it off
SU–YA–PA.
Fine...

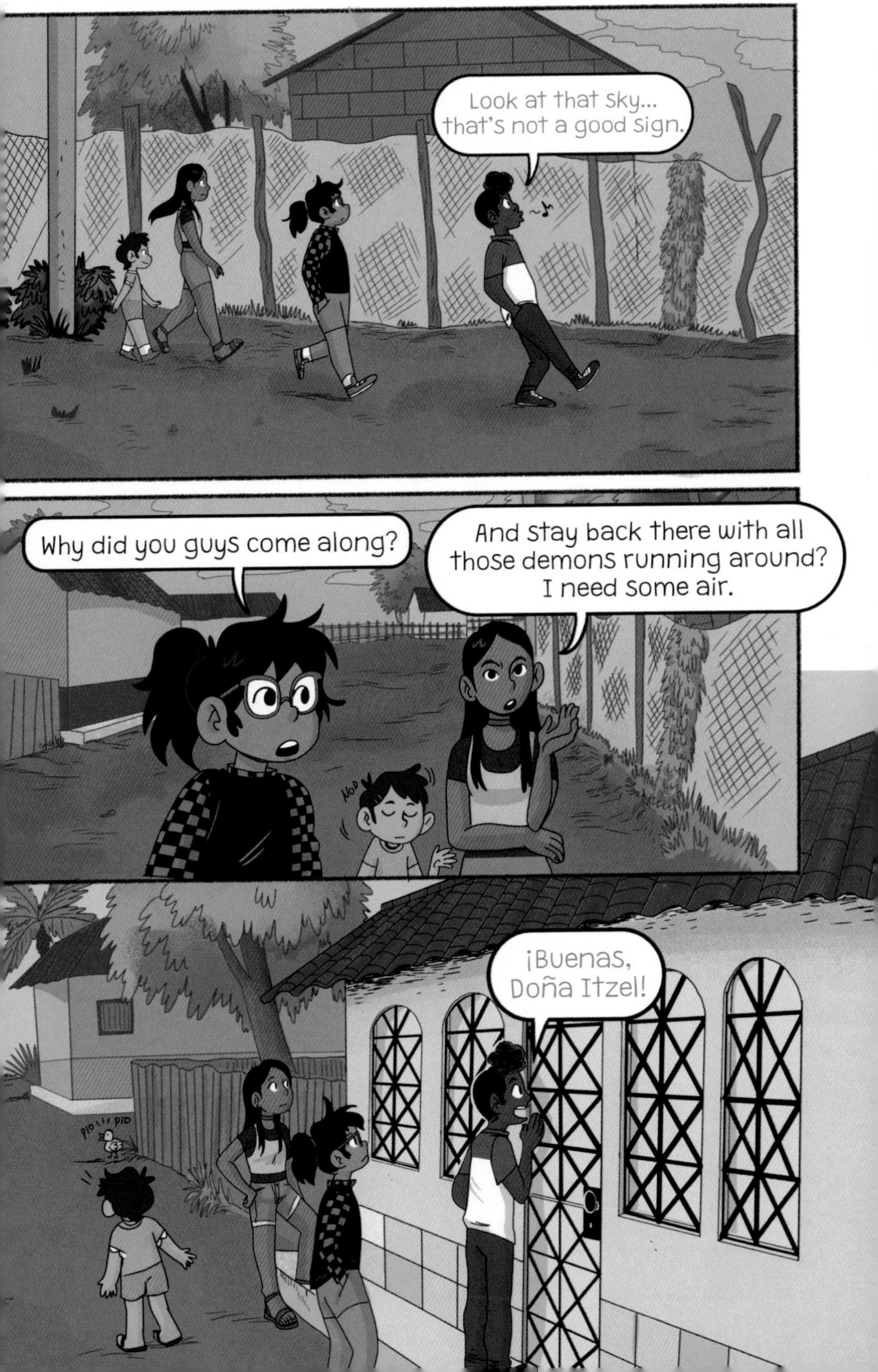
Look at that sky... that's not a good sign.
Why did you guys come along?
And stay back there with all those demons running around? I need some air.
NOD
PIO PIO
¡Buenas, Doña Itzel!

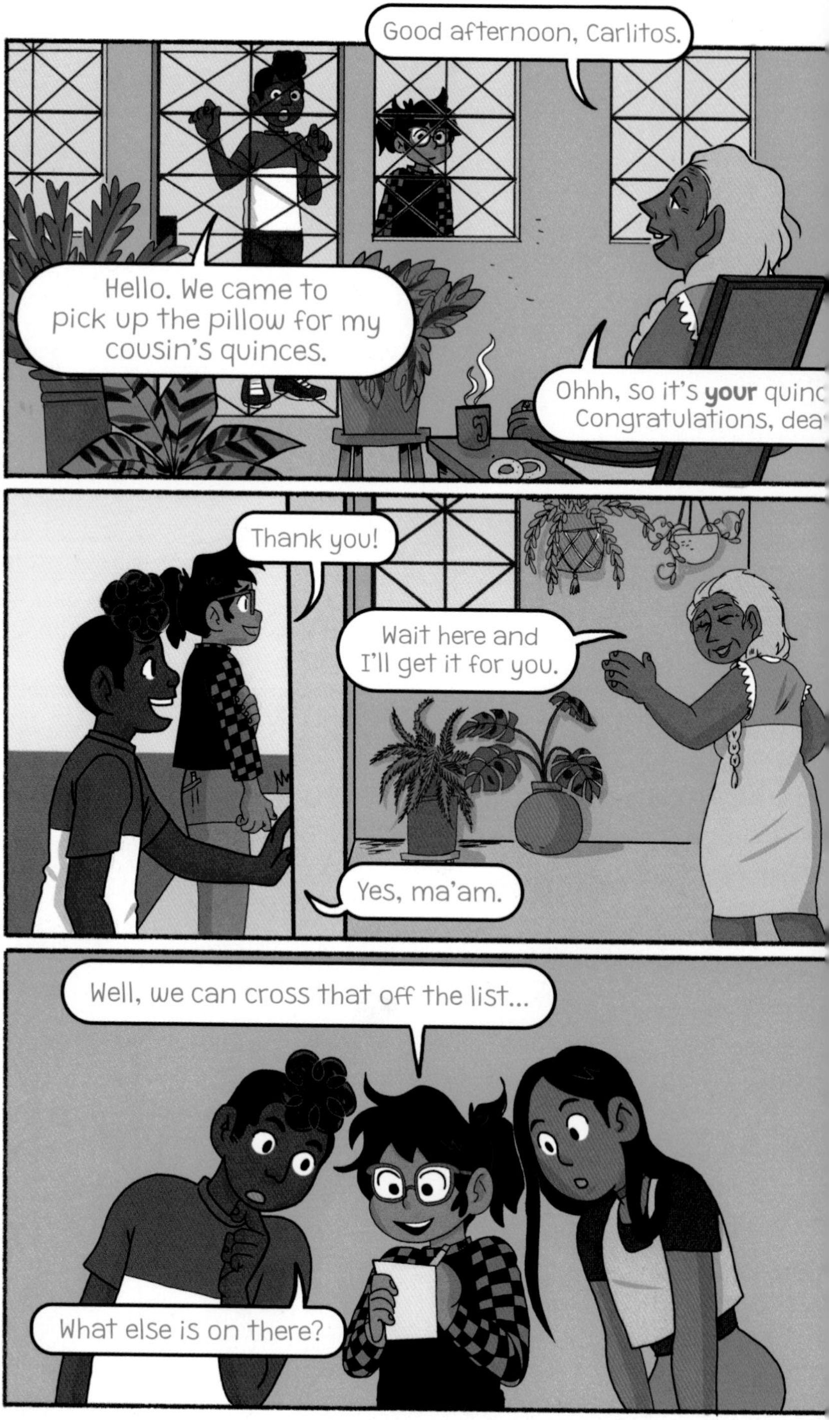
Good afternoon, Carlitos.
Hello. We came to pick up the pillow for my cousin's quinces.
Ohhh, so it's **your** quinc
Congratulations, dea
Thank you!
Wait here and I'll get it for you.
Yes, ma'am.
Well, we can cross that off the list...
What else is on there?

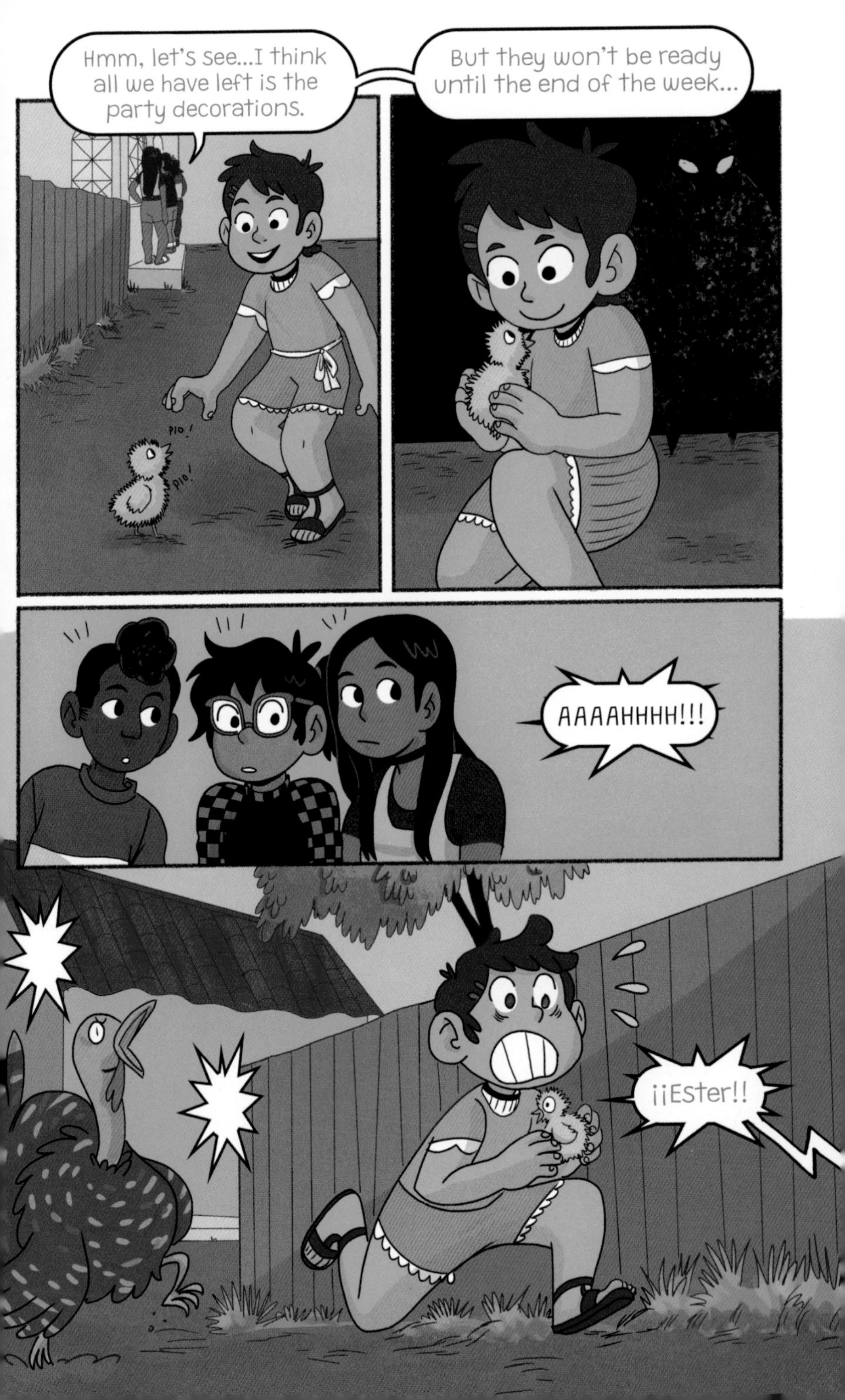
Hmm, let's see...I think all we have left is the party decorations.
PIO!
PIO!
But they won't be ready until the end of the week...
AAAAHHHH!!!
¡¡Ester!!

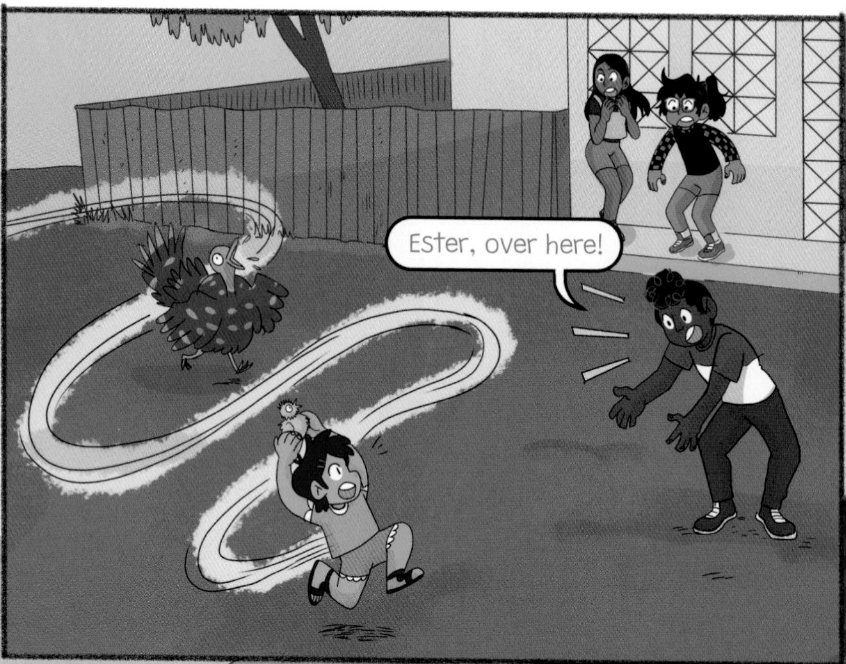
Ester, over here!

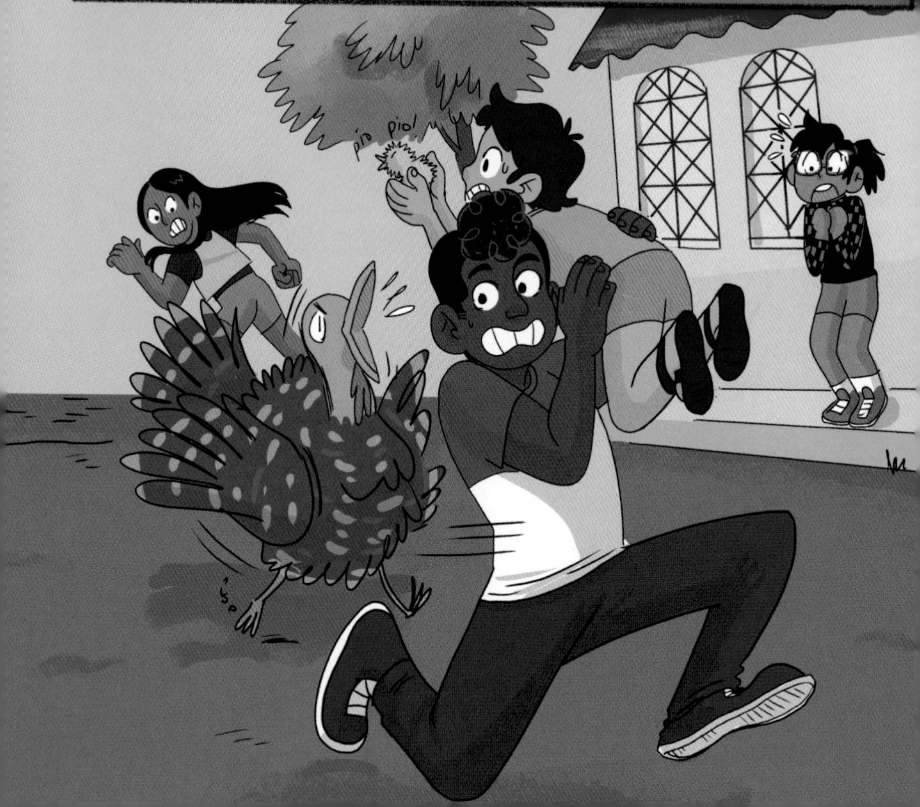
pio pio!

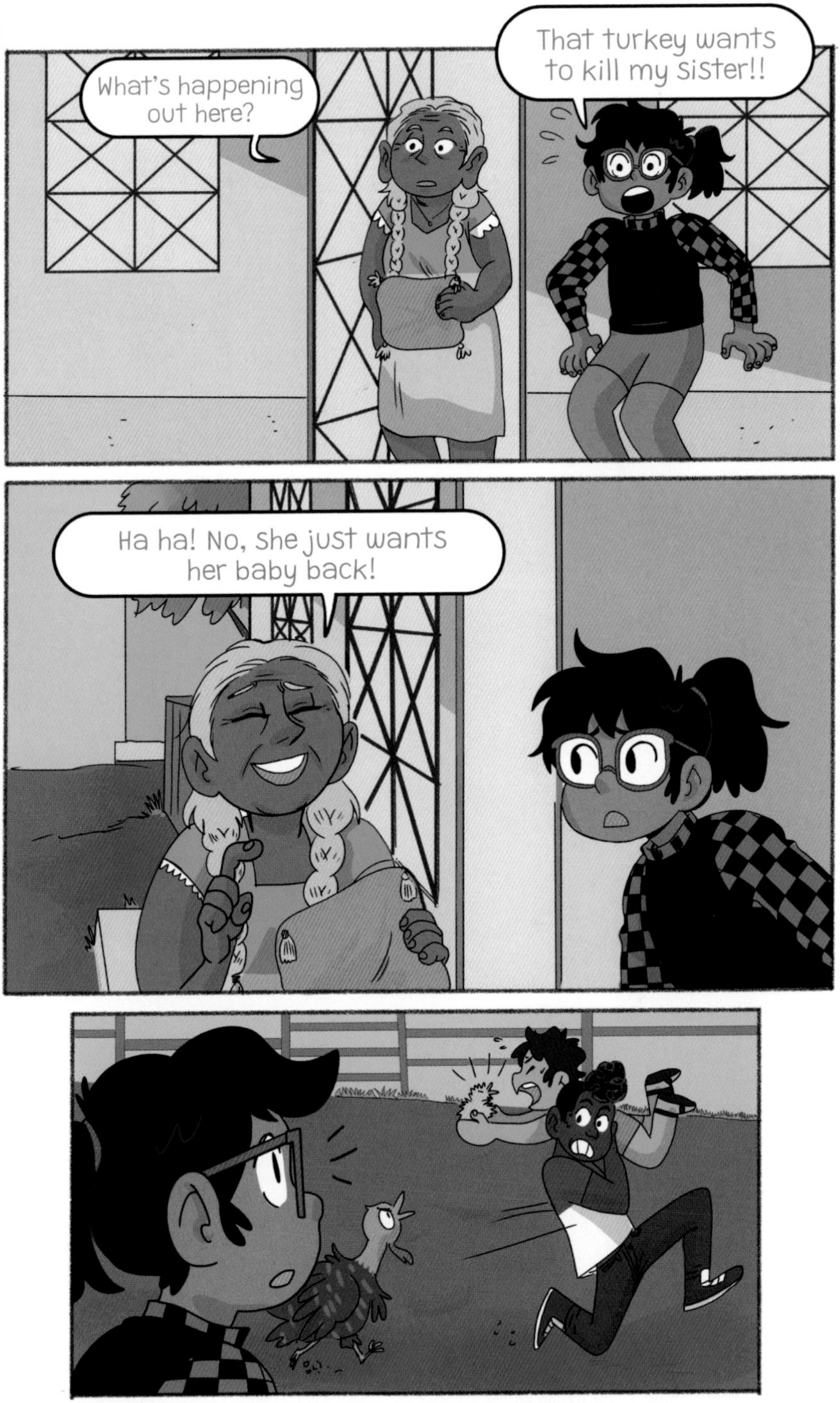
What's happening out here?
That turkey wants to kill my sister!!
Ha ha! No, she just wants her baby back!

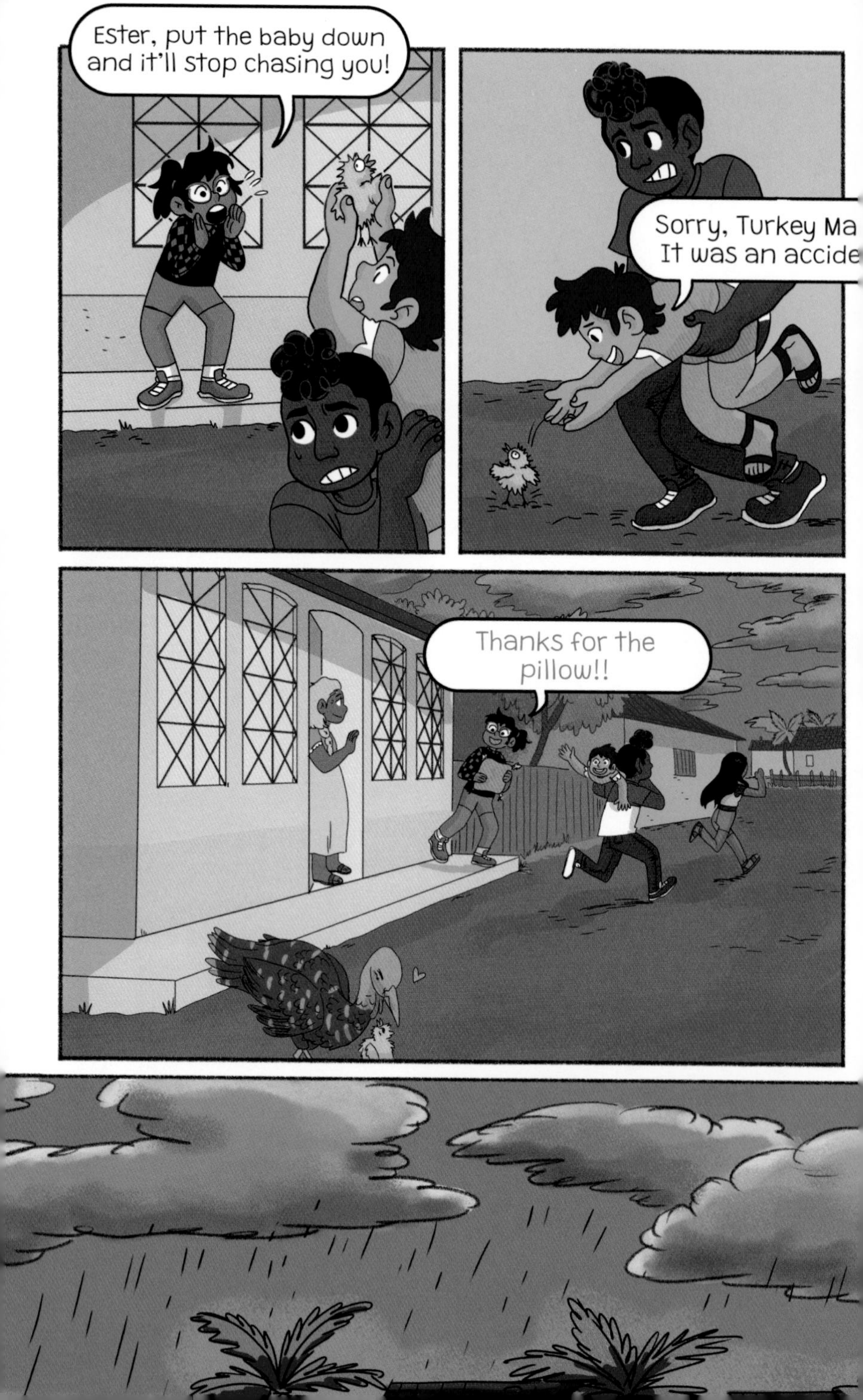
Ester, put the baby down and it'll stop chasing you!
Sorry, Turkey Ma
It was an accide
Thanks for the pillow!!

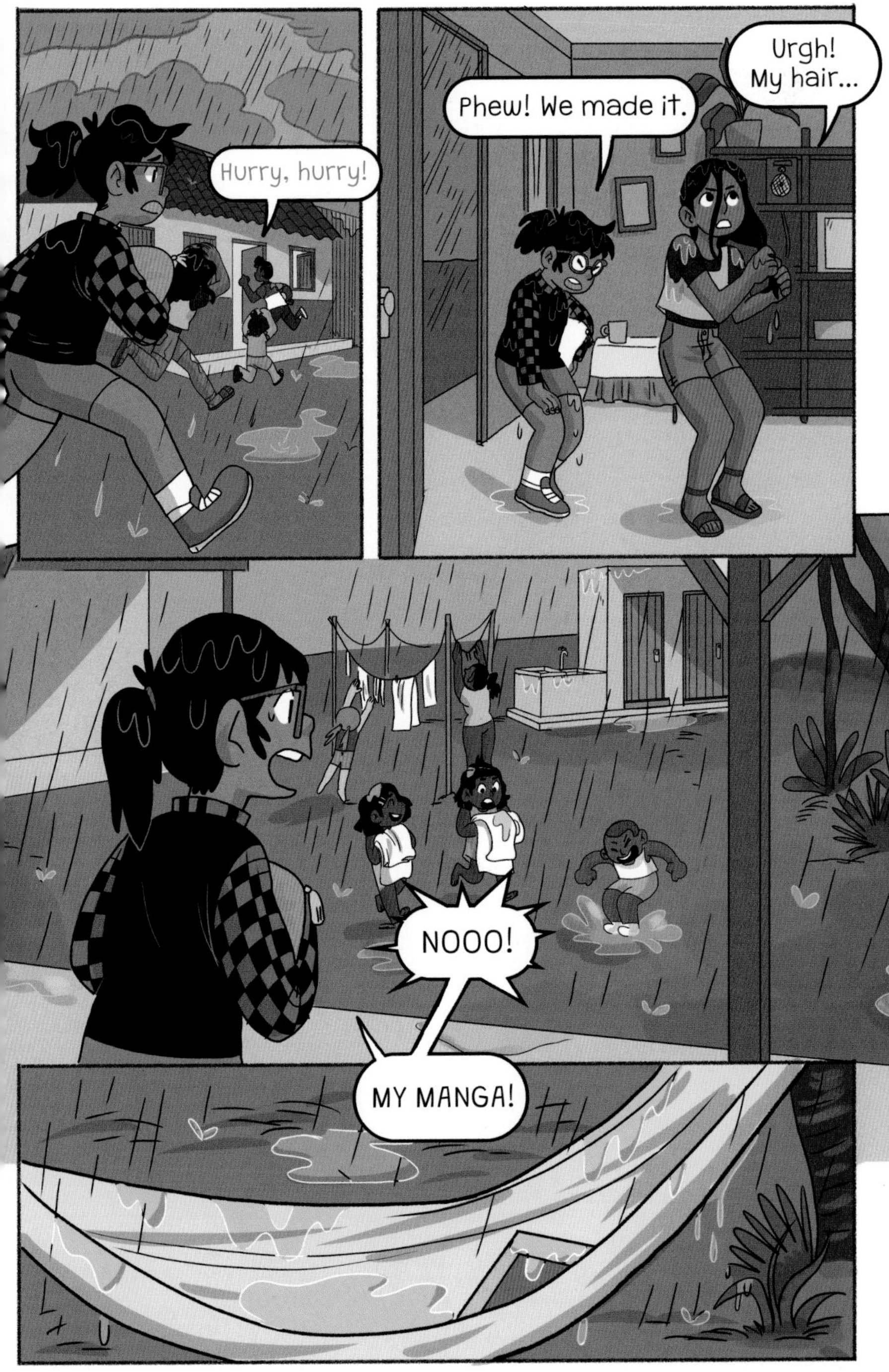
Hurry, hurry!
Phew! We made it.
Urgh! My hair...
NOOO!
MY MANGA!

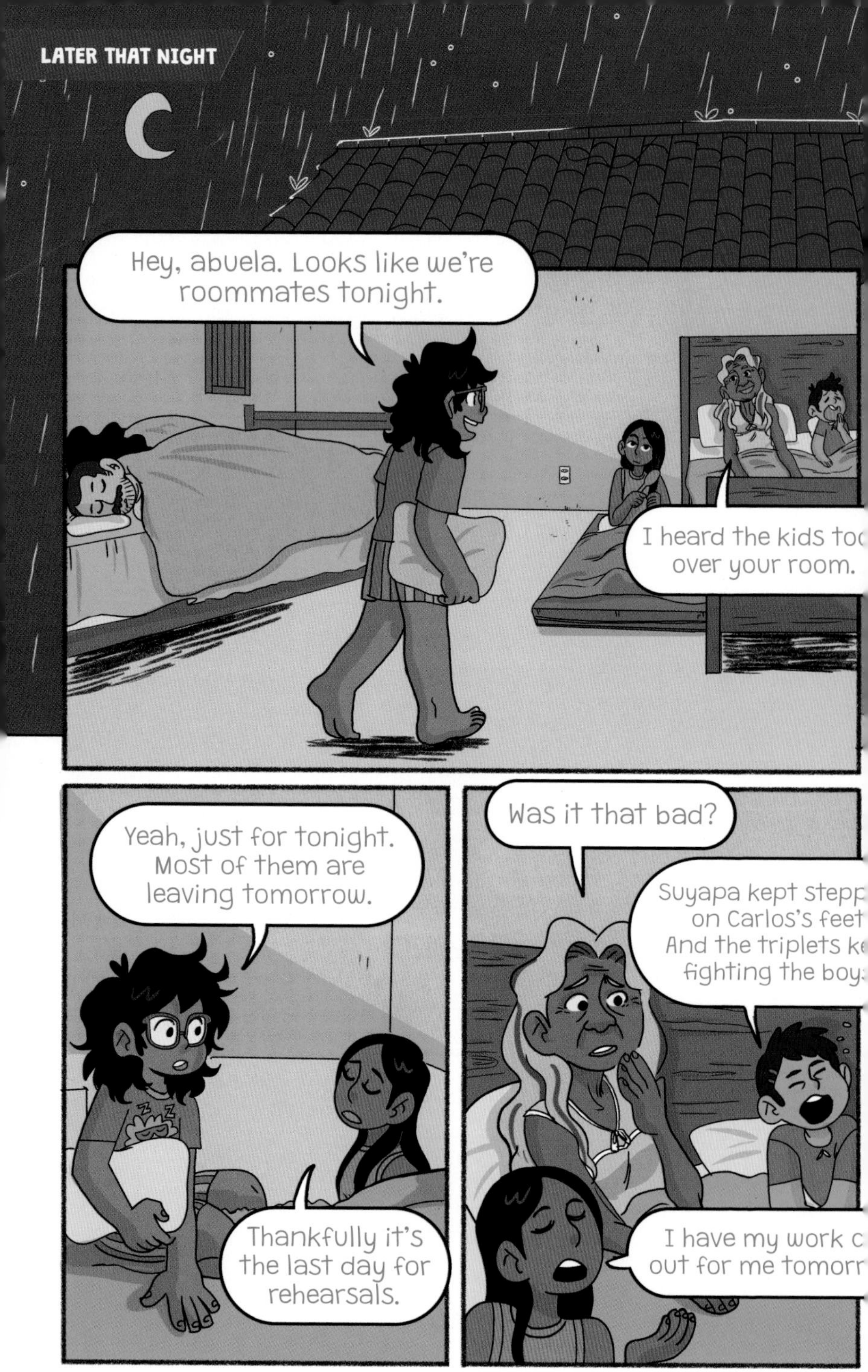
LATER THAT NIGHT
Hey, abuela. Looks like we're roommates tonight.
I heard the kids to
over your room.
Yeah, just for tonight. Most of them are leaving tomorrow.
Thankfully it's the last day for rehearsals.
Was it that bad?
Suyapa kept step
on Carlos's feet
And the triplets k
fighting the boy
I have my work
out for me tomor

Well, the dance is super complicated...

No, it's not, you just suck at it.

Urgh, whatever.

Don't worry, you'll get better. Just work hard at it and stay motivated!

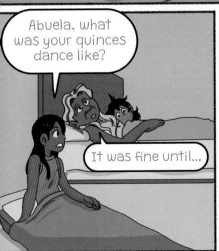

Abuela, what was your quinces dance like?

It was fine until...

I forgot my routine.

WHAT?!

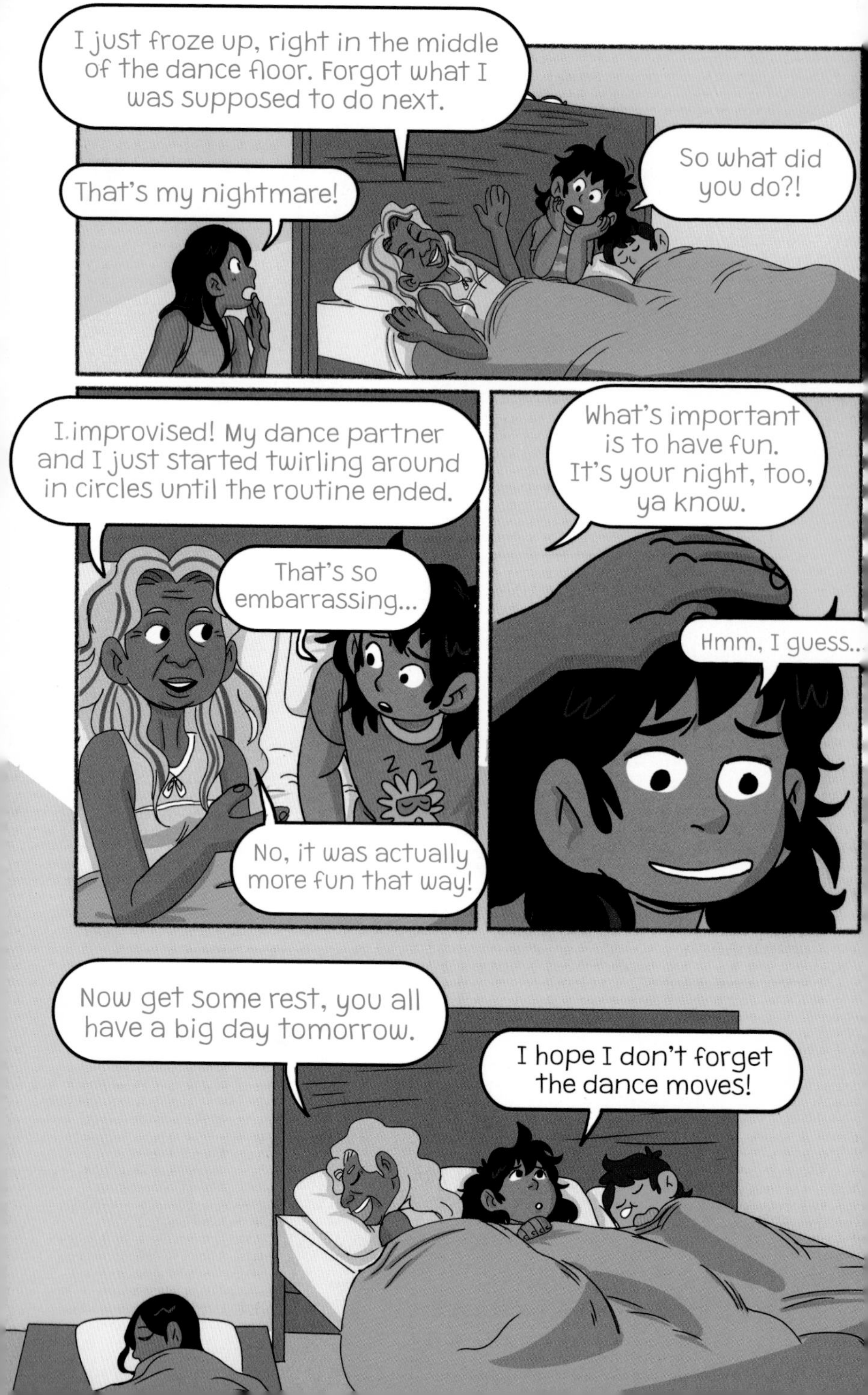
I just froze up, right in the middle of the dance floor. Forgot what I was supposed to do next.
That's my nightmare!
So what did you do?!
I improvised! My dance partner and I just started twirling around in circles until the routine ended.
That's so embarrassing...
No, it was actually more fun that way!
What's important is to have fun. It's your night, too, ya know.
Hmm, I guess..
Now get some rest, you all have a big day tomorrow.
I hope I don't forget the dance moves!

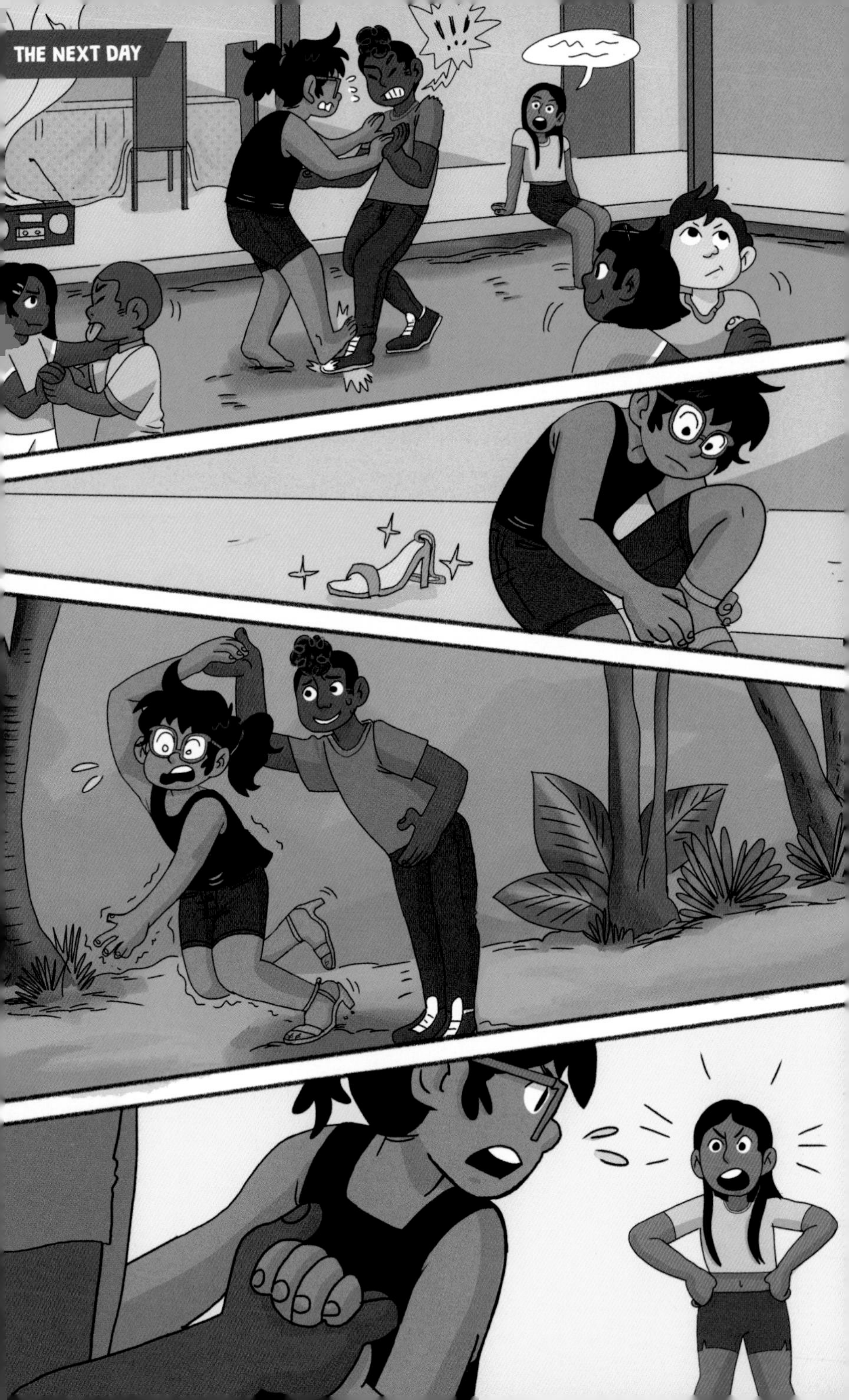
THE NEXT DAY

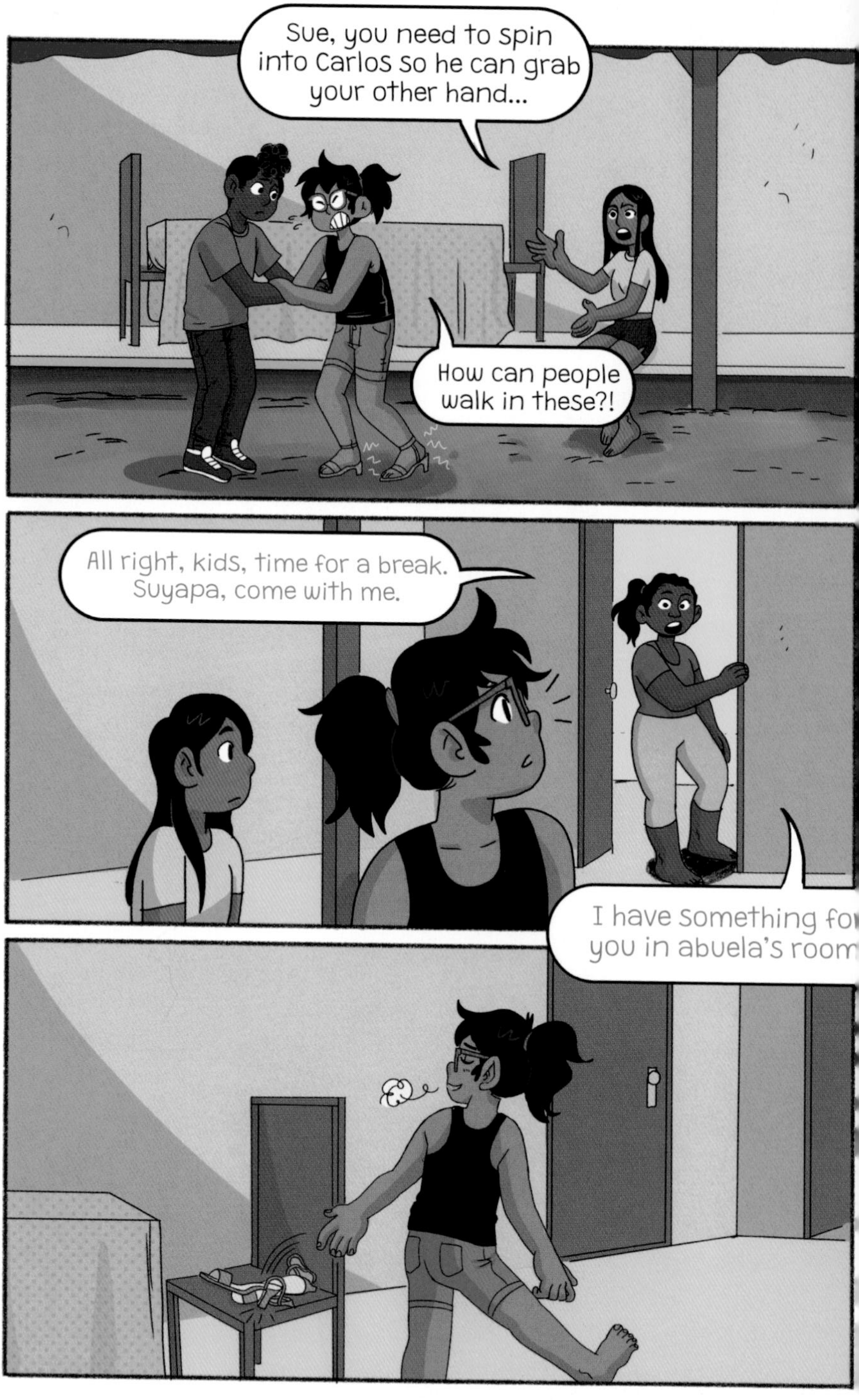

Sue, you need to spin into Carlos so he can grab your other hand...
How can people walk in these?!
All right, kids, time for a break. Suyapa, come with me.
I have something fo
you in abuela's room

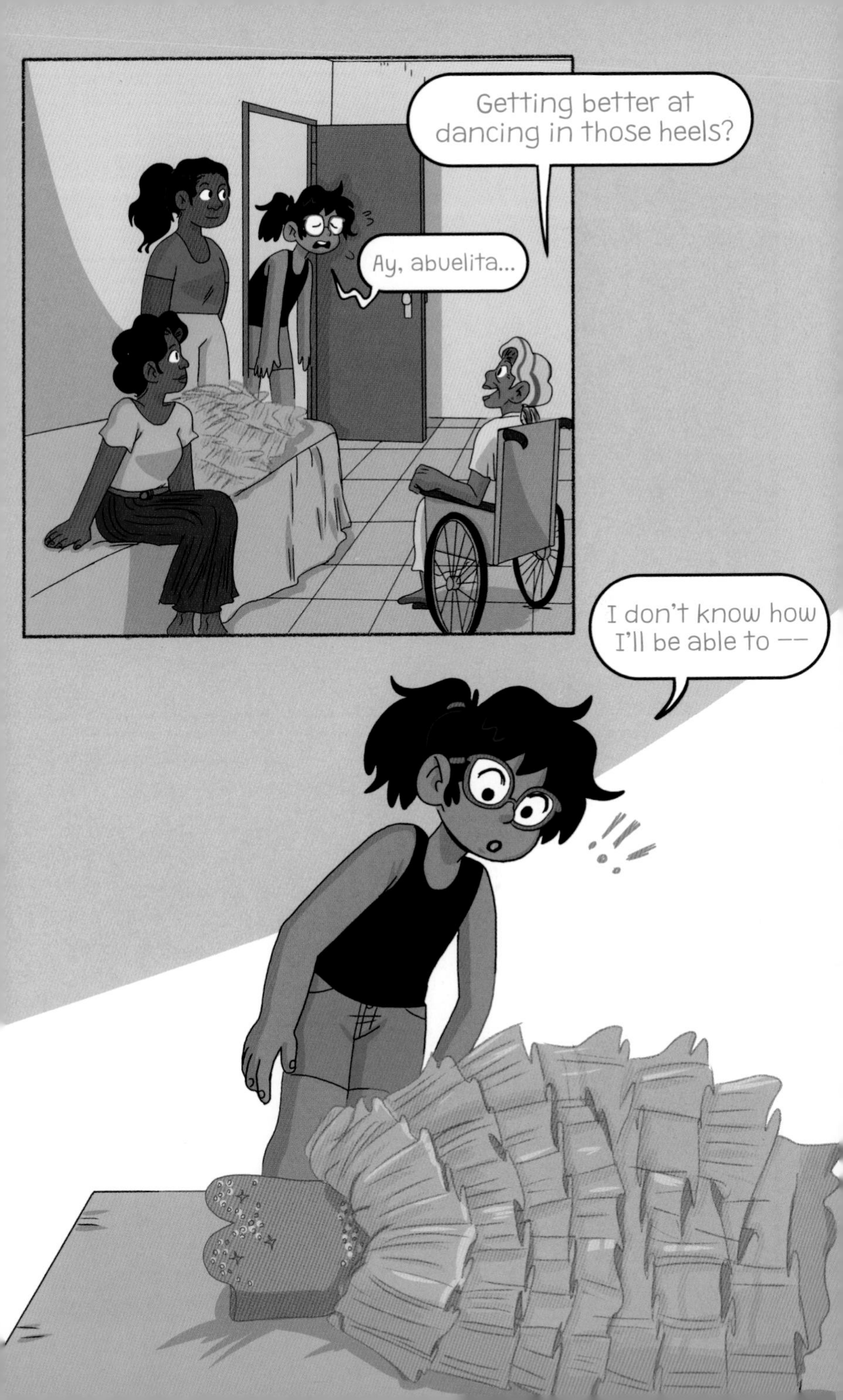

Getting better at dancing in those heels?
Ay, abuelita...
I don't know how I'll be able to --

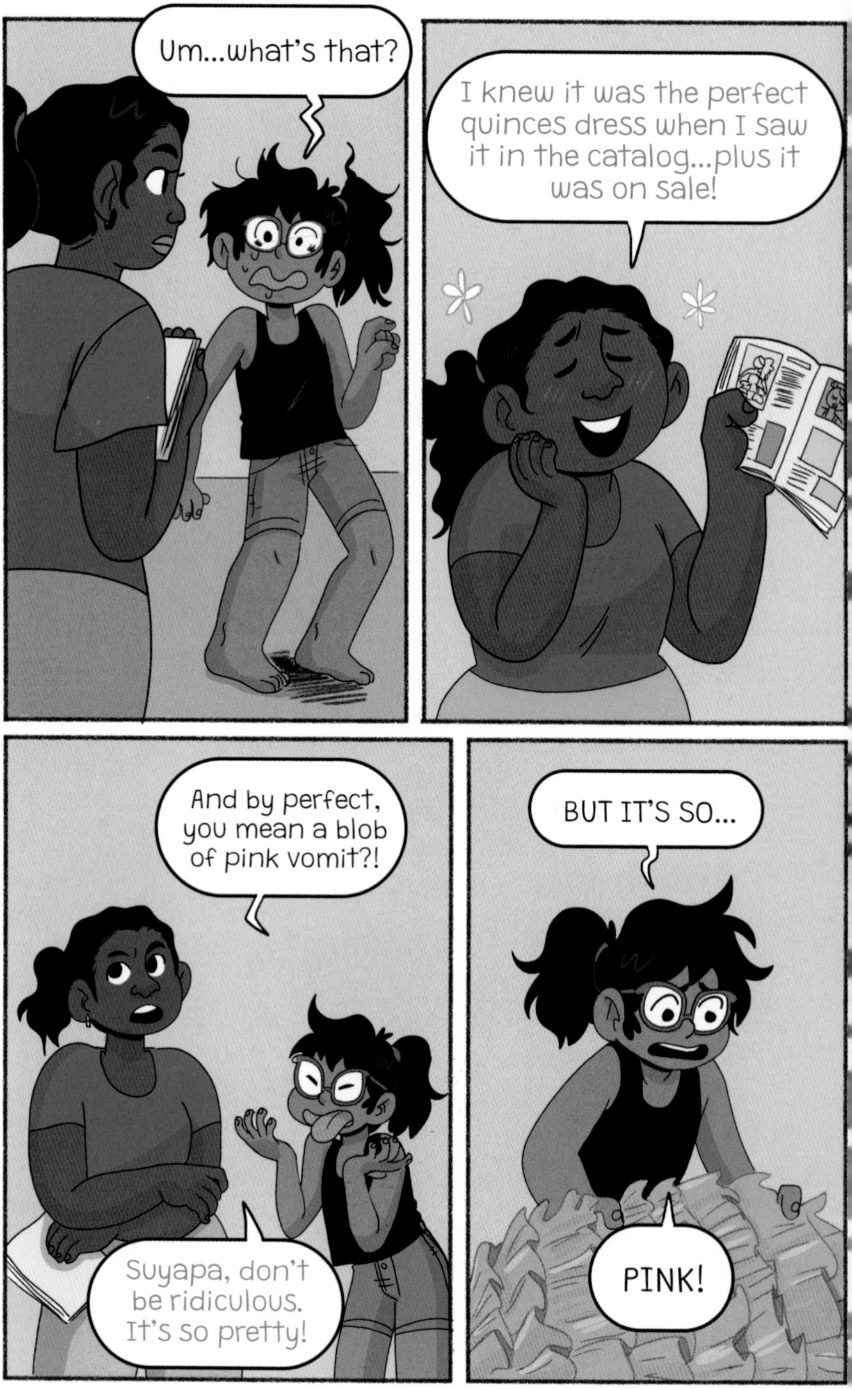
Um...what's that?
I knew it was the perfect quinces dress when I saw it in the catalog...plus it was on sale!
And by perfect, you mean a blob of pink vomit?!
Suyapa, don't be ridiculous. It's so pretty!
BUT IT'S SO...
PINK!

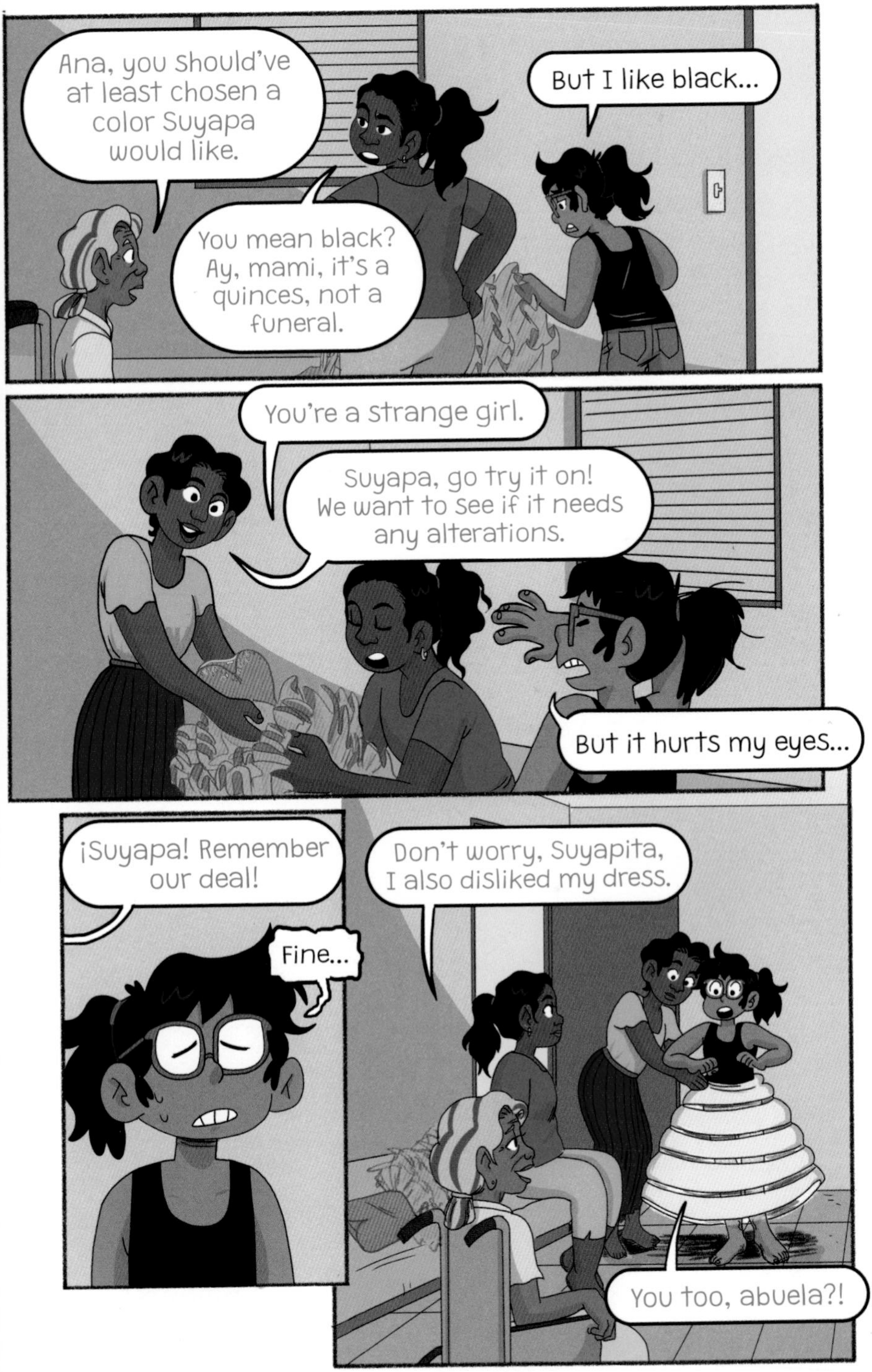
Ana, you should've at least chosen a color Suyapa would like.
You mean black? Ay, mami, it's a quinces, not a funeral.
But I like black...
You're a strange girl.
Suyapa, go try it on! We want to see if it needs any alterations.
But it hurts my eyes...
¡Suyapa! Remember our deal!
Fine...
Don't worry, Suyapita, I also disliked my dress.
You too, abuela?!

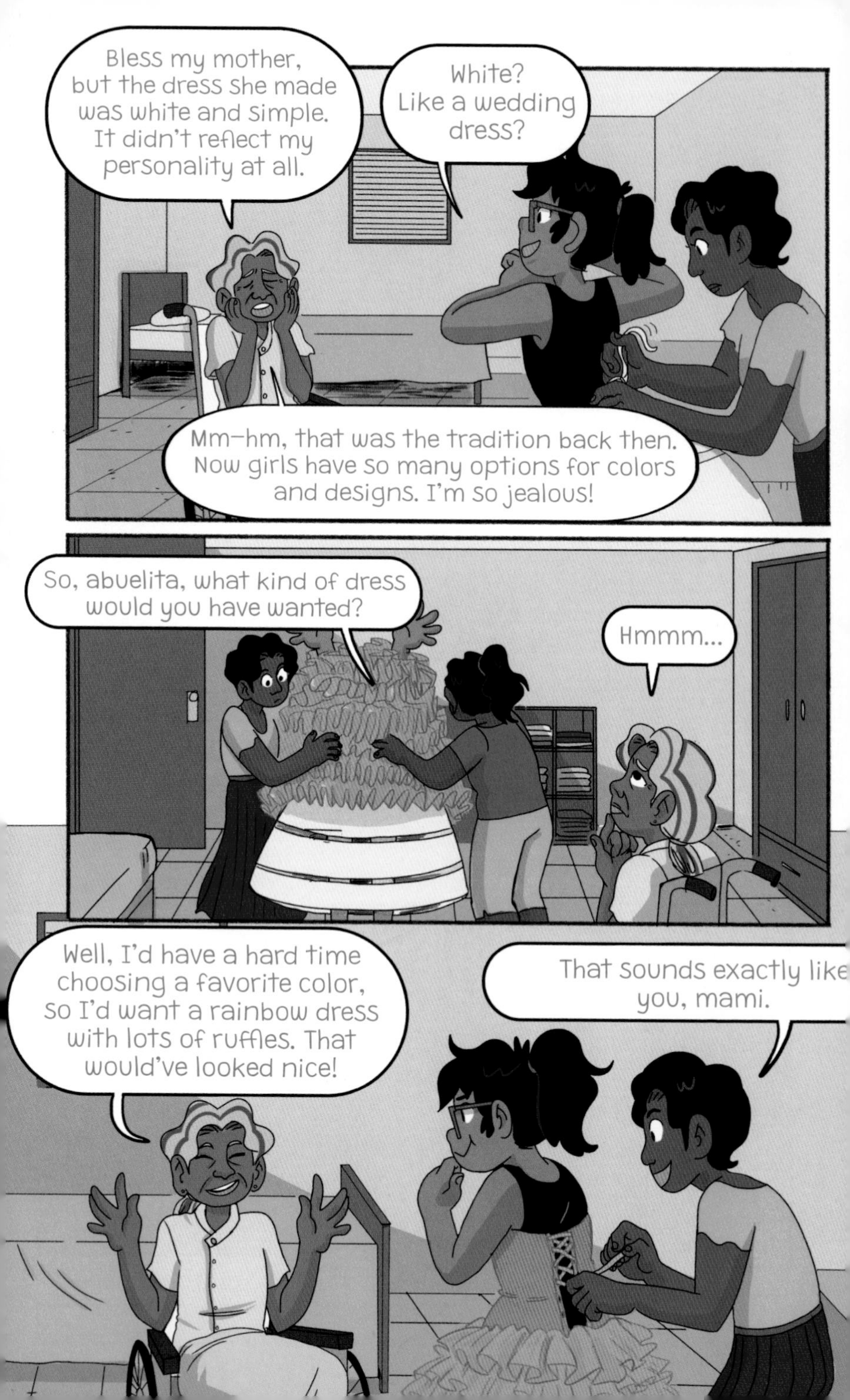
Bless my mother, but the dress she made was white and simple. It didn't reflect my personality at all.
White? Like a wedding dress?
Mm-hm, that was the tradition back then. Now girls have so many options for colors and designs. I'm so jealous!
So, abuelita, what kind of dress would you have wanted?
Hmmm...
Well, I'd have a hard time choosing a favorite color, so I'd want a rainbow dress with lots of ruffles. That would've looked nice!
That sounds exactly like you, mami.

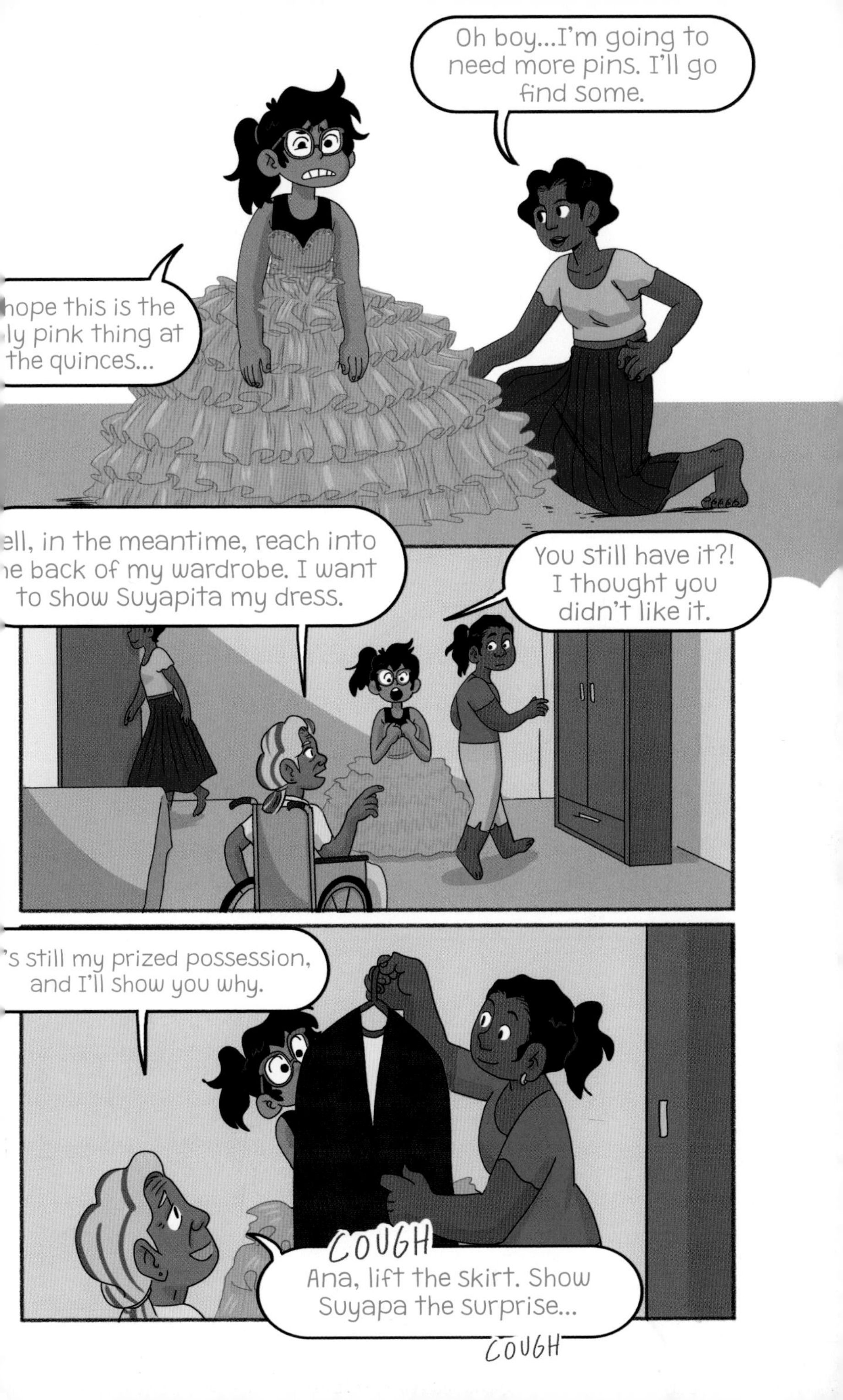

Oh boy...I'm going to need more pins. I'll go find some.
hope this is the
ly pink thing at
the quinces...
ell, in the meantime, reach into
ne back of my wardrobe. I want
to show Suyapita my dress.
You still have it?! I thought you didn't like it.
's still my prized possession,
and I'll show you why.
COUGH
Ana, lift the skirt. Show Suyapa the surprise...
COUGH

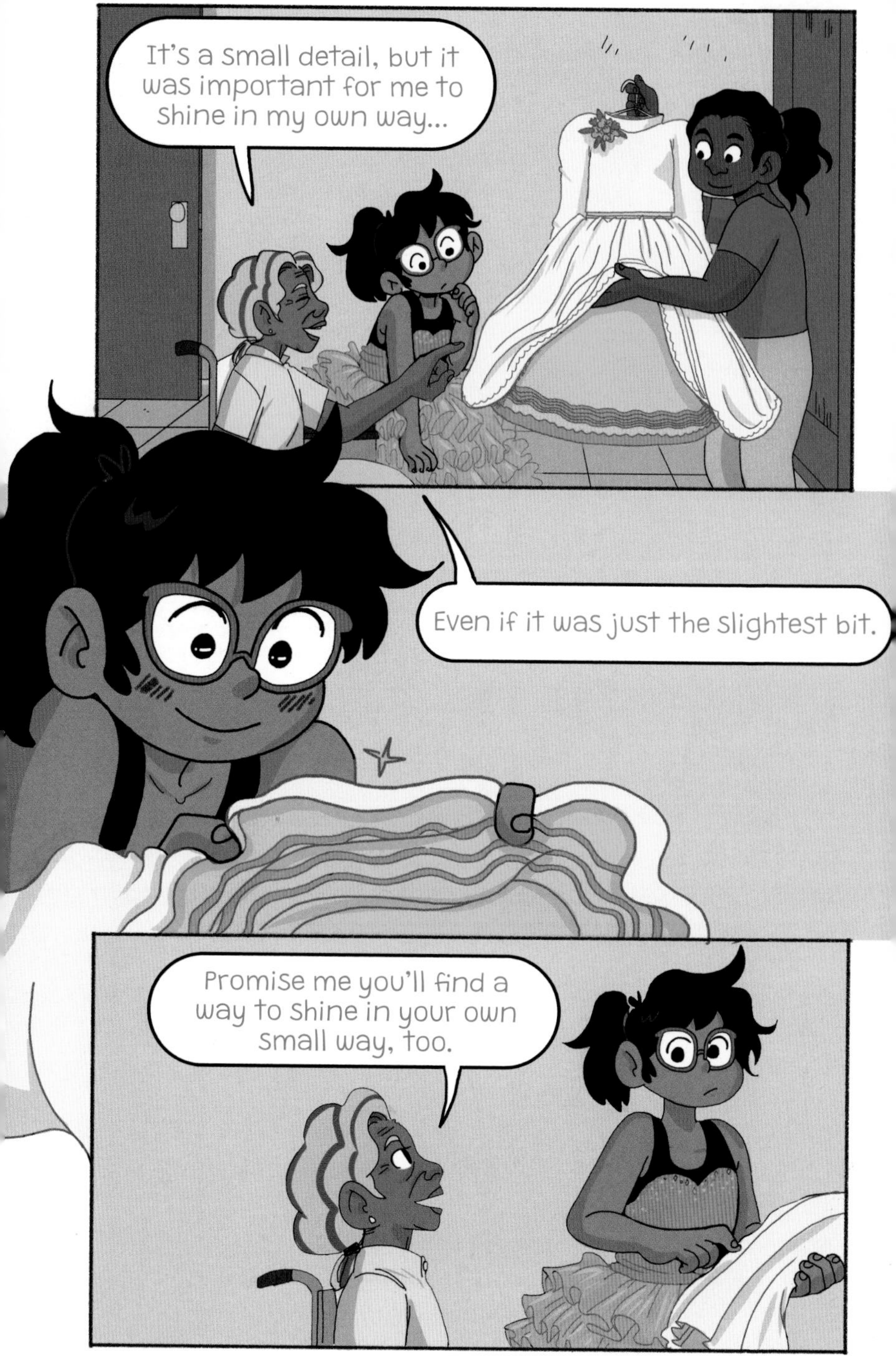
It's a small detail, but it was important for me to shine in my own way...
Even if it was just the slightest bit.
Promise me you'll find a way to shine in your own small way, too.

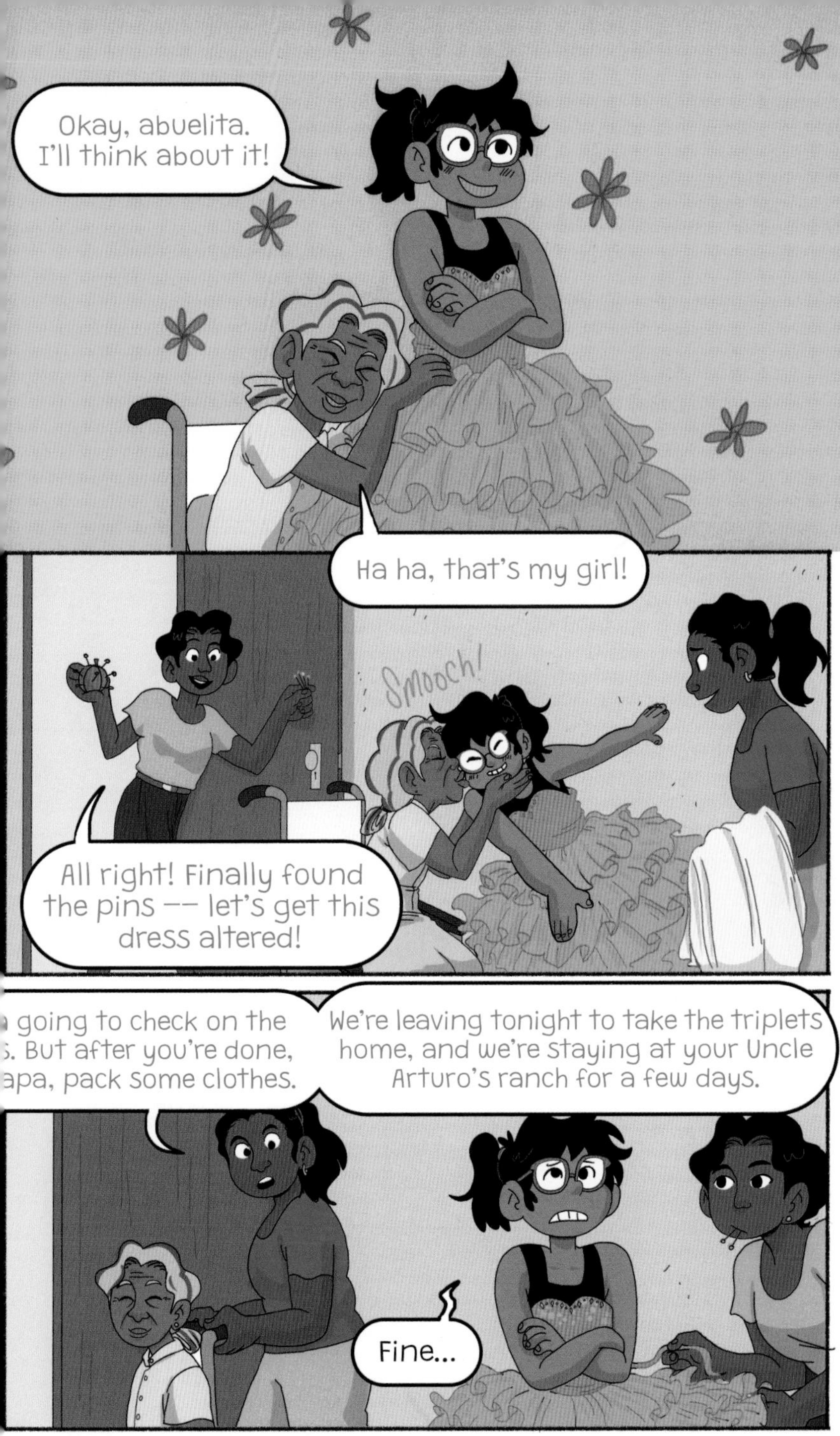
Okay, abuelita. I'll think about it!
Ha ha, that's my girl!
Smooch!
All right! Finally found the pins -- let's get this dress altered!
going to check on the
. But after you're done,
apa, pack some clothes.
We're leaving tonight to take the triplets home, and we're staying at your Uncle Arturo's ranch for a few days.
Fine...

CHAPTER FIVE

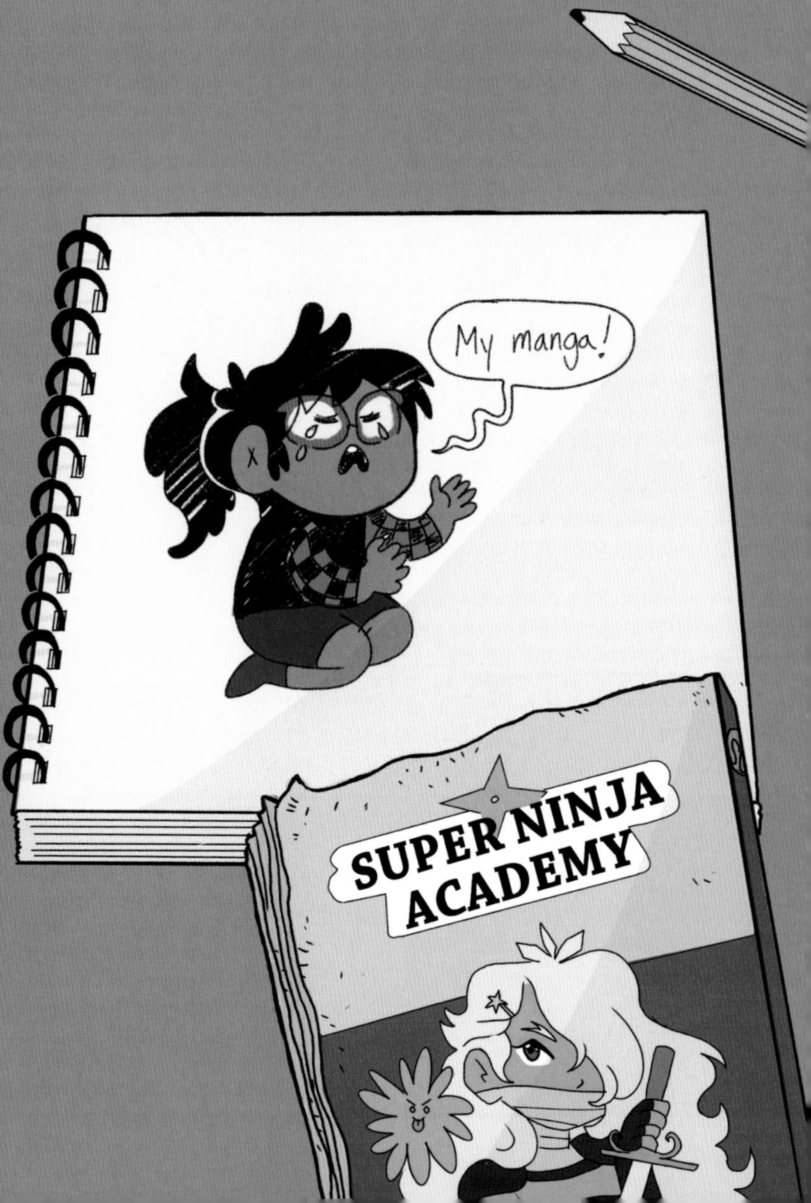
My manga!
SUPER NINJA ACADEMY

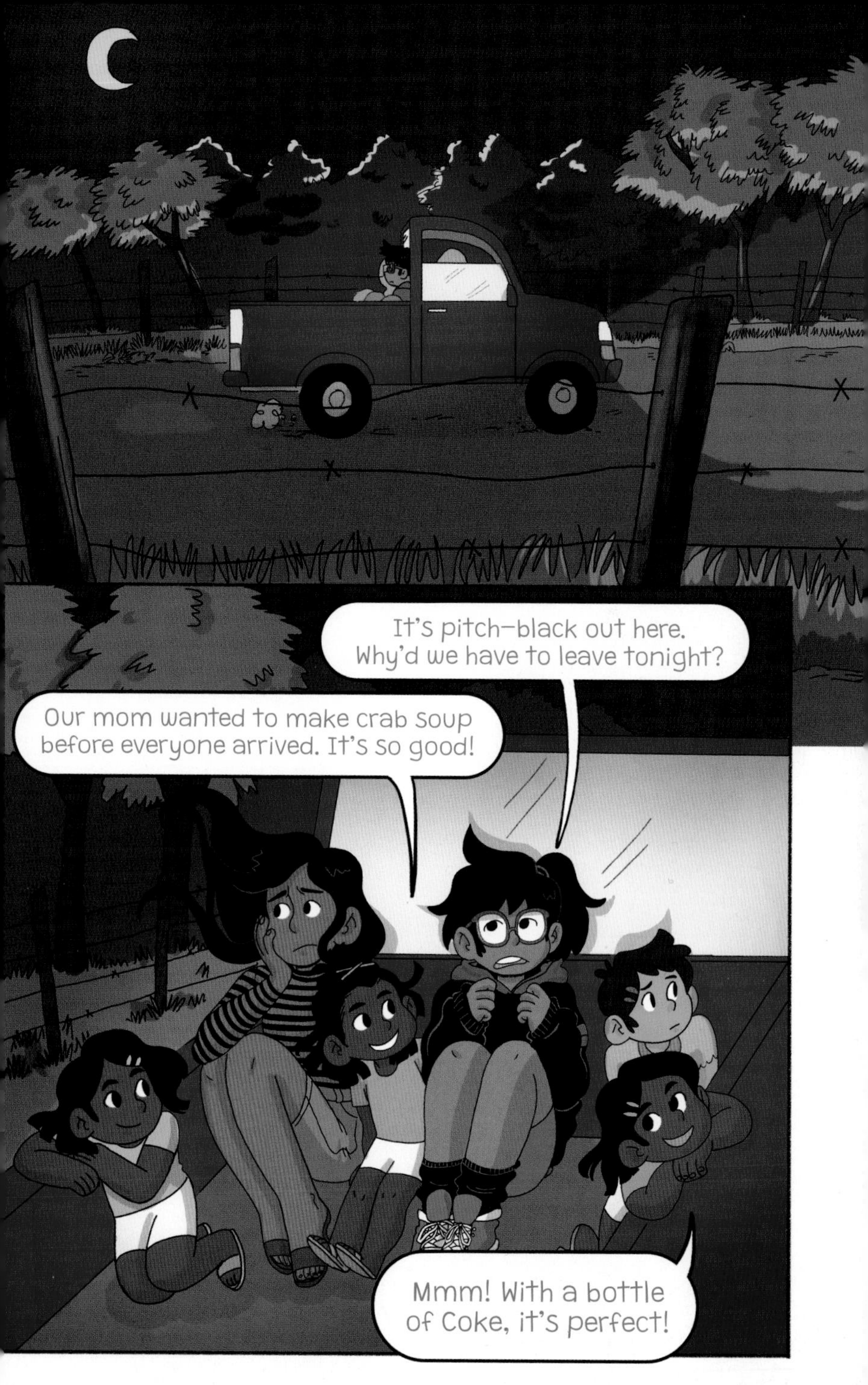
Our mom wanted to make crab soup before everyone arrived. It's so good!
It's pitch-black out here. Why'd we have to leave tonight?
Mmm! With a bottle of Coke, it's perfect!

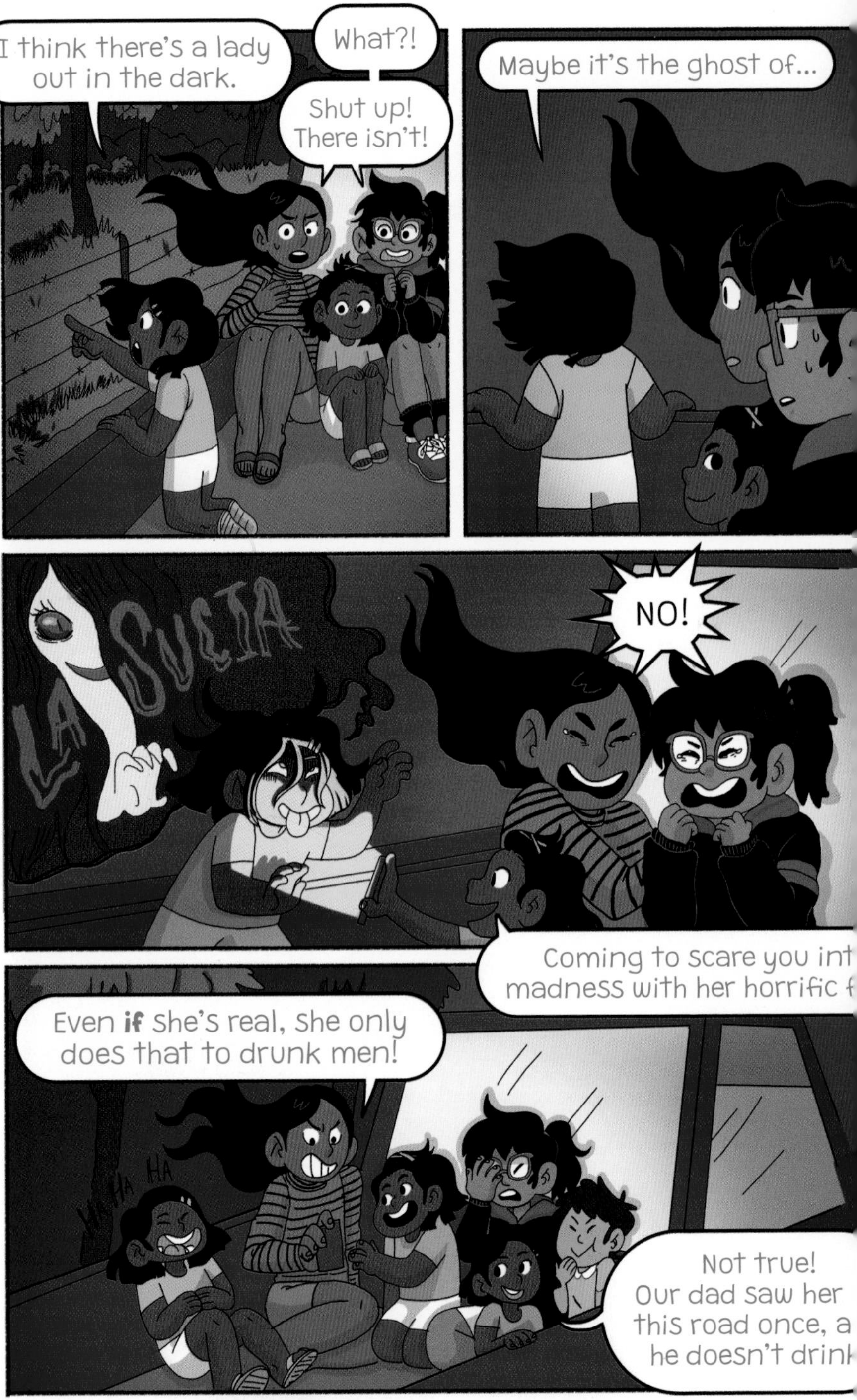
I think there's a lady out in the dark.
What?!
Shut up! There isn't!
Maybe it's the ghost of...
LA SUELTA
NO!
Coming to scare you int
madness with her horrific
Even **if** she's real, she only does that to drunk men!
HA HA HA
Not true!
Our dad saw her
this road once, a
he doesn't drin

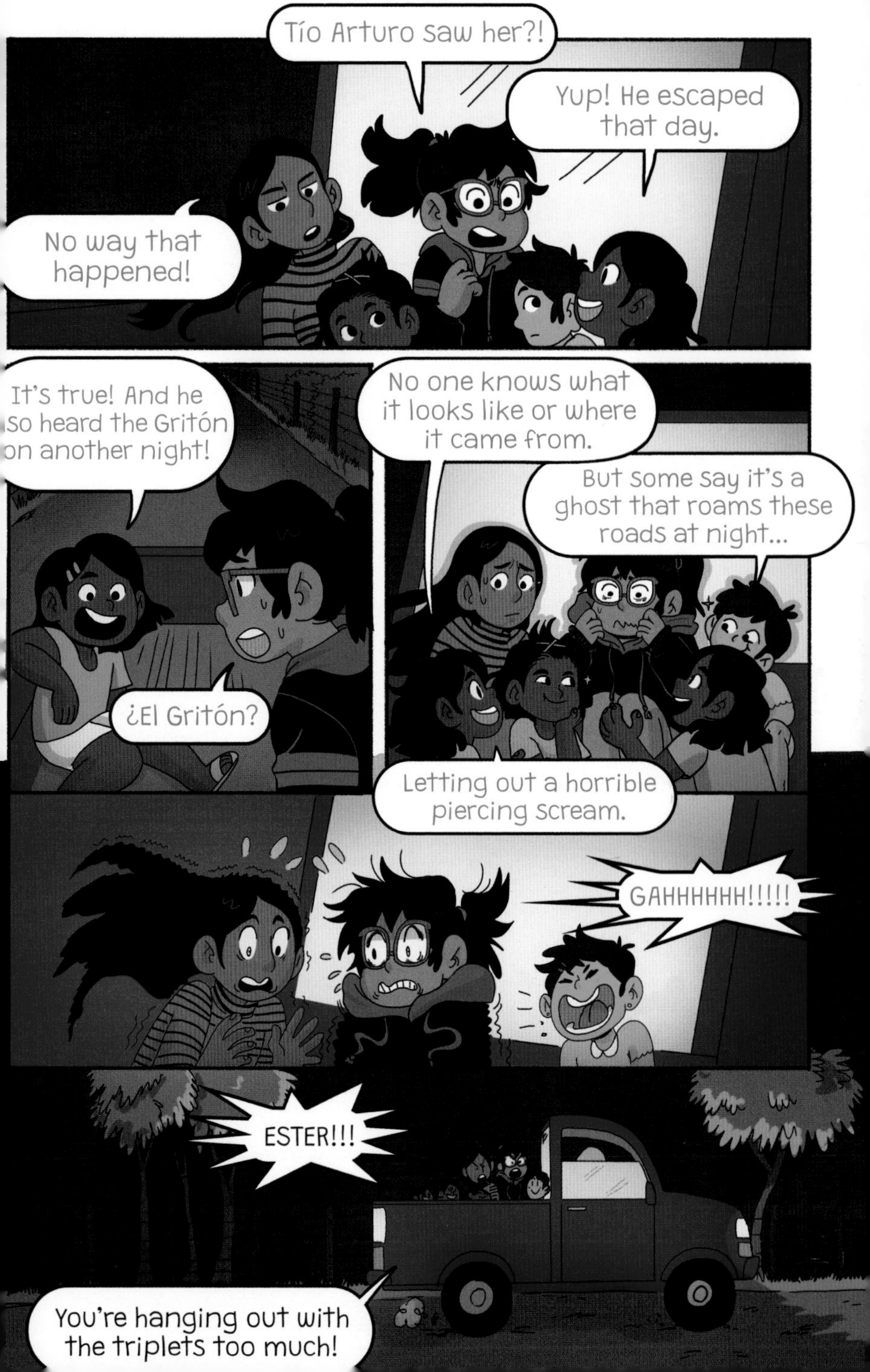
Tío Arturo saw her?!
Yup! He escaped that day.
No way that happened!
It's true! And he so heard the Gritón on another night!
¿El Gritón?
No one knows what it looks like or where it came from.
But some say it's a ghost that roams these roads at night...
Letting out a horrible piercing scream.
GAHHHHHH!!!!!
ESTER!!!
You're hanging out with the triplets too much!

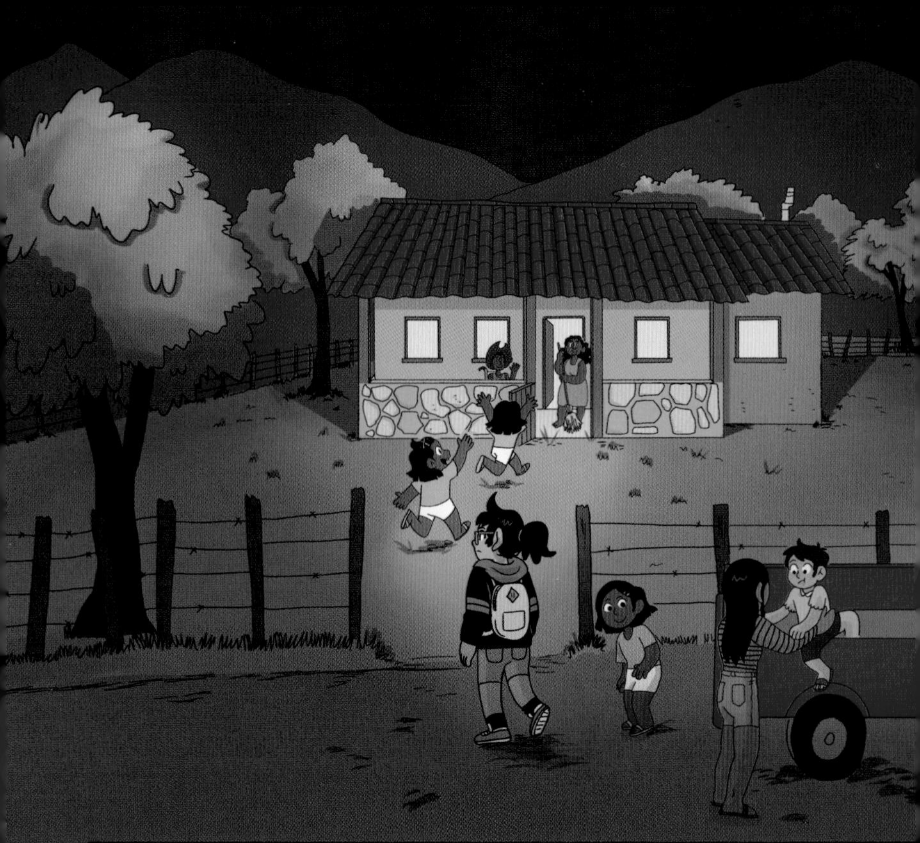

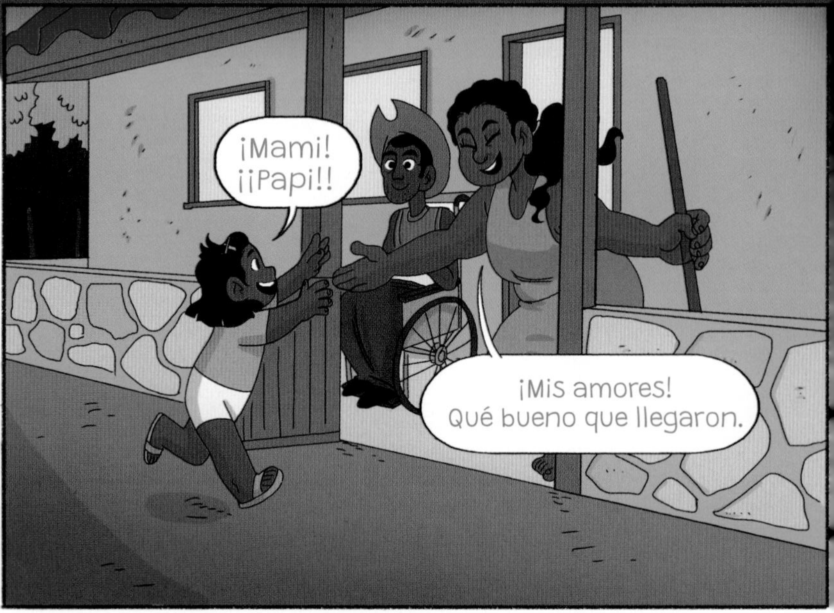
¡Mami!
¡¡Papi!!
¡Mis amores!
Qué bueno que llegaron.

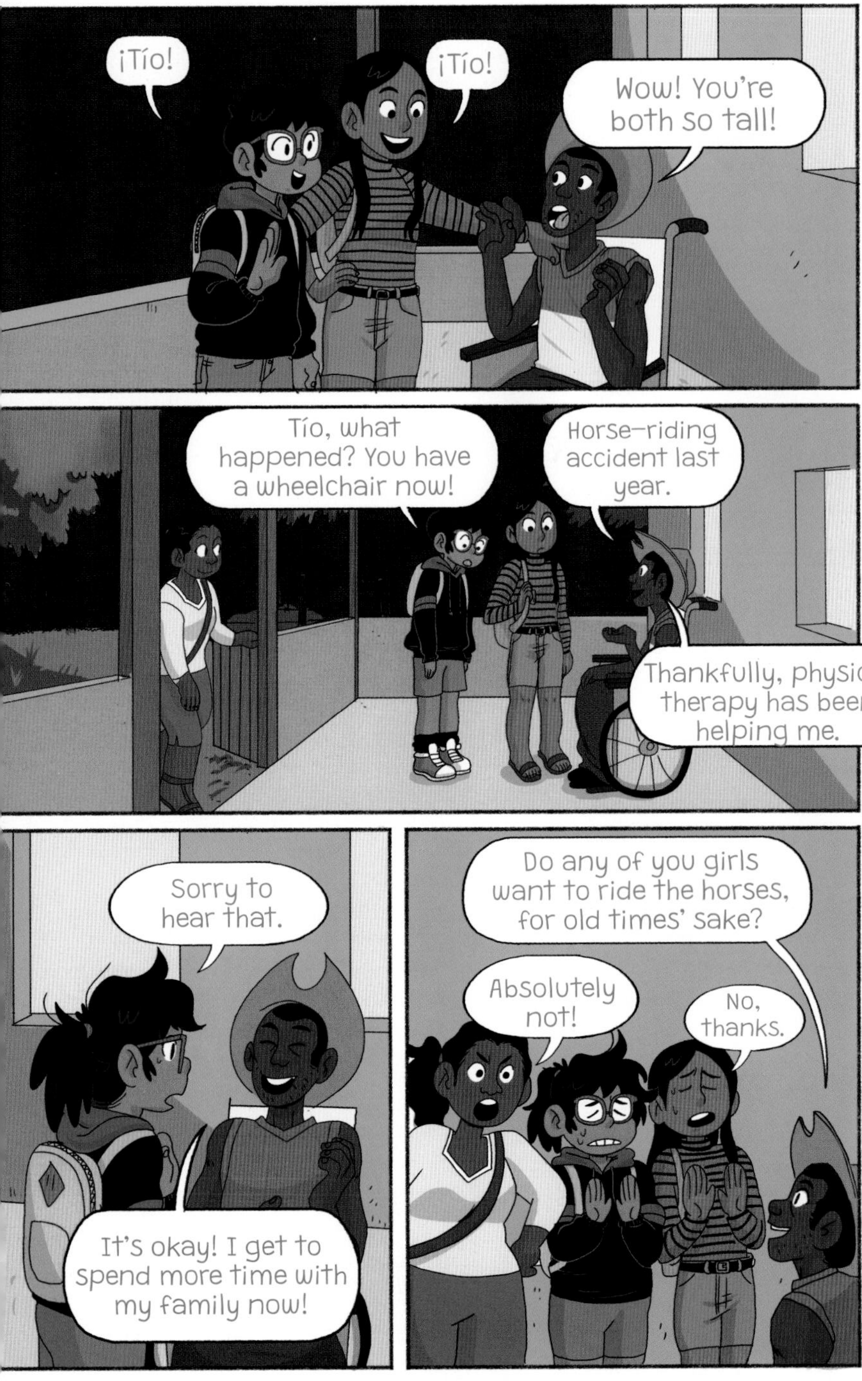
¡Tío!
¡Tío!
Wow! You're both so tall!
Tío, what happened? You have a wheelchair now!
Horse-riding accident last year.
Thankfully, physical therapy has been helping me.
Sorry to hear that.
It's okay! I get to spend more time with my family now!
Do any of you girls want to ride the horses, for old times' sake?
Absolutely not!
No, thanks.

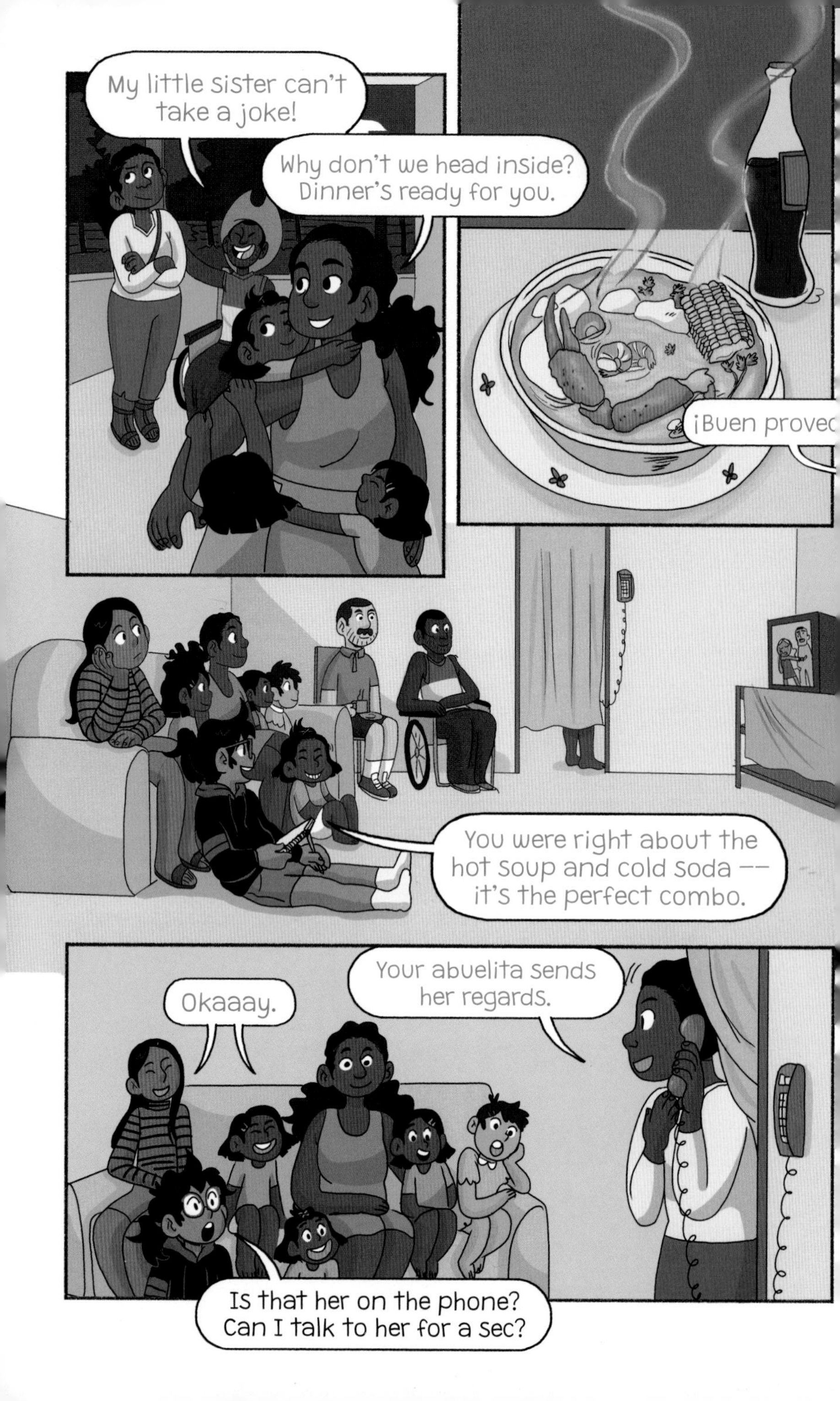
My little sister can't take a joke!
Why don't we head inside? Dinner's ready for you.
¡Buen provec
You were right about the hot soup and cold soda — it's the perfect combo.
Okaaay.
Your abuelita sends her regards.
Is that her on the phone? Can I talk to her for a sec?

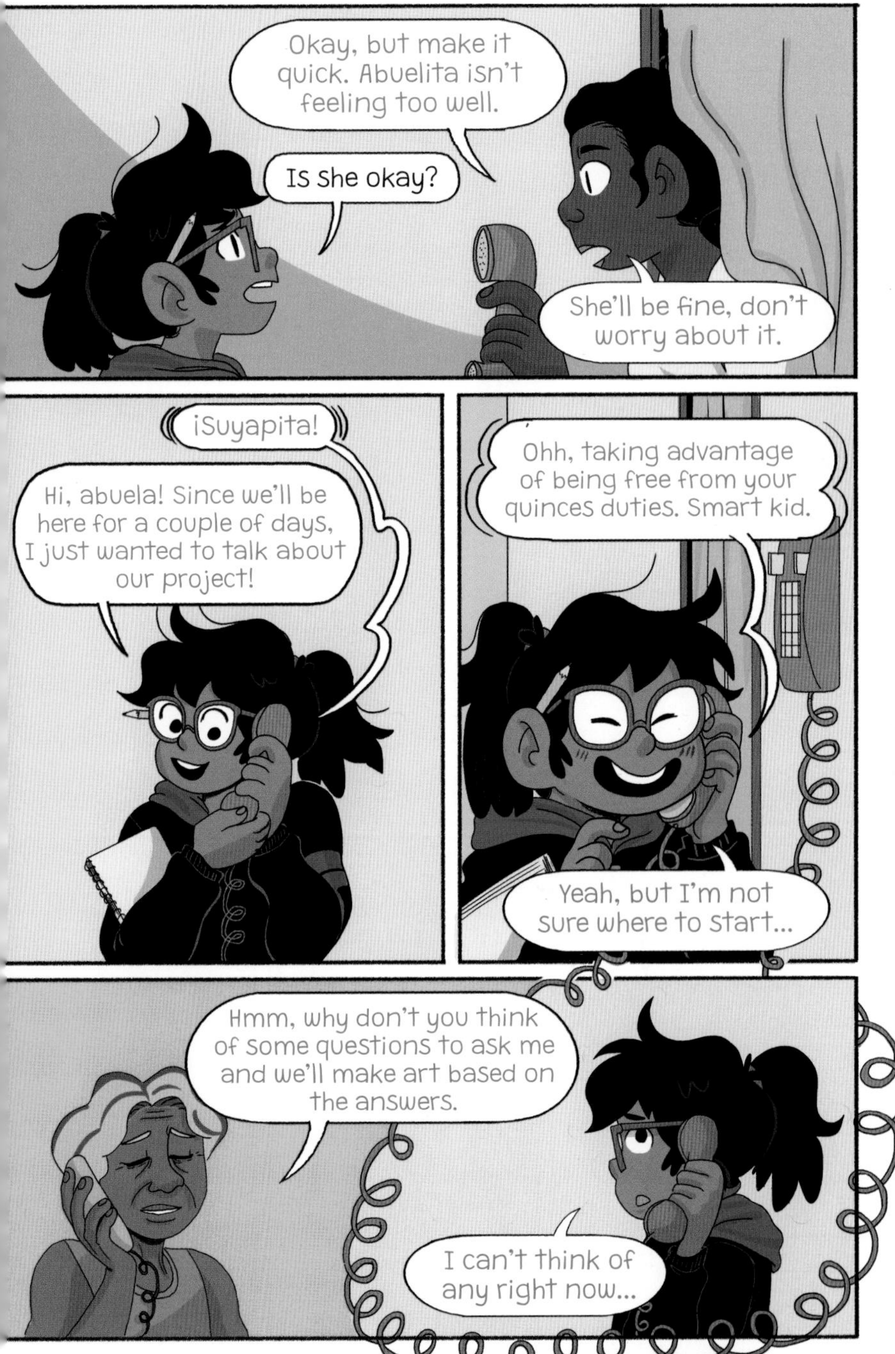
Okay, but make it quick. Abuelita isn't feeling too well.
Is she okay?
She'll be fine, don't worry about it.
¡Suyapita!
Hi, abuela! Since we'll be here for a couple of days, I just wanted to talk about our project!
Ohh, taking advantage of being free from your quinces duties. Smart kid.
Yeah, but I'm not sure where to start...
Hmm, why don't you think of some questions to ask me and we'll make art based on the answers.
I can't think of any right now...

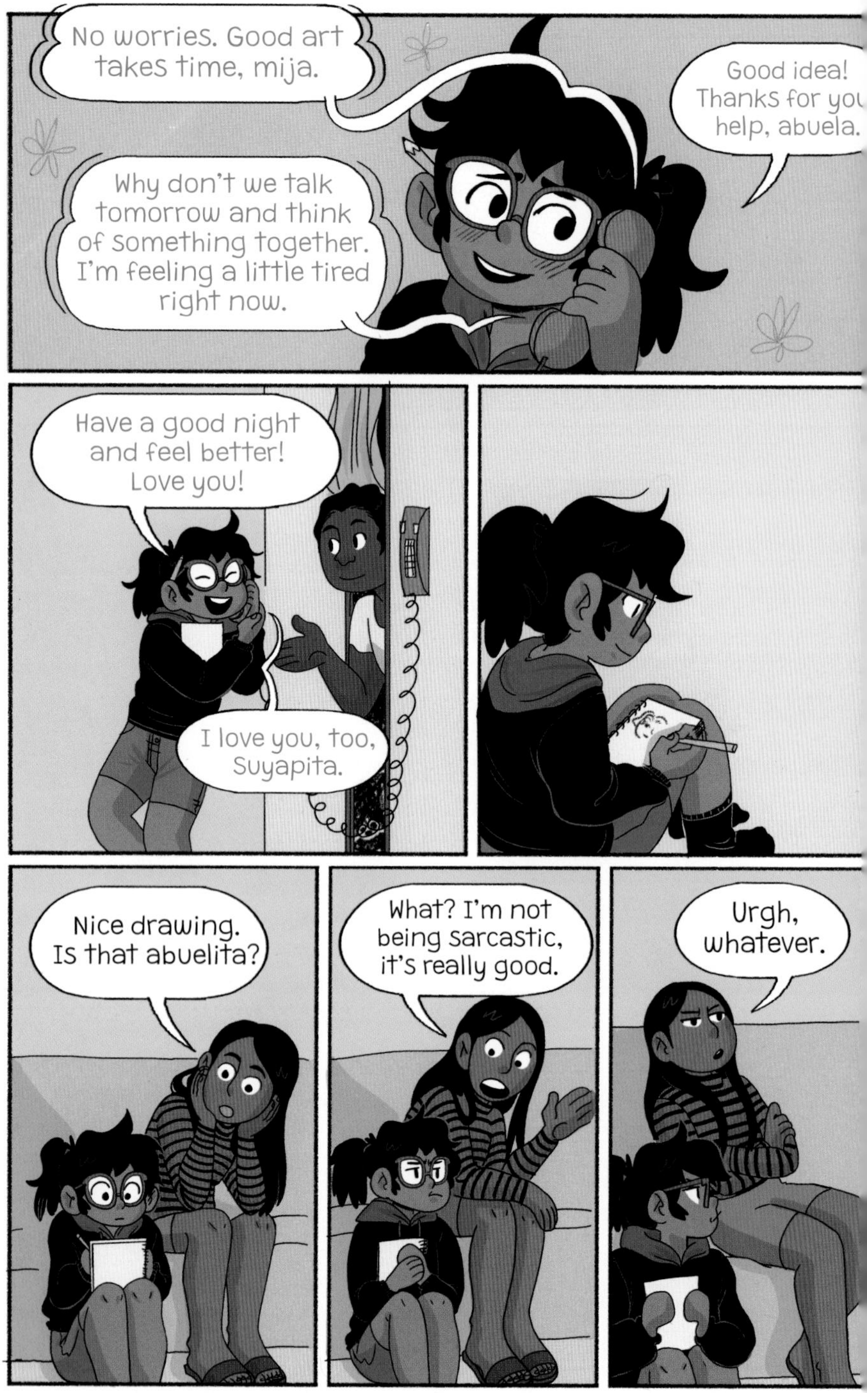
No worries. Good art takes time, mija.
Why don't we talk tomorrow and think of something together. I'm feeling a little tired right now.
Good idea! Thanks for you help, abuela.
Have a good night and feel better! Love you!
I love you, too, Suyapita.
Nice drawing. Is that abuelita?
What? I'm not being sarcastic, it's really good.
Urgh, whatever.

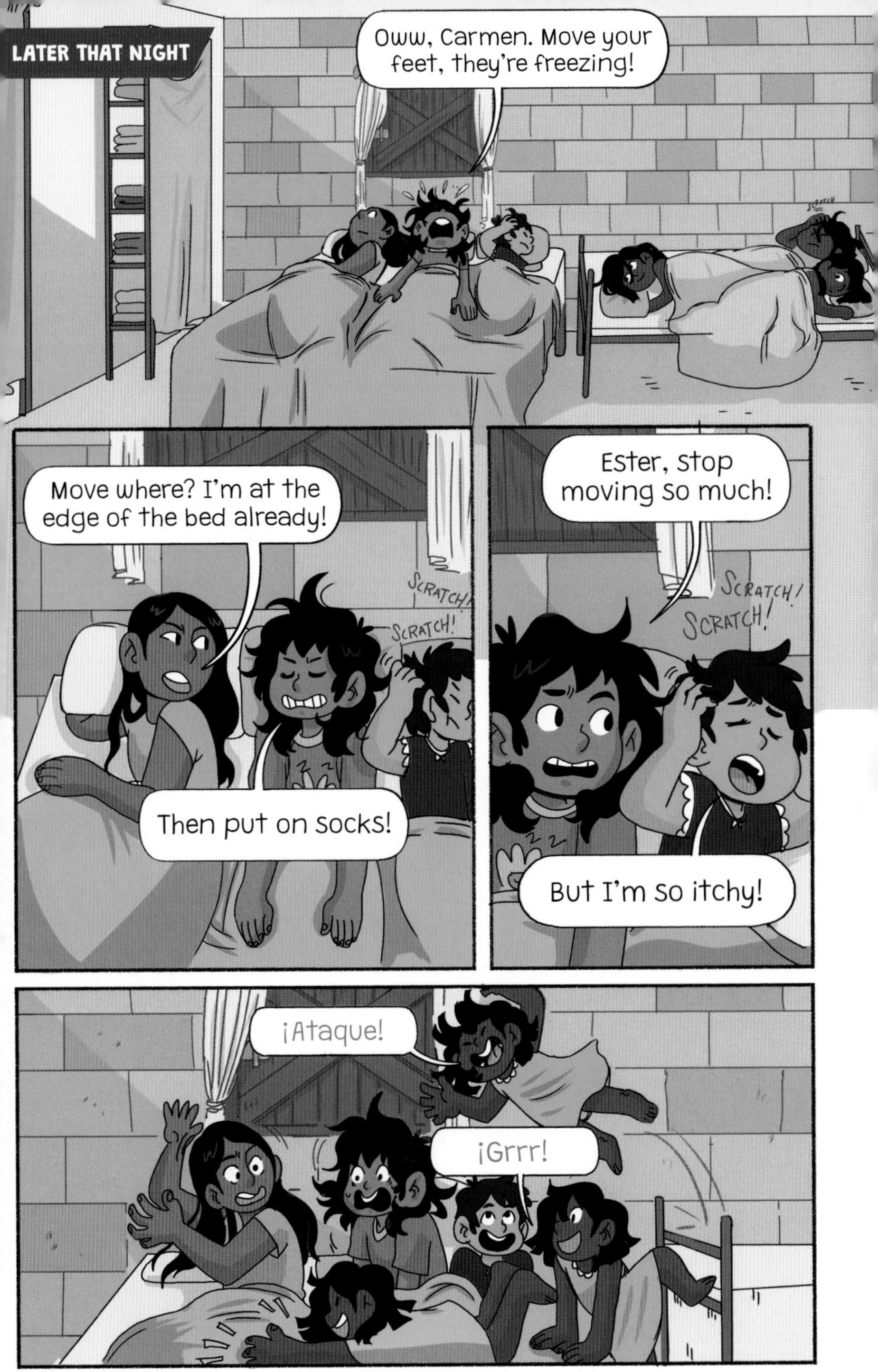
LATER THAT NIGHT
Oww, Carmen. Move your feet, they're freezing!
SCRATCH
Move where? I'm at the edge of the bed already!
SCRATCH!
SCRATCH!
Then put on socks!
Ester, stop moving so much!
SCRATCH!
SCRATCH!
But I'm so itchy!
¡Ataque!
¡Grrr!

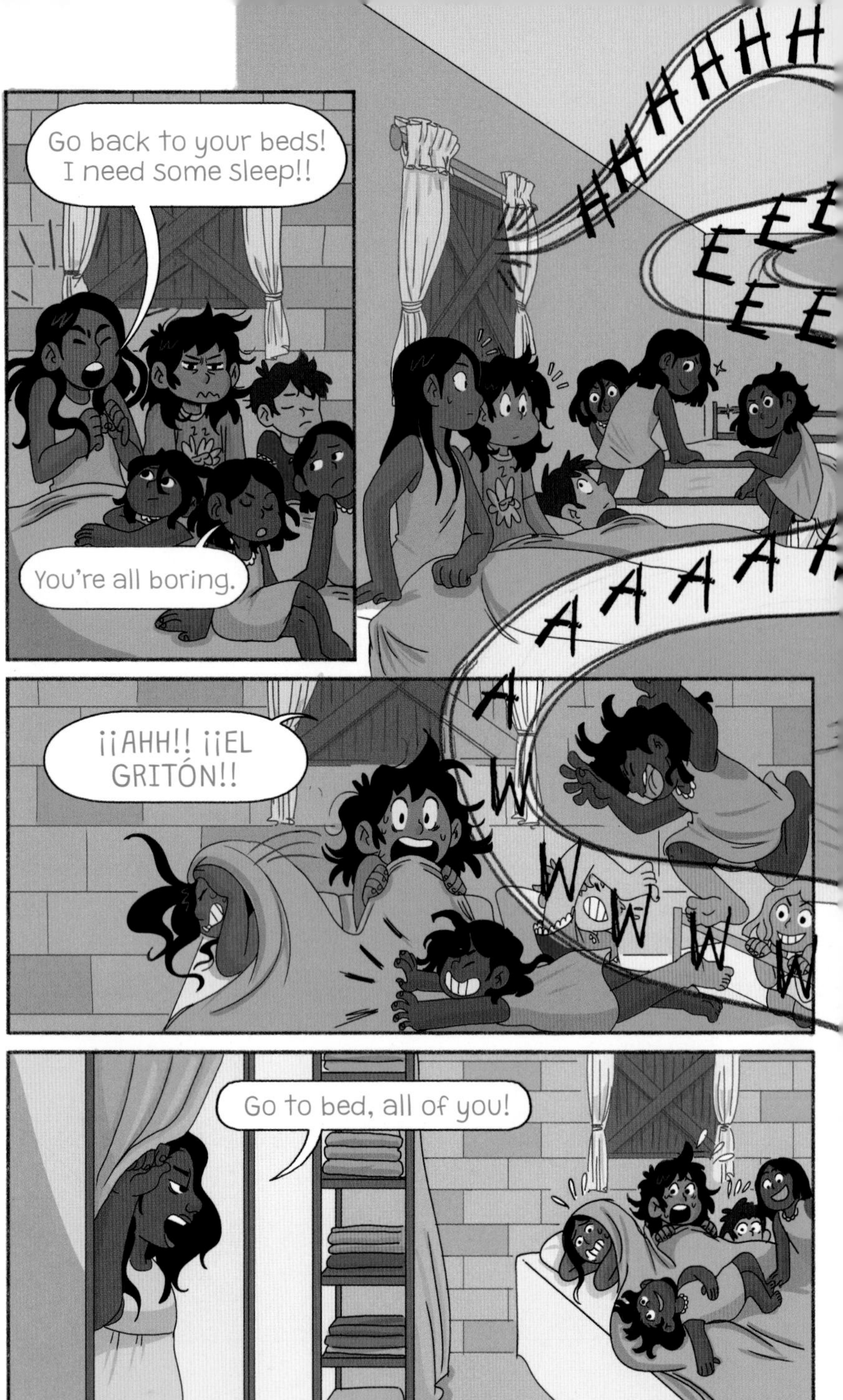
Go back to your beds! I need some sleep!!
You're all boring.
AAAAAAHHHHHHEEEEEE
AAAAAAWWWWW
¡¡AHH!! ¡¡EL GRITÓN!!
Go to bed, all of you!

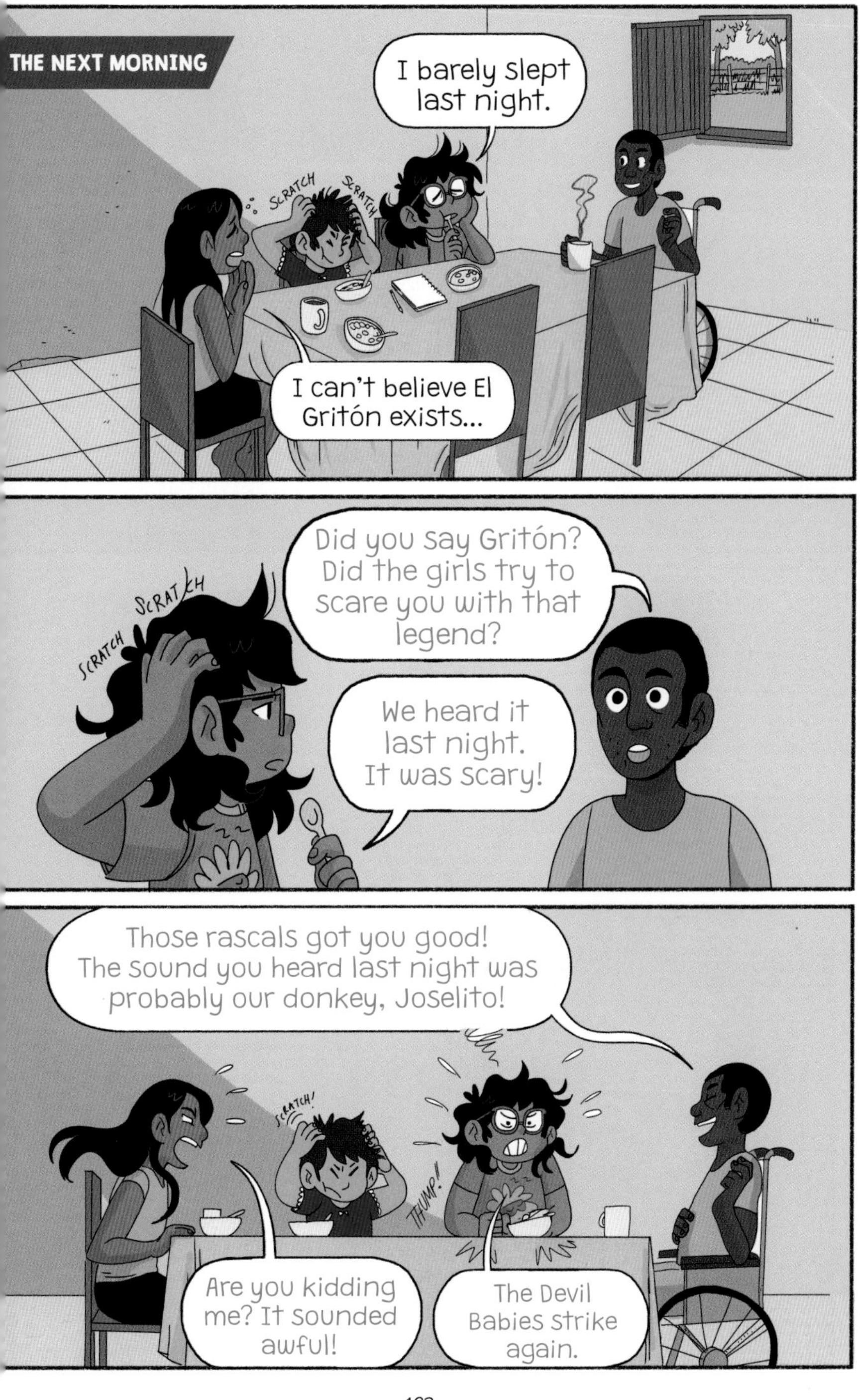
THE NEXT MORNING
I barely slept last night.
SCRATCH
SCRATCH
I can't believe El Gritón exists...
Did you say Gritón? Did the girls try to scare you with that legend?
SCRATCH
SCRATCH
We heard it last night. It was scary!
Those rascals got you good! The sound you heard last night was probably our donkey, Joselito!
SCRATCH!
THUMP!!
Are you kidding me? It sounded awful!
The Devil Babies strike again.

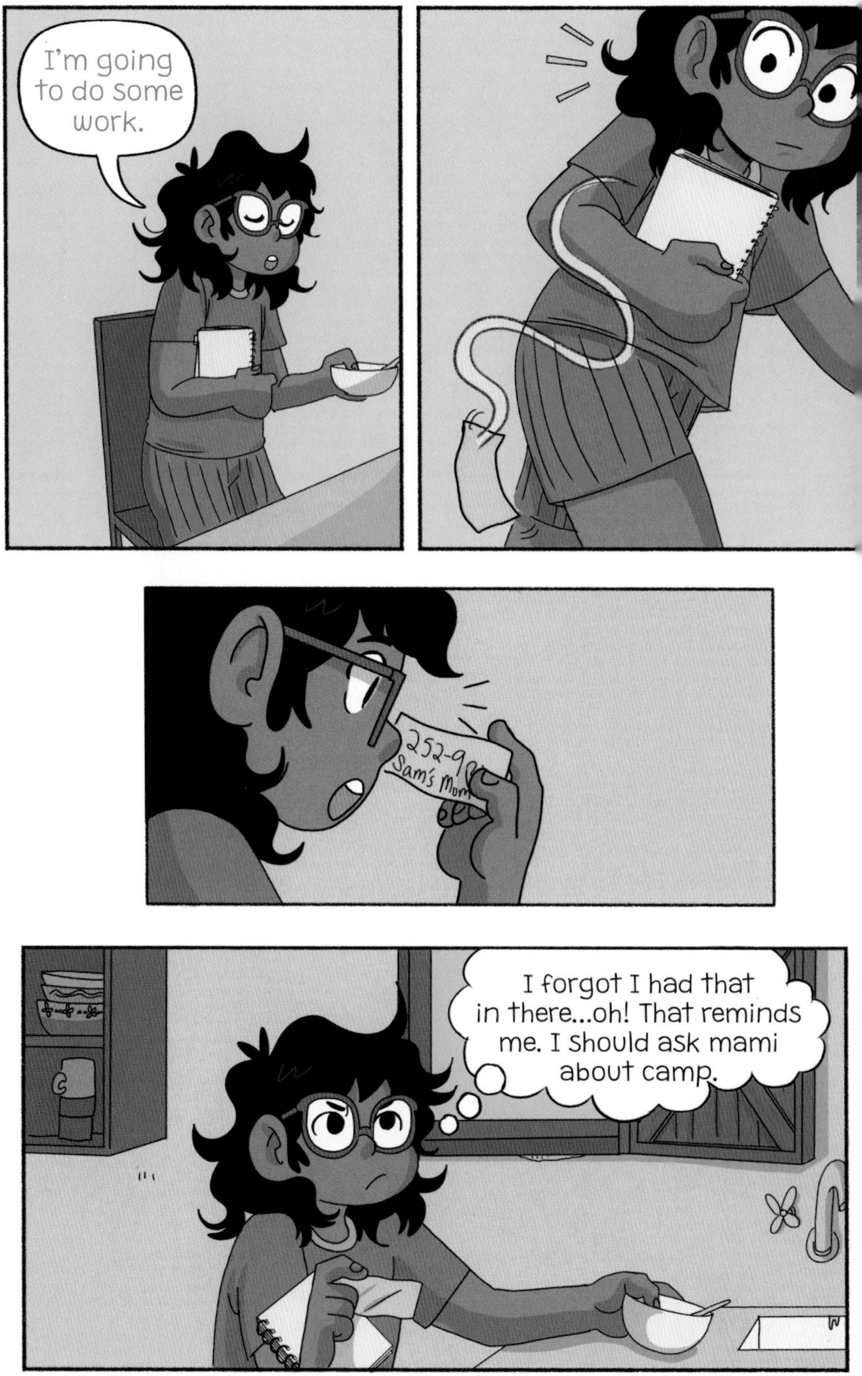
I'm going to do some work.
252-9
Sam's Mom
I forgot I had that in there...oh! That reminds me. I should ask mami about camp.

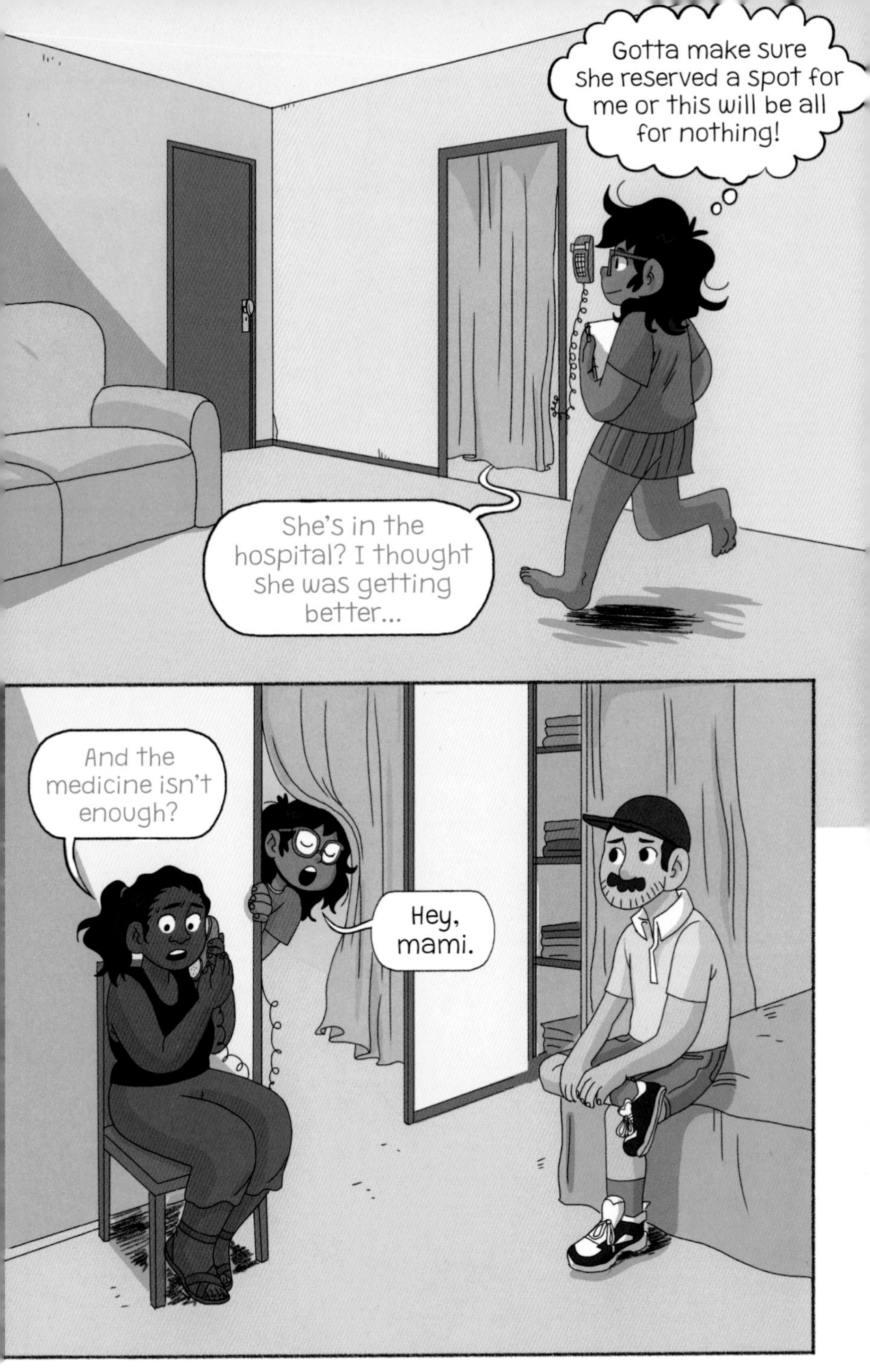
Gotta make sure she reserved a spot for me or this will be all for nothing!
She's in the hospital? I thought she was getting better...
And the medicine isn't enough?
Hey, mami.

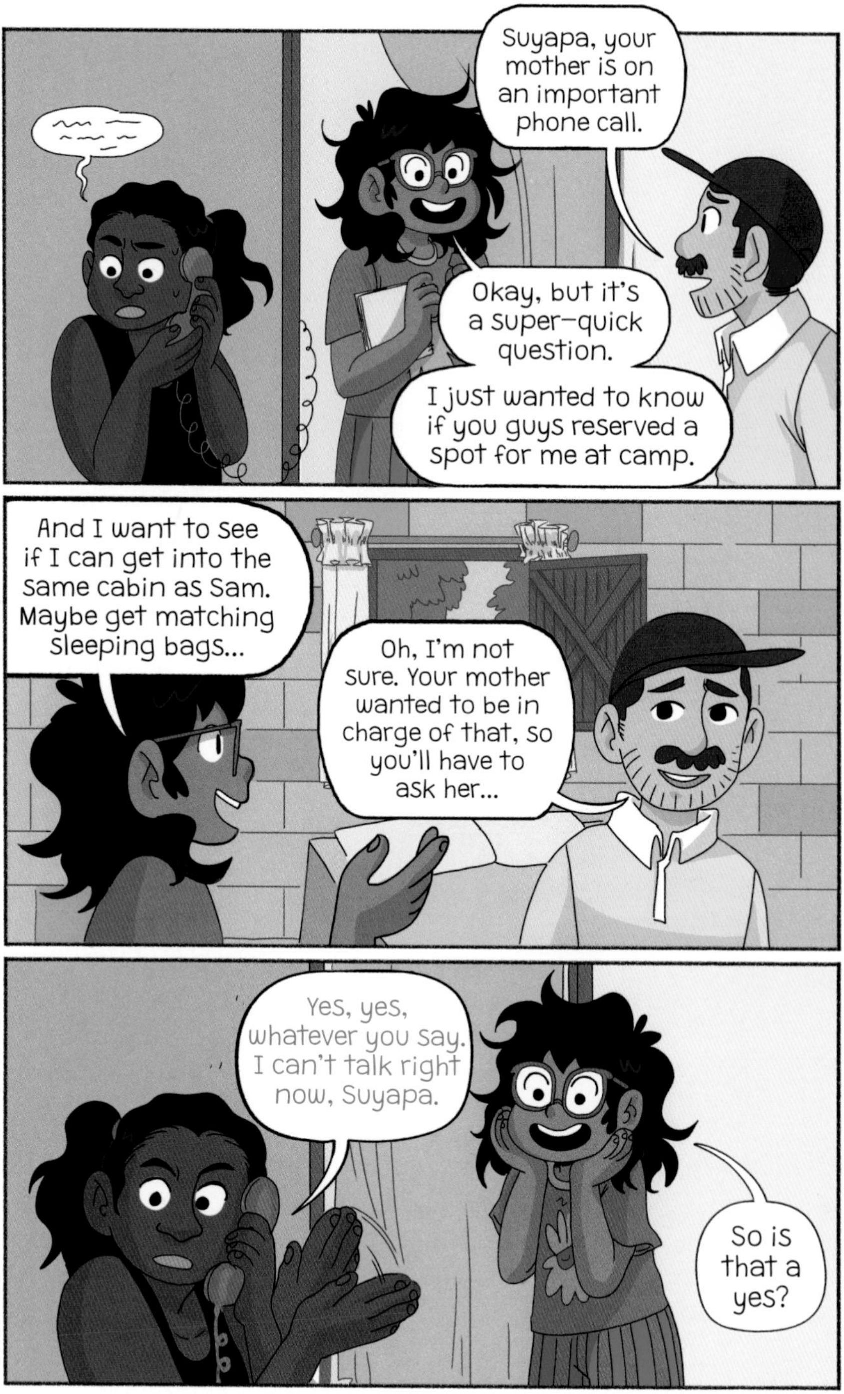

Suyapa, your mother is on an important phone call.
Okay, but it's a super-quick question.
I just wanted to know if you guys reserved a spot for me at camp.
And I want to see if I can get into the same cabin as Sam. Maybe get matching sleeping bags...
Oh, I'm not sure. Your mother wanted to be in charge of that, so you'll have to ask her...
Yes, yes, whatever you say. I can't talk right now, Suyapa.
So is that a yes?

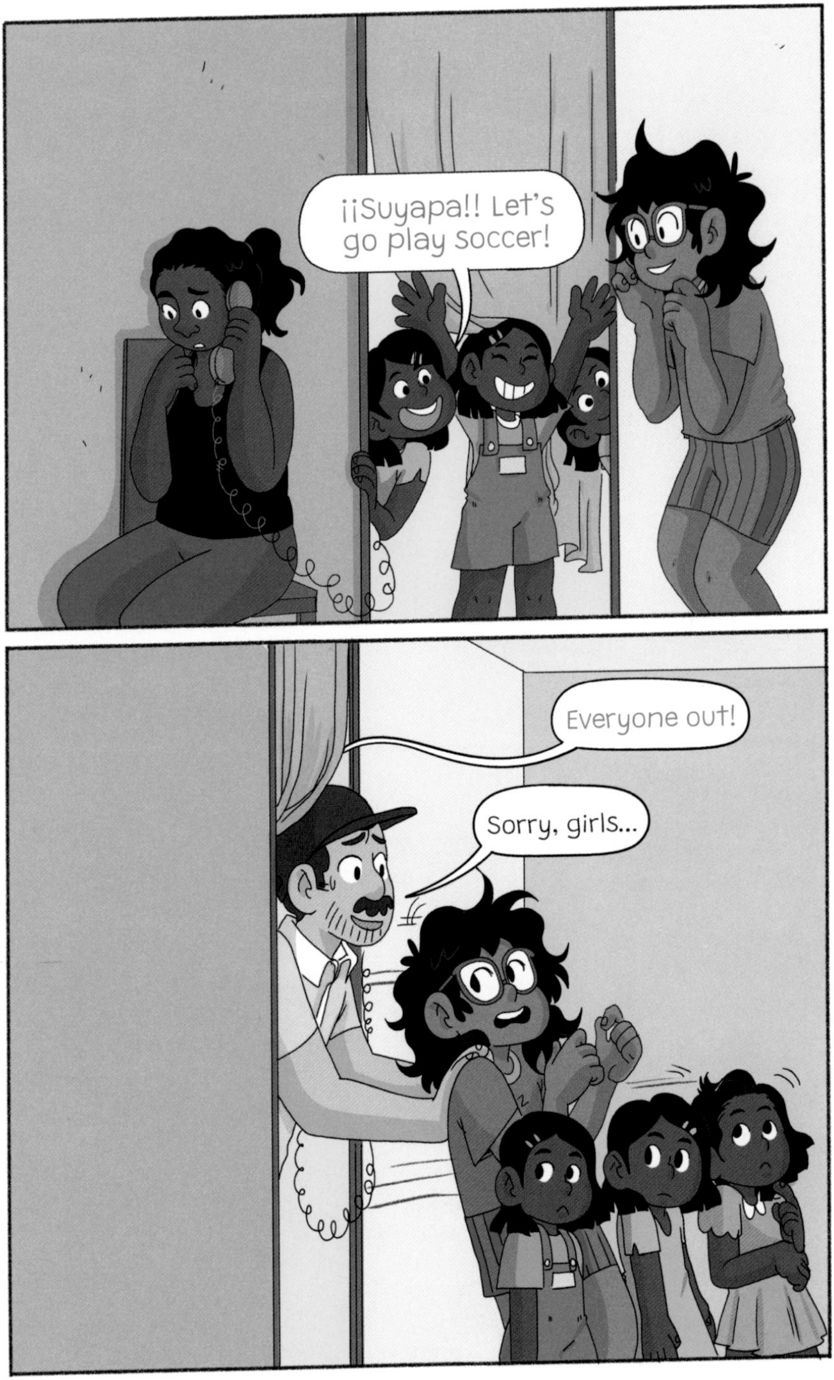
¡¡Suyapa!! Let's go play soccer!
Everyone out!
Sorry, girls...

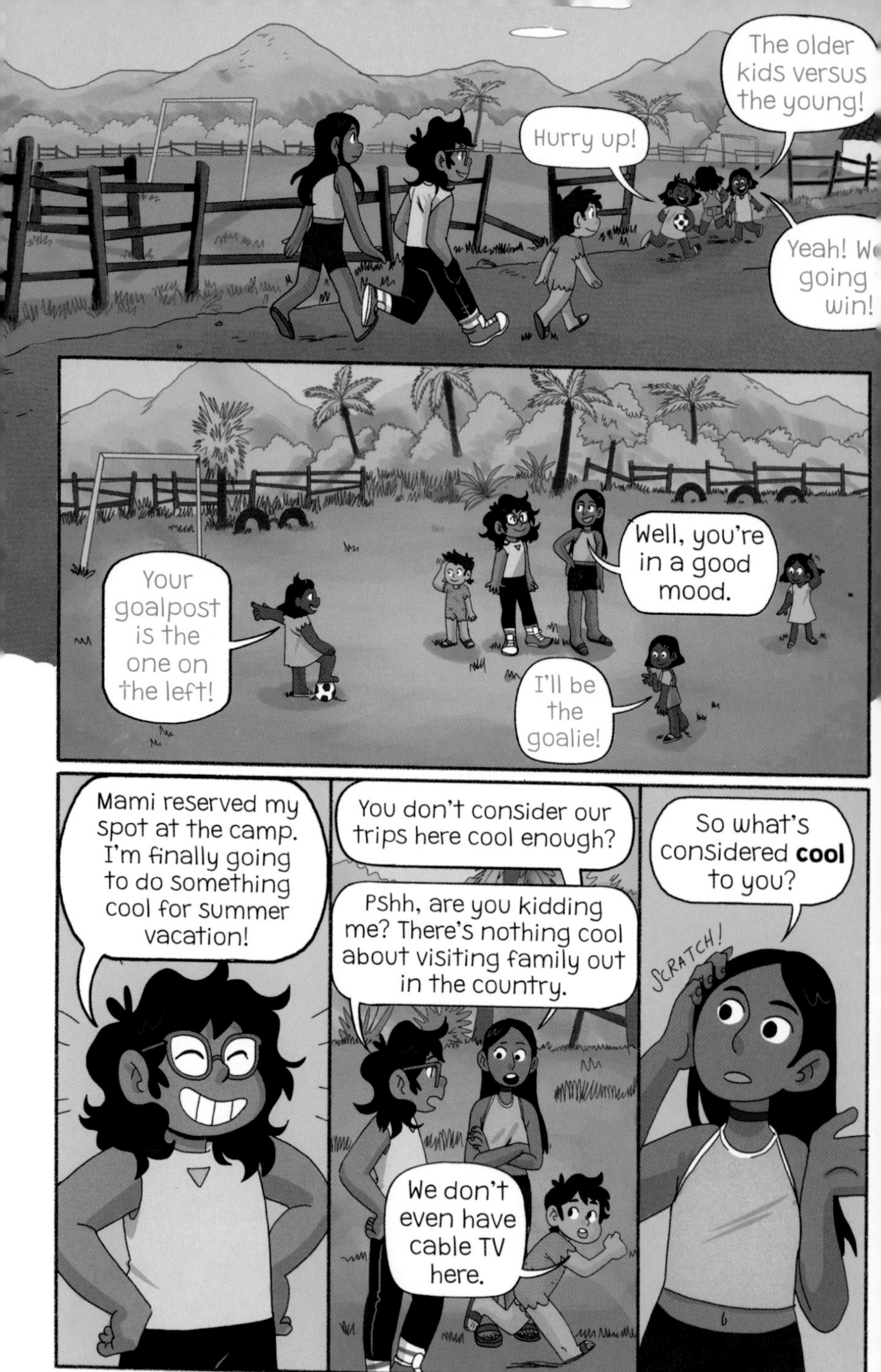
Hurry up!
The older kids versus the young!
Yeah! We going win!
Your goalpost is the one on the left!
Well, you're in a good mood.
I'll be the goalie!
Mami reserved my spot at the camp. I'm finally going to do something cool for summer vacation!
You don't consider our trips here cool enough?
Pshh, are you kidding me? There's nothing cool about visiting family out in the country.
We don't even have cable TV here.
So what's considered **cool** to you?
SCRATCH!

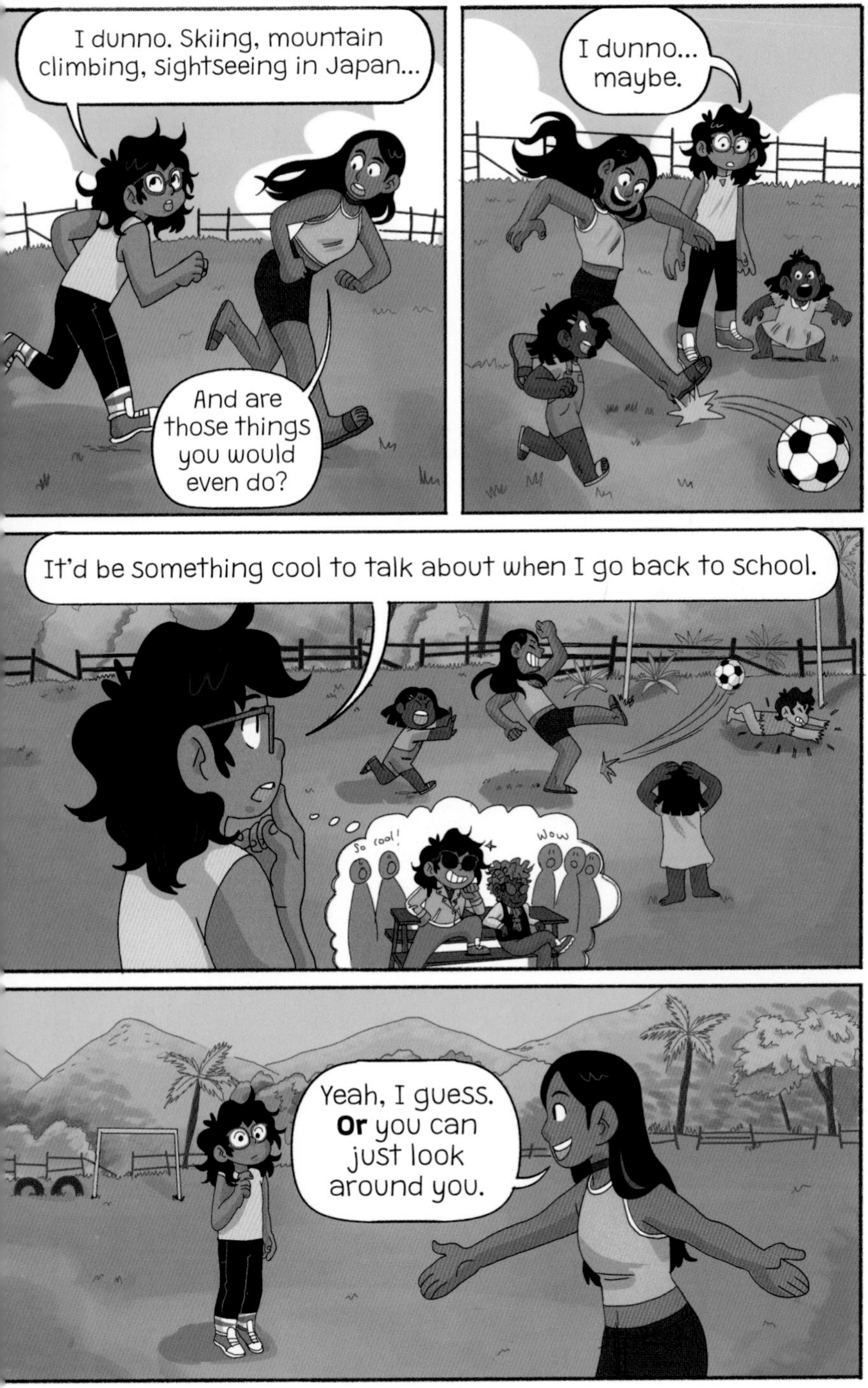
I dunno. Skiing, mountain climbing, sightseeing in Japan...
And are those things you would even do?
I dunno... maybe.
It'd be something cool to talk about when I go back to school.
So cool!
Wow
Yeah, I guess. **Or** you can just look around you.

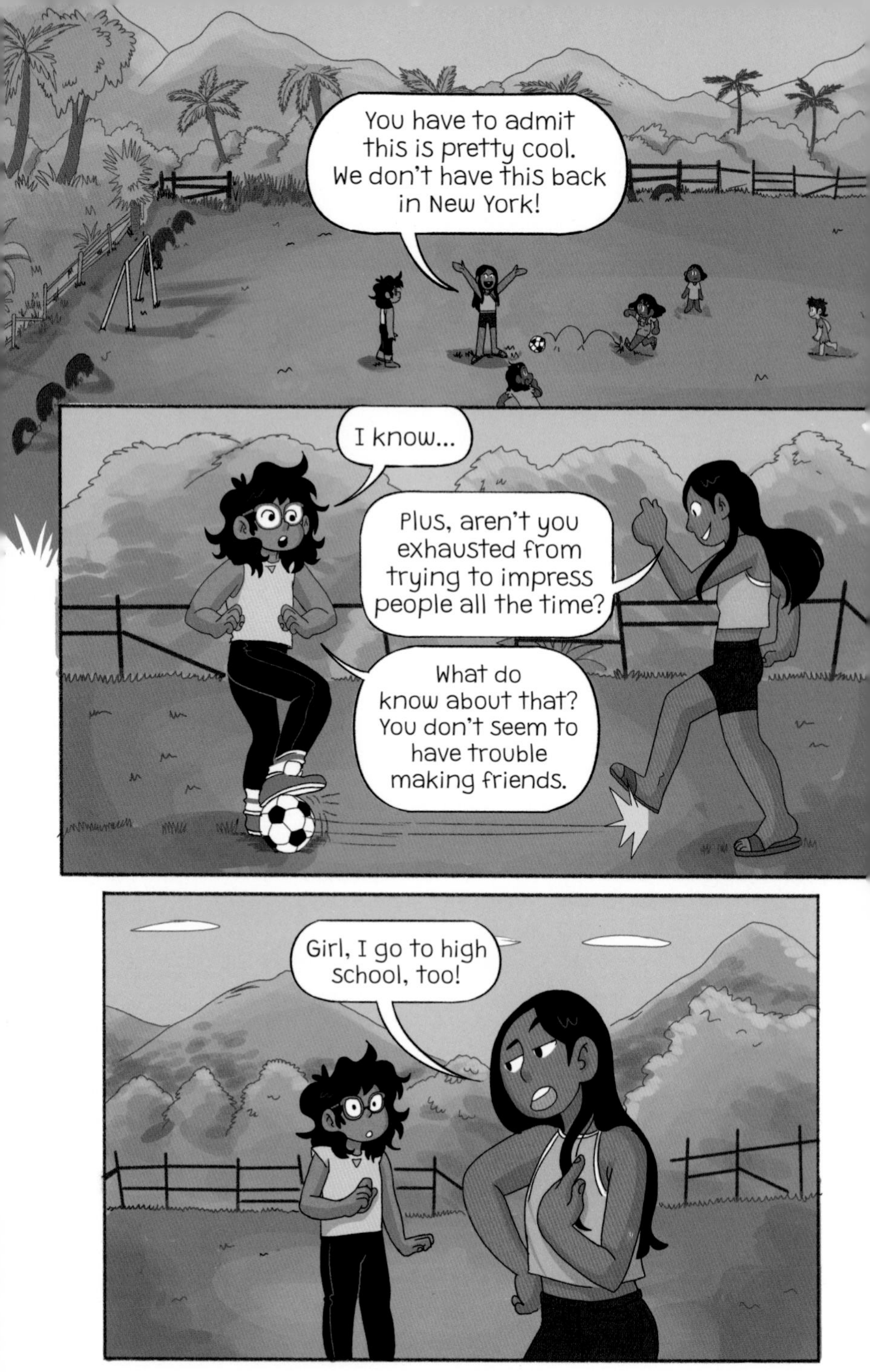
You have to admit this is pretty cool. We don't have this back in New York!
I know...
Plus, aren't you exhausted from trying to impress people all the time?
What do know about that? You don't seem to have trouble making friends.
Girl, I go to high school, too!

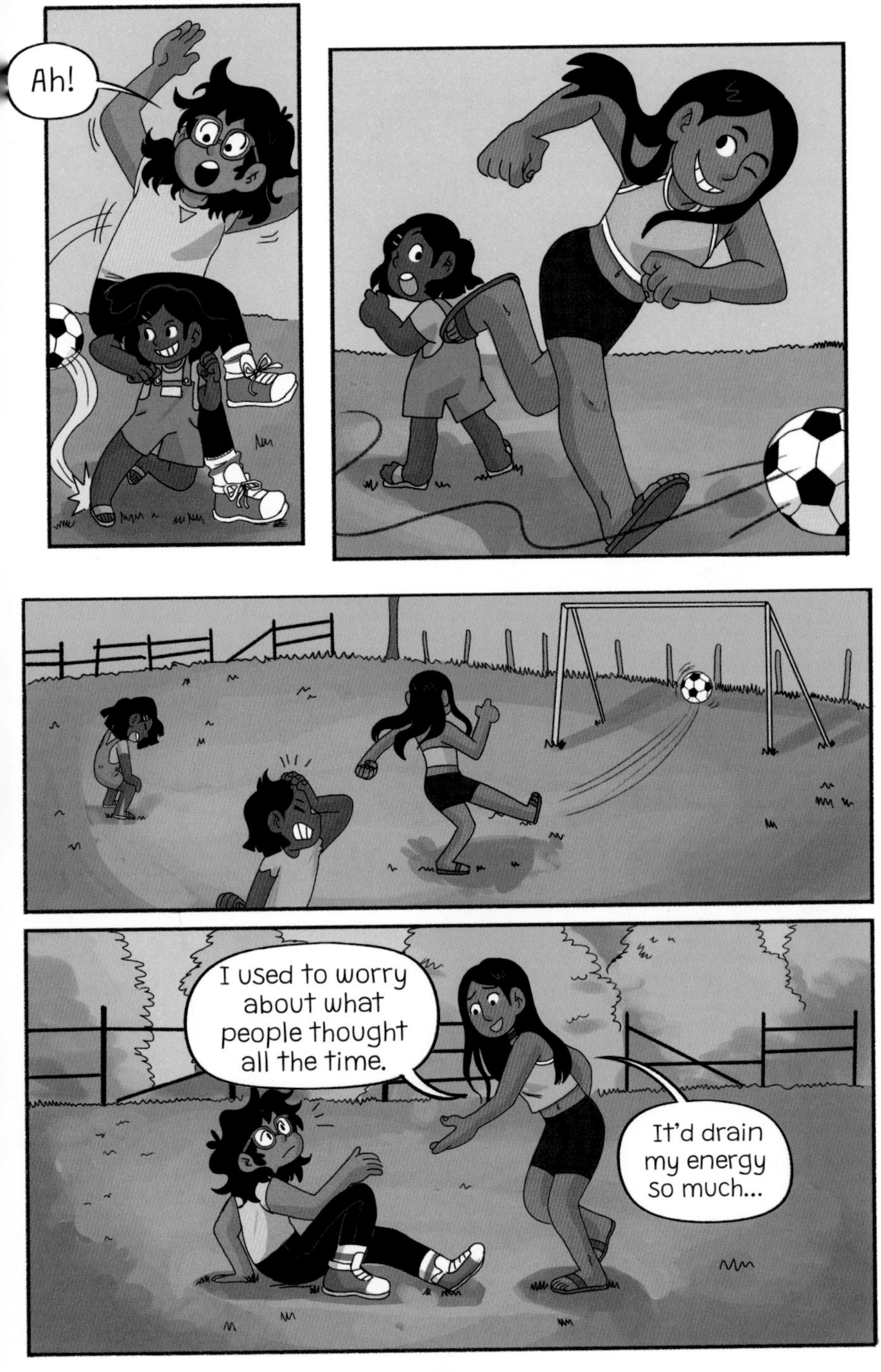
Ah!
I used to worry about what people thought all the time.
It'd drain my energy so much...

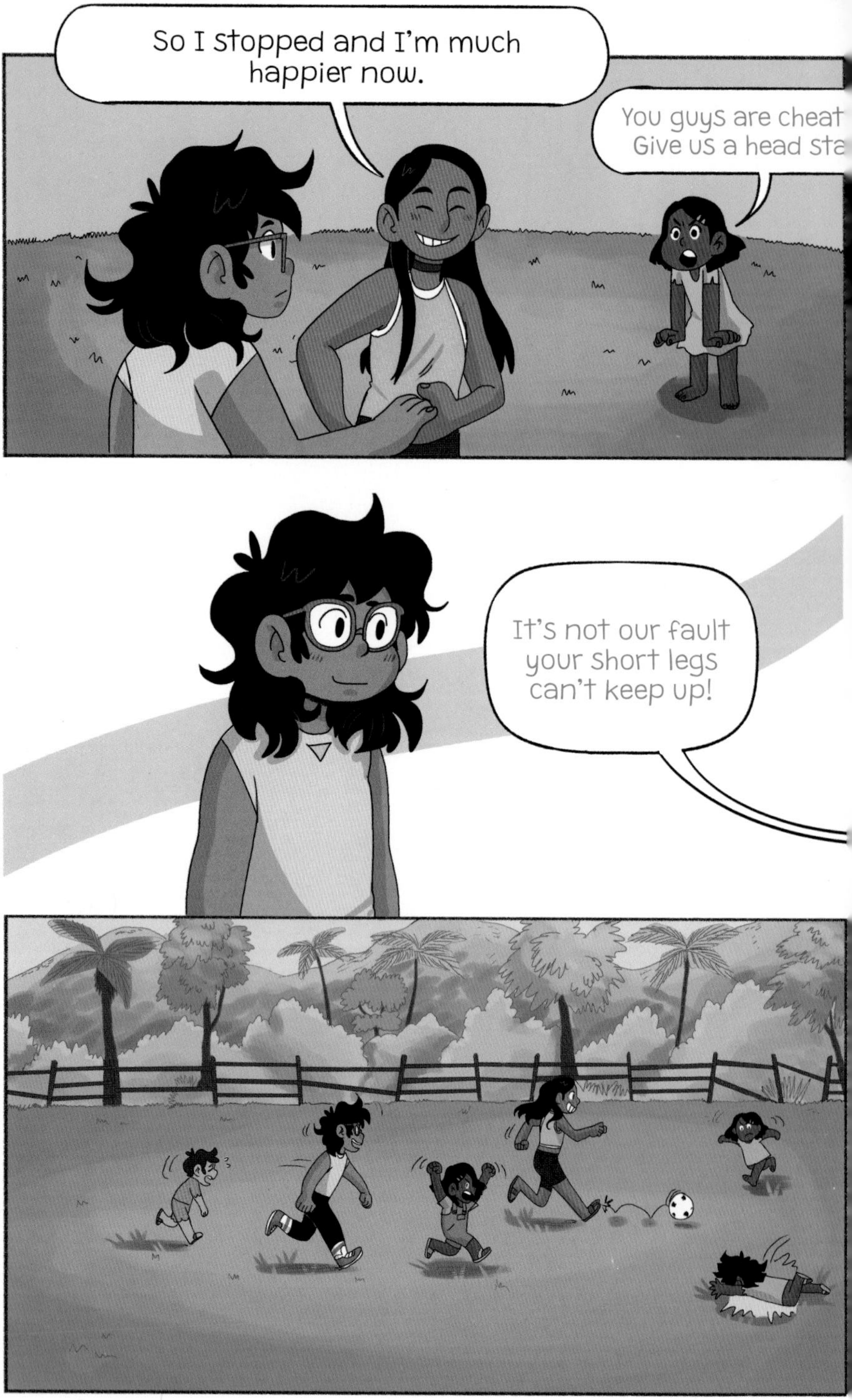
So I stopped and I'm much happier now.
You guys are cheat
Give us a head sta
It's not our fault your short legs can't keep up!

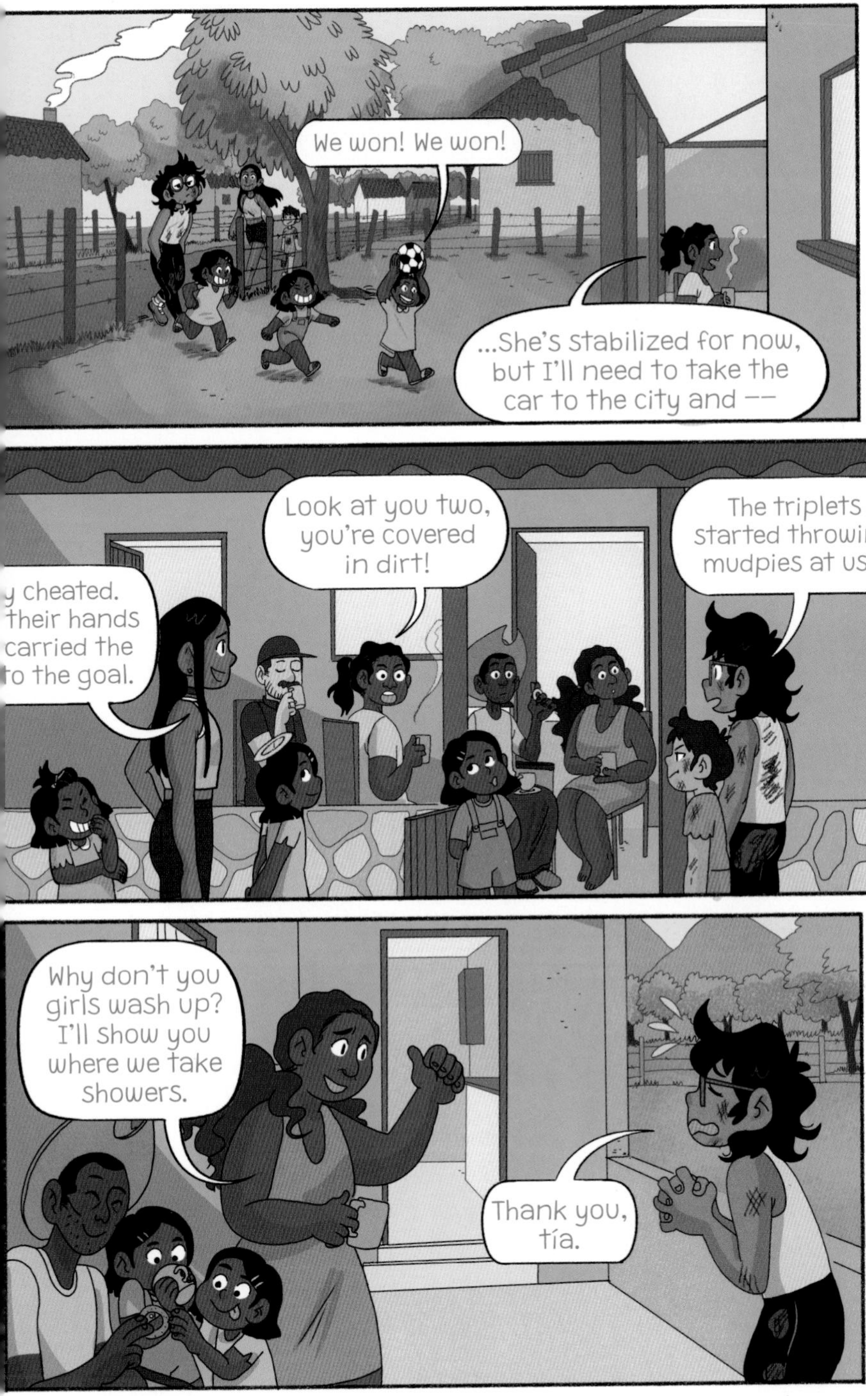
We won! We won!
...She's stabilized for now, but I'll need to take the car to the city and --
y cheated. their hands carried the to the goal.
Look at you two, you're covered in dirt!
The triplets started throwing mudpies at us...
Why don't you girls wash up? I'll show you where we take showers.
Thank you, tía.

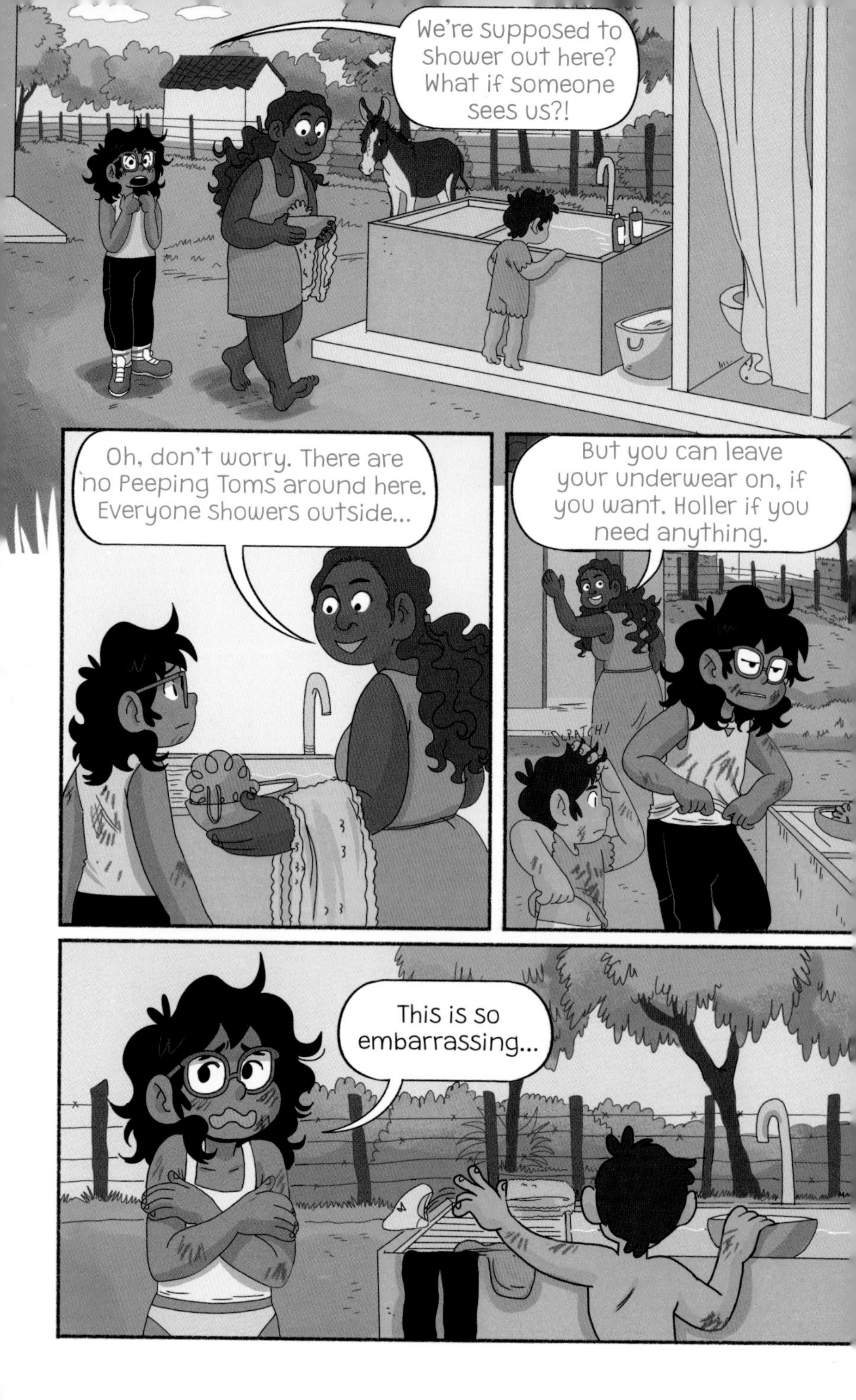
We're supposed to shower out here? What if someone sees us?!
Oh, don't worry. There are no Peeping Toms around here. Everyone showers outside...
But you can leave your underwear on, if you want. Holler if you need anything.
SCRATCH!
This is so embarrassing...

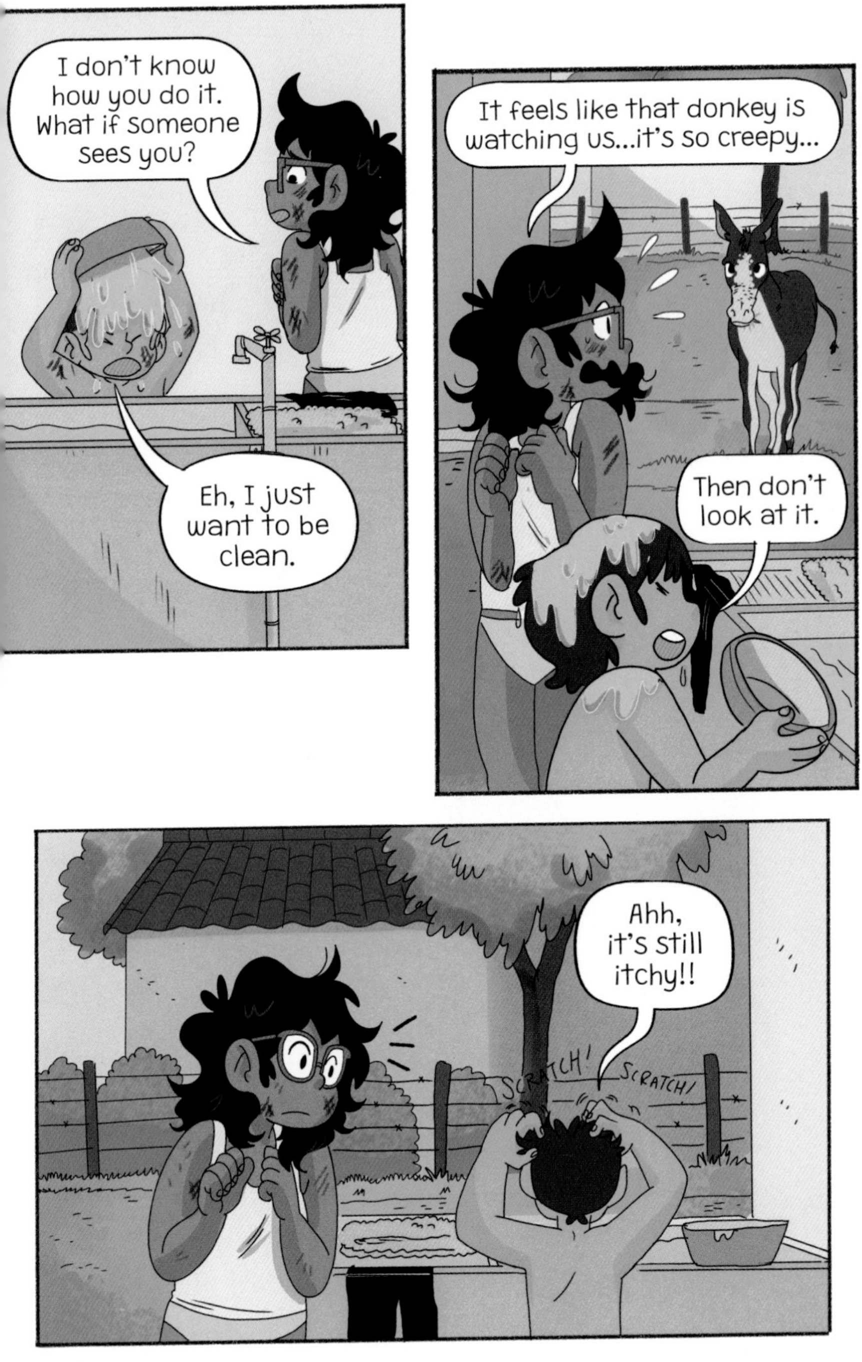
I don't know how you do it. What if someone sees you?
Eh, I just want to be clean.
It feels like that donkey is watching us...it's so creepy...
Then don't look at it.
SCRATCH!
SCRATCH!
Ahh, it's still itchy!!

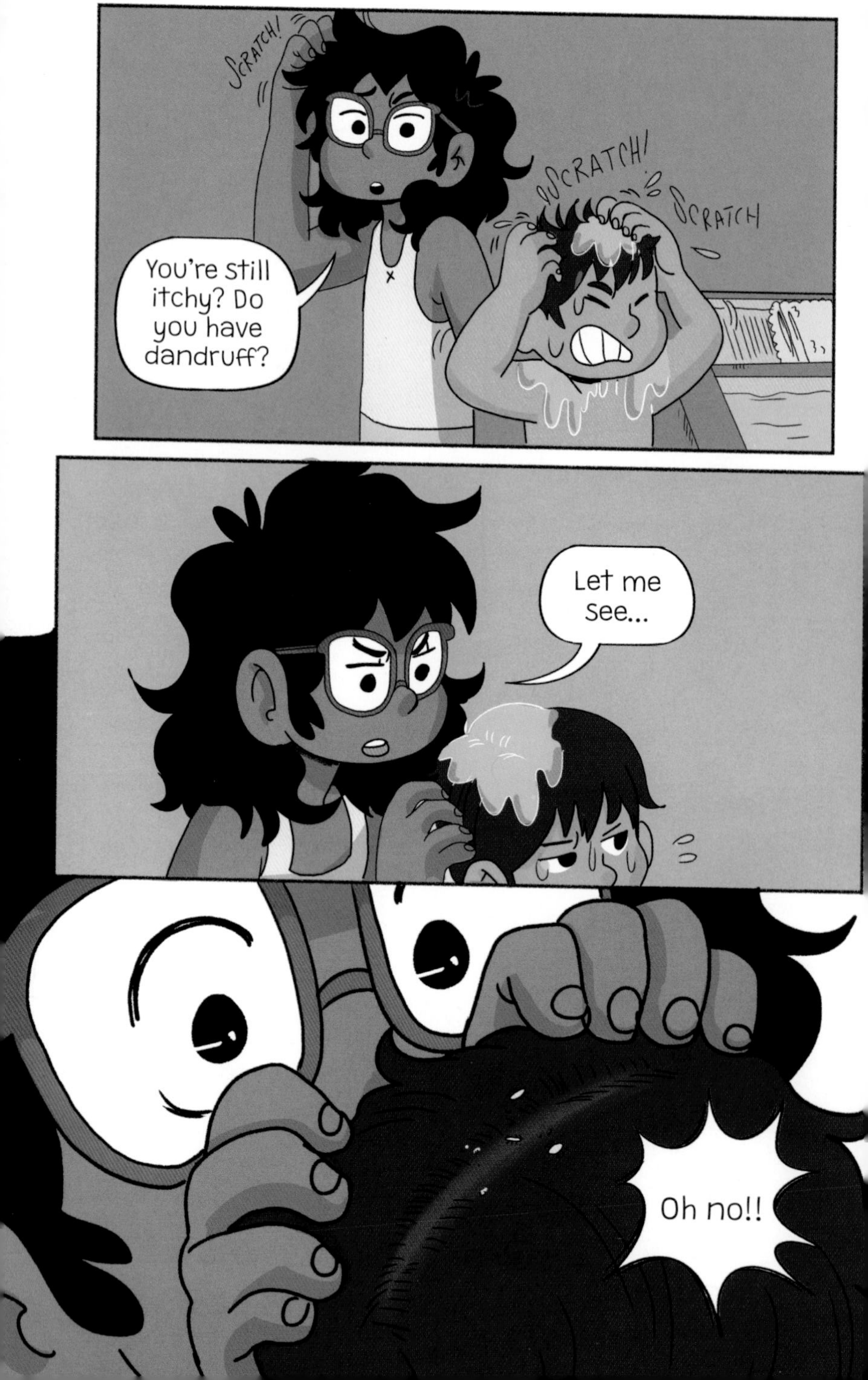
SCRATCH!
SCRATCH!
SCRATCH
You're still itchy? Do you have dandruff?
Let me see...
Oh no!!

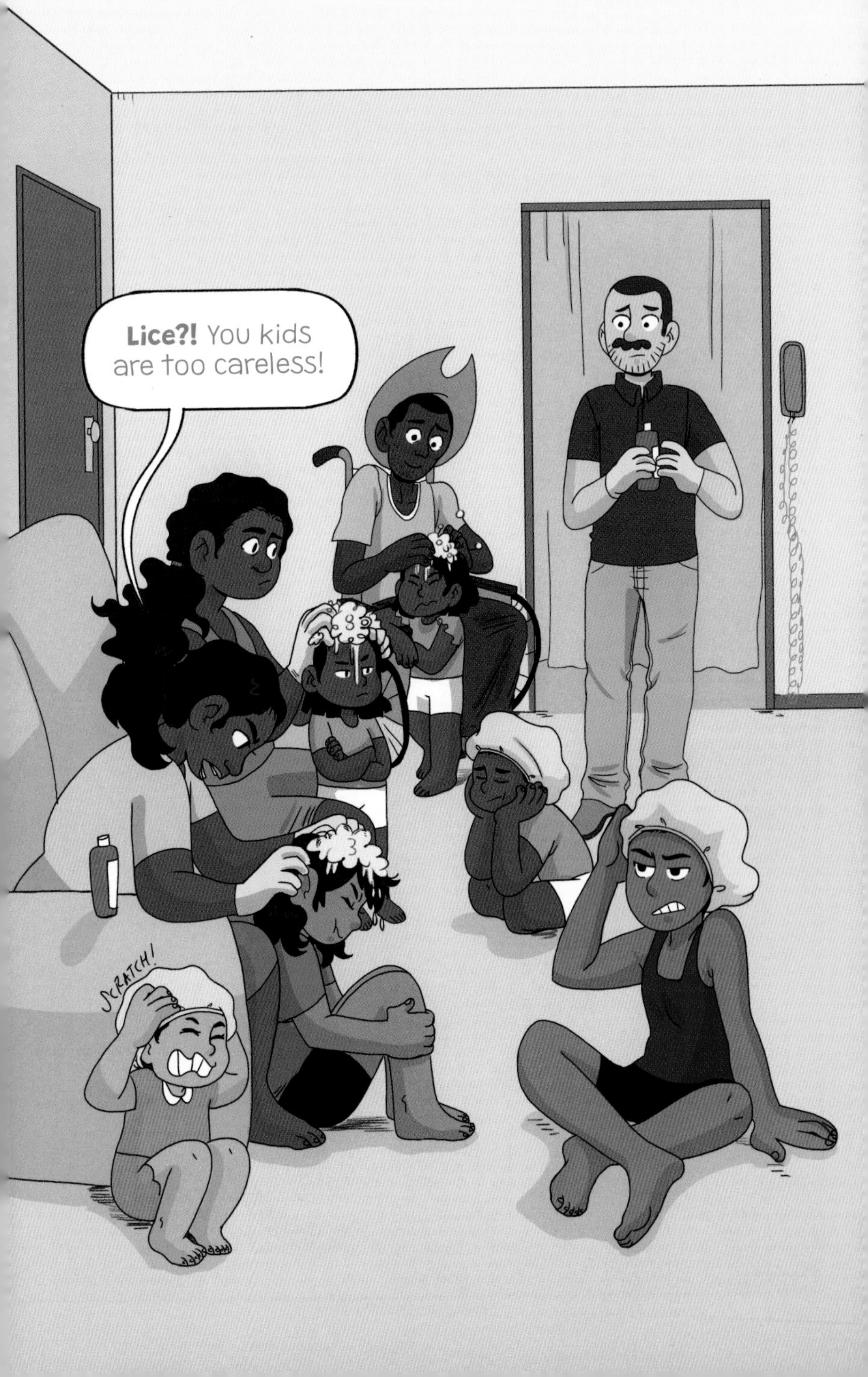
Lice?! You kids are too careless!
SCRATCH!

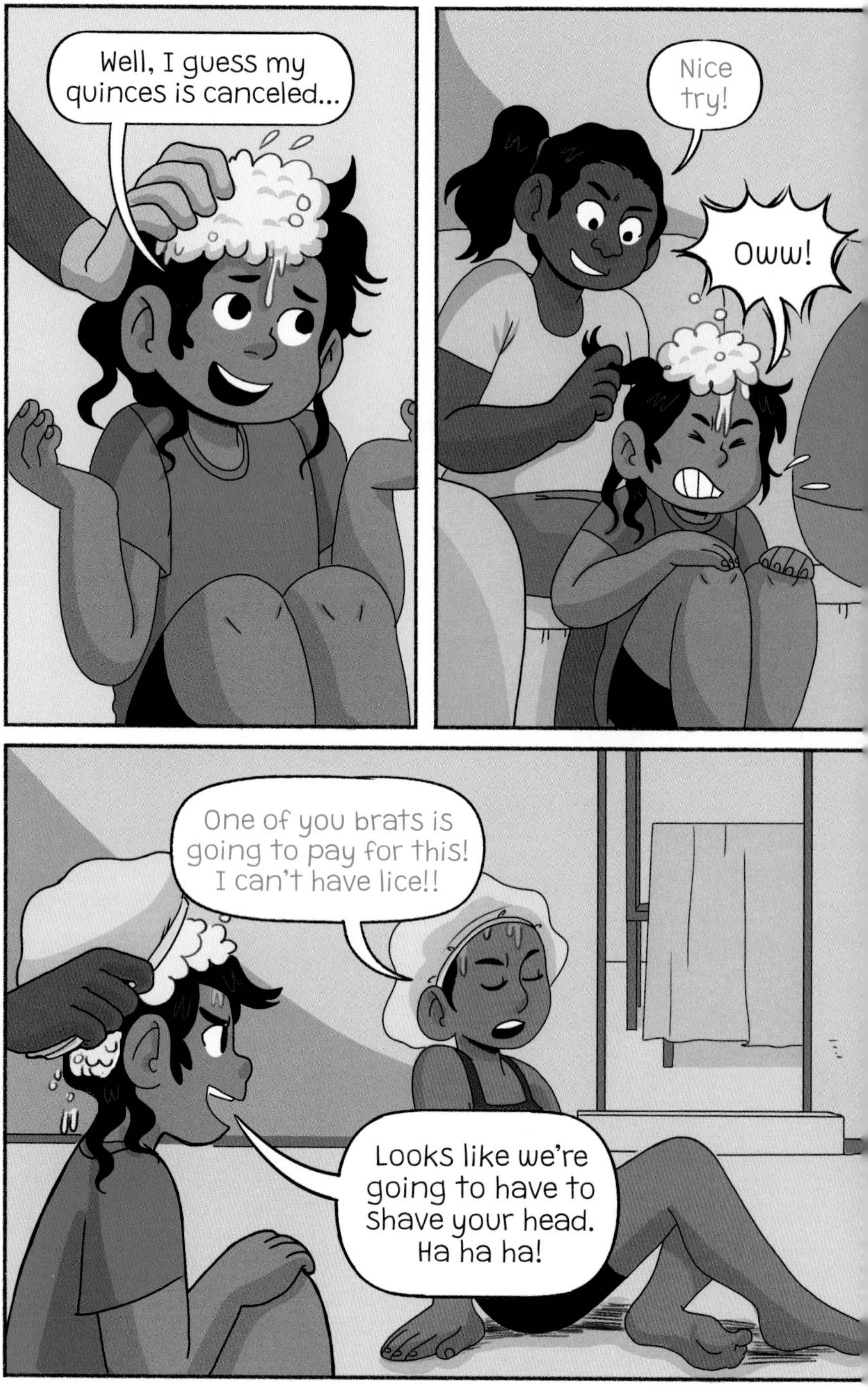
Well, I guess my quinces is canceled...
Nice try!
Oww!
One of you brats is going to pay for this! I can't have lice!!
Looks like we're going to have to shave your head. Ha ha ha!

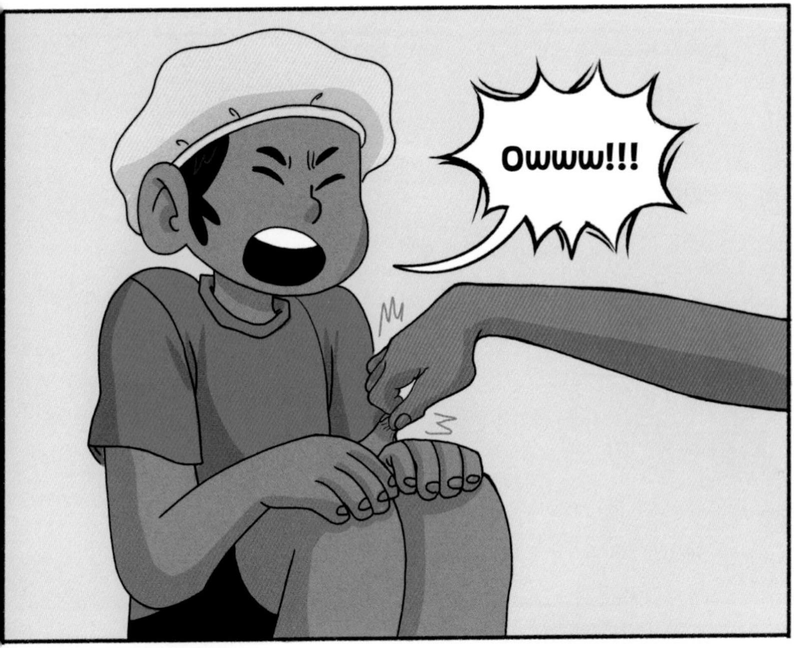
Owww!!!

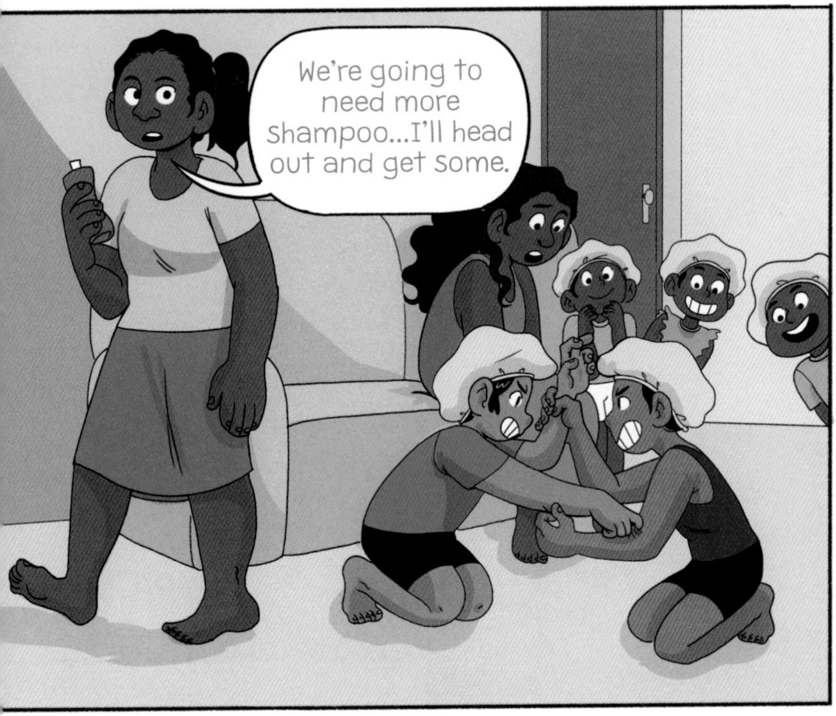
We're going to need more shampoo...I'll head out and get some.

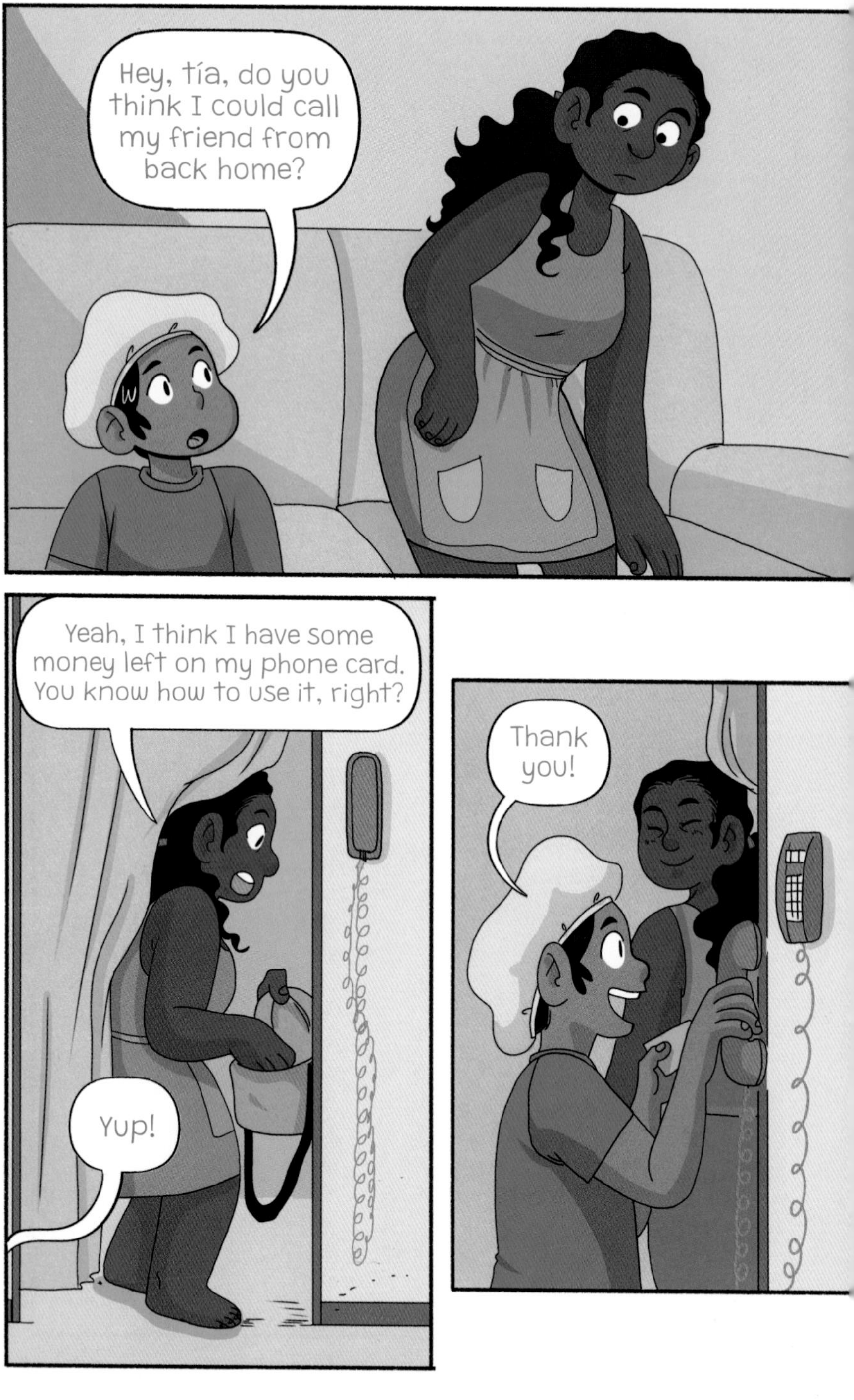
Hey, tía, do you think I could call my friend from back home?
Yeah, I think I have some money left on my phone card. You know how to use it, right?
Yup!
Thank you!

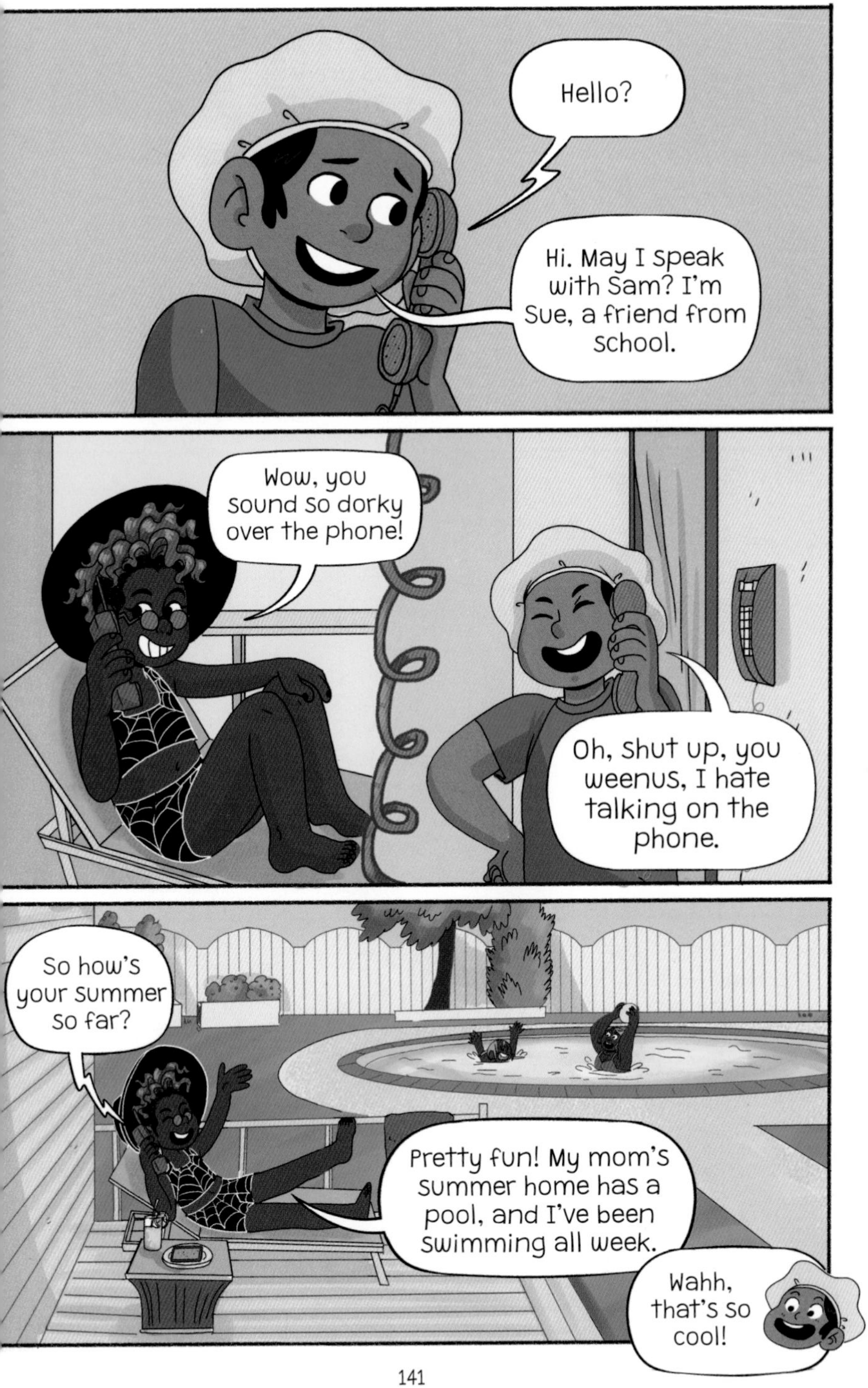
Hello?
Hi. May I speak with Sam? I'm Sue, a friend from school.
Wow, you sound so dorky over the phone!
Oh, shut up, you weenus, I hate talking on the phone.
So how's your summer so far?
Pretty fun! My mom's summer home has a pool, and I've been swimming all week.
Wahh, that's so cool!

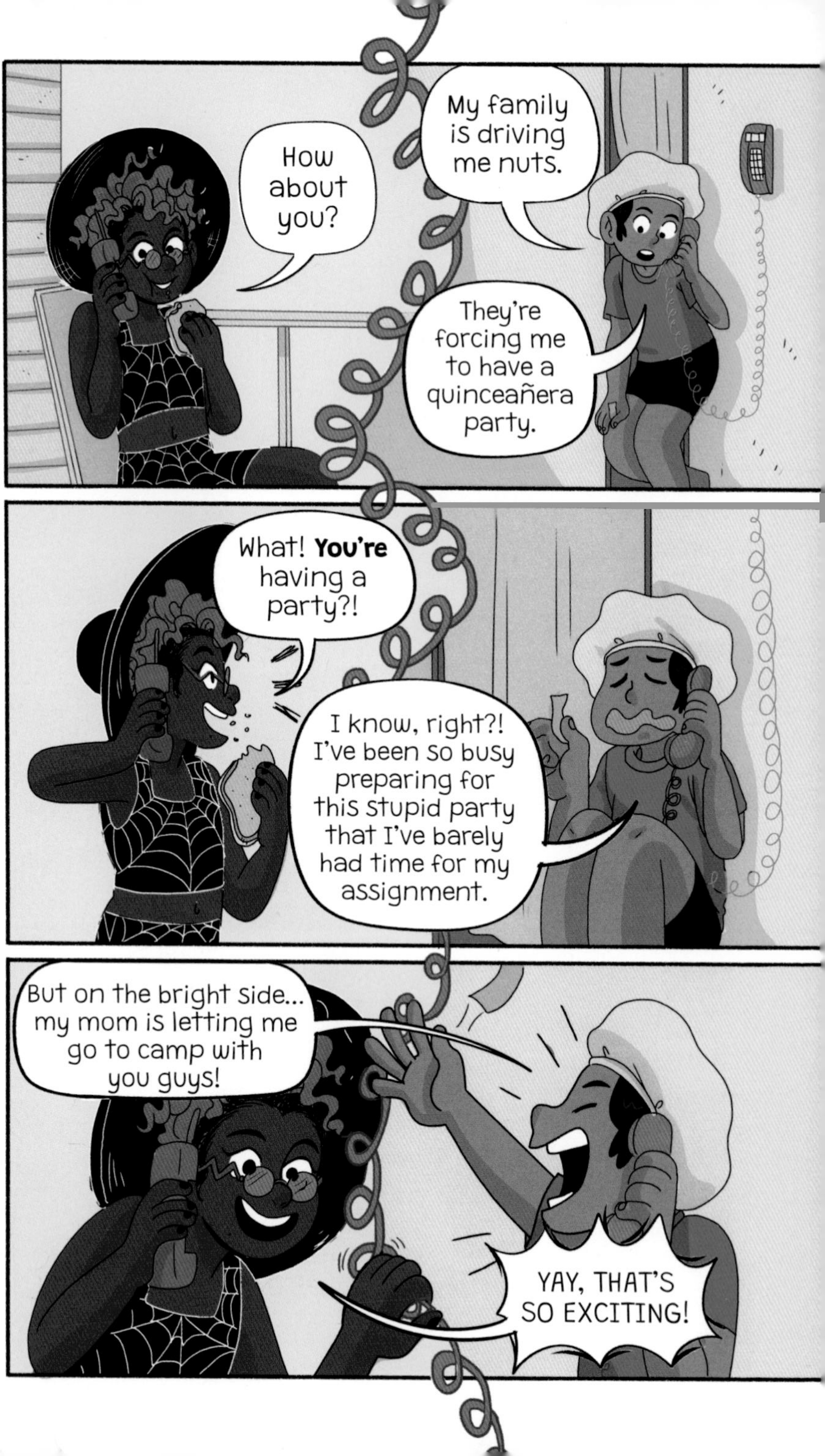
How about you?
My family is driving me nuts.
They're forcing me to have a quinceañera party.
What! **You're** having a party?!
I know, right?! I've been so busy preparing for this stupid party that I've barely had time for my assignment.
But on the bright side... my mom is letting me go to camp with you guys!
YAY, THAT'S SO EXCITING!

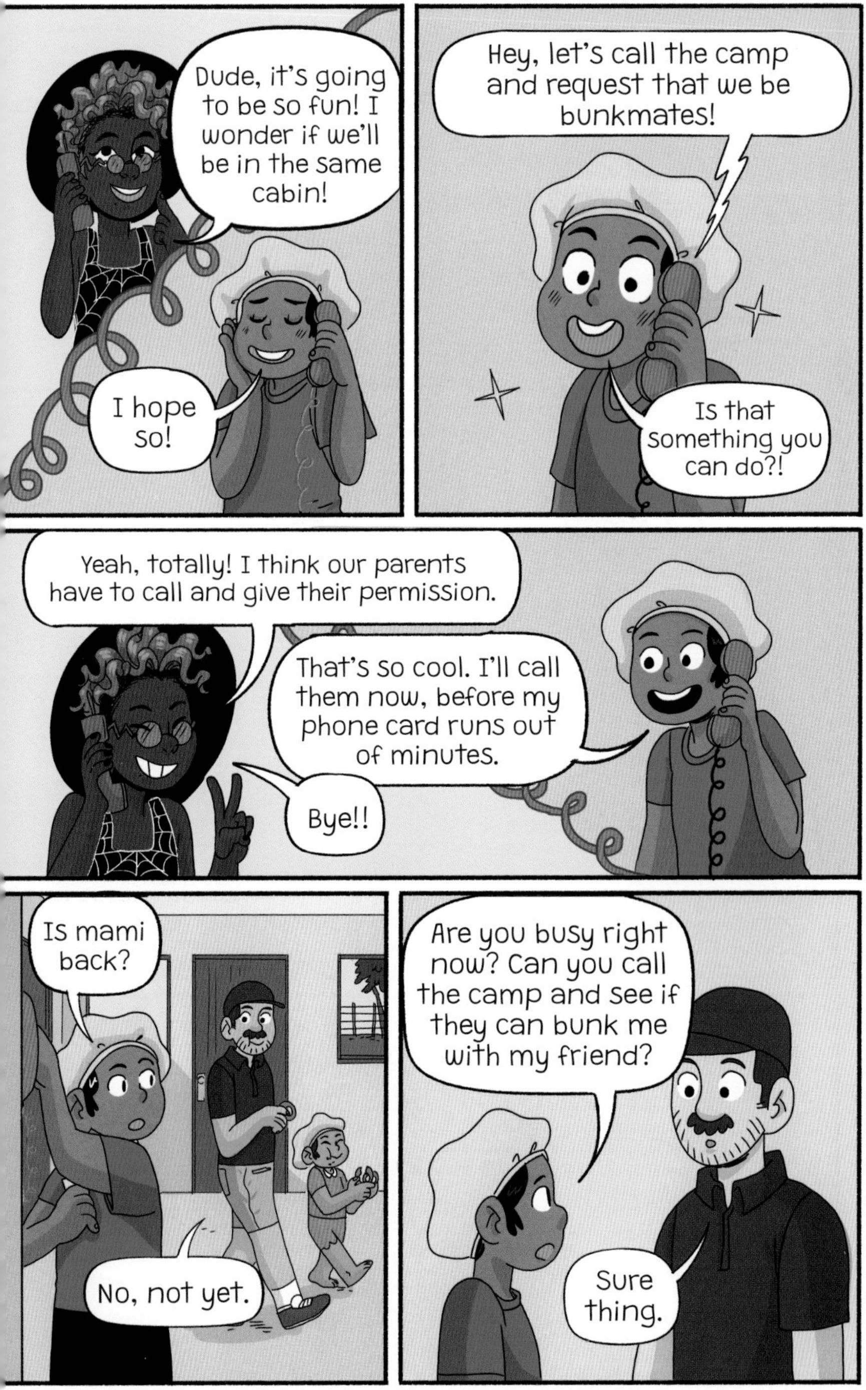
Dude, it's going to be so fun! I wonder if we'll be in the same cabin!
I hope so!
Hey, let's call the camp and request that we be bunkmates!
Is that something you can do?!
Yeah, totally! I think our parents have to call and give their permission.
That's so cool. I'll call them now, before my phone card runs out of minutes.
Bye!!
Is mami back?
No, not yet.
Are you busy right now? Can you call the camp and see if they can bunk me with my friend?
Sure thing.

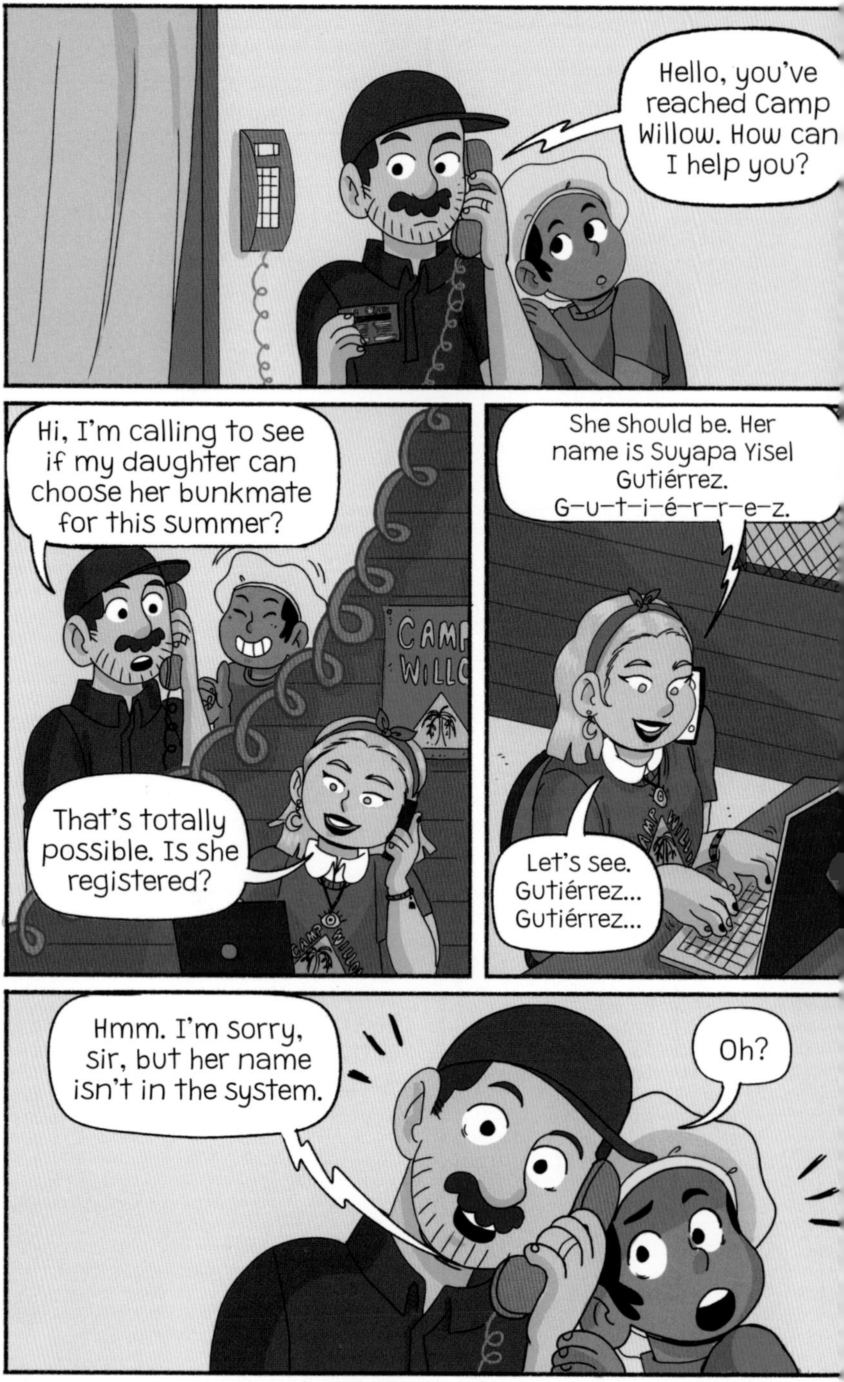
Hello, you've reached Camp Willow. How can I help you?
Hi, I'm calling to see if my daughter can choose her bunkmate for this summer?
That's totally possible. Is she registered?
CAMP WILLO
She should be. Her name is Suyapa Yisel Gutiérrez. G–u–t–i–é–r–r–e–z.
Let's see. Gutiérrez... Gutiérrez...
Hmm. I'm sorry, sir, but her name isn't in the system.
Oh?

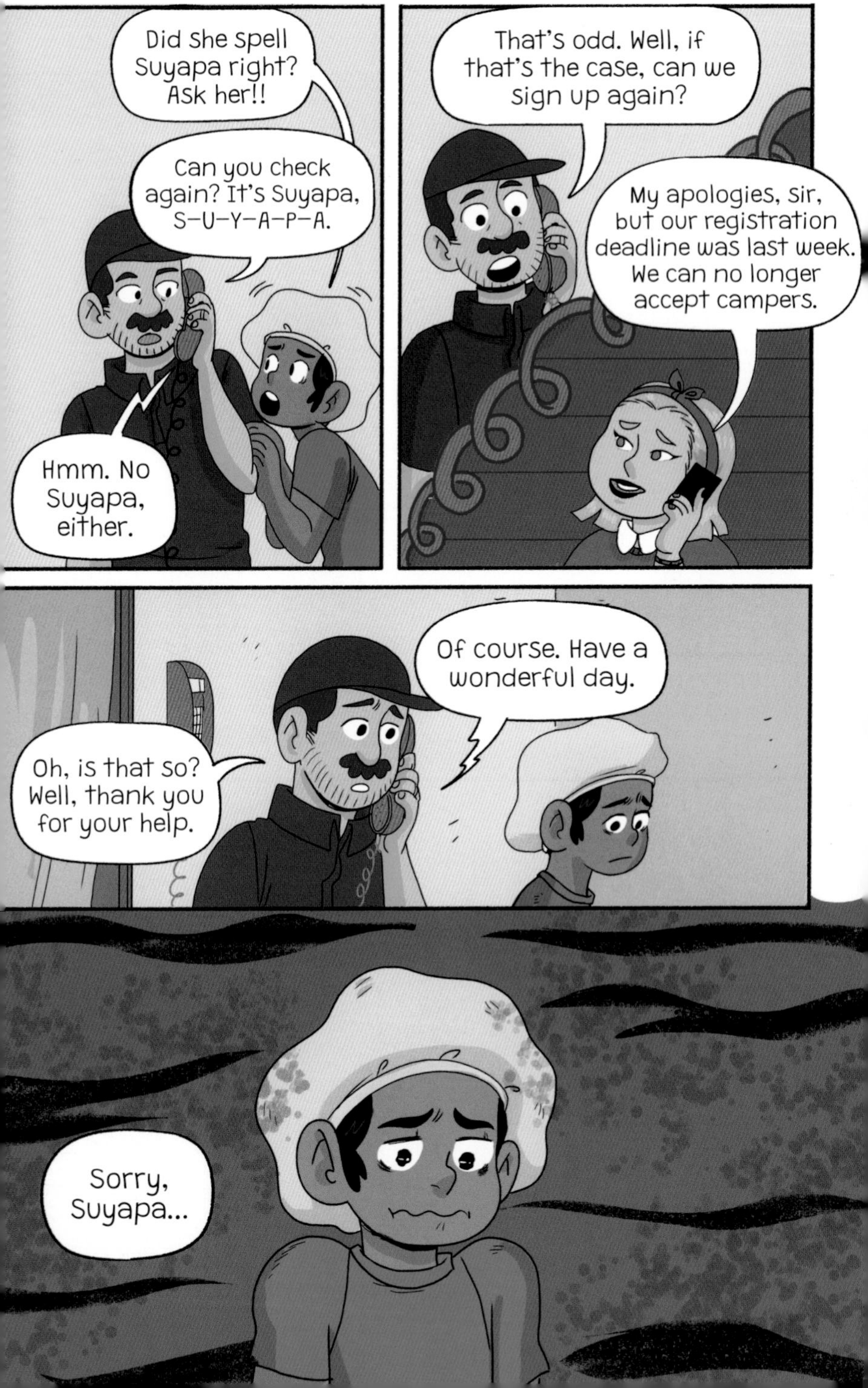
Did she spell Suyapa right? Ask her!!
Can you check again? It's Suyapa, S–U–Y–A–P–A.
Hmm. No Suyapa, either.
That's odd. Well, if that's the case, can we sign up again?
My apologies, sir, but our registration deadline was last week. We can no longer accept campers.
Of course. Have a wonderful day.
Oh, is that so? Well, thank you for your help.
Sorry, Suyapa...

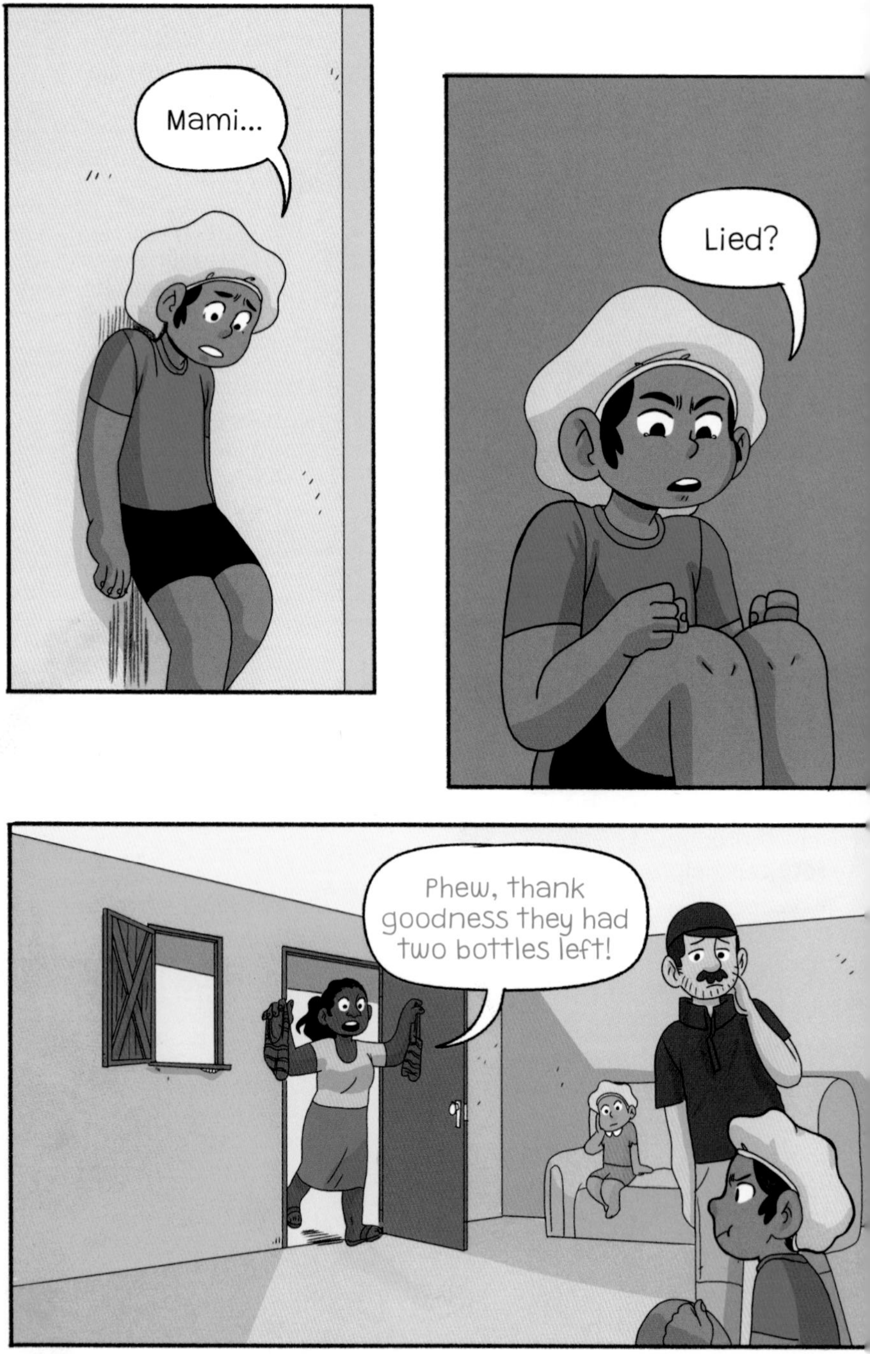
Mami...
Lied?
Phew, thank goodness they had two bottles left!

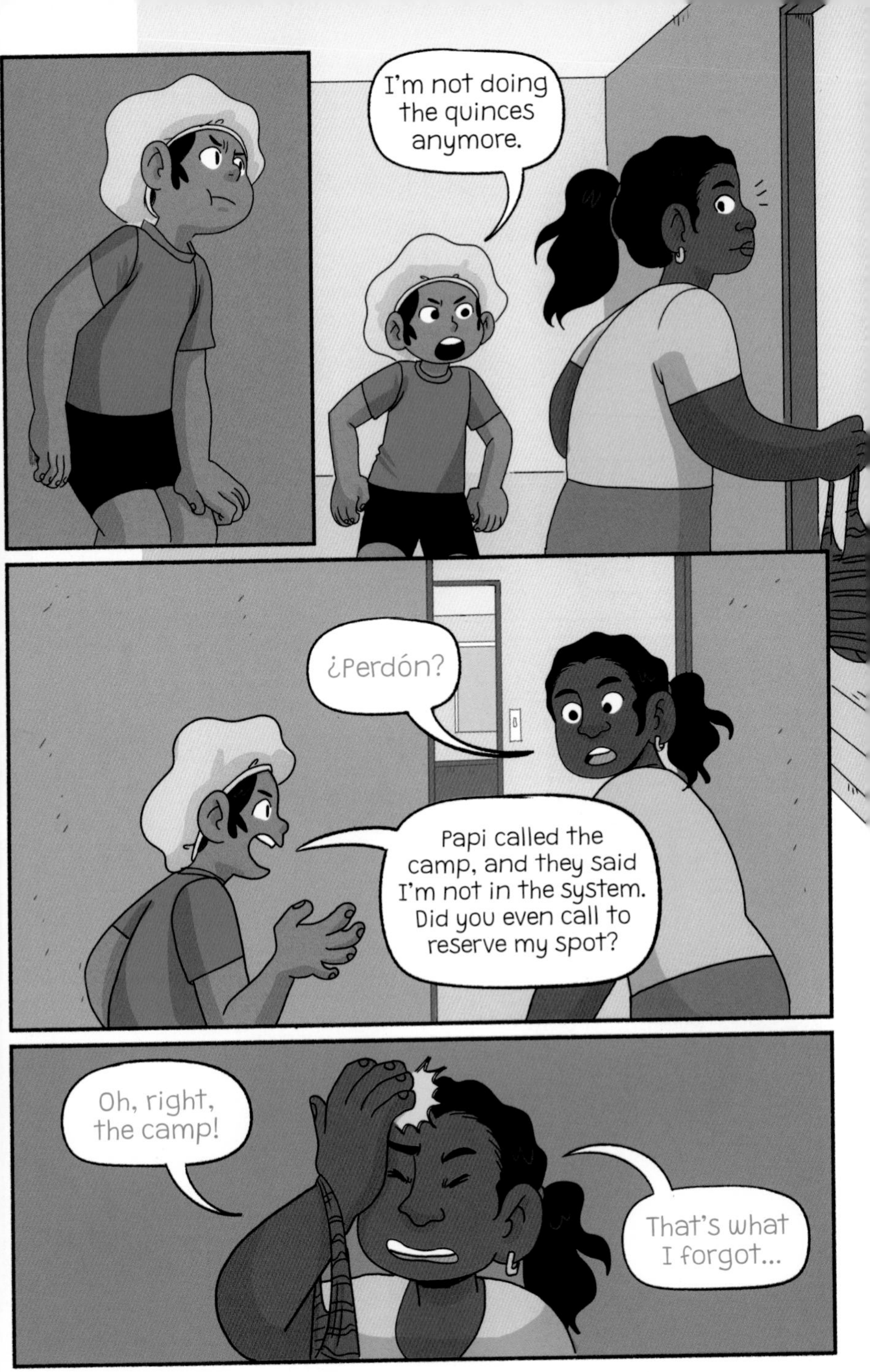
I'm not doing the quinces anymore.
¿Perdón?
Papi called the camp, and they said I'm not in the system. Did you even call to reserve my spot?
Oh, right, the camp!
That's what I forgot...

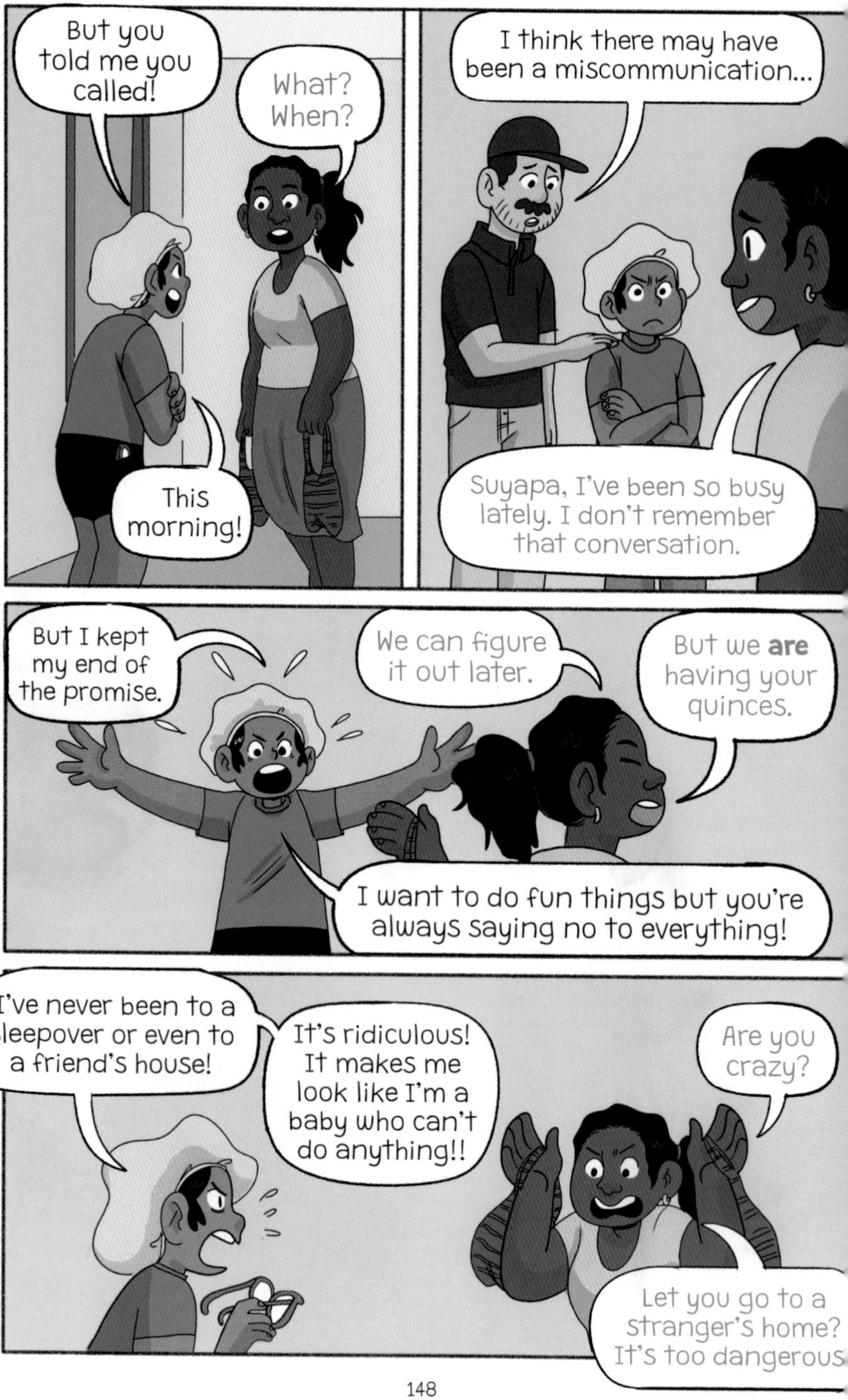
But you told me you called!
What? When?
This morning!
I think there may have been a miscommunication...
Suyapa, I've been so busy lately. I don't remember that conversation.
But I kept my end of the promise.
We can figure it out later.
But we **are** having your quinces.
I want to do fun things but you're always saying no to everything!
I've never been to a sleepover or even to a friend's house!
It's ridiculous! It makes me look like I'm a baby who can't do anything!!
Are you crazy?
Let you go to a stranger's home? It's too dangerous

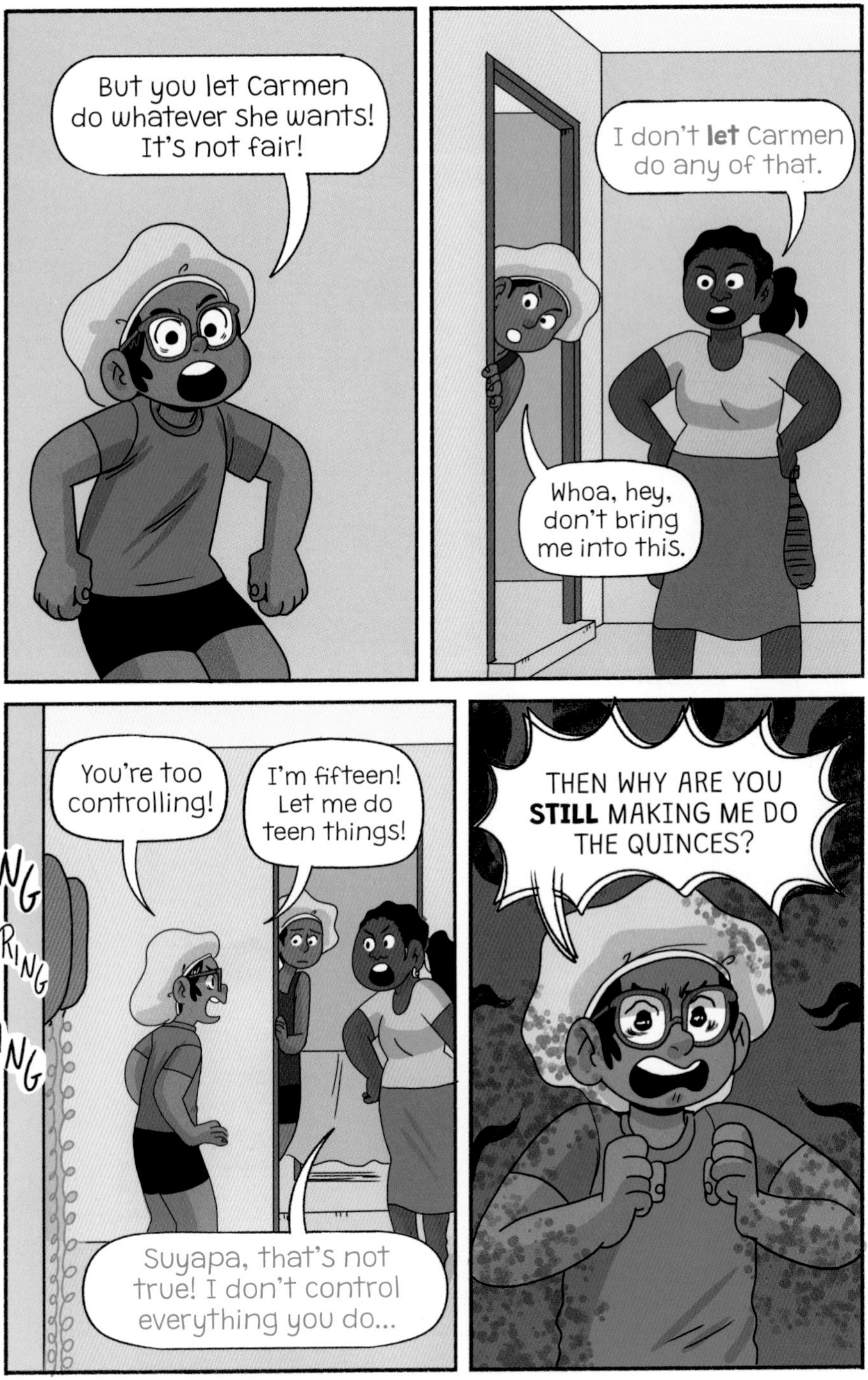
But you let Carmen do whatever she wants! It's not fair!
I don't **let** Carmen do any of that.
Whoa, hey, don't bring me into this.
You're too controlling!
I'm fifteen! Let me do teen things!
NG RING NG
Suyapa, that's not true! I don't control everything you do...
THEN WHY ARE YOU **STILL** MAKING ME DO THE QUINCES?

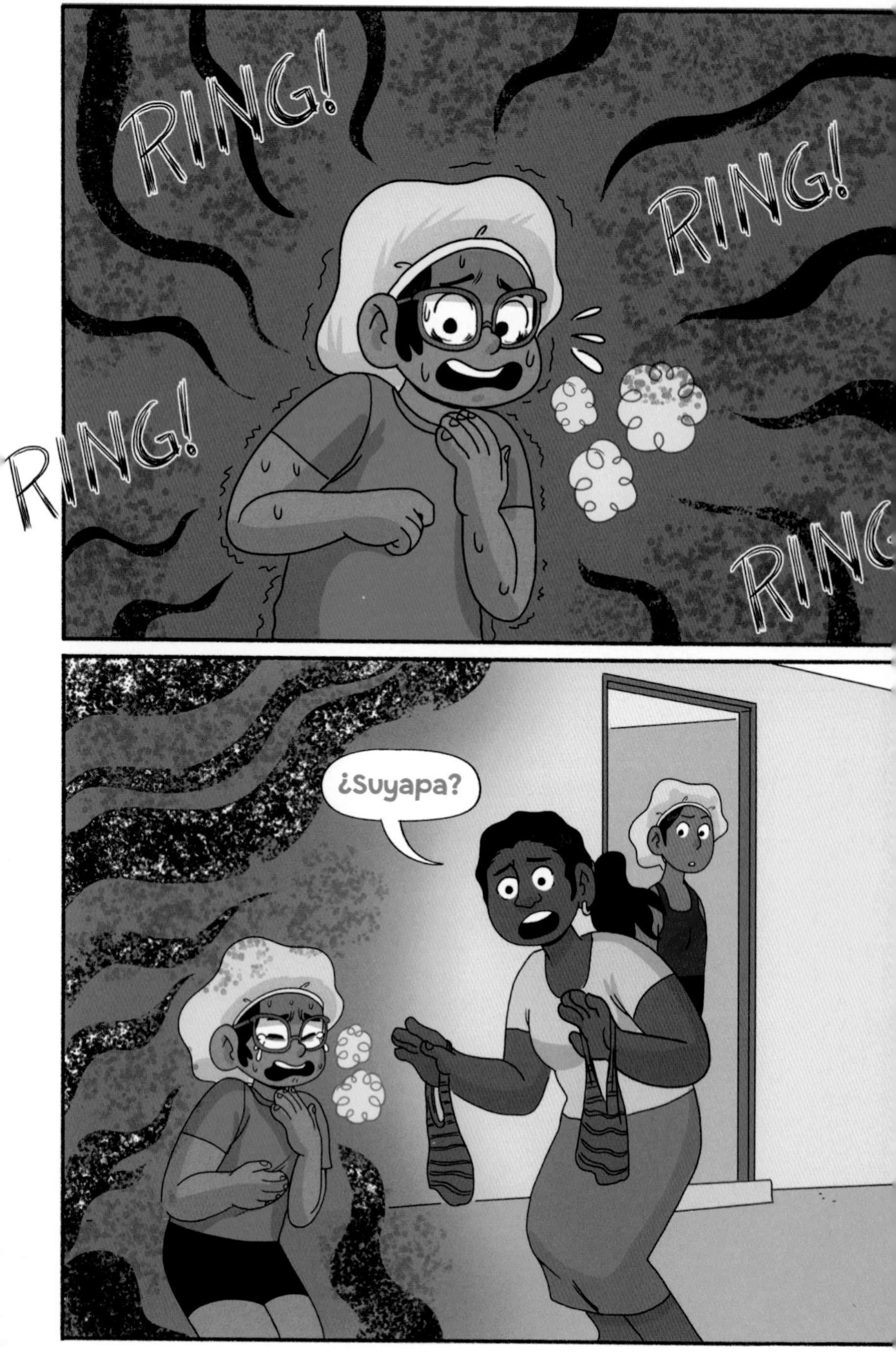
RING!
RING!
RING!
RING
¿Suyapa?

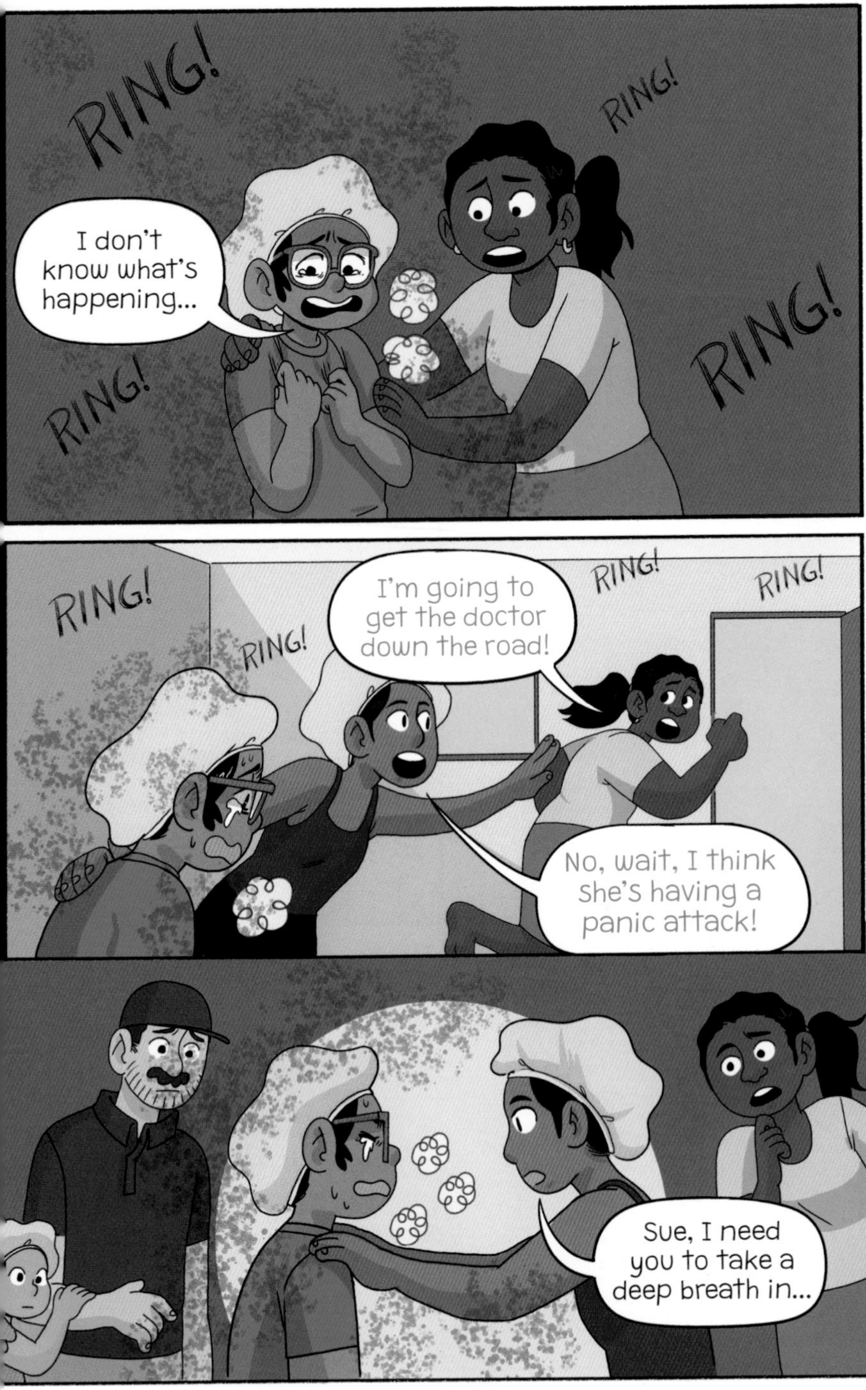
RING!
RING!
I don't know what's happening...
RING!
RING!
RING!
RING!
I'm going to get the doctor down the road!
RING!
RING!
No, wait, I think she's having a panic attack!
Sue, I need you to take a deep breath in...

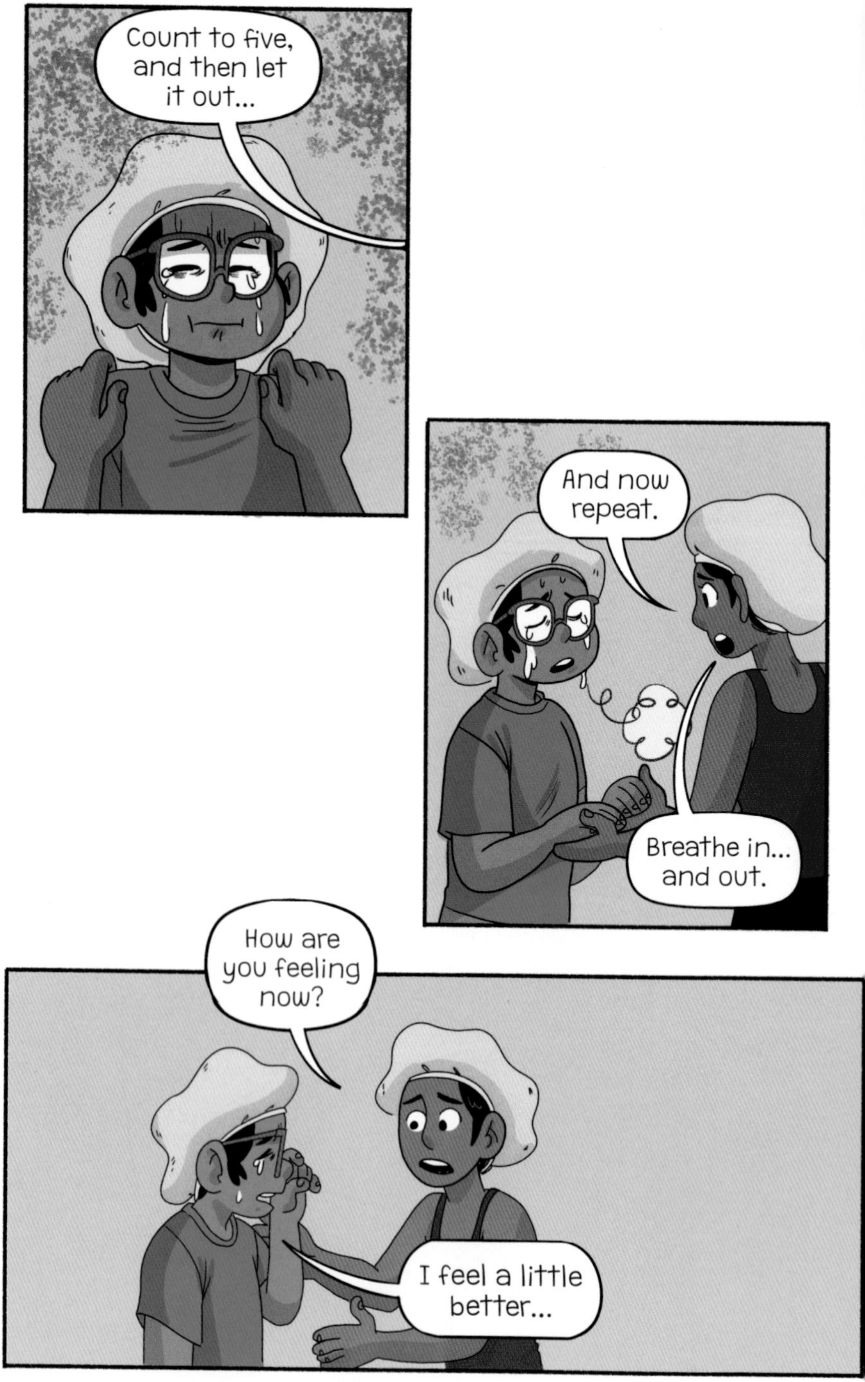
Count to five, and then let it out...
And now repeat.
Breathe in... and out.
How are you feeling now?
I feel a little better...

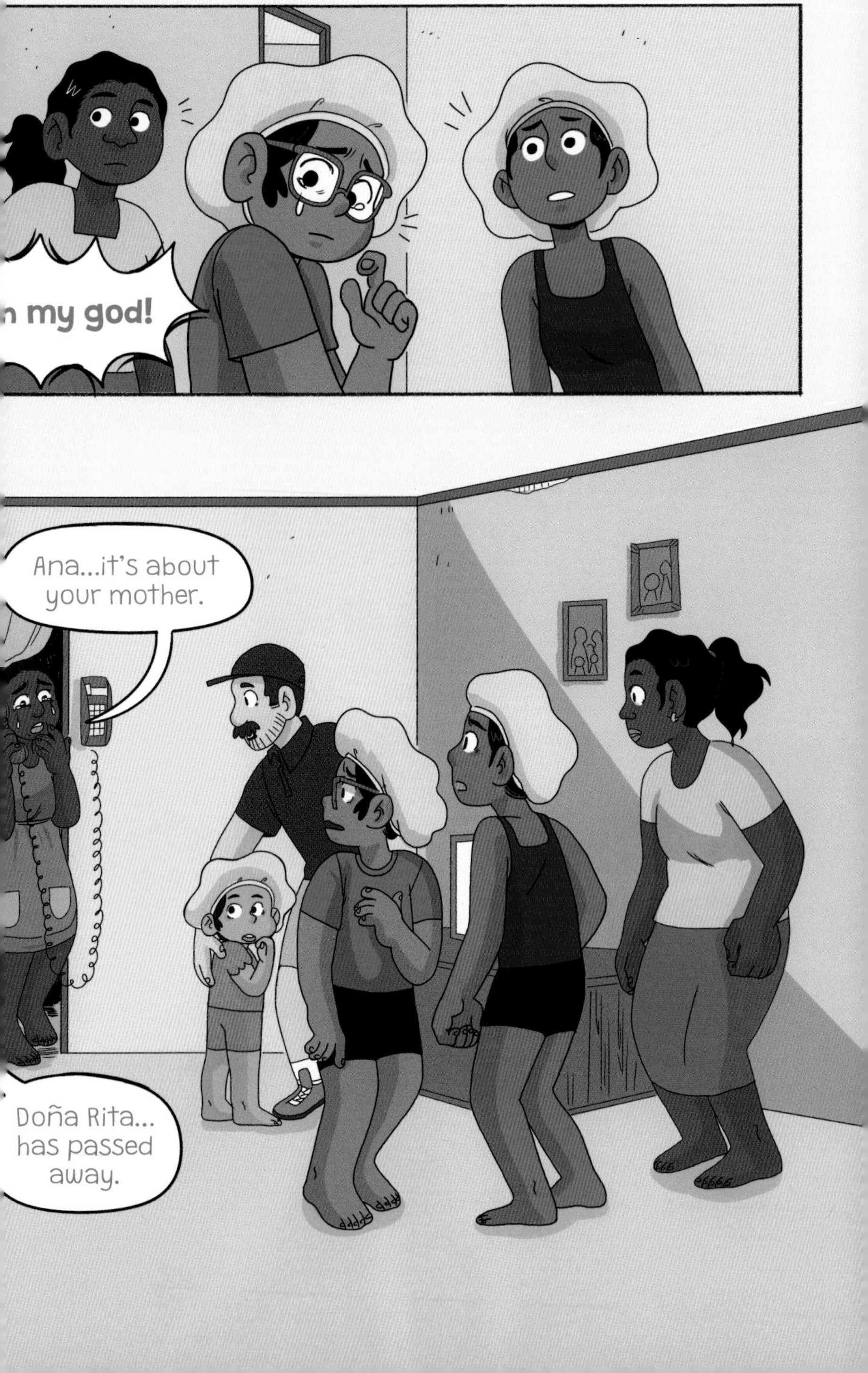

n my god!
Ana...it's about your mother.
Doña Rita... has passed away.

CHAPTER SIX

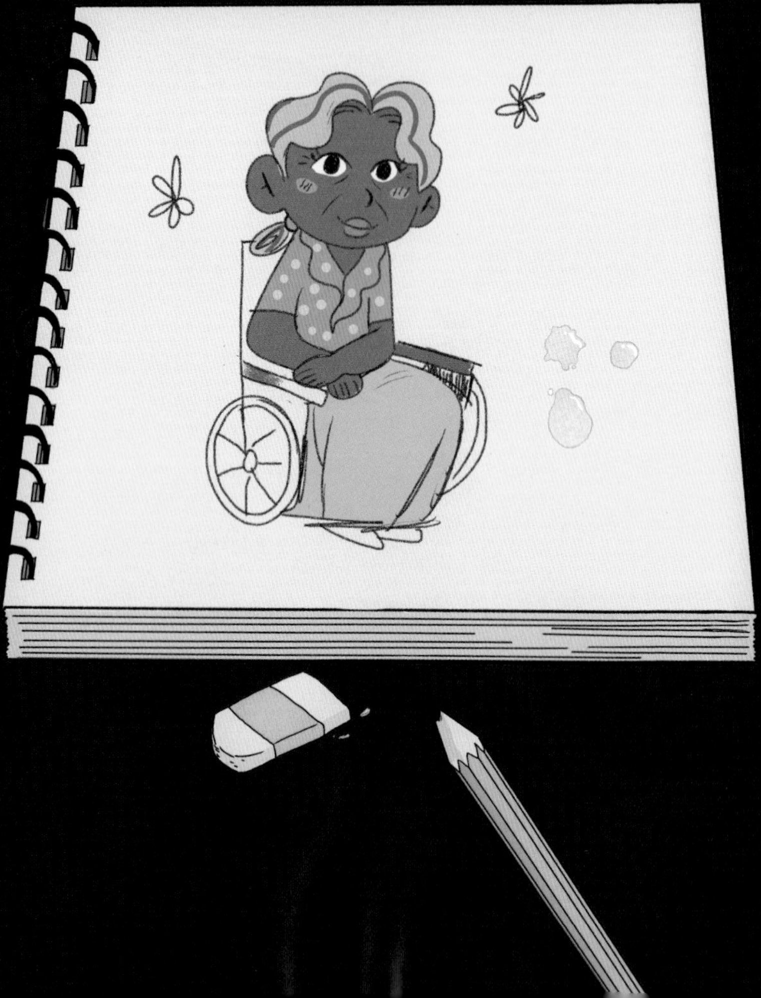

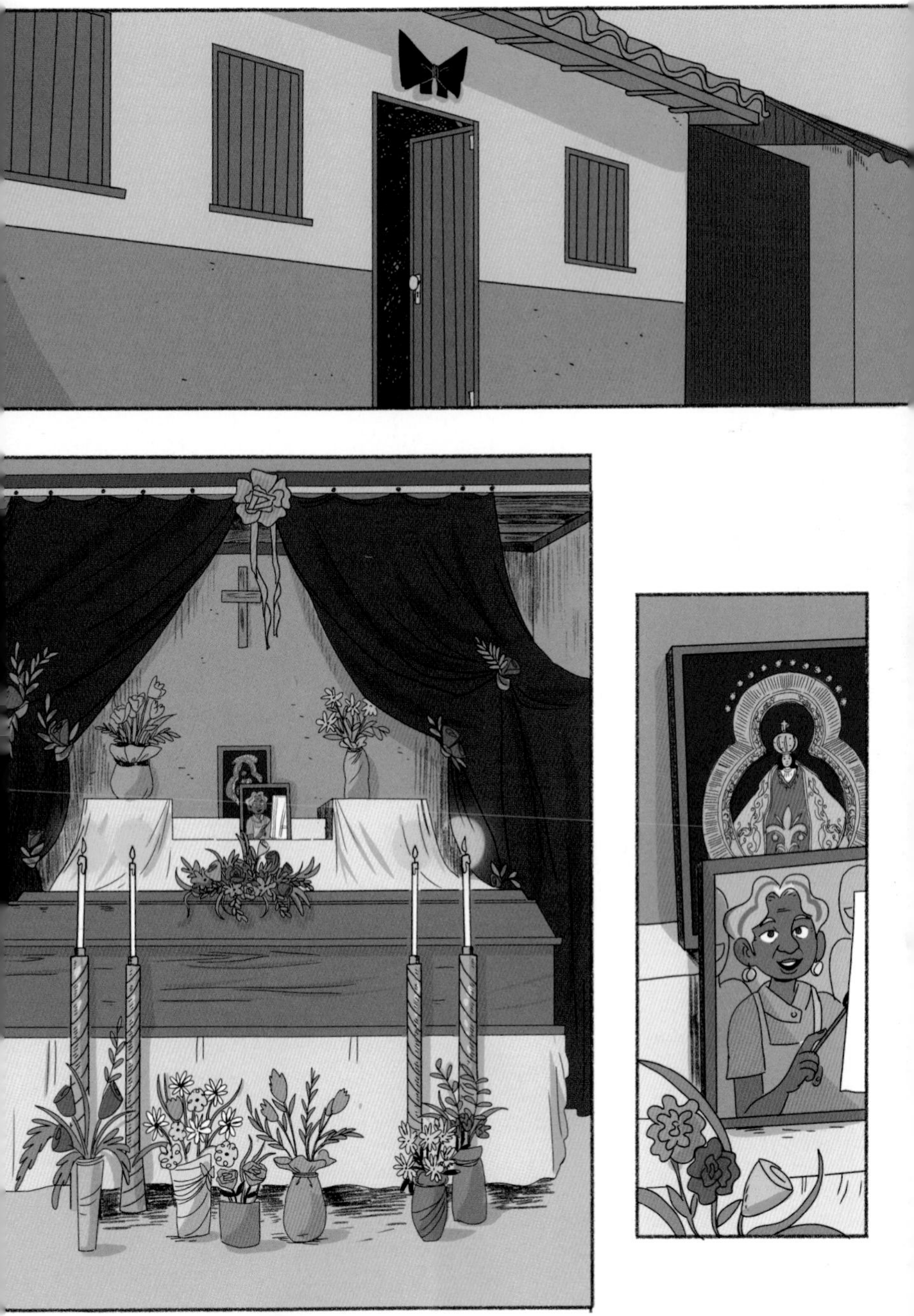

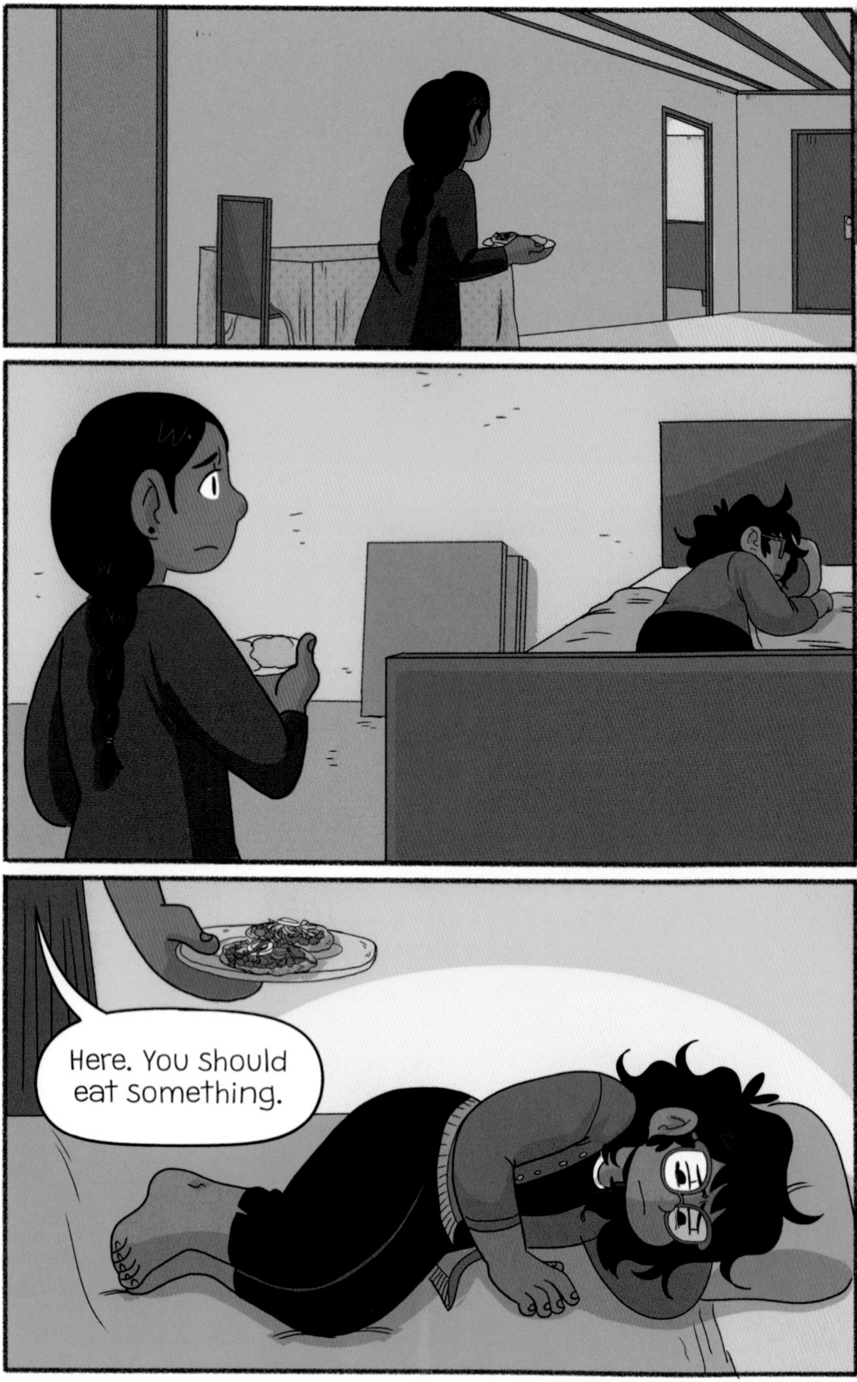
Here. You should eat something.

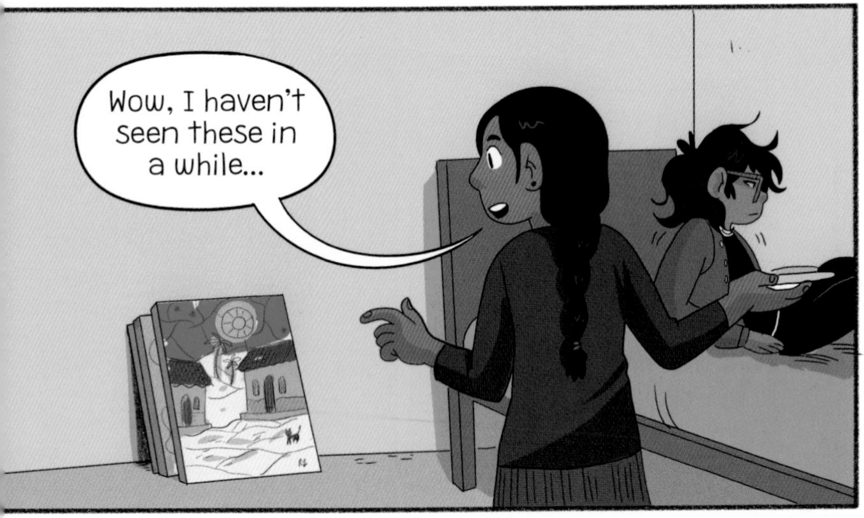
Wow, I haven't seen these in a while...

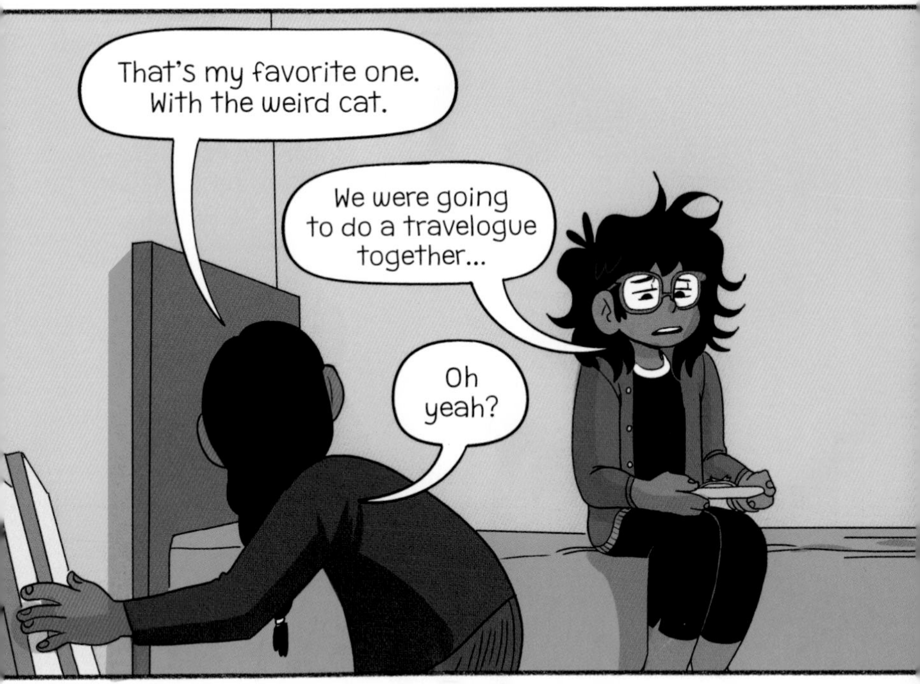
That's my favorite one. With the weird cat.
We were going to do a travelogue together...
Oh yeah?

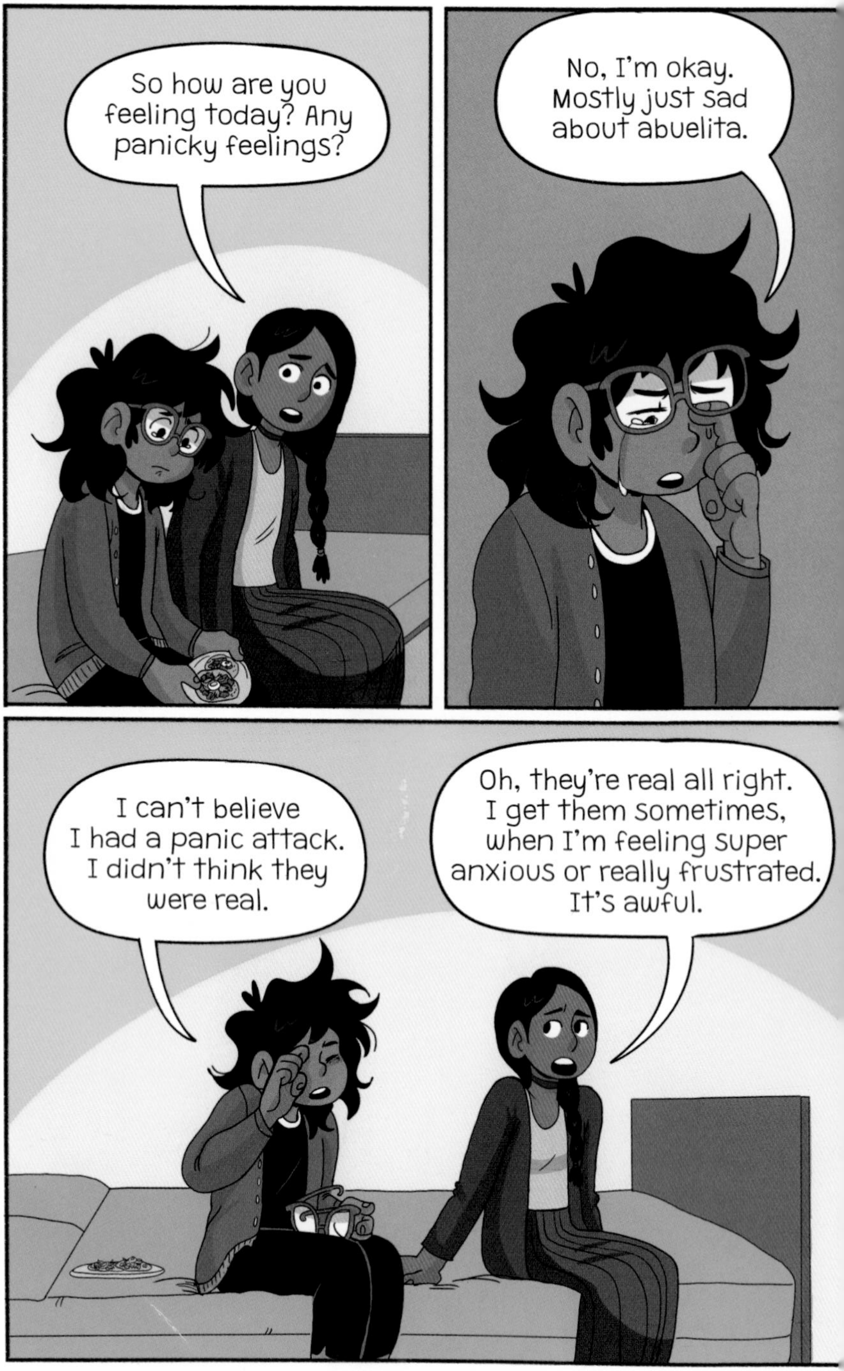
So how are you feeling today? Any panicky feelings?
No, I'm okay. Mostly just sad about abuelita.
I can't believe I had a panic attack. I didn't think they were real.
Oh, they're real all right. I get them sometimes, when I'm feeling super anxious or really frustrated. It's awful.

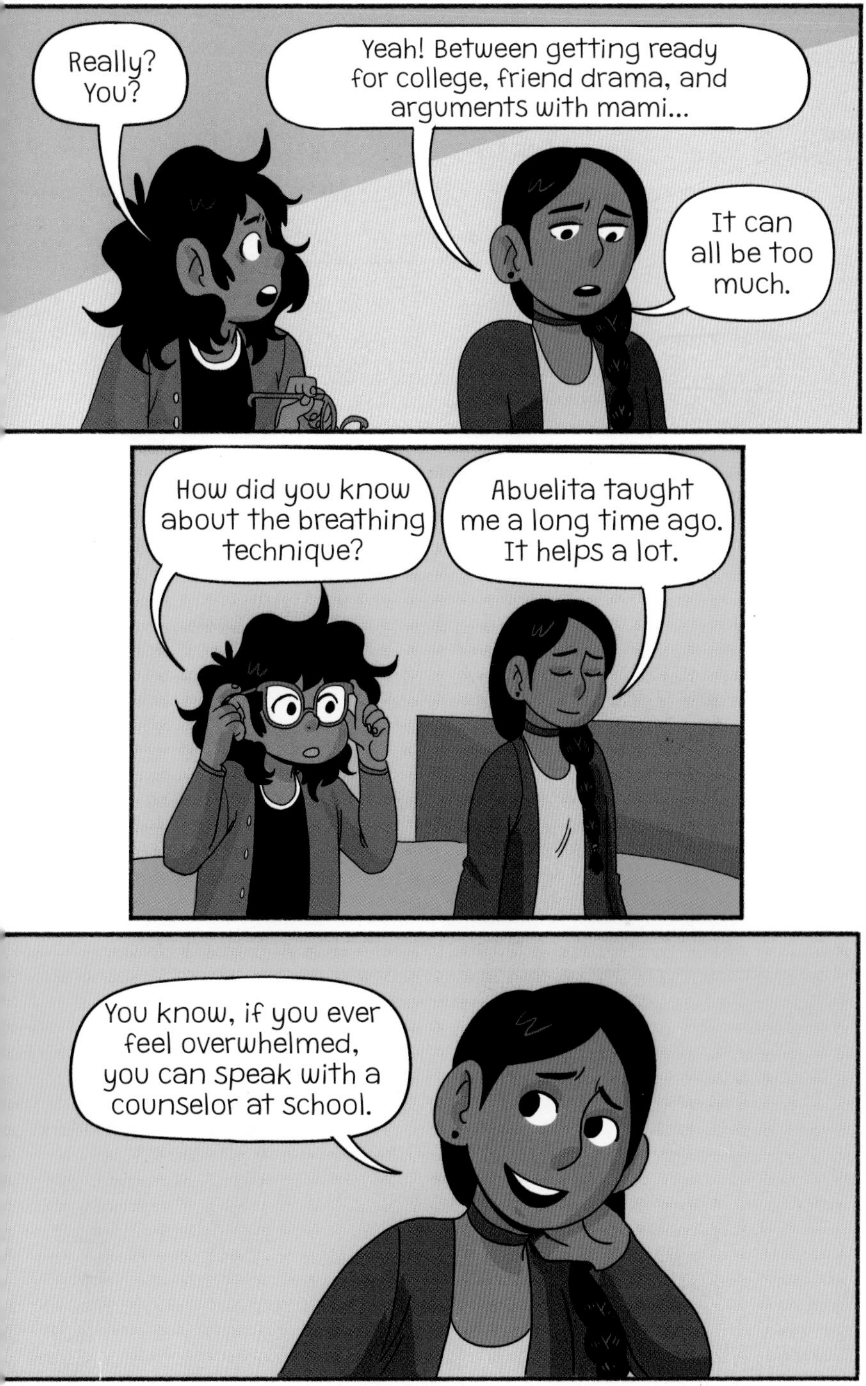
Really? You?
Yeah! Between getting ready for college, friend drama, and arguments with mami...
It can all be too much.
How did you know about the breathing technique?
Abuelita taught me a long time ago. It helps a lot.
You know, if you ever feel overwhelmed, you can speak with a counselor at school.

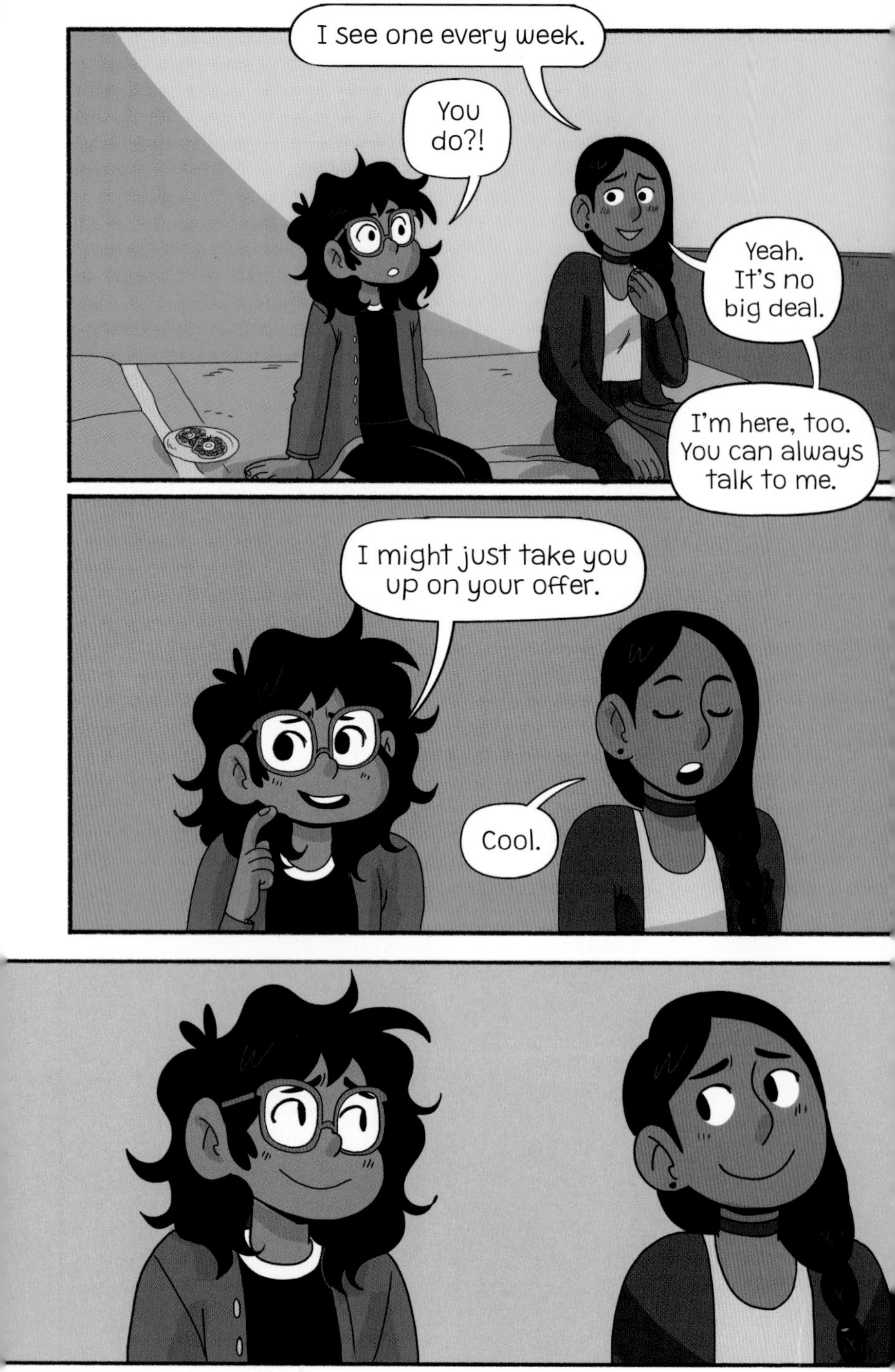
I see one every week.
You do?!
Yeah. It's no big deal.
I'm here, too. You can always talk to me.
I might just take you up on your offer.
Cool.

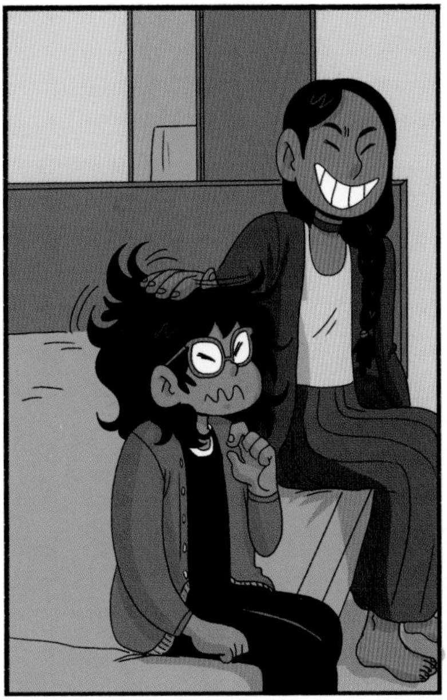

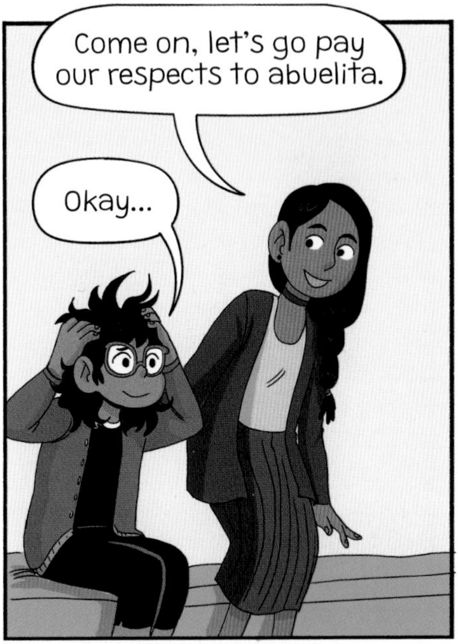
Come on, let's go pay our respects to abuelita.
Okay...

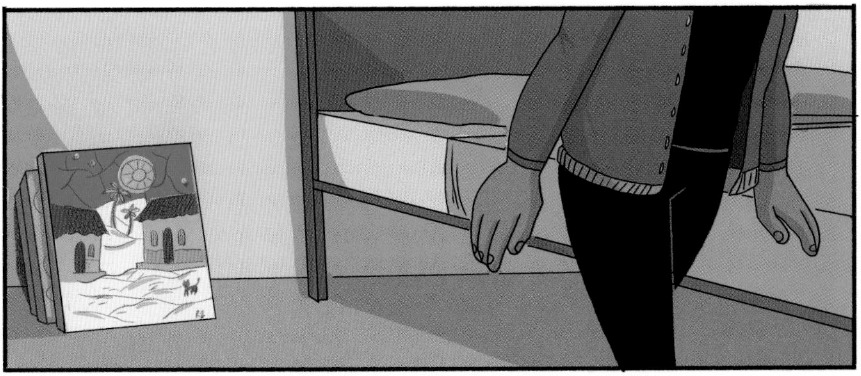

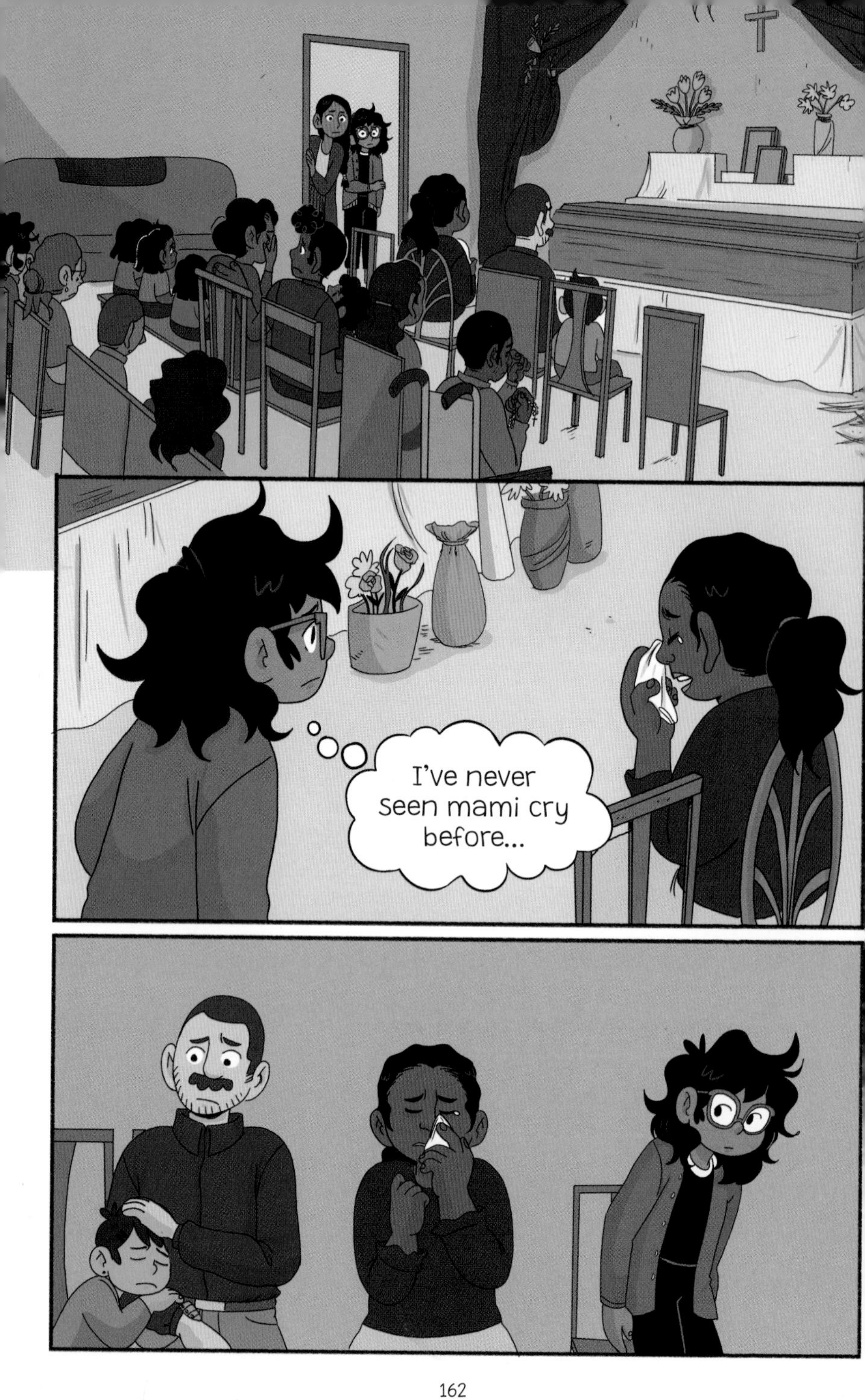
I've never seen mami cry before...

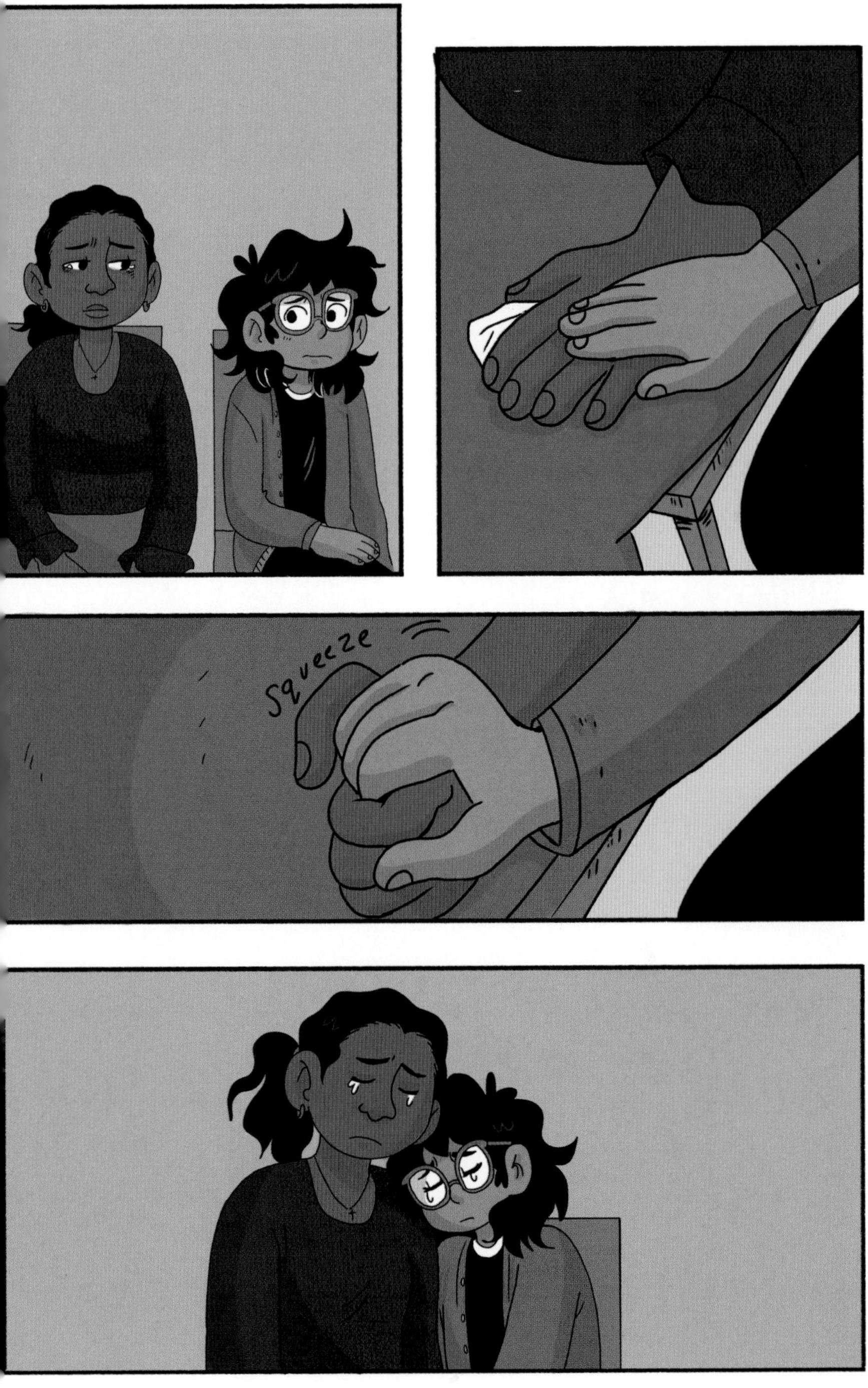
squeeze

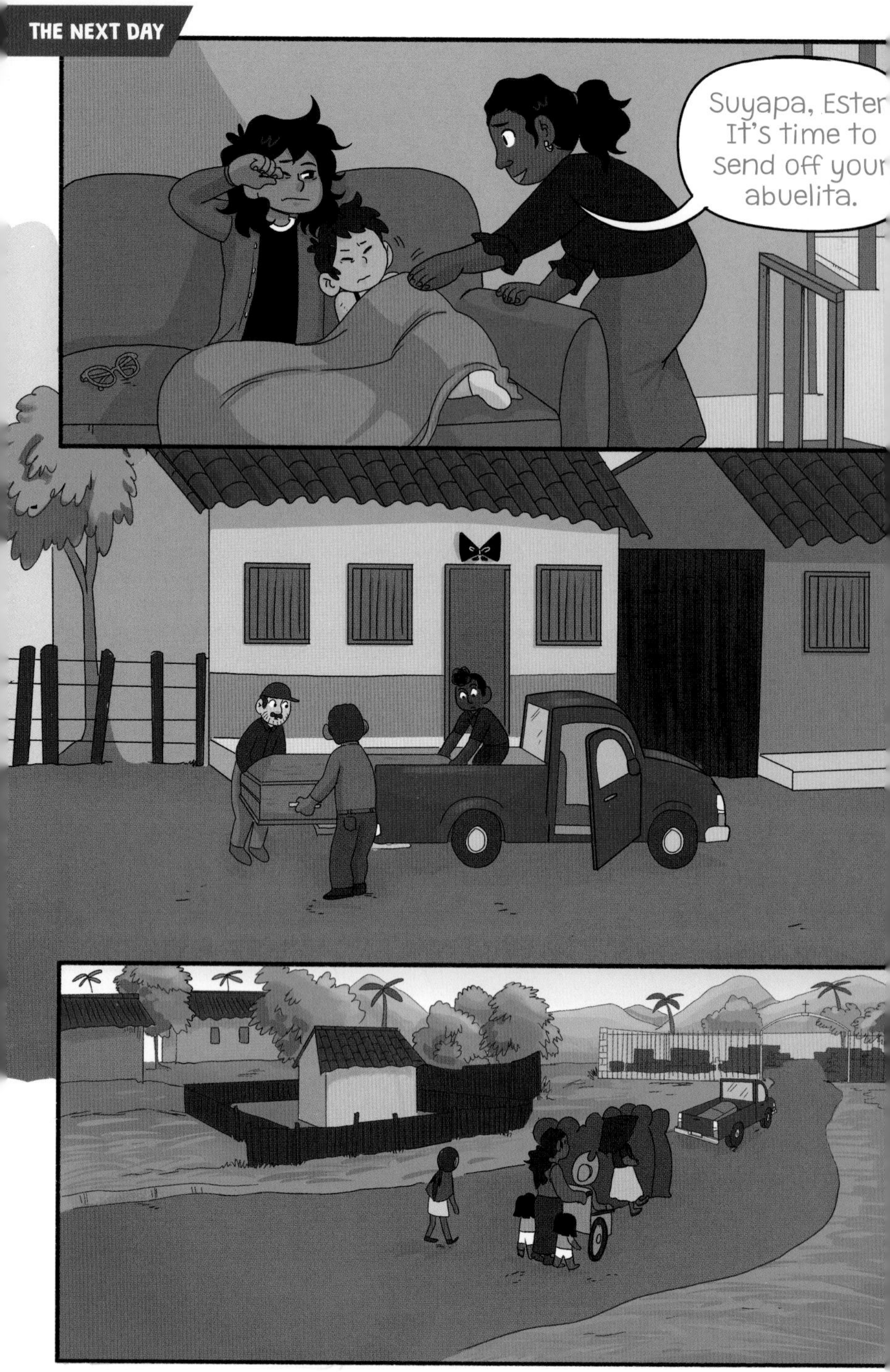
THE NEXT DAY
Suyapa, Ester It's time to send off your abuelita.

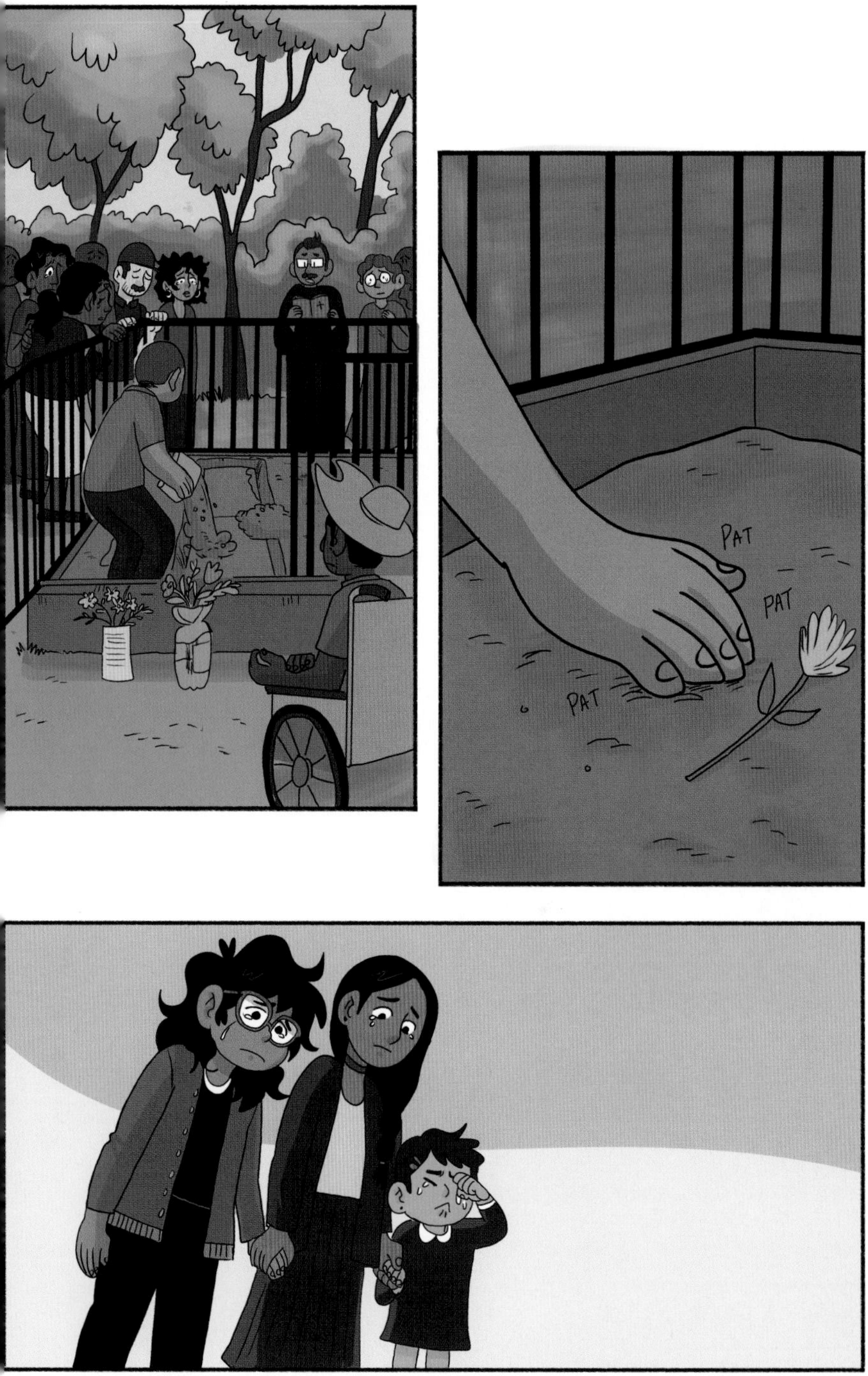
PAT
PAT
PAT

CHAPTER SEVEN

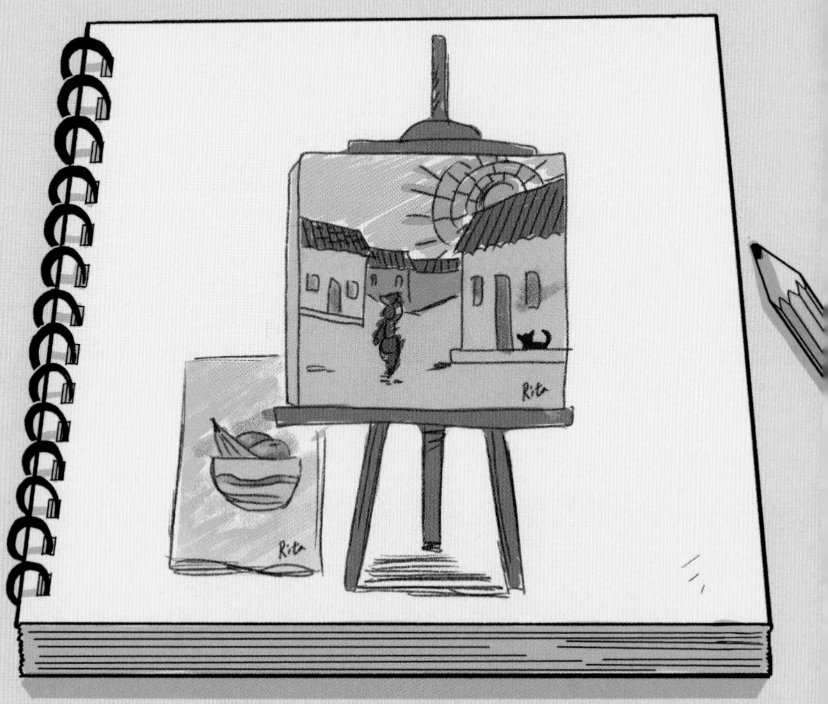
Rita
Rita

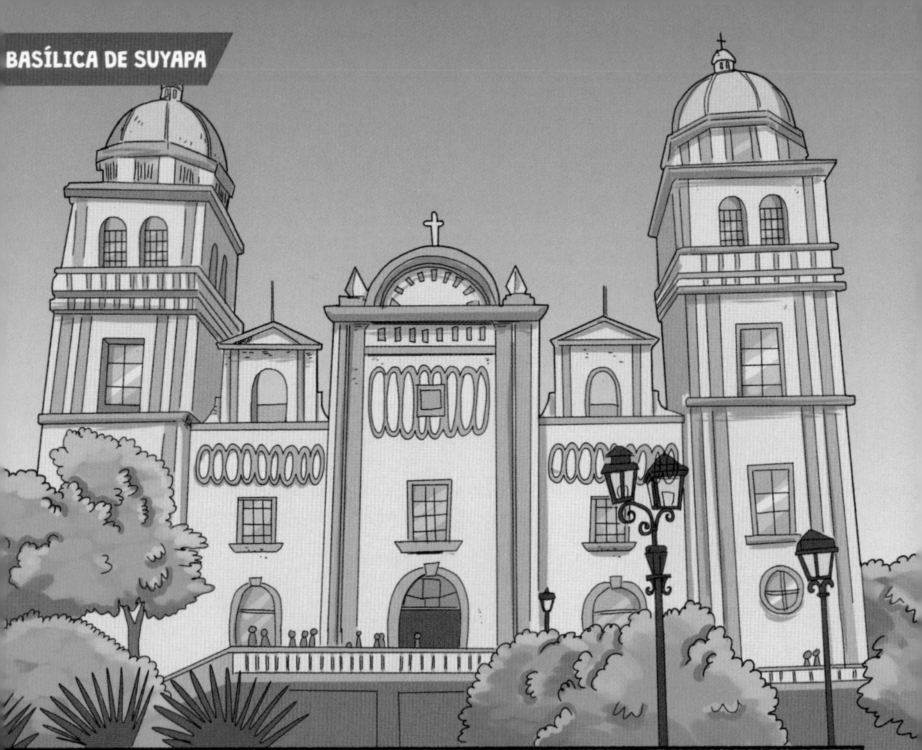
BASÍLICA DE SUYAPA

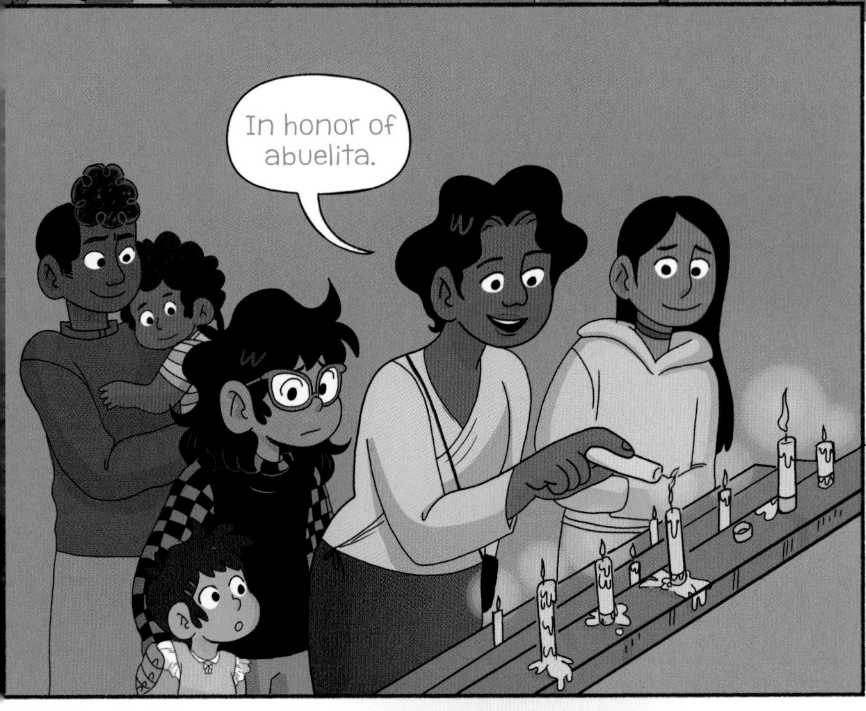
In honor of abuelita.

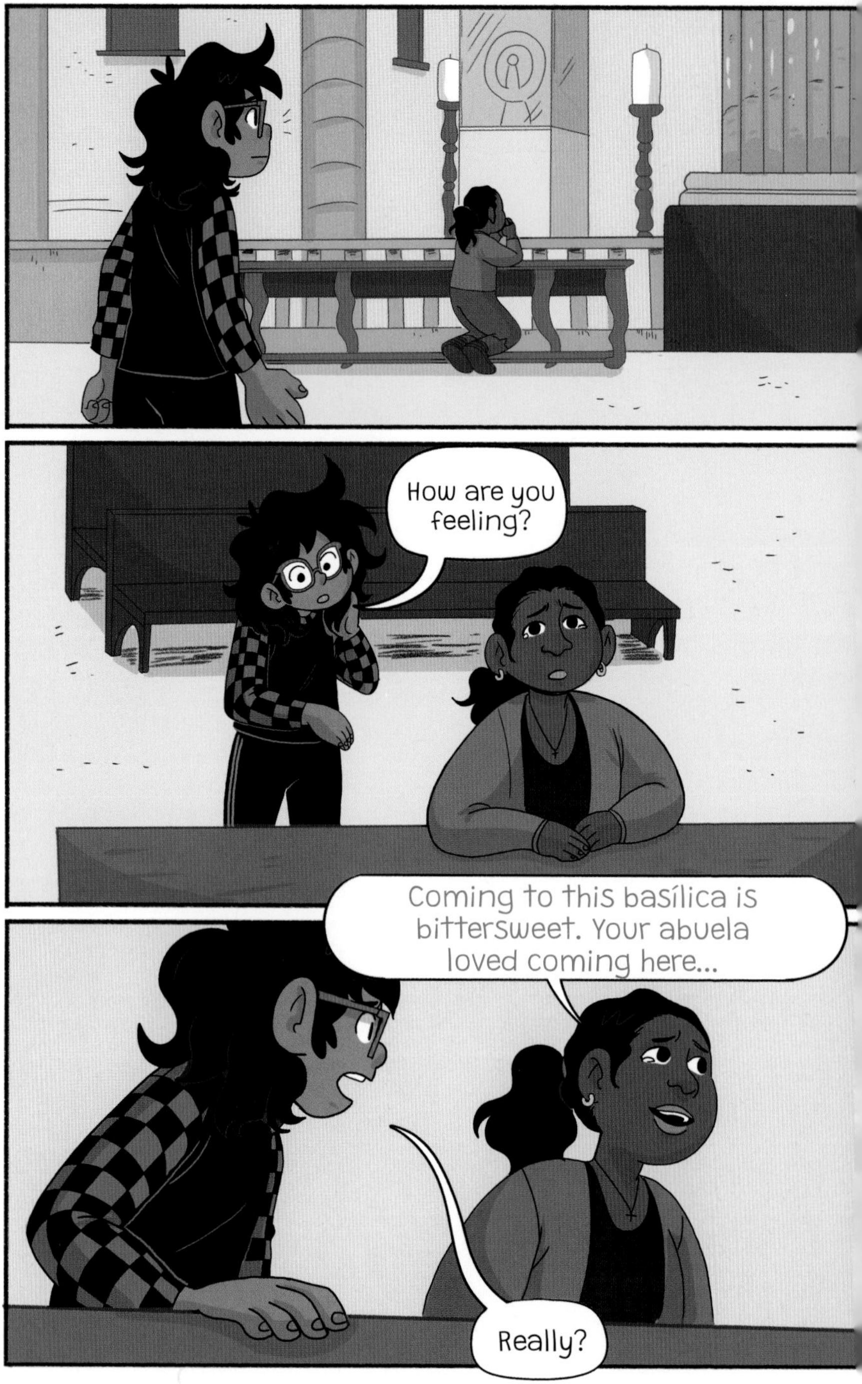
How are you feeling?
Coming to this basílica is bittersweet. Your abuela loved coming here...
Really?

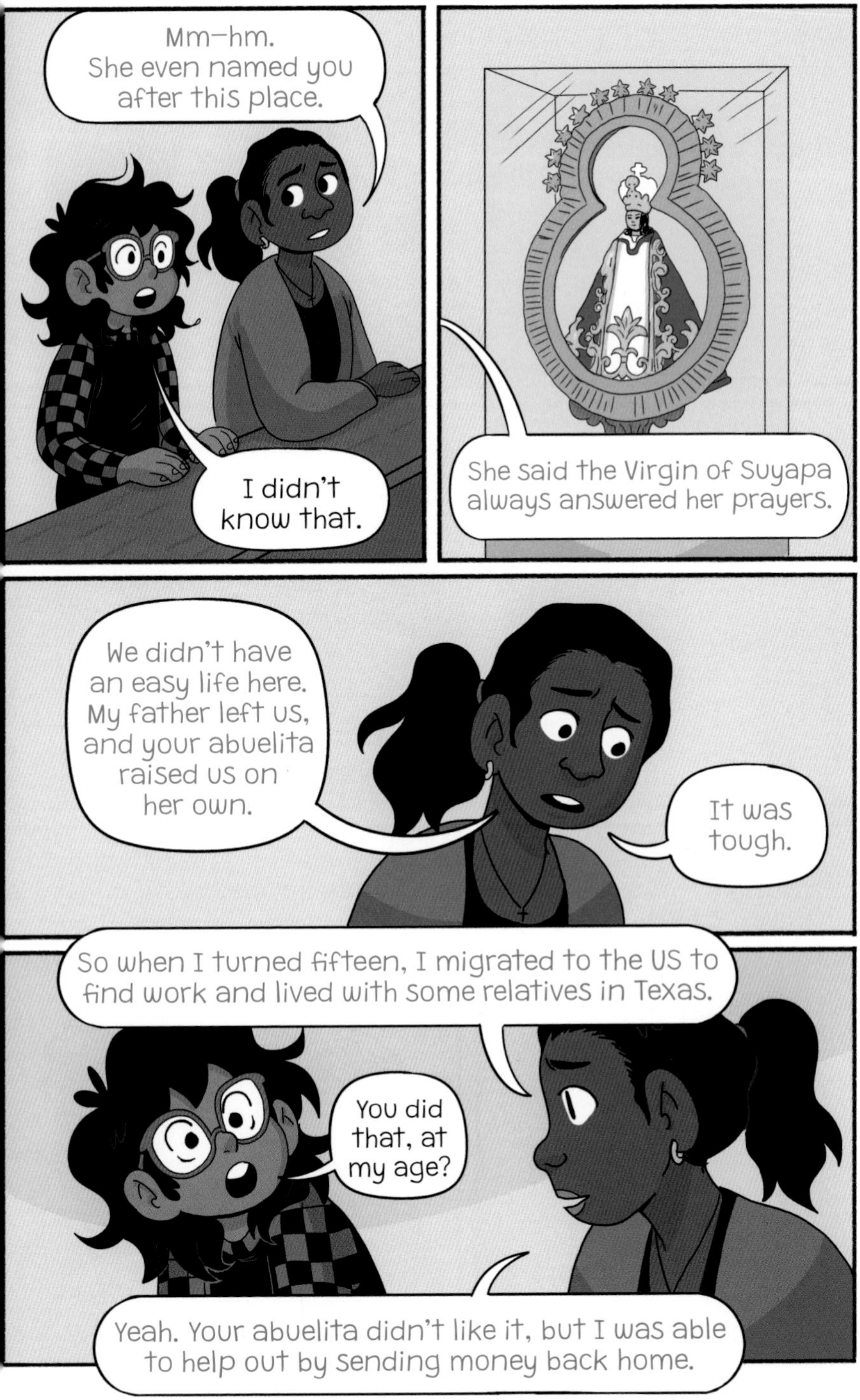
Mm–hm. She even named you after this place.
I didn't know that.
She said the Virgin of Suyapa always answered her prayers.
We didn't have an easy life here. My father left us, and your abuelita raised us on her own.
It was tough.
So when I turned fifteen, I migrated to the US to find work and lived with some relatives in Texas.
You did that, at my age?
Yeah. Your abuelita didn't like it, but I was able to help out by sending money back home.

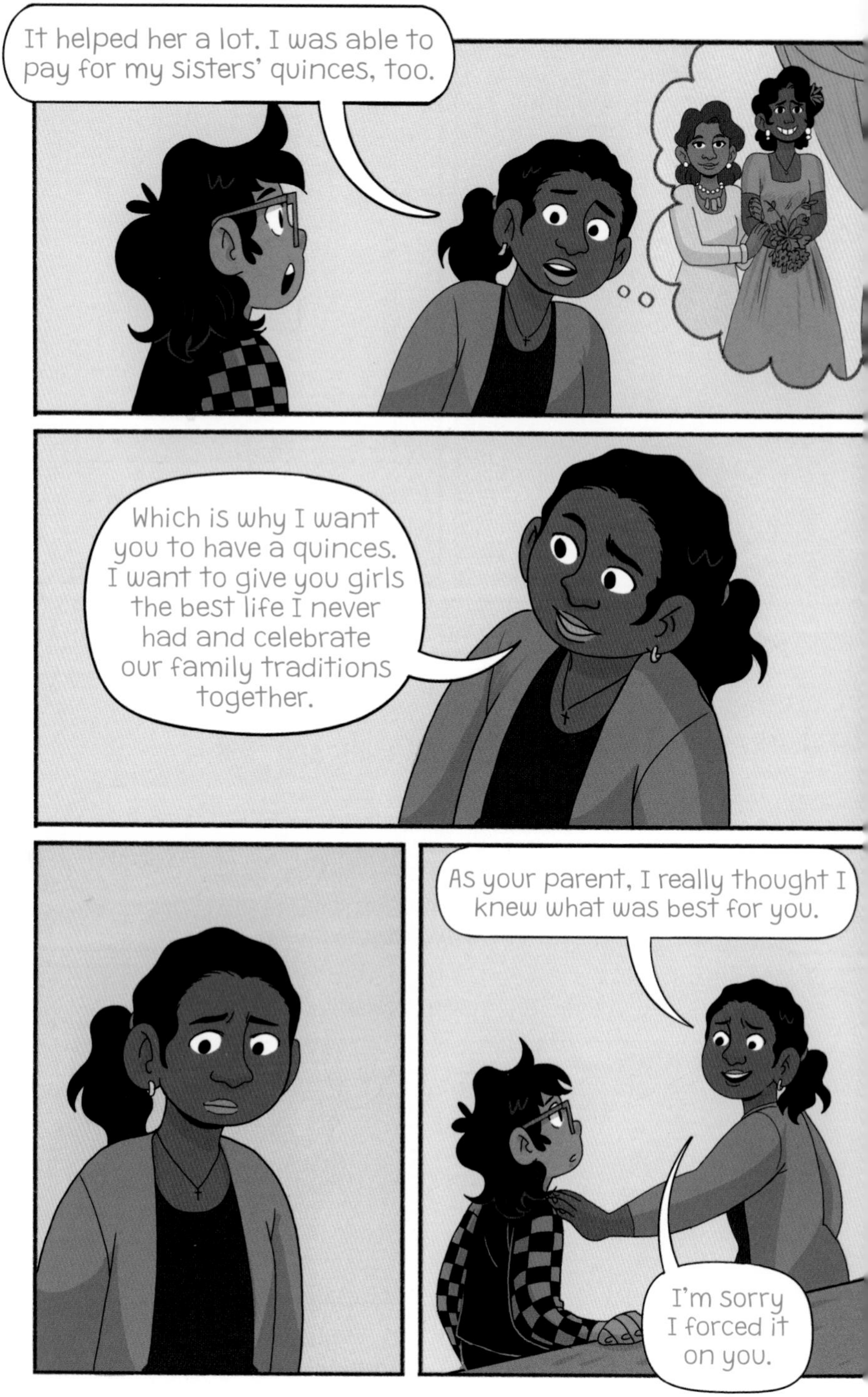
It helped her a lot. I was able to pay for my sisters' quinces, too.
Which is why I want you to have a quinces. I want to give you girls the best life I never had and celebrate our family traditions together.
As your parent, I really thought I knew what was best for you.
I'm sorry I forced it on you.

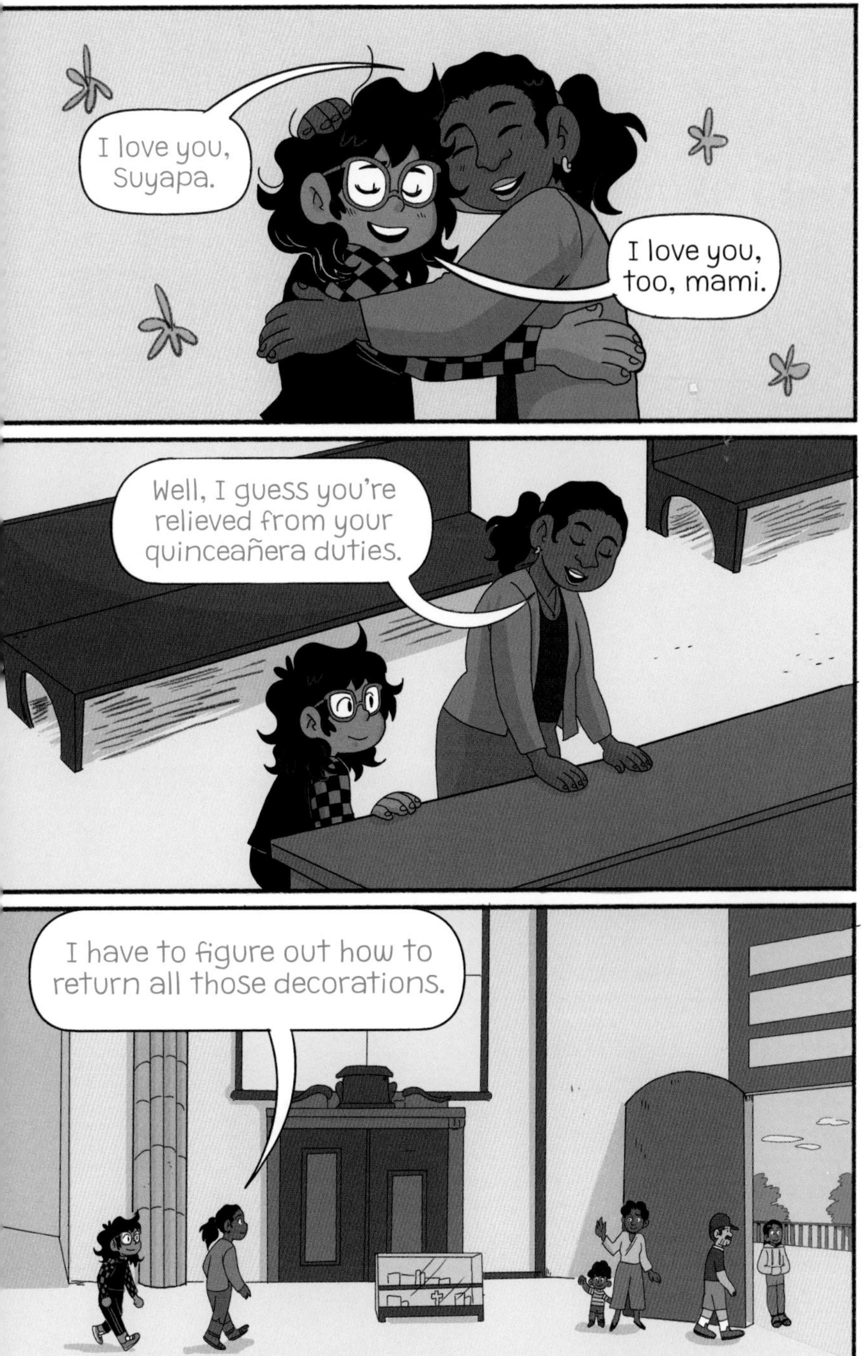

I love you, Suyapa.
I love you, too, mami.
Well, I guess you're relieved from your quinceañera duties.
I have to figure out how to return all those decorations.

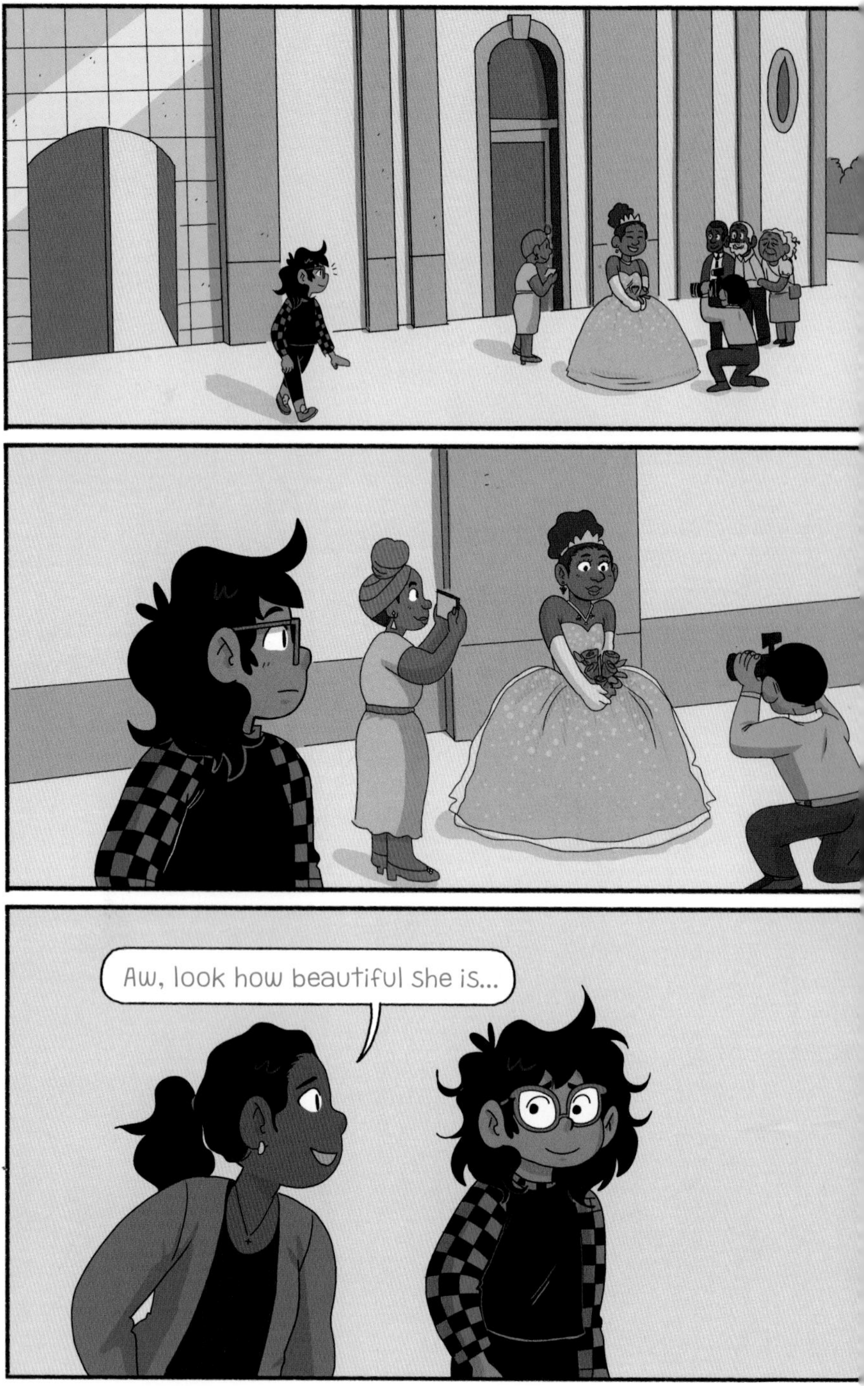

Aw, look how beautiful she is...

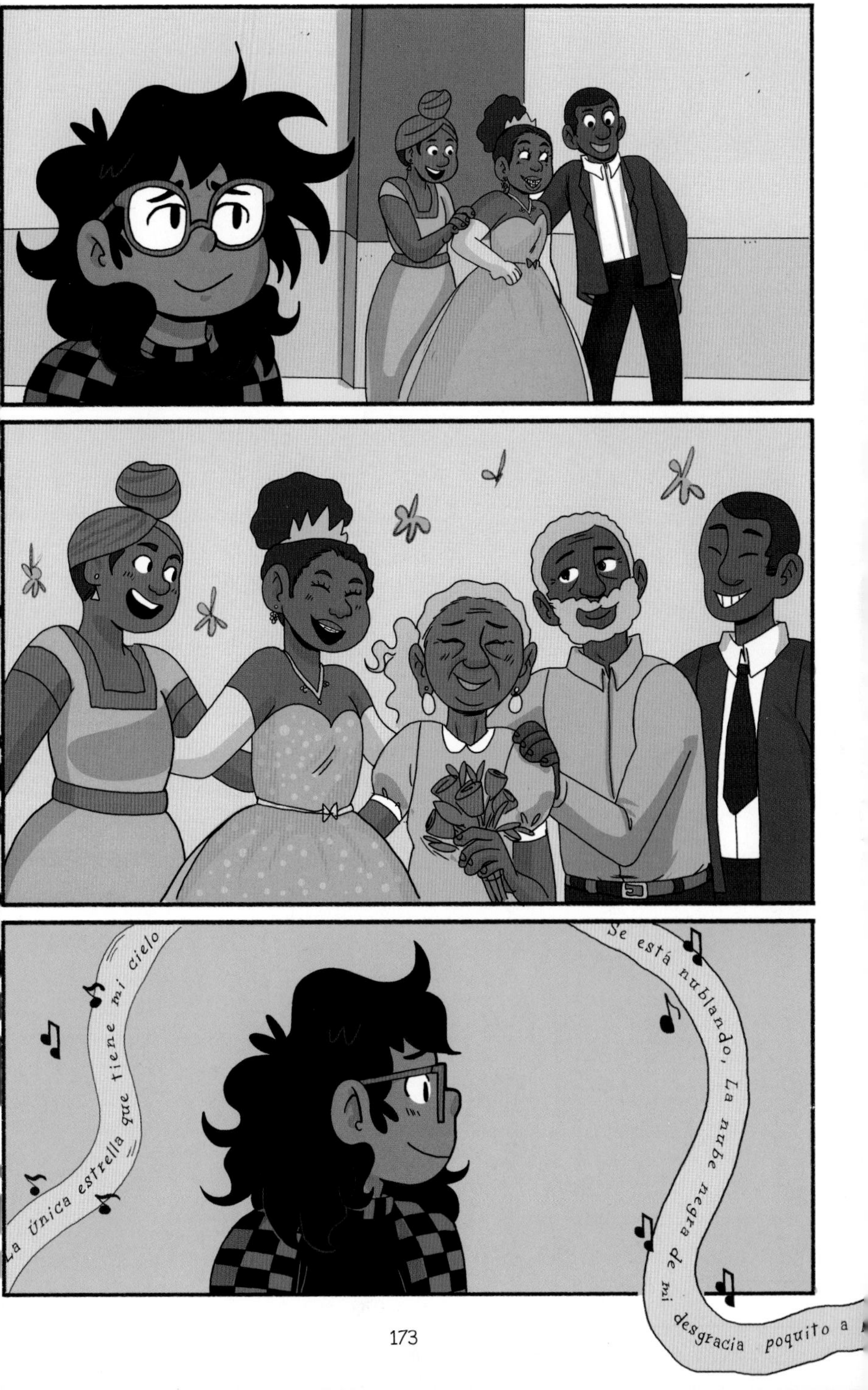

La única estrella que tiene mi cielo
Se está nublando, La nube negra de mi desgracia poquito a

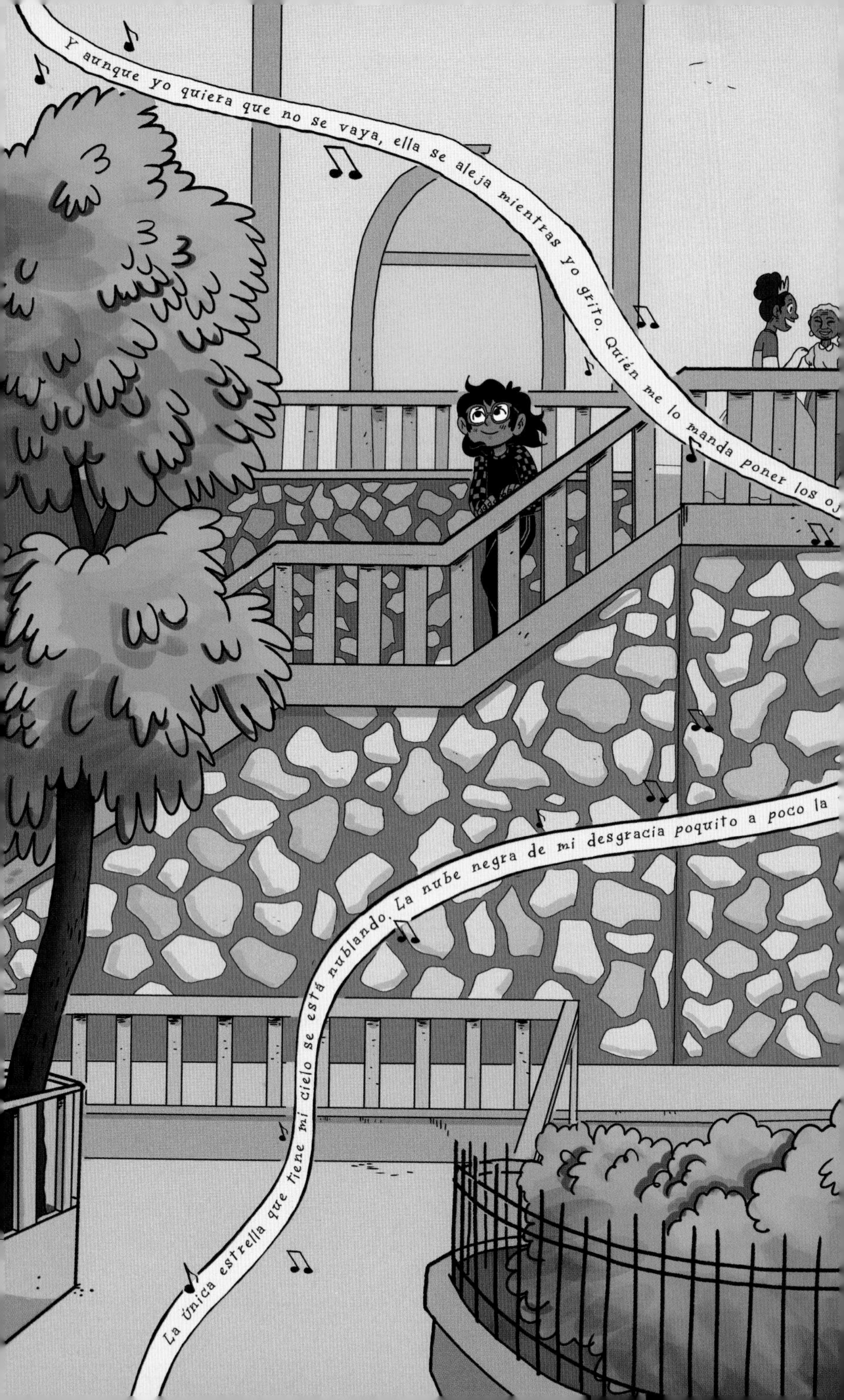
Y aunque yo quiera que no se vaya, ella se aleja mientras yo grito. Quién me lo manda poner los oj
La única estrella que tiene mi cielo se está nublando. La nube negra de mi desgracia poquito a poco la

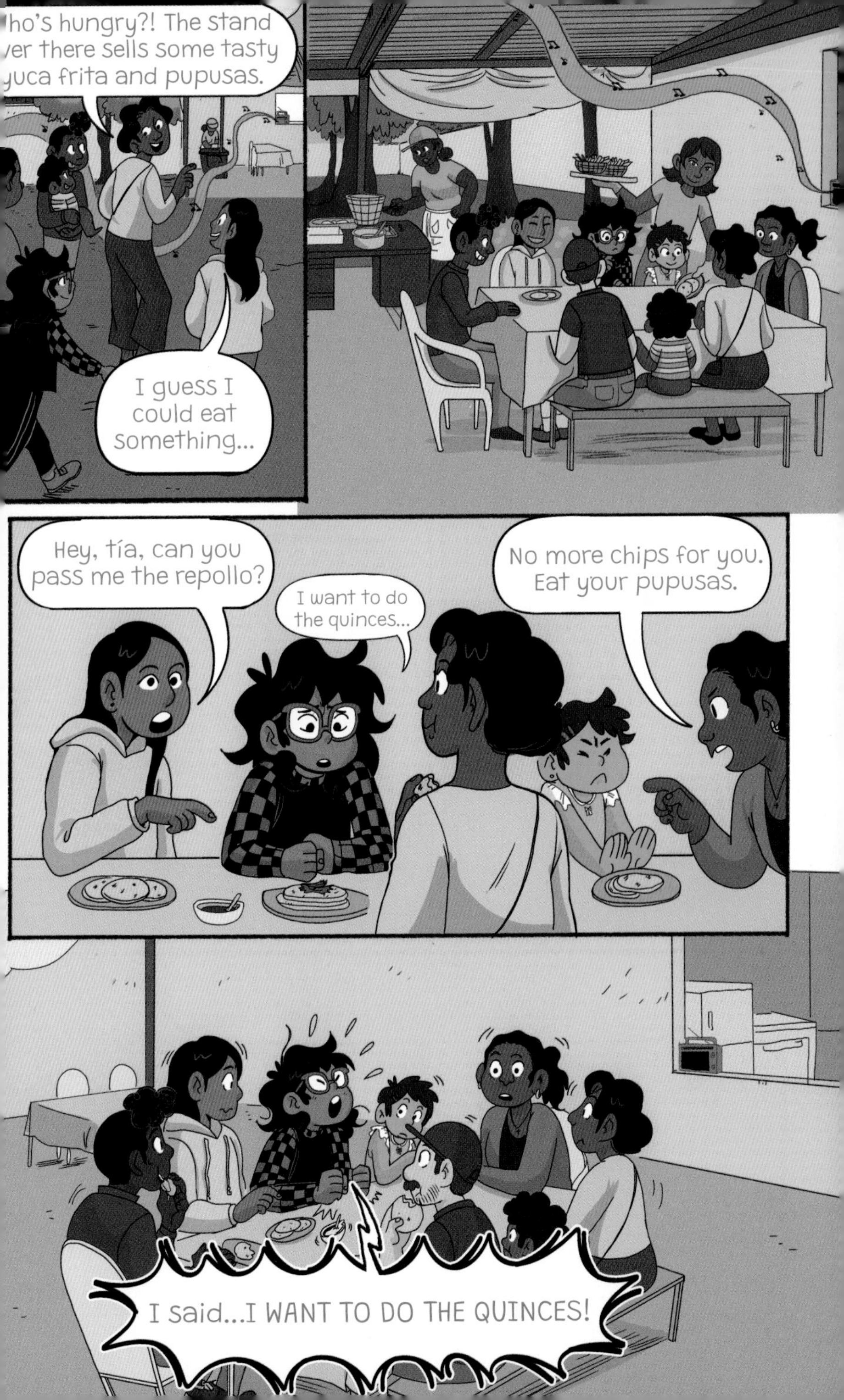
ho's hungry?! The stand
er there sells some tasty
uca frita and pupusas.
I guess I could eat something...
Hey, tía, can you pass me the repollo?
I want to do the quinces...
No more chips for you. Eat your pupusas.
I said...I WANT TO DO THE QUINCES!

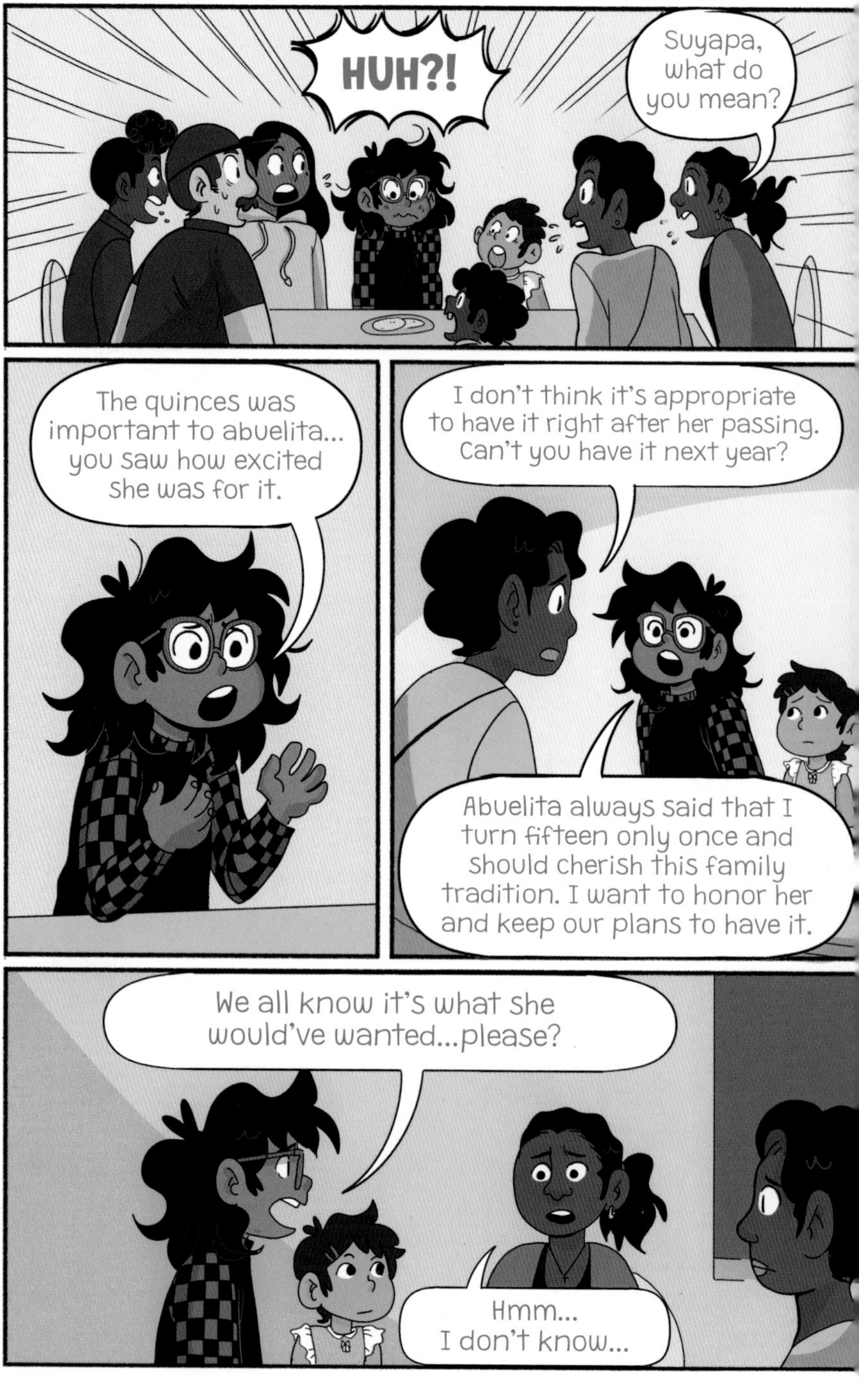
HUH?!
Suyapa, what do you mean?
The quinces was important to abuelita... you saw how excited she was for it.
I don't think it's appropriate to have it right after her passing. Can't you have it next year?
Abuelita always said that I turn fifteen only once and should cherish this family tradition. I want to honor her and keep our plans to have it.
We all know it's what she would've wanted...please?
Hmm... I don't know...

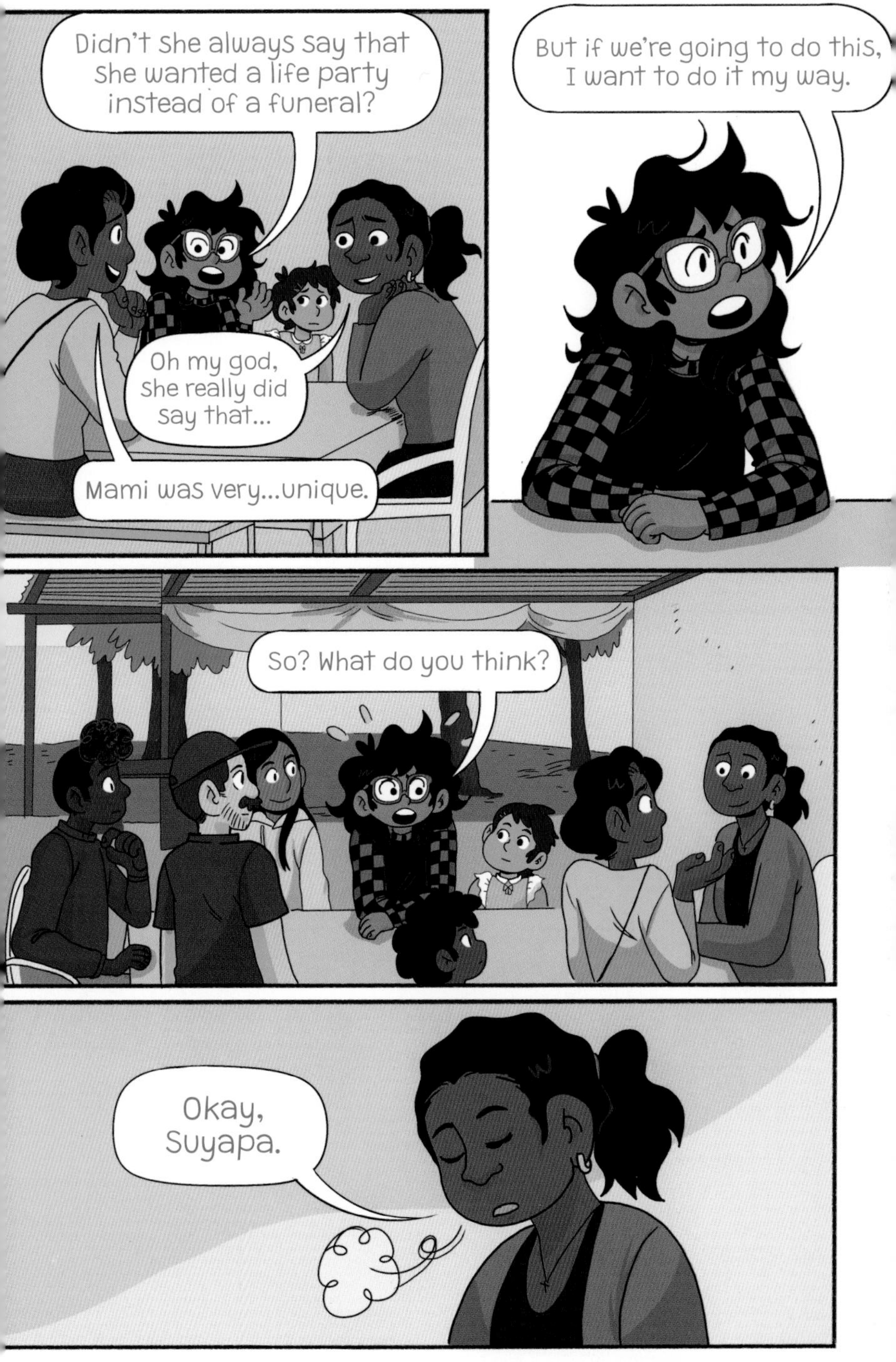
Didn't she always say that she wanted a life party instead of a funeral?
Oh my god, she really did say that...
Mami was very...unique.
But if we're going to do this, I want to do it my way.
So? What do you think?
Okay, Suyapa.

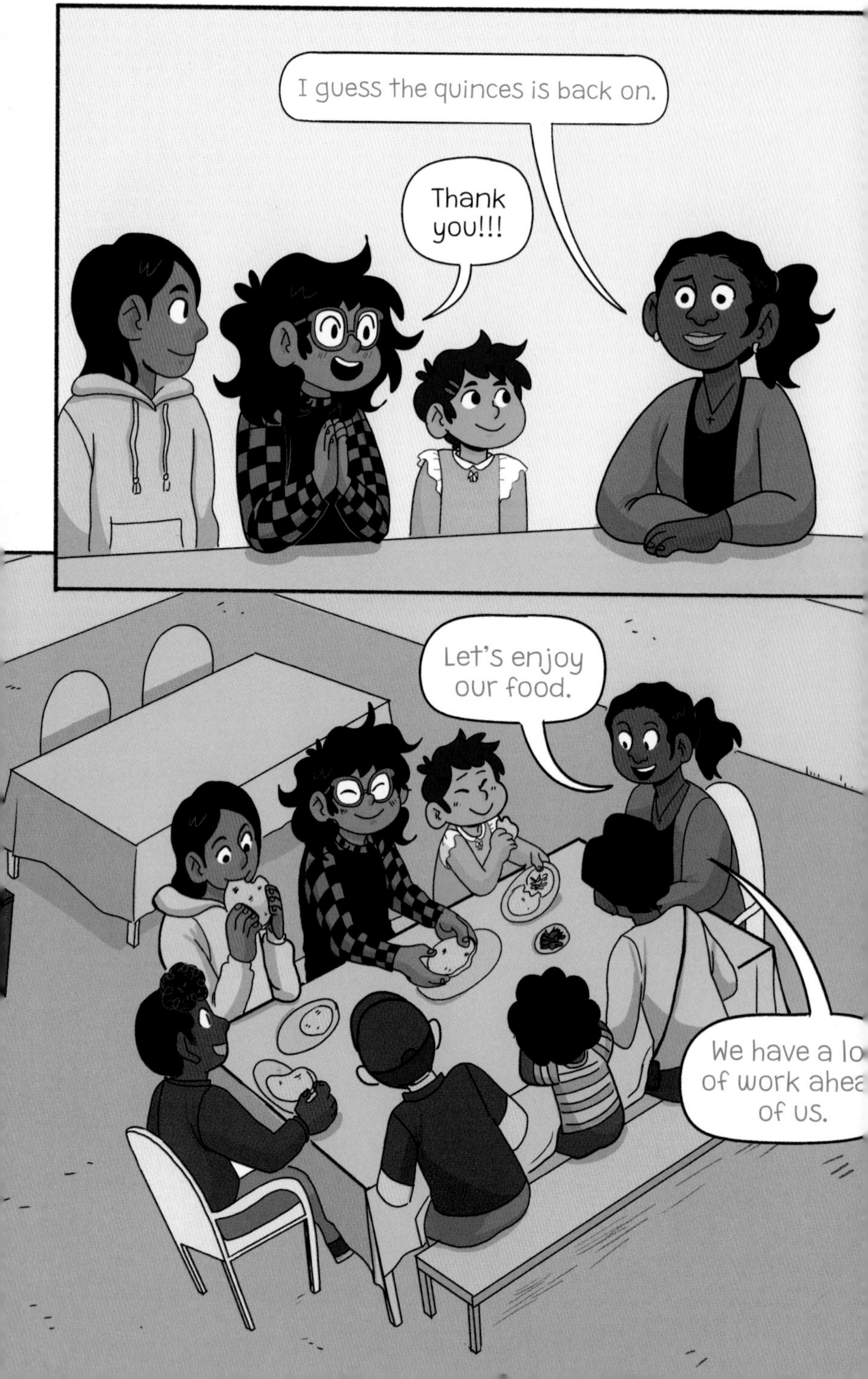
I guess the quinces is back on.
Thank you!!!
Let's enjoy our food.
We have a lo of work ahea of us.

CHAPTER EIGHT

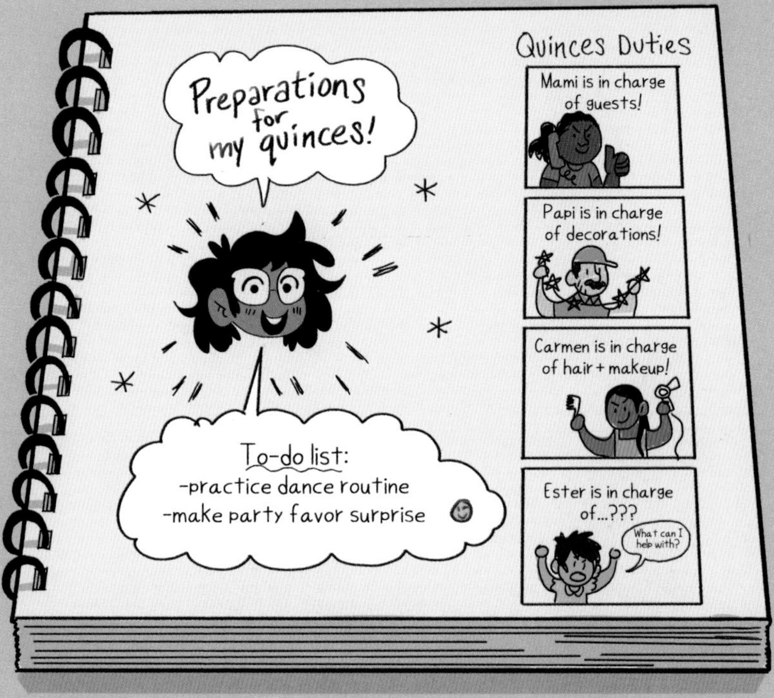
Quinces Duties
Preparations for my quinces!
To-do list:
-practice dance routine
-make party favor surprise
Mami is in charge of guests!
Papi is in charge of decorations!
Carmen is in charge of hair + makeup!
Ester is in charge of...???
What can I help with?

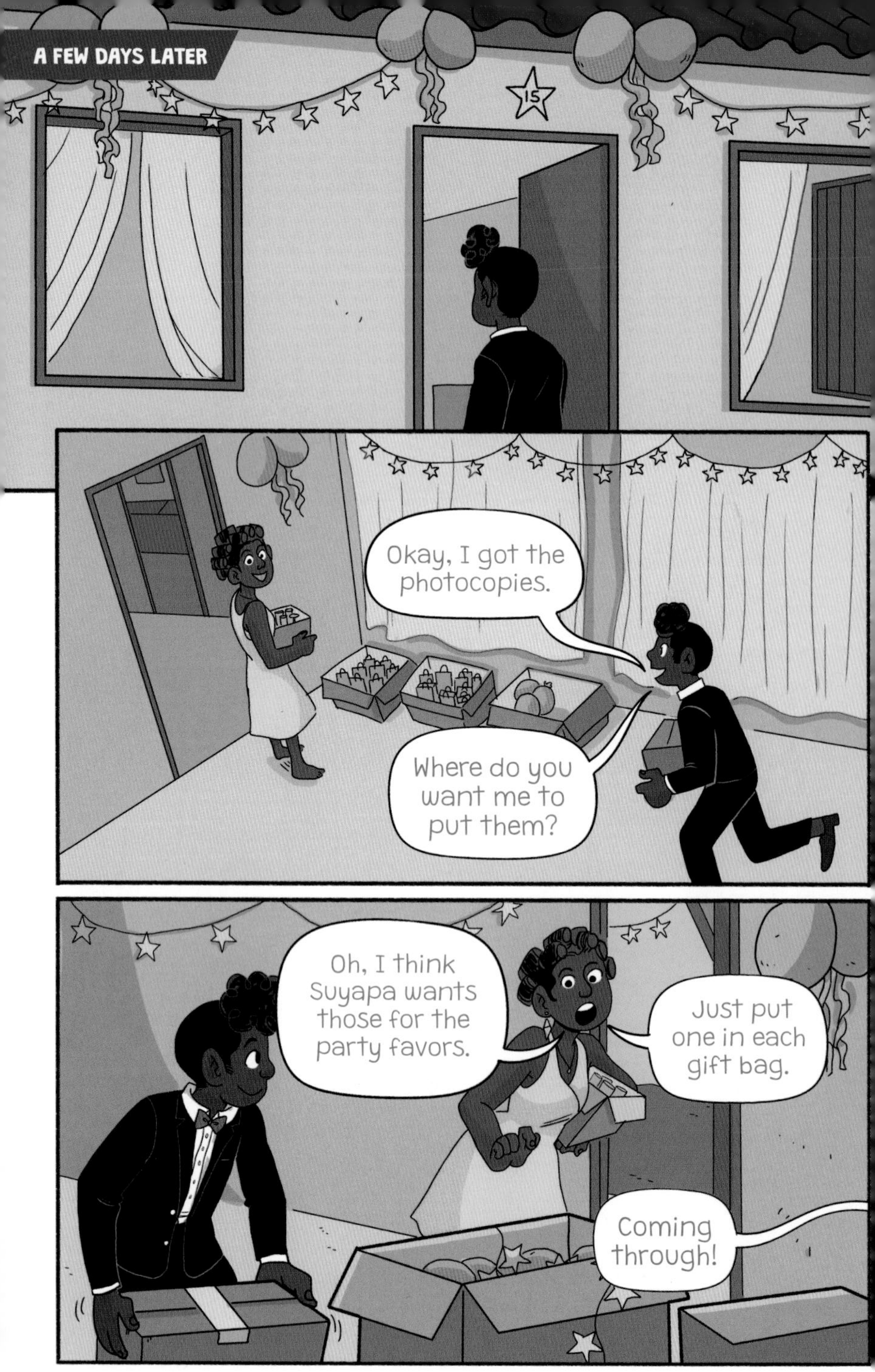
A FEW DAYS LATER
15
Okay, I got the photocopies.
Where do you want me to put them?
Oh, I think Suyapa wants those for the party favors.
Just put one in each gift bag.
Coming through!

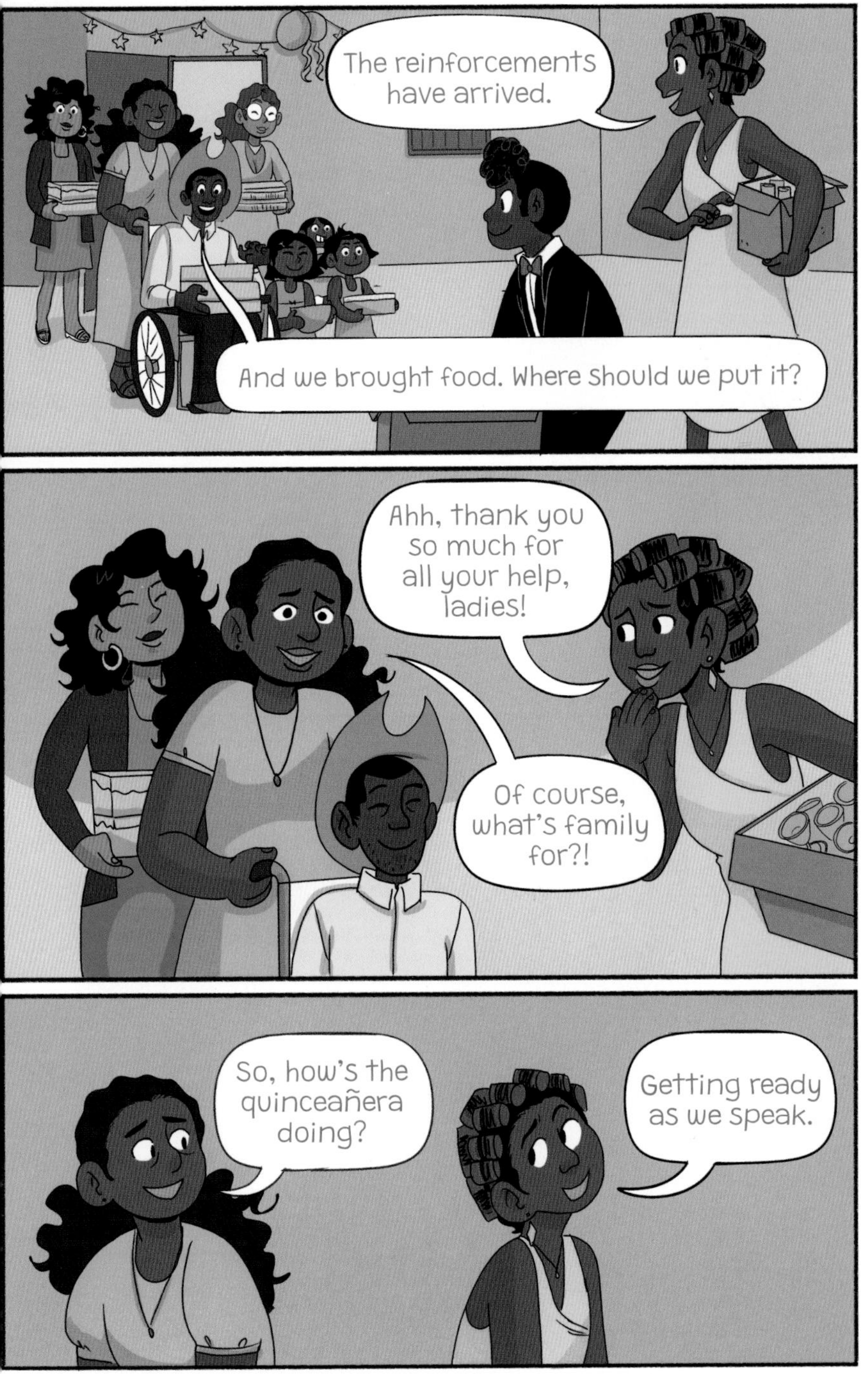
The reinforcements have arrived.
And we brought food. Where should we put it?
Ahh, thank you so much for all your help, ladies!
Of course, what's family for?!
So, how's the quinceañera doing?
Getting ready as we speak.

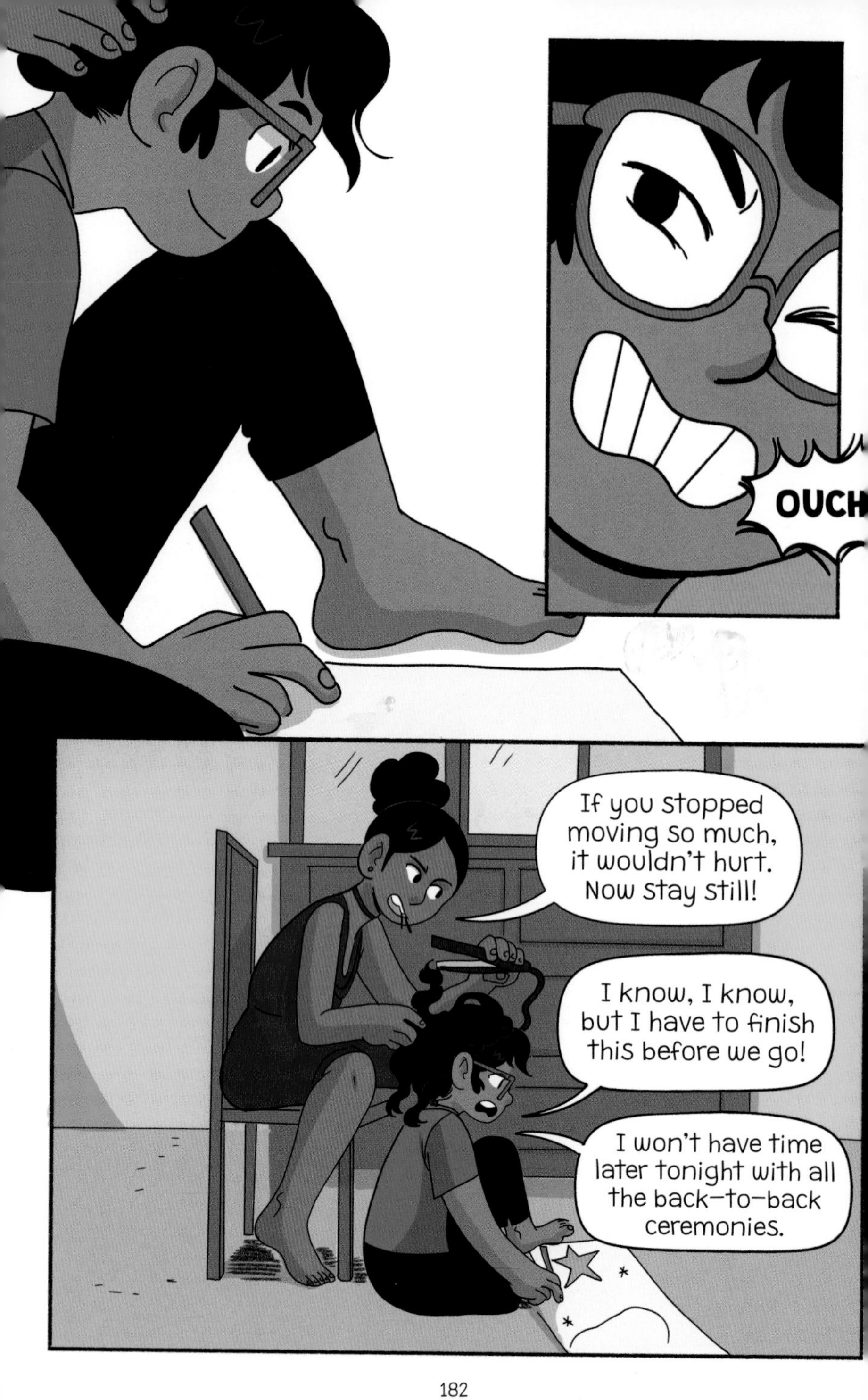
OUCH
If you stopped moving so much, it wouldn't hurt. Now stay still!
I know, I know, but I have to finish this before we go!
I won't have time later tonight with all the back-to-back ceremonies.

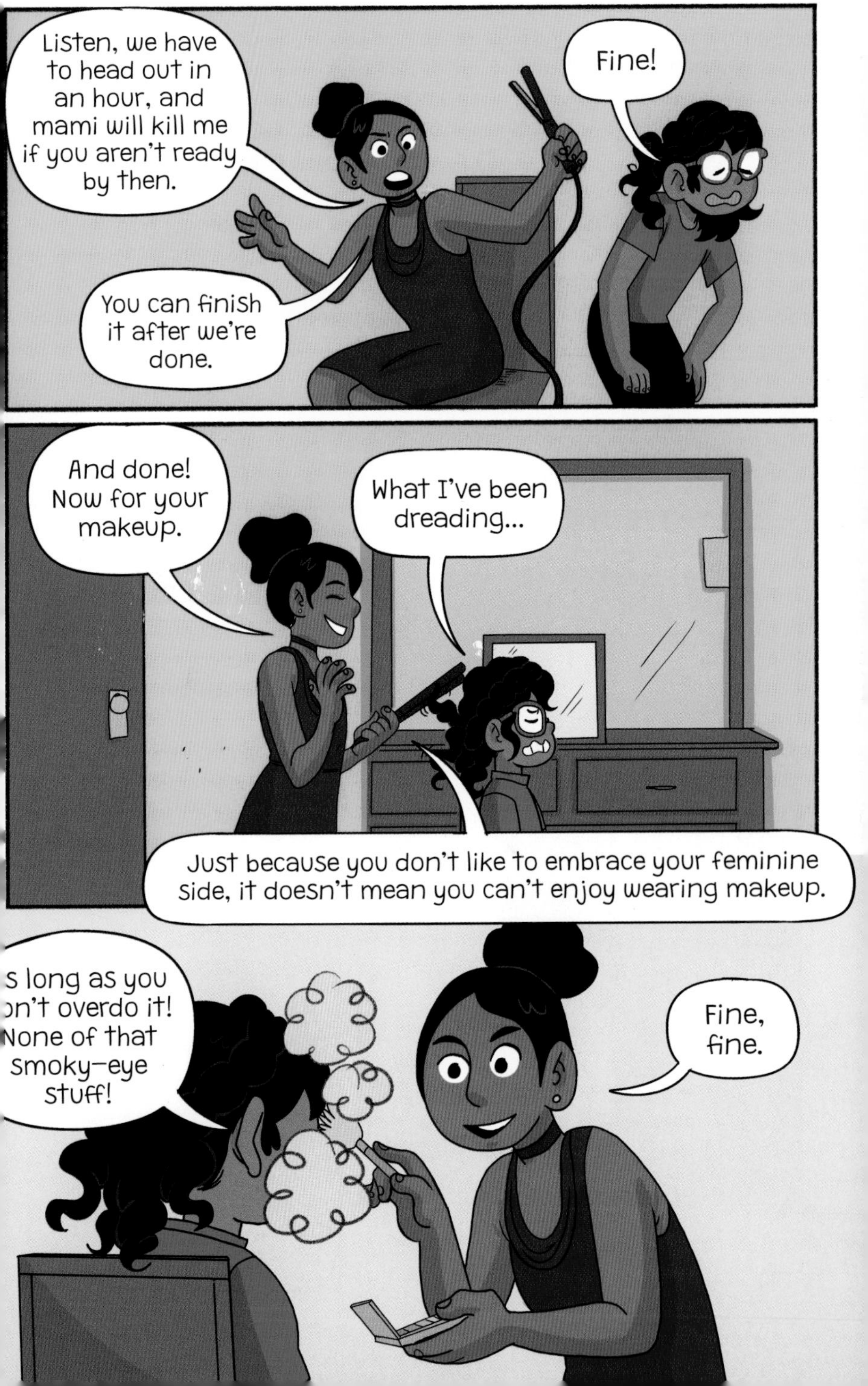

Listen, we have to head out in an hour, and mami will kill me if you aren't ready by then.
Fine!
You can finish it after we're done.
And done! Now for your makeup.
What I've been dreading...
Just because you don't like to embrace your feminine side, it doesn't mean you can't enjoy wearing makeup.
s long as you on't overdo it! None of that smoky-eye stuff!
Fine, fine.

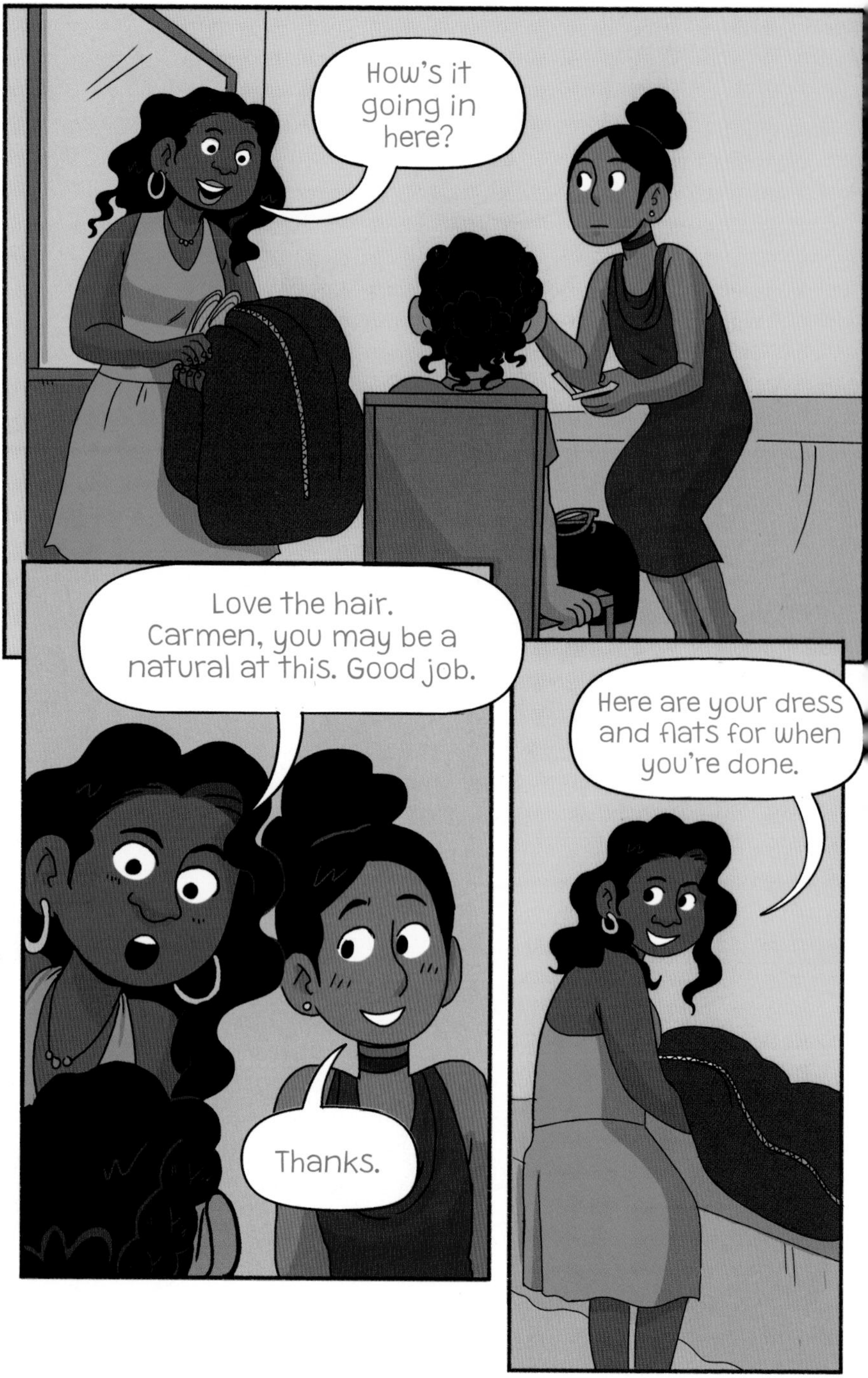
How's it going in here?
Love the hair. Carmen, you may be a natural at this. Good job.
Thanks.
Here are your dress and flats for when you're done.

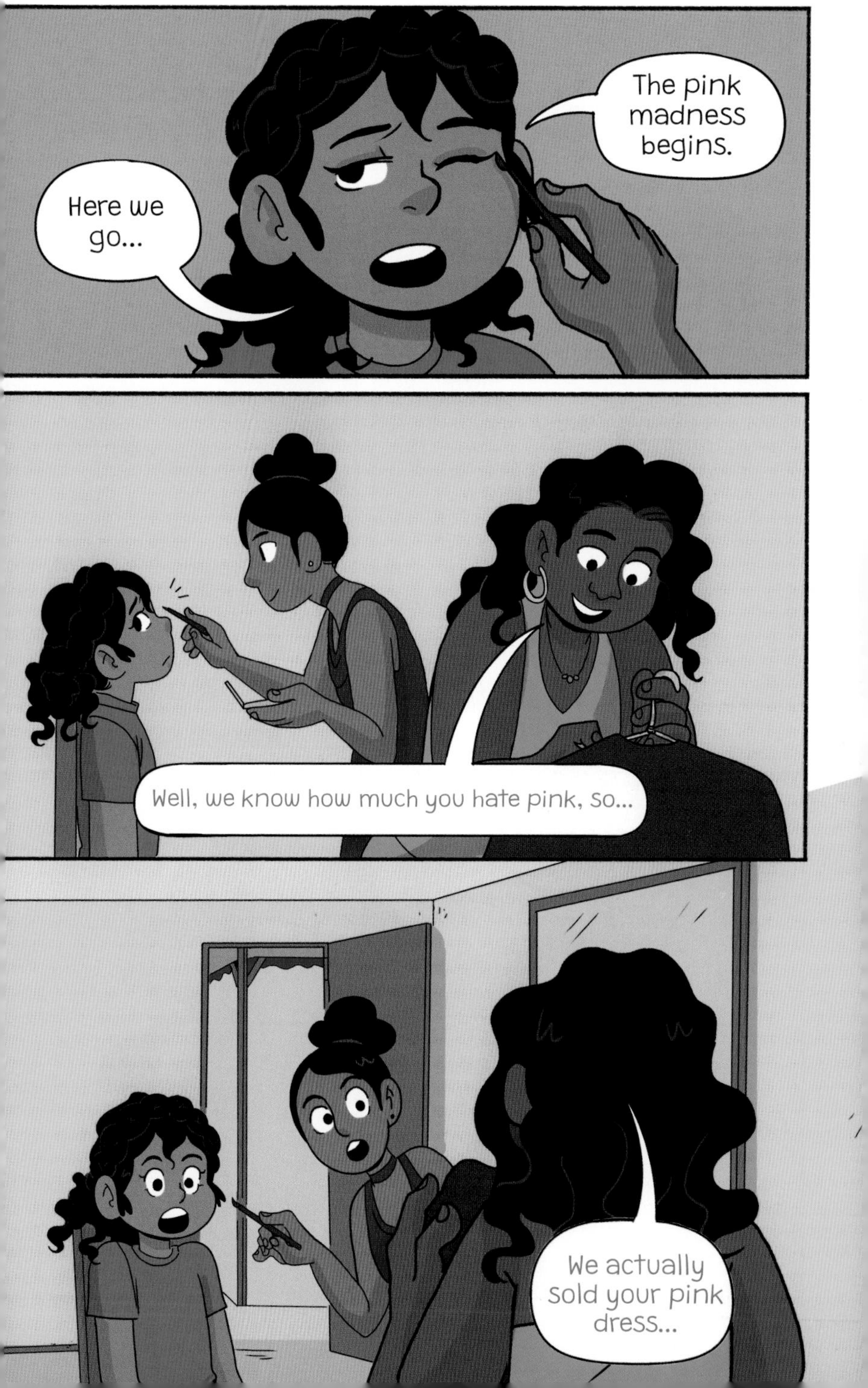
Here we go...
The pink madness begins.
Well, we know how much you hate pink, so...
We actually sold your pink dress...

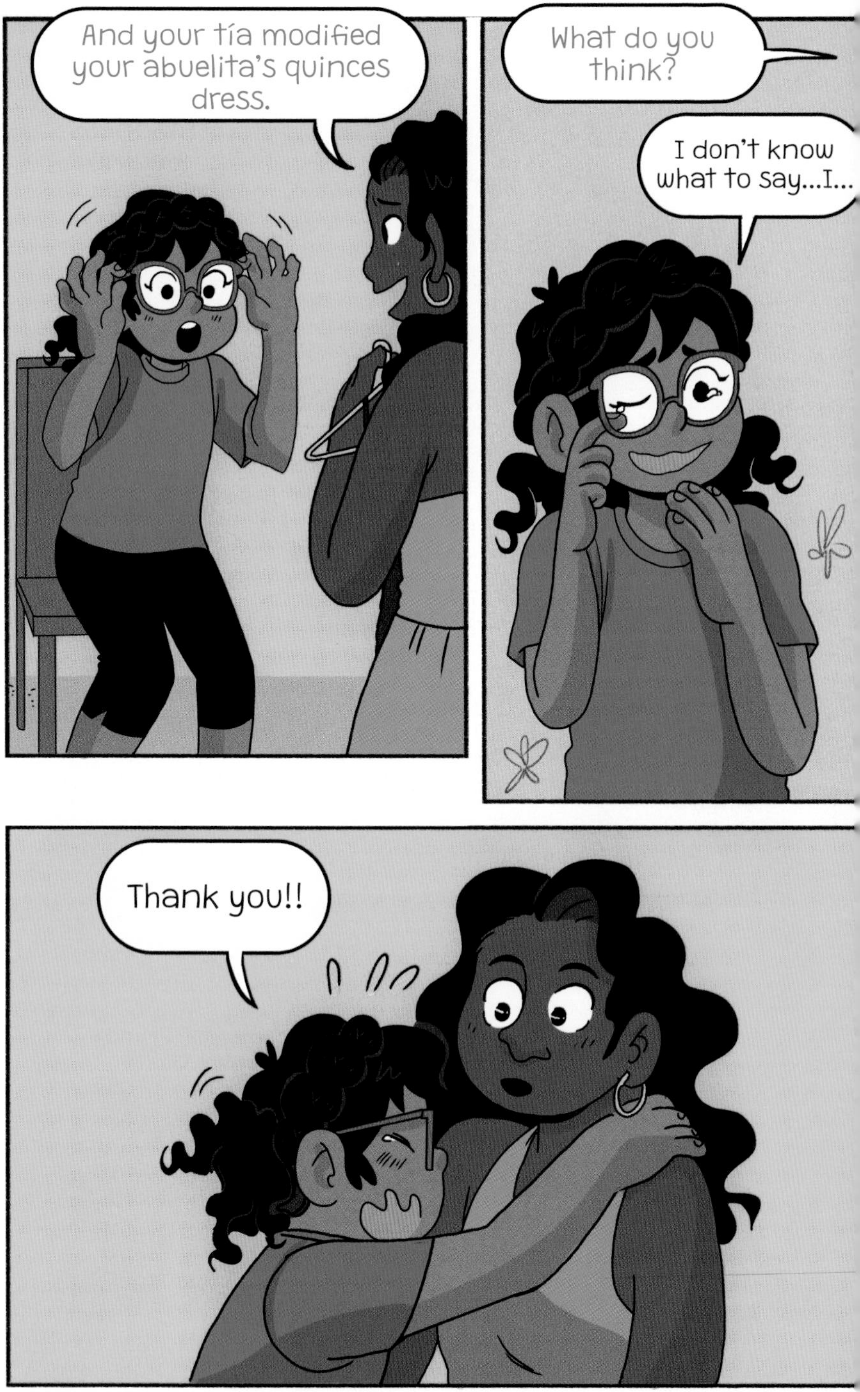
And your tía modified your abuelita's quinces dress.
What do you think?
I don't know what to say...I...
Thank you!!

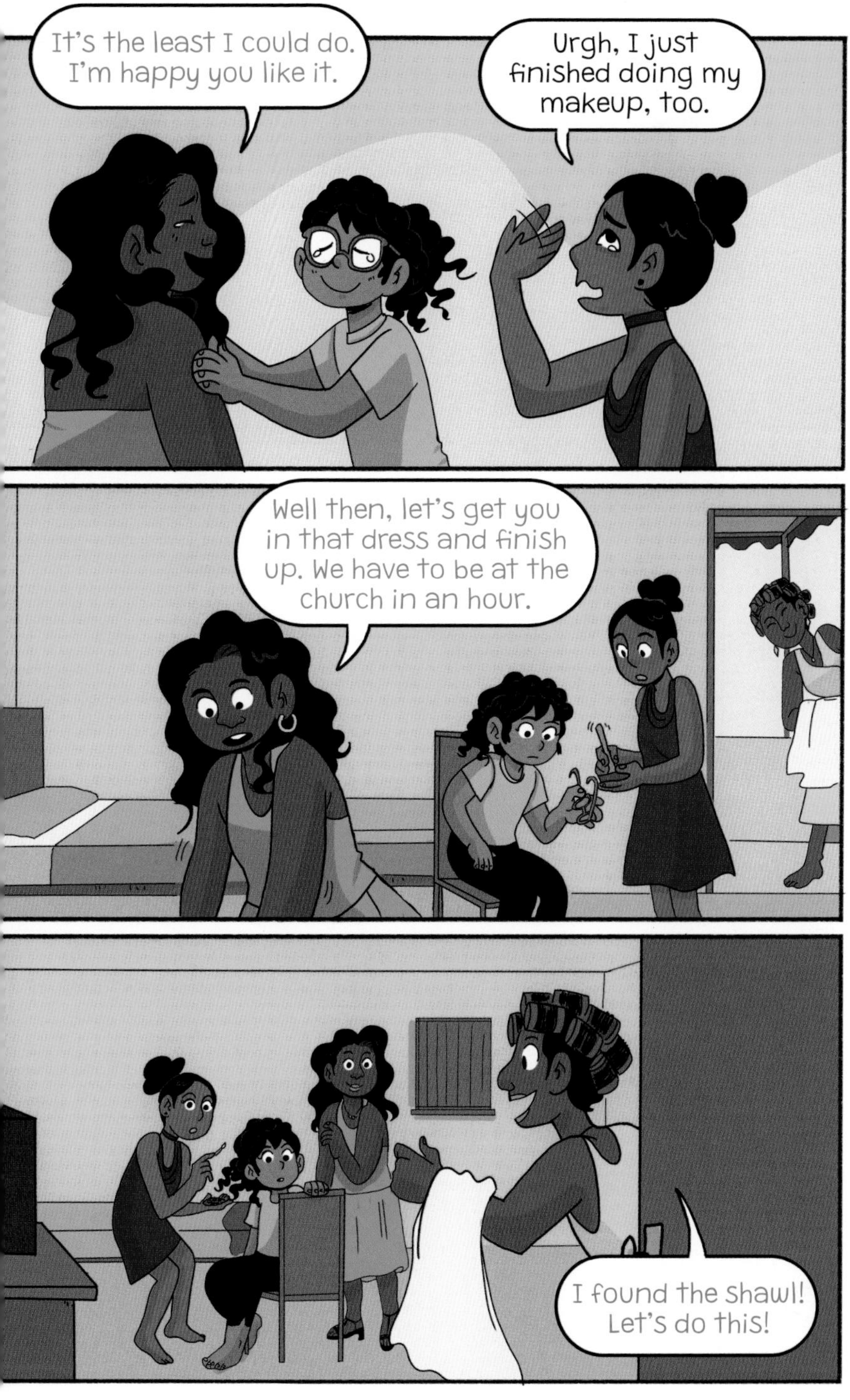
It's the least I could do. I'm happy you like it.
Urgh, I just finished doing my makeup, too.
Well then, let's get you in that dress and finish up. We have to be at the church in an hour.
I found the shawl! Let's do this!

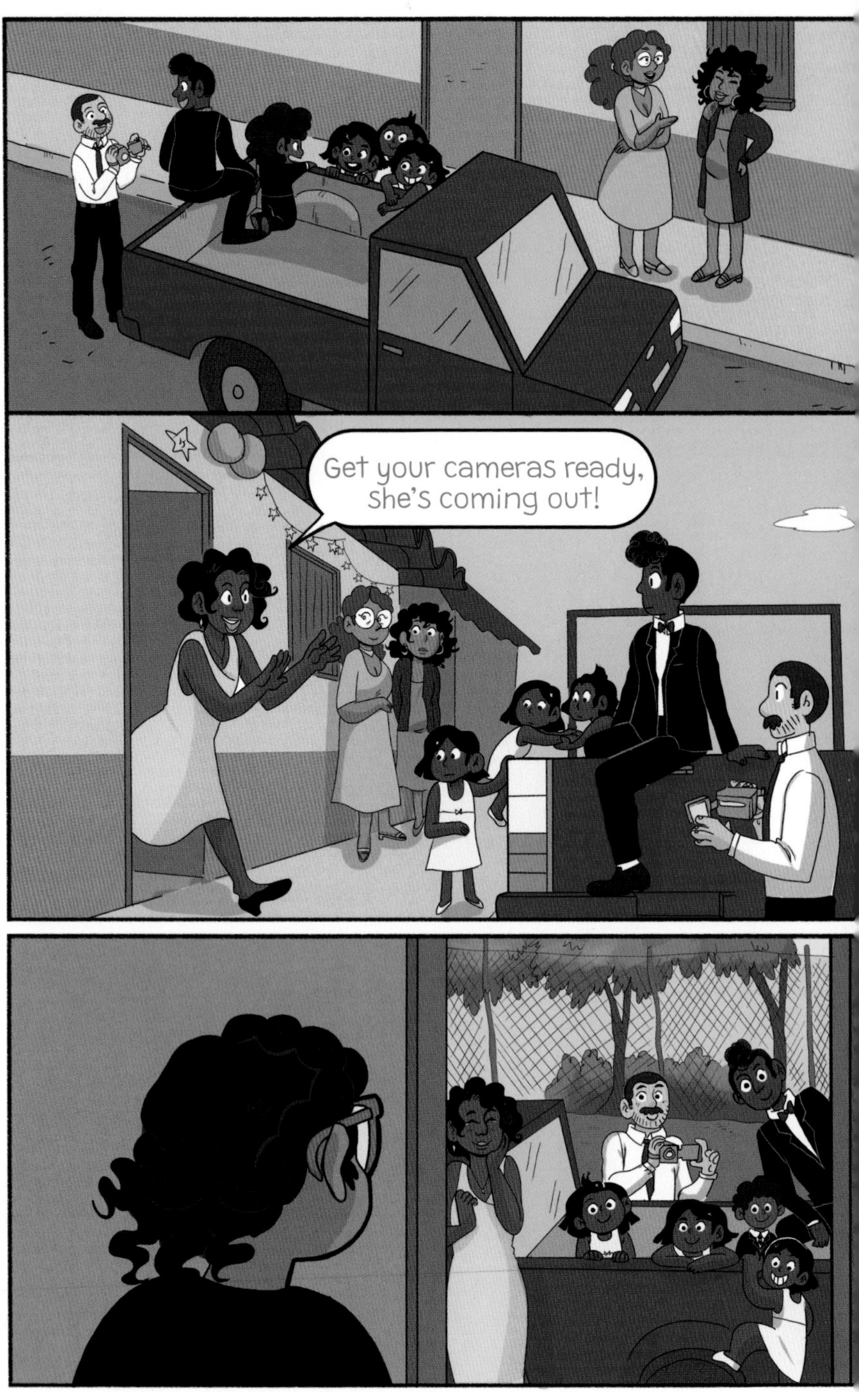
Get your cameras ready, she's coming out!

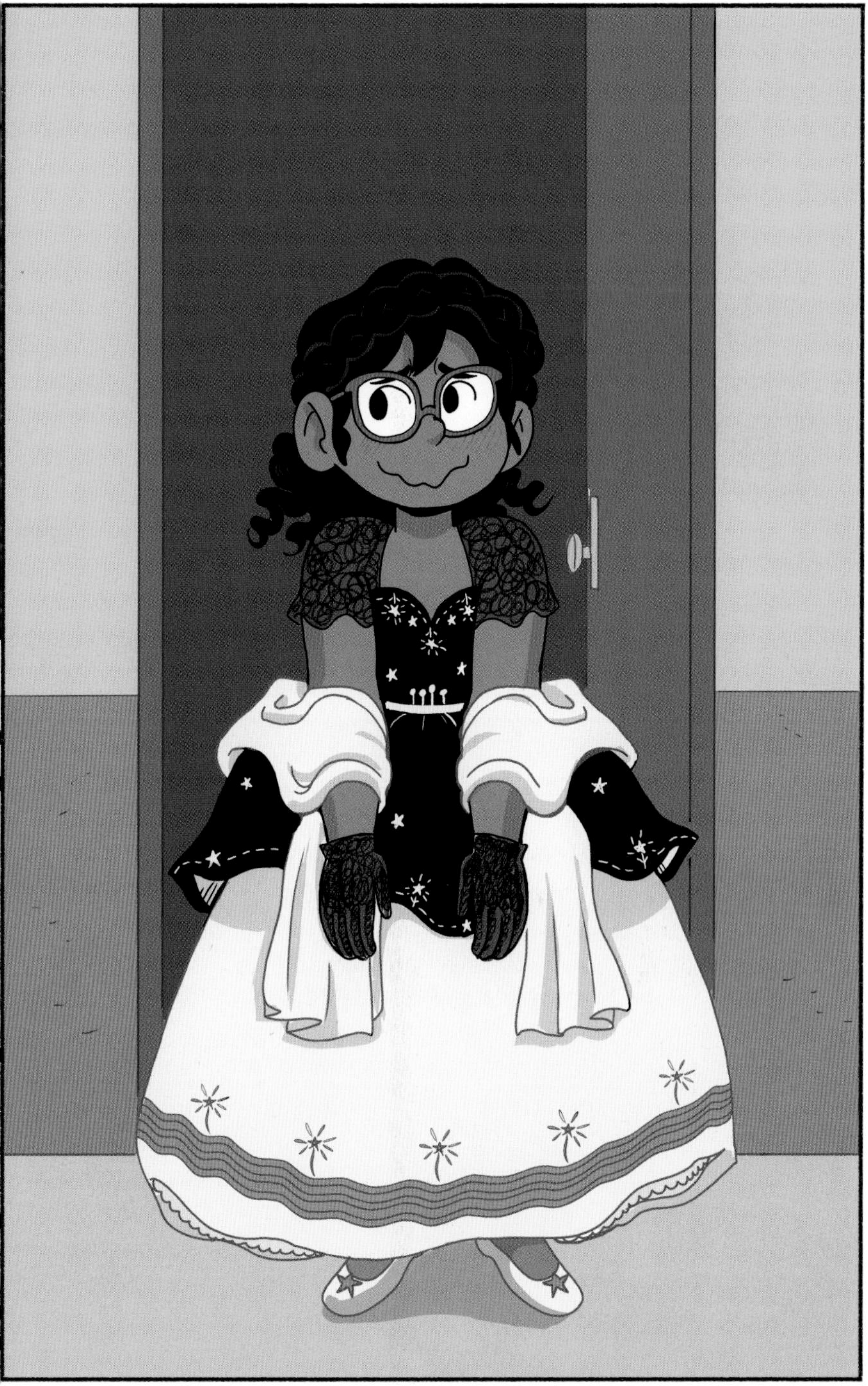

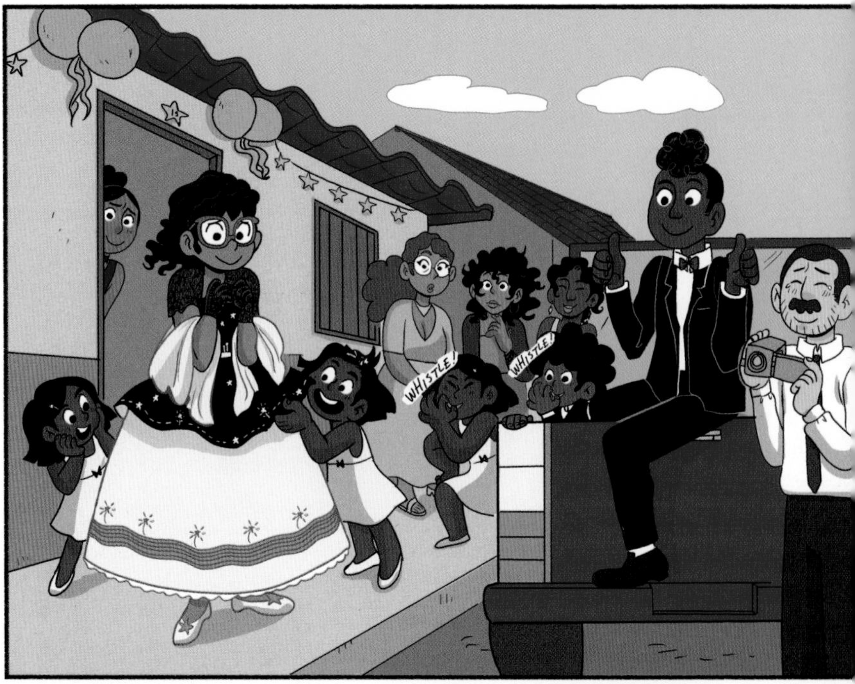
WHISTLE!
WHISTLE!

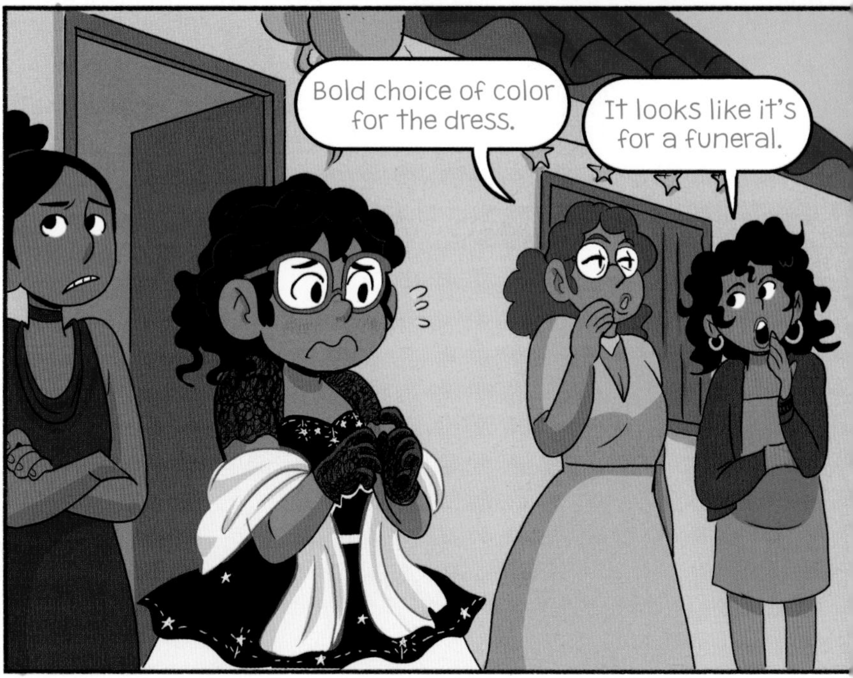
Bold choice of color for the dress.
It looks like it's for a funeral.

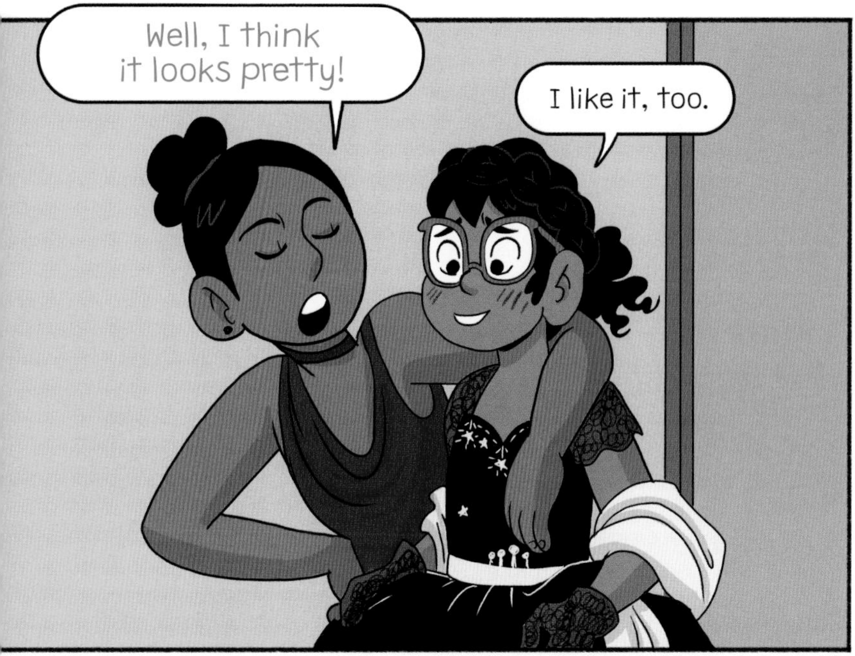
Well, I think it looks pretty!
I like it, too.

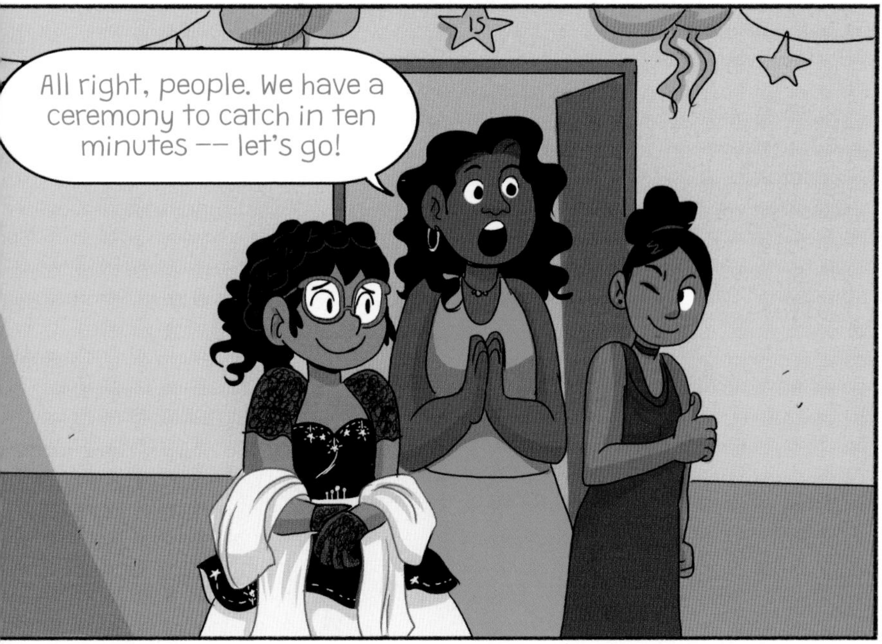
15
All right, people. We have a ceremony to catch in ten minutes -- let's go!

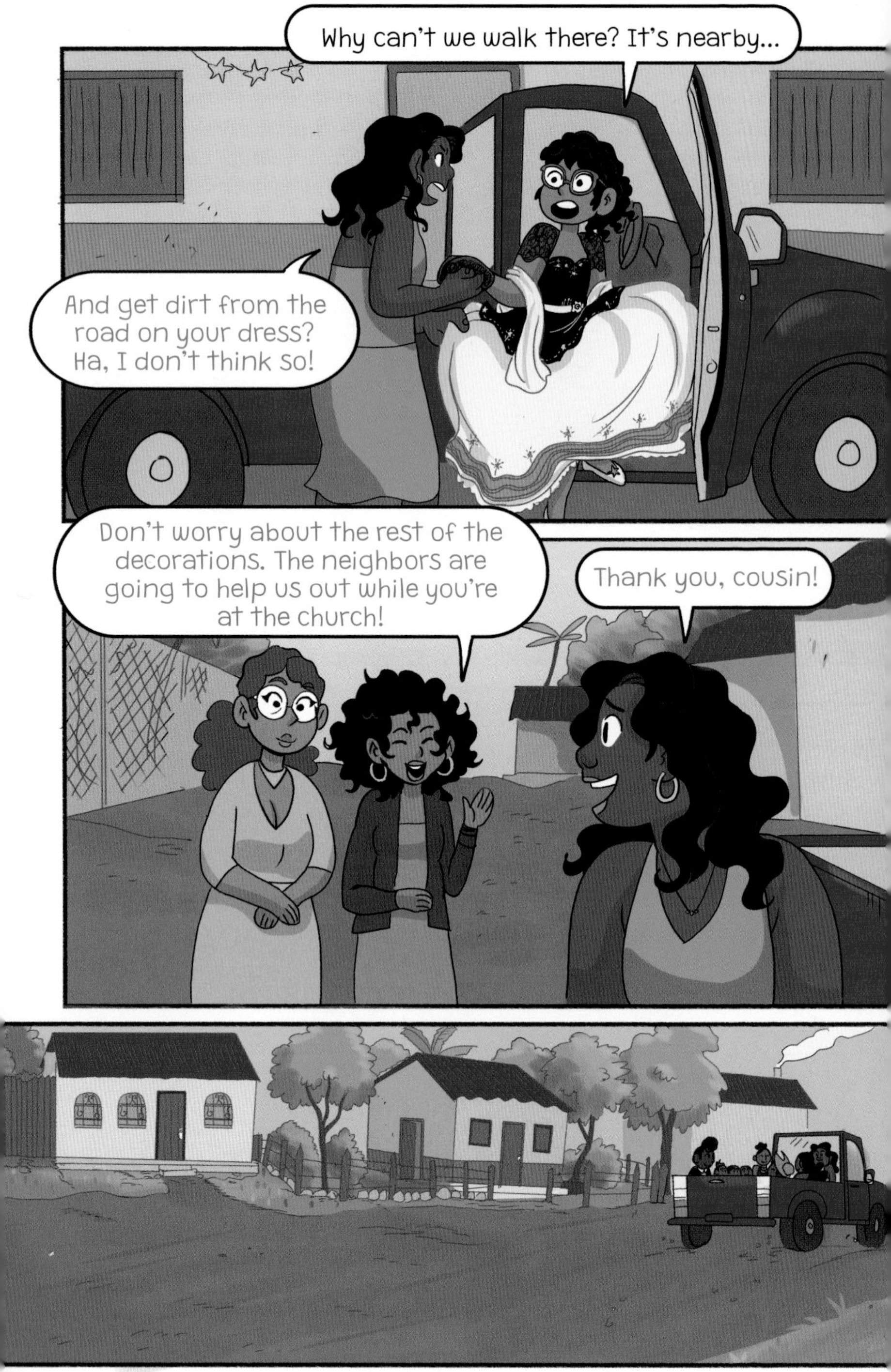
Why can't we walk there? It's nearby...
And get dirt from the road on your dress? Ha, I don't think so!
Don't worry about the rest of the decorations. The neighbors are going to help us out while you're at the church!
Thank you, cousin!

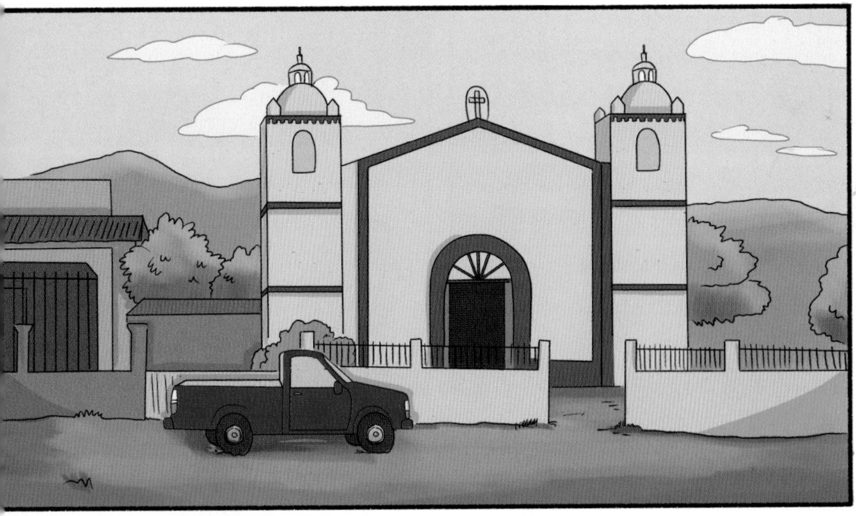

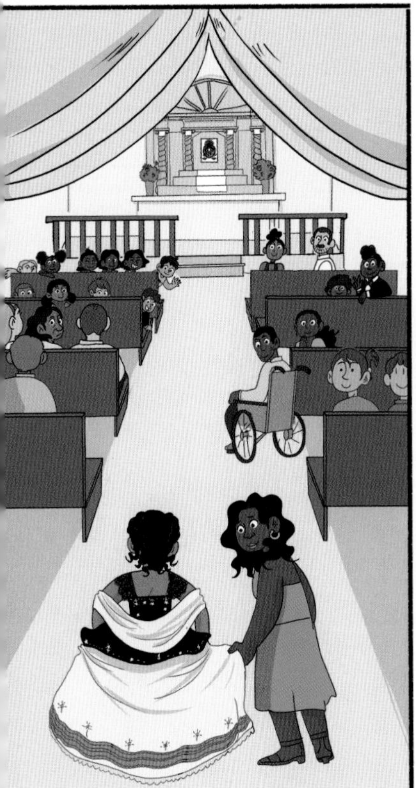

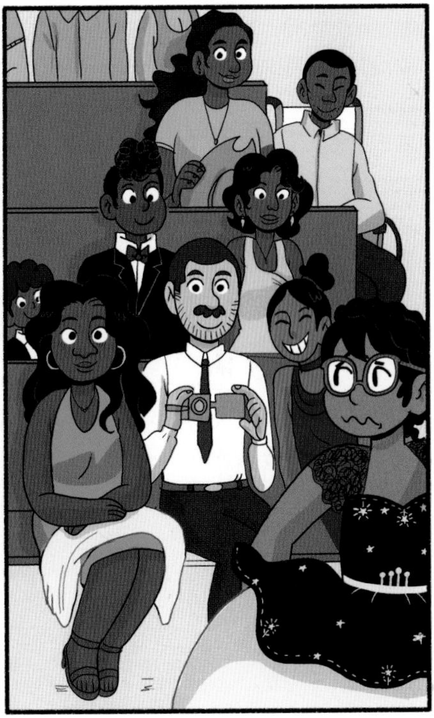

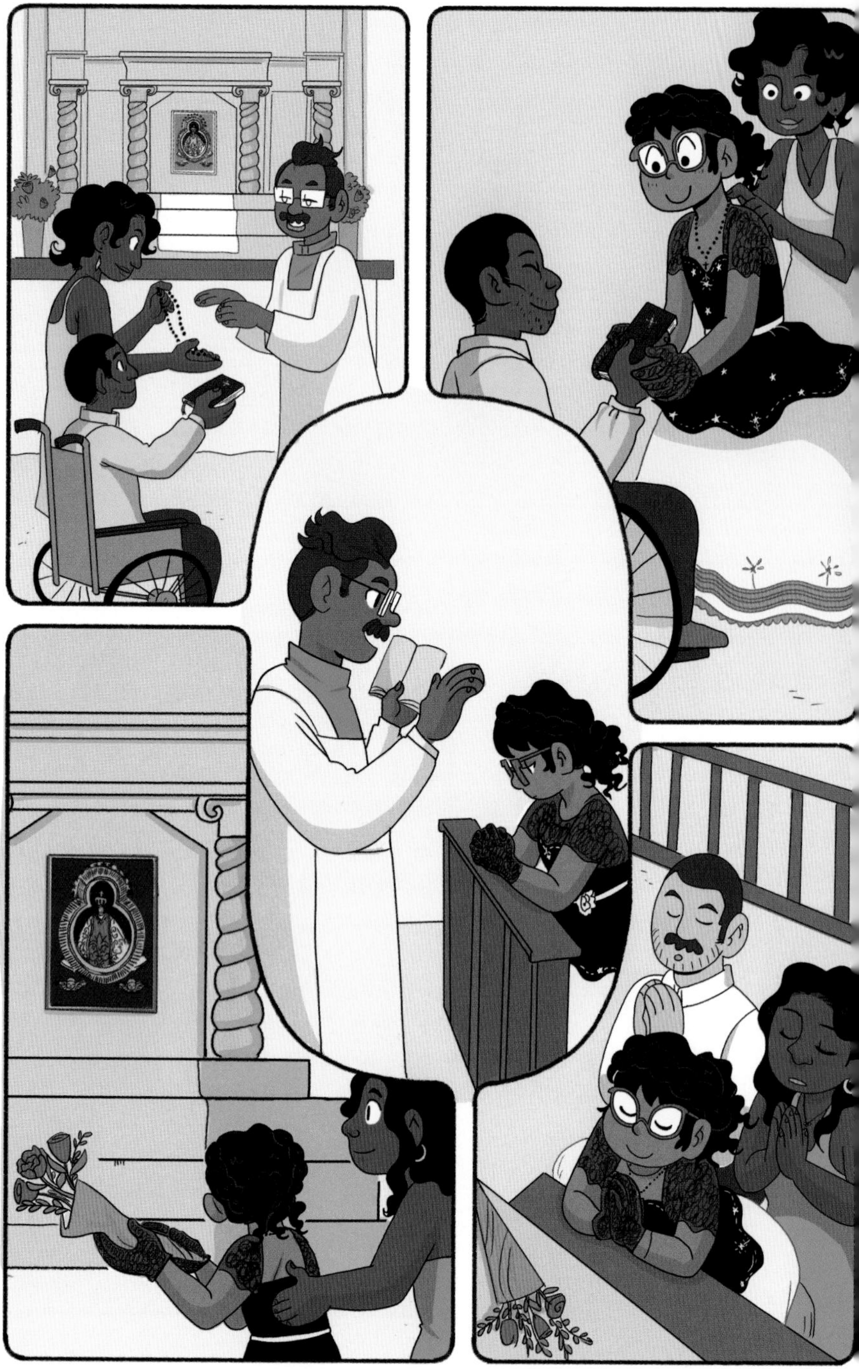

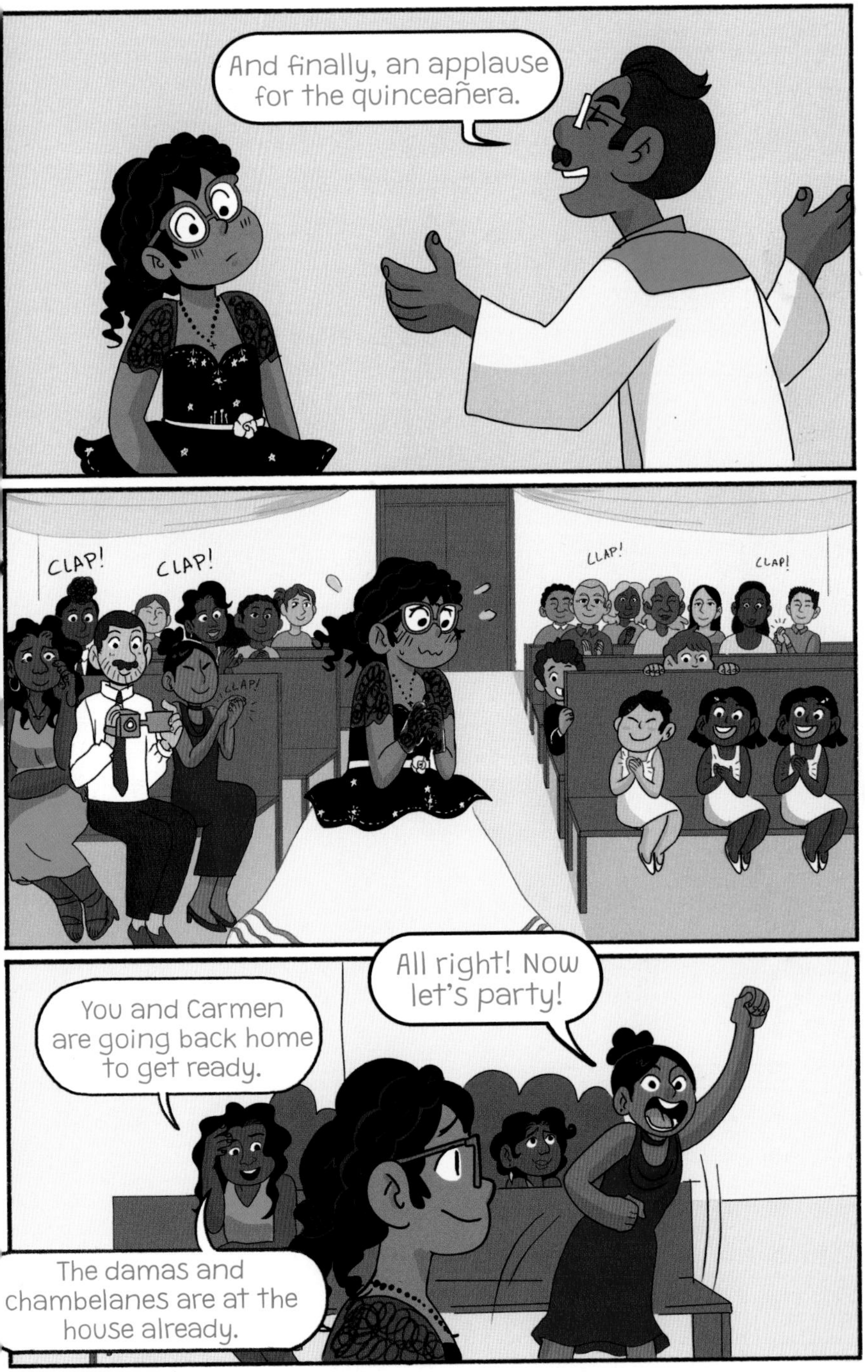
And finally, an applause for the quinceañera.
CLAP!
CLAP!
CLAP!
CLAP!
CLAP!
All right! Now let's party!
You and Carmen are going back home to get ready.
The damas and chambelanes are at the house already.

CHAPTER NINE

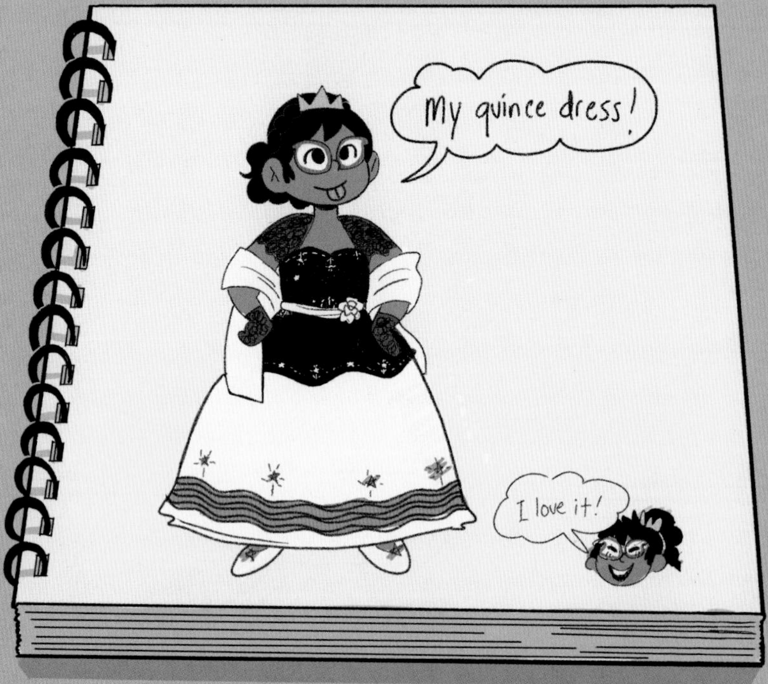
My quince dress!
I love it!

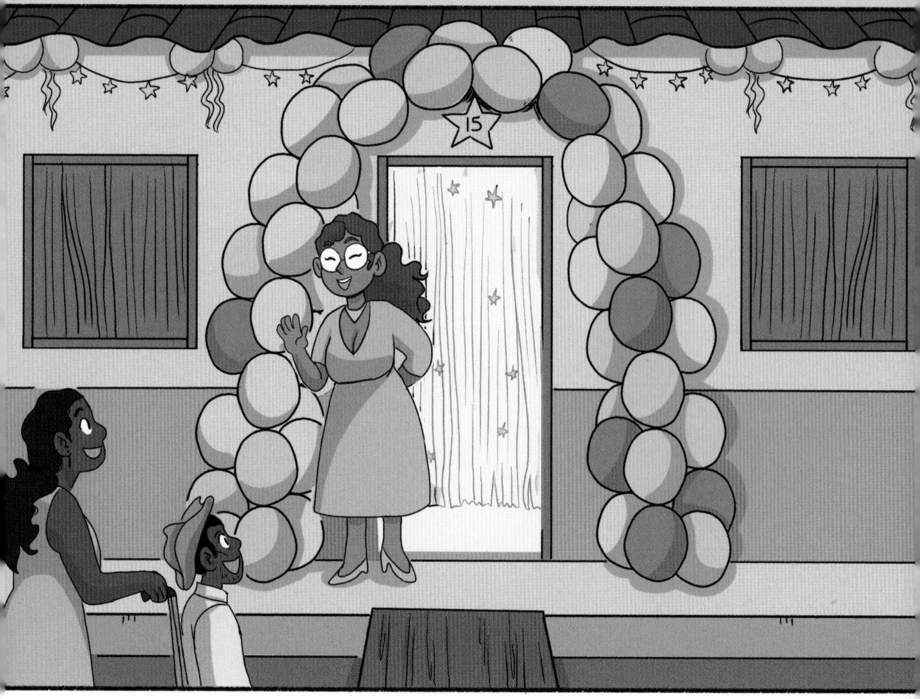
15

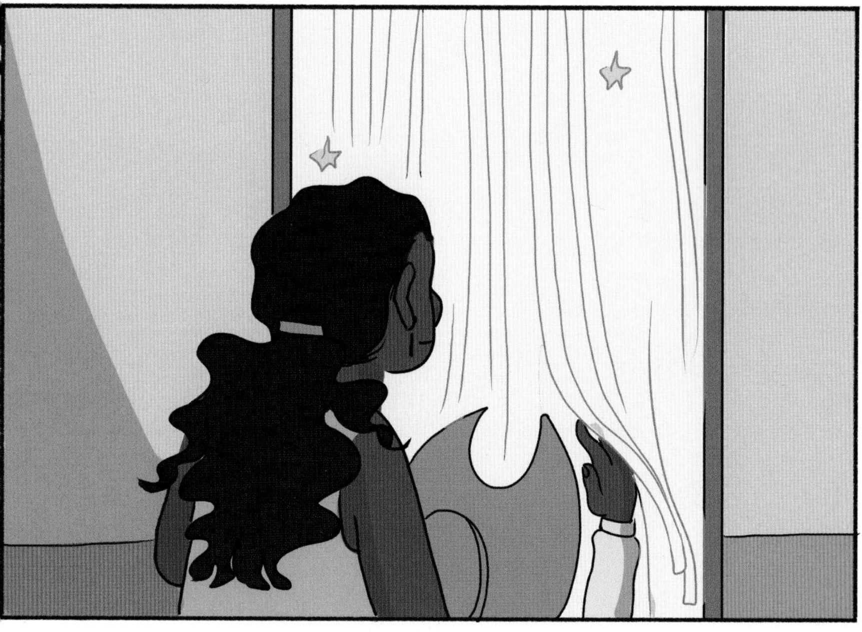

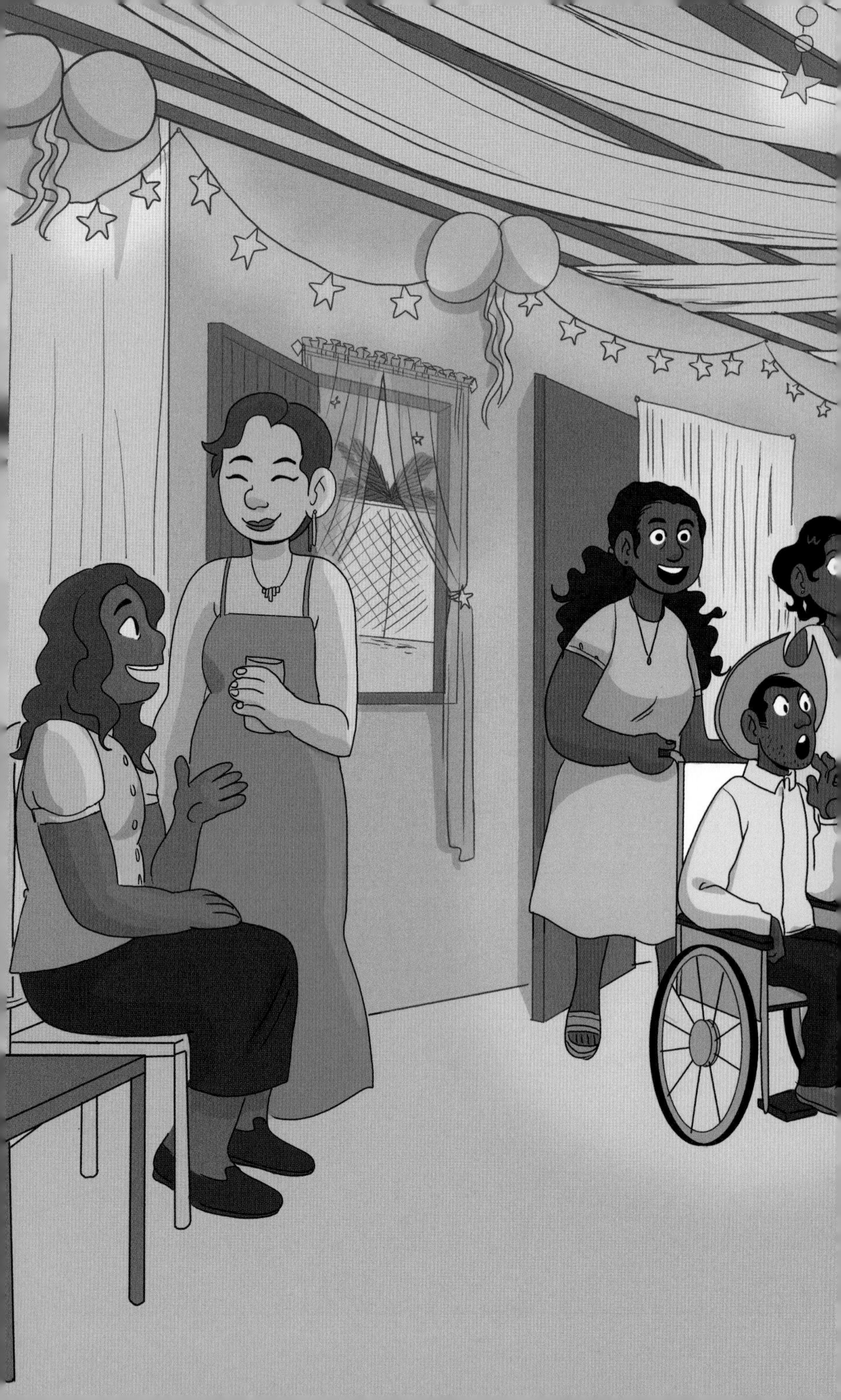

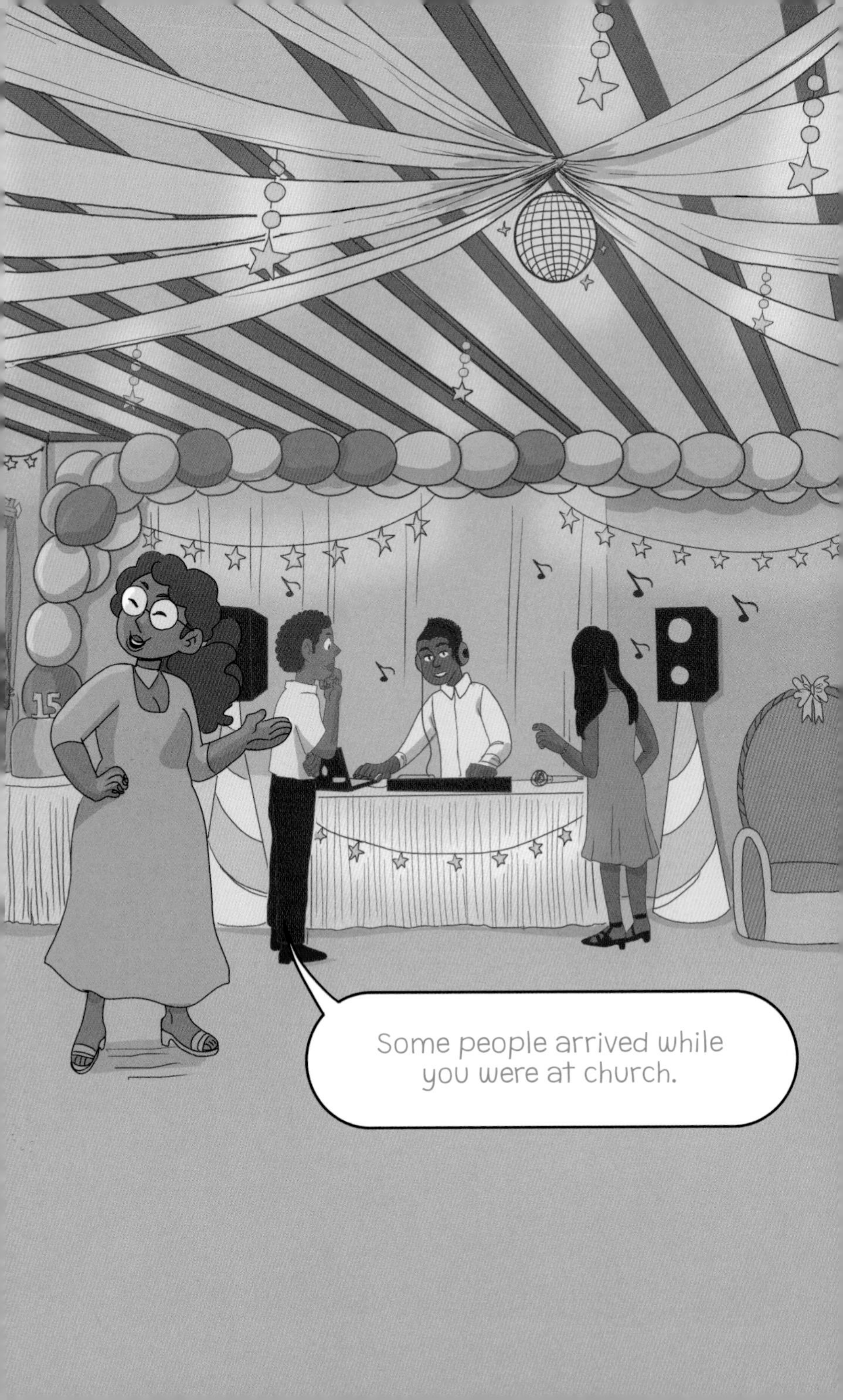
Some people arrived while you were at church.

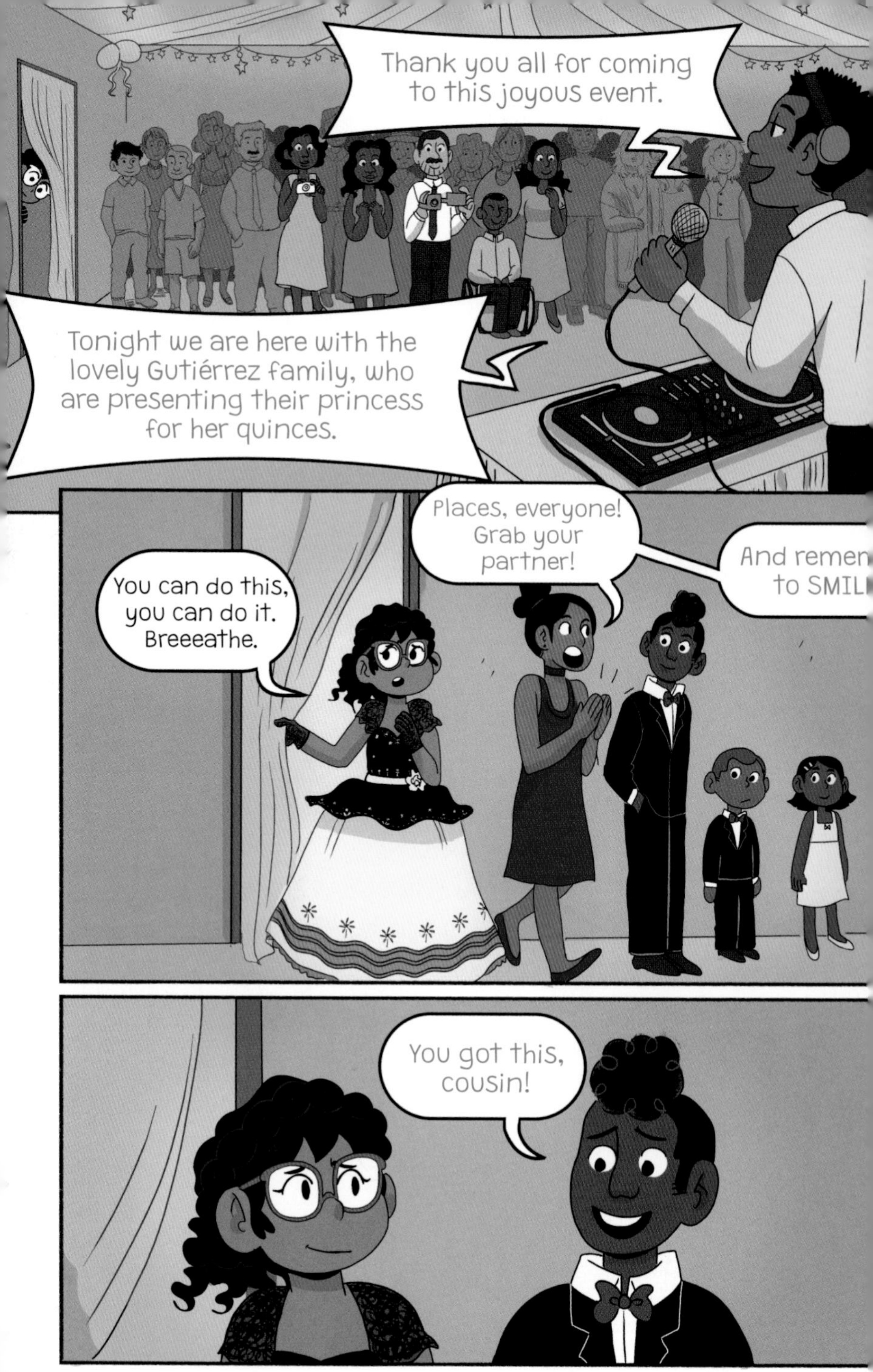
Thank you all for coming to this joyous event.
Tonight we are here with the lovely Gutiérrez family, who are presenting their princess for her quinces.
You can do this, you can do it. Breeeathe.
Places, everyone! Grab your partner!
And remen
to SMIL
You got this, cousin!

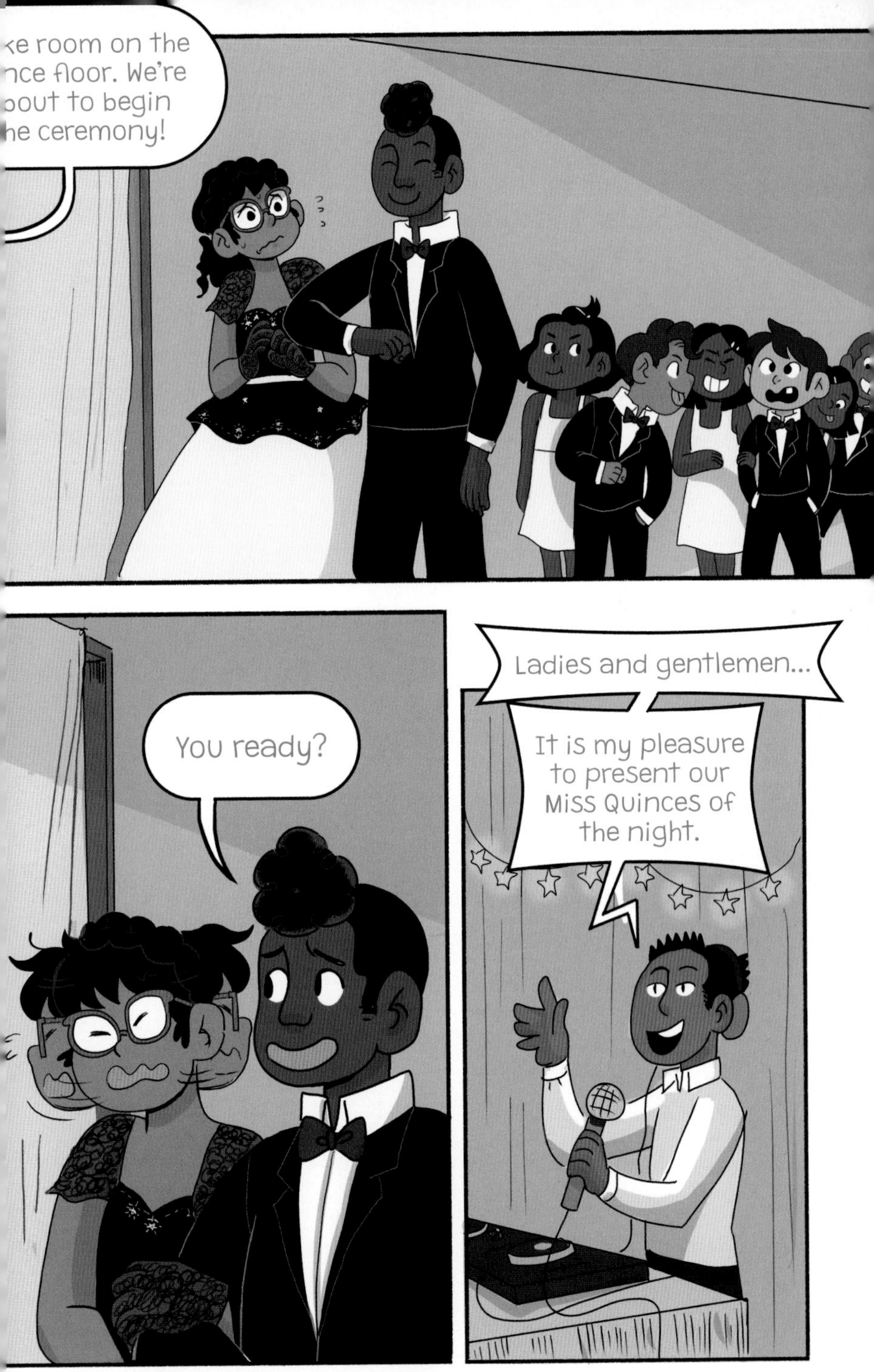
ke room on the nce floor. We're bout to begin he ceremony!
You ready?
Ladies and gentlemen...
It is my pleasure to present our Miss Quinces of the night.

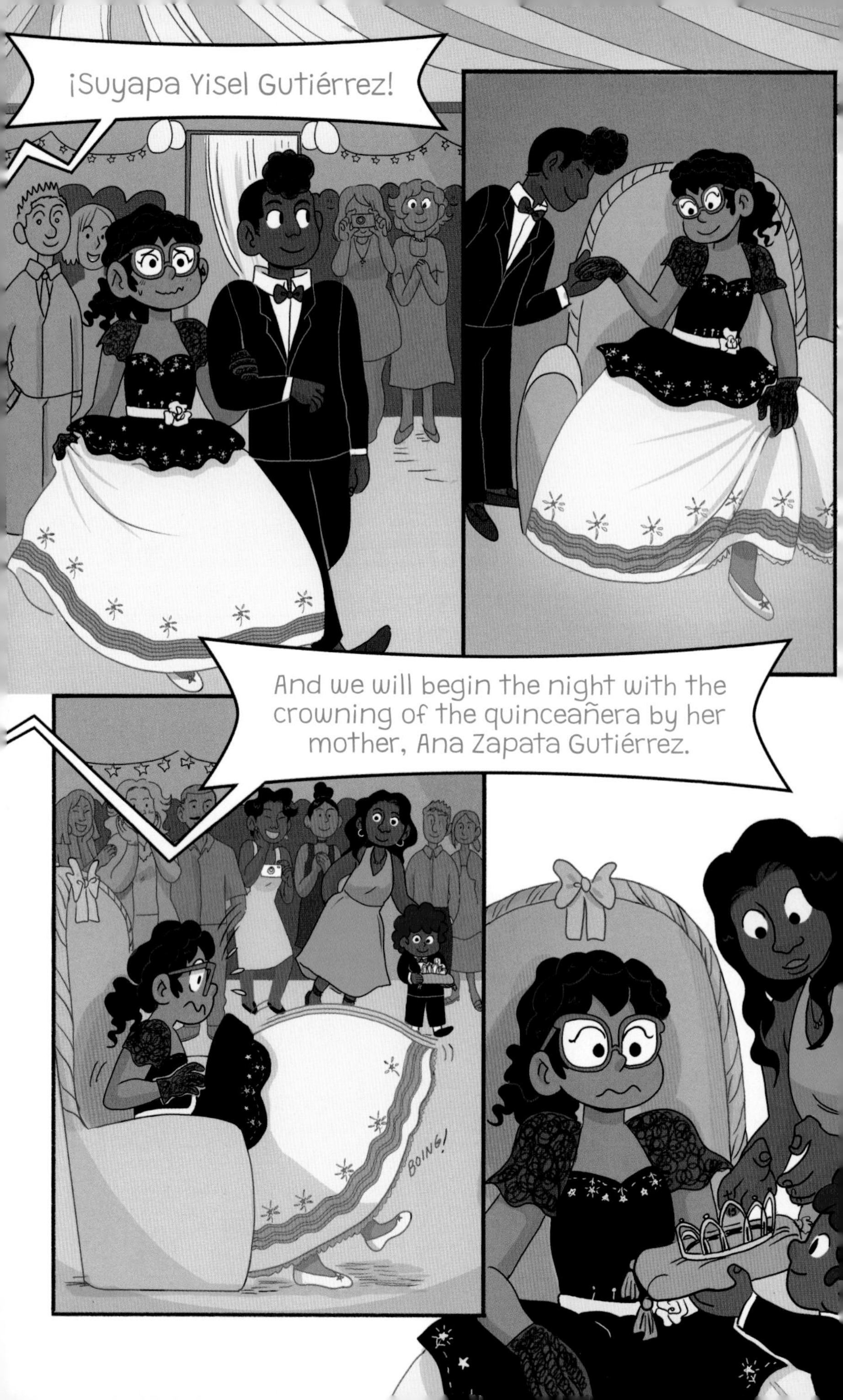
¡Suyapa Yisel Gutiérrez!
And we will begin the night with the crowning of the quinceañera by her mother, Ana Zapata Gutiérrez.
BOING!

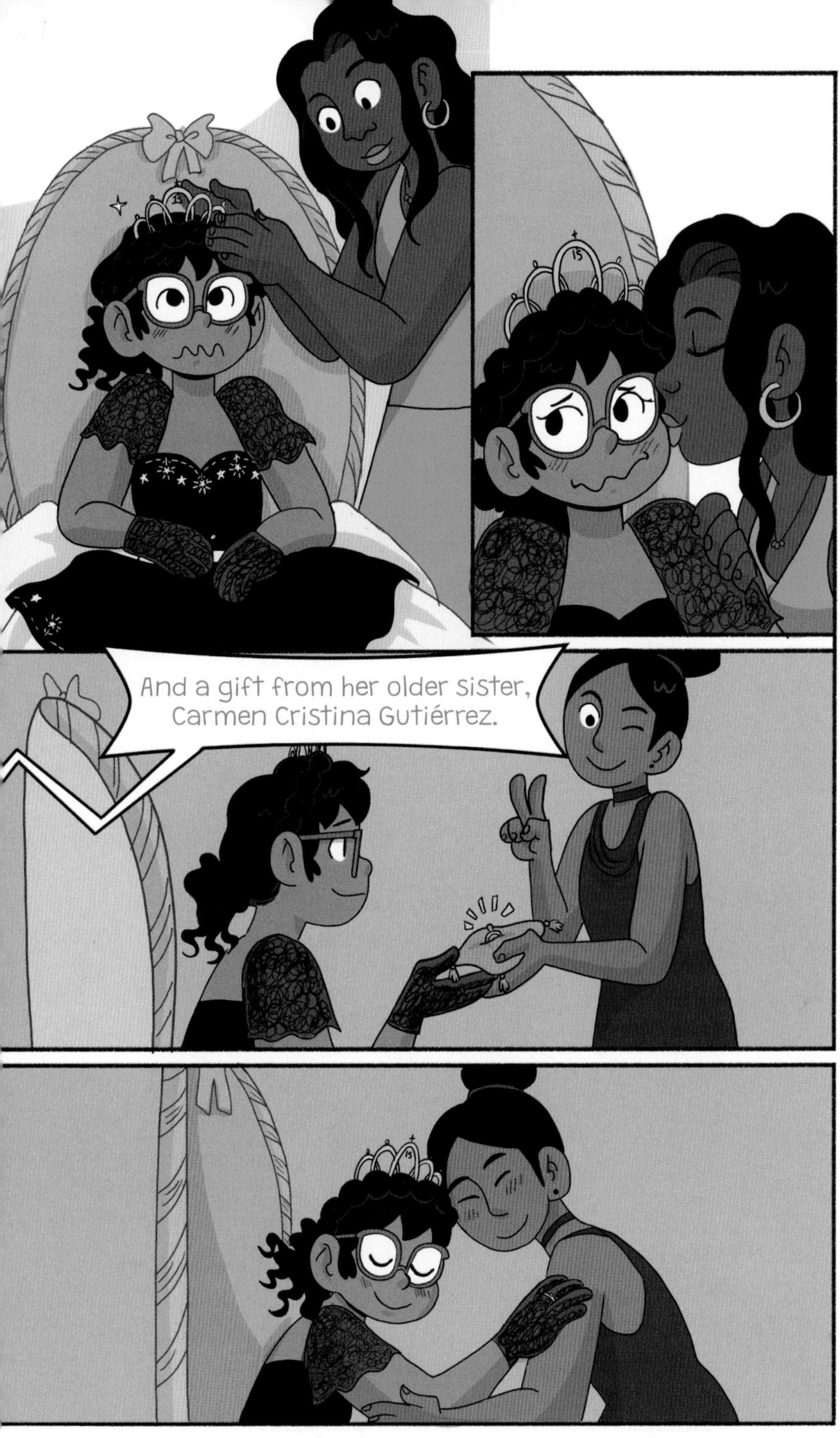
And a gift from her older sister, Carmen Cristina Gutiérrez.

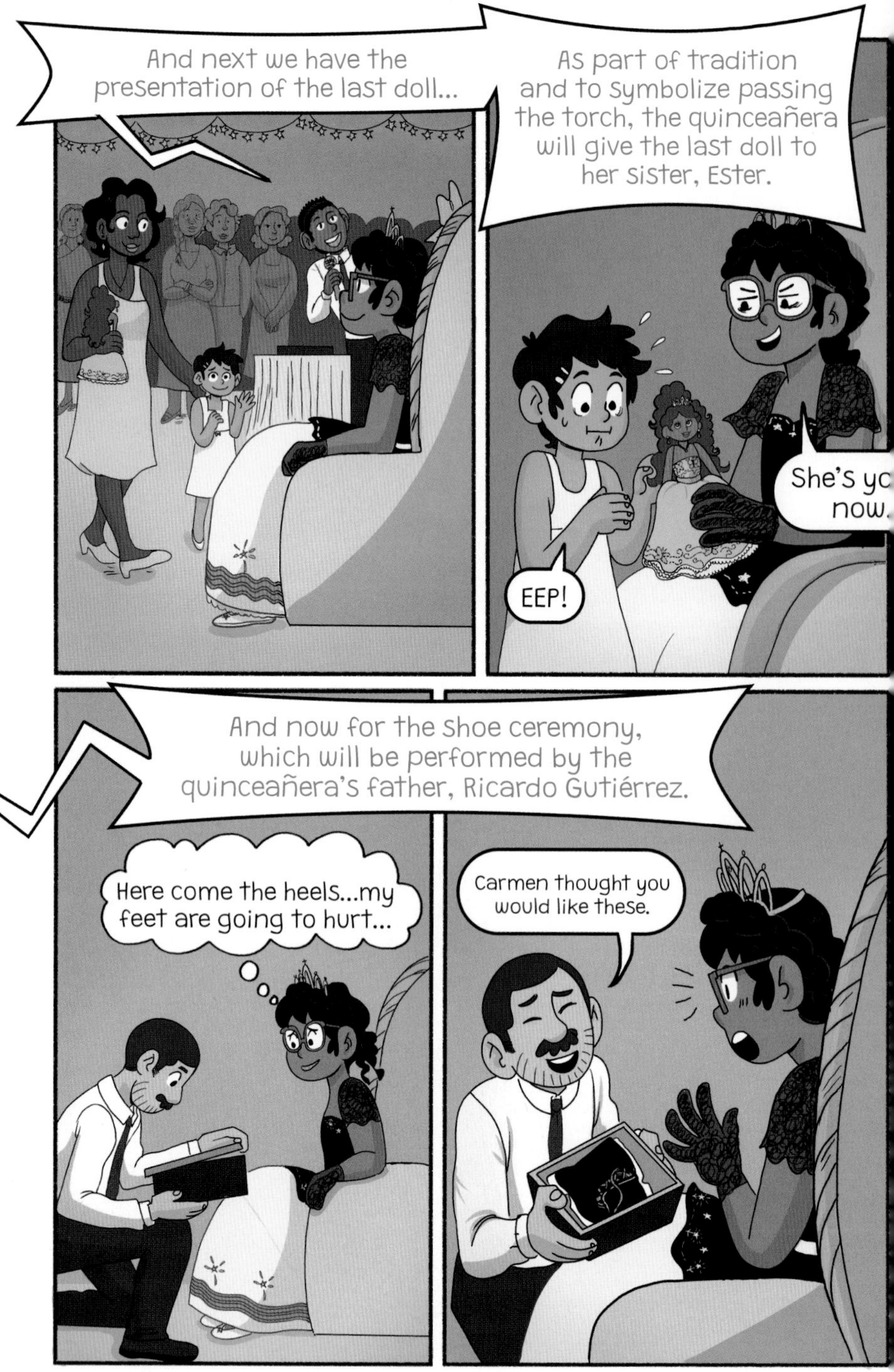
And next we have the presentation of the last doll...
As part of tradition and to symbolize passing the torch, the quinceañera will give the last doll to her sister, Ester.
She's yo
now.
EEP!
And now for the shoe ceremony, which will be performed by the quinceañera's father, Ricardo Gutiérrez.
Here come the heels...my feet are going to hurt...
Carmen thought you would like these.

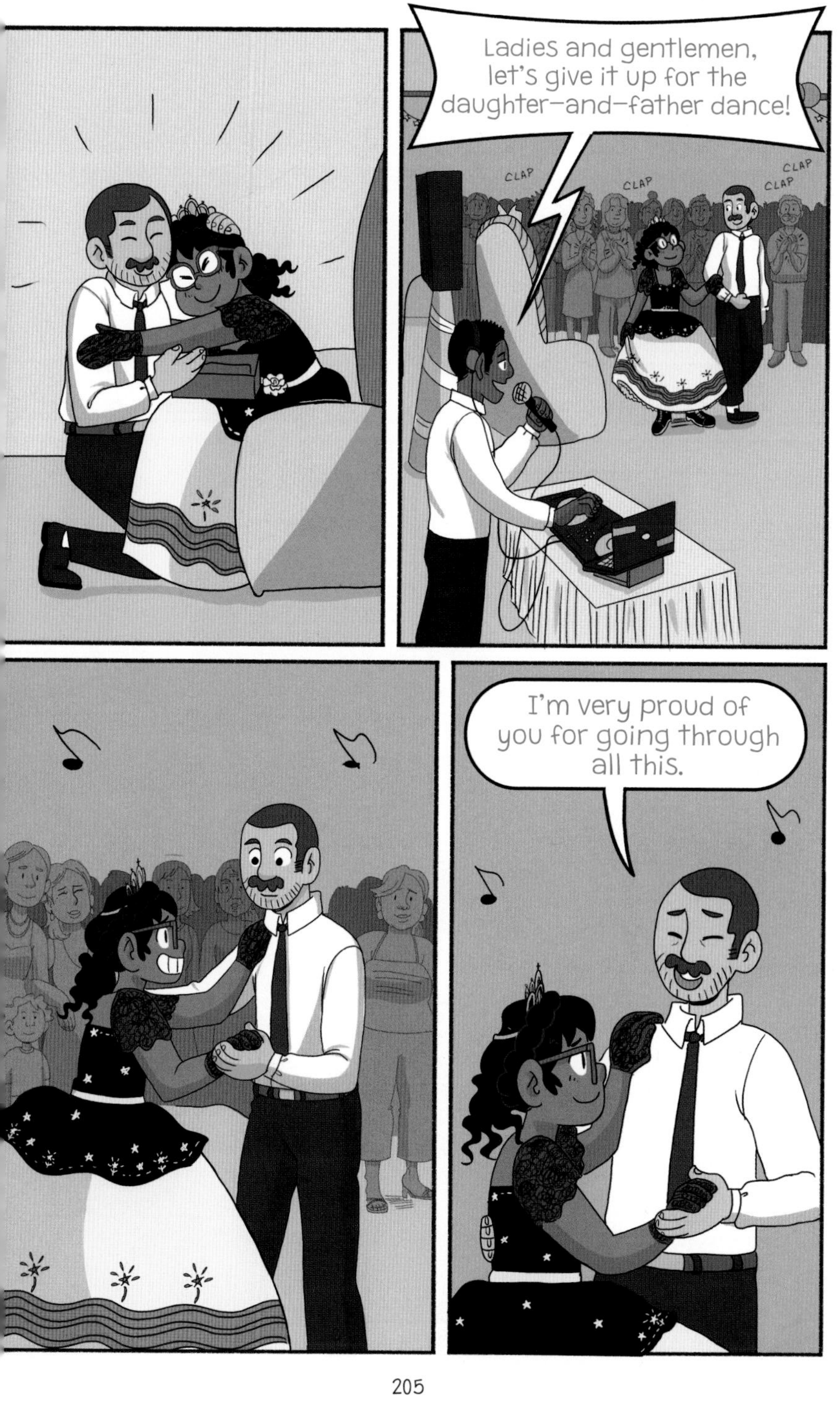
Ladies and gentlemen, let's give it up for the daughter-and-father dance!
CLAP
CLAP
CLAP
CLAP
I'm very proud of you for going through all this.

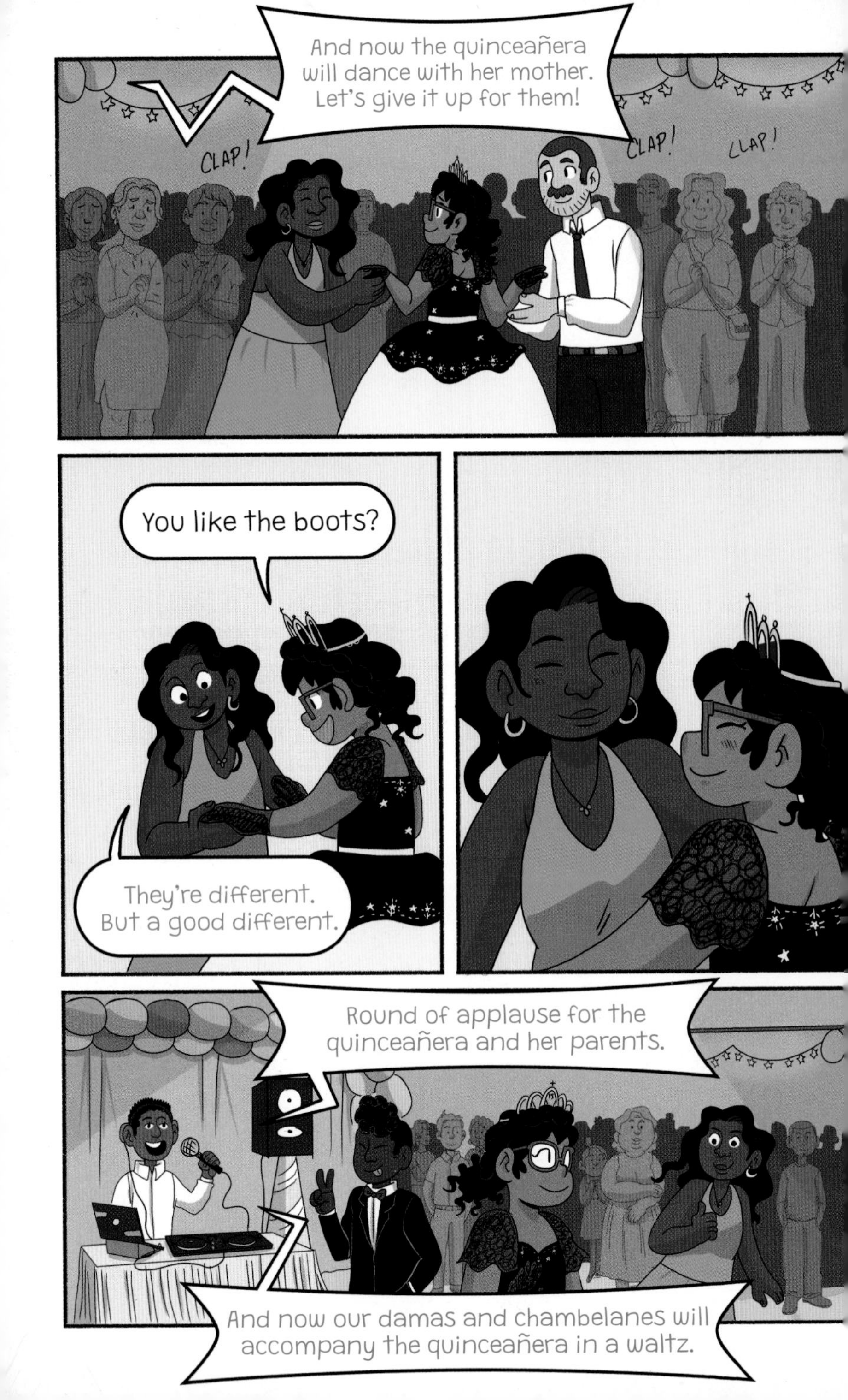
And now the quinceañera will dance with her mother. Let's give it up for them!
CLAP!
CLAP!
CLAP!
You like the boots?
They're different. But a good different.
Round of applause for the quinceañera and her parents.
And now our damas and chambelanes will accompany the quinceañera in a waltz.

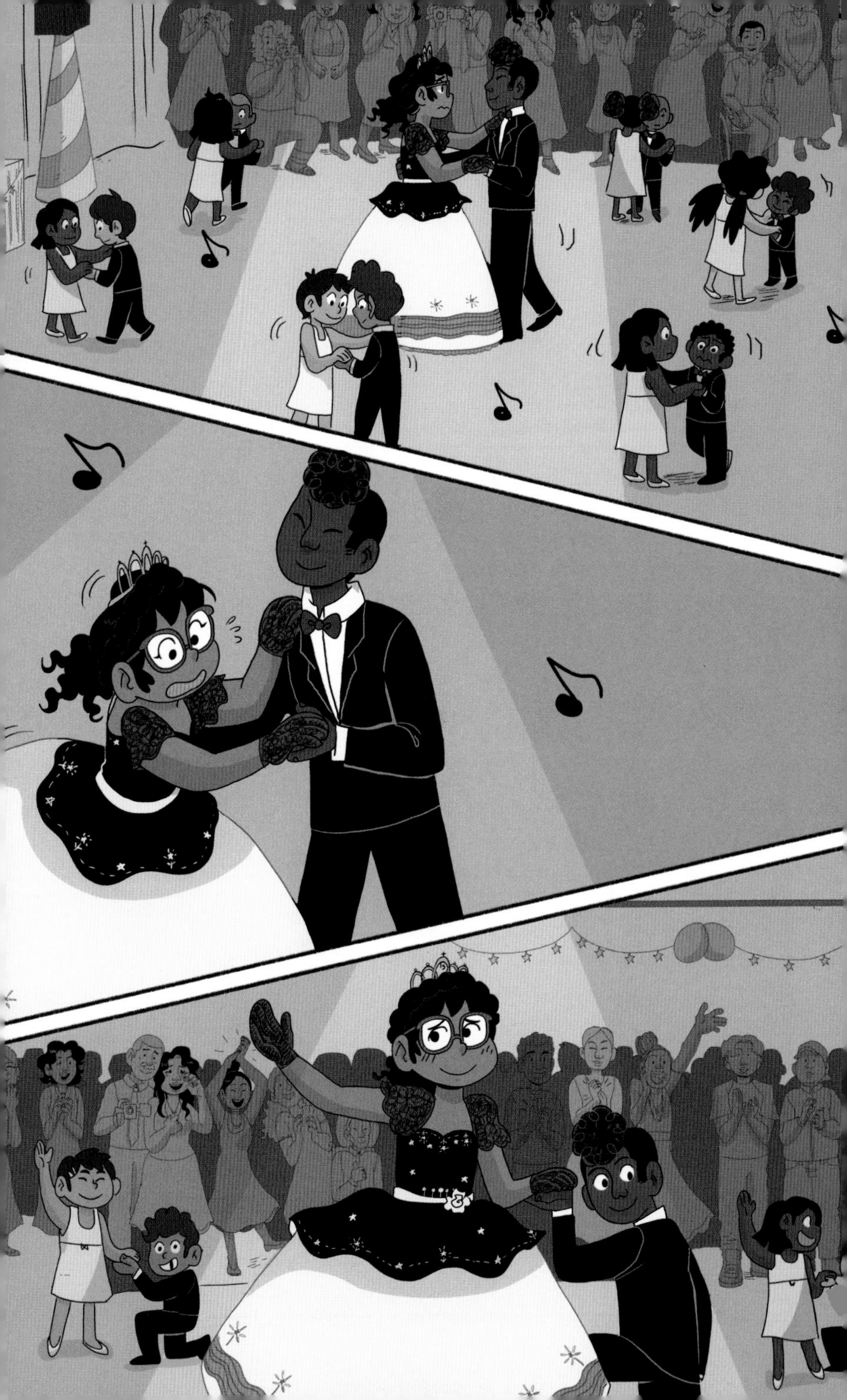

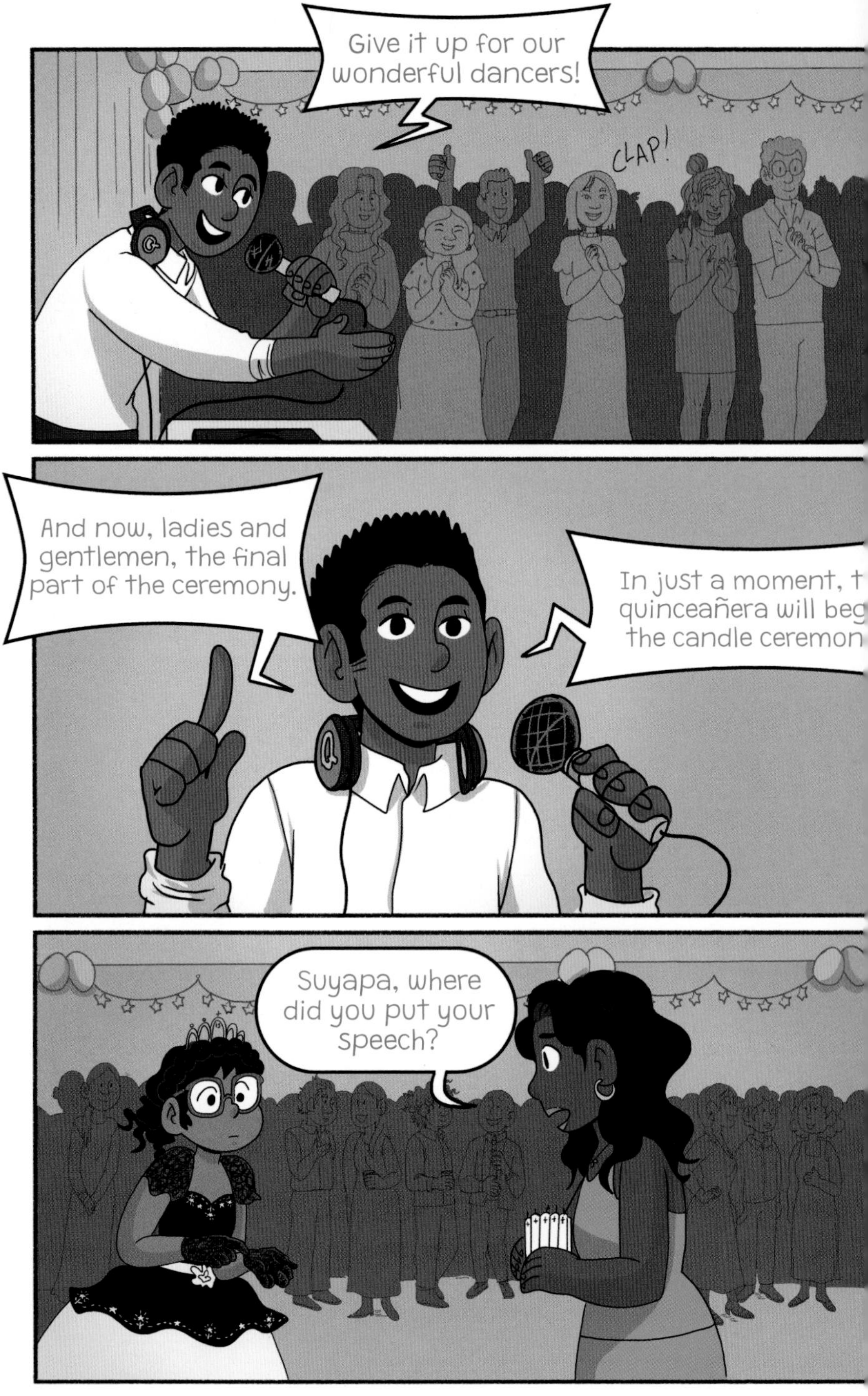
Give it up for our wonderful dancers!
CLAP!
And now, ladies and gentlemen, the final part of the ceremony.
In just a moment, t
quinceañera will beg
the candle ceremon
Suyapa, where did you put your speech?

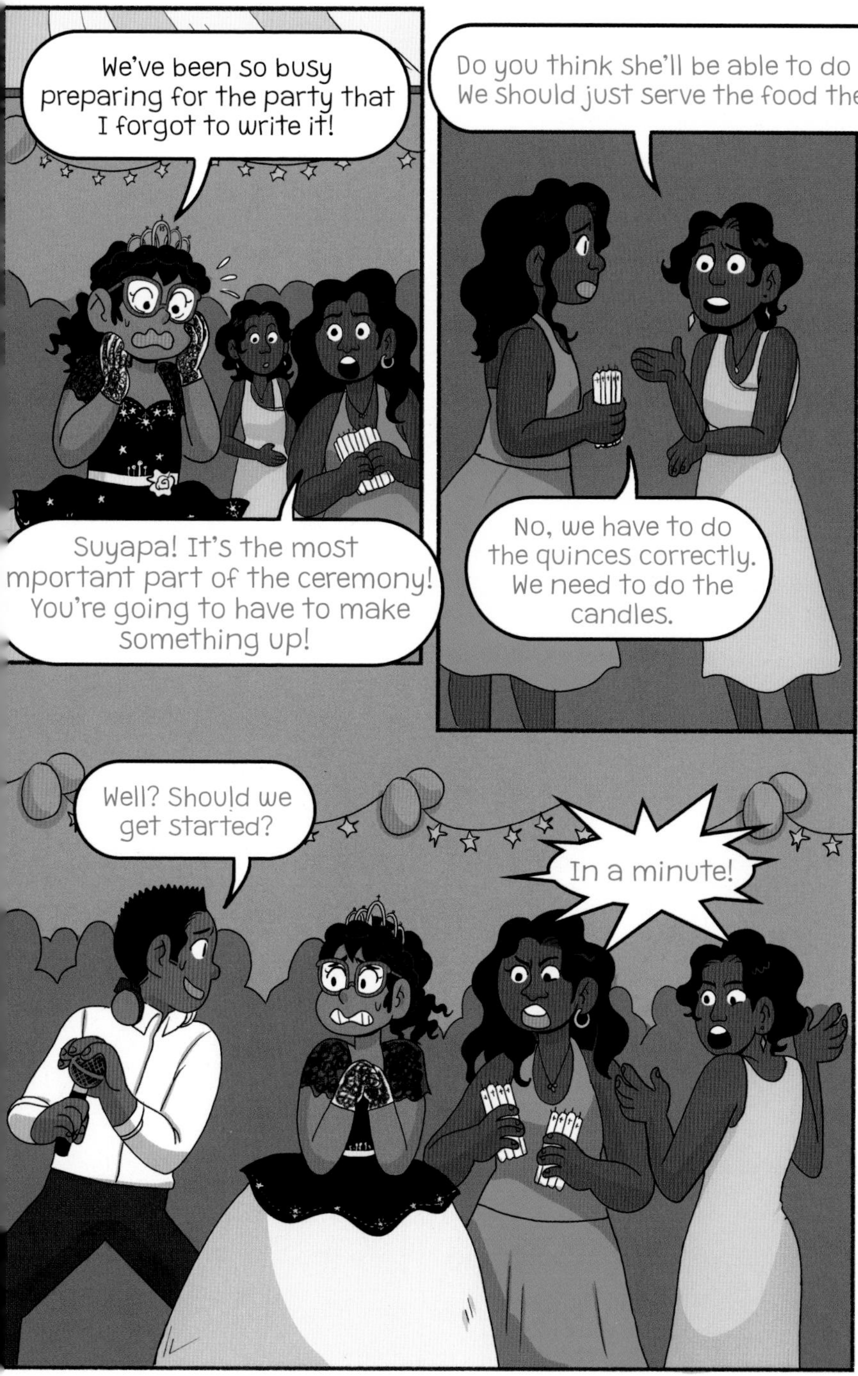
We've been so busy preparing for the party that I forgot to write it!
Suyapa! It's the most mportant part of the ceremony! You're going to have to make something up!
Do you think she'll be able to do it? We should just serve the food then.
No, we have to do the quinces correctly. We need to do the candles.
Well? Should we get started?
In a minute!

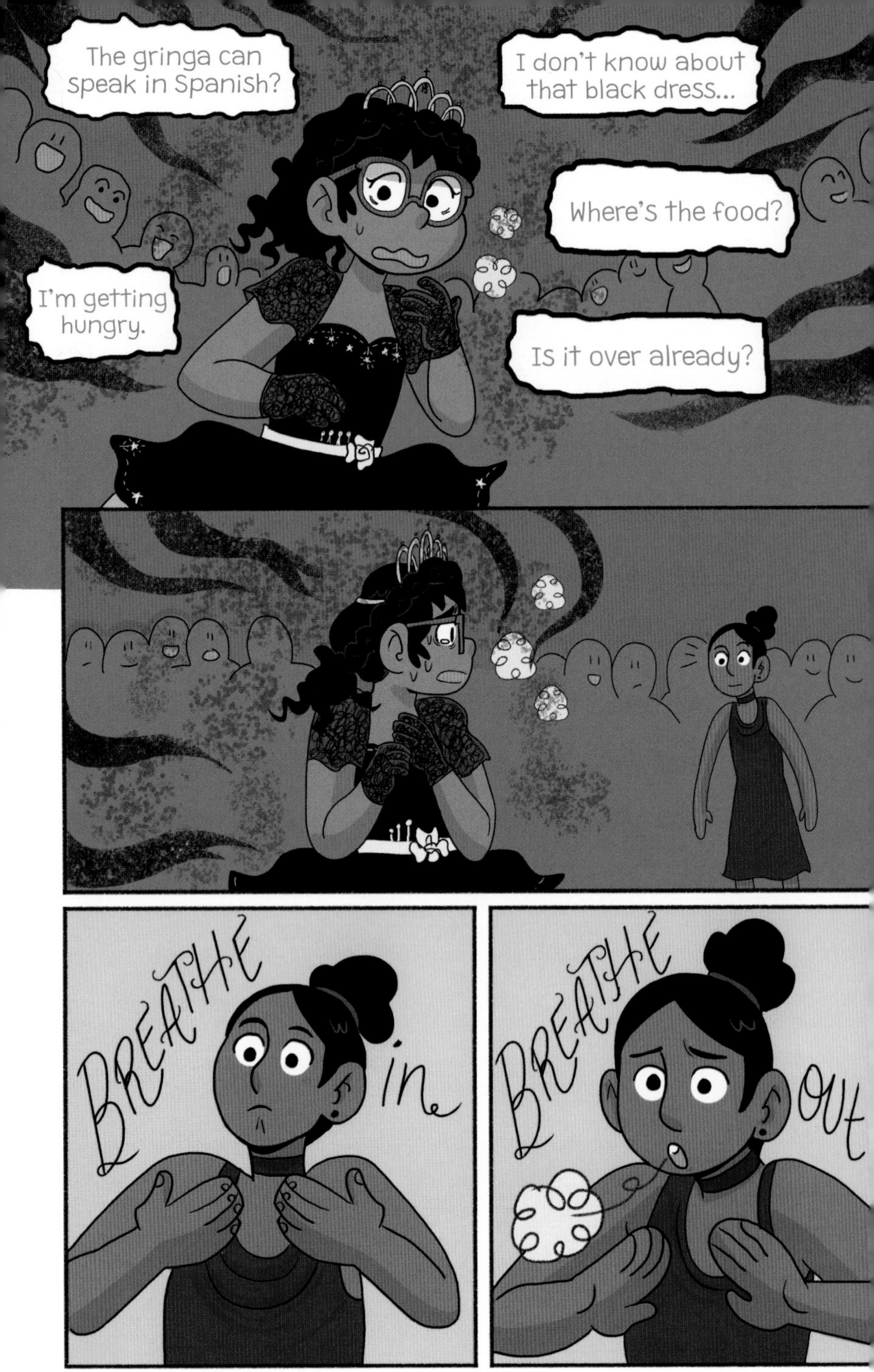
The gringa can speak in Spanish?
I don't know about that black dress...
Where's the food?
I'm getting hungry.
Is it over already?
BREATHE in
BREATHE OUT

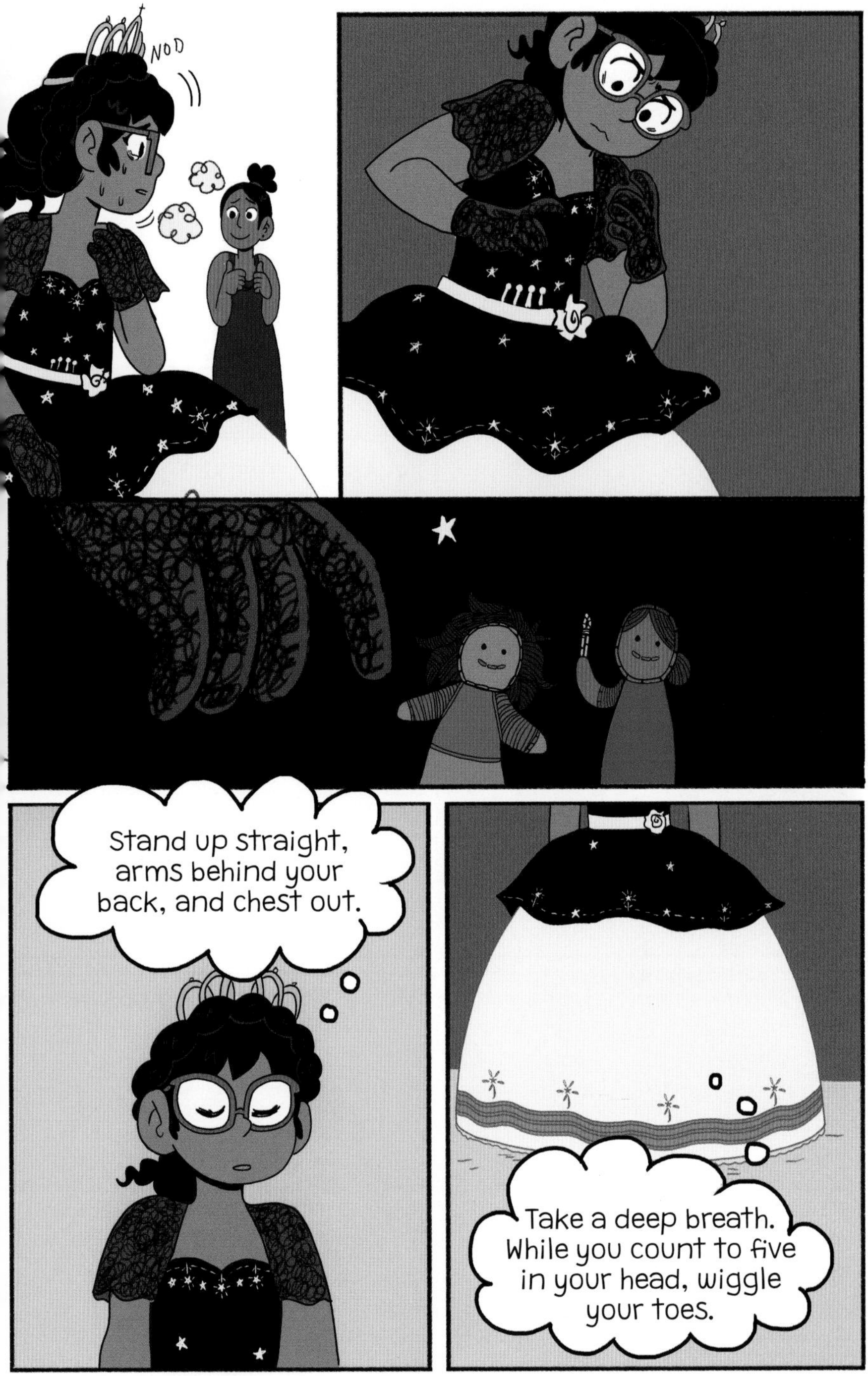
NOD
Stand up straight, arms behind your back, and chest out.
Take a deep breath. While you count to five in your head, wiggle your toes.

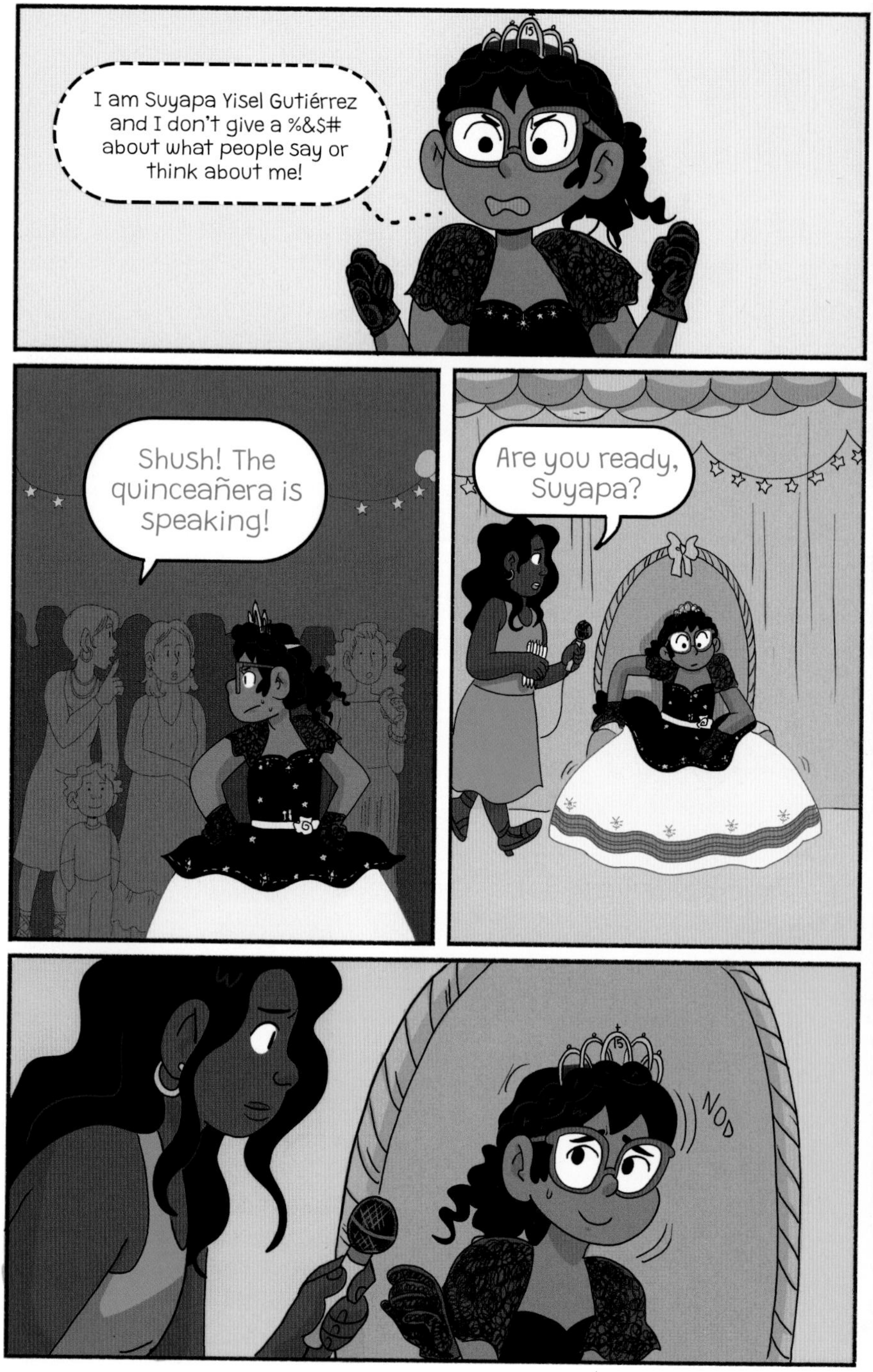
I am Suyapa Yisel Gutiérrez and I don't give a %&$# about what people say or think about me!
Shush! The quinceañera is speaking!
Are you ready, Suyapa?
NOD

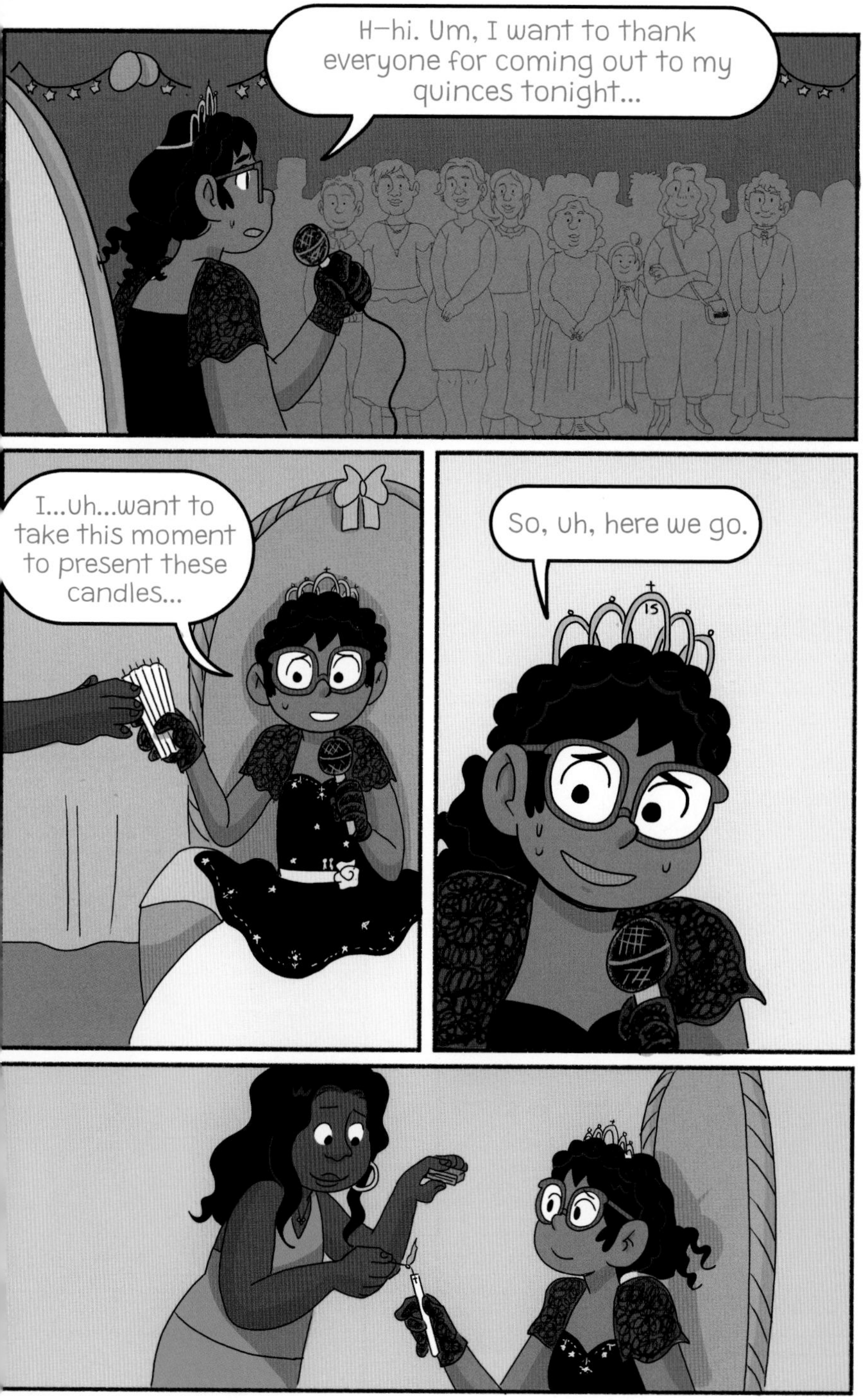
H-hi. Um, I want to thank everyone for coming out to my quinces tonight...
I...uh...want to take this moment to present these candles...
So, uh, here we go.
15

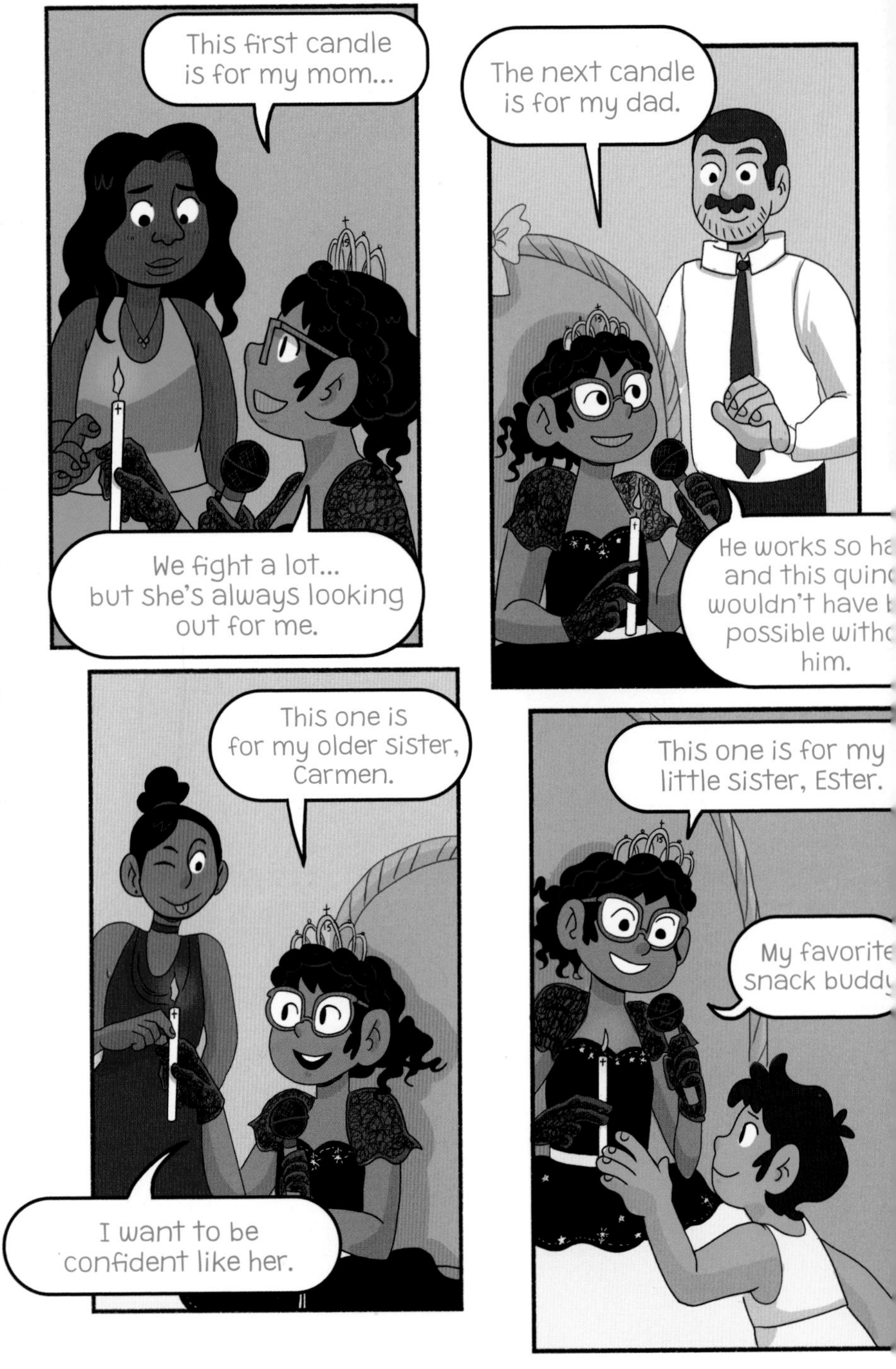
This first candle is for my mom...
We fight a lot... but she's always looking out for me.
The next candle is for my dad.
He works so ha and this quin wouldn't have possible with him.
This one is for my older sister, Carmen.
I want to be confident like her.
This one is for my little sister, Ester.
My favorite snack budd

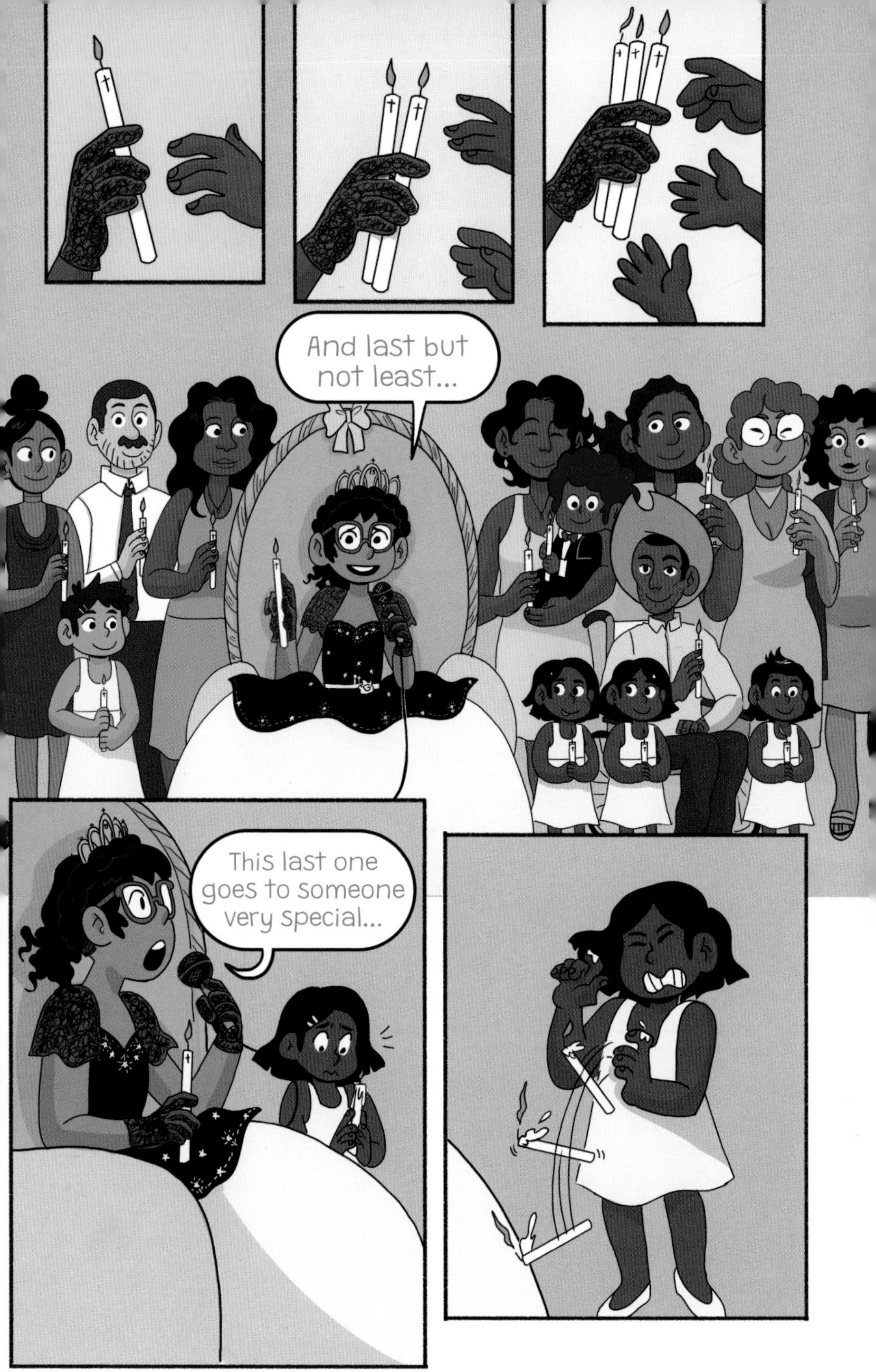

And last but not least...
This last one goes to someone very special...

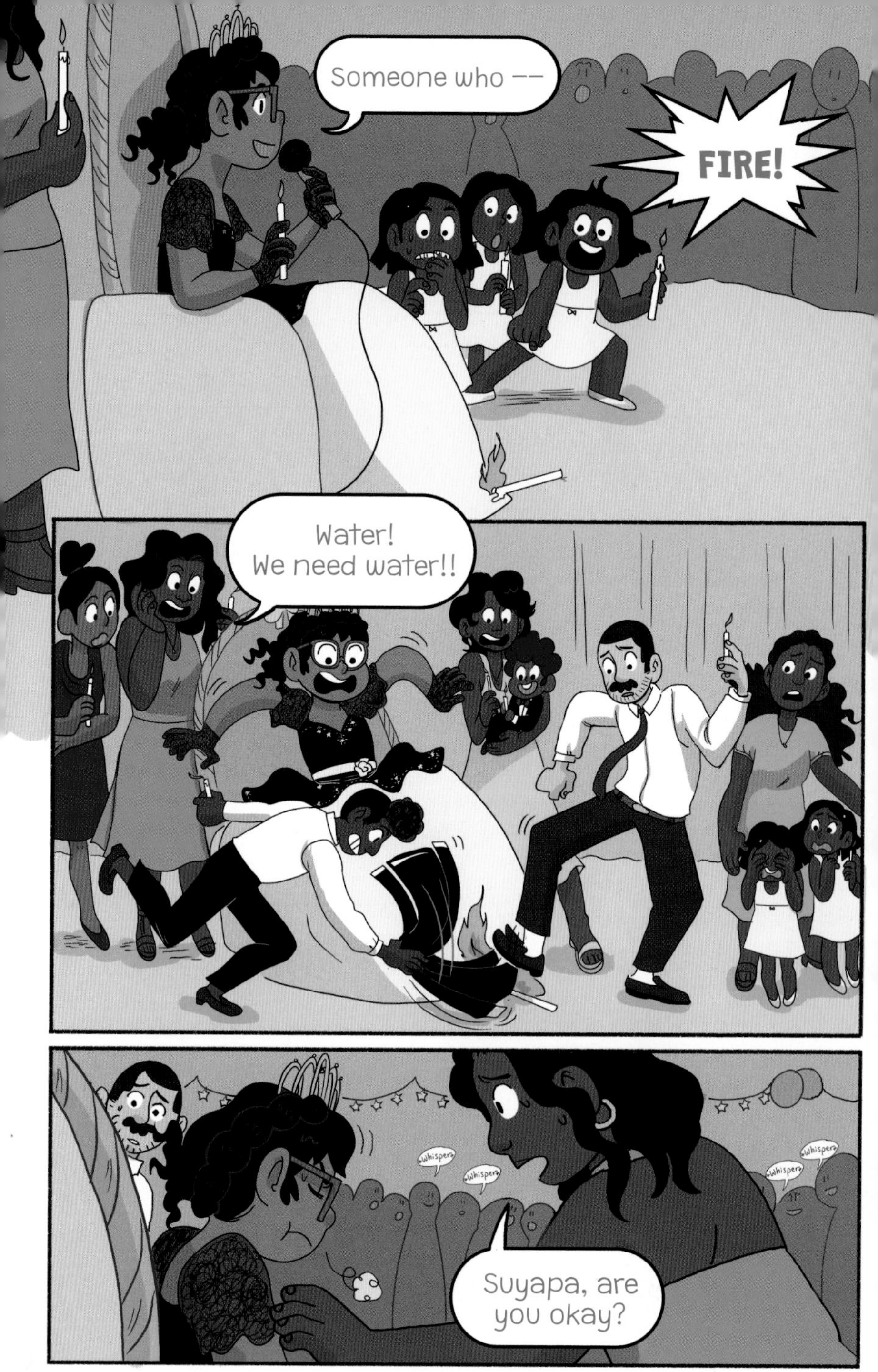
Someone who --
FIRE!
Water!
We need water!!
Whispers
Whispers
Whispers
Whispers
Suyapa, are you okay?

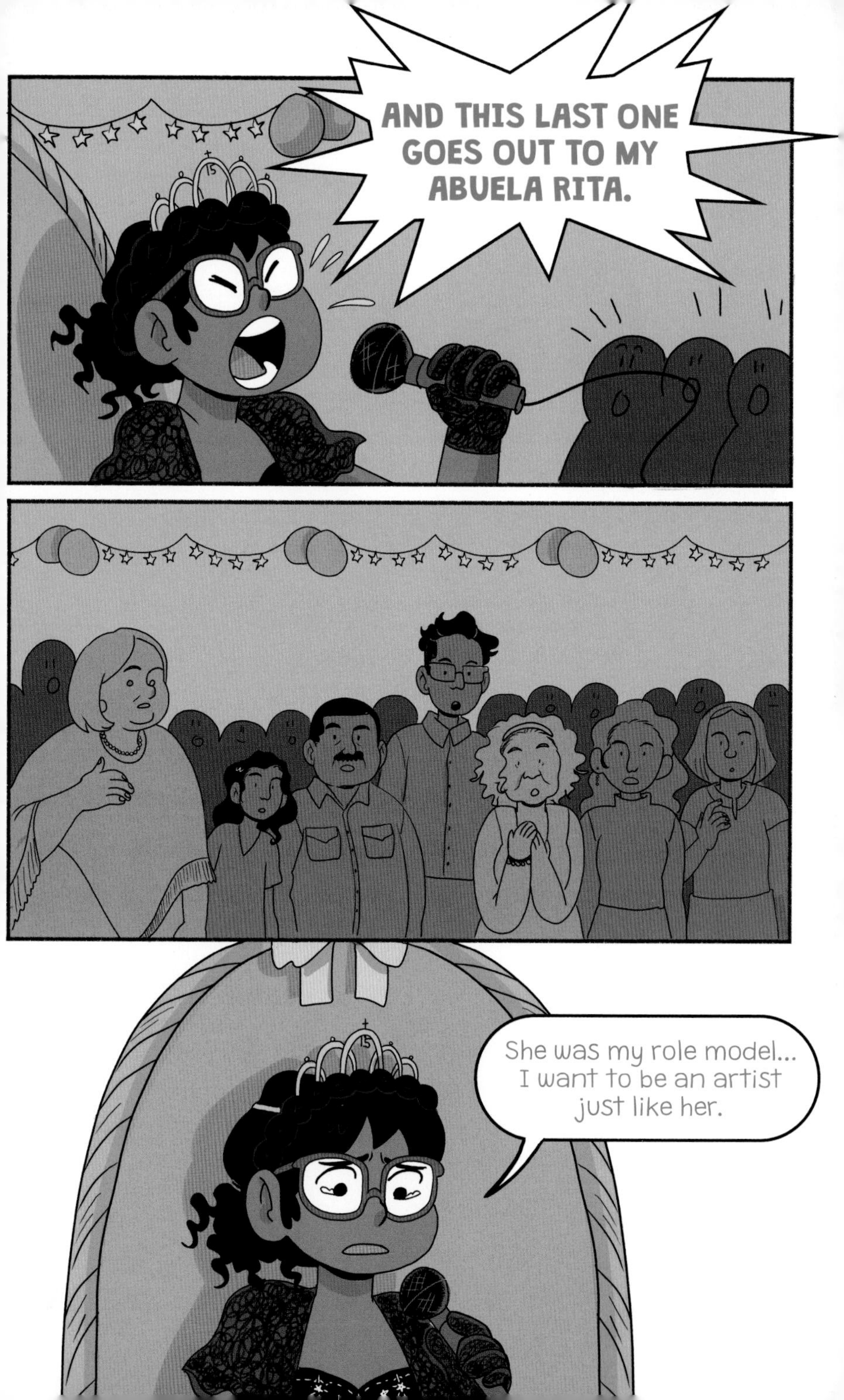
AND THIS LAST ONE GOES OUT TO MY ABUELA RITA.
She was my role model... I want to be an artist just like her.

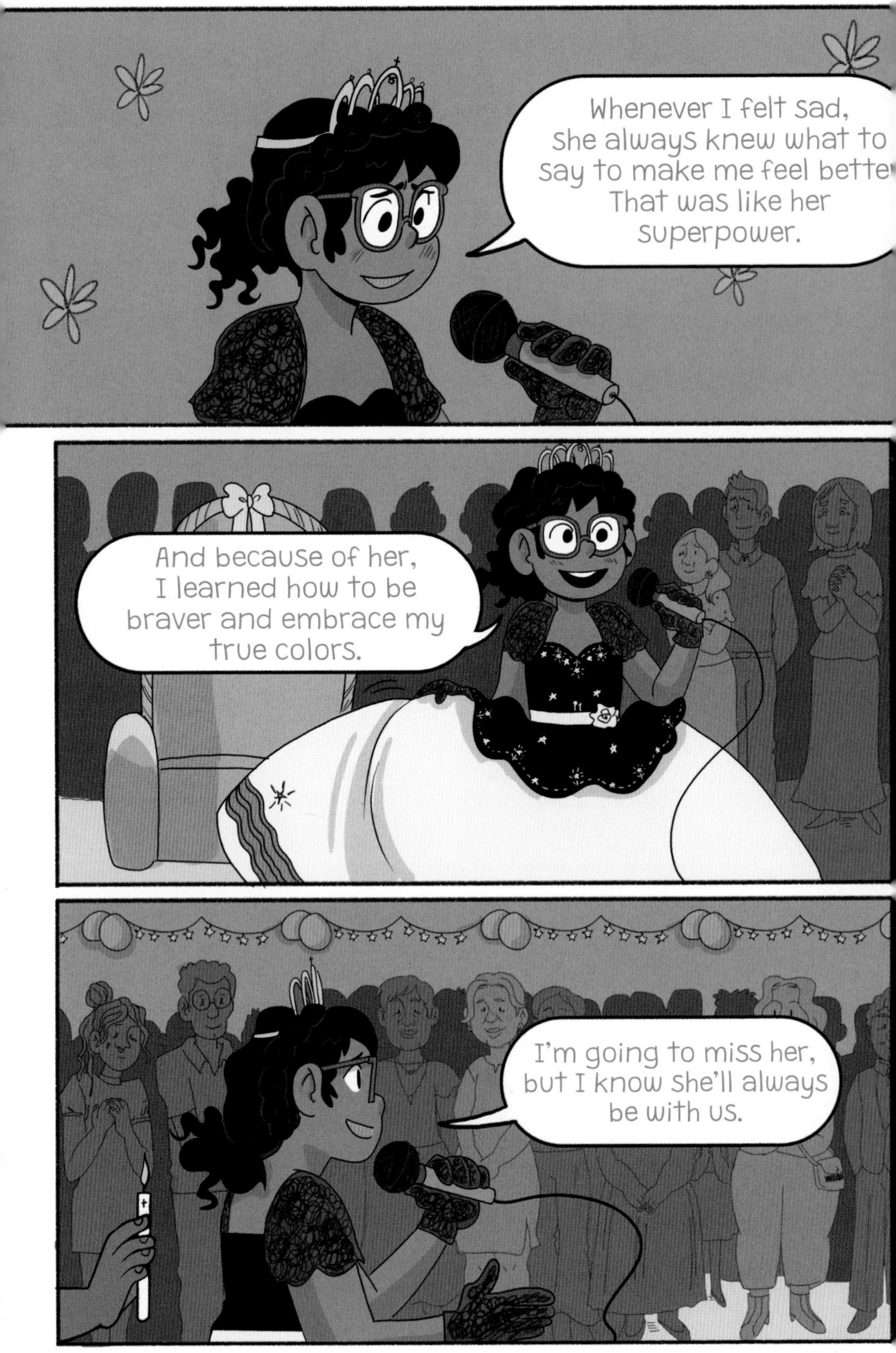
Whenever I felt sad, she always knew what to say to make me feel bette That was like her superpower.
And because of her, I learned how to be braver and embrace my true colors.
I'm going to miss her, but I know she'll always be with us.

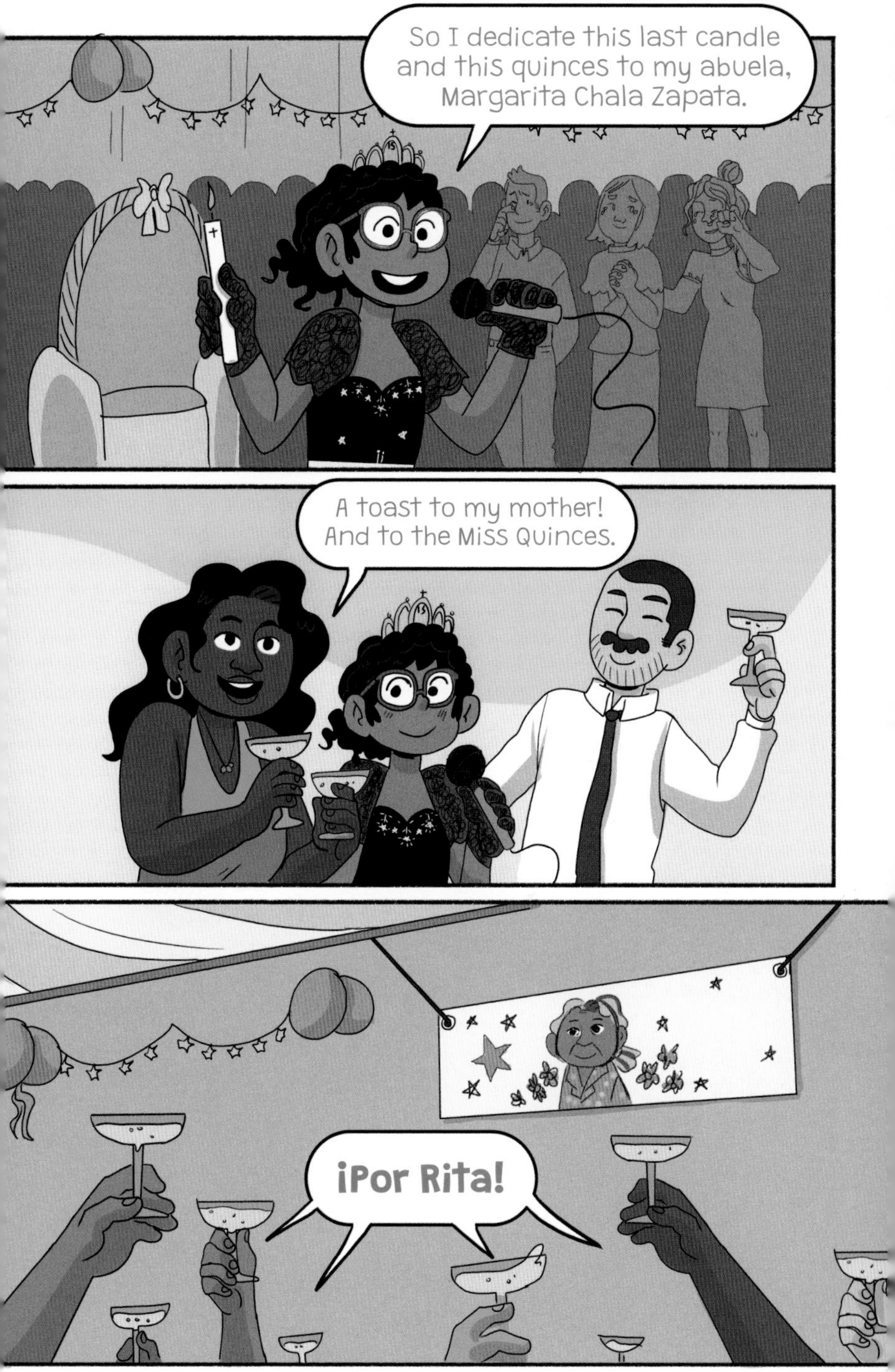
So I dedicate this last candle and this quinces to my abuela, Margarita Chala Zapata.
A toast to my mother! And to the Miss Quinces.
¡Por Rita!

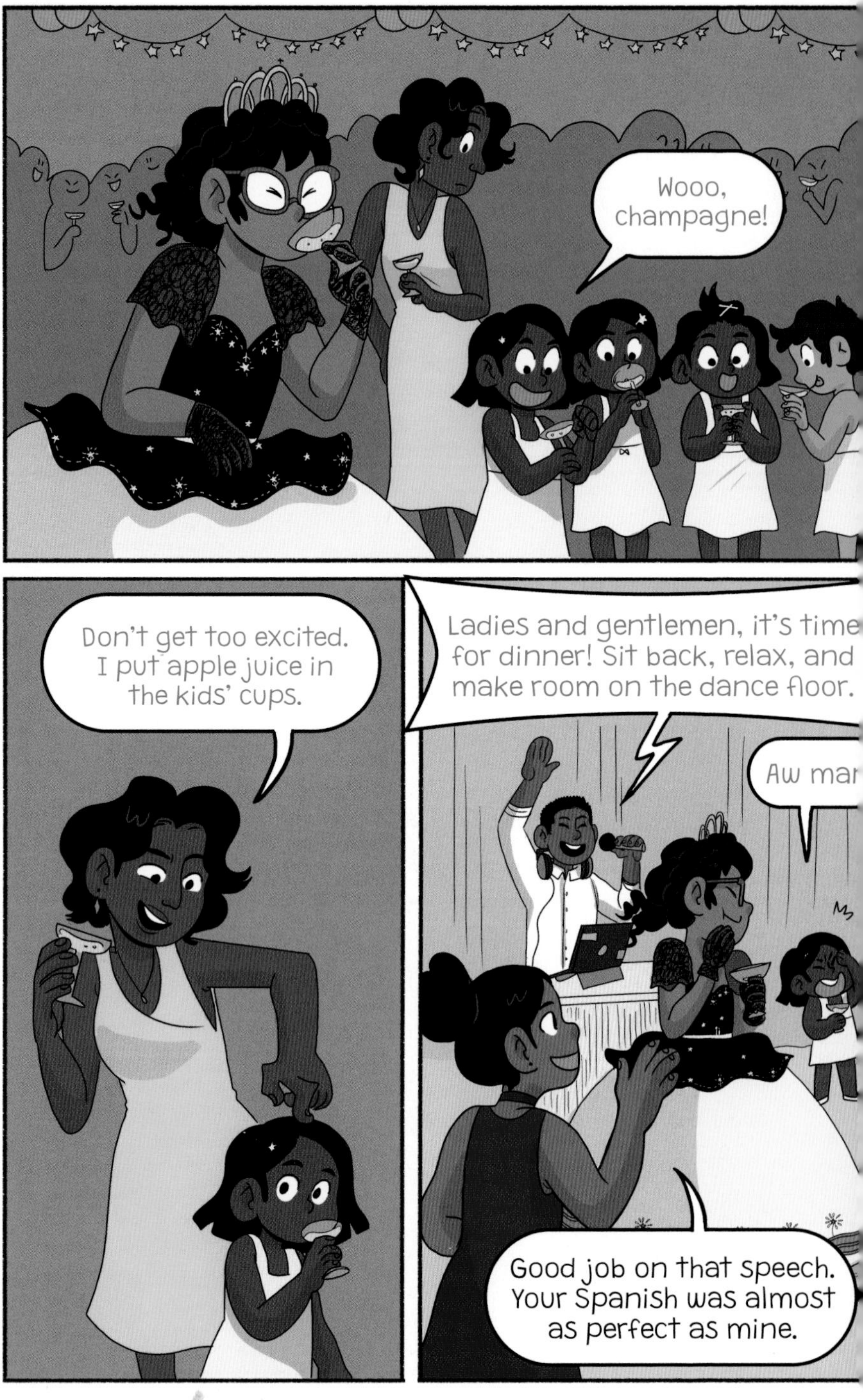

Wooo, champagne!
Don't get too excited. I put apple juice in the kids' cups.
Ladies and gentlemen, it's time for dinner! Sit back, relax, and make room on the dance floor.
Aw mar
Good job on that speech. Your Spanish was almost as perfect as mine.

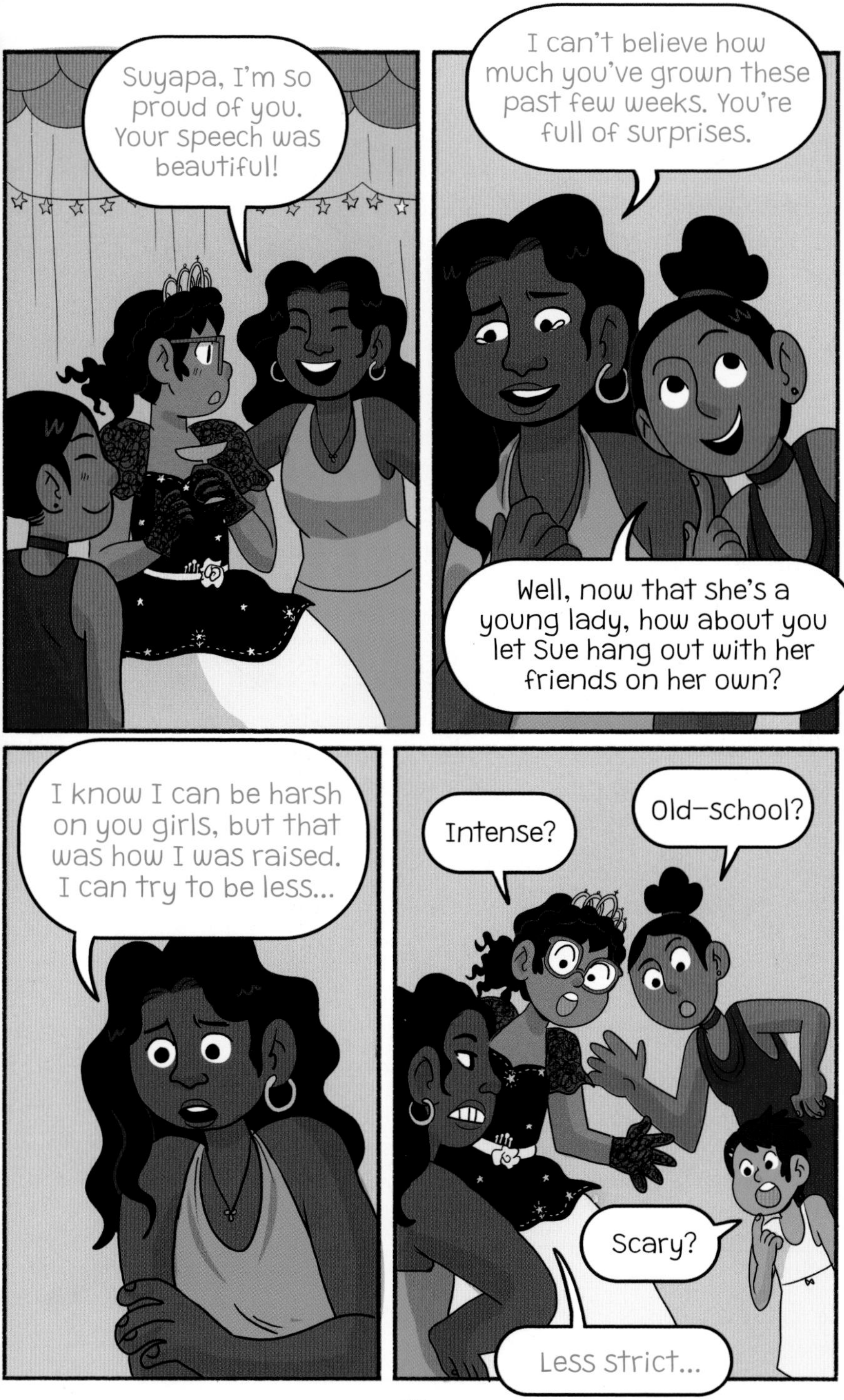
Suyapa, I'm so proud of you. Your speech was beautiful!
I can't believe how much you've grown these past few weeks. You're full of surprises.
Well, now that she's a young lady, how about you let Sue hang out with her friends on her own?
I know I can be harsh on you girls, but that was how I was raised. I can try to be less...
Intense?
Old-school?
Scary?
Less strict...

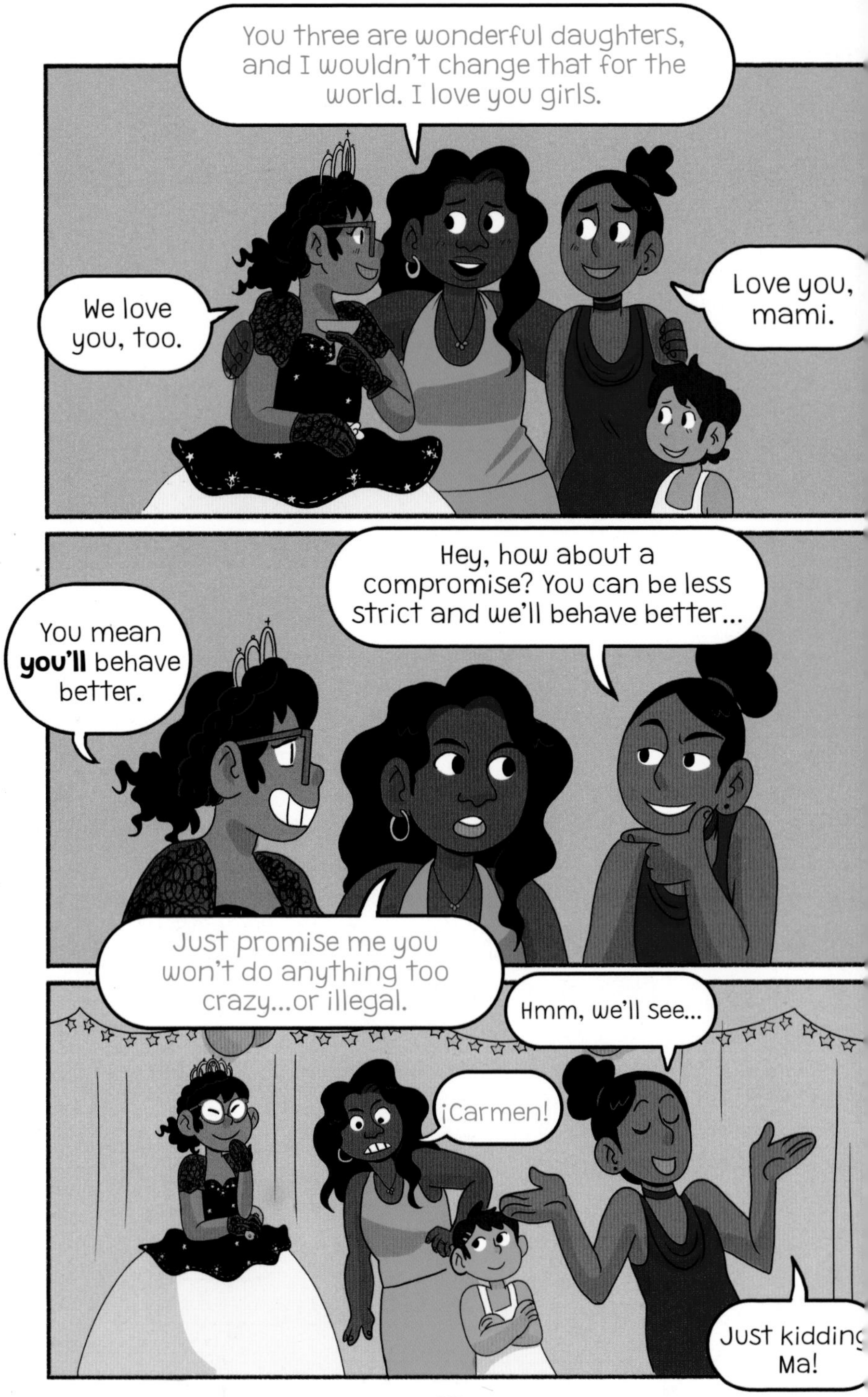

You three are wonderful daughters, and I wouldn't change that for the world. I love you girls.
We love you, too.
Love you, mami.
Hey, how about a compromise? You can be less strict and we'll behave better...
You mean **you'll** behave better.
Just promise me you won't do anything too crazy...or illegal.
Hmm, we'll see...
¡Carmen!
Just kidding Ma!

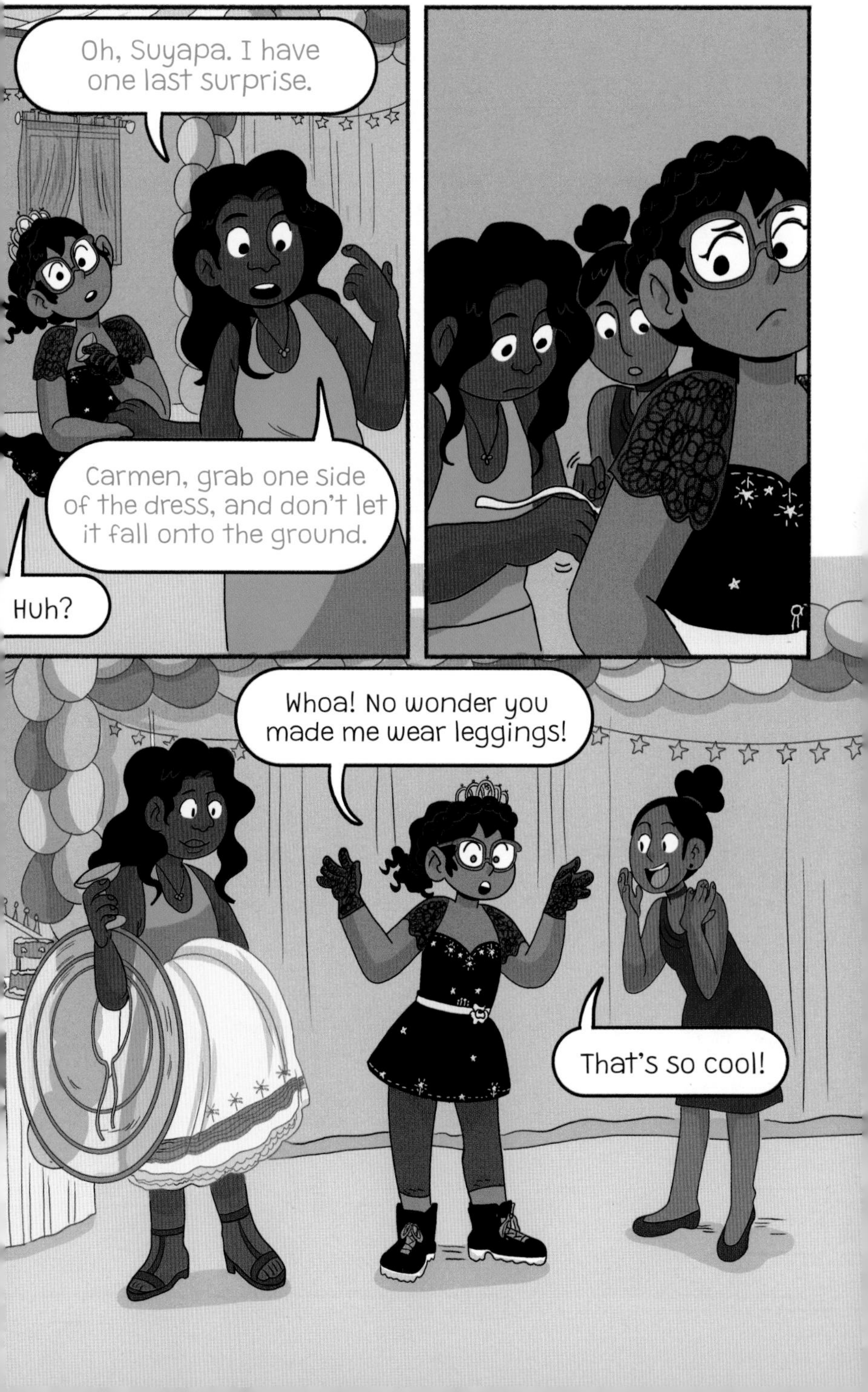
Oh, Suyapa. I have one last surprise.
Carmen, grab one side of the dress, and don't let it fall onto the ground.
Huh?
Whoa! No wonder you made me wear leggings!
That's so cool!

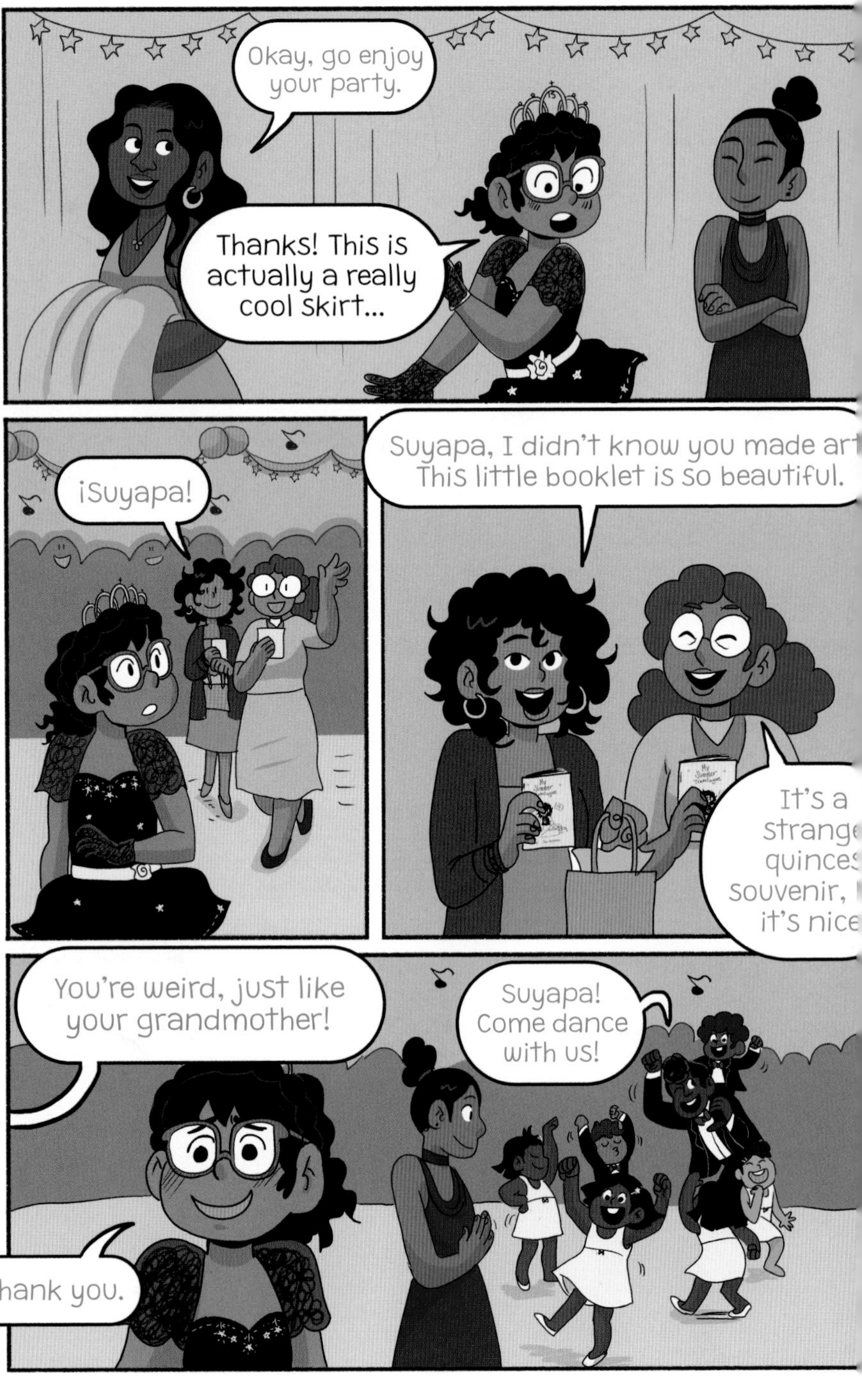

Okay, go enjoy your party.
Thanks! This is actually a really cool skirt...
¡Suyapa!
Suyapa, I didn't know you made art. This little booklet is so beautiful.
It's a strange quinces souvenir, it's nice
You're weird, just like your grandmother!
Suyapa! Come dance with us!
Thank you.

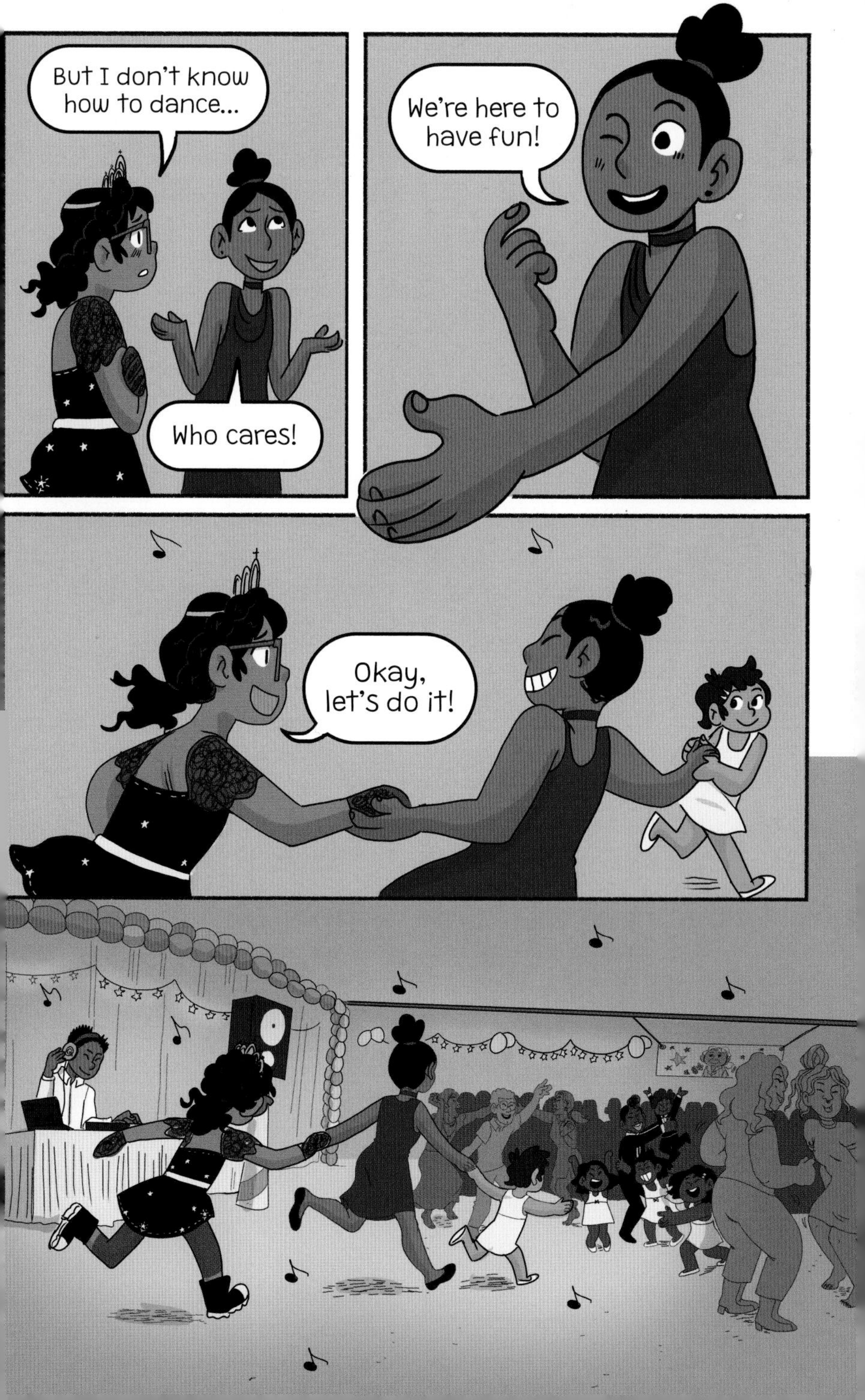
But I don't know how to dance...
Who cares!
We're here to have fun!
Okay, let's do it!

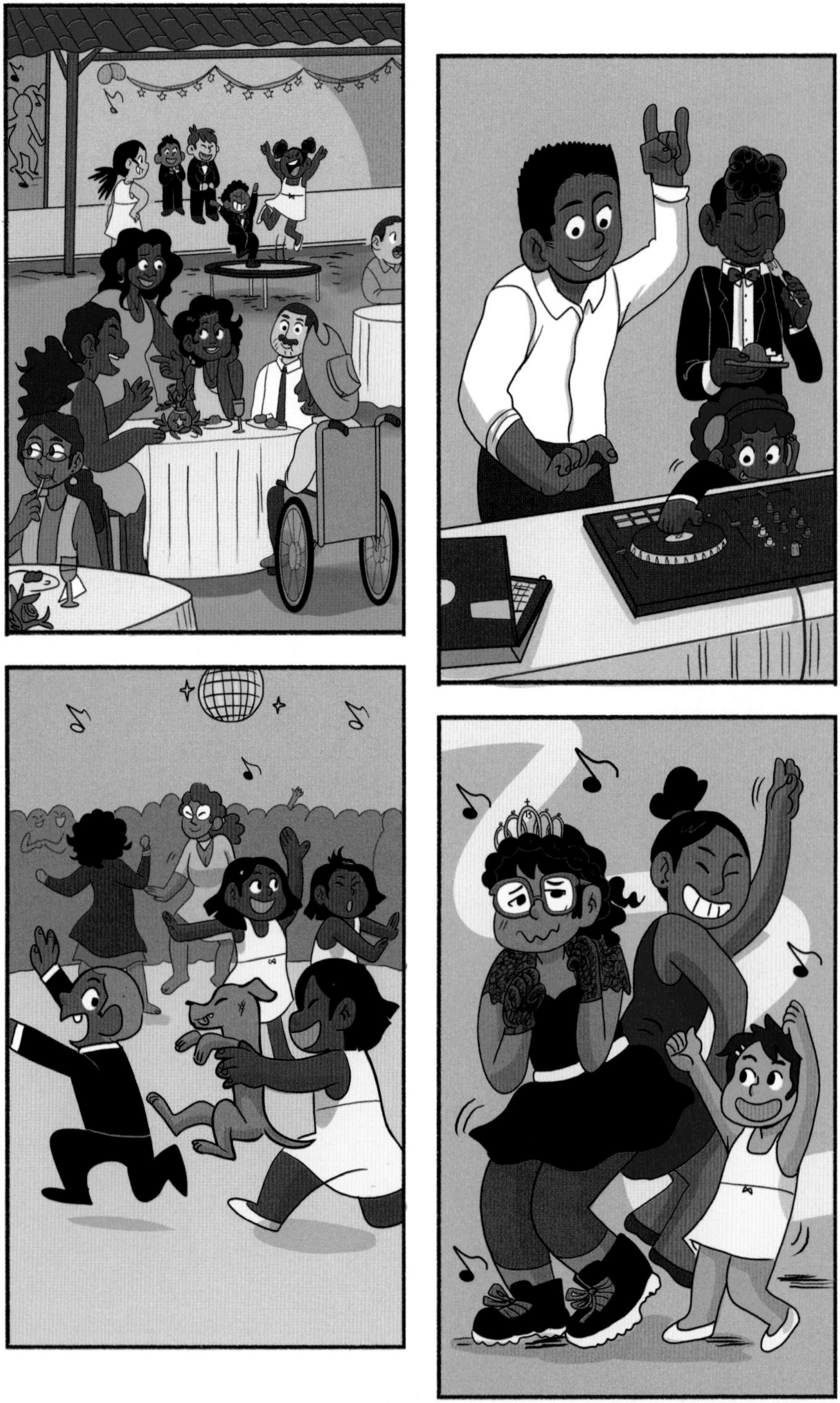

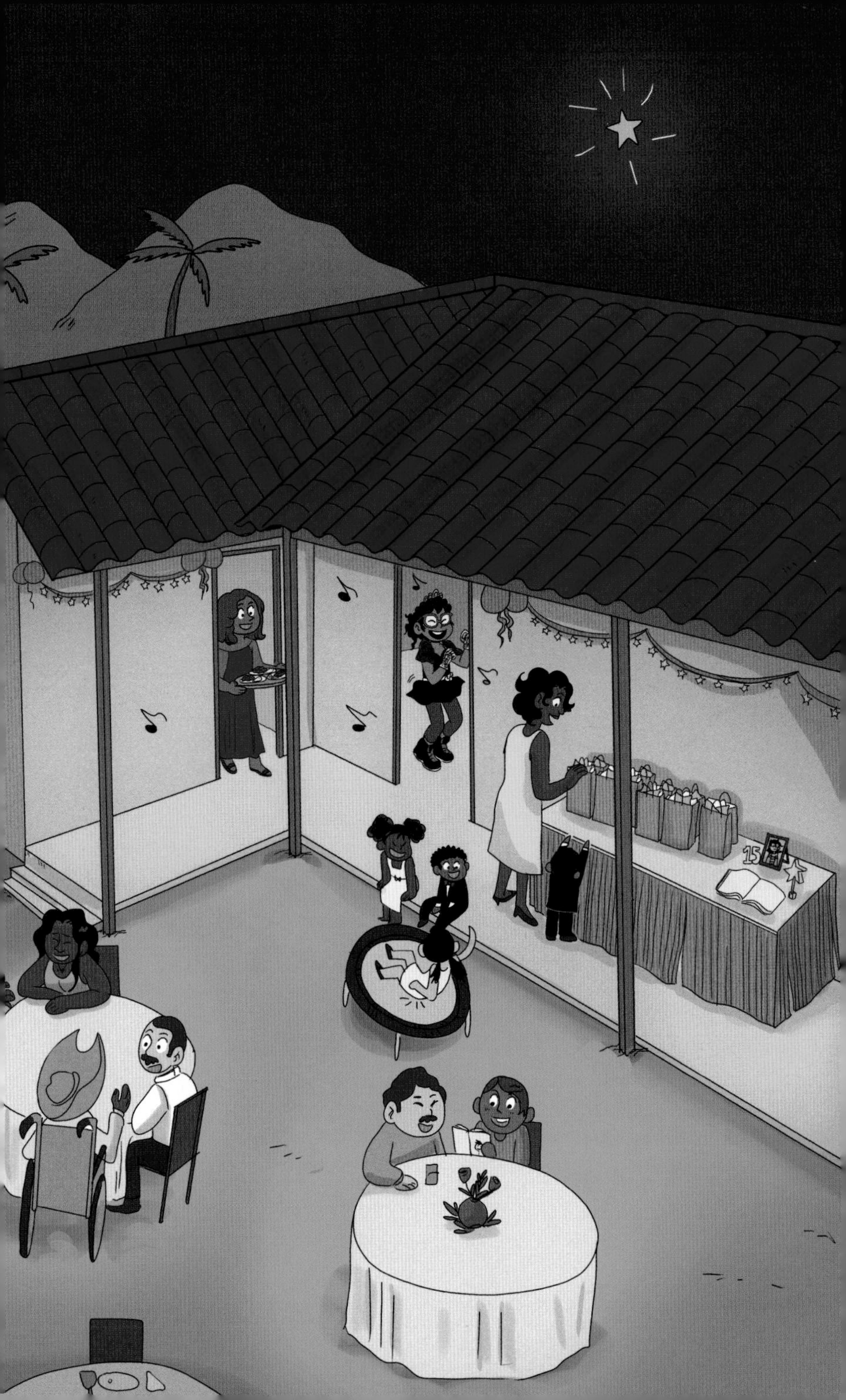
15

CHAPTER TEN

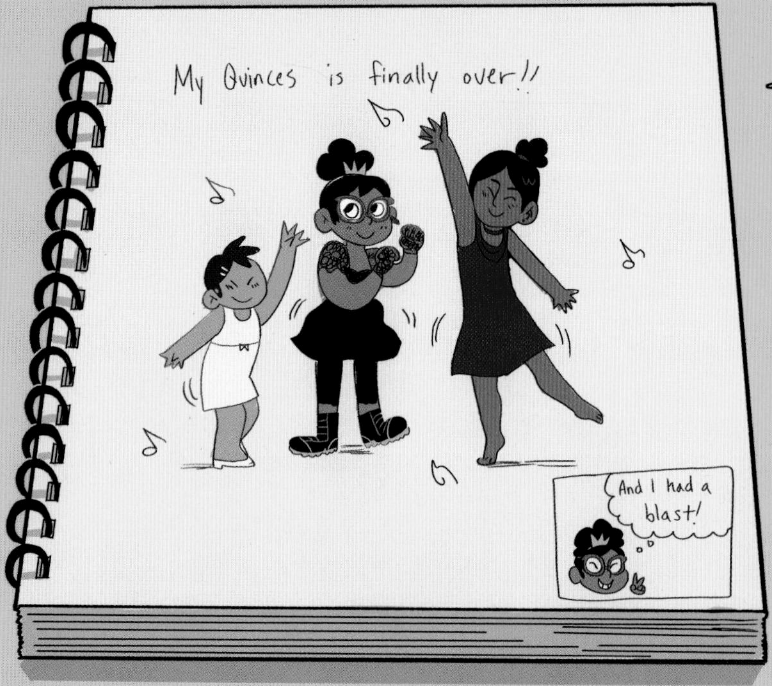
My Quinces is finally over!!
And I had a blast!

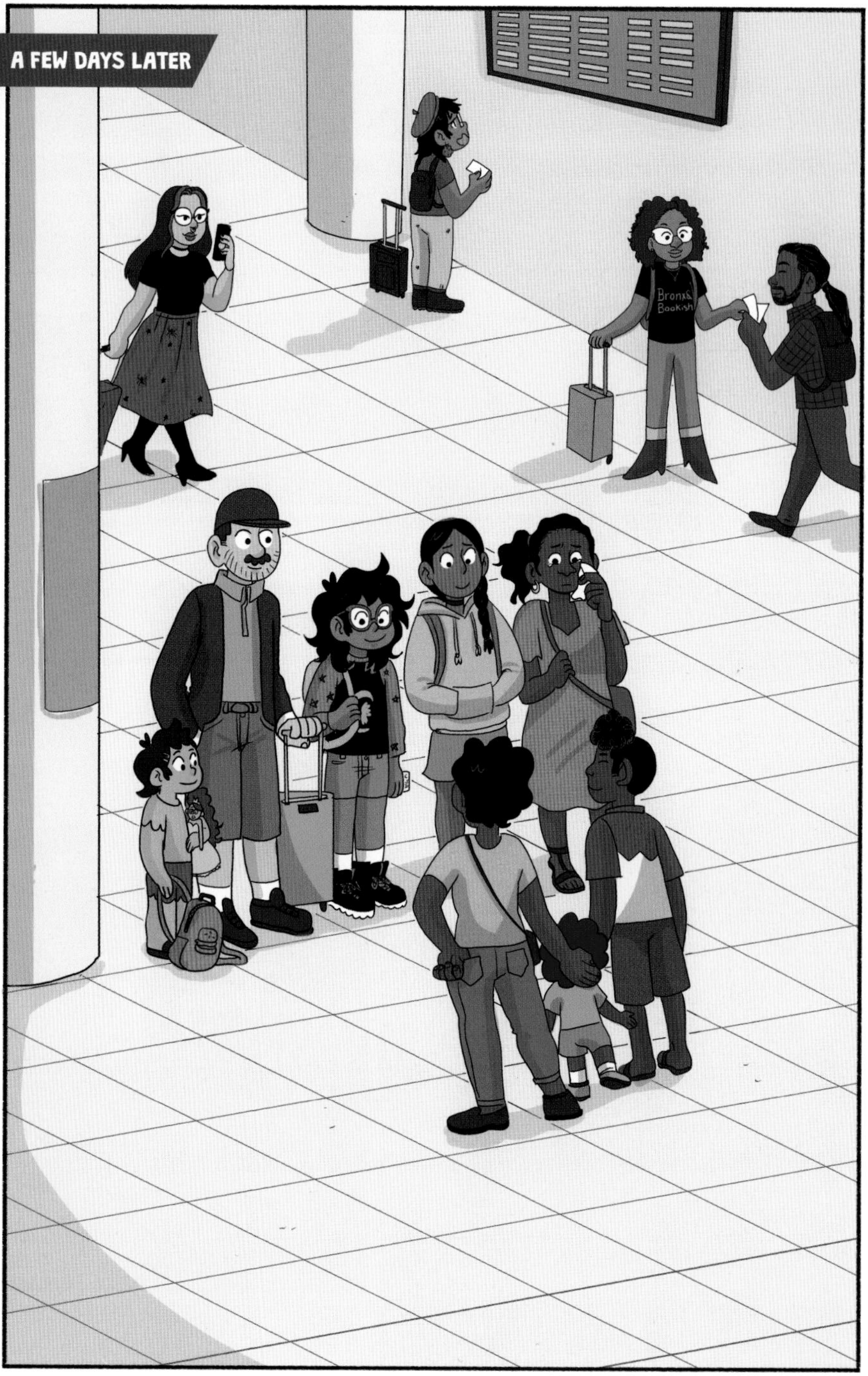
A FEW DAYS LATER
Bronx&
Bookish

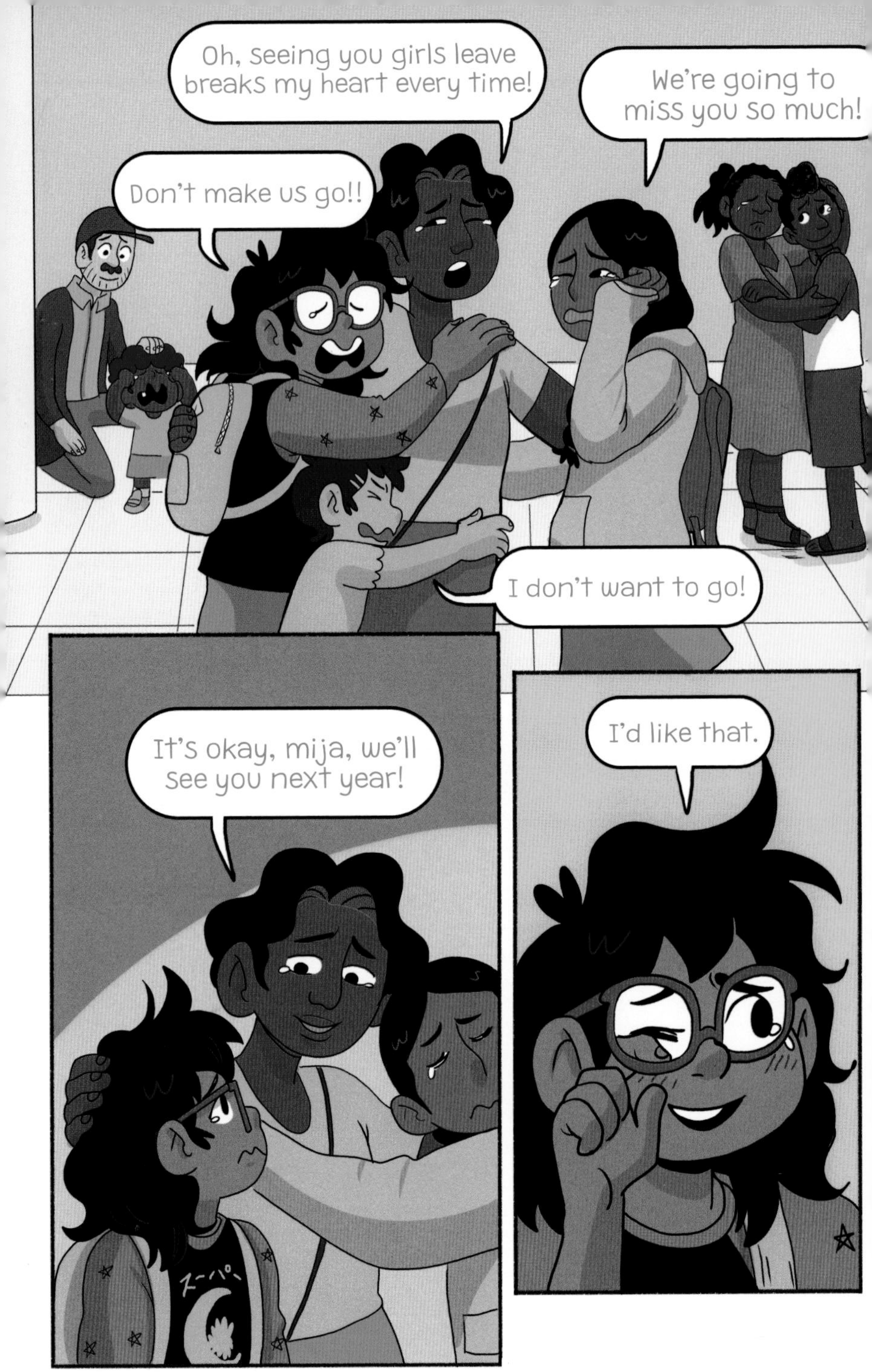
Oh, seeing you girls leave breaks my heart every time!
We're going to miss you so much!
Don't make us go!!
I don't want to go!
It's okay, mija, we'll see you next year!
I'd like that.

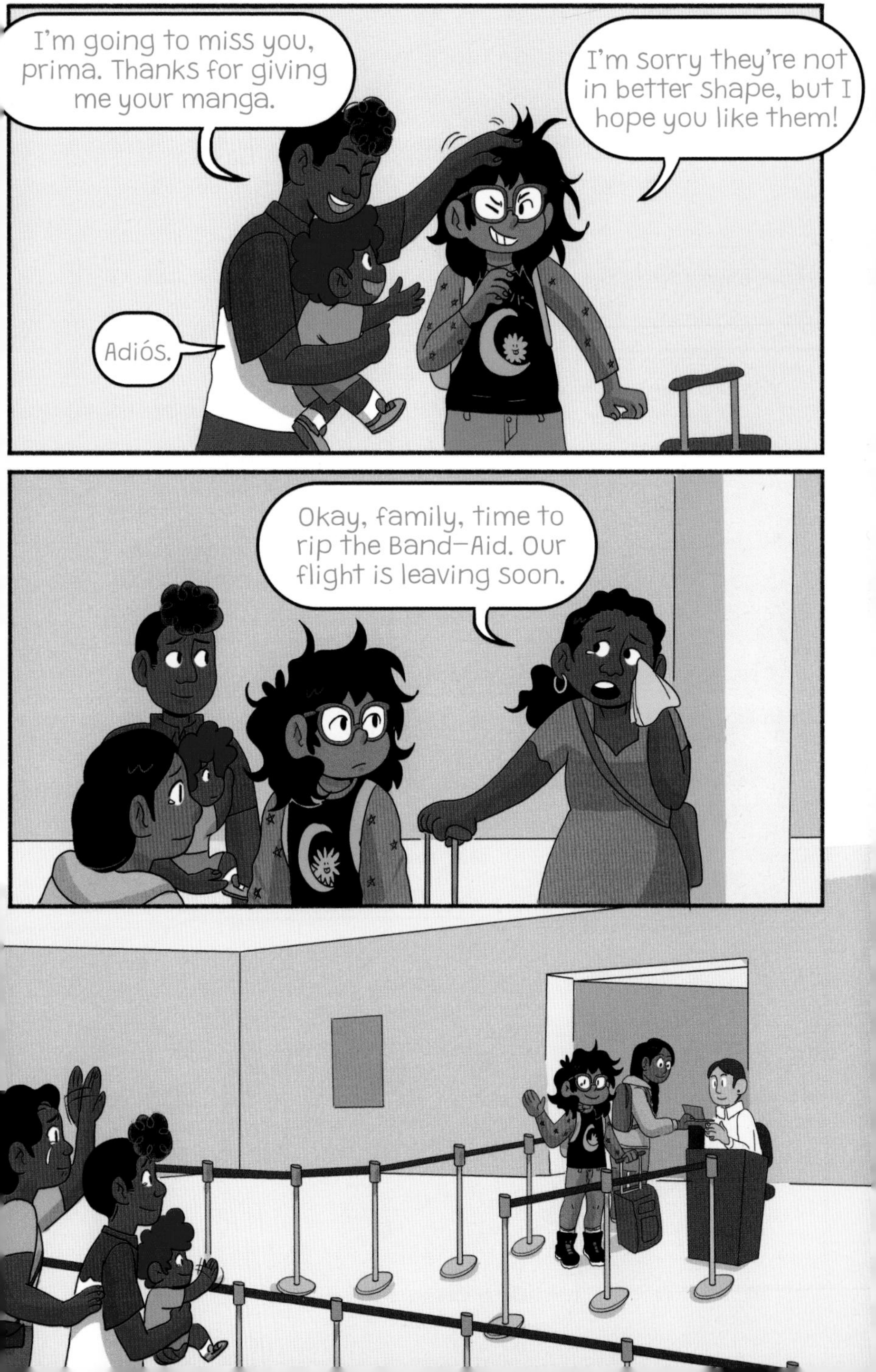
I'm going to miss you, prima. Thanks for giving me your manga.
I'm sorry they're not in better shape, but I hope you like them!
Adiós.
Okay, family, time to rip the Band-Aid. Our flight is leaving soon.

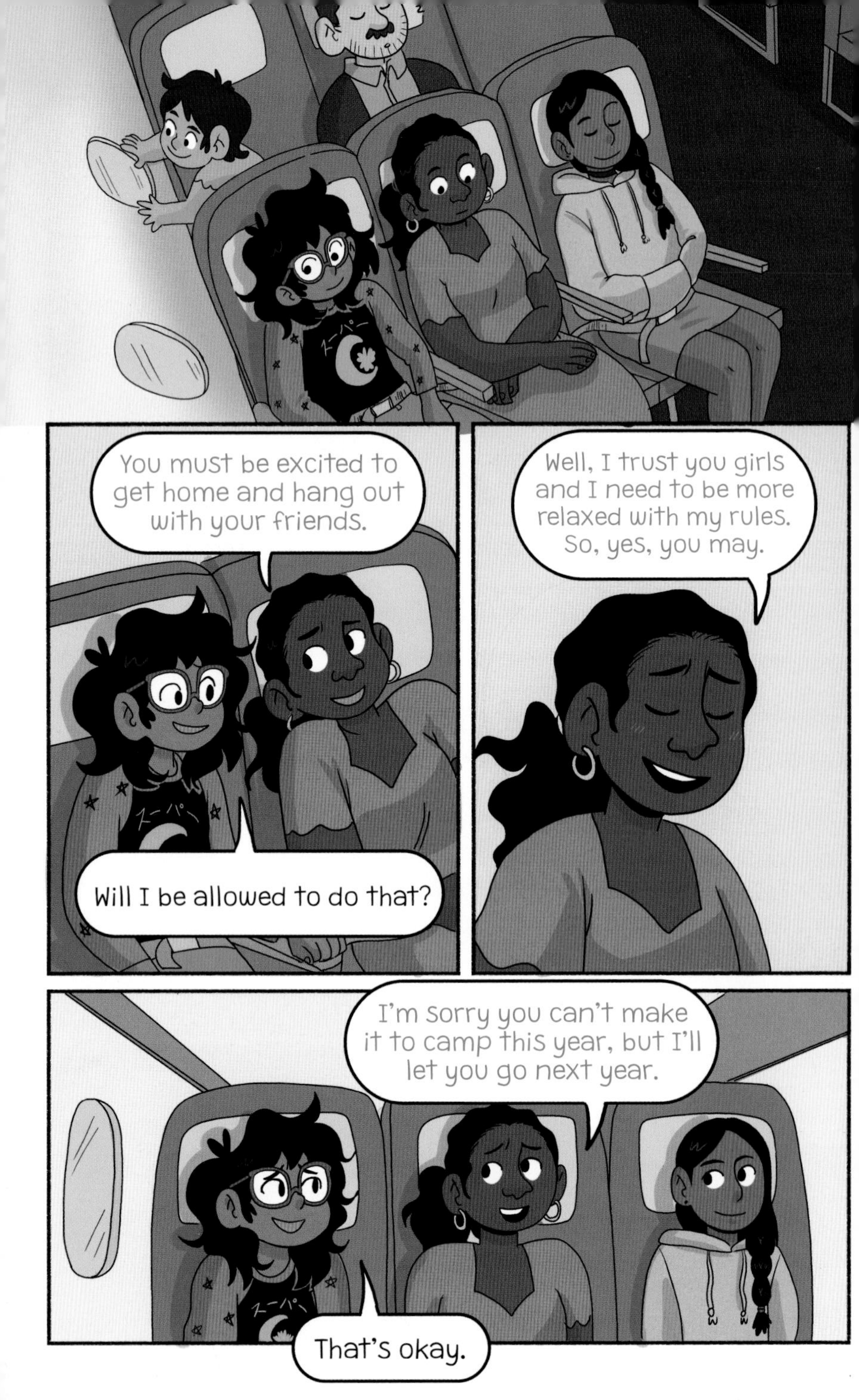
You must be excited to get home and hang out with your friends.
Will I be allowed to do that?
Well, I trust you girls and I need to be more relaxed with my rules. So, yes, you may.
I'm sorry you can't make it to camp this year, but I'll let you go next year.
That's okay.

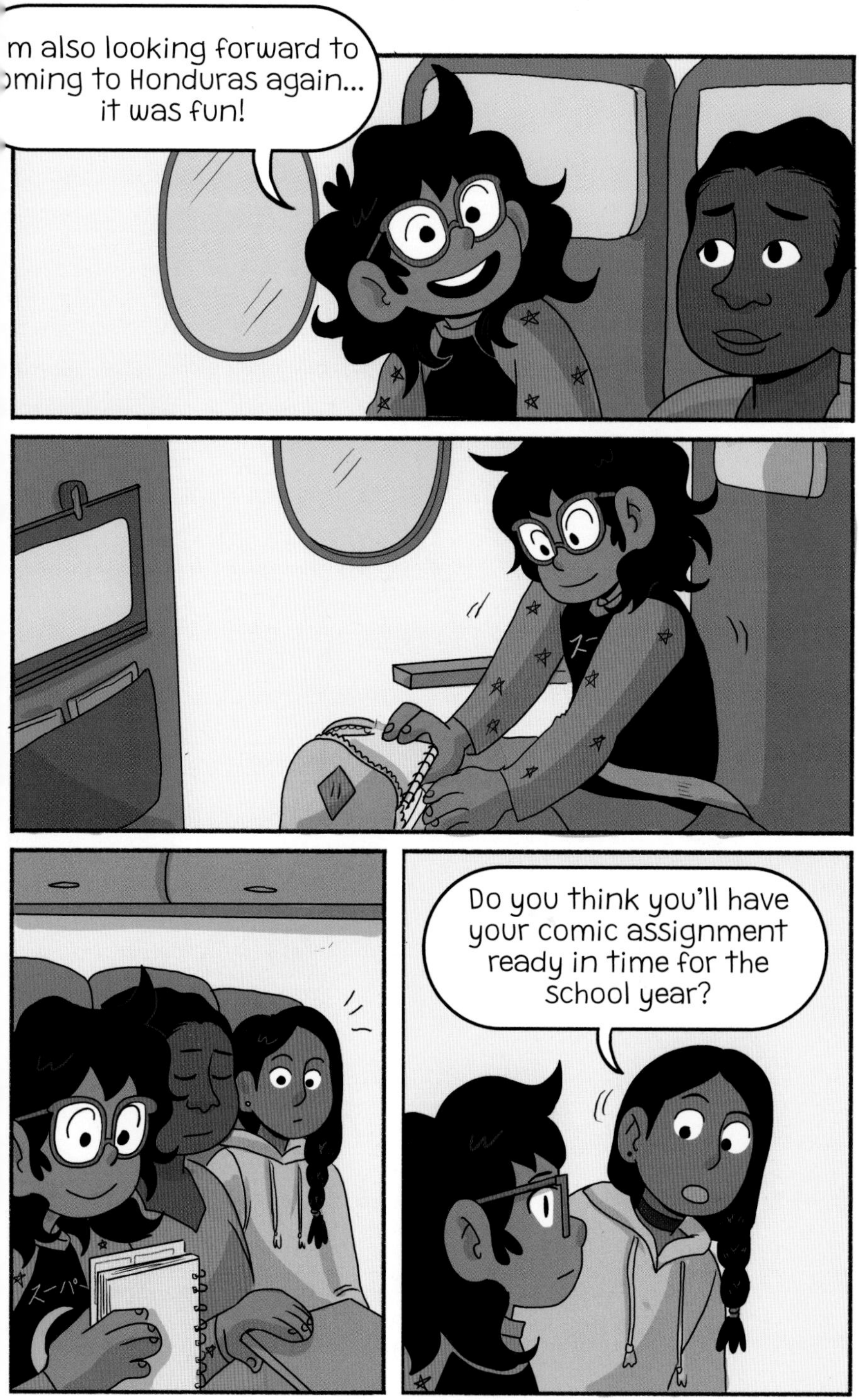
m also looking forward to
oming to Honduras again...
it was fun!
Do you think you'll have your comic assignment ready in time for the school year?

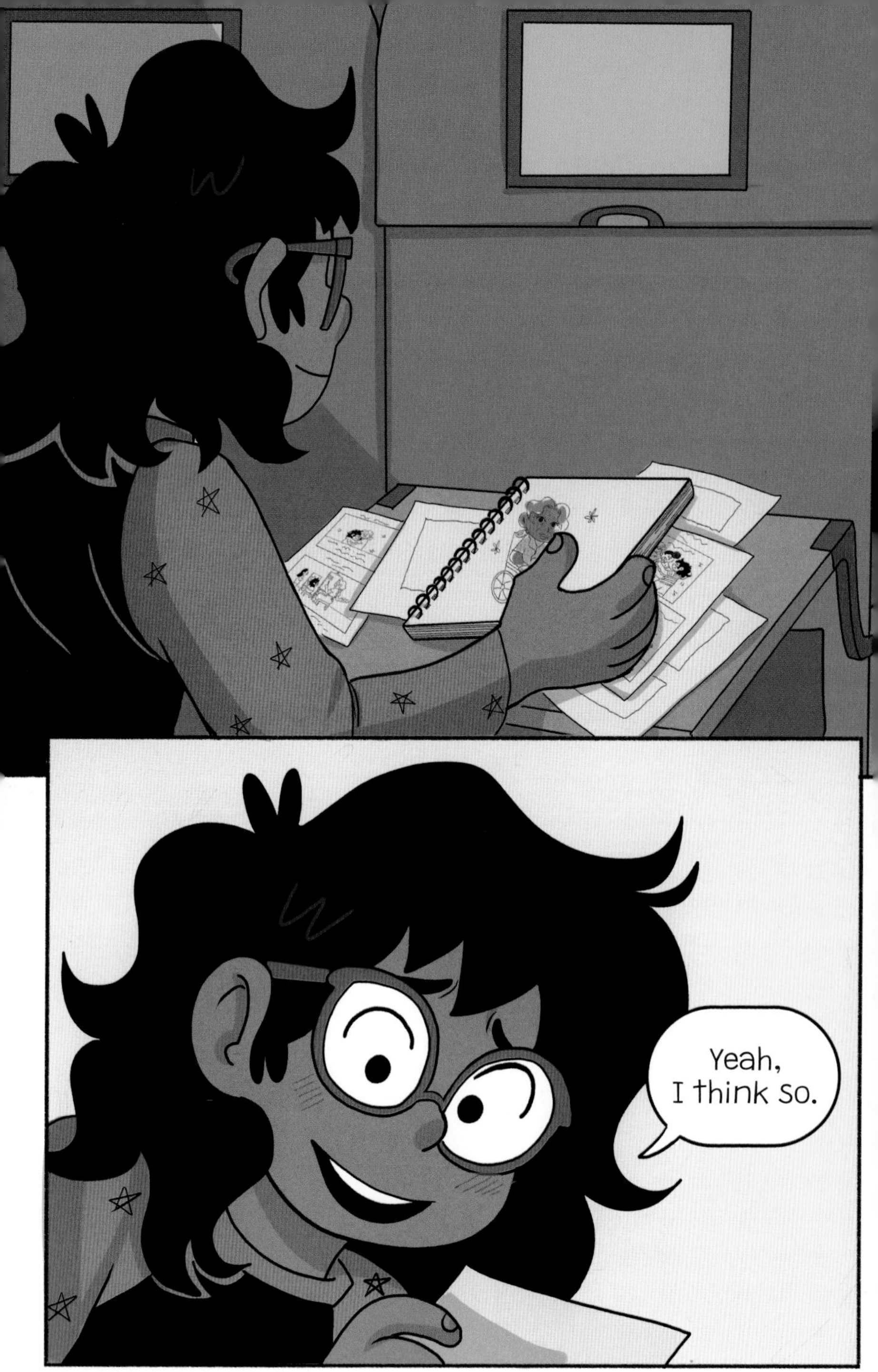
Yeah, I think so.

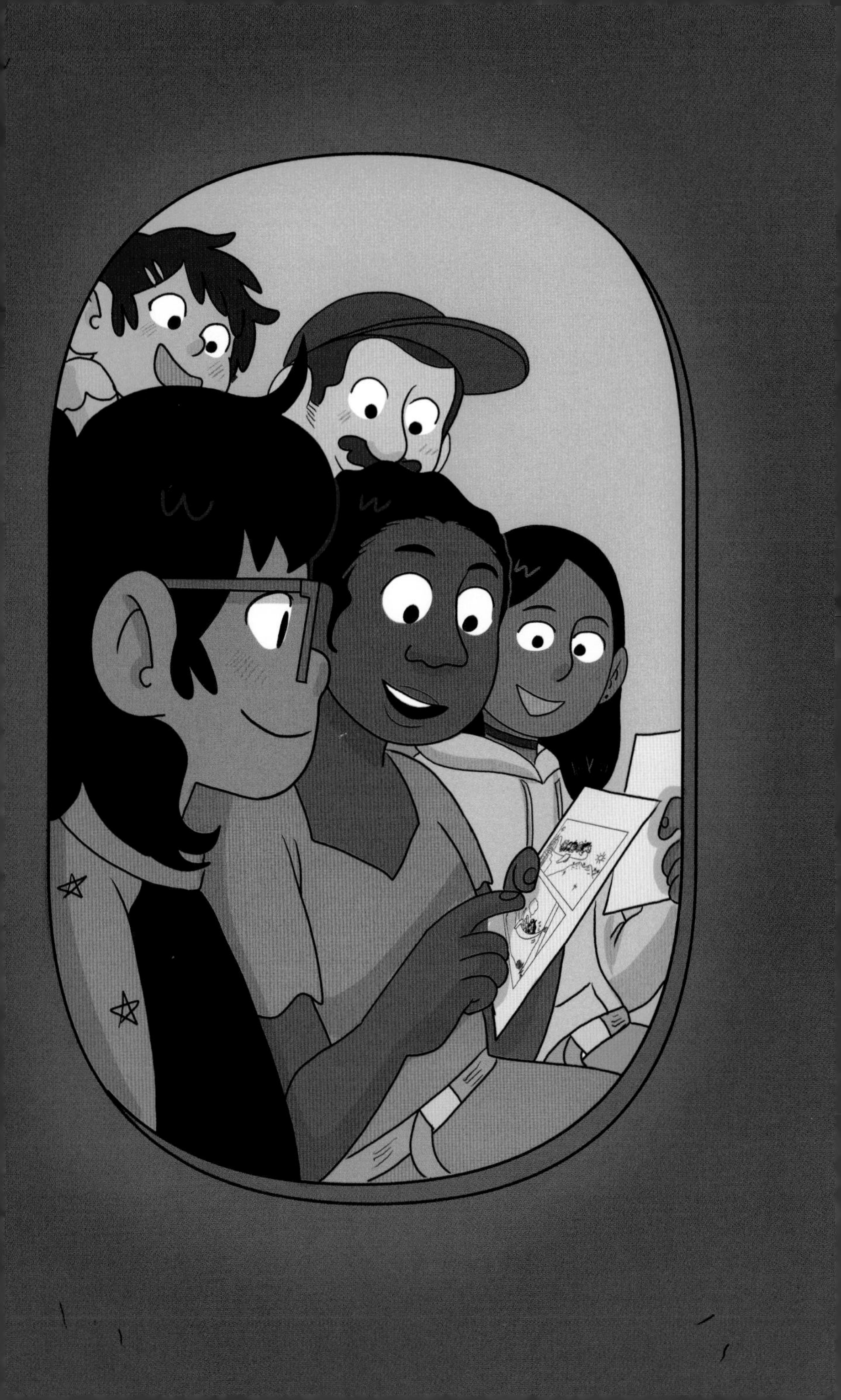

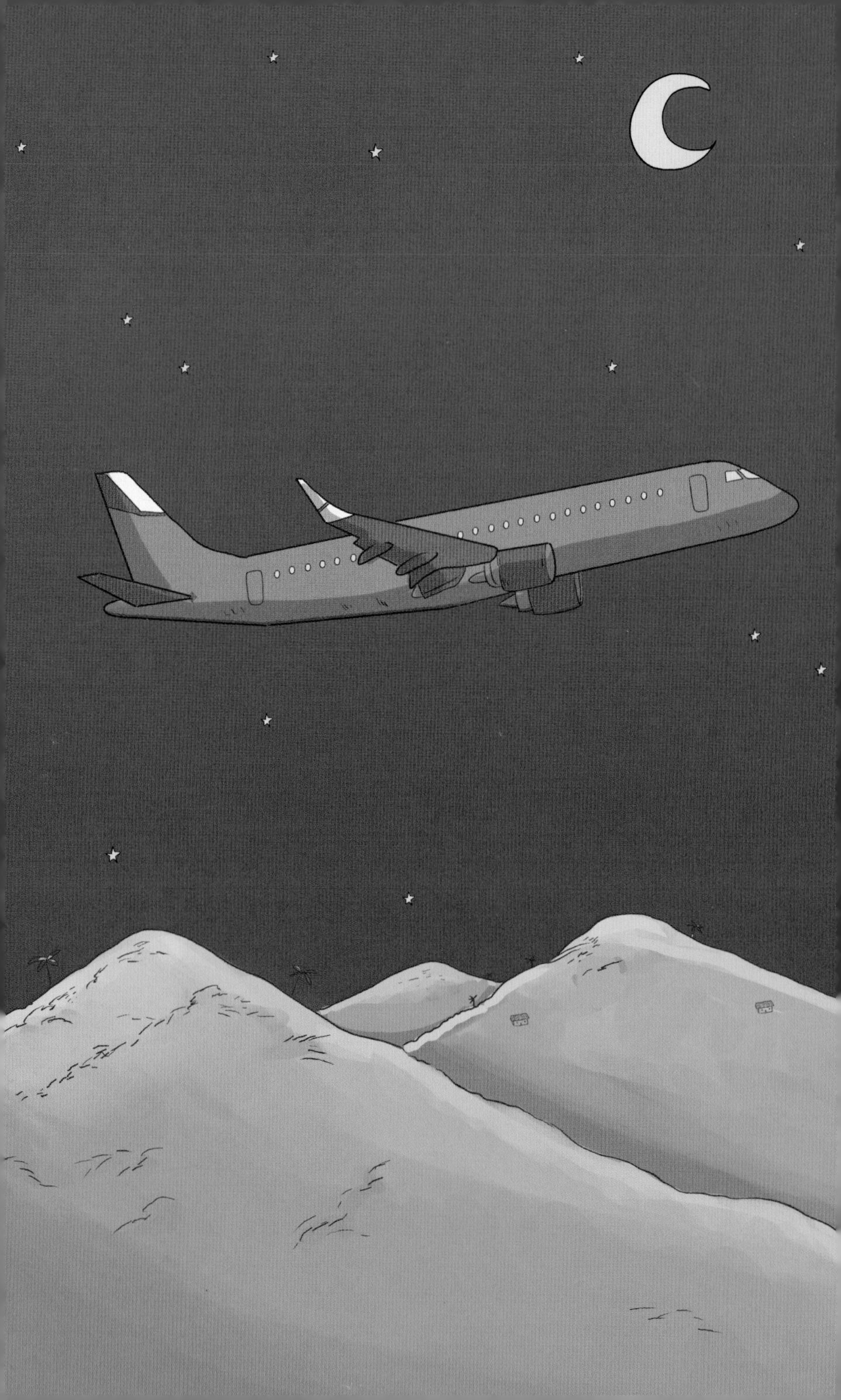

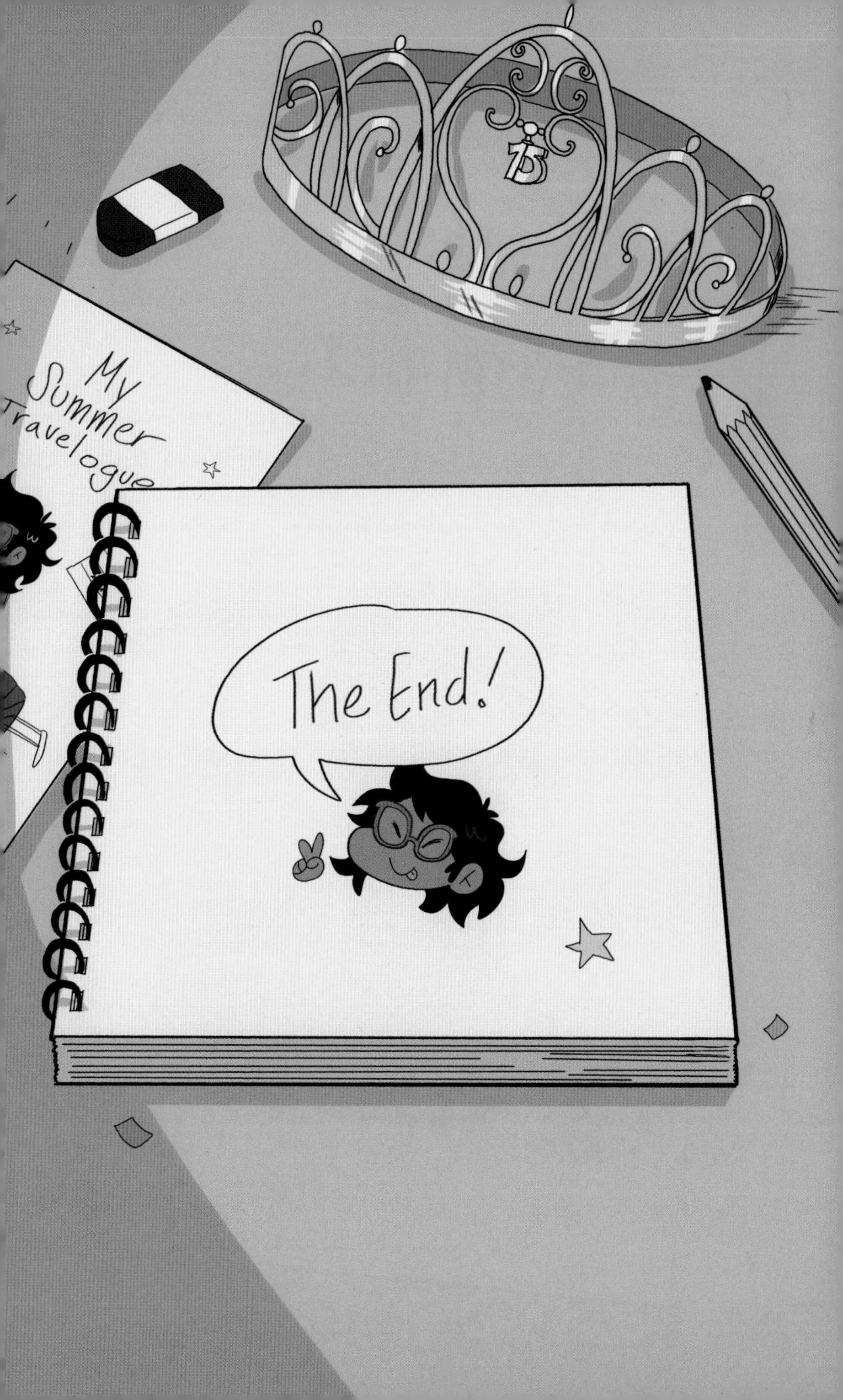
My Summer Travelogue
15
The End!

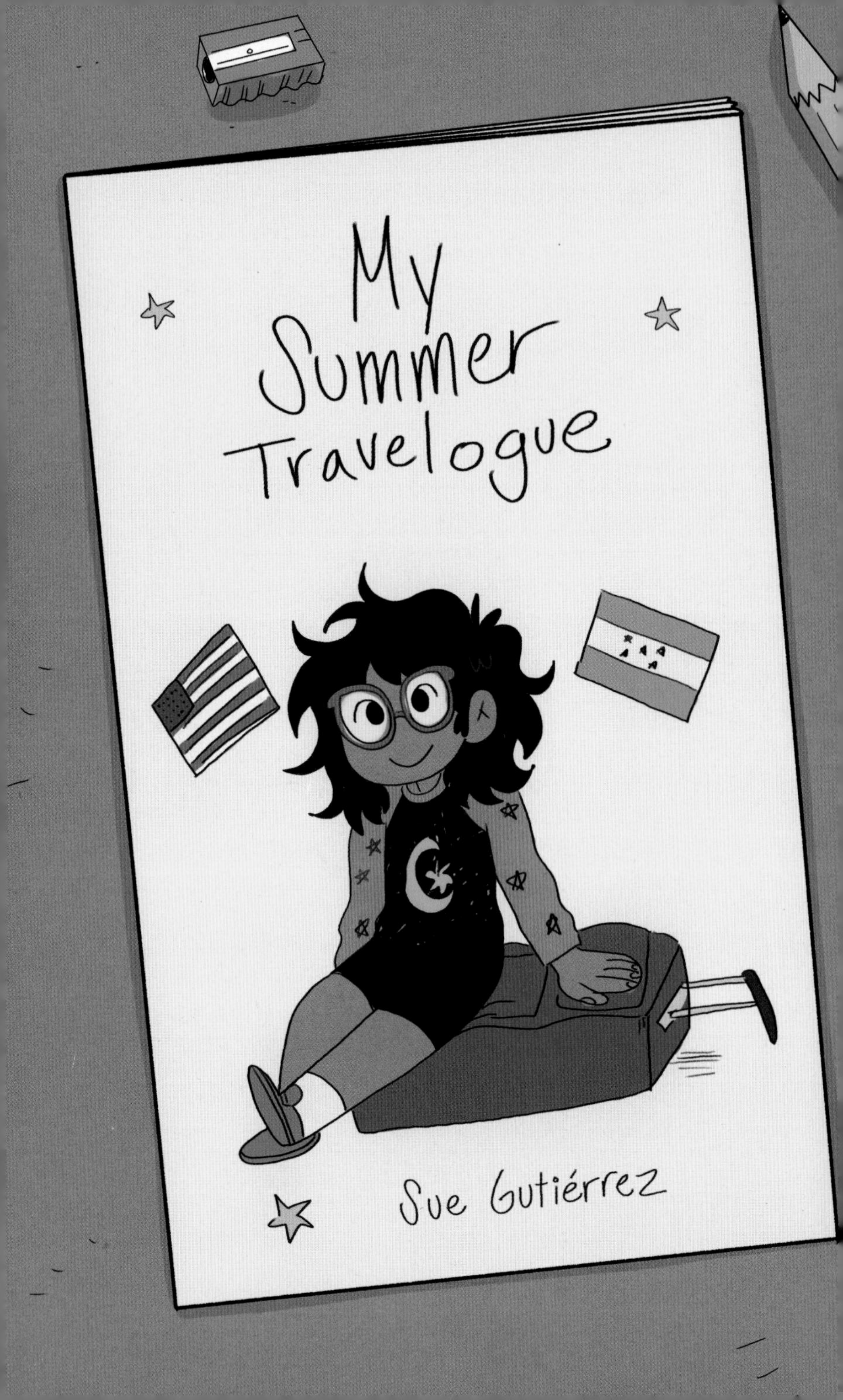
My Summer Travelogue
Sue Gutiérrez

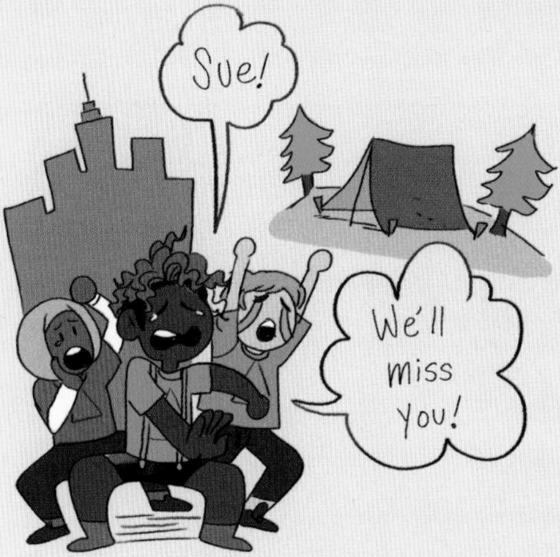
Sue!
We'll miss you!

This summer, the one thing I really wanted to do was go camping with my friends.

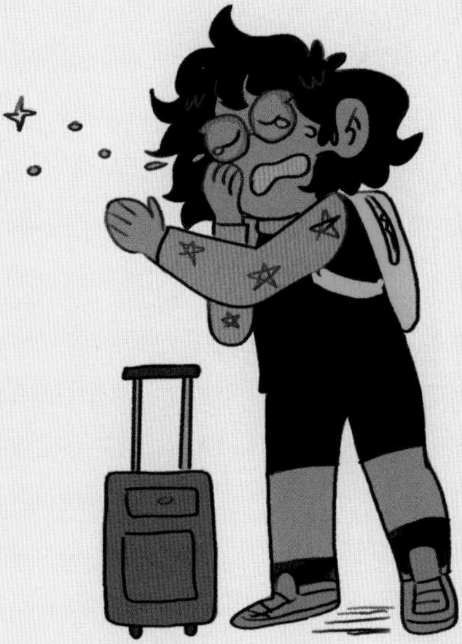

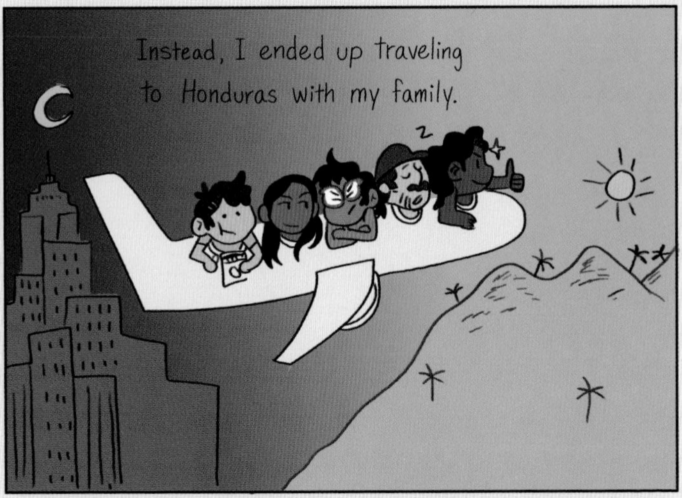
Instead, I ended up traveling to Honduras with my family.
Z

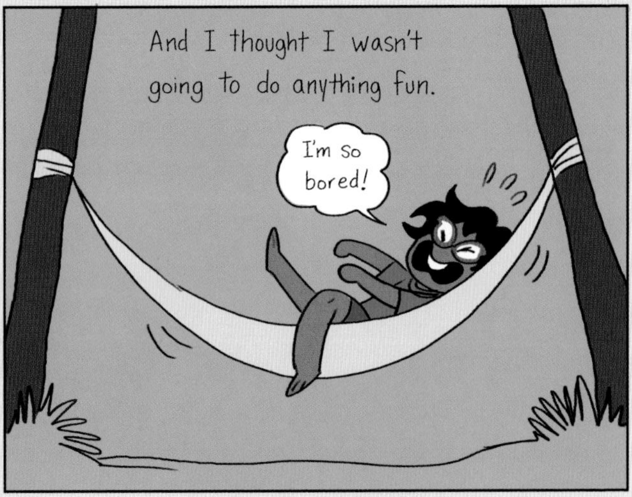
And I thought I wasn't going to do anything fun.
I'm so bored!

But to my surprise, my vacation was full of adventures like:

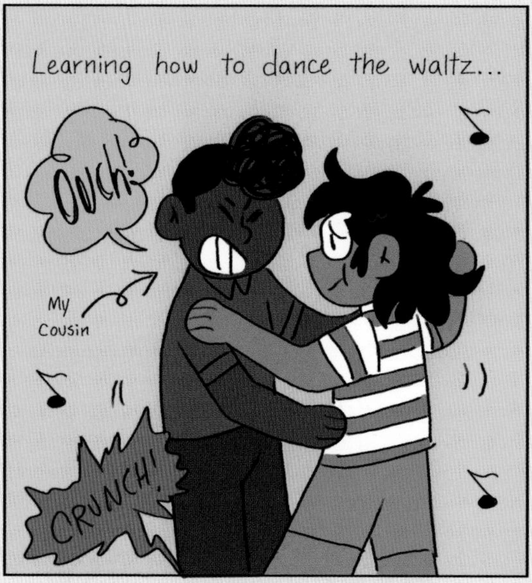
Learning how to dance the waltz...
OUCH!
My Cousin
CRUNCH!

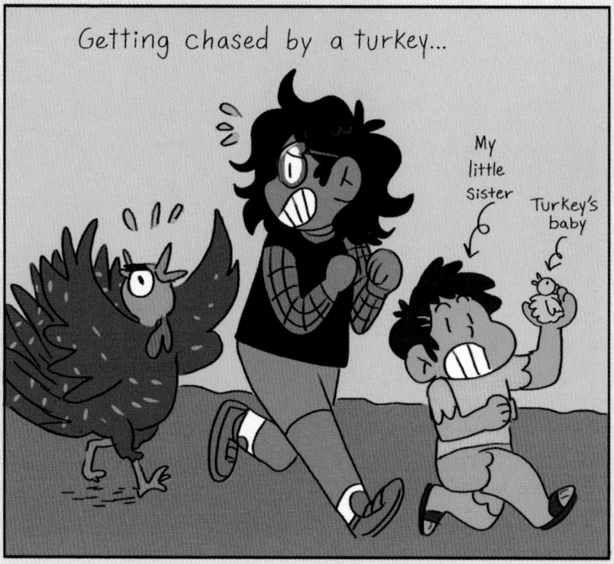
Getting chased by a turkey...
My little sister
Turkey's baby

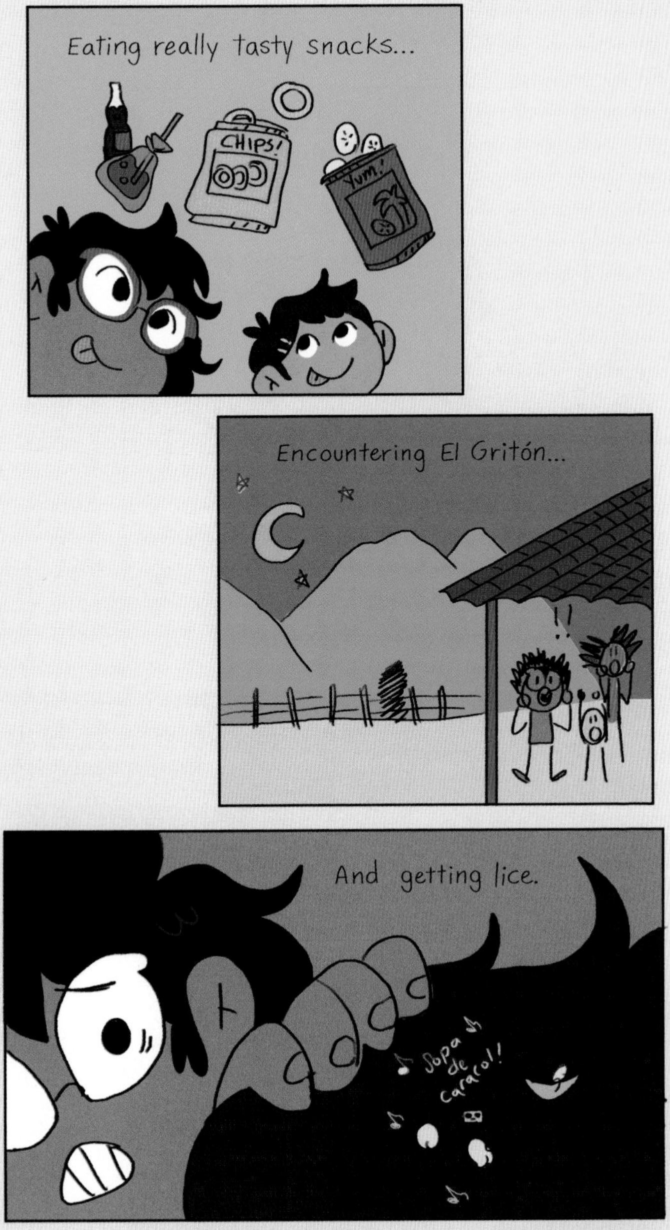
Eating really tasty snacks...
CHIPS!
Yum!
Encountering El Gritón...
!!
And getting lice.
Sopa de caracol!

Overall, I had the best time
with my abuelita, Rita.

Although I don't speak Spanish fluently
like my sister and my mom,
abuelita understood me really well.

She was weird like me and
she didn't want to change that.

She's the reason why I like art today.

She taught me how to embrace my weirdness
and let it shine bright in my own little way.

We will miss you, abuelita.
From one star to another...

You will always be loved.

Thank you for making
my last summer with you special.

−Suyapa Yisel Gutiérrez

Growing up in the United States, it was really hard to find any positive representation of Latine characters on TV or in movies. I didn't see much of the struggle that most Latine-Americans like myself faced during our adolescent years: the experience of "Ni de aquí ni de allá" (neither from here, nor from there). In other words, the lack of total belonging while being perceived as too American for our family, and too Latine for Americans.

As an awkward, nerdy teen trying to assimilate to my American social surroundings, I already felt like an outsider in my own immigrant household. Not being able to speak proper Spanish or share the same interests as my party-loving family, it's no surprise that we had a difficult time understanding each other! And just like my character Sue experiences, it was a struggle trying to forge my own identity within these two cultures. But, also like Sue, through the celebration of my quinceañera in my family's homeland, I was able to connect with my family and understand the cultural importance of this coming-of-age ceremony while embracing both aspects of my identity.

So, in a way, I created the story that I wished I could have read while growing up as the "weird kid." I want to show readers that it's okay to embrace your "otherness" and wear that identity with pride, like a shiny tiara. <3

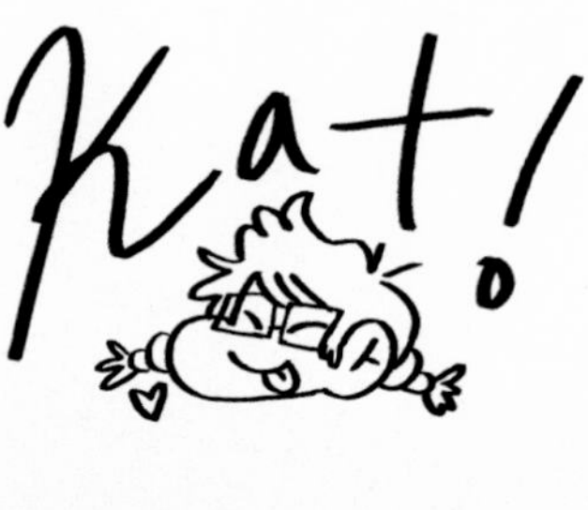
Kat!

A few notes about quinceañeras!

Whether it's an awkward stage in a young Latina's life or the day she's been dreaming about since she was a little girl, it's safe to say that a quinceañera is a very important celebration for many Latine families around the world. A tradition that dates back hundreds of years, quinces have come a long way since the Aztec and Maya versions of this coming-of-age ceremony. Eventually, with Spaniard influence, Catholic traditions were introduced, which most families include in their ceremonies today. And guess what? Marking the transition from childhood to adulthood isn't just for girls! Families sometimes hold quinceañeros for boys. Ultimately, everyone celebrates their quinces in their own fun way.

At the church

The quinceañera's day usually starts at the church, where the priest holds a religious ceremony surrounded by the young girl's family. Her godparents (or padrinos) accompany her, and serve as mentors by helping her stay on a path of spirituality and guiding her to become a reliable and responsible member of her community.

During the ceremony, the quinceañera is given traditional items that are blessed by the priest, such as the Bible and rosary that Sue receives. Then the quinceañera gives her bouquet of flowers, which symbolizes new life and beauty, to the Virgin Mary.

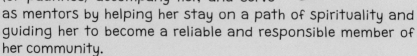

At the party

Unlike the church ceremony, the reception entrance is usually flashy and grand! The court of honor (Corte de Honor) consists of fourteen girls (damas) and boys (chambelanes) who have been chosen by the quinceañera. They escort her into the venue.

Parent-Daughter Dance: A heartfelt dance performed by the quinceañera and her parent or guardian as a symbol of guiding her from childhood to adulthood. It's one of the more emotional parts of the party, and someone will most likely cry. (I did!)

Examples of traditional quinces waltz songs:

"Tiempo de Vals" by Chayanne
"Quinceañera" by Thalía
"Vals de las Mariposas" by Tommy Valles
"De Niña a Mujer" by Julio Iglesias

Perfect for the parent-daughter dance!

The Waltz: Considered to be one of the highlights of the quinces, the waltz must be performed well, so the quinceañera and her court practice for months in order to perfect it! And if she's lucky, after the waltz there might be a fun surprise dance (baile de sorpresa) that the court choreographed and prepared just for the party!

Last Doll Ceremony: Symbolizes the quinceañera's exchange of her childhood for responsibility and womanhood. Since she can no longer have childish toys, she passes on her "last doll" to her younger sister, if she has one.

Aside from the performances, another important part of the ceremony is the presentation of the quinceañera gifts, which each hold a significant and religious meaning. Here's a bit more info on the gifts that I included in Sue's story:

Tiara: A callback to the traditional tiara veil of the young girl's first communion, the quinceañera now wears a tiara as a symbol of being a princess of God. She may receive it at the church ceremony or at the party.

Ring: A reminder of the quinceañera's commitment to God and her parents.

Heels: The switching of flats into heels, usually by the quinceañera's father, represents the young girl's transformation into adulthood as she walks into a life filled with responsibility and maturity.

Whether the quinceañera ends up being a big party at a venue or a small intimate gathering at home, it's an event that requires a lot of planning! It's up to the family to work together and pull this event off. Thanks to my family and old quinceañera magazines, I look back fondly at the memories of my own quinces.

There's always that one aunt who is the life of the party!

Acknowledgments

Although I've been making comics and zines for a while, I still can't believe this book exists! As a kid growing up in the projects, I escaped into books for hours at the Scholastic store on Broadway. I never thought that I'd be given the chance to have my own books on shelves one day, so I'm honored that Scholastic gave me the opportunity to develop this story into something much more. Thank you so much!

I'd also like to thank . . .

My parents and sisters for letting me daydream for hours and indulge in creating comics at a young age. Thank you for pushing me to pursue my own dreams and teaching me how to get out of my comfort zone, starting with my own quinces when I was an awkward fifteen-year-old. ¡Los amo!

I'd like to thank and honor my bisabuela Mamita, who was a big inspiration for Rita. She passed away during the summer of my quinces, but I still have fond memories of her always being there for us. She was the most kind and strong-willed woman I've ever met. The universe is lucky to have an additional star in the sky. <3

My cheerleading team, Gloria and the Maldonado family, for sticking with me as I worked hard on this book. Thank you for always believing in me and encouraging me to follow my path no matter what. And to my cute pups, Mac and Roni, thanks for your cuteness and kisses.

My friends from the comics and zine community—thank you so much for being an inspiration of talent and compassion. I miss you all dearly! But especially my chosen family: Delta, Steph, Kelly, Moony, Sam, and Tim for always checking in on me and providing support in the most special ways possible. I love you!

My amazing agent, Linda Camacho, who is the most driven and intelligent Latina I know. Thanks for always having my back and believing in me from the start.

My editor, Cassandra Pelham Fulton, and my art director, Phil Falco, who believed in my vision and helped nurture this project from the start. Thanks, also, to David Saylor, Megan Peace, María Domínguez, Emily Nguyen, and everyone at Scholastic who worked on both the English and Spanish editions of this book. It wouldn't have been possible without all your hard work! Thanks!!

My awesome design team, Shivana Sookdeo, for her wonderful design work and title logo; Mariana Azzi for their superb coloring skills; and DUS'T and Pablo for assisting me with lettering. Thank you all for helping bring my vision to life!

Most of all, I want to thank my partner, Pablo A. Castro, the best cartoonist and person I know, for their expertise, incredible heart, and, above all things, their invaluable support during this whole process. Thank you for believing in me and my capabilities and for being my source of strength. I'm proud to be your partner!